Philip Boast is the ~~author of~~ ... secret truth of the whereabouts of the body ~~in~~ *Resurrection*, the fate of the lost gospel of Judas Iscariot, and *City*, a panoramic epic that was the story of his thirty pieces of silver. He has also written the Ben London trilogy, *London's Child*, *London's Millionaire* and *London's Daughter*, as well as *Gloria* and, most recently, *The Foundling*, all of which are set in London. He is the author of *Watersmeet*, a West Country saga, and *Pride*, an epic novel set in Australia and England.

Philip Boast lives in Devon with his wife Rosalind and three children, Harry, Zoe and Jamie.

Sion

Philip Boast

HEADLINE

First published in 1999
by HEADLINE BOOK PUBLISHING

First published in paperback in 1999
by HEADLINE BOOK PUBLISHING

10 9 8 7 6 5 4 3 2 1

ISBN 0 7472 5960 7

Typeset by
Letterpart Limited, Reigate, Surrey
Printed and bound in Great Britain by
Clays Ltd, St Ives plc

HEADLINE BOOK PUBLISHING
A division of Hodder Headline PLC
338 Euston Road
London NW1 3BH
www.headline.co.uk
www.hodderheadline.com

For Derek
who knows what he did

Whoever slanders the Congregation shall be excommunicated from among us and return no more.
Judas the Galilean, Community Rule at Sion, AD 4

There was much else that Jesus did; if it were written down in detail, I do not suppose the world itself would hold all the books that would be written.
Gospel According to St John, 21:25, AD 100

If anyone shall say or think that there is a time limit to the torment of demons and ungodly persons, or that there will ever be an end to it, or that they will ever be pardoned or made whole again, then let him be excommunicated.
The Synod of Constantinople, AD 543

'Do you not know, daughter, who you are and who I am? You are she who has nothing; and I am He who is everything.'
Catherine of Siena, 'The Orchard of Sion', c. 1375

No 14,587   Published in London and Manchester

Daily   22 December 2012   *3Eu*

NEWS & STAR-LEGION

DEDICATED TO THE PEOPLE OF EUROPE

WHY?

FROM OUR SPECIAL REPORTER

EXCLUSIVE

CULVER, ISLE OF WIGHT

Early this morning tragedy again struck the beleaguered Culver Cliff Hotel, already ba__ **damaged in last week's cliff fall. Owne__ Brewer said, "One minute we__ huge explosion and th__ beach feared dead or__ World War II landmine. The Army issu__ Captain Julian Trevrizent was instant__**

Mystery surrounds the events leadi__ disaster. Survivors flown to Queen Mary Hos__ of Professor Mary Dumazulu, America's__ __emost paleontologist from University of Mid-W__ and Professor Michaels had made an astonishing

discovery in a cave, unconfirmed.

However local people insist that Professor Michaels was "in a state of high -ment" and had told drinkers of "find of -time or anyone else's.

The Ministry of Defence and American Embassy declined to comment on "rumours and media spec- __tion" and the family __zent were also __omment.

However rumours pers__

dragon-like fossilised skeleton of a underneath

also unconfirmed.

Barman Ted Drisco__ last Tuesday abo__ book

unknown.

65, 434, 2__ extinc__

'ARAM MENAHT MEN__

THE HOLY LAND – 9BC

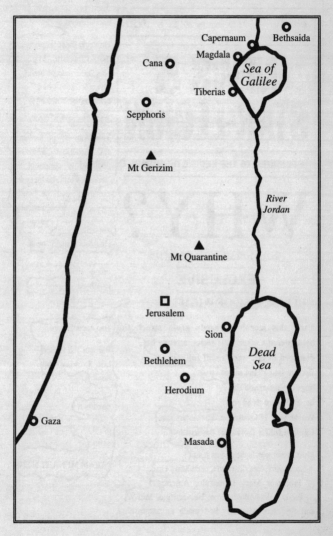

MARE MORTIS

The Dead Sea

WEDNESDAY 19 JUNE 9 BC, 6:04 A.M.

Forget what you knew. God is dead, for He has forsaken us.

I, Mary the Rainmaker, prophet, abandoned by the God of my fathers, gagged, bound hand and foot, set adrift by the priests of Sion in a rudderless boat on a lifeless sea, know this now for certain: there is no God.

There is no Jesus Christ.

Hear me, O Sion: soon the sun will rise above the dry hills, without God; soon my life will end, without God.

Soon my little boat will sink.

Hear my truth, O Sion. Here is the meaning of my death, my terrible lonely death. God will never send His Son to be our salvation in this world. There is no Messiah. There is no freedom, no end to time, no hope for us. Without Jesus Christ there is no judgment. No forgiveness. No peace. No glory. No Heaven.

God made Heaven and Earth, but the Devil made this world.

In this world Abraham did not find Jesus Christ our Anointed Saviour, the Virgin's only Son, reigning in right-eousness and perfection, eternal, universal, in Jerusalem as has been foretold in other places from the beginning of time; only Melchizadok the king-priest, fallible, demonic (I remember him well, his wheezing breath, his spit crusted in the corners of his crafty smile as he offered bread and wine), squatted raddled and serene on his throne of blood, merely human, as are we all. That was some two thousand years ago; but nothing has changed, and never will change. The

1

prophecies of Nahum, and Micah who wrongly foretold our Saviour would be born in Bethlehem, of Isaiah, Jeremiah, Malachi, Zecher, Ezekiel, and the psalms of David, are worthless dust.

Our Saviour has not come.

There is no Jesus Christ for us, for you. Here, *here*, is Hell. We live in Hell, you and I. Our children in this hellish abandoned world are born beyond redemption, born sinful, born to grow and suffer and die like us amid the torments of Hell without hope of salvation. As I do. Your time will come, my friend.

The old woman's heel slips. Seawater bubbles around her in the boat.

The Rainmaker's grandchild is born in Galilee today. I know everything about this old woman. I know her talent is a curse. Once she was beautiful. There is nothing I can do for her, she is trapped (as the priests here tell us) in the prison of her body, and her aged body will surely die. Everything beautiful rots or is taken from us, everything good perishes, life turns to dust.

I have seen more than I can tell, and lived more than I can say, and I wish I was blind. Deaf. Dumb. Stone.

I am poor Mary, dying, but I am more than Mary too.

I am immortal, like you. But old, monstrously old. Almost as old as time, it feels. My heart's hard and cold as iron. That's the only difference between us, you and I. My age, power, knowledge. Ah, knowledge! There's nothing I don't know, no despair I haven't known, no life I've not lost in pain and suffering.

But I was young once, in love. His name was James. A name without meaning, merely a man when I was merely a woman. We had no child. By now his age is as monstrous as mine, his heart as hardened and as cold, no doubt. Seeking the brief warmth of blood in his despair, as do I. But when we were young, we had each other. We thought love lasted for ever, and we dreamed.

Now I know this world itself on which we find ourselves is Hell.

Listen to me. How much do you know of yourself? No, how much do you *really* know? Do you know enough to live? Do you know that as the sun rises beside Sirius above those

2

dusty cliff tops into the hard blue arch of this cloudless sky, the sun's blazing orb will begin to disappear, and darkness will fall in daytime?

I know.

Listen, listen. This is my story that I must tell.

Do you see me now? Do you see the body of this old woman, dying, condemned? After a hard lifetime wandering from village to village, meditating in caves, living on scraps, the Rainmaker's skill has failed her, the God of her beliefs deserted her. There will be no rain. The Rainmaker is infected by my bitterness, my despair; she has lost her faith. Do you hear the rattle of her breath, the creak of the tiny rowboat as it turns aimlessly in this or that sigh of the dawn wind? Her grey head is cricked uncomfortably inside the bow of the boat, the gag pulled back so tight each brown stump of tooth is bared, a heavy bag of stones tied to her scrawny neck, her wrists knotted (too tight) to the seat, her right leg hanging awkwardly over the stern. Her left leg, even more awkwardly, she has twisted and cramped under her so that her heel plugs the hole chopped through the boat. The gopher wood's rotten and a little water seeps around her heel, and squirts powerfully at her slightest movement, so now she lies unmoving except for her heart and lungs and her staring terrified eyes which move from side to side as the light grows. But there is no escape.

From this situation it is painfully obvious, as the priests of The Poor intended, that only God can save her. The Poor are encouraging her, you may say, to believe in Him. They mean their God, of course.

Blessed are The Poor, for they shall inherit the earth.

But I know more than they, and more than this old woman.

I know that this earth spins around its sun.

These people have no word for nature; but her old eyes see the sun spread its fan of light like a glowing lid from the hilltops of Idumea to the cliffs of Judah on the other shore, Herod's kingdoms under Rome, so that here between them the Dead Sea containing her little foundering boat seems for a moment to inhabit cool deep shadow, deep blue, indigo-deep, and reminds her again of her home village by the Sea of Galilee and her daughter, Leah. But Galilee is life.

3

No place could be more different. The Rainmaker, gnawing terrified at her gag, straining at the ropes with all her strength, bitter salt water squirting around her heel, is the only living creature. No birds, for there are no fish, except dead fish floating from the mouth of the Jordan, washed down and drowned by the salt. Lifeless desert above the cliff tops, lifeless sea below: a perfect place for priests. See the sun's light on that parched strip of yellow-green along the western shore, the place local peasants call *Qimrôn*, or Qumran? The great stone buildings built there, distant, but as pure white as pillars of salt? The Essene priests call their ancient holy monastery Sion, which means command, order; and there they live, mostly without women, in total subjugation to their zealous Order which regulates their lives to the most intimate detail. They call themselves the Community of the Lord, Nazarenes, the Sons of Men, the Salt, the People of God. The Meek. The Poor.

The Poor! Their chief priest, the Righteous Teacher, has the richest library in the world. But they have no rain. The Rainmaker is a woman, unclean to them, sexual, concealing (like all women according to their priestly scrolls) a multitude of sins in her skirt, her heart a snare, even her dry wrinkled breasts and withered *gula* (the Rainmaker bore her share of grief a generation ago) a fearful trap to tempt and defile the scrubbed male organs of the righteous and circumcised Elect: a *woman* should be admitted to the holy of holies of the Sons of Men? Never. She's kept outside the monastery walls, exiled with the other women in the desert outposts called Emmaus, or Jerusalem, Bethlehem, Nazareth, Egypt, Damascus – even Galilee, for within its boundaries *Qimrôn* is a microcosm, almost a map, of all the lands of Sion – and by the women's wooden huts in the south-western quarter she draws her circles in the dust, day after day, and makes her prayers, the *shabten*. Bring them rain, O Lord.

An old woman, chanting. She has the keys to rain, is permitted to take the name of the Lord in vain: but to make rain it's necessary to have pure water nearby. A thousand details must be right.

Above all, faith. The leap of faith. Day after day.

Rain will not come. There is no rain, there is no Lord.

4

The crops wither, but taxes must be paid: at collection tables round the dry fonts and baptismal pools the peasants who can't pay their rents and tithes have their worthless land taken from them. Tomorrow they'll be beggars or bandits, they won't eat kosher, defiling themselves, living outside the Law. Beyond the monastery walls their women and children are already wailing, the peculiar sound this culture makes, their sound both of faith and desolation.

They cannot blame their God who tests them, but they can find someone else to blame: the rainmaker who failed. A woman rejected by God. A martyr.

The boat drifts further out to sea, sinking.

At last the knot slips, and the old woman, merely an old woman, a creature of blood and bone and gut, spits the gag from her mouth. Her mouth opens. That's it, girl! Fight them to your last breath, scream your defiance! But she lies silent in the seawater slopping into the boat, listening. Whose voice does she hear? Mine?

The wailing of the people and the prayers of the priests carry faintly across the water, the smoke of sacrificial offerings rises over Sion, the Field of Blood runs red with the gifts of atonement. But there's no sign of clouds. Nor will the Rainmaker's martyrdom bring them, I know.

The cedar forests that once covered this land are felled, the ring of fertile soil around the Dead Sea turns to dust under the hoe. The River Jordan brings less water from Galilee than the sun drinks, so the Rainmaker's boat floats seven hundred cubits below the level of the Mediterranean. These people say the Dead Sea is bottomless, an entrance to Sheol that lies beneath us, everywhere, as Isaiah foretold, a limbo of the dead that moves to meet us at our coming. *I* know the black sea bed is almost exactly another thousand feet below us; I knew it when it was dry grass, part of another continent.

These ordinary people believe there's no return from Sheol, that death is death. The grave cannot praise them, death cannot celebrate them, they go down into the pit and cannot hope for their God's truth. They believe in King David's psalm, that the dead praise not the Lord nor any who go down into the silence of the grave. For them, in death there is no remembrance.

But the priests at Sion believe that an immortal soul is trapped inside the prison of each human body. For good souls – they mean their own, having lived sanctified lives of the utmost dedication to virtue and purity – there waits a home beyond the ocean. That's true, though I vouch there's more rain and snow and heat there than they'd wish, and horseflies and mosquitoes as big as your fist; and they could sail there in their own lifetime, if only they knew. They believe although *they* are redeemed that ordinary people, like this old woman, will fall to the dusty emptiness of Sheol for ever and undergo eternal punishment.

There is no saving her, and she knows it.

Her lips move. Yes, defiance, rage! But instead, it is a prayer she utters. 'I am a woman who has no strength, free among the dead, like the slain that lie in the grave, whom You remember no more: and I am cut off from Your hand.' One of the psalms? She accepts what is happening to her. No rage, no disbelief, no fury. Calm submission.

I think I know this voice. It is like my own, from long ago. Faith. Acceptance. Hope. I wish I had it. But I know it is a lie.

Here in this world made by the Devil, God has forsaken us.

This world of demons. The demons were here long before Man, long before Woman. Long before grass grew on the plains of the earth. The dragon, Leviathan, knew this planet long even before us, old when even I was young. I know this; I have seen him.

Here, we are the unsaved.

The sun strikes down from the hilltops across the sea, already hot, burning dry the Rainmaker's face and eyes. She can't see the darkness chipping into the sun's orb, not yet, but I know it's there.

Again she whispers. 'I am dead, I shall not live; I am deceased, I shall not rise.' Abandoned. She means people abandoned by the God of her people, *Yhwh*, whose name is too holy to say in full. The foolish woman still prays to the remorseless God who extinguishes her!

'But Thy righteous dead men and women shall live in righteousness, together with my dead body shall they arise; and the earth shall cast out the dead.' I know this is what the Poor believe; she's been listening to half-baked rumours handed down round the women's campfire. The Rainmaker senses the light change, night falling by day: the sun half gone, bitten like a fruit. She raises herself, ignores the water gurgling round her heel into the boat. Lifts up her head against the weight of stones, gasps a breath in awe and terror. She believes she sees, by the shrinking of the sun, the coming of the Hand of God.

It's not God, it's nothing but orbital mechanics! You and I know the eclipse is only the new moon, invisible, passing between the earth and the sun. A blackened lens would show the corona of the sun around the moon's jagged rim; simple science and a little arithmetic would reveal the size and distance of the moon from the earth and overturn every belief.

Odd darkness falls.

Faintly the prayers of the 'angel', the priest standing at the *gnomon* sundial on the monastery roof, carry across the calm water. He's praying for rain, not a rain of water but Divine rain to sweep the Romans away and the Gentiles away and Herod the king of the Sadducees and Pharisees away. It's exactly the first hour of the day, seven o'clock, the eclipse at its darkest. Stars spread across the daylight sky. Hear the terror of the people! The moon in the sun! But the angel chants his prayers without fear. These priests observe the movements of the sun and stars precisely, for they believe Heaven and Earth are God, and a prayer or sacrifice or ritual offered to Him at the wrong time is unholy. Long ago in Egypt and across the ocean they made the sky their clock. They knew this would happen. They still believe their knowledge, holiness and righteous living will bring about the advent of the Messiah.

The Rainmaker splashes, jerks at her ropes like a hooked fish, cries out in terror. The planet Lucifer, *Stella matutina*, the morning star called Venus by the Romans, stands out bright and clear beneath the black sun: these priests teach that Sheol is ruled by Lucifer, son of the morning, day-star, who fell from Heaven and from God.

The sun reappears as a crescent now, the blinding horns of light growing longer, pointing down at Lucifer. Even I could almost believe such an astounding sight to be a prophecy, something more than a coincidence of the celestial dance. But prophecies do not prevail; only the laws of science.

The Rainmaker lies unmoving, stares up at the sun and moon and starry sky. Salt water flows into her ears, makes bitter bubbles at the corners of her mouth. 'I see how the winds stretch out the vaults of Heaven and hold their station between Heaven and Earth. They are the pillars of Heaven. I see columns of heavenly fire and among them I see columns of fire fall beyond all measure of height and depth.' Is that what she actually sees or some other long-dead prophecy that will never come true? 'Beyond the abyss I see a place without Heaven above, nothing below. No water on it and no birds; a wasteland. Now I see seven stars like burning mountains, and when I ask about them the angel tells me: "This place is the end of Heaven and Earth. It has become a prison for the stars and the host of Heaven. The stars which roll over the fire have transgressed the Lord's commandments in the beginning of their rising, for they did not appear at their appointed times. And God is angry with them and has bound them for ten thousand times ten thousand years until their guilt is appeased." '

This is what baffles me: their faith. These people, somewhere in their hearts, keep faith with their God though God deserts them. There is no God, *I* know, but the chanting, righteous, purified priests have utter faith that there *is*. Even the ordinary folk outside the walls have fallen silent, faithful. They too, homeless, suffering, unclean, unsaved, believe their insignificant tiny lives – we shall never hear of them again – are somehow part of something huge and important. That there is a reason. Something true.

Gleaming Lucifer winks from sight, touched by the invisible moon.

The knot slips, the Rainmaker pulls out her hand from the rope that binds her. That's it, girl! Live! Push your skirt into the hole, stop the water, bale out the boat! Use your hands as paddles to reach the far shore, no one will ever find you in the wilderness.

But she stares up, motionless, superstitious. What passes through her mind? Does she think that for the few moments that Lucifer is hidden, evil is erased from the world? She

8

makes no attempt to untie the bag of stones from her neck. No attempt to stop the water rushing into the boat.

The moon slips down towards red Sirius, brightest star in the sky. What does this geometry mean? She wants to know the truth. But there's no truth to be found here, the eclipse is merely an optical illusion, depending from where in the world she watches!

The last of the moon slips from the sun, the stars wink out, the sky's a blinding cloudless glare.

The old woman stands up in the sinking boat.

If I believed in God, I would want to believe in a God who would show this old lady a little mercy now. A few drops of rain, some small sign of grace. Sentimental, perhaps. I know a miracle is impossible, but just one grey cloud will do. A single breath of hope.

Nothing happens, of course. Except the old woman makes this happen: just before the sea flows inevitably over the sides of the doomed boat, of her own free will she steps forward. Will not go meekly down. Steps out as though to stand on the water, plunges down, plummets down dragged down by the stones, the stones around her neck pulling her down into the deep black water, her arms and legs flailing like fish in her death agony as she drops into total darkness towards the bottom of the sea. Her eardrums burst, silence falls. Still she will not let her breath go.

I know this lonely forsaken moment of death a million times. But this old woman's last thought turns to love, and a bright picture comes into her mind of her daughter Leah grunting and sweating in childbirth, and yet joyful too, a halo of sunlight round her hair. Her baby's head peeping between her legs is blinded by blood and mucus. *I* know the death vision is caused simply by chemical endorphins rushing into the old woman's brain; yet it seems so real. So very real. It's actually happening, right now, in some small village in Galilee, and through the flapping window-curtain comes the smell of drying fish, the bitter tang of indigo dye, the calls of fishermen and dyers, someone shouting prices, a shekel for half a dozen. Footsteps, a bearded black-haired man comes in, I hear his low question. 'Is my wife not dead yet? Let the child die. Cursed is the child that kills the mother.' But a woman's voice replies, 'By God's will all is well.' The mother, Leah, screams, the father pushes his purple-stained fingers through his curly black hair, groaning, I hear a babble of voices shouting. There's more, but pure awe, pure terror, rushes through me: I'm convinced the old woman is being granted a sight of something *actually happening*, and I have glimpsed a power far beyond my imagination, something beyond explanation, impossible in this world, something I can only call a divine mercy. Perhaps a glimpse of the Hand of God.

There is a divine mercy after all.

The old woman sees much more than I. Despite the darkness and the crushing weight of water I sense her smile. No terror in her, only this smile that greets an old friend. Her smile opens, bubbles pour from her mouth, of her own will she sets her spirit free.

And I, of course, am born again.

This time it's different.

BOOK ONE

Mary
Magdalene

Save me, O God;
for the waters are come into my soul.
I sink in deep mire where there is no standing;
I am come into deep waters, where the floods overflow me.
I am weary of my crying, my throat is dried:
my eyes fail while I wait for my God . . .
For God will save Sion, and will build the cities of Judah,
that [the Poor] may dwell there, and possess it.
The seed of His servants shall inherit it:
and they that love His name shall live there.

Psalm 69:1–3, 35–36

MARE VITALIS

The Sea of Life

GALILEE, WEDNESDAY 19 JUNE 9 BC, 8:04 A.M.

I'm gone. I struggle. This time I'm powerless. Seized.

I'm alive.

I'm blind. Can't move a muscle, bound hand and foot, imprisoned on every side. Can't breathe, my head held in a bag, blood pushing into my mouth and nose. I'm in the flesh; I *am* flesh. Everything of the womb, warmth, home, comfort, is gone, my journey has begun, I can't turn back! I'm trapped! The thunder is my own heart, my heart in my body beating as fast as a bird's, a hundred and fifty whirring beats a minute at least, and all around me I feel the deeper thumping rhythm of my mother's distressed heart, the heavy pulse of her veins and arteries around my body. The squeeze of her muscles comes, she contracts around me like a vice.

I'm being born.

I am Mary the Rainmaker's last sight: *I* am the child she witnessed. This is a miracle, surely. But a miracle is impossible, if there is no God. Unless life itself is the miracle; but life is simply genetics, evolution, mutation. I know. I've seen it.

But now these are just long words, far away.

This is what it feels like, this, it's really happening! I'm panicking! The squeeze tightens, my mouth opens, my mother's blood and slime fills me, I hear my soft bones creak. Through her body I hear my mother screaming, shrieking in her agony, my little body is tearing her flesh apart. My head slips forward, her screams gasp, she groans, the squeeze falters and she relaxes, her rushing heart slows. She's exhausted.

A rough hand touches my face, the fingertips bitten smooth: the midwife, then. She twists at my protruding head, pulls.

My shoulder's stuck. I'm going to die. The pull comes again, harder, distorting my face. One huge finger slips inside my mouth, I feel my lip tearing but have no way of showing pain. Footsteps, the fingers are taken away, the filth of childbirth and the foulness of his wife, my mother, are revealed to the husband. My blood-blinded eyes can't see him but I remember the man I saw in the death vision. Bearded. Curly black hair, purple-stained fingers. His enormous voice booms, 'Is my wife not dead yet?' No response from the midwife; everything to me is my mother's thudding heart, the frantic flutter of my own. My father's booming voice returns. 'Let the child die. Cursed is the child that kills the mother.'

My mother moves. She speaks but cannot. The intimate thudding of our two hearts together.

Then the midwife says bleakly, 'By God's will all is well.' She knows what she must do.

Her great hands slide past my head, she holds something hard, a midwife's stick. She forces it between my mother's flesh and my own. I hear and feel my mother's screams coming to me through the meat of her body, but I am soundless in my agony. Mother, Mother, help me. The next contraction tightens anyway, the pain is beyond belief. The stick knocks my ribs one by one as it slides forward, probes between my shoulder and my elbow, finds the angle. The midwife grunts, gives a sudden twist, and I hear my arm break.

Agony explodes through me like burning fire. This is what she means by her God's will: her stick bends my dislocated shoulder back out of the way, she prises my bloody body from my mother's womb into my father's arms. He gives a cry of revulsion, spattered. I struggle to cry out, choking, feeling the strange alien hairs that cloak his rough skin and the smell of him, fish and smoke and bitter dye.

My eyes peep open.

The slime drips from my ears, I hear the buzz of the

14

world around me, hear shapes flapping noisily in the doorway and windows, the hiss of breaking waves from the brightness outside, the superstitious cries of shapes like my father out there who think they saw God in the darkness of the sun, and I suppose the eclipse is finished ... but nothing's important, only my pain. 'A girl!' my father's huge voice booms in disgust. He must find money to burn a pigeon at least at the altar to thank God for my birth, he cannot afford a sheep or a lamb. And he may not lie again with my mother for many weeks; the birth of a girl defiles the mother more than the birth of a son. He averts his eyes.

'All's well,' the midwife says busily, then dares lift my broken helpless body from his arms. A kindly woman, with her own lips she sucks the blood and mucus from my mouth, rubs my eyes clear with the hem of her skirt. 'Look at her eyes!' She peers, what does she see? My eyes are the colour of indigo, violet-blue. She looks startled, as I find my voice, at the loudness of my infantile cries of fury, pain, desolation. My terrible newborn pain. She twists my arm into my shoulder, searching for the socket, pushes. Pushes again, frowns. Binds my broken elbow tight.

Cuts the cord, and I feel myself moving as the midwife turns to my mother. 'She's an angry little thing, this one!'

To my eyes my mother is an unfocused shadow in the bleary glare of the room, but I discern her shape sit up with the help of other women, and she holds out her hands towards me. I feel her nipple forced to my lips. Her warm arms want to enclose me. 'Miriam.' But I will not take the breast, I don't want to be Miriam, and I will not stop crying.

So this is life. I remember. I hate it.

Why am I here? Why was I born?

There's no reason for me except that my father lay with my mother. By chance one of Caleb's million billion seeds sparked one of the myriad eggs inside Leah, and I grew inside her as randomly as an ear of wheat. Human only because Caleb and Leah are human. A female by blind chance, the fall of the chemical dice in her womb. I was born in blood like any mammal, like a calf, or foal, or mouse, or you.

15

But *why* am I conscious, aware that I am myself and no other? Look at me, such a small frail baby to suffer so much! How can such a little girl as I be made to suffer such pain? My right arm stiff as a stick, my infected shoulder knobbly with arthritis, the joint grinding like an old woman's. I might have grown up not in pain, but then I might not have been born at all.

A few minutes ago, it seems, I had wisdom and the gift of prophecy (because knowledge of our past shows us our future, our terrible empty future). I understood all mysteries and all knowledge. Everything was certain, the weary orbit of the earth, the sterile patterns of the stars, the thermonuclear holocaust that illuminates the sun.

Now I have nothing. I am a child, I speak like a child, I understand as a child.

House. Mother. I must have her for everything. I learn to focus my eyes. I learn to reach out my hand. I learn to eat, to control my bowels, to crawl towards the light.

Soon the house is not enough. I crawl towards the sea, drawn by the rush of wind and waves. Early morning, the sea sparkles like jewels under the rising sun. Later fishing boats make patterns in the deep windless blue of afternoon. My mother screams, finds me, hugs me tight, smacks me, kisses me, clamps me to her breast. Good. I'm hungry.

I'm using her, her mother-love. I know I can get whatever I want. She gives milk to me, not to my father. She slips small fruit pieces to me, not him. I lie between them in their bed.

After the fire at the fish tower my father no longer smells of fish and smoke. He works where he can in the indigo fields, beyond the world I know. While I play a man comes to my father's house, Mother hands him her silver rings and earrings, closes the coins he gives her in her fist, and she weeps. For the first time I look at her, really look at her. Her arms, fingers, ears look strangely bare: my mother looks old.

It is spoken in the Mishnah, 'If two sit together and interchange words of Torah, the Divine Presence abides between them.' My mother, then, is my teacher. She explains the truth: 'God makes the sun rise.' To her it's obvious. She sighs, speaking to me simply because I am a child. 'God makes the middle of the day, He makes the setting sun.' To her these are literally facts of life. He made our sun for us, He made our sea, we try to live up to Him. 'And what God gives, Miri, He takes away.' Insects, worms and invisible demons have eaten my father's field of red soil. His crop of indigo flowers blacken in the drought. He breaks his back carrying buckets from the lake, but God wills that the flowers die. What sins does he conceal inside his body like invisible worms and insects, to be punished so harshly? Before hard times he was a dyer like his father before him, like my mother's father. Watching me play without a care in the world makes my mother both happy and afraid. Her daughter born during the darkness of the sun. Afraid for me, for what will happen to us.

The sea is what I love best, its restless waves hurrying like living animals, their sparkle, their fresh watery scent. At night, the rhythm of surf. A child dreams of life, not God. I love the clean wind blowing my hair growing long and dark, the wet lick of spray on my tongue.

Names, now. Galilee I know. Our Sea of Galilee's longer than my eye reaches, but not as broad. The sea of life, full of freshwater fish, two hundred fishing boats beached along the sand and pebbles each Sabbath morning. From our Dalmanutha shore the fields spread up like fingers, green, golden, crocus-yellow, indigo-blue, among the steep dust-blowing hills of the district. My father's field is sold but it is still our people's land, Mother says, our land and sea, our special Galilee made for us and given to us personally by God. We are chosen by Him to dwell here. She is chosen, I am chosen, she believes each of us in this God-soaked land has a personal covenant with God. Tears run down her cheeks. Everything has gone wrong for the Jews. For our sins, our failure to live up to Him, God gives over our land to lesser peoples, obscene peoples, profane Kittim who do not worship God, only gods. Mother curses their smooth faces: 'A Gentile does not die, for he has never lived.' How she hates them – and she is nobody! Yet she does. I play quietly, my tongue mumbling baby-talk against my unformed palate. But I understand every word she says. And one thing I know. To my mother, in my own small, complete way, I am simply her life.

And each day, I grow.

The Gentiles who have taken over our town know it by a Greek name, Tarichae, that my father and mother will not utter. Sadducee scribes travelling from Jerusalem write the name Magdala. Our Jewish quarter, the poor quarter named after the tower for smoking the Greeks' fish, is called the *Migdal Nunayah* which means the Tower of Fishermen in Aramaic, our spoken language which, as my palate closes, the muscles of my tongue are learning to speak with such speed.

I can say my name aloud now. Miriam.

But to my mother I am, like most children called Miriam (such a popular name), called *Miri* – Mary, that is. Mary simply means *one of us*, of our family. A name only for kin, uncles, aunts, once my grandfather walking from Sepphoris, and of course my mother and her closest friends – but believe me my mother has so many close friends! Close friends up and down the street and round the back (she averts her eyes from the houses of the rich Greeks), and leaving our stone house she pulls me quickly past the ramshackle wooden dwellings which flood in an easterly, then turns inland towards the square where Jewish market stalls flap their roofs like sails in the sea breeze. Every day – I'm about three years old – my mother tugs me along to a whole town meeting of everyone she knows closely, this buzzing sisterhood of women so big they make the sky dark and might tread on me with their huge dusty brown feet. They're the pampered daughters of Sion whose babble rises to Heaven, pushing and shoving, their smell as bitter as sweat and sweet as herbs, proud, generous, miserly, self-opinionated (some daring to wear rings of gold in their noses which the prophet Isaiah condemned), pounding clothes, picking carefully through vegetables (to eat a caterpillar brings down the wrath of God), fetching water at the drinking-well: now the pecking-order of daughters, mothers, grandmothers, crowding forward to the centre where the older women hold court. My father's mother is long dead, and Leah's own mother the Rainmaker is believed dead, no one knows where. Mother has no one to put in a good word for her. Her rings are gone, but see her pride in showing off her possession to them – me, her toddling daughter! Miriam's so pretty, Miriam's so clever, listen how

Miriam talks! I won't talk, I'm busy holding a stone in my mouth. Solitary me. Difficult me. I will get a smack.

Mother will never have another child. I am all she has. Her love for me, my power over her, is total. But only over her.

The apparent chaos of the square is a mass of invisible rules. The grandmothers observe the pale circles on Mother's arms where she wore her bracelets. Their eyes miss nothing. Their ears listen as she falls silent. There is much I do not know. My father cannot pay his debts. We are not up to this side of the square.

Mother pulls me home. 'Don't pay any attention to them, Mary! They're dry cunts!' she weeps while I play. It's herself she's talking to, her humiliation. 'Dry cunts, that's all they are!' She wipes at my dry face with her skirt, then wipes away her own tears. She says the dirty, forbidden, truthful word again, thinking I can't understand.

One day, much hotter, Mother encloses my hand in her own and strides along the black canyons between the black basalt houses. I slip from her grasp, play at hiding, then run after her broad, swaying, comforting, motherly backside between the beggars and the boys gathering goat-dung, horse-dung, donkey-dung, the best. It's *tetramenos*, the fourth month, the sun at its highest, so the sun says I am four years old exactly (the Sadducee priests whose chanting comes from the synagogue, the school or *shul*, use the moon for their calendar which makes me forty days older). This is the rough left-hand side of the square, furthest from the limestone *shul*-house with seats around the walls for when the Torah is read for the instruction of rich men's boys. Here on the left-hand side the urchins know better than Mother how pretty I am, twist my stiff arm and look with innocent faces when I cry. 'Quiet, Miriam, I'm busy. Give me some peace.' Mother leaves me in the dust to play with dirty-faced girls like myself while she talks. A boy bigger than us twists my elbow, I cry out, then put a stone in my mouth so that I am silent. These are rough women bringing up rough children but Mother devours their company like a greedy Greek devouring food. Still talking she prises the pebble from my mouth and I pop it in again as she turns away. She talks with her hands, eyes, body too, as well as her

19

voice! So quiet when at home in my father's house and under him in his bed, how she is herself in public! So silent when my father's in his house, how she complains about him here, among her new friends! All these women pounding and picking, shouting and complaining, and their complaints are all about their men. A man hurries by, ignoring us and ignored. This angry sisterhood, frustrated, contentious, indiscreet, impoverished, remains strangely invisible to them, the masters by night and in the home. By day their men scrounge for jobs, demean themselves with any sort of work for scraps, work repairing nets, cold wet work aboard a boat, hot dusty work hoeing the dye fields, bitter smoky work in the rebuilt fish tower. Worst, no work at all. But at home, with the closing of his door, each man however low is king.

I look around me and I begin to understand. The Greeks and Syrians cut Jewish labour cheap to the bone. After a day's work salting eels, food forbidden to us but not to the Greeks who flaunt their smooth pagan faces and scented bath-houses and stalls selling polluted blood meat, my father falls to the floor of our house like a dead man. He can no longer keep up appearances. His coat and beard crusted white with salt, his hands slimy with eel blood, he cannot remain the man he is and also a priest making sacrifice at the altar in his turn. His loss of face is withheld from me but it's impossible to keep a secret from a child. I see my father grow old, his dryness of faith making his body a living tomb. The salt draws the moisture from his flesh and turns his skin to leather. My mother's complaints fall silent. She has no money to bake bread. She lies beside him where he lies.

VIRI GALILAEI

men of Galilee

One day we help my father walk from our stone house to a wooden shack by the sea and cannot return home. Now this hut is all we have. My father lies on the rocks and stones, an old man suffering and not knowing how to repent. How has he so offended his God? By sacrificing at the wrong hour or with the wrong knife, or a stuttered word? Has he coveted a woman not his wife? Tongues wag, and Mother takes in washing for rich Greeks, and endures. I sit on the beach with a sea-smoothed pebble in my mouth.

Each day now my father, a white-haired shadow of himself, hobbles with his stick and listens outside the *shul*-house to the lessons and obscure disputations there. But one day he returns home with a spring coming into his step and I overhear him talking to my mother, and behind his words I catch his excitement. 'I saw a new man there today.'

'Today,' comes Mother's tired voice, working. 'Where?'

'Outside the *shul*-house. The people call him the Galilean. He's one of us.'

The Galilean. Curious, I drift silently into the doorway.

'Does he pay?' comes Mother's voice from the shadows. 'Does he give out work?'

'You should hear him speak,' my father says. 'Stop washing. Come and listen.'

Mother says, 'I'll stop washing when you start a job.'

Insolence to his face in his own home. But my father is a changed man. 'The Galilean,' he repeats. 'Judas, the Galilean.'

21

'Take that girl with you,' Mother says angrily, smoothing some Greek's tunic with a stone warmed by the fire. Breaks off to point at me. 'Why won't she talk? She does it to spite me.'

Father winks at me. 'You come with me.' But it's winter, the square and *shul* empty except for cold wind. Next morning my father keeps his promise and we return together. Now that Mother works rather than him, reversing the usual scheme of things, it is my father I am growing closer towards, and I stand in his shadow in the thin morning sunlight. A few people arrive, then more, then a large hurrying group. A man climbs the steps of the *shul* and turns. Raises his voice as though speaking to a crowd not a few scattered peasants. 'Thus saith the Lord: Who has brought pollution into the camp of Israel?'

It is an accusation. Even a child sees that from the stir among the people, as though the wind has blown between them. Pollution is such a powerful word, meaning uncleanness, evil, something against God. He is accusing them. Provoking them. The man on the steps waits for a response, but none comes. He demands, 'Are my countrymen cowards?'

'Cowards?' someone growls, but another says, 'Let the rabbi speak.'

My father bends down, whispers. 'Do you see Judas the Galilean, Mary?' I see the rabbi between the cloaks and legs in front of us: tall – he looks huge to me – with ragged black hair, ragged beard, the toes of his sandals peeping below the hem of a washed but threadbare white linen garment. Over this seamless, bleached, ancient gown the Galilean wears a cloak of yellow linen, not wool, and he carries a staff. 'An Essene monk,' my father murmurs in my ear. 'He wears only linen because it is made from flax, which grows from the pure living earth not the blood of an animal. His sandals are of wood and rope, not leather. He eats no animal and will not wear one.'

'Monks? They're not all monks, them.' Toothless Likhi the *shohet*, a Jerusalem slaughterer in his youth, pulls my father's sleeve. 'No, they live among ordinary folk, mostly. It's their duty, part time anyways. I remember 'em from Jerusalem, the Essene Gate. The most religious live in a fortress near the Dead Sea.' He sniffs, tousles my hair. If only he'd let me listen, but no. 'They've elected the Galilean their high priest. Their zadok.' I forget the other voices and stare up at old Likhi's moving lips with a child's rapt concentration. I remember telling you of that other zadok, Melchizadok, king-priest of Jerusalem in Abraham's day. The title's that old; older than Egypt, older than Noah the first zadok. Later, in the way of things, it became a name. Then Zadok the son of Ahitub anointed Solomon to be king against King David's command, won, and became head priest over his rival Abiathar – and the name *Zadok* had come full circle, was a title again. After Ezekiel's prophecy trusting in the house of Zadok as true Jews not to lead the people astray from God, the high priests were called zadoks, Keepers of the Covenant, Pillars of the World, for hundreds of years. Others called them troublemakers, fanatics, zealots. Pharisee traitors opened the Temple gates to Roman soldiers and the vegetarian zadokite priests were butchered as they calmly prayed and made their drink-offerings to the Lord and burnt incense, true Jews. Thirty years ago the Romans and King Herod installed Sadducee and Pharisee collaborators in the Sanhedrin council. Herod outlawed the title *zadok*. In Jerusalem Herod appointed his own meat-eating High Priest, or Priest-Messiah, to be Priest-Christ (their word for Messiah is Christ) over *his* people – three senile old men in the past year.

But if Likhi is right, this forceful Essene rabbi Judas has revived and renewed the zealot title of Zadok for himself even to the cloak of crocus-yellow. Only one step short of open rebellion against Jerusalem.

'Zadok,' Likhi whispers to my father. 'The Righteous One, the Pillar of the World. Reminds you, eh? Great days, they were. The Law pleased God.'

My father says uneasily, 'It's dangerous talk.' But he likes it. Look at all these shabby cloaks. The rich are not here. The poor soak up Judas's every word.

'My countrymen must be cowards,' the Galilean says fearlessly, 'cowards if they work under the Romans and the Greeks and call King Herod their lord. King Herod, who has not a drop of Jewish blood!' These words are treason, but he speaks Aramaic not Greek or Latin, and the Roman soldiers guarding the granary door yawn, bored. 'Our king has not one drop of true Jewish blood in his veins!' Eleven younger men range themselves in front of the Galilean on a lower step. Apostles, or guards against stones. Their number is always eleven to symbolise, under their leader who is the twelfth, the twelve tribes of Israel. Someone says at least three of the apostles are the Galilean's sons – another Judas, supposedly born in the provincial capital Sepphoris, another brother called Matthias, and the youngest brother, Simon, no older than fifteen but fierce. At least one of the other apostles, by his very long hair, is a Nazarene – a man who gains strength, like Samson who pulled down the temple at Dagon with his bare hands, by drinking only purified water never wine or beer, and leaving his hair uncut.

'The Galilean's not really from Galilee,' Likhi whispers dismissively. 'From the Golan, they say. Gamala maybe. Their hair's got red in it.' But newcomers arriving from the lake, fishermen mostly, hear the Galilean's name and take him for one of their own.

The Galilean calls out to the gathering crowd, 'In spring comes the Passover.' The people murmur, looking forward to the spring. 'Passover, the time when we remember the Lord saved His people from Egypt. When we remember Father Moses leading them to safety in the wilderness and receiving the Word of the Lord, his face burnt by the glory of the Lord.' The Galilean lifts his arms, raises his voice above our heads. 'The Passover is *our* Passover, when we offer up our thanks and our sacrifices as a sweet savour to the Lord in thanks for our deliverance.' He growls: 'Our Passover, when you will pay your taxes to Rome!'

The people fall silent, uncertain where this change of tack leads, how they should follow. A baby has fallen asleep in its mother's arms, dribbling, but I pull to one side so that I can peep round the mother's hip. I see spit in the Galilean's beard, his mouth moving. 'Yes, you'll pay your Passover taxes to Rome. You'll pay your harvest tax to Rome, and your head-tax to Rome, and your tithes to Rome, and plunder the riches of your land into the grasping hand of the Roman emperor who calls himself a god, *our* god!' The Galilean shouts: 'My countrymen, you are cowards! You are cowards if you submit to paying taxes to Rome and submit to mortal men as your lords instead of the Lord your God!'

The crowd push forward, but the Galilean climbs a higher step. 'One day soon, we shall plunder the riches of the Romans. One day soon, the Divine rain shall wash them back to Rome.'

A heckler shouts, 'How soon is soon?' A ripple of agreement runs through the crowd: prophets proclaim the end of history every day. The hip obscures my view; I crawl between legs, sandals, gowns, sit playing in the dust at the front.

The Galilean warns his heckler, 'I say to you, those who doubt me shall be killed for tolerating pollution in the land of Israel.' He reaches into his gown. 'And as for death, it is better to die gloriously than live a polluted life.' He pulls out a curved knife of the oriental sort, a *sica*. 'In the land of Israel are three groups of Jews. The Sadducees. The Pharisees. The Essenes.' The Galilean raises the knife so that it flashes in the winter sun. 'Now there is a fourth way!' The crowd shouts excitedly at the sight of the knife, an illegal weapon under Roman law. 'I am the way. The Fourth Philosophy is the way. We—' His arms stretch out to include the heads of his apostles below him, the knife glinting. 'We are the sicarii!'

The sicarii is not a name I remember hearing, ever. What's it about? This world makes its own path.

The eldest son, the one called Judas of Sepphoris, cries out to the crowd: 'Yes, we are the sicarii! We suffer for you, we are the true Jews, we are your brothers. Are you Greeks? Romans? Syrians? No, you are Jews. I call on you as Jews!' The Roman soldiers are coming over, alerted by the sight of the knife. My father tries to reach me but a swirl in the crowd carries him away. The Romans have drawn their swords, calmly cracking Jewish heads and shoulders with the flats of the blades as they push forward through the crowd. They're used to dealing with crazy Jewish disturbances; they don't understand what it's about and don't care. Judas of Sepphoris cries out again to us, covering his father's escape: 'For you, our brothers, we true Jews endure tortures and dismemberment. For you, brothers, we have been burnt and torn in pieces. We have been force-fed food forbidden us, camel-meat, slugs, and our brothers have been skinned alive in Herod's dungeons to make them blaspheme the Name of the Law-giver. But our brothers scorn those torturing them and give up their souls to the Lord as soon as they can! Why? To receive them back again after death! The Lord in His mercy will most surely raise us to both breath and life again, seeing how we give up our lives for the sake of His Laws.'

'Life after death,' a man behind me spits. 'They're lawyers.'

Judas of Sepphoris shouts: 'We must prove ourselves worthy of our brothers and welcome death, so that in His mercy we shall be received back again.' I stare up at his face, and he notices me. Judas stares from the step, silent because everyone is shouting now as the crowd mills around me, the solid mass breaking up into legs, arms, scuffling feet, and someone screams. A woman trips and more women trip over her, then they pull down men too.

Suddenly Judas reaches down from the step, lifts me to safety in his arms, and a man falls heavily where I sat.

Judas of Sepphoris whispers to me. Trying to make a child understand. 'We of the Way are above pain. Torture us and we smile. If our torturer strikes us we offer him the other cheek. We cannot suffer.'

'Come, brother,' Matthias says urgently. Then he calls to someone else, 'Menachem, come!' The soldiers are close now, their brown varnished armour gleaming brightly through the dust and struggling bodies below us. But I listen only to the words of Judas. *The King of the Universe, the Lion of Judah, will raise us up to new and everlasting life.* I'm hearing in a corrupted form almost the words that I was taught long ago, of Jesus Christ who saved us; but not here.

Judas shakes me, and I snap out of my daydream to dust, screams, the cold wind of this hellish place. The Galilean's son stares calmly into my eyes. 'Who are you?'

I can't reply. My pebble fills my mouth; I spit it into his hand. 'Miriam.'

My spit revolts him; he recoils. I feel the steps beneath my feet as he stumbles backwards, then his brother Simon lifts him, and I glimpse the bloody curve of the knife beneath Simon's gown. What does this mean? There's too much for

26

me to think about. A woman watches anxiously, her red hair bound in tight ringlets. Is she Judas's wife? A child of my own age stands beside her, his hair the mother's bright red, his hand held tight in hers. Judas of Sepphoris's son?

Judas of Sepphoris turns away, shepherds his family to the safety of our Magdalene alleyways and courtyards where the Romans will never find him. He stops. Looks back at me with those large brown eyes of his. Does he feel ashamed to be running away where I, a child, am staying? He shouts back: 'I call no man Lord!' Then he is gone.

In the empty square a few bored Roman soldiers stand scratching themselves by the body of the Jewish heckler killed by Simon's knife. The centurion shakes his head in disbelief, and I catch the Roman word for death. A Jew killed by Jews. It makes no sense to him.

Other shapes lie flattened in the dust where they were knocked down. Where is my father? One wears my father's robe. I shake him and his body does not move, or rather it moves too easily. I kneel beside him until his flesh stiffens and the touch of his dead meat and blood makes me filthy. I know death so well that I thought I was beyond grief, but my glands open and the hormones rush through my body and I weep. Dimly I hear my mother coming and her screams, but I am weeping and cannot stop. I am no longer a child.

Being four and a half years old, I no longer lived only for the present moment. Only babies do that. I remembered yesterday. I knew myself: Miriam the daughter of Caleb the dyer, once priest, once fisherman, no other. Deceased. I knew what hurt me and I knew what eased my pain. I had a particular sense of myself, of what was me and what not-me. I had memories. I remembered that day.

I woke screaming and weeping in the night, remembering what had happened, my father's robe slipping from his face as I knelt beside him. His terrible empty face. Nothing there. Gone.

My father died on that dreadful day and part of my mother died too, though she didn't have the strength to tear her clothes or show her grief. But something inside her flattened and became grey. She dulled. All humans and

27

animals have a soul whether we acknowledge it or not, and my mother's shrank that day, and dimmed, and she grew old inside herself. She no longer cared. We had no fire in the hut and we were cold. She was no longer the woman my father had married. There was nothing I could do; I hated her. The one day she had not gone gossiping to the square, the *one* day, my father had gone instead to hear something worthwhile that interested him and so he had died not her.

I more than hated her, I despised her. I wanted nothing of her in me. I wanted to grow up nothing like her.

'Did you love him so much when he was alive?' My mother's low voice came out of the dark. I heard the usual night surf through the thin walls but saw nothing of her. I had not slept and lay on the reed mattress exhausted as usual, wakeful as always, my knees drawn up to my chin. At last my mother's unbearably irritating whining voice came again from the dark. 'Now he's dead you're all tears for him, but you didn't show them when he was alive.' I wouldn't listen to her, I blamed her, it was her fault. 'Mary, the Lord gave your father a hard life, but he loved you.'

For the first time I spoke. 'Now he's dead you're saying this.' My voice broke. 'I loved him, not you.' I turned over and squeezed my eyes shut, trying not to see my memory of her lying tenderly beside him where he lay. It was no good. I put my hands over my ears.

But she was somewhere nearby, kneeling close to me. I couldn't shut out her whining whisper.

'Your eyes were cold when you looked at him, Mary.' The moon drifted from a cloud, silvering the sea that moved beyond the walls. Truly this was a house of sticks we lived in, full of gaps where the wind blew and the moon and sea shone through, not a home. From the earth floor her shadow reached out a hand towards me. She whispered, 'You have strange eyes, Mary! You're a strange little girl.' Had Judas of Sepphoris thought so too? I groaned. My mother was trying to shift the blame for my father's death to me. If only I had not gone with him, she was saying, he would not have died. In my fifth year as I was, my heart understood her perfectly.

Finally she said: 'Mary.' She wanted me to speak even if I said terrible things to her. She was lonely, hungry for the warmth of words that had sustained her all her life. I spat at her but she did not recoil. 'Stop it,' she said. I would have hit her if I could, I bunched my hands, but then I knew what would infuriate her most. I scratched up a handful of earth from the floor and pushed it in my mouth. 'Stop it!' she said.

I grinned. She couldn't make me do anything.

She said: 'Mary, don't.' Her hand flew, slapped me. We stared at each other amazed. What hurt was that she had never slapped my face before. She sat back on her heels looking shocked, then the moon went in and I jumped at her, where I thought she was, slapping at her with my hands and kicking with my bare feet, and my dress tore where she caught hold of me, but I struggled free spitting earth, kicking, punching. I wished I was my father with enough strength to kill her.

'Miriam.' My mother wrapped me in her arms, hard. 'Listen to me, Miriam. He's dead. Your father is dead.'

Oh, what love we small creatures give our parents! They take everything we have. She believed my father's fitful, flickering soul had been spirited to Sheol, the limbo where nothing happens and never will: she believed the dead are dead. She never prayed for my father; to her it would have been silly and superfluous. She simply honoured his memory. She didn't believe the King of the Universe would raise him up to eternal life, she'd never heard of it. But I'd heard Judas of Sepphoris, the lawyer, son of the Galilean, say those words aloud. And heard him claim that the God of the sicarii would raise His followers to life again, seeing they had given up their lives for His Laws.

I thought of my father's poor soul, probably hardly stronger than a spark, clinging to some sort of existence in the vast darkness below this world. So many humans have lived by now, in the forty thousand years since Man inevitably arose on this world, that for those with eyes to see they are dim swarming clouds like fireflies, their screams of agony and loss no louder than the squeaking of bats. And in that sea of almost-death only the strongest have learnt the strength to swim upward in their confusion towards the faint light of the sun.

By looking at Judas of Sepphoris, I had learned something of myself.

What had he seen in me? There was the mystery. He was only a man.

I whispered, 'My father's alive. He's with the fireflies.' Nothing my mother could say would change my mind. I clung to my grief with all the intensity of a child. The sound of footsteps walking past our hut made me burst into tears. No one knows grief as sharply as a child, grief that feels as if it will last for ever.

Grief does last for ever; I know. We never grow out of grieving: I know.

And with my grief came my anger. Grief and anger ran in the blood of my body, rushed with my heart when I woke, tossed and turned me in my sleep, filled my nightmares. It was better to be awake. My mother's poverty made us outsiders; I would be an outsider even to outsiders. Other children my age begged. Sarai's mother cut off Sarai's hair and bruised her face, I saw it, and Merak lay covered with sores that leaked chicken's blood. There were gates for begging and around them collected the children, the old, the sick, the blind feeling their way along the walls, the maimed crawling or dragged, the bedridden laid to beg at dawn and picked up at sunset. I sat against the wall in full good health yet coins were tossed at me. I learnt that people hurry past beggars with averted eyes, fearing what they will see, and that charity is cheap.

Other children my age were trained to steal, but I learnt the craft myself. The fingers of my left hand were long and naturally quick. Despite my stiff, clumsy right arm I learnt to slip through crowds like a draught. Too small for an adult to notice, too low to catch, I dodged pursuit as nimbly as a hare. I knew each turn, alley, stair. Often I spent a silver coin on roast lamb, or honey, or bread, standing on tiptoe to attract the stallholder's eye, before I crept home. My mother lay thin as a skeleton on her reed bed. But usually it was dark and I need not look at her.

I was always quiet, and I always worked alone. Thinking only of myself, I thought no one noticed me. One day near the fish tower – I remember the smell of the smoke like remembering my father's smoky smell – suddenly some boys surrounded me. They were dirty as I, barefoot, clad only in rags, but you probably remember from being my age how huge and dangerous a gang of ten-year-olds look. I wasn't afraid, I met their eyes. The eldest stuck his finger against my chest. 'You. Not here. This here's ours. Greeks' street to the fish tower's ours. You get off.' He didn't like me looking at him. He wasn't bright, but someone noticed my right arm and twisted it. I felt my joint tear, I heard it inside myself. The pain burst out. I bit my tongue – two pains do not hurt as much as one – and I made no sound. I crept and lay in a doorway too angry and ashamed to go home that night, and the next morning I was dizzy with fever. Someone who knew of me, Sarai I was told, pushed me home but I don't remember why. She had never spoken to me before, let alone helped me. I remember shouting at her, 'Leave me alone.' I remember the odd sadness in her distorted face, the shrug of her shoulders as she turned away. We were not friends until years later.

I remember the smell of earth and wood, home, my mother putting her cold dry hand on my forehead, murmuring, 'Where have you been?' I spat at her but the spit fell back on my face. 'Don't be dirty,' she said, but her breath smelt of age and defeat, not mine. She hurt my arm, believing the pain to be caused by a demon, but it would not come out. She bent down through the slats of sunlight crisscrossing the hut and tried to plant a kiss on my lips, but I turned my head away. My body was racked with sobs of rage. Her eyes gleamed. She wanted me back again inside her; my fever conjured her opening her legs, pulling me back into her mousy *gula* and the warm red closeness of her womb again where she could care for me completely: always my mother. To suckle me with her belly, making me her own again. I remembered ten thousand generations of women crouching behind her, a thousand times ten thousand dropping the issue of their bodies into the mists of time, daughters, mothers, grandmothers fading into fuzzy low-browed shapes more like monkeys than women, but all with the same gleam in their eyes, the same loving kiss of a mother to her child.

'Sleep,' she whispered.

ECCE VIRGO CONCIPIET

behold a virgin shall conceive

When I awoke, everything was darkness. Time had passed. The fever had retreated from the front of my brain and my arm was numb. Someone was speaking and my mother snored. There was no one else in the hut. The voice spoke again quietly into my ear, and the sound of my mother sleeping faded into the background. 'Do not turn.' A breeze fluttered against my hair; then all I heard was a voice speaking close enough to my ear for me to feel the lips moving.

The voice whispered, 'Miriam, do not go to Sepphoris.'

Sepphoris was the name of the city beyond the hills where my grandfather lived. I'd never been there and didn't suppose I would. I whispered, 'Who are you?'

The voice said, 'I am the angel Gabriel.'

I turned my head, but the fluttering breeze moved, keeping close to my ear. I could not believe this was the voice of an angel. Moses had claimed that the Voice of God (which only he had heard) had sounded to his ears like the thunder of falling mountains. This voice was a child's, no stronger or deeper than mine.

I whispered, 'You are a demon. A mischievous soul. There are no angels.' I turned my head suddenly, and saw the angel.

If it was an angel. You would call such a faint creature a fairy. Luminous, transparent, it was a pattern of golden glow. I laughed, childishly enchanted. The fluttering breeze came from its wings; I felt the coolness of it against my eyes.

'You're real.' But when I tried to see its tiny face, neither male nor female, perfect, I saw the effort that kept it near me, and my eyebrows drew together in curiosity as I realised. 'This is hard for you.'

'Because you are small of faith.'

Its glow faded and the snores of my mother grew loud. Grey dawn showed through the slats of the walls. 'Come back!' I whispered. 'You're real. You're as real as a dream. I do believe in you, while I'm asleep.'

But I knew I was not asleep. An angel or a demon pretending to be an angel was really here, somewhere. Its golden glow returned, its wings fluttered against my ear. It gasped, 'Listen to me. There is something you must see. Close your eyes.'

It was such a ridiculous command: close your eyes to see. But I do close my eyes, and I can see a small window, with dawn just beginning to show: I'm in a room about the size of my mother's hut in Galilee, but with stone walls. An old woman sits on a stool by the dismal sheen of a fire, almost out. Her face is lined, her ragged white hair hangs over her shoulders, she breathes laboriously. Her gnarled hands rest on her parted knees, her head drops forward, she's almost asleep. Then she lifts her head with a groan of discomfort, pushes into the small of her back with her knuckles. And I see the old woman's belly hangs forward like a mound between her thighs. She's with child!

At her age. Again she groans.

The angel whispers, 'You see Elizabeth, wife of Zacharias the shepherd, a priest of the Jerusalem Temple descended from King David's great high priest, Zadok – a proud history which he has sense enough to keep quiet, though it burns his brain. Zacharias wears the turban of Aaron's priestly family, and he is a respected and deeply holy man permitted by God, by the drawing of lots, to enter the Holy of Holies of the Great Temple on Mount Sion.'

I stare at the woman, baffled, afraid she'll overhear our voices. 'She's so old! How did Zacharias get her with child? Is he old as her?'

'Older. He did not believe the joyous news I brought him. Elizabeth will bear him a son named John, not Zacharias after his father's name, as is the rule. For his complaints and disbelief Zacharias the priest is struck dumb by me and sent into the hills with his sheep until the birth. And until he names his son John.'

John. What an odd, unusual name – especially as the angel insisted on it as such a matter of importance. What new prophecy, or new destiny, was the angel trying to fulfil? I remembered many Johanans and several Jonathans, and even a couple of Johas, and traditionally Jonan the son of Eliakim was the father of Joseph the shepherd, earthly guardian and teacher of Jesus Christ – the Christ I had expected to find ruling over Jerusalem in Abraham's time, you recall, not Melchizadok. But John. The only John I could think of was John the Baptist, who by tradition prepared the way and spread the teachings of Jesus with his letters and so forth, the Epistle to the Kubnites, Athenians I and II, the Letter to the Sons of Heth, his First and Second Letters to the Philistines, many others. But Abraham had found no John the Baptist in Jerusalem any more than he'd found Jesus Christ.

But here was this small creature claiming to be the archangel Gabriel, with a childish unbroken voice and a fluttering, flickering glow.

The old woman groaned again, trying to get her big behind comfortable on the wooden stool. From outside I heard the footsteps of a visitor approaching the door. As they drew near, a delicate tread, ladylike, my curiosity became intense – who was she? But the angel came closer to my face until it seemed immense, and the brightness of it made me flinch. 'She approaches. Behold, I am the archangel Gabriel!' Its wings roared around me. 'Close your eyes, Miriam, and watch what I shall show you, which has already happened! Not here in Jerusalem. Here in a house in Galilee.'

The sun came on and I shielded my eyelids from the blinding light, the brilliant radiance filling the house where I now was. I drew a deep breath. I was seeing last year. I inhaled the warm breeze blowing through the windows, no longer winter, scented with crops and harvest. Brilliance radiated from the archangel Gabriel, the immense figure of man or woman that it now was, something above sex, its halo the sun around its head in the tall room, and the wind blowing from the slow beat of its white-feathered wings set the spinning wheel in the corner clattering. The girl by the table held a flask of water, interrupted at some household task. She did not move. But her eyes moved, and I saw her calmly observing her visitor in the glory of the power it represented. Her face was so beautiful. So intent. So unafraid. I wanted to be like her. For the first time I tried to hide my twisted arm from the angel.

She had seen an angel before. I was sure of it. She glowed in its reflection. I saw the curve of her hips and loins, her youthful eagerness.

The archangel Gabriel greeted the girl courteously with its great voice. 'Hail, Mary! Virgin highly favoured by the Lord, virgin full of grace, the Lord is with you. You are blessed above all women, and blessed above all men born until now in this world.' These were not exactly the traditional words I remembered from the Bible. Yet I witnessed the archangel saying them.

The girl, who could not have been more than a willowy fourteen or so, knew to bow her head in humble prayer: pride in such a compliment from such a messenger might be her fall. She was certain in her belief, which I was not, that the archangel was sent to her by God.

The archangel said, 'Fear not, Mary.'

Mary: the archangel addressed her as a sister, family. 'Who is she?' I whispered.

My angel's boyish voice returned, and whispered in my ear. 'She is Miriam, of the same name as yourself, a virgin presented to the Temple by her wealthy parents Joachim and Anna, who are the heirs of King David's royal line through David's second son Nathan. At her induction when she was three years old, Mary climbed unaided the fifteen steps from the Court of Women to the Temple, greeted her uncle the priest Zacharias on the third step of the altar, and was kept in the Temple sanctuary until her marriage at the age of twelve.' It seemed extraordinary that I might actually be watching the Virgin Mary, just an ordinary girl as she was now, standing by an ordinary table. Yet she believed in the archangel: look how powerful it had grown. Had it or some other angel prompted Isaiah's famous prophecy, 'Behold, a virgin shall conceive'?

My angel whispered naughtily, 'At the age of twelve, even the purest and holiest virgin pollutes the sanctuary of the Lord with uncleanness. A husband must be found. Zacharias prayed in the Holy of Holies. The Lord came to him there in the smoke and golden darkness and told him, "Call every widower to the Temple, put a stick into each man's hand." There in the Temple court a dove alighted on the stick held by a man named Yosef, or Joseph, called by his people Alphaeus which means First. He's the firstborn son of Heli whose family name is Cleophas, last of the line of King David through King Solomon; another title Joseph holds among the Essenes is *Mashiya*, Christ, the Saviour, from his power to baptise Jews into the life of the monastery. The dove was a sign of the Lord's approval. Through Joseph and Mary, King David's royal line was to be reunited and blessed anew after a thousand years of separation.'

'She *married* Joseph?' What was this? 'The Virgin Mary has married a *man*?'

'Two years ago she took the first oath of betrothal to Joseph.' Joseph I understood, though not the rest of it about the title Alphaeus, and Cleophas, and Christ. And Joseph was the son of Heli not of Jonan? Who was Heli? The angel quickly continued: 'But Joseph, being an Essene of Judah, a just and pious man, hasn't taken her. Only the most important Essenes marry at all, and the ritual requires several years of engagement before consummation. And Joseph isn't young. If he'd married a girl of twelve hook, line and sinker it would have made him a laughing stock, everyone saw that. But Zacharias wanted the best for his niece.' Naturally – the priest wouldn't be human if he hadn't seen the opportunities in such a powerful dynastic marriage, a union of the two royal Davidic lines in any child born of Joseph and Mary. Being of the Pharisee party, Zacharias hated the Romans almost as much as he hated his superiors the Sadducees, favoured by Herod and Rome.

'So how did Zacharias persuade Joseph?'

'Zacharias returned to the Holy of Holies for guidance then came out and warned him, "Hear the Lord your God, Joseph, and remember what God did to the cities of Dathan and Abiram and Korah, how the earth split and they were swallowed up because of their disobedience. Be afraid,

Joseph, unless it happens in your own house." ' Of course Joseph believed him – it was true there had been earth-quakes, not least at the great Essene monastery by the Dead Sea.

I said, 'So Joseph married her because he was afraid.'

'Is she not very, very beautiful?' My angel winked, lewd as a cupid, then withdrew from me as though I, or the world itself, had contaminated it. Yes, I think it was very hard for it to come here. If it was who it said it was.

'The child would be born a king,' I said. 'A king without a throne. What will King Herod say about that?'

'Herod shall bow down in awe.'

'He'll call it a Jewish plot. He'll have them executed.'

'King Herod is old and his days are not beyond number.'

I saw behind the show of sticks and doves to the plan. 'Zacharias the priest and Joseph the Essene, with the backing of Joachim the rich wool merchant, are plotting for the child to be a Jewish *Mashiya*?' I said. 'A Christ for all the Jews, not just Essenes but Pharisees, Sadducees, everyone?'

'*The* Christ. And He shall be more than Priest-Christ, more than King-Christ,' the angel whispered. 'He shall be the One. All Man shall see and bow down before Him. He shall save you all, every man, every woman, every child, every foreigner, every dog and every cat. He will be your salvation.' The little angel pointed its fluttering, luminous finger at the towering manifestation of itself five months ago, here in the spacious sunny house of Mary's mother Anna. 'Watch. Listen.'

The archangel was speaking in its voice as great as the wind. 'In choosing chastity, Mary, you have found favour with the Lord, therefore you, a virgin, shall conceive without sin, and shall bring forth for the Lord your firstborn son. He shall be great, and you shall call Him Immanuel, God is with us, because He shall rule from ocean to ocean, and from the River Jordan to the ends of the earth. He shall be called the Son of the Most High, because He who is born on earth in humiliation reigns in Heaven in exaltation. The Lord God will give Him the throne of His father David, and He shall reign in His house for ever, and His kingdom here shall have no end. He is King of kings and Lord of lords, and His throne is from everlasting to everlasting.'

All this sounded so familiar to me, so . . . *Christian*. Tears of nostalgia came to my eyes.

But the girl gave a shiver of dread. She had never heard words like these except in the diatribes of the prophets, and such theological and sexual concepts (where's the difference, both are immortality) were beyond her experience as a young girl, though doubtless not beyond her dreams – and by tradition the true Virgin had herself been conceived by a kiss not by sinful bodily union. But this girl's voice did not quaver. 'How can it happen, seeing that my husband is not here? How can I bring forth a child without seed?'

The angel was as frank as she. 'Think not, Mary, that you shall conceive in the manner of mankind. The Holy Spirit shall come upon you and the power of the Most High shall overshadow you without the heat of lust. As a virgin, without intercourse with a man, you will conceive. As a virgin you will bring forth. As a virgin you will nurse. He who shall be born of you will alone among men be holy, because He alone, being conceived without sin and born without sin, shall be called the Son of God.'

'The Son of God,' she murmured. She'd do it. Any girl would, if she believed what she was told. And this sheltered young lady, in a torment of unfulfilled adolescent desire as she must naturally be at her age, despite her milky-smooth demeanour, had not set foot outside the Temple from three until her thirteenth year. In the Temple she was used to the awe of gold and cleanliness and the impressiveness of great structures, devotion to God, ritual, discretion, utter obedience. The scarlet and purple threads of her portion of the Temple veil that she had been spinning still clung to her hem. She was hardly more than a child, married to a man three times her age, so I was unsurprised when she simply stretched out her hands obediently, raised her eyes to Heaven, and said in her calm pale voice, 'Behold, I am the handmaiden of the Lord, for I am not worthy of the name of lady. Let it happen to me according to thy word.'

The archangel's wing swept aside, and a ray of sunlight burst through the window, through the flask of water, through (it seemed) the virgin herself. That was all. The archangel stretched its wings in a curtsey and was gone. As the scene faded I glimpsed a plump woman who must be

Anna, the girl's mother, hurry from another room and embrace her daughter, congratulating her. Then they were gone and I was left in darkness. As my vision adjusted I saw I was back in Elizabeth's room, the gritty old woman groaning pregnant on her hearth stool, grey dawn in the high window, and footsteps tap-tapping in the street outside as someone approached.

I whispered to my angel, 'What really happened to the virgin?'

'Exactly what you saw.'

'The ray of light?'

'And the Word of God. She has conceived.' The small luminous creature pulled angrily at my ear. '*She* believed. Why can't you?'

I struggled for words. 'It's not the same when you see it with your own eyes.' Anyone would expect trumpets, hosannas, clashing cymbals, but it looked so . . . real. Almost domestic. 'How was it done?'

He was almost too faint to see in the growing daylight. 'Truly you are a demon!' the angel hissed. 'A demon in a world of demons. You don't deserve salvation.'

'I am what my life makes me; I go where my life takes me.'

'Then you have no willpower or constancy.'

'What choice do I have?'

'In your long life all you've learned is doubt, all you've gained is loss. If you no longer work to be saved, you have no faith.'

It knew who I am, who I really am. Perhaps it really was an angel.

'My name is Mary, too,' I whispered. 'Help me. If you are who you say you are, help me.'

I stare right through the angel. It's almost gone.

There was a knock on the door and I remember the tapping footsteps. The old pregnant woman cries out something incoherent in her distress, the door opens, and the young girl, Mary, lifting the hem of her blue gown delicately, her head wrapped in a white scarf, descends the street steps into her aunt's room. The Virgin, so-called, is not as beautiful as I remember, her eyes reddened by tears, her smooth white skin shadowed by unhappiness, her

39

expression withdrawn. Had she really expected her husband to believe her?

I watch the two women standing together, the curves of their bellies almost touching, yet two generations of age separating them. By her heaviness Elizabeth has less than three months to wait. Both women grow joyful now with each other's company, in their excitement building on each other loudly (and dangerously) with the usual Jewish talk of putting down monarchs and raising high the people who are low: themselves; they truly believe they hold the future of the world in their bellies. Each believes she holds the Lamb of God in her womb. They stroke each other wonderingly with the flats of their hands, yet both have known anguish. Zacharias, struck dumb and sent away; and I can guess what happened when Joseph returned from Judah to lie for the first time with his young wife.

'Joseph has put her away,' my fading angel agrees. 'It is the Essene rule that a betrothed woman should fall three months' pregnant before the full celebration of marriage, lest she be found barren. To be childless is God's punishment to the husband for some secret sin. So he must lie with her first to be sure of God's blessing. But when Joseph spoke to her as her husband and came to her room freely and erect to be with her he saw that her belly was obvious, five months with child. Yet she promised him she was a virgin.'

Bulging with pregnancy and she said she was still a virgin? What was Joseph to do, who could he consult on this most important and delicate matter? Zacharias was absent, silenced. Samuel, the Pharisee filling the old priest's shoes? Too young to be trusted by an Essene. Joseph could hardly ask advice from the high priest of Jerusalem, the Priest-Christ Joazar, nephew of King Herod's queen! And Joachim, Mary's father, insisted her incredible story was true. So did Anna her mother. They would, of course. Yet, whatever his private feelings, if Joseph was a just man (and he was) he could not expose his wife to public condemnation while doubt existed. He shut his eyes and decided that a baby was not proof of fornication. A pious man (as he was) would not blacken his wife's name, and thus his own, on mere suspicion of her fornication. He was in love with

40

her, he was desperate to keep her, but he must have been as deeply hurt as any man. So he decided to send her away to Elizabeth's house and let the two women share their tribulation together, and wait on events he knew were coming.

I almost miss that. 'What events?' I murmured.

I woke suddenly in my mother's hut by the Sea of Galilee. The surf, the cries of fishermen and *taracheutae*, salt-fish sellers. Mid-morning, and the sun spreading a brilliant pattern of shadows across my mother's face. She smiled, resting her hand on my forehead, then kissed me.

Then I woke fully and said, 'It wasn't a dream.'

What had taken me? Where had I gone? In time as well as place. I had been held by something altogether greater, then, than my own great power. You can imagine what I wondered. Whether everything the angel had shown me might be not only true but also fact. Whether I'd witnessed something happening yet beyond the laws of nature. Whether there might really, somehow, too late, be a God.

I murmured, 'Wait on events? What events?' My mother's smile showed no change, thinking I still dreamt, and she heard no reply, but I heard the archangel's voice boom in my head like the wind that shook the hut.

'*Miriam, do not go to Sepphoris.*'

'Now that my forty days in mourning for your father are over,' my mother told me, 'your grandfather is coming from Sepphoris to collect us.'

She had eaten properly, washed and combed her hair, and now she sat beside me on the beach and again reached out her hand to me. Reaching out was now her habit with me, she was always touching my warm face with her cold dry cheek as though reassuring herself of my existence, squeezing my warm hands with her cold fingers, straightening my belt unnecessarily, tightening the latchet of my shoes and infuriating me with her fussing. I was all she had. I could not love her, she needed me so. Her love was an oppression. My mother would have died for me. Unbearable oppression. I pulled away from her and hurt her.

'Collect us? He's going to take us back with him to Sepphoris?'

'I know you don't know your grandfather,' she sighed,

41

shielding her eyes against the sunlight as she looked at me, the sea breeze of Galilee flapping her hair and clothes, 'but it's the Law. Someone has got to look after me. Take responsibility for me. We're going to live in his house.' A woman cannot live without a man. If her husband dies her father must look after her. Or her brothers. Or her husband's father. Somebody. Or she must beg or be a whore. My mother, I knew, had neither the strength nor the face to simply sit, as I did, and be tossed coins.

'You should go,' I said.

She laughed. 'You! Not yet five years old, and she treats her mother like someone she doesn't need for everything!' She hugged me. Then she squeezed my cheeks with her fingers, rubbing noses, and my body responded with a childish giggle. Part of me loved it. She tickled me. 'I know how to make you laugh!' I drew back from her. Her face lost its momentary animation, became dull.

We stared at the crisscrossing sails, the dun far hills rising above the blue sea-haze.

'I know you don't know him,' she repeated. 'But you will. He's a just man, your grandfather. You will grow to love him.'

On the contrary, I knew Levi the dyer all too well. Mary the Rainmaker was married to him for thirty years (technically she still was married to him, since her death was unknown) and, believe me, she'd never grown to love him. I remembered him as sultry, tall, decisive, handsome in the eyes, the sort better seduced than married. His lovely bald, circumcised cock. But they did marry, both young. He couldn't live with a woman of spirit, and she couldn't live with a man who couldn't think for himself. Levi completely lacked talent, spark, originality. But he was persistent. And that cock. The Rainmaker gave him Leah his daughter and left his house, and Levi dragged her back. She wandered in the desert and he found her. She went into the town and he fetched her. He beat her to teach her, naturally, and each time he taught her better, until one morning she put out the light of his left eye with her fingernail which she had sharpened in the night. She walked away from him and made her name as a prophet drawing her circles in the dust, drawing rain, and he did not follow her again. Except in his

42

mind, day after day, when she was his first thought and his last, as he saw her in his blinded eye. To him she was still alive, still unforgiven. That's the sort of man Levi was: that's how well I knew him.

But I had wanted him, that first time, as much as she: had I by love, as well as by doubting God, been the Rainmaker's damnation?

Having grown up crushed under her father's thumb, Leah married a man as much as possible like her father. But now Caleb was dead and the forty days was over. Leah had none of her mother's spirit, she wouldn't run off into the desert. It was back to Father for her. That was all she could think.

'We could stay here,' I said.

'Where?'

'Here. Magdala.' I pointed at the sooty, mossy, reeking fish tower. '*Migdal Nunayah*.'

'Oh!' she cried, cuddling me. 'You don't know anything!' She kissed me and hugged me. 'I'd love to eat you! We'll be so happy in Sepphoris!'

'I don't want to go to Sepphoris.'

She sighed.

'I heard the angel tell me,' I said. 'Miriam, do not go to Sepphoris.' I embellished it. 'The angel told me, "Miriam, Miriam, do not go to Sepphoris!" ' My mother covered my mouth angrily: silence. I turned my head away. 'But I did hear it.'

I stood on the edge of the sea. She followed me and brushed the blowing hair out of my eyes. 'I didn't hear anything. Mary, don't let anybody hear you talk like that.' She spoke so close that I felt her warm breath on my eyes. 'It makes trouble. People will think you're strange.' She was thinking of her own mother and how unhappy she'd made everyone who loved her. Which was only Leah, in truth. But I realised Leah still loved her mother's memory intensely. Sometimes this world works in such happy and unhappy ways it's difficult to believe it's so random. So completely chance. Difficult, sometimes, to believe in such complete abandonment. Why are the good punished and the wicked rewarded? Because that's the way this world works. Leah was no worse than most but she'd suffered much. Perhaps she didn't wear holiness on her sleeve as much as she

43

should; Levi, a violent and misunderstanding man, was a priest, and holy, and respected, and owned his own house with a courtyard.

'Don't let people think you're strange,' she murmured, stroking me. 'Don't hear voices as my mother did! You're normal and mine and I love you.' She trembled. So afraid for me. So loving. So undeserving of unhappiness.

I stood in the water to get away from her, the waves washing my ankles. She didn't scold me for wetting my shoes. 'You'll like Sepphoris,' she called. 'You'll be happy there.'

I stood in the waves, and my grandfather did not come that day. He did not come the next day either. The morning afterwards, my mother called to me over and over (I would not come to her quickly) to witness an extraordinary sight: smoke blew across our hilltops from far away. Work was being done on the Sabbath. I played, but I knew better than she, for fields burn with a white or bluish smoke like bonfires, and this smoke was dense, black, oily. It came to us all day as a fine mist, the smoke of burning buildings, towns, flesh, far away. I knew this smell, I licked it on my tongue, I knew the taste of death. Killing was the work done today. War is legal on the Sabbath. Rumours flew, and people began to run.

As always, the sea would be safe. Along the beach fishermen piled their nets and snares into their boats, took aboard the possessions of anyone who could pay, and counted their money. Soldiers guarding the armoury beat any who came near, and the poor, who had no property to defend or save, gathered round the *shul*-house until the soldiers scattered them. My mother came home with a bruised face. The Jews were fighting the Romans in Sepphoris, capital city of Galilee! No, Herod's soldiers were killing Jews in the streets and the Romans were confined to barracks, seeing who won. I thought of my grandfather Levi and hoped he was dead. I thought of Judas of Sepphoris and wondered if he were there with his father the Galilean, and imagined the sicarii with their curved knives fighting in the streets of Sepphoris. They'd kill Jews who didn't join the rebellion. I tried to remember the names of the other men I had seen, Matthias, Simon, and I remembered the woman, young Judas's wife, watching quietly with her son. But perhaps I was wrong, and the sicarii were not involved at all. During the afternoon heat I made money from the rich women sent by their husbands to be on the beach (and make sure the fishermen didn't sail away with their wealth) by selling them cups of water, which amused my mother no end and set her shaking her head at my cleverness, since the fat crones could dip it from the freshwater sea for free. But these scented loathsome creatures, the Rich, were momentarily too flustered to think for themselves. One woman fat and white as a worm stroked my long black hair, looked into my eyes and laughed to her friend, 'She's so pretty. Couldn't I take her for mine?'

The other woman watched me. 'Damaged goods,' she said spitefully. She twisted my arm and I screamed. 'Told you, Athaliah. You have no taste.' I ran away with my pain, I knew not where.

It was dark when I found my way back, and a donkey stood outside our hut. The cargo had been unloaded from its back but not the big empty baskets. The donkey drank thirstily from my cup. I fetched another, watching the firelight flicker from inside the hut. Mother never had a fire. I didn't want to go in. The donkey stood asleep. I could hear a man's voice droning.

I ducked through the tattered wool flap of the doorway and stared. I hardly recognised Levi now he was my grandfather not my husband. He was still tall, but stooped, grey as a sheet, his skull and chest fuzzed with grey hair. His right eye was as I remembered, round and dark, but his left eye stared like a white ball with blindness, and his grey face was lined. He looked like his father, and he smelt of fear. Dust. But mostly fear, its smell as sweet as spilt blood, as though he had made sacrifice. 'Hotheads!' he said in his high voice. He had walked through the Sabbath, no doubt, and now he was drinking wine. There was a jumble of goods in the corner. 'All I own. Hotheads!' he repeated, then glared at me ferociously with his one good eye, but it felt to me he saw inside me with his white blind ball.

'Children stare so!' my mother apologised, washing his feet. 'Miriam, this is your grandfather.' I was not supposed to speak, must hide myself quietly in bed.

'I won't go with him,' I said. 'I won't. The angel told me not to go to Sepphoris.'

'Angel!' My mother gave a high, anxious laugh. 'She's a dreamer.' She made a private face like a snarl at me.

'An easy command to keep, that,' Levi muttered to his wine. 'There's no Sepphoris to go to.' He grunted: 'Burnt. Hotheads! Our great buildings burning and falling, and we were proud of them. Men crucified along the roadside, blood everywhere. Disgusting.' He slurped again while my mother dried his feet, that dreadful white eye staring at me as if in blame. 'Men I knew. Customers. Suppliers. My own servant was taken, not fast on his feet. You should have heard the screaming. No, let the child hear it.' He made a ghastly screaming sound in the back of his throat, spattering wine. Then wailed again, a fading gargle like the rattle of a dying man. 'Like that.'

'Go to sleep,' my mother warned me. I knelt on my bed, the reeds hard under my knees.

'Taxes,' Levi grunted. 'That's all we cared about, why not? Taxes, getting blood out of stones, we had no more to give, did we? A third taxes, a third tithes, a third donations, a third offerings, what more had we to give but our blood? The blood of our young men, anyway. We were reasonable in our demands, the priests were on our side. There was talk of taking King Herod to court under the Law. We had a case, even the king must obey the Law. Pleased with ourselves, we were. The matter would go forward in the proper way. But then poor scum pushed to the front, someone shouted out that someone was cutting throats, and people with knives jumped up before the priests and shouted down us good Jews and accused us of bringing pollution into the land of Israel, of cowardice, saying we should plunder the riches of the Romans, and—' He buried his face in his cup.

'We are the Way,' I said.

'That's right,' he said, thinking my mother had spoken. But she abased herself on her knees, whispering to his clean white feet, 'I'm sorry, forgive Miriam's tongue, that's the rubbish she heard the day her father died. She was with him in the square. She hasn't recovered; she has nightmares.'

Levi hardly heard her, he heard only himself. We were

shadows, his women. 'Anyway,' he muttered, 'the mob broke into the armoury, swords, spears, turned the city into a butcher's stall. In the dark I got away with all I own, except bits and pieces and my dyeing vat, and that's too heavy to carry. And my pots. A few trinkets I buried only I know where. I've been all day in the mountains; look how the sun's burnt my neck! Got to Arbela before I left the smell of blood behind me. I'm staying here. I'll look after you, yes, I'll look after you!' He nodded for my mother to drop more wood on the fire. 'I'm going to need a servant.' My mother rubbed his neck with oil.

I had obeyed the angel's command, we were not going to Sepphoris; but it seemed Sepphoris had come to us. There would be refugees by the thousand.

'Rough hands, you've got,' Levi complained. He pointed at me. 'Let her do me. Gentle.' I rubbed his stinking neck, childlike, obedient. A man's smell never changed.

As I rubbed I murmured, 'Will the soldiers come here?'

'It's over,' he said sleepily. 'The Galilean's on the run for his life. He's high in the Golan by now, if he's got sense. They'll never find him there.' After any rebellion the losers fled to the wilderness of Upper Galilee and either hid out successfully or committed mass suicide. 'At the inn by Arbela, I met this salt merchant from Jerusalem. All the fuss spread from Jerusalem, see, so what he says is kosher. The Galilean had two sons, Judas of Sepphoris and the other, Matthias, and he'd sent them to Jerusalem. Herod's dying. His sons are all plotting against him, and their wives, and his wives, and all of them backstabbing each other too. So Judas of Sepphoris saw his chance, jumped up in front of the worshippers at the Great Temple. Herod had ordered that golden statue of a Roman eagle to be put up over the Temple entrance, that big staircase. A golden eagle, a blasphemy, a pagan idol, flouting the Law. But Herod had done it and all believers had to pass beneath the eagle however thick they covered their heads. And at last here was young Judas shouting to the crowd telling them just what they wanted to hear, pull down the Roman eagle, strike your blow for freedom under the Law, be free under the Law and slaves to God not Herod, not Rome, earn your reward from God for your righteousness. And if they kill you, what better death than dying as true Jews to keep and observe the righteous Law of your fathers?'

Righteous, that word again. The zadok, Righteous One, Pillar of the World. I remembered the staff Judas the Galilean, the zadok, had carried. Not really a staff, a sceptre. The Law promised: 'A Star will rise from Jacob, a Sceptre to rule the world.' One day Jerusalem, not Rome, would rule the world.

I murmured, 'Did the crowd tear down the Roman eagle?'

Levi was almost asleep. 'Of course. They were worked up, they'd do anything. Then Romans surrounded them with drawn swords. Their eagles are gods to them. Each Jewish man knew he'd die, and each Jewish woman knew she'd die, and their children would die too, and quietly they gathered together and bared their necks to receive the blades. They would die for the Law. But the priests talked among themselves. They stepped over the Roman eagle and parleyed with the centurion. "Better a few should die than many. Judas and Matthias and their sicariot followers are guilty of sacrilege in their zeal for the Law. Take them but spare us." So the Romans nabbed Judas of Sepphoris and his brother Matthias and other sicarii, tortured them, pulled the skin off their heads together with the hair, crucified them, took them down and burnt them alive, burnt their followers, and spared the crowd.'

'Praise be,' my mother prayed. She frowned at the tears she saw in my eyes. She blamed the sicariots for my father's death, but Judas had looked into my eyes, and I did not. 'Go to sleep,' she said, and I wiped the last of the precious oil from my hands on to my face and lay down.

I heard Levi saying glumly, 'For the damage done, they'll count every head in a census. They always do. Every man punished with a poll tax. Each man to take a personal oath of loyalty to Caesar, and to Herod, and pay for the privilege. Our property itemised, everything we own examined to the last grain of barley.' He yawned, lay down, and my mother covered him with a blanket. 'I'm staying here,' he grunted, and slept.

I couldn't sleep. I pulled my knees up, put my thumb in

my mouth, and lay staring up. He kept me awake with his sleeping.

Next day Levi closed the door behind him and started burying the stuff he had brought with him under the hearth. I watched him through the gaps until he beat me. But nothing else happened. Not then. And never in daylight.

on did ne, are not liketh up. He after mr age and you.

Then he law come of the those learned men are cursed.
Cursing the mother had become with that und he had begotten,
and trembled him through the ears never so close for the
multitude multitude.... Not their child were brought the

MYSTERIUM FIDEI

the mystery of faith

PASSOVER, 13 APRIL 4 BC, 7:00 P.M.

My angel did not look after me, was not my guardian. My
body was a child's body, my heart a child's heart, my tongue
a child's tongue, and my strength was no more than a child's
strength. Perhaps my angel was just a dream after all, an
invisible imagined friend such as children treasure as
though they are real. But he was not my friend. He had
warned me as sternly as a priest: 'Miriam, do not go to
Sepphoris.' He did not tell me why; he did not protect me
from my grandfather Levi; and I was an ordinary child, a
child full of secrets of what was done with me in the night. I
could not speak of Levi's hands and caresses any more than
I could speak of the angel; there was nothing I could say
because nothing would be believed. In this situation, in this
lost and evil world, there is no truth except silence. I
wandered in the fields and among the sheep folds as mute
as Zacharias. I stole. Begged from the pilgrims streaming
out of the gates. Anything to keep me from home. But now
the town was quiet and business was poor as the Passover
festival approached, with so many pilgrims gone on the long
journey to the Temple in Jerusalem.

Extraordinarily, as human lives never last more than
seventy years, in the season of green shoots the Passover or
Pesah is still celebrated by these people. One thousand three
hundred seasons of spring have passed since Akenmoses, as
I recall his name – the Egyptian prince who spoke not a
word of Hebrew or, at first, Aramaic – led the Hebrew tribe
out of Egypt where Abraham led them, where they never

should have been in the first place. But still the memory of that time lives on, handed down alive from father to son, mother to daughter so that in each generation, as the Haggadah says, each man and woman feels as though they personally came out of Egypt. These Jews, and I'm brought up as one of them, believe vast forces shape their lives, that time rushes forward towards a purpose: its end. But I wanted to go out stealing.

But that morning my mother wanted to keep me at home, to make a game with me of hunting down every crumb of leaven in our hut – we eat no risen bread during Passover. Levi came in carrying the lamb he had bought, to be ritually sacrificed and eaten with bitter herbs. He talked to himself as usual, grumbling at the price, pretending to ignore me, a child, but noticing me with his whole body and his white blind eye, circling me as he worked, repeating the story of how the Jews were enslaved long ago by the pharaoh in Egypt, and how they marked their doors with lambs' blood so that the wrath of God passed over their houses, and the plague He sent to free His people killed each firstborn Egyptian child but spared His chosen race. Saved by the lamb. As a child I listened, dizzy with the long words, but instinctively I understood. To me it was yesterday. Sunburnt, stumbling, foreign-sounding, his eyes anointed with black *kohl* in the Egyptian style like a harlot, Moses had only just in time (his own name was simplified at that moment) learnt the name of God, *Yhwh*. Until then the Hebrews had thought the name of God was El, or El-Shaddai, or El-Olam. Sometimes He was called the Shield of Abraham, or the Fear of Isaac. But it was Moses in the Egyptian mountain who made the Covenant with God, and brought God into Sion; the Arch of the Covenant itself was Sion. Even the wilderness of the exodus, therefore, was Sion. And the wilderness was beautiful. But Levi ate like a pig.

I watched him. The fifth cup of wine is called Elijah's Cup. My mother opened the door so that the prophet Elijah could return and drink the cup, if he wished, answering all questions and inaugurating the Age of the Christ when all disputes and wars will cease, heralding the age of true freedom and Peace. Levi belched coriander and horseradish.

I jumped up before the cup could be poured, ran out into the darkness, left my mother calling behind me. The sound of the sea and the wind in the plane trees and cypresses roared loud over me. I ran between the houses into the fields of barley under the stars. The stars changed their patterns in the sky under the slow, immutable laws of gravity, inertia, momentum and time. The patterns were much changed by now, but above the last faint glow in the west my eye picked out Sirius, the Red Star of the Greeks and Egyptians and other peoples too across the ocean and the world, even the People of the Isthmus and, to the north, the land of the Nephites where Jared, Lehi and Mulek were led five centuries ago and more by the breath of the Lord; some still worship Sirius there.

I felt my feet crushing the soft shoots of barley as I ran backwards and forwards in the fields. There's no God to be found here. Yet I looked back as I climbed and saw the town silent below me, the doors patiently open for Elijah's return, the candles of faith flickering as bright as the stars above me, so that Magdala looked like a map of the sky printed on the earth.

I climbed up above the fields on to steep rocky slopes. Up here the bare mountains were crumbling away, limestone and sandstone, in time not much harder than butter. I remember when this dried land was green forest, a forest of spreading cedar making half the globe green. Men and women lived before speech in the caves here, made their families here, died here. I did, ten thousand times. I knew them.

But now I am flesh again. Actually in the flesh. I *am* flesh, I cannot be anything but this child I am. These pale blurs in the dark are my childish hands, pulling me higher among the rocks. I grope for a handhold, pull myself to the summit, and pale light washes over me. I turn.

A full moon is rising in the east. I sit on a rock, my legs dangling, and watch the line of moonlight ripple slowly down the slopes below me, falling to the Sea of Galilee. The sea shimmers like a silver dish under the moon. One by one the stars in the sky are obliterated by the moon's glare. The moon of this world is unnaturally large, and contains warnings still, but its craters are too small to be seen by the naked eye. And for now the huge planet Uranus is no more than a speck somewhere deep beyond the earth. It won't rise until daylight, invisible to my eye. Far to the north, over upper Galilee, a faint star slides from the jagged, moonlit horizon as smoothly as though carried on wings.

It's beautiful. Silent. Angel's wings.

It bursts into silent flame, a shooting star. No. It lasts too long. A comet; no, not fuzzy or feathery like a comet. This star radiates light in the shape of a cross, rising with a clear untwinkling brilliance, its message as clear as a pointing finger. I put back my head, following the star dizzily as it passes overhead, its radiance dimming the moon. I can't tell how far I am away, it's something like nothing I've seen in real life: the star overhanging the land below me like a picture or a painting, but it's real. This immense illumination, brighter than the sun, the whole green growing land glowing as if in joy beneath the star in the night: I know what star it is, and what it means, and so do you.

We all know this star. This painting is so familiar, the Star of Jerusalem which beckons the faithful along the way to Jesus Christ, which stretches its light over the Madonna and Child in the scene we all know from religious paintings and icons, Nativity tableaux, childhood plays: the Star above the paint or plaster or wax figure of Joseph the shepherd son of Jonan, standing his vigil in a room with walls of gold, the Holy of Holies in the Temple; and beside him the Virgin illuminated with glorious radiance from the Holy Child in her arms, Jesus Christ, the Son of God, born as a man from a ray of light through her body – the Child's face already adult and wise – ready to be laid in His cradle on the ordinary 'lady's bedstraw' which symbolises His humility. The ox and the ass watching over Him, again showing His humility. His cradle is always draped with the purple robes and golden insignia of King and Priest of Jerusalem which await Him, and propped against His cradle stands Abraham's sceptre, which led the Chosen People from Haran to Jerusalem, symbolising the salvation freely offered by the Christ Child which is His gift to us all, the kingdom of Heaven to which He will lead the faithful and the saved; and of His people, not one shall be unsaved.

I reach up my hands towards the Star; I think I can

almost touch its light. My ears hear the harmony of the hymns of the angels which carry the Star, can almost hear the words of their worship and praise of the Lord. The sight and the sound are so glorious that tears well up in my eyes, and the moment of adoration is so glorious and pure and transcending that I could never really have imagined what I feel: O God, let me see this moment with a child's eyes for ever, let me hold on to this for eternity!

But the Star passes above me, slips by me, I cannot hold it or hear it, and darkness falls. The Star passes towards the south, and stops in the sky there. I stand on the mountain and weep as though my heart breaks. There's nothing but the moon and the wind.

Still the Star does not move. From the south end of the sea, the River Jordan wriggles between the glowing hills like a golden serpent towards the Star, illuminated by its radiance, the distance made so clear that the curve of the earth, as I hold out my arms, stretches up from my fingertips and rises high above my head as though I am flying.

I *am* flying. I see the illuminated land pass below me with the eyes of belief. I believe. I know for certain what I see. The night air rushes past me but does not touch me. The sun rises but does not burn me. The Star, its radiance undimmed, gleams gently beside the sun at midday. I hear the voices of people working below me, their endless grumbles, the tinyness of their lives; they do not look up and see the Star over Jerusalem. I fly above the River Jordan, camels drinking along its banks, women washing, carrying water. I see the roofs of the village called Ephratah near Jerusalem and overlook a whitewashed courtyard, and in the courtyard a soldier swings a baby by its feet and smashes its head against a corner of the wall.

The soul leaves the shattered skull like a whirling spark, flies past me unknowing, blind; I cannot catch it. Gone. Then I scream, unheard, and I remember the prophecy: a king shall be born in Bethlehem Ephratah. Soldiers trooping the streets wear the brassy armour of Herod, dust clinging to their red hands and boots and swords. They move forward among the houses of Ephratah pulling children from their mothers, cutting throats; more children are pulled from houses, too young to walk. The eldest are killed. Herod has seen the Star, and he won't tolerate a rival king, whether sent by the God of the Jews or not. The soldiers are killing the firstborn, any child under two years old. The mothers kneel, tear their clothes, show their breasts, but the soldiers cannot stop, and the screaming of the women rises over them like the screaming of a great flock of birds. From the last buildings the soldiers pull out children by the heels. A burly grey-haired sergeant works with a will. He must have children too, but he knows his duty. The women shriek and beg and offer their lives, but he says calmly, 'Six days ago King Herod executed his own eldest son.' I believe it; it is not the first time that Herod, the grandiose megalomaniac with ten wives, ordered his own children executed. Someone screams that King Herod himself is now dead. The soldier shrugs it off. He knows nothing ever changes. 'Following orders, that's all. King Herod's got lots more sons. Long live King Herod.'

Madness! Everything I see and hear is madness. King David was born in Bethlehem, not here. Micah's prophecy of the birth of Christ has never come true and never will. 'Out of thee, Bethlehem Ephratah, shall He that is to be the ruler in Israel come forth.' Never! Bethlehem's some other village of no account somewhere on the road from Jerusalem to Herodium, but because of the prophecy rich greedy women travel from Gaza, Caesarea, even Galilee to give birth to their children there, so the innkeepers and midwives and wet-nurses of Bethlehem are the richest in Judah, after those of Ephratah and Jerusalem. May the God of the people of this world forgive these women for their pride and deceit. They deserve this punishment; they live in sin and deserve sin. But their children did not.

I'm blown forward like a leaf on the wind. Below me a woman runs in the desert, her baggy clothes and white hair flying – I know Elizabeth, wife of Zacharias the Temple priest. Her girdle flaps open, showing me the thin baby she holds to her breast; she strokes his head, kisses his face, John. Her baby was born and named John, as the angel foretold. But did the angel foretell this terror? Sand blows around her in the growing storm. Through the clouds of dust along the road come brassy glints of reflected light: armour, soldiers marching. The old woman has nowhere to hide. Crouches down behind a rock, but there are too many soldiers, she knows she'll be seen. In blind panic she pushes on the rock with the flats of her hands. Its base moves; the ground slips forward. She lies down in the hollow, the wind covers her and her baby with sand, and the soldiers march past complaining about the wind and their thirst.

The storm blows me away, rain falling past me now as if in response to the soldiers' prayer. Below me dust gives way to mud, wet fields to the desultory fires of rubbish-tips. The muddy roads draw together; the sunless walls of Jerusalem rise up in front of me streaming wet. The massive greystone blocks flash silver with lightning, and the battlements rush below. I look down, see the Star's illumination reflected in the golden roof and pediments of the Great Temple built by King Herod for his Jews, and men and women and Temple virgins running among the courtyards and staircases and colonnades, and behind them soldiers with drawn swords spreading forward from the gates, a vast dull silent scene of despair and death. Then someone shouts, 'Zacharias.' Zacharias is one of the six thousand Pharisees who refused to take the oath of loyalty to Herod and to Caesar. The priest stands on the steps of the Temple sanctuary, holding a child in his arms. A eunuch shouts up the steps, 'Speak, Zacharias, and live. Is the Child the One? Is this the child John, the Christ who was promised you?' For a moment I'm terrified, truly terrified, that the baby is Jesus brought from the Holy of Holies by some frightful error or mistake. 'Is he the One?' But Zacharias will not or cannot speak. The soldiers' swords slice him down, Zacharias's blood trickles over the sanctuary steps and spreads out in the rain, the child is beheaded and thrown in the blood, and the soldiers move forward on their business.

The child was not John. I saw the baby John saved in the desert, and he will be the Baptist, if his God wills. But where, in all this mayhem, is the baby Jesus who was to be born beneath the Star?

Below me I see the gold roof of the Holy of Holies at the centre of its maze, gold wires stretched above the golden shingles so that pigeons cannot defile its cleanliness in the eyes of God. Where is Joseph? Where is the Virgin?

I look up. The Star that shone through the clouds and rain above Jerusalem is gone.

It's true. There is no God. But I had almost . . . wondered.

The wind blows me hither and thither. As evening falls the storm blows away southward, red cloud tops roiling in the red sunset, the land shadowed below. Lightning still flickers along the road towards Bethlehem.

And there is the Star. The Star hangs in the sky over Bethlehem.

A last gust of the wind picks me up. I rise up and fall down through the clouds into the gloom below. Ten thousand stragglers on the road, groaning with cold and wet. Men and women pushing forward through the mud, their cloaks soaked and heavy with rain, filthy to the knees, and a solemn drum beating the dirge. I see a child's face upturned in awe, so close that for a moment I think I see my own face. What does the child see? Then the child's mother snatches her away, and a great golden wheel ploughs forward through the mud and stones.

Black stallions, their teeth dripping foam, black plumes whipping in the wind, are dragged back with sliding hooves. Behind them, attached by golden harness, a huge gold funeral carriage stands in churned mud on wheels of solid gold. The casket three times the size of a man is gold and ebony, gold pillars support the gold house that shelters it from the last of the rain, and on the roof stands a huge gold eagle. Whips crack; slaves push from behind with bare feet slipping. In front more slaves tug at ropes with burnt hands. Their cries and grunts and the neighing of horses fill the evening air, and slowly the great carriage, creaking and grinding, again moves uphill to the beating of the drum.

It's King Herod's funeral cortège. The king's bones won't reach Herodium tonight. After the storm the soaked and exhausted mourners will be lucky to reach half way, to Bethlehem. The carriage reaches the summit, almost rolls back on the slaves, then rumbles downhill towards the lights of the village. Men accompanying the procession on horseback or carried by slaves in swaying palanquins send their servants ahead to prepare rooms.

And suddenly I understand. Joseph must be here. Despite

57

his Essene humility, Joseph carries the royal blood of David in his veins. He's not a man of self-importance but he *is* a man of importance. Despite his high rank he's not rich himself – the Essenes hold their wealth in common – but their monastery is enormously wealthy. At Sion by the Dead Sea, with the king's permission, they sell baptism and the forgiveness of sins to Jews and Jewish pilgrims from other lands. During Herod's lifetime the monastery channelled millions of shekels to his treasury and his building projects, and in return he favoured them and protected them from their enemies. Joseph, with the rank of David, must show his respect. He cannot have stayed back in Jerusalem.

He's here, somewhere in Bethlehem.

Where? A thousand faces in the gloom. The flames of torches. The inns of Bethlehem lining the road, people pushing inside. Soldiers guard the funeral carriage of the king. The road emptying now, quiet and dim except for a bonfire or two blowing in the cold wind, slaves shivering in the smoke that goes with what heat fires give. There's no shelter, and one scarred captive from a forgotten war looks up as a flake of snow lands on his nose. He puts out his tongue for more, smiling.

Gently the snow falls. Out of the snow, a donkey plods forward beneath the Star. On the donkey's back rides a woman, sidesaddle, wearing her blue cape. I recognise her. Behold the Virgin. Miriam, fourteen or fifteen years old, her husband Joseph beside her, his hair white with snow, is in the last extremity of her pregnancy. She says something meek, he replies angrily. They've lost their servants, obviously. 'Have you seen Joachim?' he asks someone, but no one has seen an old man. Joseph does not know what to do, and the snow falls. If Miriam's God is the father of her child, why has He abandoned her now? She won't ask that question, and her face is calm and full of faith, beyond pain. But by now even Bethlehem is full, everyone either drunk or asleep, and Miriam – a child herself! – and Joseph have come to the end of the street.

Near the ruins of the shrine to Tammuz I see a stable that even the slaves missed, so tumbledown it seems no more than the entrance to a cave under the snow. Joseph walks straight past it, then stops helplessly. 'There must be somewhere,' he says. There is, it's the stable right in front of his eyes, but he can't see it, and the donkey turns to carry its burden back the way it has come. 'Stand!' I call. The donkey stands still, and Joseph stares at me, straight at me. She'll have her baby on the donkey's back if he stares much longer. 'Look,' Joseph whispers. 'Do you see? It's a young boy dressed in white.' Young boy indeed; I look down and see myself, flat-chested, but unmistakably a girl, stark naked.

For the first time in my life in this body, I am without pain. My twisted arm does not hurt; it is not twisted. I am perfect.

Joseph's young wife rests her hands patiently over her belly, a crescent moon of snow. Such calm faith in herself, in her God, is beyond my understanding. I should be screaming with contractions. I reach out my hand, my bare shining hand, she takes it and slides easily down from the animal, and I lead her into the only place there is to go, the stable. There's no illumination here except my own, it's as dark as a cave, earth floor, dirty straw in one corner, a stone manger along one wall. And there, with incredulity, I see an ox and an ass patiently waiting. 'An ox and an ass to watch over Him, symbolising His humility.' For the first time I begin – no, not to believe – at least to hope. Begin to dare to hope.

What a mess! No cradle, let alone one draped with purple and golden insignia. No lady's bedstraw, only matted stinky animal bedding. And this stable or part of a cave is very definitely far from the glory and mystery of the Holy of Holies. Joseph returns carrying some flickering lamp which an enterprising innkeeper sold him for a shekel, the cost of a good room. Miriam lies down on the straw, settles herself calmly, but even as Joseph hangs his cloak over the doorway to protect her modesty he can see it's time for the midwife. He hesitates, smiles at her, tries to ignore me, leaves the lamp beside her, pats her hand and goes off to do his duty.

The moment he's gone light fills the stable. Dirt's banished, the bedstraw shines clean and fresh. Miriam gives a great cry. I no longer recognise her, she's a woman clothed with the sun, in her labour she is as bright as the desert sun at midday. Even I shield my eyes.

From the midst of the light, from an immense centre where there is no darkness, Ezekiel's golden archangels, Armozel, Oriel, Daveith and Eleleth, flow down into this world. They are *in Barbelo*, said to be the feminine form of the highest God. Their faces are terrified. Utterly terrified. Only the harmony to the glory of God and the paeans of praise offered up by their heavenly prayers seem to sustain them. One angel flutters, falls, touches the shadows. The illumination redoubles, the fallen broken shape is lifted gently and returned to the storm of light and gold. Not the dull worldly metal of Herod's funeral carriage, but this gold everywhere above, this pure light, this gold that is the adoration of Heaven.

And jewels. Riches beyond measure.

The Virgin gives a great cry, not of pain, but of awe and wonder.

Through the clouds of gold and jewels and adoration the angels carry down a human baby, down, down, and lay him in his shadow. This baby is as naked as I, but with a penis, the tip hidden, uncircumcised. A perfect baby boy. He bawls like a healthy baby boy, too, bunching his fists, screwing up his face, and expels something green from his bottom. Perhaps Miriam doesn't notice yet, for she kneels down in front of her baby instead of picking him up, a mother worshipping her newborn child, finding him wholly marvellous and beautiful. She counts his fingers and toes without touching, adoring him. Indeed he has beautiful feet. He cries at her hungrily, sensing her full breasts under her cape, but instead of feeding him or touching him she whispers to her baby, 'Are you the One?'

The baby mewls with all his strength, reaching as best he can for his mother's lovely overhanging milky breasts.

But she has to know. 'Are you His Son who will lead us?'

I feel the fabric of our universe move slightly, bending, as though something beyond everything that we know touches the warp and weft of creation and squeezes it, stretches it, just a little. As though the night sky is no larger than the inside of a child's play-ball. Every natural law I know, stars, numbers, the pull of gravity, the velocity of light, is over-turned for an instant by that hand. And I feel inside me the immediate Voice of God.

'You are my servant.'

I hear God.

I've seen people who say God speaks to them. I've seen people who believe deeply, who *know* He does. Many of them. Thousands of them. I have believed. I have myself been a prophet, as you know. And no one should know more of God than I. I told you I was near Moses – no one was closer to him! – when he claimed he heard the Word of God inside him. You remember that he said the Word of God sounded like the thunder of falling mountains. He believed with all his heart that God spoke to him there in the mountain which now bears his name. I know exactly what Moses heard, a sound made by Man; but perhaps even that sound is God, because Moses believed God was everywhere, in everything. And surely, if there is a God, God is in everyone. And perhaps – if there is a God – what Moses found in Mount Musa, incredible though it seems, was part of God's plan. Meant to happen. Who can say? Who knows what God knows? Not I.

The Voice I hear now is more. More than falling mountains, more than the holocaust of unshielded nuclear fires that burn inside the sun, much more: louder than the fall of an insect's wing. This calm quiet Voice of utter, inner peace.

'You are my servant.'

Miriam stares upward, her face glowing. She hears it too. Even the child is silent, eyeing the breasts without a sound, then gazing calmly into the glowing air.

Then everything is as it was, just a stable. We gasp together, let down. The feeling of loss, emptiness, mortality, is almost unbearable. It's over, like a death. Miriam touches her child sadly. He clings on to her finger with his fist, a perfect baby boy dirty at one end and hungry at the other.

You are my servant.

But which one of us did He mean? The child? The Virgin? (If she really is a virgin – *she* believes it!) Me?

The stable's growing dimmer; no, it's me who fades. Fading away. Joseph dares to come in. He's been waiting outside the cloaked doorway, afraid of the light. 'I brought the midwife,' he announces anxiously to his bride. He wants certainty, reassurance, he has to know exactly what has happened. But Miriam just smiles. It's a mystery.

61

'Look,' she says. 'I have my Son.'

Joseph glances at the boy. I see the struggle on his face. He wants to believe her. He does love his smiling wife, just a child herself. But he has to know. 'Don't smile. Let the midwife examine you.' Still Miriam just smiles at him, the picture of health. She wants him simply to believe. He insists. 'In case you should need her skill for your cure.' His tongue has slipped. 'Your care. To look after you, Mary.'

'Your love for me is speaking,' she decides. 'Call your midwife then.'

Faint though I am, everything turning to shadows, I recognise this cheerful figure who bustles into the stable: it's Salome, the same midwife who birthed me and broke my arm, my arm which is now beginning to hurt me with its old nagging pain. Whatever peace I've been blessed with is leaving me, draining away with the light. Salome drops her bag of tools with a grunt. She's put on weight. With Galilee so poor now a midwife must follow the work. Clumsily she kneels between the Virgin's ankles, smiles kindly, would rather talk about the baby, but Joseph has given her orders outside. 'How are we? What a lovely boy! Had much pain, dear?'

'No pain. Only joy.'

'Really, that's nice.' Salome eyes the breasts full of milk. 'All right if I touch you, dear?'

Salome's large knobbly hands – how well I remember them! – part Miriam's thighs beneath the skirts and make the examination. The midwife's face changes. 'She can't be. Lord have mercy on us! No blood, and she's tight as a piss-hole, pardon my saying so. How'd you do it, dear?'

'As a virgin I conceived,' Miriam tells Joseph gently. 'As a virgin I brought forth. A virgin I am, and your wife.'

'You are,' Joseph says faithfully, but that's a lie. An unconsummated marriage is not a marriage. But he wants to believe her so badly.

'Don't be a silly old fool, master, pardon my saying so!' Salome pushes forward her hand to find the trick. 'I've birthed a thousand babes and believe me the only special thing about it is they live, at least sometimes they do. What's this?' Her voice changes, then she cries out with pain. She pulls back, falling, rolls in the straw. The hand that explored the Virgin's secrets is withering like a claw.

She holds up her arm, screaming. The blood is sucked from her fingers, exposing the wrinkled veins that map the back of her hand. The ox lows peacefully, then returns to its hay. I shall never forget that brown leathery skeleton of the midwife's hand drying and crackling on the end of her plump white arm, and her screams. 'Oh Lord help me it hurts!' No one touches her. Appalled.

'God has punished her,' Joseph says, shaken.

Salome looks straight at me. She knows me. 'Are you one of my children, I who got no children of my own? Save me.' She crawls towards me, the faint fading remnant of me. 'Don't go, angel! I've done my best all my life, and lived in fear of doing wrong, believe me!' She blubbers openly. 'Cared for the poorest, sometimes, and not a shekel to show for it. Took nothing from a widow left with child, and as for orphan girls there's more than one I got out of trouble, and I never turned anyone away who needed me. Forgive me for testing her virginity, for my sinful disbelief. Forgive me!' She raises that dreadful hand in supplication.

I would do it if I could. God knows I need forgiveness myself for not believing in Him. She begs, agonised. 'I had to try her. Anyone of my profession would. For a virgin to conceive and give birth is impossible, but now I believe! I do believe!'

I wonder if everything is possible, even this. Can this baby child, kicking, wailing, smelling, dribbling on its swaddling clothes (which are too tight) actually and factually be the Christ Messiah, the heir to the royal blood plotted and planned by Joseph, and also the pure Son of God promised to the Virgin, heralding the perfect age of Christianity? Perhaps there is a way to know.

I put forward all my strength, see my glow reflected in her eyes. I order her, 'Salome, go to the Child. Touch Him with your hand, and He will cure you because He is the Saviour of the world.' I mean, of course, *if* he is the Saviour of the world.

Salome does as I tell her: kneels, touches the shawl in which the swaddled baby is wrapped. He looks at her with the blue unfocused gaze of all babies, and her hand heals. I see it. The blood and fat flow back over her bones, the healthy colour of her flesh returns, her hand grows as pink with health as the baby's cheeks. She gives such a loud shout that she makes him cry.

She forgets her tools and cloak, and rushes out into the snow crying aloud at the top of her voice, shouting aloud with wonder and joy of her disbelief, her suffering, her cure. Any people still about think she's drunk. Someone throws a stone, a group of drunks shout insults, but a few wander along to the stable. This is what they see: exactly what you expect.

The Nativity tableau, though without the gold walls and the crib of purple and gold, and without Abraham's sceptre, which must be dust long ago. And instead of royal purple Joseph wears his seamless white gown, an Essene priest – his travel cloak still covers the doorway. But the bedstraw and the ox and ass are here, which if you think about it is more likely in a stable than the Holy of Holies; and now three cloaked pilgrims approach through the whirling flakes of snow. They can only be the three Magi bearing gifts, traditionally silver, balsam and precious galbanum incense.

In the stable I'm hardly more than a shadow among the shadows, and my arm is agony. But I recognise their faces as they put back their hoods. The first Magus is Judas the Galilean.

'So the rumours are true. A baby. In Bethlehem. And a virgin, no doubt, as she claims. You must disprove her.'

Joseph shakes his head. 'I cannot. The midwife swears it also.'

The Galilean grunts angrily. He too wears his seamless white Essene garment beneath the disguise of his Persian cloak, which is woven with stars. Like the Essenes, the Magi of Persia are avid astrologers, close observers of the sun, moon and stars, the times of coming and going. Greeks and Romans regard these observant, skilled pagans more highly than Jewish prophets who claim passively to receive knowledge directly from God; King Herod often uses the Magi. A magician is a good disguise for a priest. Ragged black hair, white strands in his beard, the Galilean looks a little like Joseph. But Judas, dusty with travel, has strong cheekbones and a hawk's eyes, slitted, suspicious, almost black.

His two eldest sons are crucified; he's a hunted man. But not defeated, and he may need Joseph. He leans on his priestly sceptre, greets the older man formally. 'Joseph Alphaeus, greeting.' Not *Mashiya*; Judas calls no man Christ. He hurries on, speaking as rapidly as I remember. 'Soldiers coming. Not much time—'

Joseph holds out his arm proudly towards the child, but he speaks as slowly and simply as Moses – very slow, very simple. 'Behold, a Son is born.'

'They're killing them all, cousin, even illegitimate children,' Judas interrupts without respect. He finds Joseph dull and irritating. 'Realise your danger. Zacharias is dead. Of his son John I have no word. I will support you, I will hide you, Joseph, but quickly! Herod's soldiers are killing first-born children, second born, bastards, orphans, even girls. They've started, they can't stop. Blood on their hands and in their brains, they're drunk. Save the child!'

'God will save us,' the Virgin says, but her voice counts for nothing when men talk.

'You have little time, Joseph!'

'But King Herod is dead,' Joseph says steadfastly, 'and tomorrow he'll be buried.'

'Yes, and now Herod Archelaus claims the throne, and Herod Antipas, *and* Herod Philip. They'll fight among themselves. Civil war. The last thing we need now is another king. Keep the baby safe or everything you planned is wasted. Go into Egypt.' Judas hands over a bag, heavy: gold. 'Only in Egypt, cousin, will our royal child be safe. We can hide it there, and its bastardy.' He gives Joseph an angry stare. 'Sinful man!'

Joseph says, 'My wife is a virgin.'

'Everything was perfect. You're a fool, Joseph. Couldn't you wait? The brotherhood will know you've broken the laws of betrothal. How can I hide it? You'll pray in the wilderness for a year for your sins.'

'Why should I go into Egypt?' the Virgin's voice demands from the bedstraw. 'I'm not unclean. I haven't given birth.'

Judas bites his teeth angrily. 'We won't be manipulated, Joseph. This young girl, this child—'

'My wife.' Joseph stands up for her.

'Not fully your wife under the Law. Not until she and you

both are purified. And not, if I believed your tale, until the marriage is consummated.'

'She tells the truth. A miracle has happened.'

'I've heard her story. I hope no one else does!' Judas's voice rises; they'll hear him in the street. 'The best of a bad job, a fable, a contortion for the common people which carries no weight with us true Jews. The priesthood of the Poor stands between you and God in the light of righteousness and the Law, Joseph. I am your Righteous Teacher, your zadok; do not mock me. Into Egypt you will go.'

'Into Egypt I will go, rabbi.' Joseph bows his head. I wonder if he is strong enough to prevail against the iron will of Judas without the backing of Zacharias. Joseph has fallen into the hands of zealots.

Judas tries to end kindly, but from him even kindness feels like a threat. 'Truly, Joseph the Nazarene, go willingly and humbly, for I speak with the voice of the Law.' He glances at the baby, murmurs thoughtfully: 'So this is your infant King of the Jews. We shall see. A miracle indeed, if people would believe it's a miracle. But they won't.'

He kneels, ignores Miriam, studies the baby briefly – I would not call it a prayer. 'You'll have the child circumcised with a copper knife on the eighth day, according to the Law.'

Meanwhile the second Magus comes forward. I recognise a younger son of the Galilean, the one called Simon of Samaria. Does he still carry a curved knife beneath his Essene gown? The Magi are zealots, sicariots of the Fourth Way. No doubt they have armed men posted outside, but for the first time I begin to worry for the safety of the baby whom they have agreed, for the moment, to protect. The third Magus, the youngest brother called, I think, Menachem, waits his turn while Simon bows to the newborn babe and makes his gift.

It's not balsam. I smell frankincense, one of the four ingredients of the holy incense burnt in the tabernacle. Frankincense has another meaning (all meanings are important to the Essenes, are levels of interpretation of the hidden truth), being the washing powder that keeps Essene gowns white with sanctity, pure in holiness: frankincense means the child must live according to the Essene Way. A strange gift, almost menacing in its third level of meaning: a man condemned to death, if granted mercy, drinks frankincense mixed with wine to dull the pain of execution. It seems to me that a cold wind blows through the stable, but tonight nothing dulls the Virgin's smile or her calm pride as she accepts the gifts, which to her are simply adoration of the miracle of her baby. But they are also messages of intimidation as well as of provisional acceptance and help, and Joseph stands uncomfortably with the gold hanging from his hand.

Menachem crouches to make his gift to the baby, myrrh. Like galbanum, myrrh is an ingredient in the oil which anoints a king. That's better; but, unlike galbanum which is medicine, pure myrrh is used to embalm the dead.

None of these worldly men saw the Virgin Birth. I did. None of them saw the angels. I did. These men retreating bowing from the stable are no more than politicians. Grabbing advantage, power, influence where they can, blowing with the wind and swimming with the tide. What has happened tonight may come to something or nothing; they have many irons in the fire. But Joseph kneels by his wife, kissing her hands, her face, their baby, whispering, 'Mary, Mary, Mary. I do love you.'

Love! When ever was that enough?

I look back and see Joseph and Mary, their heads illuminated with haloes of light, sitting round their new baby in the straw, the ox and the ass watching over them, but I am very faint. I have no strength now, only pain. A faint draught blows me helplessly into the darkness, where an old man stands leaning on his stick, his face turned into the glow that shines from the stable: Joachim, the Virgin's father. Even as I watch, he smiles and turns away into the snowy night beneath the Star, and I never see him again.

Quails flutter from the snowy bushes, and I drop weakly to the ground. And for the first time I realise it isn't snow. Here's a miracle for anyone with eyes to see. But no one has seen. This snow is *manna*, bread from God, the bread of life that sustained Moses and his people in the wilderness coming out of Egypt. I taste it for the second time, a single flake of unleavened bread on my tongue, and its strength shoots through me. I rise into the air. I can do anything. I can change the world.

Screaming, I fall back to the mountaintop.

AEGYPTUS

Egypt

Was it really supposed to be that way? Bethlehem? A married Virgin? And the terrible business of the soldiers murdering the babies, and the Holy Family sent to hide in, of all places, Egypt? But so much else was right: the Holy Child's touch cured the midwife's hand, and the Magi were there although they were not quite the three wise men I expected (but it's said a Magus can do magic and has learnt unearthly powers), and the angels were beautiful, and the snow. Most of all my feeling was right. It felt as though God was there in the stable. It was more than a cute story. I was part of it, among it, it happened around me and to me.

And then falling, screaming.

I lay on the mountain where I had watched the moon rise. The sun was setting, evening falling. Where did the day go? My face and arms and legs were blistered with sunburn, the sun had shone all day on my unconscious abandoned body like a fire. My thirst was so great my lips cracked, my tongue stuck to the roof of my mouth. I heard the scrape of footsteps, the rattle of rocks sliding downhill, the grunt of a man's breathing. A shadow fell over me in the last of the light, then Levi my grandfather lowered himself over me, and I knew what he would do, but the child in me did not. I screamed. Again he forced himself on me, heavy and violent. He slobbered on my face in his affection, kissing me, caressing my wriggling sunburnt flesh with his rough sandy fingers, murmuring how he loved me, little creature, lovely little creature, and his blind white eye stared down at

68

me as though it would burst in the ecstasy of his passion as he tore me, and his seed spurted like cold barley porridge.

I screamed and screamed and he covered my mouth with his shoulder. 'Don't say a word.' He crushed me with his weight. 'Your mother knows all about it. Don't say a word or I'll tell her you were no good. You don't want to be a bad little girl.'

I wanted to be very bad, I wanted to do something very bad to him, but all the child in me could do was cry. I spat up at his face and he had to wipe it off. He heard someone coming, put his head to mine, his finger between my eyes. 'Remember.' I bit his finger but he laughed, full of himself, and swept me up in his arms. 'She's found!' he called. 'I found her, Leah. She's here.'

My mother was furious with me. 'Don't you ever go off like that again!' She smacked me, kissed me, cried over me. 'Is she ill? Look at her poor skin, look what the sun did to her.' She smacked me again, on the back of my shadowed leg which was white as a fish. 'What did you think you were doing, out here all day?'

'I was in Jerusalem.' I clung to her, shivering now darkness fell as we made the descent. 'I was in Jerusalem and I saw them killing the babies.'

'Sun's got in her head,' my mother wept. Levi tried to carry me but I shrieked at him. 'She's not herself,' my mother apologised. 'I can carry her. She's ill. My poor baby.' More kisses. 'Out all day on the Feast of Unleavened Bread, I'll never forgive myself.'

The unleavened bread. 'I saw it snow in Bethlehem,' I murmured. 'The snow was unleavened bread. I saw angels and a baby born in a stable who will be our Saviour.'

'She's sick. I wouldn't believe a word she says,' Levi told my mother. 'Not about anything. She's a dreamer like her grandmother was, your girl. Killing babies!'

I whispered, 'They're killing them because King Herod's dead.'

'He's not dead,' Levi said. As we came between the fields my mother could carry me no longer, put me down. Levi offered to carry me but I screamed at him again and he pretended to laugh. 'She's not right in the head, your girl.'

'She's all right.' My mother kissed the top of my head.

'You can't let her talk like this,' Levi warned. 'People will think she's got a demon in her.' All I could see of him in the dark was his eye. 'Demons in her.'

'Shush, shush!' my mother said, terrified. 'She hasn't. She isn't. She's just a child.' We came into town and someone shouted at us to be quiet.

'Haven't you heard the news?' someone called. 'King Herod's dead. They're killing anyone with a false claim to the throne, even the children.'

We got home. My mother looked at me fearfully. 'How could she know?' she whispered. She was afraid of me. 'How could she have known?'

She put a little oil on my burns, rubbing lightly with her fingertips, but now we both instinctively realised the distance between us. As distant as mousy, meek Leah from her own mother. As often happens in families, we were blood but we were far apart. We'd never understand each other. She would never understand me at all.

I went to bed and curled up, turned inward on myself, my hands tucked into my belly, holding my secrets deep within me. Come dawn, I was gone.

I begged until my cup remained empty. I stole until the traders threw stones at the sight of me. No one knew the courts and alleys and back-doubles of Magdala as well as I, but something had gone out of me. I learned to endure beatings in silence, I expected them, I hung mute and uncomplaining when I was caught and punished. I grew tall for a girl of six, but thin. My arms and legs were sticks, my hair was long but lank. Bruises covered my body. Levi beat me when he found me in my mother's house, for my disloyalty to her, for hurting her. As you must know, indifference to suffering enrages. How can a criminal who does not respect punishment be punished? Only by greater and greater harshness. My mother wept but I hung limply from his fist; I suffered worse beatings in town. But some folk remembered I was Caleb's daughter and how I began, and they took pity on me, showed me kindness, called me into their homes, and I stole from them until they grew wise and closed their doors.

When I was seven years old I was old enough to steal from younger children, even boys. I learnt to bruise my face as Sarai did, and sometimes I wore my hair like her, imitating her. Though a child she was old enough, despite her broken jaw, to parade for men. She showed me how to turn a man into money, especially the husbands of her mother's friends, those her mother wanted her especially to meet. Sometimes it was fun. Children learn quickly, and men's desires are simple.

When I was eight there was little we didn't know about the husbands, tradesmen and priests of Magdala. The priests talked of sin and judgment, traders of money, husbands about their wives. With my twisted arm and my torn, disfigured vagina I would never make the living Sarai did. Levi had scarred me. She learned to use her body. She was ugly but she wore red lips and nipples like the older women in the top storeys by the town wall and the fish tower. 'Who cares what you look like in the dark, anyway,' she said. Her mother died but Sarai got a red gown with yellow stripes that reached almost to the ground, and wore her hair in rings. She knew she'd meet a man who would marry her and she'd have children (she'd had several already, dead, quick) who would live, and Sarai knew she would live with her family in a good house with white walls, and her husband would come home at night. She was killed in an alley and I found her. I was nine years old.

I took her clothes and sat on the beach with a pebble in my mouth, remembering when I was a child. My mother paused behind me, carrying an armload of washing for a Greek called, I think, Apollos. She wanted to say, 'Look at you! And your hair like that!' But then she said nothing, and walked on her way. I was alone again.

Alone is how I'm happy. Magdala's pretty, circled in its fields of flowers, touched by the blue line of the sea along one edge, the sandy mountain tops blowing dust against the sky. Here, looking back from a headland, the sea breeze pulls the rings from my hair so that it flies like a crane's wing from my head, tugging me as if to make me fly again, and I remember my innocence.

I never heard any more about Bethlehem or anything that happened there. I hardly thought of it, a dream I had when I was four years old. A dream, as always in this world, that was part of a nightmare; I was never free of Levi and his groping hands, his secret contaminating winks as though I, his victim, were his willing accomplice. And I was. His demon was in me, Levi was always in my thoughts. I could never really run away. Nothing good would ever prevail here, sin is born in us here, and guilt. However far I walked into the hills, I still circled Magdala, drawn home to what I feared and hated most. Because that's the way this world works. It's home.

There's no escape. I'm myself. I'm flesh. I can't unravel myself, I can't un-be who I am. Each morning I wake up and I'm merely Miriam, Mary, and another day of my life has started. I must piss and shit (out of sight of Levi if possible), eat and drink, survive. That is life.

But sometimes I do think of Bethlehem and the Virgin and the Child. It seems like another earth, a beautiful earth. The ox and the ass adoring Him. The storm of gold and the terrified angels and the child Christ coming down who has been prophesied to these people here, and the Voice of God affirming Him.

But it's so difficult to remember it here, in the real world where I'm filthy inside.

Did Joseph lead the Holy Family into Egypt, as he had been ordered by Judas? I never dreamt of them, I never really flew. Then one day I heard the word 'Egypt' chattered and laughed by the women in the square, filling jugs at the fountain, and the splashing water swept their words away. Then I picked out the word Sotinen, a city in Egypt. A miracle there witnessed by Affrodosius, the Roman governor of the city, so it must (the women said) be true: a mother had taken her child into the temple at Sotinen and the stone pagan gods had bowed down before Him. If the fable was true, could they be telling, however incoherently, something of the Holy Child Jesus Christ, Son of God, I had seen come into this world in a stable? I listened to the women gossip. More laughter, but some took it seriously. Three hundred and fifty-five statues of gods, apparently, and each statue had bowed down in adoration of Him until it broke on the temple floor.

Really? Three hundred and fifty-five statues? This was zealot propaganda, Judas the Galilean or one of his sons, a thinly veiled attack on the Jerusalem Temple. Essenes hate the Temple. The Jerusalem priests' lunar calendar proclaims the dates of Temple rituals, sacrifices and holy days throughout the land – they believe the Temple *is* Israel. There's only one Temple because there is only one God. God is physically present inside the Holy of Holies exactly as He was present in the Arch of the Covenant carried through the wilderness, the Throne of God placed in the first Temple by King Solomon. But everyone knows a lunar year is only three hundred and fifty-four days and a few hours on top. The solar calendar so important to the Essenes gives a year of three hundred and *sixty*-four days exactly, so to them the rituals to God's glory, witnessed by God in the Jerusalem Temple, are performed on entirely the wrong days. To the zealots the Temple calendar's mutilation of the worship of God is sacrilege, an apostasy as grievous as working on the Sabbath: an affront to God and the Law. The most sacred rites of Atonement are observed in the Temple on the wrong day, the Sabbath is made ludicrous. Any Jerusalem priest would understand exactly what was meant by a dire prediction of three hundred and fifty-five statues falling.

But here in the sunlight, the women enjoyed it as a story of gods falling down at the feet of a little boy. They had children of their own.

A doctor said, 'Remember the prophecy of Isaiah: "Behold, the Lord will come upon a swift cloud, and He will enter Egypt, and all the handiwork of the Egyptians shall be moved at His presence." '

But another year, I heard something that did send a chill through me. It was such a simple story that at first I believed it no more than the other. I overheard it as Levi haggled for a donkey, blown with staring ribs and a hanging head though it was, but affordable. Levi kicked its knees. 'Ten shekels.' But they won't take shekels even in the Jerusalem Temple, and out here in Galilee the seller was sure to insist on Roman. I wouldn't have trusted him; he had a cruel mouth of teeth like yellow fangs. 'To you, Levi old friend, thirty denarius.'

Levi scratched the dust from his head, calculating. Thirty denarii was worth about half as many shekels, but the moneychanger would take his cut and it was late in the day, not much competition, rates would be high. 'Twenty denarius, you thief.' The donkey wheezed while they haggled and I tried to lie down in the shade but Levi snatched my hand, held it. He stuck on twenty-four and the thief on twenty-six. Levi followed the man's eyes. 'Twenty-four, thief, and my daughter's kiss.'

The thief summed me up. The two men spat on their hands and the thief took me behind a wall and covered my mouth with his own, searched my clothes for breasts but I was flat chested, much too young, and when he fumbled me below I hissed at him like a snake. 'Hurry it up.' Levi eyed the sun. The thief complained, 'She's not kissed me yet, not proper.' So I kissed him where he wanted until he got what he wanted, I spat, and I told Levi part of the donkey was mine. 'And I'm not your daughter, you fucker.' Levi slapped me round the head. I don't know what he told people about my mother. His wife, probably. Levi was so incredible, so common.

I walked the donkey after the thief and my grandfather to the moneychangers at the *shul*-house. Thirsty, it kept pulling towards the fountain and I kept slapping it. 'Bought it off an Egyptian,' the thief bragged at Levi. 'Least, that's what his wife said he was. Can't help being nosy I can't, it's my nature. Always asking too many questions. I'll be the death of me one day.' The moneychangers looked up from their rugs and silver pots, the first called his offer. 'Twenty-four denarius, give me twenty shekel.' Levi found someone cheaper. The thief prattled, '*She* wasn't Egyptian. Gorgeous.' He cupped his hands like breasts. 'Asked about her, you know, can't help it, and someone said you keep away from that one.' Levi demanded of a moneychanger, 'Twenty-four for twelve.' The moneychanger (I knew him well, Sallu, I'd stolen from him often) flicked his beads, slapped down the coins. 'Done.'

'You got a good deal there. I know Sallu, he's stupid,' the thief said. 'Always going out of business, that family.' He slipped the coins in his belt, and the donkey was Levi's.

'Did you have her?' Levi said. 'The Egyptian?'

'No. Turned out she's a Nazarene, along with her husband. No wine or beer, sanctimonious as priests. And well guarded; when push comes to shove you have to fight 'em all. You want to hear it or not?'

'Spend some of that donkey-money at the tavern,' Levi suggested.

I was about to take the donkey home by myself, but as the two men settled on the bench I heard the thief begin: 'Dragons.'

I know dragons. I know the dragons in this world. I mean more than Leviathan, the dragon of whom I have spoken, blind in the deeps of the ocean, ancient when even James and I were young.

I hung around behind the two men, waiting while they drank their wine. The donkey chewed a bush. 'Dragons,' Levi prompted. 'Don't tell me. She fed her husband to the dragons and fell in love with you, you thief.'

'I wouldn't touch her, not me.' The thief shook his head. 'This is what they said in the town. In the desert, she's travelling back with her husband from I don't know where.'

Levi nodded. 'Egypt?'

'All right. Them and their three sons, a few years ago.' Three sons? This wasn't the family I was thinking of. Time for home. I pulled the donkey from the bush but it clenched its teeth. 'They found a cave to shelter in for the night. Deep dark cave. Dragons came out of it. I mean real dragons, claws and teeth, breath of fire. Spikes along their backs. Each dragon as tall as ten men. Like huge lizards, real dragons.'

'More wine,' Levi said. 'How'd she get out of it?'

'She didn't.' The thief stirred his wine with his finger. 'One of her little boys stood in front of the dragons.'

'Got you. While they ate him the others escaped.'

'No, I saw him. I don't know children – four or five years old. He put up his hands to the dragons, and the dragons lay down in front of him.'

'You hear this sort of story all the time,' Levi said. 'It's being in the desert does it. Addles brains.'

Yes, you hear of demons all the time. There are demons everywhere in this world, all around us, inside us, everyone knows that. Immortal souls, the Essenes believe. But you don't hear of dragons. A dragon is altogether more.

Levi said, '*Then* they ate him?'

'No. He commanded the dragons to hurt no man, and no

woman. He commanded his mother and father not to be afraid of them.'

'And the dragons went away?'

'The dragons went away.'

I didn't know whether to believe it or not. Dragons, I believed that. But the rest of it, I don't know.

'It's the prophecy,' called an old fellow from another bench. These people never have a conversation in private, someone always interrupts, knows a better story. 'It's the prophecy of David. "Praise the Lord from the earth, ye dragons; ye dragons, and all ye deeps." ' Another prophecy. This world makes its own rules.

I had to ask. 'Did the child say anything to his mother or . . .' I could not say His father . . . 'to her husband?'

The thief looked at me with disgust because I had taken his semen, the oil of life, in my mouth. 'Yes, he did, not that it's any of your business. He piped up to them not to be afraid, because he was perfect. Perfect, he said! I'd've given him a good clout round his big head.'

Perhaps. But so many coincidences.

I asked, 'What town were you in?'

'Where there's money to be made, of course. Sepphoris.'

'That's a coincidence!' Levi said. 'That's where we're going. Sepphoris.'

I remembered years ago, a childish dream, déjà vu.

Miriam, do not go to Sepphoris.

DE NAZARENI

of Nazarenes

WEDNESDAY 12 JUNE AD 4

That stern warning no longer meant anything to me. I was old enough now to do whatever anyone told me not to do. Even if it was an angel. Rather, I was enticed. My blood was full of hormones, my body stormed with emotions of anger, self-hatred and despair that infected my thoughts, coloured my whole being. Breaking rules attracted me (these people have so many rules, laws, Thou Shalt Nots). And now I was old enough to wonder *why* an angel should be so anxious to keep me away from Sepphoris. Traditionally Sepphoris has nothing whatsoever to do with Jesus Christ. It's never mentioned. Not to go to Jerusalem, that I could understand. But why was Sepphoris forbidden me? Was I supposed to be so overawed by the revelations granted to me of Jesus's divinity in the manner of His birth that I would simply do as I was told without question?

A child would. As a child, I had not gone to Sepphoris. But now I was eleven years old, and pubic hair grew over my scar as though hiding sin. Blood trickled from me with each full moon, changing me. I was not in the mood to be obedient. God had not talked to me.

By the Dead Sea, God told Lot's wife not to look back when Sodom was destroyed, and she did, and she was turned to a pillar of salt. That God ruled by the fear of His word: obey Me or be destroyed. I could not worship a God of fear; to me that was not what He should be.

I wondered what was there at Sepphoris it was so important I should not see.

My mother watched me with worried looks. She could not stop me roaming along the shore or into the fields and even the mountains sometimes, so she believed me mad. She had never done such things. She always knew her place, was always meek, she never lost faith in her God however badly He punished her – and surely she cannot sensibly have thought a life as hard as hers was anything but punishment. Yet sometimes when I woke in the fields or on the beach, as today, she had found me and I felt her hand stroking my hair, and she kissed me and said, 'But I have you.' My God, she had so little! But even a mad daughter is better than nothing I suppose. In the square tradespeople stoned me on sight, and in the outskirts giggling children followed me twisting their arms like mine, carrying one shoulder higher than the other, sometimes rolling their eyes and talking to themselves. I must stop myself doing that. Older boys lounging on the walls followed me with their supercilious gaze, hungry for the holes in my body, curious, their moist tongues flickering in disgust and temptation: 'Look, Mary's a whore!' I forgot to tell you whores are also called by their familiar names, for contempt. The greater the lust the greater the contempt that follows. 'Mary'll do anything you want!' And they threw stones too, desiring me, fearing me.

I'm no whore. As you know, that is the one thing I cannot be.

But I'm everything else. Oh, I don't care.

Dull though she was, my mother loved me. She stroked my hair with a hand as gnarled by work as an old woman's. With her white hair she did indeed look old enough to be Levi's wife. 'I know you don't want to go to Sepphoris,' she murmured. 'I know your voices told you to stay in Magdala.'

'Angel!' I contradicted her spitefully. 'It was an angel.' She'd never understand.

'All right. Angel.'

'That's better.'

'But you see, there's so much building work in Sepphoris now. King Herod Antipas is having the whole city rebuilt!' People called Antipas king because he threw around the money he raised by punitive taxation, the census. Really he was just a petty prince, a tetrarch, the third and youngest brother but as cruel, crafty and grandiose as his elders. He ruled only a quarter of his father's kingdom but he was clever as a fox with the Romans. The eldest brother, Herod Archelaus, ruled the most important half of the kingdom around Jerusalem, but less cleverly. Herod Philip got the far shore of Lake Galilee and the Golan, and he and Herod Antipas competed in building cities to show off their wealth and attract trade and men of learning and holiness to their palaces, including Magi. My mother said eagerly, 'In Sepphoris your grandfather is bound to get work! It will improve him no end. You'll see. A job will give him back his pride in himself and he'll be kind and happy and so we'll all be happy.' She smiled rosily. 'In Sepphoris we'll have a proper house with stone walls and you won't have to go out. No one will know about you. I'll keep you secret at home and look after you.'

'Sounds like Heaven,' I said ironically, but it was a slip of the tongue. To these people Heaven is a place for God and His angels, not for ordinary people.

'Just the two of us. You'll get better.' My mother blamed herself for everything bad I had done. She stroked my twisted arm with tears in her eyes. She even blamed herself for that. What an endless capacity for guilt these people have. Even if they weren't sinners they'd want to be; they love guilt enough to roll in it.

'I'll go with you to Sepphoris,' I said, catching her off guard. I wanted to go. After all, it had been forbidden me on the highest authority, and forbidden pleasures are the most pleasurable.

'Promise you won't run away.' Her eyes widened. 'What?'

'I'll come with you to Sepphoris,' I said. I jumped up before she could hug me, walked back to the hut, and a hand grabbed my hair. Levi had dug up the hearth, heaping soil over the floor. There was nothing left in the hole. I'd sold anything of value he'd buried there years ago. He beat me unconscious with his fist.

My ribs were broken when I awoke, my body a living bruise as well as my face. My nose was swollen, broken, dripping slime and blood that ran up my forehead into my hair, for I was hung over the back of the donkey, my hands tied beneath its belly to my feet to stop me slipping off. The tight knots stripped the skin from my wrists and ankles as the donkey swayed agonisingly through the day, dust puffing from its hooves to my face, the sun coming down like a burning hand pressing on my bottom and spine and the back of my head. The donkey wheezed and stank, buzzing round its nose and arse with flies, and when we stopped at a pool I heard Levi drink thirstily. My mother's hands trembled too much for her to give me water from the ladle. Her weak trembling fingers worked at the knots for hours, it seemed – she was too afraid to cut Levi's rope – then finally the knots did give way and I flopped to the ground. I heard a fractured rib snap. On my elbows I crawled through the dust in agony to the water's edge and stared at my reflection. My face was pulp: black eyes, my nose like bruised fruit, my lip split into my cheek showing broken teeth inside. I hardly recognised myself. Levi gnawed a bone of lamb beneath a nearby tree. I looked at him and croaked. My mother said, 'Don't make him angry.'

I croaked at Levi, 'I hope you roast in Hell.'

He grinned, not realising what I meant. These people have no idea of Hell. Sheol or Gehenna was as far as his imagination went: eternity as pale dusty boredom. He picked the bone clean, came across smiling, kicked me, dragged me to the donkey before I could drink. Beat me furiously for making him drag me. No ride for me this time. He rode, and I staggered behind. The sun fell and I clung on to the donkey's buzzing, swarming tail. And so I came to Sepphoris.

And I was neither struck down by God nor turned to a pillar of salt for coming here. Those things don't happen in real life. But my grandfather was quickly lost in the confusion of new buildings and shacks springing up in the city he'd once known so well, and when he called out to someone asking what road this was, the reply came out of the dark: 'Nazareth.'

That answer threw Levi into a bad mood right from the start, because he knew perfectly well it was Sepphoris. There's no such place as Nazareth. I staggered over broken bricks and fell down in the ruin of a yard. Levi had evaded the census tax but at the cost of his property; his house was a ruin inhabited by beggars. He beat at them with a stick and they ran into the dark. Levi settled with my mother at their fire and I lay by a remnant of wall where he would not think of me. 'But she's just a child,' my mother said, and he remembered me and came over and beat me. 'Don't annoy him,' my mother begged. I was too weak for him to hurt; I thought he would kill me. With all my strength I tried to get up, and he kicked me to my feet.

'Wine,' he said. 'Then bread. Then dig.'

No doors would open in the dark. 'No wine here,' someone shouted from the tumbledown house beside Levi's. No wine at the next house either, or across the track. I saw my mother moving in the firelight. She had a little wine she had saved, and Levi drank it. She set about toasting balls of bread over the fire. 'Where have you been?' she asked me angrily. 'You know he likes things just so.' Levi pointed. I found a piece of broken pot and dug with my sliced hands bleeding on the sharp edges. From the ashy earth came a small box, then more pots; by sunrise a handful of gold coins, the bag rotted away; later copper bracelets tied by rotted rope; and by noon I uncovered a corner of the stone dyeing vat. Who ever would have stolen that, far too heavy to carry? But Levi was jealous of his possessions. He managed to find a door to wedge in the wall. The house had no roof, but already he'd made it a kind of prison. 'You stay inside,' he said.

The last sound I heard was children playing. I slept.

The next day I could not move. My body was swollen and without strength, a mass of bruises. My eyes were puffed shut; I was blind. Strangely enough Levi ignored me, and though I heard his footsteps at various times and felt his stinking breath as he examined my face, he let me lie. He'd been successful. He'd subdued me.

My mother brought me dates to suck, but I felt her looking at me reproachfully. I had made life much more difficult for her. I managed to spit out the date stone and a broken tooth. Somewhere the children were playing again, fighting, running, then laughter. A few moments of quiet then I heard another scream, more fighting. I picked out the sound of a baby crying then the shouts and cries of a

toddler, a girl I think. All from the same house? I thought
so. Their mother calling them then shouting at them, and
the sounds of smacks. Silence. Now Levi's voice negotiating
with someone for a pitched roof, putting those gold coins to
good use. He wanted clay tiles in the Roman style, *tegula*
and *imbrex*. 'Not too much straw,' I heard him warn Zeno
the tiler, a Gentile, 'and properly fired, not dried in the sun
and put up cracking. I'm nobody's fool.' Half frozen during
the night, I crawled into shadow during the heat of the day,
burning, one eye barely open. Every other house along the
track had a flat roof so Levi's sloped tiles would stand out,
Romanesque, sophisticated, superior, attracting rich trade.
The walls would be rendered with mortar, whitewashed,
encouraging good customers who valued style. Perhaps
turmeric eggs on the table, wine. A selection of cloths in
seventy-two colours (the traditional dyers' number meaning
'many'), and balls of wool graded for weaving and carpets.
Nothing too fancy for Jews, the best stuff inside for Greeks
and the traders whose caravans of camels and mules braying
under huge loads plodded on the road all day, slowing here
on the turn uphill to the city wall – cities live atop immense
mounds of their own filth and rubbish and shit. Merchants
arriving fully laden from Syria, Idumea, Galatia, even
Iberia, all smacking their lips at the sight of shitty Sepphoris
and its wealth. They would buy as well as sell. Levi was
lucky. They would meet him first.

My mother washed the stiffened blood from my face until
it hurt too much. My ribs stabbed me with each breath and
she didn't know what to do about them. 'They'll be all
right,' she decided. They weren't; they were healing
crooked. I wept, exhausted by the pain and frightened.

A sloped roof meant complicated woodwork to support
it, but there was so much work in the city that carpenters
were all rich men on high pay. Levi found a man nearby
who might do the work. 'You're a proper carpenter, right?'
Levi demanded. 'Know your job?'

A man's deep, slow voice replied using almost the same
word as carpenter. 'I'm a master.'

'Never mind that, can you make a joint without wasting
my money on nails?'

'I can do the work, neighbour. It's close to home.'

Sepphoris was a building site, and just as merchants and suppliers were drawn here like locusts to honey, so were itinerant builders and tradesmen from Alexandria, Antioch, anywhere over the Empire. My mother already spoke of robberies, extortion and violent gangs. Hammers and trowels rattled all day, taverns and whorehouses rattled all night. The carpenter obviously lived in the suburb from choice. 'I prefer to work near home.' He was not a good negotiator, stand-offish; I could almost hear Levi's fingers tightening on his purse-strings. 'I have a young family, you see.' Again that slow, familiar voice.

I sat up, gave an exclamation of pain, slipped back. Was it? I was almost sure it was him.

Silence now. A shriek from next door, a smack.

'All right, you, you can give me a price,' Levi said. 'Better make it a low one.'

The deep slow voice said, 'Let me examine the job.' Joseph's voice, I was sure. All Essene monks go out into the villages at certain times of the year. Having taken their vow of humility, they support themselves – having no money of their own – by humble toil. The Poor humbly learn of simple truths living daily hand to mouth with the real suffering poor, and instruct them in wisdom in return: they are Sons of Men learning from and instructing ordinary men and women here in the real word: us, the unclean, the filthy with sin, the illiterate, the debased, the criminal, the unbaptised. They are teaching the merely human to raise their eyes above the soil of the earth. For months each year the white-clothed Nazarenes of the Community at Sion live away from their monastery and preach throughout Judah, Samaria, Galilee, God's own land of Sion populated by God's chosen people.

His chosen people in desperate need of redemption and salvation, defiling and insulting their God by worshipping Him on the wrong days, by the moon not the sun. Not an opinion the Essenes dare preach out loud among the Pharisees and Sadducees; but there were other ways.

I heard a ladder creak. A head of long swaying hair appeared, and then that familiar bearded face stared down from the top of the wall. Shocked at the sight of me, he almost fell back; I think for a moment he had thought I was

83

dead. A person who lives by Nazarene discipline is contaminated by death, must cut off his hair and begin his purification all over again, or lose the virtue which is his strength; you know what happened to Samson, the Nazarene who lost his strength when his wife Delilah cut his hair.

Joseph pointed his blunt forefinger. 'Who is she? Is she well?'

'She's no one. She's my daughter,' came Levi's irritated voice from below the wall. 'Can you do the work or not?'

Joseph forgot about me. He blew out his cheeks, estimated distance and angle. 'I'll have to find the wood. It's scarce and expensive here. And I won't buy in town. My health.'

'I'll buy it,' Levi said impatiently. 'The man isn't born yet who can cheat me.'

Joseph named his price. It was so cheap that Levi gasped before covering his pleasure. 'Deal!' He spat on his hand to seal the bargain, and Joseph looked at him with utter revulsion. For a moment the gap between the two men was as wide as the Jordan.

'That man's a fool!' Levi told my mother that night, before screwing her, turning over and going to sleep below the stars.

I lay awake. If our neighbour was Joseph, the earthly guardian of Jesus Christ, who were the children I had heard playing together?

Infuriatingly, the courtyard of their house had high walls, rough and peeling though they were. The gate was slatted wood, showing only snatches of movement beyond. Sometimes I glimpsed fleeting shapes running, pushing. Heard excited calls, games. Shrieks, a baby crying. Angry shouts. A month passed until I walked without pain, and my curiosity grew almost unbearable. What a mysterious family they were. Fortunately the track to the well led past their gate.

Each morning my mother gave me the bucket and I limped four hundred dusty cubits down the hill to the well, and at least a thousand back uphill, it felt like, with my heavy slopping burden. Boys from the town had quickly found out about the little Nazarene community round here and picked on them. I suppose with my long hair I looked a little like a Nazarene. Boys overturned my bucket, ran off with it, taunted me because I could not catch them. Girls pulled my hair. I hated the girls. They were much worse than the boys; none of them showed me a moment's compassion. But one of them was slow, and I caught her hair and bit her cheek. She squealed like the pigs the Greeks eat, that squirt their shit on the road as they are driven terrified past us into town, leaving a brown trail of desecration among our houses. She fell into the shit and I screamed, good, I'd bite her again. After that the girls stoned me too. I was a troublemaker. Their mothers accosted my mother and tore her shawl for my crime. So I fetched water when it was still dark, before dawn.

At first light each day as I returned (except the Sabbath and the day before), Joseph climbed on to Levi's roof and worked patiently through the daylight hours. I watched him. Did he believe his simple toil improved him? Joseph was exhausted, and his bushy hair made him look heavier than he was. By sunset his white robe was stained with sawdust and toil, and as he came down the ladder I saw his thin white legs. He prayed more than he ate: only a little bread at the sixth hour. Was this the Joseph I remembered, a prince, husband of Mary? I watched him chew his bread. He avoided me because of my sex, not meeting my eye. To Essenes women are as low as Gentiles, unclean, the tenth grade.

He was a terrible carpenter. Without the support of Delanos the Essene paymaster Joseph would never have made ends meet. He measured logs by eye as though expecting God to make them right, and they were always too long or too short.

He glanced at me as he worked and crinkled his eyes, noticing me and forgetting he should not. Usually religious people are full of pride, but once he carried my bucket, making himself humble to the point of abasement. Yet he lived in that good solid house with a courtyard, all paid for by Delanos from money gathered by the Essene tax collector, a man called Matthew.

I watched Joseph at noon prayer to his God, overheard his slow deep voice of faith as I crept around him. He was a simple as well as a humble man, but that made him no less powerful.

'Lord,' he prayed, 'You are the Master and Guardian of all things. Even here in the dominion of Satan, nothing happens to any man unless it is Your will. I believe everything is foreordained by You, I believe nothing happens by chance. Without You there is no love. Without You a child is not conceived. From You comes all that is and all that shall be.' I lost his voice for the squealing of pigs on the path outside. He put his hands to his head. 'Let me in accord with Your glorious design accomplish my task without change or stumbling . . .' His shoulders shook, and as I came round in front of him I saw that Joseph was weeping. His voice choked. 'It is written by the rabbis of the Law that the sins for which we shall be forgiven shall cause our Christ to be put under an iron yoke, and our sins shall cause Him to be made like a calf whose eyes are dim, and we will choke His spirit under the yoke. And our Christ will be bruised and wounded by our iniquities. And whatever man or woman will not admit that our Christ suffers for our iniquities, shall endure and suffer them for himself and herself for all eternity. Lord, forgive us.'

Tears streamed down Joseph's cheeks. He could not stop. His tears trickled like shining beads down his long beard, snot dripped from his nose. Blasphemy for an Essene at prayer, with their strict rules against spitting and the foulness of any discharge from the body. He couldn't help himself.

He twisted his body away from me, hid his head under his robe so that his God should not see him in this state. I had never sensed such loneliness, such desolation, like a desert he carried inside his soul, as though this world was no more than a shadow. What terrible wickedness had he found, or loss of faith? My hand fluttered at his shoulder, but my touch was unclean.

'Guide me, Lord,' Joseph cried out. 'Guide me in what I must do!'

I backed away from him to another room. But I thought about him all night.

Something had gone wrong, I was sure of it. Where was Mary? What of the Child? Were they still in Egypt, or had something worse happened? And surely Jesus was an only child? Was Joseph's house looked after by a housekeeper, was it the housekeeper's children I heard playing? What a racket! The more they were kept inside, the more the little horrors played up. Next morning, as I returned with the slopping bucket, it sounded as though the elder boys were torturing the younger ones. Several times on other days I'd heard things broken, bowls probably, and a stool I think. This morning I heard the woman weeping. Joseph was away fetching wood. I stopped.

A woman weeping is a familiar enough sound, after all. I've made my mother weep often enough. Why didn't she let them out to burn off their energy? The children taunted each other, out of control over some game or possession. I heard the woman's scream of rage. She'd had enough. I looked round, then put my eye to the slats.

An eye looked back at me. 'Mother, there's someone at the gate!'

The running footsteps of more children, more eyes staring at the slats. I stood, flustered. It was too late for me to escape. Several jumped up to see me better, little fingers grasping the slats like prisoners, childish voices whispering excitedly. The mother called, 'Who is it?'

An older child's voice said confidently, 'It's only the witch from the next house, Mother. She needs help. Shall I let her in?'

A toddler squealed, 'It's the witch!' The others cried out to see.

'Mother? Shall I open the gate?'

'No!' she said. 'Tell her to go away!' But it was too late. The gate swung wide, and there they were, the boy who had spoken looking at me with a clear brown gaze, his brothers and sisters around him. Very handsome he'd grow up, with his level black eyebrows and hair all curls like that, the sort of face that caught you right away, made you look at him. I vaguely noticed the others milling around me, touching my clothes, staring up at my face, but this boy looked at me so directly that I could not think what to say. 'I'm sorry,' I muttered. 'Forgive me, I didn't mean—'

Without looking down from my eyes the boy called, 'She

thought I wouldn't see her, Mother. She was peeping. I saw her.'

The round-eyed toddler with red cheeks said, 'She's so ugly.' He began to cry. I wondered if I should pick him up.

'I'll do it.' The mother held her scarf across her nose, hiding her face, but I recognised her eyes. How did she know what I was thinking? She took the toddler impatiently, jolted him to make him quiet, would not look at me. 'Well? What do you want?'

'I'm Miriam,' I said. For the first time in my life I was shy. 'I have the same name as you.'

'You're looking for work? We have no money!' She put her hand on the gate to close me out. No, no. I said something quickly.

'I saw your baby born in the stable.'

The Virgin stared at me as though I were mad, and her scarf slipped. In her early twenties, she was a woman a lifetime older than the girl I remembered. Her skin was dry, the lines in her face caked with grey dust, her dark hair stripped of its youthful cared-for shine. She no longer needed to find a husband. She'd had her children and she looked like any harassed mother I've ever seen, any of them up and down the road. What else had I expected?

'I'm sorry,' I blurted. I was sorry for her. She'd started off her marriage with such high hopes. Those early days must seem like just a dream now. A girl's romantic dream.

'You keep saying you're sorry, Miriam,' she said. But she was lonely because her hand still did not close the gate. 'All my babies were born in a stable.'

Of course Joseph loved her. It was not a loveless marriage. How could I ever have thought so for one moment? They were human, not divine; I had denied them the greatest human attribute. 'In Bethlehem?' I said.

'Yes, in Bethlehem. Of course.'

All of them! 'I could help you look after them. I wouldn't mind.' I shuffled, intensely aware of my appearance, my twisted shoulder, my cheekbone that had never healed properly. I tried to smile with my lips closed, not showing the teeth that Levi had broken.

'You have lovely hair,' she said longingly. 'I had hair like that once, when I was young.'

88

'I comb it every day.' The boys groaned. Woman talk.

She asked, 'How old are you, child?'

'Eleven. Just twelve now.'

'Just twelve. You should be married. I was.' She handed me the toddler, and he hung on to my neck. I wrapped my arms around him and the child touched my cheekbone wonderingly.

'I'm not pretty, mistress,' I said. I remembered how beautiful and beautifully innocent she had been, all I am not, stained by living and death and all I've lost; not innocent or in love since the earth was young. 'I'll never find a husband, mistress.' More mocking groans from the boys. But I had to be among them, I had to *know*. Would their mother trust me near them, an outsider, not Nazarene, not an Essene – and thus not, to her, a true Jew? To the beliefs of her sect I was a common Jew lost to Satan and Belial. But I could not discern her thoughts even when she looked into my eyes. 'You have strange eyes.' Indigo-blue, you recall; eyes do not change. She shivered, as though remembering them from somewhere. 'I almost . . . I almost think you are an angel, Miriam.' Essenes believe in angels, *kedoshim*, though Sadducees and Pharisees do not believe; Zacharias had been struck dumb by the archangel Gabriel for his disbelief.

I laughed, 'Angel!' and she smiled at herself. 'Still,' she said, 'we do believe that a person's soul, fallen from the heavenly ether to this world and chained in a foul soiled body on the earth, looks out like sparks of Heaven through that person's eyes.'

At first it had felt odd to think of this ordinary-looking woman as the Virgin (how had I expected her to look?), but now as she recovered her composure and spoke to me of things with which she was familiar her natural dignity returned. She inclined her head to welcome me through the gate, stepped smoothly backwards. Years of devotion in the Temple had taught her how to move with flawless delicacy and control. But not how to be a mother – the babble of the children rose to an angry squall, interrupting her thoughts as she tried to speak, and the boys pushed and shoved at each other to be closest to my side. The toddler I carried, victorious in his position of eminence, stuck out his tongue at them.

'I'm Joses, me,' he whispered, 'you can carry Joses all day.' His name so startled me I almost dropped him – for a moment I thought he said Jesus. But Joses was much too young, two, three years old.

'I'm Jacob.' The boy who had opened the gate shut it behind me, and I looked round for the eldest child in the yard. Surely I would recognise the Christ-child, Immanuel. Would He wear His halo? How would a perfect child look? Perhaps that was why His mother kept the gate always closed, protecting Him from admirers. No; He would not be what I expected. God must altogether, in every way, exceed my expectations. Surely any preconceptions of Him, the Son of God, the real God, were ridiculous. He must exceed them by His very nature.

He was born a man. The baby I had seen in the stable looked simply human. So he must look like an ordinary child, not an angel. At least until the time of His Recognition came.

Which one of them was called Immanuel?

'My father works on your roof,' Jacob said loudly. He must be seven or eight but he looked older, tall, almost as tall as me. She fed them well. 'My father's an important man.'

'Our father,' one of the other boys said. By size he might be a twin of the first, but not by his look. He gave me a smile as shy as my own.

The confident boy wasn't having it. He threw a punch. '*My* father!'

'Silence, Jacob!' their mother warned. 'You two!'

The two elder boys exchanged punches, kicks, rolled in the dust. The boy who I had thought, wrongly, was shy now fought back with an anger equal to his brother's. Goodness, they were rough! Jacob was stronger but the other, thinner, made up for it with wiry quickness. Struck, his long arm flew out in return, drew a thread of blood from Jacob's nose.

'That's Joshua, the rough one,' Mary said. 'I'm so sorry about this. They're wild. Their father won't control them. I don't know what to do with them.' She put her hands to her head, screamed: 'Stop it!'

Joshua smacked Jacob's nose for the second time. The

blood stuck to his fist and Jacob's eyes streamed. It was hateful. It was a game to them but Levi's violence filled my mind, I felt his blows inside myself, happening again. Joses slipped from my arms to the ground; he wanted to join in. I stepped in front of him towards the older boys. 'Please,' I said. 'Please don't.'

My head was struck, by Joshua's elbow, I think. I tripped into the sand, falling on my twisted arm. The boys drew back, appalled.

'You hit her!' Jacob said. 'Mother, he hit her.'

'*You* hit her,' Joshua said. 'I never hit her. Why's it always me?' He looked at his mother with tears in his eyes. She shouted at both of them, 'Stop arguing!'

'Yes, stop.' Jacob elbowed his brother. I knew they'd side against me.

'It was her fault,' Joshua said. 'She must be stupid.'

They helped me to my feet. 'It wasn't hard,' Jacob decided. 'I can't even see where it was, can you? Besides, she's used to it. Look at her bruises.'

'She must be clumsy,' Joshua said. 'I think she fell over between us, that's all.'

'She tripped,' Jacob agreed. He grinned at me and I couldn't help grinning back. The brothers tousled each other's hair. 'It was her fault,' they decided.

Their mother told them coldly: 'Go into the house. Wash yourselves. Pray for the Lord's forgiveness for what you have done.'

Joshua said, 'And especially for Miriam's forgiveness.'

Jacob threw back over his shoulder, 'She's tough.'

'For a girl,' Joshua said, 'but boys are tougher.' They raced each other to the doorway.

Mary stared after them. She said: 'What have I done? I've already failed them, haven't I.' A mother is defenceless most of all against her own children. They slip between the gaps in her, are her and yet not-her. Mary had given them the freedom denied to her in her own childhood. They took for granted something which was very hard for her.

She sat in the shade of the scrawny lemon tree, motioned me to sit at her feet, examined my head with quick touches of her fingertips. 'Joshua's elbow's not the worst thing to have happened to you, child.' She dabbed balm on my

91

temple. 'My own mixture. The Essenes are great healers, it's how they got their name, *Asayya*. Healers.' Her voice ran on. She gave a pretty little smile and the years lifted from her face. How lonely she was, seeking out the company of a child of twelve years old! She wasn't originally from a Nazarene family – Joachim and Anna were ordinary Jews – and for a toddler to enter the Temple of the Sadducees and Pharisees as a Virgin aged three, as Mary had, was to enter a kind of death. She was a child without a childhood. Obviously she had no idea how to deal with children; they wore her out. Yet her eyes shone as Joses ran past with his little bottom flashing out of his tunic. 'And Joses's little brother is Shimon, Silas we call him, there are so many Shimons.' As a mother she thought to love them was enough, however wild they were. 'My youngest are twins.' Her eyes lit. She loved to talk about her family. 'Oh-oh, hear them? They've woken early!' She fetched two swaddled babies from inside the house, let me hold one, showed me the other. 'This is Thomas, which means twin. He's the eldest. Sometimes we call him Didymus.' The baby grinned at me.

'Didymus?'

'It's Greek for twin. He understands it. The sound makes him laugh. Look.' She tickled him, and the baby chuckled and writhed. 'Tickly-Didymus. Isn't he clever?' The twin I held inserted its finger curiously in my mouth. They were ordinary children; this was an ordinary family. 'She's a girl,' Mary said proudly. 'My second. I named her after me. Miri.' Another Mary. 'You saw my first girl running about earlier? What a difficult one. I named that one after the midwife who birthed her.'

'Salome,' I said. Mary – I could no longer think of her as the Virgin – looked startled at the accuracy of my reply. Then she laughed. 'Yes, Salome! Do I shout so loud at her? You must have overheard me.' But again she gave that look into my eyes.

Here was my chance. We had covered all the names and there was no child here called Immanuel, but usually the first male was given the father's name. 'I suppose your eldest son is named Joseph?' I asked obliquely. 'Have I met him?'

'My husband—' But there was a knock at the gate. Mary dropped Tom in my lap and went to the latch, piously covering her head with her scarf. 'Oh, it's you, Matthew. Come in.'

A man's voice, deep, with a learned accent, spoke Hebrew. 'I looked for my brother. Is the Alphaeus not back?'

'Joseph will be back soon, rabbi.'

'There are the preparations to discuss for the Feast of Tabernacles.' Matthew must be Joseph's younger brother. Perhaps thirty-five years old, his hair lay in shiny black curls across his white linen shoulders. His white gown was immaculately starched. At his throat hung the copper symbol of a dove, which revealed to initiates (the Rainmaker observed these people for many months), Matthew's rank as an Essene levite, or priest. A levite of the rank of dove was circumcised but celibate.

Mary said, 'Tabernacles?'

'Arrangements to be made for the journey. Money. Protection. Donkeys. The twins will find the journey long and trying.'

'Rabbi, must they go?'

'All shall attend at Sion during Tabernacles. It's the Law, Mary.' A husband's brother was permitted the intimate use of the wife's name. Brothers were inextricably close. Back in the days of the levirate a brother must marry his brother's widow and father a child on her. For him to fail to do so was the sin of Onan, punished by *halitzah*, public humiliation. As a celibate Matthew was forbidden ever to marry, but the formality remained, part of the invisible web of custom that binds these people together as tight as strands of rope. She bowed her head, overruled.

Backing away before him, she welcomed her dignified visitor into the chaos of the courtyard. Took his foul pig-shitted sandals in her hands, washed his feet, slipped the thongs of a clean pair of household sandals between his toes. She seated him among the cool fragrant shrubs in the corner across the yard. No vines had been trained up the bare sandstone walls. Her face still hidden by her scarf, she hurried into the house.

Matthew ignored me. He spread rustling scrolls, papers,

records, lists of accounts on the bench, examined his complex work with practised flicks of his eyes, made brief notations with his stylus. Obviously he was a scribe, a polite word for a tax collector – these people give all their property and income to their Community, and receive in return. I cuddled the twins and watched Mary return with two bowls of water, one with mint leaves, another containing sliced lemon, and set them on the low table beside him. No beer or wine for a Nazarene. She cleaned his fingers with the lemon water, dabbed his face. She left him and as he sipped the mint water the table rocked on its uneven legs. He put out his hand to steady it, frowning.

Mary knelt at the gate, scrubbed his dirty discarded sandals. The yellow slime clung to her fingers and she looked sick. I laid the twins in a crib and went over.

'I'll do it for you,' I said, kneeling beside her.

'Isn't this a terrible place?' she whispered, jerking her head at the invisible world beyond the walls. She'd tied up her hair to avoid contamination with her work. 'it's worse than Gehenna. Pig—' She could not say the word, though it is the most familiar word of all to mothers with young children. I giggled. 'I believe we live in the Hell of Babylon,' she whispered seriously. Her words struck so close to my own thoughts that I stared at her, then covered my interest with scrubbing. *I believe we live in Hell.* She was anything but ordinary, it was the first time I had heard a Jew speak of Hell. She was only a human, but her soul was large. 'At Sion, by the Dead Sea, even the air is pure. The sun washes the air and sand and salt with its cleansing rays. There is no dirt. But here is nothing but dirt, Greeks, Gentiles, the Rich and pigs, and daily the Law is broken.'

'The Law?'

'The Law that teaches us how to live. I mean the Essene Law, righteous living. In all my years in innocence at the Temple,' she murmured, to herself as much as to me, no more than a child, 'I believed I was doing good, serving God by adoring Him in the ritual and liturgy every minute of every day. Now my husband and people like Matthew assure me that everything that I believed and did is wrong.' She put down his cleaned sandals carefully, then washed her hands three times and made me wash my own.

'Anyway, you have your children now,' I said, 'so you're probably too busy to care!' She laughed, looked into my eyes. She loved to talk about her children more than she knew how to deal with them. We sat with our heads close together, she and I, talking in whispers like this, trying not to disturb Matthew's work or the sleeping twins. In many ways beneath the skin she was still the Virgin, I realised, beneath the demands of age and mortality she remained a child inside herself, as self-contained as the walls that enclosed her house. An innocent child-adult, whereas I am her opposite, an adult in the form of a child. The sun moved the shadows around the mess her children had made of the yard. I saw Jacob and Joshua watching us from a window. 'Those two look like twins,' I said.

'My eldest?' She shook her head. 'Yes, I often think so, but they're not.' Matthew put down his stylus and she hurried to him with a platter of dates and other fruit. He arranged his gown, ready for the day's lesson, and she beckoned Jacob and Joshua from the house. The boys sat cross-legged on the ground at Matthew's cleansed feet, their heads turned up to him, and I heard him speak. 'Children, every scribe who has learnt of Heaven is like a householder who brings from his box of knowledge things new and old. Let us begin . . .'

Mary sat quietly beside me. 'It's all so different from what I imagined,' she sighed. 'My life. So very different.'

I watched Jacob and Joshua learning. Matthew instructed them, 'God shall reign over the whole world from Mount Sion. The enemies of Israel will learn by their fate to bow down to Israel.'

'Does that mean we'll win, rabbi?' Jacob asked eagerly. 'Will we beat the Romans? Is that the prophecy's meaning?'

'Each year the nations of the world shall come to Sion on pilgrimage to attend the Lord's enthronement at the Feast of Tabernacles.'

'And the Romans too?' Jacob asked. 'Will they bow down at our feet – I mean God's feet?'

Matthew tapped Jacob's head reprovingly. 'Patience, Jacob. The Lord will help us. But first, listen, for thus says the Lord: 'I will not feed you: he who dieth, let him die; and he that is to be cut off, let him be cut off, and let the rest eat every one the flesh of another.'

'Who is he?' Joshua asked. 'Who is the other?'

Matthew said: 'This is the prophecy of Zecher, written down for us five hundred years ago, and anyone with two good ears must prick them up.' Joshua laughed indiscreetly, touching his ears. I could tell he loved the picture that came into his mind. Matthew frowned, then continued. 'First, the Lord took His sceptre, Beauty, and cut it asunder to break His covenant which He had made with all His people.'

'The Ark of the Covenant that Moses found!' Jacob interrupted quickly.

'That God gave to Moses in the mountain,' Matthew corrected him, but gently. 'Not *Ark*, it is Arch. We say Arch, the Arch that connects the two pillars of the Covenant, priest and king, Zadok and Christ. The pillars of gold, the metal of Heaven. The Arch whose pillars are joined by a box of acacia wood and beaten gold that contains within it the Way to the Lord and the Voice of the Lord. The Arch that we carried with us everywhere, the Arch that defeated our enemies in battle, the Arch that Zadok placed in the first Temple for King Solomon, the building "not built by the hands of men", destroyed by the soldiers of Babylon. But Zadok had hidden the Arch where none but Zadok would find it.' Jacob paid close attention to every word. But Joshua's eyes wandered to the wall, to the babies, to his mother and me talking; he wanted to overhear our prattle. Matthew slapped his head.

'Ow,' Joshua said. 'Sorry.' He remembered the correct phrase. 'Forgive me, rabbi, for I have sinned.'

Matthew ignored him. 'So, Jacob, more than five hundred years ago the Lord broke His covenant with the Jews. He hid the Arch from His people. The soldiers of Babylon sold us into slavery. The Romans, the Kittim, conquered our land. The Pharisees and the scholars have taken the keys of knowledge and hidden them. They have not entered nor have they allowed the Poor to enter. But we Poor of the flock wait on Him, faithful in our rituals to Him, knowing that before the end of the world we shall hear the Word of the Lord. And the Lord says, "If you think good, give me my price; and if not, forbear." ' Matthew spoke sharply.

'Joshua! What price did the Poor agree to pay to the Lord to receive His Covenant?'

'The Poor shall pay thirty talents of silver to the Lord,' Joshua said. He had been paying attention after all. 'And His Covenant shall be renewed with us.'

Jacob pushed forward. 'And then, rabbi, the Lord shall take the thirty talents of silver and cast them to the potter in the Temple. It's in the prophecy.' The Essenes actually believed the Arch of the Covenant was still hidden somewhere in the Temple.

'Well done, Jacob,' Matthew said. 'Although "potter" may also mean a treasury, or even a melting-pot.'

Joshua interrupted, 'Or Gentiles.' He wriggled, embarrassed by Matthew's stare. 'The potter's field below Sion, where the foreigners camp.' He wilted, but then resisted Matthew's steady gaze. 'I mean, rabbi, that Gentiles are unformed clay. To be taken in hand . . . you know . . . shaped by the potter. Initiated. Ordained.'

'Foreigners are foreigners,' Jacob said. 'They aren't like us. They will never have the covenant with God. They don't observe God's promise, the Law. They can't see it, it's not revealed to them. They're blind. Only foreign Jews are allowed into the potter's field, the field of holy blood, not Gentiles.'

Matthew kept his attention on Jacob. 'By the renewal of His Covenant, what does the Lord promise to the Poor?'

'That He shall restore the royal line of David,' Jacob said. 'The heir of David shall be enthroned king as Christ, the zadok equal in rank with him at his right hand: they are the two pillars of the Arch. The most pure and righteous of the Poor, the Nazarenes, the *Notzri ha-Brit*, shall be the Keepers of the Covenant, the guardians of God's Word. There shall be no guilt in the land, purity restored to the Temple, the idols thrown down. Our cities overflowing with prosperity. A plague shall strike out from Israel at the nations of the world, they shall rot where they stand on their feet. And those who have turned to God shall mourn for Him whom they have pierced.'

'Good, Jacob. You've learnt your lessons well. And the shepherds of which Zecher speaks?'

'Rabbi, there is a foolish shepherd who will neither visit,

nor seek, nor heal, nor give sustenance. A second shepherd leaves the flock and carries a sword with the light of battle in his eye.'

Mary and I have fallen silent. I can't help looking at her rapt, hopeful face. How these people love their crazy prophecies! They believe their past creates their future, their dreadful past, yet they hope for a golden future. 'And those who have turned to God shall mourn for Him whom they have pierced.' What can it mean? They'll injure God? How can a people mislead themselves so thoroughly, how can they be so wrong? Somewhere here, I *know* (I witnessed God's promise to the Virgin), is Immanuel, Jesus Christ, the Son of God, and He shall rule over Jerusalem as priest and king for a thousand years, and save us all. I believe, I do believe it, I must. Or live again in despair. And again. And again.

'Tomorrow we shall consider the prophecies of Jeremiah,' Matthew said.

Jacob understood instantly. 'Shall I study, "Do you take this Temple that bears My name for a robbers' den?" '

'Yes, the righteous destruction of the Temple that is to come. You do your work well, Jacob.' Matthew turned back to his work. The boys played quietly in a corner, where Joseph had dug a well. A puddle remained from the last rain and Joshua scooped it into seven pools with his hands, then scratched channels with his fingers so that the water ran together again. 'That's a stupid game,' Jacob said, and I thought there'd be another fight. Fortunately Matthew had gone into the house. Joshua pushed Jacob against the courtyard wall, hard. 'Careful, careful!' Jacob taunted him. He was stronger than Joshua, muscular where Joshua was slim.

Mary followed my gaze. 'I do everything for them. Protect them. Love them. Bring them up the best I can. And sometimes I'm so ashamed of them. Louts.'

'Leave the gate open,' I said.

'I couldn't do that!' she said. 'The street. The people. The gangs. Robbers. The herds of pigs. Other children. Something terrible would happen.'

I watched the two boys push each other, expecting trouble. Joshua slipped, fell backwards in the pools he had made, and Jacob howled with laughter. Joshua jumped up, bunched his fists, his face red with anger. I was pleased he didn't have a knife. Jacob backed away from him, then laughed from a safe distance. Joshua kicked the pools to mud. He had a furious anger in him.

'Joshua!' Mary shouted.

Joshua kicked his sandals off. He threw them in the mud. I saw he had beautiful feet, with long toes and slim ankles. Panting, he picked them out of the mud and threw them at Jacob, who managed to catch them. 'Now they'll be friends,' I said.

She shook her head, but the two boys began laughing at themselves spattered with mud, circled warily, then embraced. Friends.

'If the gate was open,' I said, 'I could keep an eye on them for you.'

She hesitated, but I persisted. *All my babies were born in a stable. In Bethlehem.* I sensed the power here like the eye of the storm, as though around me whirled the winds of the hurricanes that are born in the ocean beyond the sea, that blow clear to the land of the Nephites. Here, now, was the centre of the universe. Somewhere here was Immanuel.

IMMANUEL

Son of God

Next day, the gate opened, the children ran out, and found me sitting in the dust. They gathered around, afraid of my touch.

'Why are you sitting in the dirt?' Jacob asked. He was always first.

'It's fun,' I said. They looked such clean boys. Washed. Scrubbed. 'You're afraid of dirt?'

'Not afraid of anything,' Jacob said.

'Except God,' said Joshua.

'God's angry with us,' little Joses said.

'Yes,' Jacob and Joshua said together. They circled me like animals, staring, sniffing. 'Isn't she old?' they whispered. 'And ugly. And she's so dirty!' My dirty knees, my bottom in the dust, my dusty scabby face. The boys decided together, 'She's just a living, walking sin, she's just an ordinary Jew. She stinks! We should wash her.' They grew quite frightening, prowling round me like this. A voice behind me, then speaking across the top of my head, and wherever I turned they were not quite there. Testing me.

I spoke up. 'You boys rolled in the dirt yesterday, in your yard.' I smiled at Salome, her lovely dark eyes, a girl. 'Dirty boys, dirty boys!' I taunted them. If only I could have a girl to talk to. But Salome hung back, watching the boys. She'd do nothing without them.

'In there's *our* dust,' Jacob said. 'This outside is dirt. Animals do their dung in it. It's dung-dirt, this.'

'By now the whole world's made of shit,' I said.

They stared. 'She doesn't speak like a girl,' Jacob said.

'There can't have been enough time for everything to have been defiled,' Joshua said. 'God created Heaven and Earth three thousand seven hundred and sixty-four years ago. It's easy to work out by counting the generations from Adam.'

'Don't insult God!' Jacob looked alarmed. 'That's wrong. You're a Jerusalem priest, a dog baying at the moon.' They were going to fight again.

I said quickly, 'Does it matter?'

'It matters to God,' Jacob said simply. 'Essene astrologers calculate the stars and the signs of God precisely. God created the earth three thousand *nine* hundred and *forty-five* years ago, in the month of Tishri.'

Joshua said: 'Matthew says it was the month of Nisan.'

'No! In Tishri all those years ago God first showed Himself in this world, and created Heaven and Earth. Everything is explained, all the prophecies fall into place! The predicted destruction of the First Temple five hundred and eighty-six years ago. The ordained exile of Essenes at Sion, the land of our desolation, one hundred and forty-four years ago. The return of Zadok, who hid the Arch in Jerusalem on King David's command when David was driven from Jerusalem by his son Absalom's rebellion. The coming of Christ and the fall of the Second Temple that will occur according to His scheme. The dawn of true worship by pure men will come, men deserving of salvation, not baying dogs. History, prophecies, coming together like strands drawn together on a loom, weaving the Hand of God. We shall see God and build the Last Temple to His glory, and every secret knowledge and of the universe and of Heaven shall be revealed in His *shekinah*, the dawn of His divine illumination at the end of time.'

In the silence Joshua said, 'Still, Matthew says it was Nisan.'

Jacob said, 'Matthew is only a man and he shall see what he shall see. I know the truth. Only by pure living can we see God.'

Joshua explained to me, 'Men make impurity. Waste. Dirt. Sin. Breath. Words.'

'Only the Word of God is perfect,' Jacob said. 'A man is

born sinful. Every word a man speaks is sinful, impure, filthy. Breath is filth and the tongue that utters words births them in slime.'

'Your father's a man of few words,' I said. These young brothers were formidable in their young learning, their parroted wisdom, but didn't they know how to be children? I'd seen the Holy Child born seven years and (I counted quickly) three, now four months ago; either of these boys could have passed for that age, but despite their height and strength, well fed, sheltered, protected, educated, must be a year younger at least. Despite the strictness of Matthew the levite's teaching and the obedience with which they soaked it up, to me they seemed so lively, wilful, uncontrolled. And threatening – I felt in danger from the fierceness of their childish minds, their intolerance. A man in long robes leant by the gate, yawning, bearded, his hands hidden, watching over them, precious sons of the royal line of David. It was not the herdsmen shoving between the workshops who frightened me, rough and noisy though they were, ordinary men whacking their animals with sticks, shouting oaths and curses. These two children, little boys half my age who knew much of learning but nothing of the world, frightened me. And their guard wore a short club in his belt and a knife hidden beneath his clothes, I thought. A zealot at least, perhaps a sicariot.

'My father keeps his peace because silence is a virtue,' Jacob said. He thought I was an idiot for not paying attention. 'Listen, Miriam. Only prayers are clean, because they are not spoken, but spring soundlessly from the heart and mind which are the residence of the soul. Prayers are the soul's pure longing for God.'

But I'd heard Joseph at prayer crying aloud, defiling himself in his distress.

'Are you trying to convert me?' I said.

Joshua said angrily, 'Are you trying to convert us?'

Joses, hardly old enough to walk, sat down abruptly in the dust. He clenched the dirt wonderingly in his chubby fists. 'Dirt doesn't hurt,' he said. He rubbed it on his face.

'Now you look almost as bad as Miriam, dirty-face,' Salome scolded him, but she was attracted to me. She looked at me yearningly, as friendless as I. 'What colour is your dress?' She didn't know colours. I put my head close to hers. 'Rust-red, like rusty iron, and the bands are yellow gold!' Salome's small brown hands dared touch the weave. She laughed.

'But it's just cheap wool!'

'You'll get sores and die for touching her,' Jacob said.

Joshua said, 'How'd you burn your hands, Miriam?'

'From the well rope. In summer the water's that far down.'

'We have our own well,' Jacob said. He stared at the people milling in the street. 'They blame us because their wells are low, say we're stealing their water.'

' "They"?'

'You. Ordinary Jews.' He looked at me aggressively. 'You hate us. Call us thieves.'

'You shouldn't wash so much,' I said.

He said simply: 'It's the Law. All Essenes live in cleanliness and purity. We have to be baptised into our faith even if we are born to it.' Pride crept into his voice. 'My grandfather invented baptism. It's a holy rite, so we know who we are for sure. We're pushed under a pool of water and held down and when we're lifted up, it's by God, we're reborn. A Nazarene consecrates his body to God. Nazarene is from the word *Nazi*, meaning Prince. Each time we wash it renews our baptism, our personal oath to God.'

'You wash every day?'

'No, twice every day. Morning, evening. And before meals.'

'Everything clean and pure and fresh is holy,' Joshua said. 'Everything is part of God.'

'Only to the righteous,' Jacob said. 'My father washes seven times a day. Without righteous living, there is no God. We are the Princes of the Congregation.'

Dust rose in the heat of the afternoon; people pushed through the clouds of dust and stink like yellow-brown shadows. I said, 'No wonder people think you're different.'

'We are different,' Jacob said. 'Because everyone else lives in lies and dirt and sin.'

I picked up some stones and played pebbles and knock-knuckle with Salome. Joses tried to join in and I taught him, guiding his hands. The two elder boys stood looking round them awkwardly, then Joshua crouched, touched my knuckle. 'How do you do it?'

Jacob crouched beside him. I smiled. They'd forget themselves in games. I knew we'd be friends as long as we played.

'Like this,' I said.

How wrong I was.

But at first it didn't seem as though anything was wrong. That I would be a friend, not an enemy.

Oh, I lay awake in the night thinking about them, couldn't stop! Lucifer the morning star rose to announce the dawn before I realised that my rope-burnt hands no longer hurt. By first light I examined the shiny scalds of my fingertips. No scalds, no burns. Gone. The tiny whorls of my fingerprints, my individuality, were perfect. Each one. Perfect.

Which boy touched me? I couldn't remember. None of them. All of them. Mary had put balm on my head the day before, and that itched still.

My fingerprints were as perfect as the day I was born.

A visit to the well soon changed that. The wet rope scalded my fingers, a stone cut my hand. 'Stick with your own people, girl,' a toothless woman said. Her sons held my arms. 'Want trouble, girl?' I didn't want trouble. 'Want to be sorry, girl?' Another son sloshed my bucket at the well, but it bounced from the wall. They pushed my neck against the ground and I knew worse would come. I wriggled, clawed, bit into the fleshy part of a leg, was rewarded with a squeal and a jerk that nearly pulled the teeth from my gums. Someone dropped my bucket over my shoulders, blinding me, and tripped me, kicked me. 'That's the friendly warning, girl,' came the crone's voice through the bucket. 'We're respectable. We don't like your sort round here. Nothing good ever came out of Nazareth.' A note of irritation crept into her voice. 'Come away, Hobab. Stop your noise.'

She had seen me with Joseph's sons, and because of my long hair she thought me a Nazarene.

When I was sure they were gone I pulled off the bucket, shrieked curses after them. 'I'm one of you, you bitch! I'm not with them!' Blood ran from my nose like brown date-honey, pulling flies.

I felt my face. I couldn't show myself to Jacob and Joshua. Ashamed, I did what I always do: I ran, dropped the bucket and ran, ran away alone into the blighted fields. Wandered, roamed, was accosted by cropworkers at harvest in any fields worth harvesting, ran away again, hid out the day in the broad shade of a terebinth tree. It was in the branches of a terebinth tree like this, I remembered, that Absalom fleeing from David caught his long hair and swung agonisingly 'between Heaven and Earth' before being speared to death by his father's men. It was long ago. When stars showed between the branches I returned home quiet as a mouse across the stubble fields. Levi, who'd waited even more quietly for the creak of Joseph's ill-fitting door, caught me and beat me with his savage, silent, skilful blows for the loss of the bucket, then gave vent to a great yawn of boredom, and went to sleep.

I sharpened my fingernail in the night, but I was too young in body and brain to actually thrust it in his one remaining eye. I remembered it was necessary to prise open his shuttered eyelid first, and I remembered his peeping sleepy eye and then the hot salty spurt of jelly, the flopping and squealing of his body, but I was not yet a mature woman. Too hard for a child. I sat beside the snorting dreaming mound of him with my hand raised, but then I crept away. I tried to hide in the house. I wasn't Levi's prisoner, I was prisoner to the boys next door. Because of them I could not leave him. Jacob and Joshua drew me to them with the fascination of sweet honey.

The moon rose late. I climbed among Joseph's half-finished roof beams and looked down on the miserable draggle of dwellings and workshops lining the moonlit road. Beyond them stretched moonlit fields, waste ground, loose rock. The Nazarenes were busy before cock-crow, shadowy figures spreading out from the houses of the Community into the wasteland beneath the moon. Beyond a certain distance they stopped as though crossing a line, and each man settled down in his own patch, at prayer I supposed. While the moon shone they left their heads uncovered, but at the first gleam of the sun they covered themselves with white cloth. One by one they returned, and began their day's work.

I collected water in another bucket, burning my hands again. Stayed inside, too ashamed to face the children that day.

Joseph would not look down at me as he worked on the roof. Blood and bruise is unclean. All day he would not look down at me. He knew what Levi did to me but his heart would not believe it.

At dawn next day I watched for them all from his place in the roof timbers. No one. Silence and stillness, Sabbath-quiet, in the Community while busy Sepphoris awoke, markets yammered, merchants haggled, dogs scavenged. A cat slipped along the top of Joseph's wall and a boy's hand beckoned it. The cat ran to the hand, purred against the fingers, rubbed its face lovingly into the palm. I watched the cat roll on its back, the fingers scratch its chest. Then a voice called, the hand was snatched away, the cat fled. I saw nothing more. The gate was shut all day.

Next morning, before dawn on the Sabbath of the Temple, the Community spread out as usual into the wasteland to pray, and the gate was open all day though it was our day of rest, and I heard the boys fighting.

Next morning I sat cross-legged at the gate until it opened. I spread my shells in front of me. 'I saw you working on our Sabbath. And fighting.'

'Our holy days aren't always the Temple's,' Joshua said. 'I told you we're different.'

'It was me told her that,' Jacob said.

'How different?' I said. 'Give me a precise example.'

'Holier,' Jacob said. 'We live by example. We excel by example. Prayers are our sacrifice, not animals. The Temple's day starts in the evening, by the moon, as night falls, which is obviously wrong. Our day starts every day at dawn, by the sun.' He watched Joshua play the shell game with me (I told you this land was once under the sea) but he wouldn't play himself. Salome brought Joses out to watch. Only us children, no guard. Jacob knelt closer. 'Middle shell, Joshua.'

Joshua tapped the shell with his finger. I turned it over. Nothing. 'I knew it wasn't that one,' Joshua said. He crossed his legs, rested his elbows on his knees, watching me. 'Watch the shells carefully,' I said, sliding them. 'Tell me

106

why you don't go out to pray on your Sabbath.'

Joshua glanced at the shells. 'Pray?'

'I watch you go out. You cover your heads against the sun but not against the moon.'

Joshua laughed. He pointed at a shell, but Jacob said, 'Not that one, the left.'

Joshua's finger moved obediently to the left. 'That's not going out to pray. We shit.' He touched the leftmost shell. Empty.

'She's cheating.' Jacob said. 'How's she do it?'

I lifted the shell Joshua had moved towards first, revealed the pea. 'No trick,' I said. 'Why go out all that way to relieve yourselves?'

'Two thousand cubits. It's the Law,' Jacob said. 'And since God allows us to walk no more than one thousand cubits on the Sabbath, we can't relieve ourselves on the Sabbath.'

'So, therefore, we don't eat the day before.' Joshua touched a shell. I knew it wasn't that one.

'Not that one!' Jacob said.

Without looking down Joshua lifted the shell, revealed the pea underneath. He grinned into my eyes. 'I wanted to win.'

'You cheated,' I said.

'Like you.' He hid the pea, circled the shells. 'We carry a trowel to cover our bodily waste so God doesn't see our filth. We don't cover our heads against the moon because the moon is already stained, pockmarked, defiled by its closeness to the earth. Miriam, I sometimes think I can touch the moon, when it rises above the hills.'

I said, 'So do I.' He nodded. He knew I understood.

'The Temple dogs hang all their prayers from the moon,' Jacob said. 'The same moon that makes women unclean. No wonder we despise them.'

Joshua touched a shell. I said, 'Wrong again, empty.' He turned it over, showed the pea. Quickly I turned over the shell I'd really put the pea under. Another pea. Joshua's grin didn't change. He hadn't taken his eyes off mine. Distracting me while his hands were busy. 'If day comes before we finish, we cover ourselves so we don't show our backsides to the sun.'

'The sun is holy to you?'

Joshua shrugged. 'Some men say God lives in the sun.'

'God is in the Arch of the Covenant,' Jacob said. 'Like a prisoner beneath the Temple, profaned, Sion in Sion. His Word cannot be heard in this world.'

Joshua said, 'I believe we are surrounded by holy angels.'

He turned over the remaining shells. A pea under each and every one. He grinned.

'If there were holy angels everywhere,' Jacob said, 'they'd be disgusted by us. Our filth. That we live in sin. That we break the Law. That we will not let God save us. They won't be on our side until we live in righteousness, and keep the covenant of obedience to God.'

'But still, there are angels,' Joshua said.

'Those are demons, idiot,' Jacob said. 'They deceive you. You're a fool.' Joshua punched him and the brothers rolled on the ground, scattered the shells, knocked Joses over. Salome cried. I jumped up and pulled Joses to safety. I was so angry that I kicked at the fighting boys. 'Stop!' I kicked again and Joshua said, 'Ow!' He rolled, stood up, and I saw rage at me flood into his eyes. I mean eyes full of rage like blood and fire. I saw the rage come into him and fill him. I stepped back smartly, almost fell over Joses. I dropped to my knees then got up again. Joses started crying too.

Mary called quietly from the gate: 'Joshua.'

He turned to her, then back at me. The colour of rage left his eyes. His shoulders sagged slightly.

Mary called, 'Joshua, come in now. Pick me some mint leaves.' She might have said hyssop. Or garlic. I can't remember. I was holding my breath. Joshua went from sight behind the wall and I breathed out. Mary touched my elbow, taking Salome and Joses. She looked where Joshua had gone. 'It isn't his fault. Joshua. It's not his fault, Miriam. It's mine.' She gave that strange, innocent half-smile I thought I knew so well. 'We shall not see you for a while. During the Feast of Tabernacles. We must go on a journey but we shall return one day.' She gathered the two children under her breasts, bent her head over them tenderly, walked them back through the gate.

Jacob stayed with me, sitting up slowly.

Then he got to his feet, breathed heavily, wiped the blood and dust from his lip. He stared through the gateway, all his mind on Joshua, Joshua, Joshua.

I asked. 'Where are you going to? Where will your journey take you all?'

He glanced at me. 'To Egypt.' He pushed past me. 'Egypt.'

I called after him, 'Jacob, who is the eldest?'

He turned, stared. 'I am. I am the eldest.'

He went through the gateway but I called after him, 'Jacob, what of Joshua? He's younger than you? How much younger than you is your brother?'

Jacob stopped. He clenched his fists, nodded after his mother. 'Don't listen to a word *she* says. She made a cuckold of my father. I am the rightful heir. Joshua isn't my brother. He's her bastard.'

NOVA HIEROSOLYMA

New Jerusalem

Next day, they were gone. All the high-ranking Essenes, gone. The departure of the Branch of the Nazarene Community, the Princes of the Congregation, left the suburb silent and deserted except for a few guards and wardens and the mass of unimportant people. Then along the trail passed Essenes of the Naphtali tribe and of Manasseh, the leading families openly headed on their long march by Judas the Galilean and his son, Simon, heavily guarded. The best priestly families of the Essene tribes of Zebulun, Asher, Issachar and Dan (which was the tribe of my father) passed by, and all over Galilee the village Essenes of Bethsaida, Capernaum and Magdala and the ten towns of the Decapolis obeyed God's command to gather for Tabernacles, turning their footsteps southward. Not westward to the sea, the way to Egypt: a single day's sail, with a brisk lucky wind. No, they went south on foot, following the River Jordan and the sun towards Jerusalem and the wilderness of Judah, hallowing the time of tents that Tabernacles remembers. I watched them pass all day, hundreds, perhaps a thousand. To Jerusalem would be a hard enough journey on the children and old people. To Egypt would leave many dead of heat, exhaustion, disease, the rest picked off by bandits, terrorists, soldiers and the taxes of King Herod Archelaus which draw blood from stone; survivors abandoned at the mercy of innkeepers and merchants who would demand a shekel for a sip of water. Only a few stragglers would reach Egypt, and fewer would return.

Evening came and Levi beat me – I'd forgotten to fetch water. I ran away into the dark. I'd lost them, my family. Nothing else mattered.

Jacob's dreadful condemnation of Mary his own mother echoed in my head. *Don't listen to a word* she *says. She made a cuckold of my father. I am the rightful heir. Joshua isn't my brother. He's her bastard.* Blasphemy (if Joshua really was the Son of God), but legally true. The words echoed in my head because Jacob was right: Joshua was illegitimate. Joshua's birth did not count. He'd been born outside completed wedlock. He was not King David's legitimate line, he was the bastard, he counted no more than any other king's bastard – Herod had hundreds, and his wives deceived him by foisting the children of their lovers on him. To make matters worse Joseph himself had denied his fatherhood of Joshua by sending Mary away, allowing the rumours to circulate, doubts about his paternity to escalate. Some said Joshua's father was Pantera, a Temple guard. By law Jacob (though I found out he was more than eighteen months younger than Joshua, born the twenty-third of September of the following year) was the true-born son, legally the eldest.

Jacob, the legitimate heir. The Prince of David.

Jacob had Joseph his father's rugged build, his muscle. Jacob was clever, righteous, dedicated to the Law. Jacob was his teacher's favourite, a leader. Jacob would make a fine and ruthless prince. But Jacob was not Mary's firstborn child that the angel had foretold.

I remembered the archangel Gabriel's promise to Mary when she was fourteen, hardly older than myself now: *You shall bring forth for the Lord your firstborn son.* They were both firstborn! Joshua according to God's biological will (had I not seen His angels, heard His voice?), Jacob according to the Law of men.

I held my hands to my head. No wonder Joseph cried his prayers aloud in his torment, and buried himself in dull work. The man was in an impossible position. Had God spoken to him too, assured him that Joshua was the Christ? I didn't know, but Joseph himself hadn't believed for sure, or he wouldn't have insisted on the midwife's examination, would he? Joseph, kept outside the stable until the end, had glimpsed at most only the aftermath of the miracle.

And Jacob was growing up as sensitive of his status as any boy. *My* father! Who wouldn't want to be the Christ and King, and reign in peace over Jerusalem for a thousand years, and live for ever at God's side in Heaven?

But traditionally, as you know, Jesus Christ had no brothers or sisters, but was sent to earth as an only child – which *firstborn* fits equally well, first and only Son. But Joshua (if he was somehow renamed Jesus) and Jacob were part of a family of five brothers and two sisters. Was I seeing a plan of God to assert Himself against all the odds in this world, or a conspiracy of Satan to prevent Him? A battle between them, between good and evil? Two brothers' stories are famous in the Bible, where the younger brother always triumphs over his older brother or brothers. Yacob stealing Esau's birthright, or Yassuf of Egypt against his wicked elder brothers. Jacob pitted against Joshua, Joshua against Jacob: who'd win?

Nothing would surprise me in this world. Anything could happen.

This I know. God, if He exists on this hellish world, is logically the perfect being and cannot create imperfection. Evil, on the other hand, cannot create perfection. Perfection (except perfect evil) is the one thing the Devil cannot do. The appearance of truth, yes. The feeling of happiness, yes. The joys of delight, yes, yes, yes. The perfect unbesmirched reality of Christ, no. Never.

But those two boys were so human! Educated, yes. But human!

Traditionally we are told that Joseph the widower, the Guardian of Christ, had sons and daughters only by his anonymous first marriage – the 'kinfolk' of Jesus, His 'stepbrothers' and 'stepsisters'. Jesus was born in Jerusalem and brought up in the city of Nazareth. But here in the horrible city of Sepphoris in the Nazarene ghetto, all Mary's seven children were born in Bethlehem and Nazareth does not exist. *Nazarene* is a political and religious label. A man who actually came from a city called Nazareth would be called a *Natzrati*, a Nazarethite. Never a *Notzri* or Nazarene.

No, I saw no Jesus Christ the Son of God here – Joshua,

with his mad rages, his violence? Jacob with his zeal for the Law, his jealousy? Neither of them fitted. Both were tainted.

But this world is not perfect. This world is imperfect. This world is unsaved, it is not Heaven and Earth (despite Jacob's insistence) in the course of creation by God starting three or four thousand years ago; this world is the fallible filthy spinning world of men, formed by gravity and dust and chance four billion years ago and lit by the blind nuclear furnace of the sun.

Yet I lie on my back and I reach up, and I can almost touch them, almost touch the stars with my outstretched hands: salvation, perfection, reason, explanation. Almost.

When the sun rose I sat up in its golden rays striking across the ground. I had forgotten about my fingerprints, but now I examined them again. Scarred, burnt, dusty: but for a day, they had seemed perfect. Perhaps that was the dream. There are no miracles, we all know that.

When I took the bucket to the well, Hobab waited for me with a look in his eye. A stained cloth was wrapped around his leg where I'd taken the bite out of him. 'I can run faster than you!' I shouted, turned, ran, and a stick whipped me full in the belly. I dropped on my knees between his brothers. Choking. Winded. My hair was pulled and I was dragged forward across the bucket, the rim digging into my hips. 'She's used to it,' Hobab said. 'This is how she likes it.' I kicked out and my legs were seized. Hobab forced himself forward into my body and I felt my scar tear. 'Don't hurt,' I begged in my agony. A hand covered my mouth; I neither screamed nor breathed. 'Leave some for me,' a voice said. I jerked like a landed fish, Hobab gave a high laugh of pleasure, and a picture came into my mind of the stones of Magdala, a fish jerking and flapping suffocating in the dry dust in the orgasm of death.

'Your turn, Kedar, you pig,' Hobab said. 'God, I feel good!' He limped to my head, I saw his bandaged leg, he lifted my head by my hair. He said something, his mouth moved, as my body was pierced and demeaned by his brother, I know not what. My head dropped in the dust, the sun rose in my eyes, and my spirit fled in horror from what happened.

I looked down on my dusty body folded over the

upturned bucket, hairy Kedar behind me bent over me like a dog, his brother pale Shibah nervously waiting his turn. Suddenly the wind gusted sand in their eyes, blinding them, only for a moment.

In that moment my fist was taken up in a cold adamantine grip, my screams were stifled, and by my hand I was pulled out of myself like a hare out of its skin.

Below me my shape dwindled. My poor pathetic body humped over the bucket shrank from sight, and I understood my suffering was unimportant. Through my long, wild, flapping hair I dared to look beside me in the rushing air, and a golden angel was holding my hand. 'Stop them,' I said.

The angel put his cold golden finger to his cold golden lips. 'They will never stop, Miriam.'

This angel was muscular, complete, powerful, uncircumcised, and between his massive thighs swung testicles of wrinkled gold. His wings, a mass of golden feathers, beat at the sky. He whispered in my ear. 'Look beneath you, Miriam, and see Heaven and Earth, and be warned.'

Between my feet as we rose I saw the whole of Sepphoris shrink small on its hilltop like a closing eye. The ring of poverty and dirt and rubbish tips winked closed, the roads wriggling outwards like tiny veins were swallowed. My horizon spread across the bare harvested fields and the desert, and then the land lying green and yellow between the vast violet haze of the Middle Sea and the blue teardrop of the Sea of Galilee, and I saw the blue Jordan winding like a tear southward, and the golden pillars of Jerusalem, and dusty Anathoth where the prophet Jeremiah was born who went with the Jews to exile in Egypt. The Jordan, the river joining sea to sea: below me I saw its destination, the Dead Sea like a deathly mirror of Galilee sunk deep beneath the desert.

The angel whirled me on thundering wings down towards the salty pinnacles and burning brown cliffs of this gigantic pit, and we fell between its sides towards the shore.

I whispered, 'You're like no angel I've ever seen. Are you a demon sent to destroy me?'

He held his golden finger to his golden lips. 'You shall not fall.'

I shouted, 'Are you a demon or an angel?' The angel smiled. His face melted like golden wax into an expression of pity. Such pity. But his grip held me like iron, not gold. I stared into his golden eyes and saw no reflection of myself.

I whispered, 'God, help me.'

The angel, if angel he was, fell with me through the air. 'Behold, the land at Sion.'

Spreading out beneath me I saw the white buildings at Sion, the monastery rooftops white as salt. The boundary walls enclosing the land rushed outward as I fell. The outposts and camps scattered apparently at random in the desert around the monastery are in fact precisely placed, each degree named and graded in its Order and Command. I've told you before; the wooden outbuildings of Jericho, the caves called Nazareth and Emmaus across the stream, Jerusalem and all the others, this land *at* Sion precisely mirrors the land *of* Sion, the land given to the Jewish people by God in His Covenant. But this is land made by men only for men, each 'village' and 'city' and the precisely measured angles joining them sacred with esoteric meaning to the priests at Sion.

And here is Egypt. Of course.

The angel stops me with great thrusts of his wings. Below me a woman prays, her prayers shimmering in the air. I can't see her face but I know her by the way she kneels, her children with her. She is Mary. The Holy Family never went to Egypt; are not in Egypt now. Egypt is here, in the safety at Sion, not a long and dangerous journey to another country. Egypt, the camp at Sion for families, unclean quarters fit only for marriage, women, children, sex. Mary kneels outside her wooden hut, her head bowed, her arms extended in prayer. I recognise little Joses beside her, mimicking her prayers as seriously as he can. Joshua, Silas and Salome are also with her, the babies Thomas and Miri laid in the shade. Where was Jacob?

Joshua's face is shattered. His eyes closed. Rejected. He'd lost out to his younger brother.

Also sitting in the shade I see an old woman, heavy, white-haired. The last time I saw her she was hiding her baby beneath a rock from Herod's soldiers: Zacharias's widow Elizabeth, the mother of John.

Where's Jacob? I remembered Jacob saying that history, 'prophecy' – and remember to these people their history *is* prophecy – was coming together like strands drawn together on a loom, 'Weaving the Hand of God,' he'd said. So where has Joseph taken Jacob his son, and why has he left Joshua here with his mother? One look at Joshua's face and I know the answer.

No woman capable of menstruation is allowed to set foot in the holy ground within the salt-white battlements of the monastery itself, Jerusalem. The mysteries and parables are denied her. No blind man may enter Jerusalem, neither may any man enduring recent sexual intercourse, nor any man suffering dirty dreams, or nocturnal emissions, and no lepers are permitted, or any disease, neither any man deformed by demons at birth or maimed or disfigured in war, nor any man born of fornication out of wedlock. The list is long. God, being perfect, may only see perfection; and only the high priest, living in celibacy, whole, cleansed, sinless, white to the last tooth, is perfect enough and worthy, if God wishes it, of seeing God.

But there's no Holy of Holies here at Sion. By God's ancient command His people are allowed only one Temple for their worship: only the great Temple of the Sadducees and Pharisees. And, since the First Temple of Solomon was destroyed to the foundations on that site nearly six hundred years ago, no Arch of the Covenant is to be found even there. But I remember Matthew the levite telling Jacob that God would reign over the world from Mount Sion where the Temple stands, and then Israel's enemies would bow down to Israel. *Mount* Sion! Here at Sion the angel has dragged me down into an inverted image of Mount Sion, a pit sunk deeper below sea level than Mount Sion rises above it. Here, so far down, the air is breathless and boiling, reeking of sulphur and pitch and hot springs and more like Hell than Heaven.

I call out to Mary, but the angel smiles; I've no voice. To Mary there's no thunder of the angel's wings, the dust does not fly up around her. But as the angel's shadow ripples across the rocks and passes over her, she shivers and clasps her shawl tight. Then I am swept away on the angel's wingbeats, and the distance takes her.

116

Settlements along the shore flash beneath my feet: sheer cliffs pocked with caves like eyes, palm trees, scythed fields and the headlands of Sodom, platforms set out for ritual contemplation, pilgrim camps on level ground separated by precisely laid out paths. Unclean areas, latrines, ponds for washing. Here's the potter's field, busy with tents and olive-wood booths for Tabernacles, no one showing in the heat of the day. The battlements of Sion rise up blindingly white, the vaulted arch of the gateway *Qimrôn* stands tall, the many baptismal pools enclosed within the walls glitter like silver coins below me in the sunlight. Other pools and wells are shadowed by the jigsaw of courtyards, squares and esplanades whose organisation is an ascent, a progress towards sanctity. At the centre is the library and scriptorium where scribes copy sacred scriptures and the many, many rules of the community. Beside it I see the meeting hall. Beyond that, a two-storey building I do not recognise. Then it comes fully into view.

Amazingly, I'm seeing something that resembles a Christian church, in this world where Christianity has not occurred.

Not a synagogue. This pure white building is complex in shape, once modelled on the maze around the Holy of Holies perhaps. The humans of this world, influenced by the teachings of a Greek, Plato, otherwise unknown, believe that the pure forms of everything in this world are to be found in Heaven, and that earthly buildings are only shabby copies, gropings-towards, the endlessly ascending architectural perfection of Heaven. So the Essenes feel free to copy the Holy of Holies of the Great Temple, whose position on Mount Sion they revere but whose meat-eating priests they despise. Now their whole church building is the maze, with the Holy of Holies moved to one end not the centre. Instead of being totally dark, filled with the smoke of incense, the Essenes allow daylight through high windows to illuminate the gold leaf on the wooden panels. Again I'm amazed: this is a building for a whole congregation, not just a single priest. The vestry is full of people, these people groping towards Christianity.

The hour has come. 'Angels', novice priests reciting prayers whose timing is governed by the *gnomon* sundial on

117

the roof, throw open hatches, and the sun reveals rows of bowed heads below, the prayers of the congregation rising into the sunlight. The zadok, Judas the Galilean, wearing his golden cloak over starched white linen, stands on a raised platform above the heads of the congregation, a pulpit below the opened roof. Incongruously there is a vault and a furnace on one side, spouting flames despite the desert heat. The Galilean raises his arms and priestly sceptre into the open glare of the sun, a glorious sight, his cowl and wide sleeves whitened by frankincense whose clean fresh scent of sanctity rises to me in the shimmering air. No sacrifices, no atonement by burning or blood here, only these perfumed prayers, this intensity of worship.

A voice cries out: 'Hail to the Zadok!'

Judas the Galilean speaks. 'No one given knowledge of the Covenant shall enter the Temple to light His altar in vain.' Raises his voice, and now I see Joseph stands on a pulpit to one side, just coming to the afternoon sun, wearing a crown, the Star. On the altar between the two men is a menorah, a tall seven-branched gold candlestick, its flames burning olive oil. 'Thus says the Lord. If anyone shall do evil to the Congregation, he shall be excommunicated from among us, dead in the sight of the Lord, and he shall return no more.' Where in the Bible is Judas getting these words from? Nowhere that I know. 'Whoever slanders the Congregation shall be excommunicated from among us and shall return no more.'

The congregation in the tiers below him murmur the Christian response, 'Amen.' But to me it sounds like 'Amun', the sun-god of the Egyptians whose name I've heard worshipped and hailed a thousand times in the desert at Thebes and Karnak and along the Nile.

A voice cries out: 'Hail to the Christ!'

Joseph stands in the sun. He presses his fingers to his lips, doubting, hesitant. Still trying to change his mind, to draw back. He glances at the Galilean, who responds with a sharp, impatient nod. Get on with it. Inside himself, Joseph believes God's truth. He believes in Mary his wife, he has faith in her fidelity and knowledge. He believes her child Joshua is born of a virgin, is the Son of God. But this is politics. Survival.

'Joseph!' the Galilean warns him. The Essene community would never accept a Christ born of fornication.

'Behold,' Joseph proclaims, 'I have a Son.'

Jacob. No!

Jacob stands up, walks to the platform, waits below his father, bows his head to the Princes of the Congregation, the seven ranks of Michael, Gabriel, Sariel, Phanuel and other old men. Then Jacob turns, is publicly confirmed in the eyes of the bishops, presbyters, 'angels' and 'beasts' and all the lower grades of the Poor as the legitimate son of Joseph and Mary. But he's too young to be anointed or baptised formally into the life of the congregation. Jacob's training won't begin until he's eighteen, taken into Grade Twelve, and not until twenty-one will he enter the monastery as junior novice, receiving his first baptism. Not before the age of twenty-three will he be initiated into the drink of the community, wine, at the Sacred Meal; and not until his twenty-ninth year will he complete his monastic education and enter into the sanctuary.

And with the death of Joseph, Jacob will be anointed the Christ.

I stare at my hand dwarfed in the angel's golden grip, the golden muscles pumping in his body, the golden feathers streaming back and forth with the beating of his wings, his golden pubic hairs fluttering and the curls on his head untwining, just a little, not quite perfect, handsome, impossibly handsome, utterly confident, and I know, I *know* I am in the grip of a demon.

Who down there below me has sold his soul? These people of the Light and the Way believe God observes them every minute of their lives and sees everything that is not hidden in the dark, or under their robes where it is too dark to see. Their God hears the secrets of every heart that cries loud enough to hear, if its sound is pure enough to rise to Him; the rest, they believe, fall to the Prince of Darkness. But they believe they worship God.

I twist the angel's grip. The angel's smile lies. His pity lies. His compassion for me is a lie and a fake. His handsomeness is fake, rotten, skin deep; below is nothing but black marble, cold iron, rust. Gold leaf. A demon of this world.

I'm right. It's a battle. A battle between good and evil.

Evil always wins in this world, as you know. As you have seen. This world *is* Hell.

'Be still, harlot.' The demon holds me effortlessly, clasps me to his cold hard chest with his enormous strength, hungry for my warmth. His flaking lips touch my ear. 'I know who you are, Mary.' His reeking breath gusts across my face. 'I know who you really are.'

Then he hisses, staring. Something's happened. Joseph points out another boy, a year or two older than Jacob but stark as a whip, eyes intense, looking each man in the eye. 'I offer for the Recognition of the Congregation – John, the heir of Zadok.'

Judas shouts: 'No! My son Simon is my heir!'

Joseph says calmly, 'I offer the boy John for your Recognition.' John. Many in the audience frown at the unfamiliar name. 'John, the son of Zacharias whom you knew, who carried the blood of Zadok in his veins. Now John carries his father's blood for us.'

The boy John shouts out his rehearsed lines bravely. 'Elect of Righteousness, Princes of the Light, it is ordained in Heaven that you will make me your banner, your interpreter of wonderful mysteries. This says the Lord.' But he's so young that many laugh at such strong words piped in a child's high, unbroken voice.

'My son Simon follows me,' Judas says dangerously. 'That is the Law.'

The Princes of the Congregation nod. 'It is the Law.'

'This matter is not finished,' Joseph says.

'This matter *is* finished,' Judas says contemptuously. He and his sons have studied the arts all their lives. They are lawyers, magicians, politicians, warriors, martyrs, not to be challenged by a boy's piping voice.

But above them the demon's grip tightens on me, his icy fingers squeeze my soul. Whatever happened, or nearly happened, down there about the boy John, it startled him. He's only a minor demon, but I'm frozen despite this hot day, motionless, powerless, terrified. I can't even draw breath. My lungs are flat.

I gasp, 'You don't dare let go of me.'

He turns his rusty golden eyes at me. I'm nothing to him. But he doesn't drop me.

'Watch, Mary,' he whispers, his voice as intimate as fornication. 'See. Live. Despair.'

The tiny figures move below me, led at prayer by Judas as Zadok, his son the zealot Simon now laying aside his disguise, the starry robes of a magus, for the yellow linen cloak of zadokite priests. His father's heir. One day Simon, not John, will wear the gold cloak of the zadok. So it seems.

Simon calls out, 'At this holy time of Tabernacles I present before the Congregation my dead brother's son. My brother Judas of Sepphoris lived bright under the eye of our Lord. He threw down the idol of the Romans, their eagle which profaned the holy ground of the Temple, and the Romans tormented him and flayed the skin from his body while he lived, and crucified him while he lived, and prised him down and burnt him alive. A martyr does not die. I present to you his son who proudly bears his father's name and the name of his father's father, Judas.' Simon rests his hands lightly on the shoulders of the boy who comes to him. I should say young man; my own age, heavy in the flesh, already furred with mannish beard on his jaw and lip. It's his eyes I recognise, brown, almost black. He noticed me in the square, the day my father died. Young Judas.

His grandfather Judas Zadok is calling for the tithes and taxes gathered for the Poor throughout the year to be collected. Below the altar I see Matthew among the tax collectors laying down bags of gold, silver, pitchers of holy oil, harvest offerings, which novices drag to the doorway in the north-west corner leading to the great vault, the monastery's treasury.

Judas Zadok holds out his arms, speaks to the congregation. 'We have done well. Soon our time will come. Soon, in our own lifetimes, we shall cast our thirty talents of silver into the Temple and receive from the Lord His Covenant, according to the words of the prophecy.' He halts for effect, theatrical as ever. 'There is a danger.' Lowers his voice. 'King Herod Archelaus, the fatted calf, casts out priests who will not pay taxes to him. Each year the taxes rise. Word has reached the king's ear of the talents gathered by the Poor for the Lord's work. Let the fatted calf beware of his greed! He shall not tax us. He shall not steal the talents raised for the Lord.' Raises his voice. 'Let King Herod

Archelaus beware! The end of time is coming! The end of his time is coming!' Spittle flies from his lips as he shouts at the top of his voice, 'We shall resist. We shall fight. We have weapons. *Our time is just beginning!'*

The congregation stirs. They'll fight. They have it in them, these religious fanatics. Fight against hopeless odds, even against Rome. Their angry, chanting voices rise up into the air.

Judas Zadok's shouts come up to us. 'It shall be according to the prophecy! Arise!' The furnace roars, thick white smoke rises, billows upward, pungent as incense; a magician knows such eastern tricks. 'Arise, and measure the Temple of God, and the altar. And two candlesticks stand before the God of the Earth, and fire proceeds out of their mouth, and devours their enemies.' What was he quoting? No Bible I knew. 'A man who is holy and true, and has the key of David, what he opens no man shall shut. I look, and behold, a door is opened in Heaven. Around the throne twenty-four elders sit, clothed in white raiment, gold crowns upon their heads. And out of the throne comes lightning and thunder and voices, and He that sits upon the throne holds in His right hand a Book with the pages written on both sides, sealed with seven seals, and no man is worthy to open the Book.'

Another handful of crystals from his sleeve, and the fire blazed with dense black flames, then red, white, green. 'He's deceiving them,' I said. 'It's tricks.'

'No,' the demon said, 'he's telling them the truth. Fragments of the truth. As you know. We each have the potential to become like our Heavenly Father, we can attain Godhood. All of us.'

Is that the truth or a lie? Truth is a weapon of the Devil, and of his demons and dragons who inhabit this world of men, no more and no less than Truth is the tool of God. The serpent had promised Eve that women would be as gods, knowing good and evil – and was that the truth or a lie?

Now Judas Zadok preaches against the Great Harlot arrayed in purple and scarlet – the colours of the Temple veil – who wears a crown of stars around her head. He preaches against the Temple and the, to him, idolatrous rituals of its priests (to him a prostitute is an idol because she is worshipped by men), and he prophesies that from the wilderness a beast full of the names of blasphemy will carry the Harlot up from the bottomless pit, and the Lamb of God will overcome her, and He will send her to perdition, and the Temple will be destroyed except for one wall, from which He shall make the foundation of the Last Temple.

'It's not in the Bible,' I say weakly.

Smoke rises around us, drifts in the sky, hangs above the sea, and we hear the voices of the congregation chanting the responses below us. 'Seven angels blew seven trumpets. The first trumpet sounded, and there followed hail and fire mingled with blood, and every third tree was burnt up, and all the green grass was burnt up. The second trumpet sounded, and a great mountain burning with fire was cast down into the sea, and of the sea creatures one in three died, and one in three of the ships was destroyed. The third angel sounded his trumpet, and a great star fell from Heaven. The fourth angel sounded, and a third part of the sun was smitten, and a third of the moon, and a third of the stars, so that neither the day shone nor the night. And the fifth angel sounded, and I saw a star fall from Heaven to the Earth, and to him was given the key of the bottomless pit. And he opened the bottomless pit, and the smoke of a great furnace ascended.' More smoke rising around me, bitter, acrid. 'And the sun and the air were darkened by the smoke of the pit. And the sixth angel sounded, and a third of the men were killed. And when the seventh angel shall sound the mystery of God shall be revealed.'

'It's just words—' I hear myself groan aloud. The demon's grip crushes me; it feels as though his fingers will meet inside my ribs. 'Not in the Bible.'

'Not words,' grates the demon's voice. 'Not the words of men. We do not bow down to creatures of clay. God is here. He's here in this world.'

I cry out, 'I don't know!'

'Liar. Woman of a lie. You do know.'

'I don't know!'

'You were shown. The archangel of God revealed His

birth to you. At Bethlehem. The archangel Gabriel, was it, or Michael, god of the Nile?'

Michael? I know no angel called Michael. But the demon knows everything and he does not believe me. The gold trickles from his skin like sweat, and the shape revealed beneath is more handsome than ever. 'Who can offer you more than this?' His full, rounded lips move. 'Love. Love that you never had. All that you have lost.'

'Stop.'

'I can give your life meaning. Your long, weary life, Mary.' His lips kiss my hair, it flies unbound like the hair of a whore. 'I can give you love.'

My eyes fill with tears despite myself. I overflow with pain. I whisper, 'Love isn't meaning. It doesn't mean anything. It's just love.'

'Give your soul for it, Mary.'

'Let me go, let me go. Drop me.'

His lips caress my ear like snakes. 'Love. Rest. Peace. Safety. The bliss of sleep, forgetting. The happiness of Heaven here, now, in this world. I can give it to you, Mary, for a while.'

'For how long?'

'For as long as I wish. Cease your suffering.'

I push away from him, and fall. But I am only air and dreams, and he holds me up with easy strength, as beautiful as a god of the Greeks. His lips touch my lips, his hands like squids suck my hair. 'What woman would not desire me?' he murmurs. 'Who could not fall in love with me?'

Below me I see the two young boys standing at the altar. No Joshua. It's Jacob standing beside John, almost close enough to touch hands. John – it had been shown me – who is born to be the Baptist, his role in life ordained by God, the forerunner who paves the way for Jesus's earthly rule as king and priest from Mount Sion: John, the right hand of Jesus, bringing the word of Christianity from Jerusalem to the nations of the earth. But something is terribly wrong, nothing is happening quite as I remember it from the Bible.

This battle. This war.

No Jesus. No Son of God. An illusion, as far as I can see.

I hear Judas Zadok preaching taxes and swords, and then he preaches words that strike me as chill as the demon's grip, a parable of a beast that comes up out of the sea. 'And the dragon gave the beast his power and great authority, and the number of the beast was the same as the number of a man.' The dragon again.

Judas reveals more secrets. 'And the number of God is 3. And the number of the created earth is 4. "His name Immanuel" adds up to 543, "in congregations" also 543. This is the Word of God and shall be His Covenant with us. One day all will be revealed to you under the sun. And the number of the beast is 666.' To these people the Word of God is coded in numbers, not Hebrew, or Aramaic, or even Egyptian. I forgot how cold I am. Numbers don't change with language; they're their own language. Roman, Greek, Hebrew, Egyptian, even the glyphs and bar-dot numbers of the Maya of the Isthmus: some arithmetics are quicker than others, but they all add up to the same result however ancient they are. God's numbers.

I looked up into the demon's face. Still offering me what he thought was love.

'You're afraid of me,' I said. I laughed. 'My God, you're afraid of me!'

His eyes looked at me as emptily as stone. I saw nothing but darkness. He was not afraid of God in all His wrath or all His glory.

'Leave them, Mary. Do not interfere.'

He hurled me down into the light. I was not above the monastery any more. I hurtled into my body thrown over the bucket, my eyes in the dust, Shibah crouched over me like a dog, tearing my anus rather than soil himself with his brothers' seed. He gave an angry, heedless cry. 'About time,' Hobab said. He pulled him away. 'Come on, Kedar.'

'Did you see me do her like a dog!' Shibah said. 'I did all right, didn't I?'

'You do dogs better,' Hobab said. 'You got her wrong hole.' He put his arms round his brothers' shoulders, laughing. The sight of me, my humiliation, disgusted and upset them. That they'd achieved what they desired revolted them, yet amused them: look at her. They'd achieved something. No one was going to interfere. No one was going to see me. No one was going to hear me. And if they did, I'd be blamed.

Kedar said anxiously, 'We should cut her hair off, like Samson.'

Hobab said, 'She's done for.' He kicked me with his good leg.

They left me lying in the dust.

A dog went past, then walked back the other way with a bone.

My hips slipped off the bucket.

I crawled, but I could not crawl. I wept, but I could not weep. I could see the shadows but I could not reach them.

The shadow moved, took shape, turned into the demon. The demon thrust his marble fingers into my hair, twisted my head so hard I screamed.

'Remember, Mary,' he whispered, and fiery breath came out of his mouth. 'Do not interfere.'

CONTRA MUNDUM

against the world

I found myself lying in the shadows. I don't remember crawling; the shadows came to me as the sun swung. Brown scabs of blood tightened on my legs, and the dried white scale of seed. Dogs licked me, filthy creatures. On my elbows I pulled myself behind a white wall, leaked fresh blood and slime in the dust. The dogs fought over me, yelping, nipping my legs. I cried but I was too dry for tears, my mouth was dust, I could not utter the word for help. The whiteness struck into my eyes. I lay against the wall of Joseph and the Virgin's house. Damp seeped under the wall from their well. I touched my tongue to the cool clinging sand. I wept. My face wept at me from a brown puddle. In my mind's eye I saw the boys at Sion, at Egypt, at Jerusalem. I thought about Joshua sitting in the desert, his face as shattered by emotion as my own, and Jacob standing beneath the pulpit being recognised as the future Christ, and John waiting beside him.

Remember, Mary. Do not interfere.

Miriam, do not go to Sepphoris.

I'd been warned by the archangel of God not to come here. Now a demon of the Prince of Darkness warned me not to interfere in whatever happened in this bad place. Yet I can't be anyone but who I am, flesh and blood. Like you, I am who I am. I'm here. I exist. I survive.

Footsteps. I flinched, tried to see, but my swollen eye closed. Kicking noises, yelps as the dogs were driven away. 'Joshua?' I mumbled, then twisted my head the other way

127

and saw Levi staring down at me. His usual rage, but worse. 'You!' he said. 'You disgusting. You disgusting. Disgusting.' He kicked me. I tried to cling on to the straps of his sandal. 'Where you been, you slut, you whore, you shame. Shameless.' He kicked me with each word. 'Shaming me.' I cried a tooth from my mouth. 'Don't you care?' Levi shouted. My fingernails broke on the straps of his sandal. 'She's dead. Your mother's dead. She fell from the roof. Now who'll look after me?'

She'd used Joseph's ladder. One end of the roof was not yet tiled. My mother had climbed up and sat on Joseph's roof-beam, the bark still on it, and at some point during the day she'd leant backwards until she hung by her knees from the beam, straightened her legs, and dropped ten cubits on to her head on the stone floor.

Had she killed herself because she found out what Levi did to me, as well as to her?

I lay with my head on the floor. The sun was hot. My mother's body stank like pig's flesh within an hour or two. When I woke she was not there, taken to the tombs as though she had never existed, except for me, and Levi's voice went on and on. 'She died without a shekel to her name,' he swore. He swore and swore. 'Look at me. D'you think dying costs nothing? Do you think it's cheap? She must have had something. Where'd she hide it?' He pinched me. 'Look at me. She give it to you? Copper rings, pieces of gold, something. Trinkets. She can't have died with nothing.' His pinches twisted at me, his swearing washed over me. 'Very well. Don't tell me. You think you can deceive me, trick me. I know you've got it somewhere.' Evening fell and I heard him going round his house opening everything, looking under everything, trying to find her fortune.

The truth was that all my mother had was me, and now she was gone.

'If you won't tell me,' Levi said, 'I'll make you work until you do.' He mistook my swollen face in the shadows. 'Don't sulk! Wash yourself. What trouble have you got me in now? Get out of my sight!'

I crawled from the back of the house into the sandy wasteland that the Nazarenes had used for their toilet. I washed myself with sand. The moon rose and I held out my arms, trying to fly. I pictured the same moon rising over the great pit at Sion, its rays falling across the salt-white rooftops and battlements of the monastery, Jerusalem, where Jacob slept, and John. I imagined the unclean quarters at Egypt and Joshua standing outside just as I was, staring at the same moon. I could not fly. My feet were stuck to the ground by my blood.

I lay on Levi's floor in a corner where he would not find me, my knees drawn up under my chin, my thumb in my mouth.

Levi found me.

One morning Hobab's uncle, Raphu, came to the house with his cousin Annas the scribe to back him up. They would not look me in the eye or accept hospitality. Raphu spoke with the moral authority of an elder. 'Levi, your name is good with us, but we hear serious complaints against the girl. She behaves with ill repute, infecting the sons of our district with lewd thoughts. Her presence disrupts public order.'

'Spit it out, gentlemen,' Levi said. 'I've lived here longer than you have. Nine years ago I saw your faces in the tax uprising. Complaints? What complaints?'

'Who complains?' I asked from behind my scarf. Raphu would not look at me; it was not my place to speak. 'Who complains against me?'

Raphu turned his back on me. 'Levi, my friend, it is said she is a . . . woman.'

Levi laughed. 'Prostitute, you mean.'

Raphu's shoulder shrugged angrily. 'If you say so.'

Levi dragged me forward by my twisted arm. 'Look at her.' He pulled away my scarf from my face. 'Look at her! Ugly bitch. Shoddy goods. She couldn't charge anything, could she? Pay the men, I should say! One look and they'd run all the way back to town.' He hid my face with my black scarf, tied it tight, only my eyes showed. 'There, now we don't have to look at her. Fetch wine!' He clapped hands, looked at me fiercely. 'Go!'

I served wine. 'All right,' Raphu agreed, 'but she is not to show herself at the well again.'

'You don't have the power to do that,' Levi said. 'To deny someone water. You're going to tax water like you tax this wine, and beer, flour, worship, everything else? The Lord's air itself, next?'

Raphu gave his little shrug. 'We hate taxes as much as you. The Lord gave you great luck to escape with your life last time. Isn't one census enough for you? My three brothers were rounded up and crucified, my shop was burnt, I was in prison for a year fearing for my life. Where were you?' The matter of the well was definitely closed. 'Another complaint, I'll have her cast out.'

'The girl is mad, that's all,' Levi said appeasingly. 'She has demons. She's harmless.'

'So are stones,' Raphu said. 'It's the hand that casts them that's dangerous.'

Levi watched them go, then gripped my wrists tight in his fists. 'I saved you. You know why.' He pulled away my veil, peered into my face with his one good eye. 'I'm the only one who looks at you. You're mine even though your body disgusts me. You don't breathe without me. Whatever I say, you do. Say yes.'

I looked away.

He punched me in the belly. 'Say yes.'

I would not look at him. He beat me until my eyes flickered in his direction. 'That's better,' Levi said. 'Yes, Levi.'

'Yes, Levi.'

'My bed's cold since your mother left. You know what to do.'

But every night, as soon as he slept, I slipped from his bed and lay beneath the stars. I sang to myself, wandering. I heard the side gate to Joseph's house rattle but there was no one there. The latch was loose. I wriggled my fingers through the gap, lifted the clasp. The yard was deserted, silent, heavy with memory. I smiled in the dark. I could almost see the boys playing, fighting together. I knew those playing days were gone. Jacob was no longer a child: he was the future Christ. Everything between them had changed. I found a broken pitcher by the well, dipped, lifted the chin of my veil, lapped the sweet water. The lemon tree rustled, bare, but the yard wall gave shelter from the cold winter wind. Once it snowed, and I lay wrapped in blankets feeling nothing, nothing at all. Perhaps this numbness is as near as I can come to the mercy of death, true death. No feelings, no dreams. But still the faint movement of my lungs, the rise and fall of my chest scratching the blankets, the slow whisper of my heart.

The Nazarenes returned in the spring, families plodding behind their donkeys, some of the women hanging on to the donkeys' tails they were so weary with their long journey. Mary rode, the most senior wife – or perhaps it was just that she held the twins – and then Jacob broke away and ran ahead on his strong legs, first at the gate. Matthew was with them. I watched from behind a rock, shy because so much time had passed. Joshua helped his mother down from the donkey, took the twins. Thomas was toddling – they'd have to watch him near the well. Miri stayed asleep in the pannier. She looked so sweet. I wanted to go over but I knew how terrifying my face would look to the baby, scarred, disfigured; she would wake and cry as soon as I came near. Jacob came out. 'I'll carry your tools, Father.' He returned inside. Hobab leaned in a doorway across the road. 'Look,' he called his brothers, 'our Nazarene friends are back.' I sank down behind the rock, heard Joseph calling to Joshua to help with the unloading, heard Joshua swear under his breath then demand insultingly, 'Why are you shouting at me, Joseph?'

'Help with the wood, boy,' Joseph said.

'You're always shouting,' Joshua said. He had grown. 'You've got no right to shout at me.'

'I've every right!' Joseph said. 'Don't say another word, you! Be silent. When you have finished the wood, fetch water.'

Joshua threw down the pieces of wood from the donkey, pulled off the saddle and dropped it on the ground. He dragged the donkey by its halter and tied it to an olive tree. 'Not in the sun!' Joseph said. Joshua dragged the donkey to a shadier tree. Trembling with anger he snatched up a pitcher and went behind the wall. I heard him fill it from the well. He gave a cry of disgust. 'There's a dead dog in the water!'

Joseph glared around him for the culprit. It was an old

131

man's squinting glare; his sight was failing. People pushed past him along the track, a man leading a camel with raw wool for Levi's bleaches and dyes, a fuller with his club and a pig-man with a long stick. Hobab and his brothers yawned against the wall in the afternoon sun, watching. Hobab called to Kedar, 'Our Nazarene friends don't know the difference between a dog and bitch.' One of the men behind Joseph, Dositheus, with a flowing black moustache, cursed and crossed towards them with long strides, reaching under his cloak. The boys melted away but Hobab saw me and grinned, then covered his face with his hands in mocking imitation of my veil. I crouched lower behind the rock and Joshua looked straight at me, then looked at Hobab.

Joshua ran towards me. He couldn't know this figure was me. I walked away with all the grace I could muster. Hobab went from sight behind his uncle's house. I hurried faster, heard running footsteps. Joshua seized my twisted arm. 'I knew it was you!'

I said, 'My Lord.'

He frowned, not understanding, then shrugged. 'Miriam. I saw you in Egypt!'

'You must have been dreaming.'

'Yes, of course it was a dream! I saw your face. I saw you recognise me. Where have you been?'

I stared up. Joshua had those large brown eyes, too large. He saw through me. No, I was fanciful. I remembered the Child's bright blue eyes; but all babies' eyes are blue. His nose was thin, not at all a baby's nose, no similarity. No distinguishing marks. Joshua's long hair was blown across his face by the wind, dense curls unravelling. One tickled his nose and he snorted it away, put back his hair with his wrist. But it came down again. He didn't ask me why I wore a veil across my face, showed no sign of noticing it.

'I did dream of you,' I said. 'You were sad. Alone.'

'Sad?' He pushed me away. 'Screw you. It was a stupid dream then!'

'I'm sorry if it was.'

He glanced round as Joseph called him. 'How did you break your tooth?' he asked, but Joseph called again, louder. Something about the dog. Mary had heard about it and she

132

was crying. Joses wanted to see; he almost fell down the well.

Joshua asked me, 'What's it between you and that boy? The one who grinned?' Joseph shouted at the top of his voice this time. Joshua had to go. Had to. Right now.

Joshua let go my arm. He took a step backwards. Then he turned and ran angrily back to his family. I saw him fetch a rope to pull out the dog, bitch, whatever it was. Anyway, the water would be contaminated for ever. I wondered how he knew my front tooth was broken.

But surely Jesus Christ would know *everything*? Even on this imperfect world He would be given perfection; perfect knowledge. I would have no secrets from Him. Joshua had not understood when I said 'My Lord'. He hadn't even known Hobab's name. He hadn't known his dream of me in Egypt was no dream but real. And I had seen Joshua's own earthly guardian, Joseph the cuckold, obliged to recognise Jacob as his heir before all men in the church, *de facto* repudiating the Virgin Birth, and thus any claim by Joshua to be the Christ. Mary had been publicly humiliated by her husband, never openly accused of fornication but tacitly found guilty of it. Such compromises are the price of politics. But surely the Heaven and Earth of Jesus Christ was supposed to be above all that. Surely everyone was supposed simply to believe in the Virgin Birth and the truth.

I crept back to Levi's house, its tiled floors swarming with apprentices and air thick with the bitter tang of dye. The roof was finished and Zeno fobbed off with promises of payment tomorrow. Levi entertained a Syrian merchant, little bowls of nuts, a dish of yellow eggs, everything busy, noisy, tawdry. Levi roared for me when he lost the deal. I hid before I was seen, but I had no hiding place he did not know.

Each morning Joseph sent Joshua with a pitcher to the well for water, the journey I'd made so often. From behind a tree I watched him hurry down and hurry back. I watched him from behind a wall. I watched him from the field ditch. He never saw me. His feet were dirty. If somebody threw a stone at him he threw it back. What, then, of Jacob? Matthew taught him lessons beneath the lemon tree. I only saw him sent for water once, but he carried two pitchers because he was stronger. Jacob was trained in Greek, but Joshua was apprenticed to Zeno the Gentile as a roofing carpenter. A Gentile! No special treatment for him, no more education. Anyone could see Joshua hated his toil. Like all apprentices he got only the poorest jobs, peeling off bark, bringing wood to the bench, holding down the work while more skilful or more speedy hands shaped the piece. Learning to do the job rough and fast and cheap. Sweeping up shavings at the end of the day. And then after work, returning home, Joshua was sent with the pitcher for more water until the house cistern was full.

Just a boy like any other boy. Nothing special about him.

And Joseph worked as a common jobbing carpenter. Made sure he was seen to be no more than a carpenter. No one noticed him. No one thought about him. But as the heat of the year increased, Joseph kept his head down, and I knew trouble was coming.

No rain had fallen during the spring. Summer was a waterless, pent-up time, the people simmering with anger like held breath while the crops visibly dried and died. Harvest was a miserable dusty business, the desert wind blowing dry and hot as the devil's breath. There was no rejoicing at the time of Tabernacles, the price of bread rose high as the sky, and taxes fell due. Judas Zadok saw this boiling pot of resentment and stirred it with the ancient cry of revolt, 'To your tents, O Israel!' This time his words fell on fertile ground and brought about the storm. Young men ran about with swords, and older people hid themselves and their possessions in the country rather than pay tax. Herod Archelaus clamped down with all the brutality Judas Zadok hoped for. Even the old men of the Temple's Sanhedrin council, incensed by Archelaus's mistreatment of priests, swallowed their pride and sent a delegation of complaint to the God-Emperor in Rome. Too late. In Jerusalem the people ran riot against Archelaus and he lost control. For a single moment Judas Zadok was victorious. His sicarii and zealots and assassins turned on the Rich, Roman and Greek traders, bureaucrats and any soldiers they could stab in the back, and burnt a few wine-taverns and beer-shops and the houses of a few collaborators. They imposed new food laws and new rules for hygiene. For a few minutes Judas Zadok stood on the top step of the Temple and looked around him, and everything he saw was his. He was king and priest of all he surveyed, the Pillar of the World. He didn't need Joseph or his childish brats or to live any more as he had, hand to mouth, in hiding and in hopes of years to come. Here and now the true Jews of the Fourth Way would kick the Romans out, and within a few years – less! – the Poor would collect or tax or loot the full thirty talents required by God for the renewal of His Covenant with the Nazarenes, the *Notzri ha-Brit*, the Keepers of the Covenant; and Israel would live until the end of time in purity and virtue in God's eyes, as the prophecy foretold, with the nations of the world at her feet.

What actually happened was that a Roman legion marched from the coast like wolves into a sheepfold, scattered Judas Zadok's followers and beheaded him, and the revolt collapsed. Defeat was utter, but rumours flew. Judas was not dead but living in the Golan. He had been seen in Galilee. From the Dead Sea he would rise to lead his people when the trumpet sounded.

In fact the Roman patience with the Jews had run thin. For decades the Romans, tolerant on religious matters, had put up with the intolerant and insulting religion of the Jews and their one Jewish God and no others allowed. Now the Romans stepped in and did what they did best. Archelaus, it was rumoured, was packed off to exile in the south of France. The proud lands of Judah, Samaria and Idumea were reduced to a mere Roman province, ruled by a Roman governor, the prefect Coponius. Jews revolted against taxes; very well, we would be taxed to the hilt. To punish us the legate of Syria, Quirinius, an expert in tax matters, was brought in to hold a second census. Jews hated taxes; very well, we would be forced to pay more tax. We would pay taxes through the nose for all the trouble and cost of our rebellion, and the more we hated the Romans who ruled us the more tax we would pay, until we learnt our submission.

It was too dangerous to fight the Romans, so throughout the winter gangs of youths led by Hobab threw stones at the walls of the Nazarene community. 'When did anything good ever come out of Nazareth,' they jeered. The Pharisee elders turned a blind eye; it was well known that the

Nazarenes were an Essene faction just as the Fourth Way had been. Tarred with the same brush despite all Joseph's quietness and humility, Nazarene men and women were beaten worse than I ever was. Still Joseph did nothing, careful to obey every law, to do no work on their Sabbath, to avoid trouble, not to stand out. He ordered Nazarenes to go out to relieve themselves only at night, but if necessary the small hatchets his people wore under their clothes, to dig the holes that hid their waste from the sight of God, made useful weapons. Joseph and his family must journey to their birthplace Bethlehem to register for Quirinius's head-tax, of course. Their departure couldn't come soon enough for me. In Sepphoris anyone could see it was only a matter of time before someone got killed on one side or the other. But then the weather changed.

After the drought came the rain. After too much sun, too much rain.

The one who started the trouble, of course, was Joshua. I saw it. It was the first marvel I saw. Oh, it's not like you imagine! Something like that, a miracle, is marvellous, yet terrible – I mean, against nature. Outside nature. Except to these people God is everything, there is no nature outside God. But, I mean, it was frightening to witness. So frightening I would not have believed it but for one thing.

It was so simple. The Sabbath. Joshua playing with little Joses in the mud after the rain. As usual I spied on them as well as I could, trying to see better, to see the mystery made plain, to see a sign I could believe in. Certainty. Such a thing, as you know, is not shown to us in real life. But I dreamed, I hoped, my eyes were open, I wanted so desperately to believe in something. I was ready to see. And there was Joshua sitting cross-legged, playing his game with the pools, making little dams to hold back the water. Joses splashed with his hands, spattering wet mud over them both. I knew their mother would scream when she saw them. Joshua would be in trouble again.

I watched him squeeze mud balls in his hands and set them in a row beside the pools like little birds drinking. Joses laughed to see it. Other small children arrived, and laughed too. They wanted the birds really to drink – they were only small children, they did not understand. Their excitement brought Annas the scribe frowning into his doorway. 'What are you doing?' he called across the road to Joshua. 'What are you doing, polluting our Sabbath with work, making toys?' He clapped his hands as though to disperse the children, then told his son, 'Fetch the boy's father to come at once.'

After a while Joseph came out of his gate. His hands and arms were still strong but he used a crutch, his knees swollen with arthritis. Annas called to him in a high voice, 'Don't you Nazarenes care it's our Sabbath?' He pointed at the twelve mud birds.

Joseph only wanted peace. 'Come inside, Joshua. You know it's not lawful to make things on the Sabbath.'

Joshua said: 'It's not the Sabbath, Joseph. Only the Temple Sabbath.'

Joseph said, 'Do as I say.'

Joshua stared at him angrily, then turned to the twelve sparrows, clapped his hands at the chirping birds. 'Go!'

The twelve sparrows flew up, and flew away. I saw them. The earth given life. But I think I would not have believed what I was seeing, which was impossible, except for the look on Joses's face. The child's look of pure childish wonder. He stared into the sky long after the birds were gone.

Annas saw only birds come out of mud birds, and like you or anyone he wondered how the trick was done. But I saw the children's faces, and I simply believed. I had seen the truth. A miracle.

'Joses!' Joseph held out his hand to his younger son. 'Come inside.'

Joshua sat alone, cross-legged, in the mud. Annas returned to his house, but his son grinned at Joshua and knocked down the clay dams with a stick. He knew Joshua couldn't get up quickly enough to catch him.

I heard Joshua say, 'Why? What did the pools and water do to you?' The boy laughed, splashing with his stick, and Joshua said, 'You'll wither like a tree without water. Your flesh withers like dry leaves, your skin dries up like bark.' The boy stopped laughing. He gave a cry. He moved his head with a great effort, looked down at himself. He had not changed into a tree. Nevertheless he groaned, turning in on himself, and fell down in the road. Annas ran out. 'What have you done to him?'

Oh yes; Annas knew. Deep inside himself, instinctively he knew. He looked fearfully at Joshua.

Joshua shrugged. 'What has been done to him, he has done to himself.'

Joseph called urgently from the gate, and Joshua got up slowly and walked to him. I heard Jacob asking excitedly, 'What happened? Was there a fight?' But Joseph shut the gate quickly.

And that is what I saw. Except for one thing. In the moment before the gate closed, Joshua looked back at me. Straight at me.

My nerve failed me. Every day I wanted to approach Joshua, see him, touch him, but each time something was wrong: it was too early, too late, or he had someone else with him; the opportunity did not arise. Yes, I lost my nerve. I crept away.

Mary's voice spoke behind me. 'I have not seen you with us, Miriam. Have you, too, rejected us?'

I crouched, shook my head, my black hood, my black veil. She had such a sweet voice, but there was iron in it. Determination.

'Stand up, Miriam.' She touched my elbow, and I stood taller than her, gawky with youth and clumsy. But she gave her small smile, and her gaze looked up at me examining the narrow slit in my veil, my peeping eyes. 'Such beautiful eyes,' she murmured. 'I still believe I've seen them before, some-where.' I looked down, shook my head. 'You've not been as long as us in this place, Miriam. Where were you before?'

I mumbled. There were many answers I could have given. She said, 'Speak up.'

'Only from Magdala, my lady.'

She laughed. 'My lady! Why this sudden formality? Are Magdalenes all so formal? You didn't use to be, Miriam. My children loved you. Why don't you play with them any longer?'

I blurted, 'My lady, I know who you are.'

She looked sad. 'We are born, we live, we can't help being Nazarenes.'

I shook my head wildly. That wasn't what I meant. But she murmured, speaking almost to herself, 'Any more than we can help who our children are, or our blessings, or change them. There is no fate. It is all the will of God.' I thought, *Is it, my lady?* But she heard Joses laughing and happiness came into her eyes. Then she raised her fingers to my shaking head, stopped me. 'Let me see you.'

I clamped my veil to my scarred face with the palms of my hands. I backed away from her.

'Let me see your face,' she said. 'Miriam!' But I turned and ran away.

And the next day, they were gone. To Bethlehem, I suppose. What I had wanted to say to her and meant to say was that I knew she was the Virgin, but I'd heard the laughter of Joses playing with Silas, and Thomas had toddled into sight through the gate, and I would have sounded ridiculous, wouldn't I? She'd have given her wise, tinkling laugh and I would've blurted out, you were *supposed* to be the Virgin, and then everything else would have come out. Madwoman's talk. You weren't supposed to have children by Joseph, he wasn't supposed to love you. No Jacob. No Joses, no Silas, no Salome, no Thomas, no Miri. He was not supposed to love you! No happiness, no brimming family for you, only duty! You yourself were conceived with a kiss, Mary, not in passion. And you, like your Son, will never die.

It was too late to say it. I couldn't have said it anyway. How could I tell the Virgin she'd done the wrong thing? She couldn't. It was impossible. Yet it had happened.

And Joshua had miraculously created the twelve sparrows. I don't recall any tradition about Jesus spontaneously making sparrows, or any prophecy about pools and dams – I couldn't remember if there had been seven of them – seven's always a significant number in the Bible. Mary has seven children. Perhaps I'm going mad, seeing miracles and being convinced by them. I don't remember a biblical miracle of Jesus withering a boy's life like an autumn tree, or any prophecy that He, perfect, would do such a dreadful thing. But I saw it happen.

Now they were gone. Their house stood empty but for a guard. Without them there was nothing to keep me here.

Not for the first time in my life, I ran away. I've been running all my life, and at that time I still thought I had only one place to run to.

I ran back to Magdala.

Let me tell you an innermost secret of my heart. There's something about a man. I'm not talking of love, which happens only once and once it dies is dead for ever. I mean the business of love, the pretence. The feel of a caress. I can pretend it's love. I can pretend the precious moment of warmth, I want it so badly. Turn roughness into passion, the passion I remember, the passion I never had as love. Turn some skinny grey face into James, some plump red whiskery face into James, turn the crushing and twisting and agonising business in some shabby room, or back of an alley, or corner of a yard, into love with James. What we never had, these caresses, is how I keep myself alive. Without love, without the memory of love, I'm nothing. I'm not stealing husbands; they go back to their wives in a few minutes, I'm forgotten, and no one ever knows. I can't show my face, ever. But to a man, all cats are black in the dark. I have the body, and the skills, and the need.

The desperate, crying need. My body is no longer the body of a child. Twisted, tormented, scarred, my shoulder crooked, my face crooked too from the blows that have been rained upon me in anger or lust, my broken jaw set crooked, my mouth full of broken or crooked teeth, my body and brain those of any young woman, my blood so awash with hormones I can hardly think in my rage, loneliness, desire, youth: I am simply human.

And yet I do think. After the night I sit on the beach all day with a pebble in my mouth and the waters of Galilee breaking around my toes, and I think.

And one day I stood and walked back between the rough volcanic houses of Magdala and took the dusty track back to Sepphoris. My feet were bare, my sandals were stolen. I'd no money for beer or wine or water, everything I'd saved was stolen, or I'd lost it. I forgot the coins sewn in the hem of my cloak until my lips were blistered with thirst, then found the stitching had given way where it dragged on the ground. At Sepphoris, Levi would beat me. Where had I been? I would have no words to answer him with, nothing to say, no defence. Joseph and the Community had returned from Bethlehem. I saw a lamp in his window. A crowd had gathered in the street, and I turned away, then heard Joseph's voice raised. 'An accident!'

I crept forward in the failing light, slipped through the shadows between the people. At the centre of the crowd a boy of twelve or thirteen lay outstretched on the ground where he had fallen down dead. I recognised him by his staring face: Hobab. I was so glad he was dead! I'd have spat on him if only I had spit. He must have been running when struck down; his body had skidded in the dust, his legs bent as though running still. The woman who wept over him was his mother, sinful woman that she had let him grow as wild as she had. Now she covered his face with her skirts as though protecting him from the coming night, and she wept for him, too late. Beside him on one hand lay a broken water-pitcher. On the other side stood Joshua, calm, reflective. I knew his calmness.

Joseph, his long hair and beard blowing pale in the wind, was intensely uneasy in the presence of death. 'Joshua, tell us what happened.'

'Hobab ran at me,' Joshua said. 'He provoked me. He knocked me with his shoulder. He spilt the water I was carrying and then he broke the pitcher with his fist.' He looked at the boys closing around him in the crowd, looked each one of them in the eye, and I knew what they did not: Joshua's calmness was a cloak laid over intense anger. 'They're always doing it. Hobab, Kedar, Shibah, Bukki, others.' He burst out, 'All you others! Pushing us around.'

'That's true!' Jacob said. He bunched his fists. 'Don't worry, Joshua. I'll look after you. Go on, anyone want to make something of it? You, Kedar? I'll give you more than a push.'

Joseph said sharply, 'Jacob, hush now!'

'The Nazarenes are stealing our water!' Kedar shouted. 'Everyone knows that!' The adults murmured agreement. Annas came forward. 'Joseph, Joseph, it cannot go on like this.'

The mother screamed, 'My Hobab was only having a little sport! Why shouldn't he, my poor baby! They deserve to be chucked out, them! Troublemakers,' she spat. 'Nazarenes.'

'An accident,' Joseph said doggedly. 'Hobab knocked himself too hard against Joshua and fell badly, that's all. You didn't strike him, did you, Joshua?'

Joshua said, 'I spoke to him.'

Cries of disbelief, mockery. Then the crowd waited, expectant. Joseph asked reluctantly, 'What did you say?'

Joshua said: 'I told him, "You shall not live your life." '

'Yes, but you didn't touch him, did you?'

Joshua said: 'And he fell down and died.'

Joseph said, 'Words cannot do that.'

Hobab's uncle Raphu stood up with the dust of mourning over his head. He put himself in front of Joseph's face. 'It is your child who, by whatever means, did the deed. Joseph the Nazarene, I accuse you for your son. Joseph the Nazarene, I blame you for your son. You cannot remain among us with such a son.'

Other voices called out, 'We accuse him! Guilty, guilty. Throw them out!' Night had fallen, and they called for candles. But I stayed on my knees at the feet of the crowd, staring at Joshua by the light of the candles already held up there, seeing his illuminated face, knowing the intensity of feeling I saw there in his eyes, the flames moving brighter in the deepness of his pupils as more candles were brought. I heard Kedar and Shibah shouting their accusations from the crowd, moving between the people so that the word spread. Soon someone would cast the first stone. But in the quiet space at the centre Joshua did not move, just stared calmly at them. The people accusing him called out for more candles. Candles and tapers of burning rushes were held up in front of their eyes but still they called for more light, seeing only darkness.

'They're blind,' Joshua said.

The people around him thought they were in fog or smoke or had lost their way, but then they began to believe him, panicking. Their calls turned to screams. They clapped their hands to their eyes and took them away, screaming, and the bright flames around them made a rushing sound in the night wind. They held out their hands to the heat, they listened to the flames with their ears, they smelt the smoke, but their eyes were blind.

They drew back, stumbling, leaving me kneeling where I

was. I saw Joseph hobble to Joshua, I heard his words. 'Why, Joshua, my son? Why have you polluted us with death?'

Joshua lost his calm. 'I'm not your son! You say so yourself!' He pointed at Jacob. 'You say *he* is your son! Him! Not me!' His fury evaporated. 'I know who my mother is. I don't know who my father is. It's not you. Ow!' Joseph had taken Joshua's ear in his fist and twisted it hard.

'Listen to me, boy,' Joseph said in a low voice. 'I'm fed up with this story. It's true you're your mother's son. But you mustn't listen to every story she tells you. We must be very careful living among these people. They're simple people and we rely on their goodwill. You're making them hate us and persecute us.'

'You're afraid of them,' Joshua said. 'You're speaking for ruffians, louts, sanctimonious old men, their loudmouthed wives. For your sake I'll keep quiet. But they'll keep their punishment.'

Joseph tightened his fist. 'Respect me. I speak to you as your father would, sternly but with love.'

'No, you're not like my father.' The tears came to Joshua's eyes. 'Who are you? It's enough for you to seek and not to find, isn't it? You're a fool, Joseph. I'm not yours. You know the truth really. You know who I am. Tell me. In your heart you *know*.'

A single drop of blood ran from Joshua's ear. It dripped from Joseph's fist.

Joseph sighed. He let go.

Jacob came across, grinned at the dispersing crowd. 'They're only blind because it's dark,' he said, then nodded at the women carrying Hobab's body away. 'How did you do that, Josh? You hit him, didn't you? Not a mark.' He grunted with satisfaction. 'Now they'll give us some respect.'

Levi was kind to me. He gave me a plate of yellow eggs and salted fish, white bread and oil. I ate in silence, trembling. He smiled, enjoying my fear. He visibly swelled with pride in the firelight as he watched me. 'Don't like that black!' he said. 'Makes you look like a leper. Puts people off.' He brought out a soft woollen gown, pretty colours, good quality. 'Here, more wine. Put this on, let's see your face.' I shrank from him, held my veil so tight I hurt my fingers. He tugged, slapped me, sighed. 'I'll throw you in that fire one day,' he said. 'Then you'll see how good a husband you get. What's it to be?' We stared at each other. He laughed and spread his hands. 'It's my misfortune to live with a devil. What have I ever done to you? Have I offended you in another life? All you do is hate me, hate me, hate me. I can see it in your eyes! You're incapable of love, you're a stone. The sight of you disgusts me, you whore, your cunt smells. I'm doing my best for you, not that you deserve it. You have no feelings. I've found you a husband.'

He moved fast, but I was on his blind side. Levi's grasping hand caught my black cloak and it tore, rotten. I shrank into the darkness surrounding the firelight, stared back. 'I'll put you on a rope!' he shouted into the dark. He tried to sound reasonable again, but he had burnt his foot. He lit one end of the torn cloak, held it up. 'Miriam? My Syrian friend needs a wife. Only occasionally. When he's passing through.' He snarled: 'I'll keep you on a rope around your neck.'

I ran away, and hid in the tombs.

It's good here. Quiet. The tombs are dry. Boulders are pushed against their crumbling mouths that dot the hillside, but persistent fingers like mine can scratch away the pebbles around them, and the rough marl, and the dust, and the shells of dead beetles, and their larvae, and wriggle inside. The dry inside, and dry bones for company. Only the latest still wet. You get used to the smell. Soon smell doesn't smell at all. The dead here are silent, mostly. But you hear other things stirring all the time, creaks, drips, giggles, cries, babbling, rising from other caves. Tombs are a place for the living too, and the half-dead, and the mad. Mad people full of suffering and the demons of the dead. Demons have to go somewhere, into worms and beetles and motes of bone-dust, breathed into the mouths of the living, our nostrils, our eyes and ears, sliding into our skin as our sweat comes out, slithering into our arseholes with the movement of our shit, slipping into us as we pee, making love to the profanity of our menstrual blood as they swim like an infection to our wombs, and from there into the testicles of men. Busy, busy, busy, the tombs.

In day the sunlight shines around the boulder that seals my chosen tomb and reaches inside like white fingers in the dusty air, fingering the slab where the body of a rich man is laid. At first he grows bigger, swelling, purple, enormous. Then time runs in reverse and each day as the blood comes out of him he melts a little, he softens, his imposing gassy belly squeaks and farts as it shrinks and sags, flows outwards, finally hangs from his ribs like an empty brown sack turning to leather, and the ribs stick through it like white fingers. At night it's cold. Even the days are cold. I forgot to mention the rich man was wrapped in a shroud at first. I need it more than he. I wrap myself round and round and round, and sit with my knees drawn up to my chin, watching for the sun to cease. Like the moon, I come out at night.

The stones move under my eyes. I see my hands crawl on the stones in the moonlight.

I drink on my knees and elbows like a slobbering animal at the whitewashed wall where moisture seeps from the polluted well. Joseph won't use it even for watering his beds of lentils, leeks, garlic, onions, the moonlit watermelons that I glimpse through the gate. Moonlit lemon tree. Apple tree. Fig tree. Those trees that I remember like another world, and sometimes Mary in her moonlit blue robe, moonlit white scarf, praying in the dark. There must be more than this darkness, but I cannot remember it.

But I try. Sometimes I come out under the winter sun, if I cannot be seen.

I hardly recognise the old man, his gleaming grey skull, her husband. Polluted by being in the presence of that boy's death, I forget what he was called, Joseph has shaved his head and beard. I remember the boy's name, Hobab. I remember Hobab hurt me once. From my place of concealment in winter's long shadows I watch, longingly, as Joseph and Jacob go about their business shaved to their shiny scalps. The old man (he looks eighty-nine years old) and his son renewing their Nazarene vows and starting again, growing in strength as their hair grows.

But it's not them. It's Joshua I watch, Joshua who makes my heart beat. No haircut for him; his hair hangs down his back, the weight of hair pulling his curls straight. I follow him with my hands padding on the stones. He still works in town for Zeno the Gentile, endures his humiliation with anger. Hardly talks back to Joseph, bites his lips. The muscles stand out in his arms as he works up the ladder or strides along the roof joists; don't cross him. The other apprentices are meek in his presence, fall silent. Joshua drinks wine with Zeno. Joshua eats a fish preserved in vinegar with Zeno, which a Nazarene would never do. The anger in Joshua! The strength! Zeno, thirty years older, is his friend. A Gentile, the friend of a Jewish boy. I wonder how long Joseph will tolerate this contamination returning to his house each night.

Kneeling at the chink in the gate, I glimpse the bright, child-filled world of Mary's happy, now-unhappy house. Beneath the sunlit fig tree my blessed, gorgeous Mary begs her husband to be calm about Joshua. 'Do nothing, Joseph. Let it go. He'll sort himself out, you'll see.' Her infinite smiling patience, but Joseph shakes his fuzzy head grumpily, she always says do nothing. She touches his whiskery white cheek gently with her fingertip, lovingly. 'Joshua's not like you, Joseph. He's not you. You have to understand.' I can feel Joseph's agony. I can feel it from here. Mary's asking the one thing of him he cannot understand about her, and never will. He is not the father of her firstborn. Only she knows who is the father of Joshua. On his deathbed Joseph will beg her with his last breath, 'Is it true?' And she will reply, 'He is all true, every word.' Joseph will die believing her, because he loves her, but he will never understand.

I didn't see Jacob watching them from the window until his face moved. A few moments later he came out of the side of the house. He'd been eavesdropping. I slipped behind the wall, then sniffed his footprints in the dust, followed them uphill. I slid between the rocks, and Jacob came in sight between the new houses. He couldn't find Joshua, asked directions. A camel plodded by piled high with carpets like a stately ship, and beyond its summit Joshua, balanced hands on hips, called down insultingly from a half-finished roof. 'Jacob! Got time off from your Latin and Greek to see some real work? Come on up.' He kicked the top of the rough-hewn ladder in invitation.

Jacob eyed the ladder, and I smelt his fear. Then he ran

up it in one breath, teetered on the top rung, and Joshua pulled him up effortlessly. Zeno worked on the very summit of the roof, the new tiles clacking like teeth as they were laid. My shadow rippled over the rubble beneath the building as I slithered towards the wall. I hid my head and the windings of the shroud under my torn black cloak, only my eyes looking up like tiny blue stones from the slit of my black veil, a shadow in the shadows.

Jacob's voice came down clearly to me, echoing, angry. 'What's happened to you, Joshua? Why do you shame us? Why do you shame my father?' I squinted. They were silhouetted against the glare of the sun, balancing on the lattice of joists and beams on which Joshua moved nimbly, and Jacob followed awkwardly. 'You're no Nazarene, Joshua. Your breath stinks of sour wine. Your sweat reeks of beer.'

Joshua, climbing to the apex of the roof, snapped back: 'Why should I not shame your father, since he shames me? He's not my father.'

Jacob said, 'For your mother's sake, Joshua, come back.' Jacob spread his arms, whether to make his point or keep his balance I could not say. 'Be pure in righteousness for your mother's sake. Return to her. Return to the fold. Be with us.'

Even looking at Joshua against the sun, from his shadow, I felt his anger and pain come down like radiated heat. 'I'm not with you. You exclude me. I don't hear your lessons.' So that was all! Jealousy that Jacob was still taught the Law, and Latin, and Greek by Matthew.

'There are other teachers,' Jacob said. 'But I shall be the Christ, Joshua. You have to understand that. You have to be at peace with this. I am the Christ when my father dies.' He climbed a few paces on the joist, wobbled. 'Careful,' Zeno called, 'the lad's not finished off the last bit.'

But Jacob only heard his own voice. 'Joshua, come back to us. Repent. Change your ways. You know what I say is the truth. It's not by words or prayers that God saves us, it's by our deeds, what we actually *do*.'

Joshua said angrily, 'I hear you. Don't come any closer.'

'Come and work in my father's workshop,' Jacob offered. 'He'll listen to me. I can arrange it. Don't work for this foreigner. Only by pure righteousness can we be saved. By working for him you're contaminating us all. Breaking one law, however small, breaks them all. Defiance brings pollution on the whole community.'

'Stand still, boy!' Zeno shouted. The beam creaked. Jacob looked down and realised his height above the ground. He swayed. Zeno reached for him, and the beam gave way. Joshua caught Jacob's wrist in one hand, grabbed Zeno with the other.

'I can't hold you both,' Joshua told Jacob. 'You're right. Actions speak louder than words.'

He let Zeno go, and pulled Jacob up.

Zeno came down shrieking, running in the air, and fell by me. His body landed across the pile of stones. I heard his neck break like a stick. His eyes stared past me, glass, empty of life. I shrank deeper into a niche in the wall.

Jacob stared down from the top of the roof. 'You killed him!' he said. 'Is he dead?'

Joshua walked down a slanted beam, jumped like a cat from the side wall. He glanced down at the dead man. 'Yes, he's dead.'

'He can't be dead.' Jacob backed carefully down the beam. 'They'll kill us! Murder! I didn't see it. I wasn't here.' He jumped down, stood with his hands to his head. 'You tried to save him. You just weren't strong enough. Is he really dead?'

Workmen pushed through the half-finished doorways. 'That's a dead 'un!' one man swore. 'Zeno, was it? Wearing his head backwards!'

Joshua touched Jacob's elbow. 'You're right,' he said, 'I don't feel any worse. Breaking all the law's no different from breaking the smallest, is it?'

Jacob flinched away from him. 'You're mad,' he muttered. His own words had been thrown back at him like a parable brought to life. Action not words. Jacob's face looked white as the belly of a fish.

'Poor old Zeno.' A workman spat the nails from his mouth with awkward reverence. 'Poor old bugger wasn't a bad sort. Sighs of relief all over town tonight, mark my words, that he never learned to count. A lot of people owed him money.'

Joshua said: 'He isn't dead.' He lifted the dead man's

148

hand. Zeno's head moved, his eyes closed, then opened. 'Up you get, Zeno.'

Zeno got to his feet, dusted off his knees. 'All right, lads, back to work. I'll never live this down,' he confided to Joshua. 'Taking a nap in the middle of the morning. Must be getting old. You just wake me if you see me doing it again.'

Jacob watched him climb the ladder, then laughed with relief. 'I really thought he was dead!' He punched Joshua half in anger, half relief.

But one of the workmen said, 'I saw him. He was dead.' He stared at Joshua and trembled. Some people living by the Nazarene Community were still blind, and word had got about. 'That boy has the power to curse.'

They watched the two boys walk away. Someone said, 'He's learning to bless, not to curse. I saw it with my own eyes. Zeno was dead and now he's alive.' Zeno yelled down, 'All you lazy buggers, back to work!' The workmen grinned as they hurried up the ladder. 'And noisy as ever, our Zeno.'

'But still,' one hawk-faced bearded man muttered, 'healing a Gentile, that can't be right. What about us?'

The boys were gone. My hands moved from the dark dust of shadows into the bright dust of sunlight, I crossed the track behind them unseen as they walked, I loped behind the houses to keep up. A woman coming from her yard saw my black clothes, the bandages showing through the tears, drew back from me. 'Leper!' But I was already gone, the wind lifting my cloak, hurrying, the dust puffing from my bare torn feet on the rocks. And I heard a mother wailing in her grief.

I hurried, hurried, hurried. In the road a thin young girl, her scarf over her face in mourning, knelt with a baby held to her breast. The baby was dead. The man with her could not make her let her baby go.

'Zeno wasn't really hurt, was he,' I heard Jacob say to Joshua. 'He was lucky. He fell lucky. He must have landed just right. Yes, that's what happened.'

Joshua walked past the mother who wept, and she looked up at him, and her baby cried hungrily for milk. Joshua walked forward sunk in thought, not answering his half-brother.

'Be a Nazarene again,' Jacob said. He fell half a pace behind, circling her, offended by the girl's exposed breast, shamelessly feeding her baby in public. Then he hurried after Joshua, running to catch up. 'Take our vows again.'

Joshua hardly noticed him. 'No.'

'Be my father's apprentice,' Jacob said. 'Don't work for a dog.' Dog was their word for a Gentile. 'My father will welcome you back. Perhaps even a few lessons. Only learn humility, Joshua.' His voice faded as he hurried to catch up, and Joshua's shadow swung across a bundle of dry bramble on the verge.

I knelt, reached into the brittle heap, and from its centre cupped a fat yellow crocus in my hands. An impossible crocus, as though spring had passed by on a December day. I ran after Joshua with the flower clasped against my chest, beneath my cloak, held it bright yellow against the windings of the shroud as I ran, held the happy laughter of the girl feeding her baby in my ears, and so I came to Mary's house.

I stopped at the gate, staring through.

Joseph embraced Joshua, welcoming him home. I heard Jacob brag, 'I brought him back to you, Father.' I watched Jacob standing behind his mother's bastard son and the carpenter, smiling as though part of their happiness. Jacob even reached out – but then he did not quite touch Joshua's shoulder, and drew his hand away. I saw the look in Jacob's eyes. He knew what he had seen, back there on the building site. He knew and did not believe it. He was afraid to believe it, to admit it. The look I saw was almost . . . terror. He knew he had seen something for real.

I stared at Jacob's eyes. I knew that look. Old, monstrously old. Knowledge, despair, and the bitter cold of a yearning heart. The loneliness, the longing for the warmth of blood. The hunger. That terrifying hunger.

Was this, too, part of the plan? What plan? Whose plan?

Was I, too, born in blood as I was, part of the plan? What should, could, I do? Something? Anything? Nothing? Even doing nothing does something. Merely to observe, as every particle physicist knows, is to participate. Influence. Change the events observed.

I ran to the tombs, crouched behind the boulder.

Remembered the bright warning and the dark warning.

Miriam, do not go to Sepphoris. I'm in Sepphoris, I can't help it! Help me! What do you want?

Now the demon's fiery breath. *Remember, Mary. Do not interfere.* How can I not interfere? By erasing myself? I could hang myself – but might that not, too, be interference?

Does my life have a purpose?

I remembered the Virgin's soft words. *There is no fate. It is all the will of God.*

But it isn't. There's wickedness in the world. The Prince of Darkness lives.

There's one way to know if something is right. I took off my cloak, my veil. The crocus fell to the rock floor, I picked it up, unwound the bandages from my body, stood shivering in my bare skin. I tied the shroud on a slip-knot around my neck, wrapped the other end round and round the boulder, and fell forward.

I woke lying naked, cold as the grave. The breath whistled in my nostrils. I had a headache. The shroud had frayed, parted, relaxed the noose just enough. No miracle, just a sharp edge of slate in the rock. Or a message that I must live.

I sat holding the wedge of slate, its grey point resting between my breasts. I would have to push very hard to slam it through my breastbone. The slate would break, fragment. My heart thudded. The fingers of sunlight splayed around me; outside it was sunset and soon the stars would come out. The pain would be very bad. My hands shook. I've killed myself before, but that was different. I'm not speaking of the Rainmaker's death – hers was a choice of which death, not death or life. I killed myself with a gun in my mouth firing through the palate into my brain, painless, merciful, instant. I blew my brain apart and I felt nothing until I looked down on myself, my poor pathetic body slipping, sliding, falling down the cave where I'd dragged myself on my elbows from my sleeping bag to the holster by the fire, the gun James used against the dreadful things that came and still come in the night in this world, monsters dreadful beyond imagination.

I couldn't do it.

I dropped the slate. This time I would try to live.

Strangely enough, as I slowly dressed myself in the shroud that had failed me, and pulled my cloak around my shoulders, and my veil across my face, and lay down to sleep with the crocus held lightly between my fingers against my cheek, it was the words of the workman that came back to me over and over, like a dream. *He's learning to bless.*

He's learning to bless.

MIRABILIA

wonders

He's learning.

I watched him every moment of every day, somehow, starving myself, forgetting even to steal food, licking the moisture from rocks. There's the gap in the gate, places to look over the top of the wall, and don't forget the side gate with the broken latch, so that I could even slip inside at night, drift from the lemon tree to the fig tree like a shadow, listen at any window, hear everything. Finger the toys left lying about by the younger children. A space behind the wood pile for the kitchen fire concealed me. There was the well, disused but not covered over, to hide in, staring up, listening, glimpsing, yearning, the stem of the crocus between my lips.

Joshua's defiance against his guardian was not ended. He would not cut his hair, not purge his contact with death, not be again a Nazarene. An adolescent, determined to be awkward as any other adolescent. I think Mary liked this rebellion against Joseph. Keeping up with the ways of her eldest son kept her husband, complaining, crotchety and irritable with Joshua though he was, younger than he really was. Joseph even walked without his crutch. He treated Joshua more harshly than his other apprentices; nothing Joshua made (the workshop fabricated roughshod ploughs at this time) was good enough. But it was difficult for the old man to find fault, because Joshua's fingers spoke to wood. Wood wanted to work for him. Whether he worked hard or carelessly joints fell into place for him and never fell apart, and for him bronze tools worked as sharp as iron. Joshua made a chest of cedarwood and it filled Mary's house with perfume. For Joseph he made a stick from an olive branch that grew in his hands into the shape Joshua had in mind, strong yet seeming too thin to support weight, solid-looking and gnarled yet graceful, lending gravity and authority to the old man who leant on it.

'It'll do,' Joseph said. He pursed his lips at Mary's silent reproof. 'Very well, Joshua, you may attend a lesson with Jacob for an hour in the afternoons.' Mary smiled to herself.

But Joshua merely said, 'Thank you, Joseph.' He never called him Father. The hurt ran too deep to heal. Joshua attended the lessons, but he had not forgotten or forgiven his exclusion – of course not! *I* wouldn't – would you?

In this the tax season Jacob's day-lessons were given by Zacchaeus, who being a levite educated like Matthew spelt his name as a Greek would, and spoke of Judaea not Judah. Joshua, of course, arrived late. 'So this is the boy who would know Greek,' Zacchaeus said unctuously, sitting beneath the lemon tree.

'I already speak Greek, master,' Joshua said, sitting cross-legged. 'Got it off Zeno the Greek.'

'A common tiler, master,' Jacob explained.

'Swearing mostly,' Joshua said. No one spoke to school-masters like this. It was all I could do not to laugh – the first time I had laughed for years. I covered my mouth, staring up at the blue circle of sky above me, listening to their echoing voices.

There came the crack of a schoolmaster's stick across a pupil's knuckles. 'Ow,' Joshua said.

'Listen with both ears to what I said. *Speaking* Greek is not what I said,' came Zacchaeus's exasperated voice. 'To *know* Greek is altogether more. It is to know the alpha from the omega, which I shall show you. It is to acquire mental precision. It is to learn learning itself.'

'Learning to be a king,' Jacob said. 'To be the Christ.'

Zacchaeus sounded a little in awe of Joseph's heir, I thought. 'Exactly, Jacob. For example, let us examine the Greek *ho theos*. As the Christ your father, Joseph, may be addressed as *ho theos*, meaning Supreme. *Ho theos* can also mean "the god" or "God".'

I perched on the rock sticking from the side of the well, my legs trembling, the filthy water slopping below me. But I heard only their voices, fascinated.

'Zeno said it often. *Ho theos!*' came Joshua's voice. 'When he dropped a tile, or banged his thumb with a hammer.'

Zacchaeus sounded testy. 'The name of the Lord is not to be taken in vain.'

'It also means Satan,' Joshua said. '*Ho theos* means Satan as well as God.' The crack of the stick on the table. Joshua had moved his knuckles in time. He said: 'Did you not know, master?'

'I did – I did not – I am sure you are wrong! What difference can it make, anyway?' Rattled, Zacchaeus struggled to recover his authority. 'You will learn to know, Joshua, that in Greek your brother's name changes—'

'How can a name change if the person remains the same?' came Joshua's voice. 'Any more than Satan, *ho theos*, is part of God, *ho theos*. Matthew taught us that perfection cannot create imperfection. This world is imperfect. Therefore God did not create this world.'

Zacchaeus muttered something.

Joshua said confidently, 'Satan, the Supreme Divinity of this world, is evil, so God could not possibly have created him. Therefore Satan is the creation of this world. Darkness, sin, filth is found only in this world. It's our duty to climb to God.'

Jacob said, 'That's why we live by our Community Rule, Joshua. A stain on one of us is a stain on all, don't you see? We must all wash ourselves with holy baptism. By clean living achieve purity and virtue. Only then can we begin to approach God, and renew His Covenant. One law-breaker pollutes us all in the sight of God, one sin speaks louder than a thousand prayers.'

'You're wrong,' Joshua said.

'Silence!' Zacchaeus was not to be drawn. 'I speak of the Greeks.' He ploughed on, 'For example Jacob's name in Greek is *Iames*, or James.'

I was stunned. I listened with my mouth open. James. I've told you of James, whom I loved. I had not thought James was a Greek name. I had just thought it was – ordinary. Just a name.

155

'And to the Greeks, Joshua, your name is *Iesous*. Jesus.'

Jesus was a Greek name, not Hebrew? Joshua in this language I'm writing, Yeshua in Aramaic, Yehoshua in Hebrew – in Greek, is Jesus!

I thought I knew everything. I realise now I know almost nothing. I pull myself up on tiptoe to the rim of the well, can just see their heads (Zacchaeus is balding) under the lemon tree as they talk and gesture.

Looking at Joshua, I can't think of him as Jesus. He's Joshua. I feel I know him so well. Each curl of Joshua's hair, the angle he holds his head as he listens to the droning of that balding bore. I really feel I know everything about Joshua, I know what he's thinking now, he's wishing a bee would land on that shiny head. But to feel I knew everything about Jesus, the Jesus Christ of tradition and the Bible, would be . . . presumptuous. A contradiction in terms. I should be so awed in His presence that I wouldn't be able to speak, I'd just throw myself on my face at His feet. Joshua's so human! He even has a fly on his neck, and dandruff. Not even a man, yet; just a boy.

And next to him, James. The coincidence of that name so familiar and loved and terrible to me. But I wonder if anything is ever coincidence. Maybe the fall of a dice is never random, and Mary the Mother of God is right: it is all God's will. Even James. After all, *I* am here.

We're all part of the battle. Even he and I.

And it would be difficult to imagine anyone better able than Joshua to look after himself. Even from the back of his head I can tell his expression perfectly. He has his wonderful smile. A bee has landed on Zacchaeus's gleaming head.

'Master, please,' Joshua asked his teacher, smiling, 'tell me the nature of the alpha and the omega, as you promised.'

'It is simple. Alpha is the first and omega is last.'

'Alpha is first and omega last,' Joshua agreed, 'but what of their nature, as I asked you?'

Zacchaeus swallowed. 'Their nature? How can they have a nature?'

'If you don't know the number of the alpha according to its nature, how can you know the beta? Without the first, how can you teach others the second?'

Zacchaeus said stiffly, 'Of course. The alpha has no secrets from me.'

Joshua said: 'Then teach us.' He shrugged, splayed his hands, the mannerism I knew so well. The bee flew away. 'Teach us the alpha, master, then we shall believe what you say concerning the beta.' He waited.

'The lesson is finished for today,' Zacchaeus said.

Suddenly Joshua leant down, drew lines from his fingers in the dust. I could not see them, only his movements, sometimes long, some short. 'The alpha has these lines, and these lines. Here is the middle mark, common to both where they come together and go apart. Here is the point raised on high, here are the trinity of three signs always in movement, balanced, made equal. Now you see the universal rule of the alpha.'

Zacchaeus gazed. 'Don't rub it out!' He dropped to his knees in the dust. 'I almost see it.'

'It doesn't make any sense to me,' Jacob said. He grinned, clapped Joshua's shoulder for exposing the teacher's gullibility by such a simple trick.

'Can't you see it either?' Joshua asked him, surprised.

I stood on tiptoe until my toes cracked. If only I could have seen those marks!

Zacchaeus backed away from Joshua. I've rarely seen such humiliation on a man's face, and never in front of a boy. Joshua called, 'Stay with us, Zacchaeus. Stay.' But the schoolmaster gathered up his scrolls and left, rubbing his stinging head, and I thought they'd never see that one again.

Next day the boys too were gone, and all the children, and the donkey, and Mary and Joseph, and the house lay cold and empty for a month before the Passover, and for a month after. My life was empty until they returned. More empty than I could have believed.

Joshua returned like water to the desert. He was no longer a boy.

It was Joshua I saw, but they brought another man with them, following behind. I scrambled beside the wall, ducked behind the rocks. Later, as Mary prepared their simple evening meal of lentils, I eavesdropped with my knuckles in my mouth from my excitement, and gradually from their arguing and raised voices I understood a little of what happened.

Joseph and Mary had travelled between the two Jerusalems for the Passover, of course. First to Jerusalem at Sion, City of the Sun, where by the solar calendar Passover fell on a different day. At 'Egypt' they found Elizabeth lying in a wooden hut, blind and crippled by infirmity. From her deathbed, carried by her son John, she uttered her oath: 'I offer my son's life to the Christ's service, as the angel foretold I would, to be His forerunner and prepare the world for Him.' Joseph guided her hand, and she pledged John's support to Jacob. Joseph's policy from four years ago, foiled by Judas Zadok's support of his own family, had finally prevailed: in the church at Sion during Passover Jacob was confirmed in his place beneath the pulpit of the Christ as Joseph's legitimate successor, and this time John stood in waiting below the empty pulpit of the zadok – empty because Judas Zadok's eldest surviving son and heir Simon dared not show his face on the roads to Sion, controlled by the Romans. A humble elderly carpenter travelled freely where a zealot, however clever his disguises, however high his intelligence and his cleverness, could not. If Simon kept his freedom and his head, he and his discredited followers of the Fourth Way might risk appearing in public to claim his dangerous inheritance – but John was Zacharias's firstborn son, his father's zadokite blood flowing in his veins directly from Noah, so his claim by nature was as strong as Simon's.

Strengthened by their success, the holy family brought John with them on their journey to Jerusalem, City of the Moon, to attend the Great Temple on Mount Sion and the Passover according to lunar practice. Here everything went wrong for them, and it was Joshua's fault – of course. Joseph was still angry because he was not recognised and formally greeted as Alphaeus by the high priest, Ananus, appointed over the Jews by the Romans. Because of Judas Zadok's disastrous uprising and defeat, relations between the Temple and the Essenes at Sion had sunk to rock bottom since Zacharias's day. Herod Antipas, clinging to whatever royal titles the Romans left him, contrived to keep a foot in each camp; Essene baptisms and initiations were still an important source of revenue for his huge building works at Sepphoris and Tiberias, a whole new city rising from the shore of Galilee. Joseph, gritting his teeth, presented Joshua in the Temple courtyard as was obligatory at the boy's age, but cast only a couple of turtledoves to the priests for sacrifice, a deliberate insult.

At his house as he washed ready for the evening meal Joseph was still angry, white with anger. Must be more than Ananus's slurs. The others washed and Joshua's ears gave the clue, as so often: still swollen red from Joseph's fist. Little Salome came out carefully carrying a single wooden grail which she placed in front of John, then Mary carried out an armful of grail bowls to the table. 'I still can't believe you did it,' she told Joshua reproachfully, slipping his bowl of lentils in front of him. 'We didn't know where you were, we searched everywhere.'

Joseph's frustrated anger broke through again. 'What did you think you were doing, Joshua, talking back to those meat-eating priests and Temple scholars? Showing off? Or have you gone over to that brood of vipers?'

Mary said simply, 'You worry me to death, Joshua. I love you. I was afraid you were dead. I would have died too, you know.'

'I was busy, Mother.' Joshua put a loaf beside him on the bench.

She spoke softly. 'We'd gone a day's walk from Jerusalem before we realised you were missing. We turned back, and with each step I thought I'd lost you. I imagined you cold, alone, frightened.' Stroked his hair out of his eyes.

'I imagined you dead!' Jacob said. He looked at John for support.

'Could have been much worse than death,' Joseph said grimly. 'Kidnapped. Sold into slavery. Defiled. There's no form of wickedness that can't be found in a city.'

'How would you know?' Joshua said. 'You never go into a city.' He was insolent, and knew he would be slapped for it. He did not flinch. His ear looked like a ripe plum.

'You were a very difficult child,' Joseph threatened. 'You're a man now. Behave like a criminal and I'll treat you like one.'

'Joseph,' Mary said gently. Joseph's lips moved with an

old man's voiceless trembling. She turned gently to Joshua. 'You never told us what matters you discussed with the Temple priests and doctors of the Law.' When he said nothing she said, 'What were they?'

Joshua burst out, 'I was on my Father's business!' He held his ear, tears showed in his eyes. And yet no anger now. Hurt. Confusion. Not understanding.

But *I* understood. Sometime in the last few days, with Joshua's coming of age, Mary had chosen her moment to tell Joshua where he came from. You're not from a father's lust and sperm, Joshua, conceived by mere wriggling mortality and chance fertilising an egg somewhere in the darkness inside me. You are special, created by God's will, His divine storm of illumination. Delivered not in blood from the meat of my womb, but carried down to this world by the golden hands of angels. You are His Son.

Hurt, confused, uncomprehending. No wonder. At this most difficult age.

What *had* Joshua said to the Temple priests? Except for the Nativity, and that He was brought up in the city of Nazareth by his guardian the shepherd Joseph, the Disputation with the Doctors is the only fact known of Jesus's life before He began His ministry and was anointed into the Kingdom of Jerusalem at thirty years of age. But what Jesus had said to the doctors was never revealed. Nobody ever knew.

'The doctors and priests said they had never heard such wisdom,' Mary said. 'Such learning and knowledge of the Law.'

John jumped up, scoffing. 'Knowledge of laws! Joshua knows nothing of the true Law!' I slipped away from the gate barely in time. John's bare feet padded, his bony arms slammed the gate closed, I lost sight of Joshua. Heard John's footsteps padding to rejoin them at the table, and then, when Joseph did not speak from the head of the table, I heard John's harsh high voice take over. 'Let us now share table fellowship. One table, one people, one God.' I ran round to the side gate, knelt, peered through the latch hole. The round circle showed John's head bowed over the food bowls.

Joseph and Mary had to bring John home with them of

course. Even though he had no one else who loved him his stick-figure had dragged his footsteps far behind their donkey, making a show of his separateness, and he'd arrived after them as if by chance. A tall boy – man, now – tall as Joshua but burnt dark brown, skinny, he'd not an ounce of fat on him. Jacob was fascinated by him: John the Baptist, ordained by God in the womb to spread the Word of Christianity, would be the Christ's most faithful disciple. No doubt about John, in my opinion: look at him, born to be exactly what he is, straight from God, the genuine article, his scrawny teenage body and wild hair exactly as the Bible depicts him. And those eyes! A prophet's eyes, hunted, haunted, dark as olives, shafted with reflected lights and promise. A believer born and bred, a spear, fanatical in his zeal and devotion. All afternoon I'd watched him striding about the place, long-legged, hard as a locust from the desert sun, mumbling to himself, pulling out his sprouting chin-hair with long bony fingers, calling Jacob James. 'James!' John's voice cawed like a bird, it made you jump, impossible to ignore. 'James!' Always James. I never heard him call Joshua's name. He ignored Joshua, making himself Jacob's constant companion. John's body twitched and twittered with nervous life; his tongue seemed sewn to his brain, cawing aloud whatever came into his mind, and Jacob hanging on every word. I'd often see John fall still in mid-step in the afternoon sun, one foot raised, tongue clicking from side to side. His eyes blazed like coals with the intensity of his thoughts, completely obsessed with himself, with God. Even Mary obviously found John difficult: a wild animal, undomesticated, not knowing friends or kindness. And what of Joshua's feelings? Poor Joshua, not even the eldest child now, John three months his senior. Jacob, in awe of John's powerful personality, ran each time he was called. But Joshua did not run to John's beck and call, or even acknowledge his presence. He ignored John. And Joshua's hair was long; he had not renewed his vows.

John's cawing voice blessed the dry lentils. 'Lord, we give thanks that You have brought us here at Your Table to share table fellowship with our brothers. And we thank You for this pure clean food, and that You see us obey Your holy commandment not to eat the blood of flesh with life in it.

We commit ourselves to utter dedication to Your Law, obeying even the smallest part of it, even to the last jot and tittle, that we may not be defiled in the whole body. We travel lightly. And at the time of our Examination and Judgment when You shall demand an account of our lifeblood and weigh our souls in Your heavy balance, You shall see that our souls are scrubbed white in righteousness, in purity and virtue, and they shall rise from our foul bodies as light as air to Heaven.'

'Amen,' Joshua said, but it still sounded like Amun to me.

John and Jacob praised the Lord. They hardly ate, but Joshua tucked in, tore open the loaf.

'Lord, bar this gate!' John spread his hands at Joshua as though pushing back a beast. 'Save us from all who are blind, and from all cripples, from all who are blemished with sores or boils, from all fornicators and from all married men who have endured sexual contamination with their wives, from all women who are fouled with the curse of blood, from all who drink wine or beer or drink water other than water made from the pure rain of the clouds, and—' he stared at Joshua, 'from all who pollute themselves by eating bread.'

Joshua chewed, swallowed. 'It's not what a man puts into his mouth that pollutes him. It's what comes out of his mouth.'

John demanded, 'Do you speak of vomit? Will you vomit up your bread after your meal like a Roman or a Greek?'

Mary saw at once. She gave a delighted laugh. 'Words,' she said. 'Joshua's speaking of words. It's what a man says that matters!'

'I know of what I speak,' Joshua said. I stared at them, those three wise children, felt the tension like swords in the air, and knew I had seen them change into men.

Someone came on the path. I slipped away and crouched beside a bush in the desert.

Jesus Christ *never* spoke of pollution. He *never* spoke anything like those lines about how it doesn't matter what you put in your mouth, it's what comes out of your mouth that matters – He never would, because He taught us that we are what we eat. And Jesus Christ would have agreed totally with John's harsh but righteous words about saving us from the blind and crippled and all the others – because Jesus Christ *does* save us.

Am I right – for this fleeting moment – to doubt Joshua? Or wrong, because the kingdom of God is not only more marvellous than I imagine, but so much more marvellous than I *can* imagine?

There's one more childish miracle I'll relate before moving to more important matters. I must have told you of the wood pile where I hid, more often as time passed, because the well was filled in towards the end of Joseph's life. But the wood pile remained. How from the close, dark, fragrant gap between the wood pile and the wall I often spied on them through the gaps, almost close enough to touch them as they passed to and fro, almost part of the family. They had no secrets from me. Tears, arguments, laughter, Salome and Miri playing with dolls they made of clay and wool, Thomas stomping about with a set of wooden play-tools like his father's, Silas and Joses almost old enough to be apprenticed – and then Joses was apprenticed, though by now Joshua ran the workshop except for 'Joseph's hour' in the morning. Joseph was almost entirely blind and deaf but Joshua always made the pieces fit for him. I often saw Joshua draw out a piece of wood longer between his hands as easily as a magician, or compress it between his palms, and drop it in place as though the tree had created the artefact. Joseph never realised that these miracles were every day around him in his workshop. Never. None of them did. All around them. Until one day, the day I almost lost my life.

At the first glow of dawn as always I slipped silently past the sealing stone among the tombs and limped in my rotten clothes downhill over the rock, careful not to be attacked, and made myself part of whatever hiding place I chose between the stones and bushes and field boundary walls, I forget which. The Community filed past me like pale ghosts in their white linen gowns, one or two at first, then many, spreading out to relieve themselves in the dawn light.

Before they returned, bringing the sunlight with them, I crept along a dry irrigation ditch towards the house-backs. The sound of stones sliding from my feet was covered by the early crackling fire kindled in the potter's kiln – not for nothing are these people called the Potters by some, though their kilns also forge spears and arrow-heads, even swords, for their word for a metalworker is the same as for a potter. More than onions lie hidden under these parched fields: a growing crop of weapons. They believe in Armageddon, the place where the nations of the world will assemble, led by demonic spirits, for the final battle between the forces of evil and the Word of God and His Covenant, which He promised to return to their Zadok for thirty talents of silver. This morning the gate was ajar; I slipped inside and crouched in the fragrant darkness behind the wood pile. Just in time! I heard their footsteps returning, and the sun showed over the wall.

Something cool and dry coiled around my ankle. My eyes widened as its shape rippled up my leg. I glimpsed scales sliding between the holes and tears in what was left of my cloak, my shift. From between two pieces of firewood the tail came out, slithering, disappeared into my clothes.

My eyes stared. My hair stood on end, each greasy spike screaming fear. But I held my breath. Felt the harsh underside of the snake grip my belly as it searched out a warm nest, its triangular head questing the warmth of my loins, now twisting upwards towards my armpit, seeking. The sweat slid down me. I felt the weight of the snake as it curled between my breasts.

I heard Mary's voice call for one of her sons. 'Jacob, the fire's cold.'

The snake straightened, its head found my sleeve, its body followed. The scales gripped my ribs and as my clothes moved the head appeared at my wrist. A viper. Its poisonous tongue flickered, tasting my palm.

Mary called, 'Joshua, fetch some wood for the fire.'

Jacob said, 'I'll get it for you, Mother.'

The viper's head moved forward, slid between two pieces of firewood into the pile. I heard Jacob's footsteps, saw the hypnotic scaly pattern of the viper's back sliding out of my sleeve. The firewood clacked as Jacob took pieces off the top of the pile, stacked them under one arm. A shaft of sunlight fell on me. His hand almost grabbed my hair instead of wood but he never saw me. The viper's tail slid from my sleeve into the firewood, and Jacob staggered back. I heard

164

him drop the wood. 'Snake bit me,' he said. I heard him call out, 'Mother!' I heard him crying with pain. It was my fault. I peered through, saw him fall to his knees. He gripped his wrist, I saw the mark on his skin, I saw his face distort as the poison worked in him. 'Mother, help me.' He swayed and lay on one hip, his head falling back. His legs writhed in the dust. 'Mother, help.' Bubbles came from his mouth. I saw Mary's blue cloak, her white scarf. She wrapped her arms around her son as his back arched.

Jacob was dying. He would die. His eyes stared up white with terror. 'Mother, Mother.'

Mary wept over him. Her tears fell on Jacob's face, mingled with his own. He was frightened. He stiffened with the poison, grew cold. His fists clenched, then loosened.

Mary called, 'Joshua.'

Jacob jerked breath into his lungs. His throat rattled. His eyes turned upwards into his head.

Joshua knelt beside him. 'Where are you going, Jacob?' He lifted Jacob's wrist. He blew on it.

Jacob held his breath, then gently breathed out. His eyes blinked, he drew another breath. Then another. He took panting breaths, tried to sit up, then did sit up. He stared at his wrist, his smooth skin. He shook his head. His whole body shook. He licked his wrist, tasted the harmless drips of poison trickling from his flesh.

'No,' he said. 'No, no, no.' Then he slowly looked up at Joshua, who was carrying the firewood inside. 'No,' Jacob shouted. 'It's not *him*. It's me. I am the Christ.' He gripped Mary's arm, tried to pull himself up. 'Tell him. Tell him I am the Christ.'

John came out. 'All the community and the congregation know you shall be the Christ.' He held out his hand to Jacob, pulled. 'Rise, James.'

And James stood up in the yard as though baptised in the dust. James he was for ever after.

But Mary had seen the miracle that actually happened: saw her son almost die from the snake bite, and be saved by her Son.

And I had seen.

SUB ROSA

in strict confidence

Politics: years later the priestly zadokite faction of the Essenes, the Sons of Zadok, claimed that John had brought James back to life from Death. The royal faction, the Sons of David, claimed that James changed the viper that tried to bite him into a dove, and the dove took an olive branch in its beak, blessed James and John both, and flew away. Neither of these things, *I* know, are in the Bible, it's all new.

And Joshua? He didn't know his gift. He felt ordinary. I watched amazed as he went about the normal business of his day, the Son of God swinging His adze along a plank of wood, the Son of God drinking His cup of water, trickling drips down His chin. The Son of God crawling with His littlest sister Miri on His back, being her donkey, she geeing Him on with stinging whips to His backside from her little stick. The Son of God being scolded by His mother for dirtying His white linen shift with the game, scuffing holes that His knees stuck through. It was quite impossible to look at a real person in this way, see Joshua sneaking pieces of bread when he thought no one (especially John) was looking, and once even a cup of wine, and see him as anything but human.

A human who had been told by his mother that he was the Son of God. Human ego and ambition stood on its head: no wonder Joshua wanted to be ordinary. Self-effacing. How these mothers love their sons. She wanted him to carry the world on his shoulders. Commonplace.

But I had seen Joshua perform miracles. Not magic: real

miracles, actions beyond science. No scientific explanation. Impossible: his touch made my burnt fingers whole to the last whorl of the last fingerprint. His shadow made a yellow spring crocus flourish in dry December brambles. His words killed and brought back to life. He blinded by seeing the blindness in people. His hands made lengths of wood perfect. And his breath turned poison to honey.

I didn't sneak into their yard again. I was ashamed. James hadn't seen me behind the woodpile, nor Mary, certainly not John who had been sightless even to the real miracle, and believed it was his own hand that made James rise up. But Joshua. In the few moments he had been outside, *he* had seen me. Joshua *knew* I hid behind the woodpile. Joshua *knew* I hid in the well. Joshua *knew* I came into the garden at night, that I stood beneath the lemon tree or the fig tree, that I looked up at his window. He knew everything that I felt. He looked into me like a clear light and made me naked. By naked I mean nothing pornographic or blasphemous, I mean his glance saw everything of me, my emotions had no lies, no secrets, no privacy.

Ashamed, I hid in the tombs.

And yet, I told myself as the sun swung its fingers around the rock, he knows almost nothing about himself. He is the one person he cannot look into.

From time to time I saw him in the distance. But I thought about him all the time.

Joseph's life ran its natural course, he weakened, and took to his bed, and when God was ready he breathed his last. I do not know if in fact, in the last moments of his life, Joseph was reconciled to Mary's truth of her child, not his, who was least favourite to him; I saw no angel. His body was taken to its tomb but not allowed to rot; it was treated in the Egyptian manner of senior Essenes, preserved in the flesh. For the forty days of mourning Joseph's body lay entire in its tomb before being taken to its final rest in Jerusalem. After forty days Mary shaved her head, and John shaved his head, and James shaved his to equal shininess and devotion, and I suppose the Nazarene younger children had their heads shaved too. But Joshua kept his hair, his youthful stand against the fanatical holiness of John and James, the mourning bands they wore so prominently on their sleeves.

Mary was a widow. Her father Joachim was long dead and Matthew the levite, Joseph's younger brother, who ordinarily would have taken over responsibility for Mary, was celibate. James was head of the family now. I spied on him with John, talking about Joshua: by wearing his hair long, showing no respect, going against the family, John argued, Joshua was going against God. Going against them was the same as going against God. They talked as Nazarenes: John said Joshua's apostasy made him an abomination in the eyes of God, he should be declared dead by his family.

I knew Mary would not allow it.

I *hoped* Mary would not allow it. But who knows what will happen in this world?

I could not bear to stay in the tombs. My gross flesh shambled heavily among the newly deceased spirits – including Joseph – in their loss and confusion; my ears heard no difference between their cries and the shrieks of madmen, the soft calls and footsteps of tomb robbers, the scuttle and squeak of mice, the clink of beetles pushing their tiny stones, the moans of dispossessed souls not knowing which way to rise from this world. Where was God? I dreamt I heard the voice of Joseph whispering, 'Why?' To that, in death as in life, there is no answer: because Jesus Christ has not saved us.

I took to the paths at the top of the hill between the houses built for the dead, some with pillars, some carved into the cliff below, but gradually the hill grew smaller and I found my way back, as always, to Magdala. I was very thin. A white-bearded man was kind, said he'd known Levi, took me in. His name was Eutropios and his house was large, of black volcanic rock, the servants mostly gone since his wife died, so I knew he'd asked me in for sex. I put my hands beneath his robes but Eutropios drew away as though I touched him with fire. As he drew back he covered his nose, not used to the stink of tombs, ordered a spiced bath to be filled for me. He pitied or despised me, not realising what I could do for him, the relief I could give his body, that in the dark I could be his wife. At his table he gave me meat and bread and I planted myself in his lap. He pushed me away with revulsion but I knew how to turn that to lust, they're all the same. I gripped him with my hips to bring him out of himself. He gave a cry, threw me to the floor. I opened my thighs for him and showed him what I'd got, hairy and ready, they can't resist it. 'I'm your wife tonight,' I whispered in the husky voice they like. He cried an oath and stumbled to the door, slammed it behind him, left me alone.

I finished the bread and the wine, curled up on the floor, and slept to the usual nightmares. Eutropios kept the door locked the next day however loud I screamed, kicked. I broke all the furniture except the table, which was too heavy. I tried to break the table all day, breaking whatever I could find against it, howling and shrieking. I howled and shrieked all night. At dawn I fell silent, because the door opened, and a shape I knew stood there.

'Found you at last,' Levi said. He held a rope. 'Wondered where you'd been, naughty little thing you.' I flew at him, shrieking, and he struck me down.

'She's a demon.' Eutropios surveyed the wreck of his room. 'Who'll pay?'

Levi grinned. He put my neck in the rope, pulled tight. 'She'll pay,' he said.

So I was dragged back to Sepphoris behind the mule, my hands tied behind my back, hauled by the noose around my neck. Travellers who saw me looked away, knowing I was a dreadful criminal to deserve such punishment, and paid respect to Levi, *shalom*, for his righteousness. Each time I fell the mule plodded forward, pulled me by my neck in the dust, strangled me. My face swelled up, the purple veins in my cheeks and nose burst. My legs writhed until I walked again, and fell again.

In his house Levi threw the end of the rope around a roof beam, tied it tight so I stood on tiptoe. 'Should've done this long ago,' he said. I screamed so he gagged me. I kicked him so he bound my ankles. I wriggled silent and hopeless as a hooked worm in my misery. He smacked his hands at last, satisfied with his handiwork.

'Yes, you'll pay.'

He turned his back on me, hungry after his long day, crouched at the fire. Prodded it with the iron poker, then lifted an iron pot on to its hook over the flames. My eyes blurred, my toes had cramped. My nose was full of blood and dust, the gag suffocated me. I lifted myself on one foot,

169

opened my mouth wide, gasped a breath around the gag. 'Mercy.' My dry tongue could not form the word. 'Mercy. Let me go.'

He glanced round, went back to his work. Poured a pitcher of water into the pot. Making pottage. He chopped leeks into the water. Lentils, broad beans for thickening.

I tried to say something but all that came out of me was formless misery. He came over. Standing on tiptoe like this I was taller than him. He pressed down on my shoulders, the rope tightened, cut off my air. 'You'll pay, you bitch.' He grinned, released me, went back to his cooking. Searched for his precious salt pot.

There was the poker. I imagined beating Levi's head in with the poker.

Levi picked up the poker, stoked the fire. He put the poker down beside him. It smoked with heat. He saw the salt pot, reached up for it.

I pushed forward with my toes, strangling. My big toe brushed the hot iron, snagged the poker a hand's breadth towards me. Next time was easier. I dragged the poker towards me between my feet, gasped. My head thudded for oxygen.

Levi added a twist of salt to the cooking pot. He turned but did not look at my feet, only into my eyes. He pressed my shoulders down indifferently. Perhaps this time he would kill me. Or next time. Or sometime later, he did not care when I died but I would die. For the moment he went back to the fire. I heard his stomach rumble; he was hungry. He found bread, took out his knife, cut pieces from a loaf. I wanted that knife!

Only the poker, and he'd stoke the fire any moment. I bent my knees, came off the ground, beginning to strangle, lifting one end of the poker from the floor between my heels. The tip clinked on the tiles. Levi glanced at the door, thinking someone was outside. I was on his blind side; he didn't see me swinging behind him. The crescent moon of Levi's white eye blinked, then he turned back to the pot. I pulled my feet back like a child swinging from a tree branch, except that I swung by my neck, my face swelling to burst, my swollen tongue forced against the gag. I swung my feet forward. Swung towards Levi. Swung back. I was losing my senses, I could hardly see. I swung my feet forward, and this time the arc of my motion almost brought the blunt tip of the poker into the small of Levi's back. If he'd turned he'd have stared directly into my tortured face.

I swung back almost as far as the wall, pushed off. I don't know whether Levi heard the creak of the rope, the rush of air, or felt the sixth sense that warns us of our mortality. Anyway, he turned. I jerked my feet forward with all my strength, the last of my strength, and the poker went in through his chest, through his heart I suppose, and I saw the blunt bloody tip come out through his backbone and heard the crack. His legs collapsed at once. He lay on his side cursing and crying and trying to pull the poker out with his slippery, scalded fingers. Got it out in the end. I teetered on tiptoe, staring down at him, then stopped breathing. Levi dragged himself on his elbows towards me. His eye glared. He slowed. He stopped. His head dropped between his bloody fists.

He shuddered, and died.

I stared at him I don't know how long. Until my toes cramped like claws. I ignored the pain. I loved the pain. I twitched the knife from his belt with my toes, bent my legs behind me – easy, they cramped in that position – and sawed, as I strangled, at the rope that bound my hands. I don't know how long it took. The room fell dark as the fire died down, hiding the body at my feet. I strangled, I sawed, I sliced my hands like meat on the bone, no sounds but the drip of my blood on the tiles and my grunts for breath. I stood on tiptoe, dripping, then I continued. I felt the strands part. When dawn showed the outline of the window, the last strand parted.

I clawed my hand around the knife handle, reached up behind me, cut the rope that held me up, and fell beside Levi. Lying beside him, I stuck the knife into him to convince myself he was dead, then again and again to the hilt to make sure. None of the wounds bled much. When I was strong enough I crawled to the poker encrusted with his dried brown blood, crawled back and brought it down on his head. I beat and beat at his head until I forgot him.

Then I wandered away.

The usual cruel sunny day, the sky a merciless harsh blue,

no wind, the heat like an oven. I limped across the dun stones until I fell down. In the valley beyond the hill was a pond. All I could think of was the pond, the banks of soft green grass, a cool sip of water against my cracked lips, my dried tongue, my parched throat. Dear Lord, one sip. I suppose it's a common prayer. The stones burned me as I crawled.

Somewhere I heard a girl laugh. An unmistakable sound. I glimpsed her hair as her slim body ran between the heat-shimmering boulders, long black hair, glossy, curly not straight as mine once was, and not so long. But she was pretty enough I suppose, with a strong nose and cheekbones and chin, strong enough to hold a sharp whippish tongue in later life, but for now she was a young girl. She laughed again, looking back, chased. I know this chase. It's the chase where she wants to get caught and, by being caught, catch. She danced backwards lightly, then laughed and ran again down the slope, carefree yet calculating, hunted by her prey.

A man's head moving between the boulders. Curly black hair pulled straight by its length, longer than hers. His voice called her name, 'Hadassah.'

Joshua's voice.

Joshua ran down through the boulders to the water's edge where, of course, she waited. She ignored him, pointed at something in the water, a fish, a leaf, but he looked only at her. Didn't he know this is how we get what we want? He stared at Hadassah with his complete attention. He seemed so young, fourteen years old, fifteen, sixteen, he never seemed any particular age, just so achingly, stupidly innocent. No trace of his anger. Just gentleness. He wanted to kiss her, all his concentration was on her lips, she pouted to entice him, then quickly turned her head away. He'd learn his lesson; what ugly beasts we are beneath our pretty skin. A dragonfly fluttered like a rainbow in the reeds and he caught it in his hand, held it in front of her eyes, let it go. A small miracle for her that she did not appreciate. But romantic, and for the first time she looked at him directly. There was sweat above her upper lip and her eyebrows. She breathed through her mouth. He leant forward with his hands behind her head, his thumbs on the lobes of her ears, and kissed her.

I stared appalled. I hardly felt my feet walking forward. I forgot my thirst. Everyone knows Jesus Christ was celibate. He never knew a girl, her cunt, her sleep, peace, family, love: all his love was of God. He reigned alone as King in Jerusalem, he never took a queen. The thought of him touching a girl, feeling worldly lust, is repellent to every Christian belief: *we*, all of us, are equal in Christ's love. Yet Joshua kissed smirking Hadassah the woman, fallible, wicked in parts, all-too-human, beneath the myrtle tree; ignorant, innocent of the ways of women. I knew exactly what she would do next, and she did. Her hands stroked his shoulder blades through his white linen shift, her fingertips touched his arm, guided his hand to her breast. She breathed rapidly, looking into his right eye and his left eye.

He said, unmemorably: 'You're beautiful.'

They all say that. He was just a man. She smiled inside herself; we always do. I limped, staggered over the burning stones. 'No! Don't trust her.' The heat swallowed my words. I could see he didn't know what to do with her. Finally she pulled a knot for him, her dress opened and her ripe young breasts stood out like baskets of fruit on sale, white melons – the bitch had powdered them – the nipples virgin-pink. He kissed them like a baby. She sighed, slipped down among the grassy tussocks beneath the tree as though delight had taken the strength from her spreading legs, enfolded him between them like a flower searching for its stalk. Her hands found the hem of his shift as she moved under him, lifted, and for the second time in my life I saw Joshua's bottom.

I limped, I ran, I screamed at them, I pelted them with earth and mud, I kicked at his white bottom, blasphemous bottom, apostate bottom. His passion destroyed everything I'd believed in once, long, long, ago. I kicked him again and again and he jumped off her and said, 'Ow!' I fell screaming on her, the bitch, I pulled her hair in a handful, I smacked at her face, I wept. I hated her so much I wept. I lost my strength and lay as I always lie, with my knees drawn up, my thumb in my mouth, and I wept as though my heart would break.

I hardly felt her scramble away.

Hadassah's voice shook. 'She should be reported to the

elders.' O God, her coarse accent, one of us: he'd been about to screw just an ordinary Jew, one of the Rich, not even an Essene, let alone a Nazarene. She shouted, 'She should be reported. They should stone her. She's the madwoman who lives in the tombs!' She shouted and shouted; I hardly heard her.

Joshua murmured: 'Leave us.'

I thought he meant me. I did not have the strength to leave anyone. I was almost dead of thirst, baked, dried out, bloodless. I lay weeping without the moisture for tears, covered my face with the torn veil in my shame, crawled to his feet, pressed my forehead to his toes. 'Oh my Lord.'

Joshua murmured again: 'Hadassah. Leave us.'

'I didn't want you anyway, limp stick you,' she swore. 'Help! Rape! You stay with your stinking friend if that's what you want. She's your level, all right. Look at my hair,' she wailed. He ignored her. She shouted some more, then step by step her voice faded, and she ran.

I clung to Joshua's ankles. His feet smelt of goats' cheese. There was dirt under his toenails. He hadn't even washed this morning with the other Essenes. I felt the bones in his foot move inside his flesh as he shifted his weight. The cartilage clicked in his ankle. So human.

He said: 'What do you expect of me, Mary?'

He remembered me. I couldn't reply, my tongue was dry meat, my head was a headache, the sun beat down on my body like an open furnace.

'Save us,' I whispered.

His bones moved again. I felt him smiling. 'Where have you been sheltering, Mary?' I knew he was calling me Mary deliberately. He was calling me his sister. Me. Filthy dirty, wrapped in grave windings and shit. Oh, help me.

I whispered. 'Save us. You'll save us. Every man. Every woman. Every child. Every dog. Every flower. Every stone. Every thought.'

He bent, his hand touched my chin. I stared up at the sun, cried out in agony in the harsh brilliance. His shadow moved across me, cool, soft. 'You're so full of hate,' he marvelled. 'How can you speak of love?'

I thought of Hadassah arching her back under him, readying herself to take him into her.

I wept. 'Joshua, Joshua, why do you always do everything wrong? Why?'

His finger lifted my chin. 'I remember you as a child,' he said sadly. 'What have you become?'

My gaze travelled up his starched white shift scented with frankincense, stalks of green grass clinging to the material, seeds, myrtle leaves, two streaks of mud showing where his knees had knelt on the soil, his belt loosely tied so that the boiling noon wind rippled the fine linen like a mirage. Above, his face looked down at me with the sun around his head. I knew there was no one else in the world for him at this moment, only me.

Fragments of green grass, a single golden dandelion petal caught in his black beard. The sun reddening his cheek-bones, the wind fluttering his eyelashes around his almond-shaped eyes. His eyes that stare into me. 'No,' I whisper. My breath comes fast. I stare into His right eye and into His left eye just as that bitch Hadassah had, and I see myself in his eyes, see how ugly my reflection is. I whisper, 'I know who you really are, my Lord.' He smiles wonderingly, still believing He's no more than human, and then His fingertip against my chin lifts me to my feet, His face examines me so close that I breathe in His scented breath deep into my lungs, see the tiny hairs quivering in His nostrils as He breathes, and instinctively my wrist brushes back His hair that the wind blows across His eyes. I see the flicker of recognition in those eyes: His own human mannerism reflected back at Him. His smile broadens, though everyone knows traditionally Jesus Christ never smiled or laughed. Nothing of what I feel is hypnotism; we're both fully alive, never more so. Every emotion I've ever felt pours through my body, my obscene filthy body.

His fingertip touches my face, the veil falls away, the wind takes it. I clap my hands over my eyes. No. I'm afraid.

'Mary. I shall see you.'

No, no, no, but the more I shake my head, the more He raises me up, the more my hands fall away, the more I see myself. My arms float outstretched beside me, I smell the stink of me, the disgusting female stench of me, everything revealed to Him as the wind flaps open the grave windings whose dirt and grease kept me warm in the tombs, unravelling them like tattered grey tongues from my foul slimy flesh, unspinning the coverings from my nakedness, legs, arms, torso, flat ugly breasts, until I stand before Him exposed in my agony of shame. See my nakedness reflected in His eyes. He stares into me and I suffer the most revealing act of intrusion I have ever suffered, worse than sex, worse than defecation. See myself as I am seen. My unwashed body a mass of sores and scars, my broken teeth, my twisted arm, the scabs festering on my hands. Imperfection. My lusts and thefts and cheats, all exposed. Everything that's been done to me and everything I do to myself. No lies. Nothing left to conceal.

'Mary.' He holds out His hands to me. 'Mary, come to me.'

No. No. I back away. The bitterness bursts out of me. 'I saw you with her!'

He smiles gently, seeing what I had seen.

He replies: 'She too was willing to love me, Mary.'

I'm so angry I scream. My lips curl, I crouch to avoid being touched. 'I hate you. Get out. Go away. You let us all down.'

But He steps forward as I step back, He steps into my footsteps in the grass with His own bare feet. My foot skids, splashes, I'm on the edge. Nowhere farther back to go. I snarl like an animal.

'You're full of hate,' He marvels. 'Hate. Jealousy. Anger. Sadness. Mary, do you have nothing, nothing at all?' His thumbs touch my ear lobes, His fingers sink into my hair, but I see no pity in His eyes, only love for me. 'Why should that girl not be willing to give her body's love to me, Mary? Am I so unworthy of her?' His thumbs caress the corners of my eyes. 'You have so many demons in you. So many contradictions.' I feel His eyes peeling back the layers of me like the petals of a flower, but this is a very different sort of love. His is not like any love I knew before. His love opens my eyes, wider, wider. And for a moment – just a moment – I glimpse something inside Him that's more, much more, than even I know (and I know almost everything by now, I thought), I glimpse this land and all its people shrinking to a grain of dust, the world to nothing, the universe no larger than a bubble in a waterfall of ten thousand times ten thousand bubbles, falling. I knew this already. But that's just the surface! There's so much more! I can see it in Him. Touch it in Him. Know it in Him.

I glimpse Heaven and Earth.

But my feet are sunk in the mud of this world, reeds scratch my legs. 'You kissed her. You can't. It's wrong. It's *wrong*.'

'Mary, Mary. Help me.' He strokes my face. My fists clench in anger. I shall burst with anger. As He strokes my eyes, my forehead, my lips, everything I feel bubbles up inside me. It's all too much, it comes out of me like vomit. I shriek. I feel myself slipping away, shrieking, screaming all my misery and pain into His face.

Blood on my lips where my teeth have bitten myself. My spittle on His skin in white bubbles; He holds my face calmly with His fingertips while my body writhes and wriggles below. I scream, 'It's *wrong*, don't you see, you can't make yourself only human. You can't! Only half of you is only a man, Joshua. You can't love a woman.' I bite down on my tongue, and it bursts in my mouth like rotten fruit. I scream blood at him: 'You are the Son of God.'

Everything comes out of me. He touches my ears, and slugs come out of my ears. He puts his fingers to my nose, draws strings of foulness from my nostrils. My bowels soil the water with black stains. His voice commands: 'Jealousy, come out of her. Envy, I cast you out. Hatred, leave her. Murder, you are forgiven. Love—' I fall limp. I feel myself go under the water, feel Joshua's hands lift me up. 'As for love, I touch you neither one way nor the other. You shall be as I find you.'

I blink. I feel myself fill with blood. I even stare at the sun. I'm clean.

'Only a man,' Joshua murmurs. 'Who can not do this?'

I stare at my hands. White, unmarked. No cuts, no scars. My tongue is whole. I touch the jagged line of my broken jaw and find it straight. My hair floats around me as soft and glossy as though freshly oiled, my skin is smooth and supple. I reach beneath the water and find my vagina no longer torn, as though He touched me even there, and I feel the tight prohibiting skin of my immaculate virginity.

'My Lord.' I bow my head, too joyful to weep for joy. I say simply, 'My Lord, You have made me whole again.'

ILLUMINATA ET ILLUMINATRIX

both illuminated and illuminator

Joshua drew me through the water after him. His white linen shift floated around us. The water reflected the sky: the blue arch of the sky above us and below. He knelt beside me in the shallows, only our heads showing, and his reflection shattered as he splashed water over his face. Only then did I realise how tired he was. 'How many devils did I cast out, Mary?'

I said, 'Seven, my Lord.' The number is always seven, for the seven deadly sins.

'Shall I be your lord?' Joshua asked, with that huge open direct stare of his.

'Yes,' I said. 'Joshua, You are the Son of God.'

'So you say,' he murmured. Water dripped from his beard. 'And so my mother says.'

He touched my twisted arm impulsively and my throbbing pain, which I have known every day since my birth, was gone. The shock of feeling nothing on that side was so great that I almost fell over in the water, as if my shoulder had been sucked into a vacuum, both of air and emotion.

He said, 'Do you thirst?' He held up his cupped hand, and I drank from his palm. At once I was not thirsty. He said nothing, weary. The water lapped around us. A bittern honked somewhere in the reed beds. A flight of turtledoves winged overhead, returning to Egypt. Still Joshua said nothing.

Then he said, 'Is it absolutely true?'

'True?'

'That I am the Son of God.'

'Yes, Joshua. Absolutely true. I saw you born.'

'I don't remember it. There are miracles all around us. I say we are all sons and daughters of God. Me. You. Everyone.'

'Your birth was different, Joshua.'

He wanted to know. 'My mother says there were angels.'

'Yes, there were angels. A stable in Bethlehem. And many miracles.'

He shrugged. 'Some people say they remember their birth. I don't.' Then he asked urgently: 'Was I born circumcised?'

Startled, I had to think for a moment. 'No.'

He doodled his fingertip in the water. 'My half-brother James, the Christ, claims that he was born with his cock ready circumcised.' He glanced at my face, returned his attention to his fingertip. 'To be born circumcised is considered a sign of extreme holiness. A sign of the Son of God.'

'You had to be circumcised,' I said. 'I don't know about James.'

He doodled for a while, then glanced. 'You know a lot about James.'

'You saw it in me.'

'I saw that you know more, much more, than you say aloud.'

'And you know nothing,' I scoffed.

'Nothing.'

'Nothing of the wonders and horrors all around us?'

He shrugged. 'I am.' He shrugged again. 'I simply am.' His hair was already drying in the sun, strands beginning to blow. I put them back for him. He looked at me steadily. 'You really are very beautiful,' he decided.

'Don't,' I said. 'I'm no Hadassah.'

'Not now,' he agreed. He added, 'I can't stop them. Girls like Hadassah. It's their God-given nature.'

'You must. You are incapable of sin.'

He sighed, looked at me earnestly. 'Tell me, will I ever overcome my birth and be the Christ?'

I laughed, sending ripples splashing between us. 'Believe me, Joshua, I know in my heart and head and in my body from your touch that you are Jesus Christ, the Son of God, and that you are sent by Your Father to save us all.'

He shook his head, then muttered, 'Our Father.' He gave a little shiver as though the water was cold. 'Mary, what does the future hold for me?'

'You begin your ministry in your twenties and in your thirtieth year you are crowned king and zadok in Jerusalem, and you rule in wisdom and benevolence for a thousand years, and bring salvation to all the peoples of all the nations of the world.'

'King *and* zadok? The two pillars of the earth, made into one? That's impossible.'

'Nevertheless.'

He shook his head. 'And until then what do I do?'

'I don't know.' I was caught out. 'Nothing is known. Not until your authority is revealed. The event some call the Recognition.'

'Shall I be a Nazarene?'

Tender feelings for him filled me. Despite his beard he was just a boy, an innocent boy. I said, 'My Lord, I do not know.'

'Shall I fulfil the prophecies?'

The prophets and prophecies of this world are beyond number. I chose the reply that could not possibly be wrong. 'Yes.'

He blew his nose in his hand, washed it in the water, doodled again. 'Matthew repeats the prophecy that the Covenant of the Poor with God will be renewed for thirty talents. Is it true?'

'No. You yourself are the Covenant between God and Man.'

'I thought it couldn't be right. A talent is an enormous sum. Almost unimaginable.'

'It's just something the Essenes believe, one thing in ten thousand, it's a belief made by men. It doesn't mean anything. You can't buy God.'

'They say the Arch of the Covenant is beneath the Temple. I thought they meant that.'

'No. The Arch was made by men. And women.'

'Are all women so wise as you?'

'Yes.'

'None of this matters. There's no future for us.' He stared

at his reflection, then broke it. 'John has an eloquent tongue, and he says the world will end, and that's true, isn't it?'

Is it true? *I* know that in fact this hot and uncomfortable sun will swell up and burst in four billion years or so, but that wasn't what he was asking, because we all know life doesn't work like that. He said, 'It's Enoch's prophecy that the world will end with the intervention of Heaven.'

'You!' I said quickly. 'Jesus Christ is the intervention of Heaven in worldly affairs.'

'Enoch prophesies the restoration of the zadoks in the year 3969 from Creation.'

He still didn't see it. 'And you will be how old in that year, Joshua?'

'Thirty. Just over thirty. I see what you mean.' He closed his eyes. 'But John will be zadok.' His eyes opened wide, irresistible. 'Can I trust John?'

'Yes. He's your voice.'

'And James?'

I sighed, and my face in the water quivered at my breath. 'No, you cannot trust James.'

'Who can I trust?'

I said, 'The one who loves you.'

He stared at me so close I thought our noses would touch.

'You,' he said.

I kissed his lips as a sister would.

He whispered, 'Where do you come from, Mary?'

'From Magdala in Dalmanutha, on the shore of Galilee.'

'Mary Magdalene,' he said. 'You shall be my constant companion.'

'No,' I told him. 'Jesus Christ has no companion. No woman. There's no Mary Magdalene in the book which you will write, the Bible. There's Mary your mother, Mary her sister—'

'My mother has no sister. Two daughters called Mary, how could that be?'

'What I'm saying is, I'm no part of your fate.'

'And if I want you to be?'

'It cannot be.'

He breathed out through his nose. He was a man. He had

hormones like the rest of us, a heart and a mind and all the rest of it. The tears came to my eyes. 'My Lord,' I said. 'I ask one more blessing before we part.'

He said heavily: 'I shall say when we part, Mary.' I drew back, the water swirling around me, from the force in his eyes.

'Forgive me, my Lord.'

'Ask.'

'All my life I've been in pain. My life is long, I've known much pain. Too much. When I was born in Magdala, my arm was twisted by the midwife. Her intentions were good, but it's always hurt. Just now you touched me, healed me, took that pain from me. But my pain was part of me, Lord Jesus.'

'Then let it be.' He touched my arm, and the old nagging discomfort flooded back to my shoulder and elbow. But his touch was reverent. 'Don't call me by my Greek name, that's for John and James, their educated tongues. And don't call me your lord between us. I can do so much more for you, Mary, and I want to, but I know so little. Are you sent by my Father?'

I ducked my head under the water by way of not answering. How could I know? Joshua had given pain back to my arm: God can create imperfection as well as forgive it. Joshua could curse as well as bless; perhaps as a child the two God-given natures were equal in him and he'd simply learnt to make his choice. So goodness can make use of evil. Without darkness, after all, there is no light.

But who else, except Jesus Christ, knows their place in Heaven and Earth? Not you. Not I.

I opened my eyes underwater, then lifted my head into the sunlight, drew breath, shook the drops from my hair. It was a mistake. Joshua watched me, his eyes fascinated.

'I shan't ask you again who you are,' he said, 'but one day I shall know.'

I'd forgotten I was naked, my full breasts swaying above the water, my pubic hairs floating in serpentine desire beneath, five years older than he. I don't suppose he'd seen a girl wholly without her clothes before me, just the bits of us that attract the imaginations of young men. Joshua reflected my smile, then stood and pulled off his wet white shift, slipped it over my head. 'We aren't alone. They're coming.'

I followed him from the water, his long white gown drying quickly around me in the evening sun. Wearing only his dripping linen loincloth and wooden sandals bound to his feet with plant fibre tightly twisted, trailing damp footprints, Joshua strode towards the people coming over the top of the hill. They were led by Hadassah, but she ignored Joshua as though she had never met him. Pointing past him, with only a spiteful glance at him, her shrill cry carried to me. 'She's her! She's the one. Murderer!'

Men ran down and seized me. Children were already picking up stones. I would be stoned for the murder of Levi. I fell to my knees at Joshua's side. 'My Lord, it's true. I killed him.'

Joshua asked them, 'What do you say this woman did?'

An apprentice shouted, 'She killed Levi the dyer with a red-hot poker, and knifed him in her frenzy a hundred times, and she beat his head in with the poker, and left him to stink in the sun all day, and now we're out of a job.' Other apprentices, who had all hated Levi alive, took up the cries for vengeance, absolving themselves of their own sinful daydreams no doubt. Madwoman. Murderess. A stone clattered past me.

Joshua came between us. 'You all knew Levi. You all knew what he was like. You all knew what he did to this girl. None of you did anything. What happened was not murder but justice.' A stone flew at my head; Joshua's hand snatched it from the air. He said: 'Very well. Show me this man whom you say is dead.' The crowd led us to Levi's house where more people waited, jostling forward around us with accusing eyes in filthy faces, gusting their foul breath through yellowed teeth.

Someone said: 'She doesn't look guilty.' I walked forward calmly after Joshua. A woman tried to trip me to make my clothes dirty; another pulled my hair, but her hands slipped through my glossy curls. A boy threw dung but it spattered the people around us, and he was pursued. The crowd drew back in front of us, closed behind us as we came to Levi's door. The door hung open as I had left it. Through the doorway I glimpsed Levi's feet sticking out of his bloodstained gown. After the heat of the day the leather thongs of his sandals cut deeply into his swollen discoloured flesh, and the smell of the rotting meat of his body wafted out to us.

I told Joshua, 'He's lying as I left him.'

Someone shouted: 'She's confessed!'

They shouted, 'Kill her!'

Joshua said, 'If there is no dead man, there is no murder and no guilt.' He commanded: 'Bring Levi to me.'

No one moved. Someone said, 'Haven't you got a nose? He stinks!'

Joshua went into the house. I followed him. The crowd followed me, pushing, then drew back in a circle. On the tiles Levi's bloody body looked like a bloated brown turd, something already eaten and digested and deposited by some huge terrible lizard, dropped discarded in a puddle of brown scabs. Each inch of bare flesh buzzed with flies. Joshua's wooden soles clacked on the tiles, then their sound fell dull when he walked on the blood. A Nazarene, lapsed or not, could never bear to put himself into such intimate contamination with death. Yet, what did I expect Joshua to do? Wouldn't I expect Jesus Christ to be here? Why, why, why do I doubt Him as soon as I can, it seems, and deny the evidence of my eyes and what I *know* to be the truth? Joshua glanced at me, then gripped Levi's gown in his fists, pulled hard, and Levi rolled naked on to the floor. His belly squeaked, swollen with gases. Someone was sick. Children laughed at the horror of it. Joshua strode to Levi's marble dyeing trough, unstoppered one of the precious pitchers, sniffed it. I knew that smell. Indigo.

Joshua emptied the pitcher into the trough, then threw the bloodstained gown into the dense violet-purple dye. Instead of taking tongs he pushed the gown beneath the surface with his bare hands.

He stood with his arms dripping dye to the elbows, faced the people. 'Any of you with two good ears to hear had better listen. The Lord is a dyer. Good dyes are called true, and dissolve into what they dye, and can't be washed out or changed afterwards. So it is with those whom the Lord has dyed with His immortal dyes. You . . . and I, yes, and I, we all have our colours, God-given. It's impossible to see any of the things that actually exist unless you become like them.' The people murmured, understanding not a word of what he tried to make them hear. Joshua reached into the trough, plucked the bloodstained gown from the purple dye.

The gown came up pure white in his hands. No bloodstains. No indigo.

The people talked among themselves, impressed. They waited expectantly for more. 'That's what I want for my washing,' one woman said. They all wanted to hold the gown. For an awful moment I thought they were going to throw money. Someone called, 'Come on, let's feel it then, show us.'

Joshua threw the gown on the tiles. Anyone could see they hadn't listened. I knew this rage in him and was afraid for the people who watched, who thought they saw an entertainment. To Joshua this was life and death – yet he was young, so young, a fierce young man working in a crowd. He walked along the row lifting the heavy pitchers of dye, crocus yellow, shellfish blue, isatis blue, threw them all into the bath, strode along the shelves snatching down precious phials of Tyrian purple, vermilion oxide, powders of red and yellow oxide and coloured lead, scattered them across the mixture in the bath. 'Seventy-two colours,' I said, understanding. He would make the gown a coat of many colours, a Joseph's coat, fulfilling some prophecy or other. But then Joshua unstrapped his sandals and stepped into the bath to his knees, wading like a man treading grapes, and the powders dissolved in bright streaks around him until all the colours ran together, sticky, black as pitch, clinging to him.

He padded from the bath to Levi's naked, bloody, crusted body. He knelt beside it, slipped his thin arms beneath the shoulders and thighs, lifted the weight, stood. A horrified silence fell except for two children playing tag. Levi's blind eye stared; the other had burst. His head hung down like pulp. Joshua turned, staggered forward, dropped the body into the dye. Some people swore, splashed, but others stared.

Joshua pushed at the body with his feet until every part of Levi was submerged. A white hand stuck out; he pushed it down. Black dye poured into the open mouth, nostrils, eye sockets. Levi's sparse grey hair floated up, then even the tip of his nose was gone.

Joshua turned to the crowd, breathing hard. 'The Sons of Men of the Community come among you not only as carpenters, or scholars, or the humblest of the humble or the poorest of the poor, but also as dyers.'

A man called out fussily, 'Preach, then. What's your lesson?'

Joshua stared. He did not know. 'I—' He looked towards me, completely vulnerable, human, unaided by divine guidance. The draught from the door fluttered my, his, white shift.

I held out my hands. 'Forgive me, my Lord.'

'Forgiveness.' Joshua shook himself as if cold. 'Forgiveness.' He remembered Levi, reached into the dye. 'Man, rise and go about your work.' He pulled Levi up by the hand, and Levi sat up naked and white out of the black dye. His eyes fluttered open, restored. He stared at the black beads of dye trickling down his hairy white chest. With white fingers he touched the white skin of his face, feeling himself. He looked up with an expression of intense fear and submission. Then he stood, and covered his private parts in shame.

'What have I to do with You, Joshua, Son of the most high God?'

Joshua looked at me. We knew he had to give an answer. He said, 'Live your life and fear God.'

Levi mumbled, 'Live my life and fear God.'

An old woman shouted out, deaf by the sound of her, 'He wasn't dead after all, there wasn't a murder, that's what he said?'

'The Magdalene's innocent,' a friend called in her ear, disappointed. 'She should be thrown in chains, just in case.'

'No, she has a sweet lovely face,' the deaf woman said. 'I can't believe she'd hurt a fly.'

'She must have broken some law,' a broad motherly woman said. 'There's always something.'

'If she looks so sweet,' the deaf woman's son shouted in her ear, 'what's she hiding beneath her sweetness? Look at her, smooth as milk! And what's going on between them, those two? What's she given him, eh?'

'We saw what you did to the dyer, young man,' called the fussy man who had called out to Joshua earlier, 'but what lesson are we to draw from it?'

I looked at Joshua. He didn't know. He was too young. He knew he was here for a purpose, but he didn't know what it was. He didn't know how to begin.

I knelt, covered Joshua's bare feet with my hair, and kissed him.

Joshua preached to them: 'See this woman. Faith only receives, but love gives.'

VIDE ET CREDE

seeing is believing

I couldn't see enough of him. Joshua was every answer to my every question. I needed to touch him, smell him, listen to him, talk to him every moment of every day. But it had been that way with me for years; and it was impossible.

I lived in Levi's house among the Nazarenes. I mentioned I've been only twice without pain, once when I was an angel called to witness the birth of Christ, once when in the lake He cast out the torment of demons and made my body whole and perfect, the physical image of my forgiven sins. But I'd asked Him to give me back my pain, imperfection, and He had done it. Levi, however, was raised perfect from the dead. Whatever corruption of the spirit had warped and twisted him into the man he had once been was gone, erased from him like his body's corruption and decay. No man was ever more kind than Levi, more gentle, more holy. He praised God aloud or under his breath every hour of every day of his returned life, he treasured each sunrise, each drop of water, each insect.

Levi begged my forgiveness. The enormity of his sins and wickedness in his earlier life overwhelmed him. He understood completely the evil he had done and been, he understood that life does not end with death. 'Forgive me, Miriam,' he begged in his calm, low voice, 'Never, though I was a priest once, did I believe that there really is, *actually* is, a God of anger and vengeance and wrath, and that He has a face, and that He will punish *me*, me personally, for eternity for my sins, not just my whole people.' He brought me wine and cakes dipped in date honey. 'Forgive, forgive.'

'I can't forgive you, Levi.'

'When I die, I shall scream in flames in Hell for ever for what I did to you.' Hell, that word again, only the second time I'd heard it from Jewish lips, the Hell of hellfire. If I didn't know better I'd say he sounded like a Christian. 'I'll go down for my sins, I know that now, I've seen it. Eternal punishment. Eternal justice. It's right.' He touched his eye that had been blind. 'My eye sees into my head. I can't shut it out. There's something missing from me.'

'Forgiveness?'

'Ignorance,' Levi said. 'I know what's coming for me.'

He smiled tenderly. For me Levi washed clothes like a woman, swept floors like a woman, cooked food like a woman, fetched water like a woman, and I lived at leisure.

I saw Joshua from a distance most days, spoke to him sometimes. My God, his troubles were larger than mine had ever been! Sometimes I saw John arguing with him, sometimes James. Mostly they ignored him, excluded him. Those two had their own strong ideas of God and the apocalypse, the coming end of time, and neither enjoyed living tainted by the company of a bastard son born of fornication outside marriage, contravening every moral belief of God and Sion. Breaking one law breaks them all, remember – and Joshua was heedless, he ate and drank what he liked, grew his hair how he liked, broke a lot more than one law. Now that Joseph, his earthly flesh and bone laid in the Tomb of the Davids in David's city, Jerusalem, could no longer protect her name Mary had lost all respect in the Community. She should be cast out, shunned – and would be, except for one thing: she was the mother of James. James would soon enter the monastery on the Dead Sea as a novice, and as the successor of Joseph would be recognised and anointed as the Christ when he 'passed through the eye of the needle' on his confirmation at the age of twenty-seven. But even as the mother of James to be the Christ, Mary trod carefully. Joshua made his own rules, but politics was a deadly dangerous profession, and she was well aware that the obstacles faced by the two legitimate heirs were formidable. John's zadokite ambitions were opposed and undermined as always by Simon the Zealot, still in hiding in the Golan with his zealot and sicariot supporters, plotting, planning, conniving to grasp the zadok's sceptre for himself; his hands grabbed as far as Jerusalem, his opponents being assassinated even in the Temple courtyards by fanatics who went as mysteriously as they came. Here in the Nazarene suburb James and John were guarded day and night by Delanos's men, and I often saw the paymaster bringing spies and men who wore cloaks over their heads to see James, their exact God and no other intensely important to each sect and faction, to live and die for. One God, but a hundred religious sects, each convinced to the death of its own righteousness.

From all this turbulent activity, Joshua was excluded. He was in the way. Delanos tried to keep him busy with carpentry and small tasks, but Mary his mother whispered in Joshua's ear: 'Do not forget who you are.' Yet I'm sure she felt he was safer out of the way. Frozen out of the councils of the Community, Joshua was more popular with the poor farmers and ordinary Jews of the district, always willing to repair a plough or a wheel while he talked with them in the evening sun. Joseph had never done that; despite his stiff humility he had always been a dispossessed king, never one of the people. But Joshua worked as easily with people as with wood. I overheard what James thought of his wayward half-brother's fraternising. 'Whoever chooses the world for a friend makes himself an enemy of God, Joshua. Making the world your friend makes you God's enemy. Keep to your own people.'

Joshua said steadily: 'Do my own people listen to me?'

And there were the girls who loved him, following him as I did but with more than their eyes, walking in front of him with their swinging hips and saucy looks, yearning, pouting, the least seductive dragging their fathers with them in hopes of marriage. Joshua was handsome, incredibly handsome because he looked so sensitive and vulnerable, but he wasn't. He had a hard long body with that long hair I loved so much, and those enormous eyes. A girl could fall into those eyes, as I had, and some did. 'Why shouldn't they be willing to give their love to me, Mary?' he'd told me, 'Am I so unworthy of them?' But now I watched them love him without jealousy – though out of his sight the girls often fought among themselves, and pulled each other's hair screaming vanity. I only desired his happiness. He had made me at ease with jealousy, with envy, with desire. To see him happy with someone interesting and vivacious for an hour or a day made me happy. He was a man. I would not have wanted him to be anything less, or loved him if he were. But he was so much more than a man, and *that*'s what I love.

There, I said it. I'm more than curious about Joshua, more than obsessed with him. I'm in love with all of him. Everything else is shadows. With him, love is all I am.

He knows.

I watched the Essenes in the desert, watched them bow in prayer to the rising sun. Joshua walked away to the workshop with long strides. I hardly noticed a shadow, not Joshua's, fall across me from the side. Someone pinched my shoulder, hard, like the sting of an insect through the linen. 'Does that hurt?' James pinched me again. 'Don't look at *him*, does that *hurt*?'

'Yes.'

James stared down at me where I sat. He resembled Joshua but his hair was not as long, and he had his father Joseph's broad cheekbones, Joseph's bushy eyebrows, as well as Mary's fine chin. He smelled of dust and sun and clean water, his hair still wet, very black and gleaming over his white linen shoulders. 'So you're the one they're all talking about,' he said.

'You know who I am, James.' I looked at him directly, opened my eyes wide. He staggered, saw into me just as I saw into him: we knew each other's look, none better. 'Still angry,' he said. 'My God, you're still angry.' Once we were everything to each other, as I told you. I was right about James: old, monstrously old in his body. I saw the knowledge all locked up in him behind his eyes, the despair, the bitter cold of his yearning heart. His loneliness, his longing for the warmth of blood, his hunger. Like mine. His terrifying hunger.

'You're just like me,' I said. 'What are you searching for? The truth?'

'Mary,' he whispered. 'Mary.' He sat on the rock opposite me as though the muscles had been cut from his legs. 'My Mary? It's truly you?'

'Yes, James, it's me. How are you?'

He made that strange little instinctive jerk of his shoulders. I've seen it a million times. Once his every mannerism was as familiar to me as the beating of my own heart. But he's always doubted me; it was he who fell, slowly, slowly, out of love with me, not me from him. He who could not love me. He's always been male, a taker not a giver. 'Still seeking the truth, are you?'

'As always.'

And he still doubts me. 'How do I know for certain it's you, Mary?'

I said simply: '*Ouranos*.'

Ouranos, the ancient male god of the sky who fell passionately in love with the female earth, Gaia. These Jews never heard of such names or their myths, though their stories of the Flood grew from them, until they thought them their own. Long, long, long ago Ouranos, Sky, drew near to Gaia the Earth and spread out around her and enveloped her in his passion. But because of his unremitting lust Gaia's children could not come out from her womb – until one of them, Time, swung a sharp sickle and cut off Ouranos's gigantic penis embedded in Gaia's body, so that her children could be born.

'Ouranos and Gaia,' James whispered. He knows. He's James, my James. He banged his fists on the hard rock. 'It's you. I should have guessed. How long have you known this is me?'

'I saw it in your eyes, James. You never could lie to me.'

'How long, damn you?' *Damn you*. The language of this world had soaked into us. Here damnation was possible, probable, certain.

'I saw your look when the builder fell off the roof, and Joshua—'

He knew what I was going to say, dismissed it. 'Zeno was drunk. He's always falling.'

'Joshua raised Zeno from the dead. I saw it in your eyes. You know it happened, James.'

He said contemptuously, 'Joshua ben-Pantera didn't do anything of the sort.' Son of Pantera, the old slander that Joshua's father was a Temple guard. 'Zeno wasn't dead. He was dead drunk. Stunned, that's all.'

'You're afraid to believe it. You saw a miracle.'

I glimpsed his pain. 'We both know there are no miracles, Mary.'

'What of the snake that bit you from the woodpile? Why didn't you die?'

'You've been spying on me.'

'On Joshua. Just as you have. You're afraid of him, aren't you? Terrified.'

'No. Everyone saw my hands change that snake into a dove.'

'We all heard the stories that were put about,' I agreed. 'And John changed the serpent, or was it viper, into the sceptre of Zadok. All that, showing that you two are the Two Pillars. But my eyes saw what they saw.'

James said: 'I am the Christ.'

'You're afraid of Joshua because everything that you and I once believed in, and lost faith in, is coming true.'

'I'm not afraid.'

'You are afraid, James, you're terrified, because *you know Jesus Christ is born.*'

'No.'

'Born here among us. Growing up among us. To be the Christ among us.'

'Tricks. Confusion. The devil's work.'

'Jesus Christ is come here to this world, James. He does miracles. He heals. He blesses.' I touched my unblemished face. 'Look at me.' But James would not, he would not touch me. Did he love me still, then, somewhere inside his aching heart, in his pain that he would not acknowledge, his loss, his guilt? Oh, James, I know you so well, even after so long! Nothing ever changes, and no one. 'Jesus Christ,' I said quietly. 'No fable, no myth. He's here among us, in the flesh. Real. Actual. I've touched Him.'

'So've I,' James exploded. 'I've held his head while he was sick, I've heard him fart, I've seen his bad manners, I've watched him turn himself into an abomination against us. A pollution. He shouldn't even have the right to wear linen. Going against us, going against God!' He leant forward. 'Leave him alone. We'll deal with him. Joshua is my mother's living shame, not your miraculous lover.' He sneered. James thought he knew everything about love now he loved God.

I said: 'Joshua was born of a Virgin. I saw it. And I saw it proved.'

'I've no doubt you thought you saw it. But in fact Joshua's father was the captain of the Greek guard in the Court of the Gentiles.'

I sighed. 'I heard she had no choice, Pantera raped her.'

'Of course, we've put that about.'

It was very important for me to understand this dangerous nonsense. 'Which side are you on, James?'

He said at once, 'God's side.'

I said carefully, 'We're not talking about any God you happen to want to believe in. We're talking about reality.'

'Yes, I believe in Him so deeply that I *know* Him. I can see His instructions, His laws, all around us in reality, Mary. His laws for nature, His Law for men. By perfect living, perfect obedience to the Law, we can attain godhood. We can be gods in His image.'

'No, you can't make up your own God any more, James! God is here. He is *here*. No more lies. No opinion. No choice. No more pick and mix, no more truth being in the eye of the beholder, only submission. Total knowledge of God means total submission. No more fabrications, sects, factions, no more politics. Jesus Christ is among us in the flesh, actual, factual, real, not to be denied. Jesus Christ, the miraculous Son of God born of the Virgin, is sent to save us. And He will save us. We shall live baptised in truth, in God's truth, a saved people. He will write His Bible, and John will spread His Word, and Jesus Christ will be crowned king and priest in Jerusalem, and peace will reign.'

I sat exhausted by my words. I said a good deal more in the same vein, and so did James. We had so much to talk about, but we were no longer in love. Our love was as cold as clinker, and we had both known it for a long, long, long time. The sun swung its shadows around us. James sat beside me, as tired as I, I think.

He said in a low voice, 'If what you say is true, why am I here? Why are you?'

I sighed. 'Good question. Why are any of us here? To witness? To participate? To be foolish or wise? To see what is real.'

'Mary, I was sent to be the Christ. I *am* the legitimate

Christ. It's God's will, obviously. Everything you talk of is of me.'

He was as mad in his disbelief as I had been, once. I said gently, 'We all know Jesus had no brothers.'

He shook his head wildly. 'You're all talk. Words, born of slime. Truth doesn't *say*, truth *does*. Freedom, deliverance, come to us through our own good works, our desire to be holy, to be close to God. I eat only vegetables grown in the wild, not cultivated. I eat no meat.'

He was off again. 'How does that make you holy?'

'Meat's the bloody fruit of sexual intercourse, the fruit of the womb. What could be farther from God? I shall never touch a woman's flesh.' He shuddered at the thought of it. He was so thin he looked ill, his knees callused like a camel's from the hours he spent kneeling in prayer. 'Isaiah foretold that I should be the Christ, celibate, eternal, bringing vengeance on the ungodly. "The Way is a man zealous for the Law, whose Time is the Day of Vengeance." I am that Man of Vengeance Isaiah prophesied. "God shall accomplish mighty works by the Holy One of His people." ' He gripped my hands. 'I am the Christ, believe me.'

'Joshua saved your life.' James simply closed his eyes. 'Very well!' I said. 'How was the miracle done? You know more science than I, how did he do it?' He had no answer except closed eyes, his mumbled prayers. 'You're touching me,' I added, and he snatched his hands away from mine.

'You're a demon, Mary,' he murmured. 'A woman.'

'I loved you once.'

'God help me, Mary, you saw me with some girl, some girl's sleeping bag—'

'Esther. Esther, her name. You haven't forgotten.'

'It was you I loved. You dragged yourself on your elbows to the cave, Mary, God knows how, your back broken, and you shot yourself in the mouth with my pistol, and your body fell to the centre of the world.' He corrected himself in the speech of these people. 'Into the bottomless pit.' Tears trickled from the corners of his eyes. 'Did you think I forgave myself?'

'I did it because I loved you. So you had with her the children I couldn't give you.'

He put his hands to his head. 'They died. They all died.'

I wanted desperately to hug him in his ancient grief, but knew I couldn't touch him now. Words, gestures, sharing, were so ridiculously small.

'I'm sorry.' I closed my hands at my sides, hardened my heart. 'Have you spent all this time searching for a way to God?'

He looked away, to the desert, rocks, anything but me.

He said, 'I never loved anyone but you.'

We looked at the desert and the rocks.

'I hate this place,' he whispered. 'I reached the end of my tether. There's no God.'

I couldn't blame him. 'Me too.' I told him the truth. 'I forgot everything I knew. I thought God was dead. And then something happened to me, in the Dead Sea. I was a woman who'd grown old and lost hope. I sank, and something happened. Something not an accident.'

He looked straight at me. 'The Hand of God. I've felt it too.'

'You felt it? The power? That you were born for a reason?'

'The son of Joseph and Mary. No choice. And the coincidence of their names, Joseph, Mary! Can't be just the fall of a dice.'

I thought about it. My mouth went very dry. 'Do you think God sent you, James?' I used the Greek phrase, *ho theos*.

'God? Yes, of course. Who else?'

I swallowed with my dry throat. 'Or the Devil?' The same, *ho theos*.

He jumped to his feet. 'Did the Devil send *you*, to make me doubt myself?'

'No. I don't know.' I thought about it some more. 'God, surely.' I had felt it was God, but how would I know for certain? 'Surely we'd know the difference between God and the Devil.' The Devil, the grand Deceiver. The Persuader. The Devil makes everything so reasonable. To sell His lies the Prince of Darkness of this world even tells the truth.

James said, 'I'd know the Devil. His is the smell which is found between the buttocks.' He was on about cleanliness and hygiene again.

'Cleanliness is sterile,' I said. 'Manure makes the flowers and crops grow.'

'God is good. God gave the Law to Moses in the desert.'

'We both know that what Moses found in the desert was not the Power of God but the power of men.'

The singsong of the Nazarene priest calling the Community to evening prayer carried to us across the sand and rocks, through the shimmering mirages in the air after the heat of the day. James knelt, held up his fists in front of his face, praying.

He said: 'I know God. God is God because He wins. God is the victor on Judgment Day. He writes the Book. Until then everything is . . . nothing. Belief. Human imperfection. Pollution.' His voice rose. 'The Jews who run away to foreign countries rather than take up arms against the Romans who rule us, they shall not be saved. Gentiles shall not be saved for they have never lived. The Sadducees and Pharisees who desecrate the Temple with their false priests, their contamination, their profanity, offering up their blasphemous worship as an insult to God, there shall be no place for them in Heaven. The Covenant shall not be renewed for them.'

I reached out, then did not touch him. James had suffered. His Hell was far worse than mine. The sun quivered on the horizon like clotting blood, the chants of the Nazarenes rose, then fell silent as the sun's light was extinguished. My last sight was Joshua walking home along the road in the failing light.

'Until we worship God properly, with good works,' James whispered, 'there will be no God for us.' He followed the gleam of my eyes, saw Joshua. 'Leave him alone!' James hissed. 'You're not to speak to him, I forbid it.' He was mortally afraid of taint, of one sin making all goodness worthless. 'Don't interfere!'

I had been warned not to interfere by both angels and men. 'The more I'm told not to interfere the more I think interference works.'

James said: 'He is the AntiChrist sent to confuse us, blind us, deceive us, and turn us on the path of wickedness and sin and despair. Unless he's stopped he'll be the damnation of our whole people, for our God shall turn from us.'

I tried to see James's face in the gathering gloom. The Ante-Christ, I know; traditionally 'Ante-Christ' is one of the names of John the Baptist, the Forerunner of Jesus who brought Christianity to Rome. But AntiChrist, against Christ, opposite to Christ, opposed to Christ, I do not know.

I shook my head in the dark, knowing James was wrong. 'The one you call the abomination,' I said. 'The criminal. The apostate. The one who eats bread and drinks wine even at your table. Joshua. You're so afraid because in your heart you know it's Him.'

There *is* absolute truth, surely. But I don't know whether James has been sent by the Devil or not, and neither does he. He searches for God. He believes I'm sent by the Devil because my love for Joshua is frankly of the body as well as the soul. Any girl would love Him that way, if she got the chance, if she had the nerve. But others would call that love fornication, dire blasphemy. So perhaps James is right. Perhaps if I were to kiss Joshua on the lips and place his hand on my breast, some secret corrupting scheme of Satan would be achieved. If I were the lover of Jesus Christ the celibate king, I would have power over him. And if Satan had power over me . . . I turned round and round.

If James was born by Satan's will, it made sense for him to want to be proclaimed the Christ. That would be a delicious irony for the Dark One: to be the master of the Christ. But where did John fit in? He was supposed to be on God's side, the Ante-Christ, the Forerunner, but was he? Joshua had no message, no heartfelt lesson to preach. He simply *was*. By John's support of James, was the will of God served or thwarted? In this titanic struggle I could be sure of nothing, not even which side was God and which the Devil. This world is a swamp.

But I could be sure of one person. The Greeks, whose ploughs and yokes Joshua constructed, merrily called him Jesus (though they patronise every Jew named Joshua by the Greek name Jesus), but I had heard his mother whisper in his ear, 'Do not forget who you are.' Mary paid Zacchaeus the teacher (presumably with money she had salted away from the Community, just as the priests salt away their talents in secret places at Sion, ready for the renewal of the Covenant) to tutor Joshua privately; or perhaps Zacchaeus, his earlier fear of Joshua replaced by a kind of intellectual intoxication, worked for free. I often saw Zacchaeus and his wife Bernice, an intelligent and wilful woman, in the workshop or the yard disputing with Joshua so that as his hands laboured, his mind learned. Sometimes the twins Thomas and Miri listened too, and Silas who loved wood more than learning. But Joshua was the centre of everything. To James and John he was the bastard son, the outsider, the rebel, but however much they hated him they could not ignore him. The workshop, his brothers and sisters, and Zacchaeus and Bernice, revolved around him. I'd seen Bernice, whom I told you was intelligent and so you knew was unhappy, touch Joshua's face, and seen her fierce intellectual doubt flooded with peace. Beautiful peace.

Sometimes I even heard Joshua say words that the Bible tells us Jesus traditionally said. I heard Joshua warn James with immense authority: 'If you fast, you will bring sin on to yourself. If you pray, you will be condemned. If you give to charity, your pride will harm your soul.'

Joshua told John: 'In the days when you ate what is dead, you made it come alive with your manure. But now you do not know yourself, and live in poverty, you have impoverished yourself.'

To Delanos the paymaster Joshua sneered, 'Congratulations to the Poor, for to you belongs Heaven's kingdom.'

To Zacchaeus I heard Joshua say, smiling, 'Have you found the beginning yet, Zacchaeus? Are you still looking for the end? You will see that the end is where the beginning is.'

And once when he was very tired I heard Joshua tell Bernice, 'You believe in me. You believe in peace. You believe I've come to cast peace like a peaceful net over the world. But I have come to cast conflict over the world, fire and sword and war.'

I knew beyond doubt, on every level, that Joshua was the Son of God sent to save us and bring the world into Heaven and Earth. Since he touched me I'd had a hundred offers of marriage from men who desired a beautiful wife with even white teeth and perfect skin, potential lovers and masters who claimed to lose themselves in my strange indigo-blue eyes, and jerked crude sexual gestures bragging to their friends when I turned my back. Men, mere men. I wasn't tempted. I roamed the dry fields and the desert paths, let the wind blow my clothes like pale wings beneath my long black hair.

But sometimes, I wondered if James was right. Surely it is right to try to worship God through goodness, good works, good actions, charity. Was God mocking me, deceiving me, by letting me believe that a man condemned by his community and his family (except his mother) as an abomination and a criminal, was in fact the Son of God? If the Devil can tell the truth, then God can lie.

I stood on the hilltop, the wind blowing around me. This is where reason takes us. Nowhere. The place where we know nothing.

But I *feel* everything. I know I'm right. I have faith. My faith is certainty.

It so happened a few months later that Joshua walked towards me on the road. Except that nothing so happens; I know now there's no such thing as coincidence. Our paths coincided exactly; I couldn't have escaped him if I tried. I ran towards him, knelt at his feet. 'My Lord.'

He touched my hair, lifted me. 'Mary, Mary.'

I kissed his fingers, his work-broken nails. I began to cry. I could not speak. It had been months since I had spoken with him. My throat closed up.

He touched my cheeks with his thumbs, stared into my eyes. 'I'm going from here. My mother worries for my safety.'

'They can't touch you,' I blurted. I thought I knew all about James and John. Their house was an armed camp of thugs and sicariots. Several times I'd seen running fights with Simon's tribesmen.

Joshua smiled because I'd interrupted him. 'Mary, Mary. I must go away. Far away. There is a friend of my mother's, he'll take me with him. A merchant from Arimathea.'

I frowned at the unfamiliar name. I've heard of Ramathaim Zophim, known as Rama, where the prophet Samuel was born. Presumably Arimathea was the same place, but I had no idea where. 'Is it far?'

Joshua looked down. His eyebrows were as fine as lines I could have drawn with my fingernails. 'Joseph of Arimathea is taking me to the end of the world.'

'Joshua, no!' Then I realised with a thumping heart that he meant only the limit of their known world, which is not so far. These people have only myths of the land beyond the ocean, which the Greeks call Oceania. Joshua meant somewhere closer, but I felt desperate. 'Your place is here.' Everyone knows Jesus Christ never left His people; the world came to Him. 'Your place is here with us!'

Joshua looked into me through my eyes, and I fell silent.

'Mary, the Arimathean's a rich man, widely travelled. His family's traded in tin father and son since Solomon's time. Tin's the metal of the land at the end of the world, the Eretz ha-Brit.'

I gaped. 'The Land of the Covenant?' Brit's their word for covenant. A coincidence, surely.

He gave the Latin name. 'Britannia. Britain.'

'You can't go!'

He frowned. 'Can't?'

'I meant you can't go overland, it's an island.'

He was curious. 'You're right, but the Arimathean's an experienced seafarer.' Then Joshua's excitement overwhelmed him, just a young man. 'To the Pillars of Hercules, that's a month's sail – longer, since we'll stop at ports on the way for pottery, wine, jewellery, factory-made stuff. Then weeks more sailing to Britannia, beyond the empire of the Kittim, to the market at Luan-dun. We'll trade at ports along the lower coast until we reach the mines where the cliffs meet the ocean.' Cliffs! I chilled, wondering if Joshua meant the chalk cliffs of the white island Vectis where Balaam the high priest met his horrible death, but no tin's found there. Some people call all Britain the White Island, since white cliffs are all that can be seen of it from the lands of the Kittim.

I looked up at his eyes. 'Your mother doesn't want you to go.'

'She's afraid for me. But she's more afraid if I stay.'

I swallowed angrily. 'Does she say this is God's will?'

'I do not know my Father's will, Mary.' He let my hair slide through his palms. 'Mary Magdalene. You don't want me to go either. Only the women care for me in my life.'

'Take me with you!' I said. Joshua shook his head, no. I

201

grabbed his head, I kissed his lips with my lips, pressed my face to his face, tasted the sweet sweaty taste of him, his lips, his skin, felt his beard warmed by the sun against my cheeks.

The ends of my hair slid from his fingers. He stepped back. 'I shall return to you before Passover next year.'

But he did not.

DE NIHILO NIHIL

nothing comes from nothing

Years passed.

James and John grew thin and harsh, went away. The house fell silent, zealots, sicariots, thugs, overnight all gone, the walls and rooms silent and empty of life. After Passover, when I waited for Joshua to return, Mary came back to her house on her donkey, only Matthew the celibate levite with her, not James or John. She saw me watching and waiting and came over.

Mary touched my shoulder kindly. I felt her infinite sympathy. 'John will not be here again.'

John? Such sympathy, when I felt nothing at all for John – I had hardly noticed him! I felt deeply alarmed – how much had I not noticed? Was John in love with me? 'You will be a widow feeling such love,' Mary told me gently. 'Both John and James, my own son, have been initiated as "angels", novices in the priesthood at Sion.'

I sat with her beneath the lemon tree. She said, 'John has taken the oath of lifelong celibacy. If he cannot have you he will have no other.'

'John only loves himself and God,' I said.

'That's true of all priests,' she said. 'It takes pride and arrogance almost beyond imagination to be a priest.' Matthew coughed, overhearing. She sent him away.

'I don't love John,' I said.

'I knew you could not!' She sounded relieved. 'It would have been impossible. From the moment of his conception in Elizabeth's womb, the course of John's life has been ordained for him by God. He is well aware of it, and lives in total submission to his fate.'

'I love Joshua.'

'No.' She repeated the word in a flat voice. 'No.'

'I know it's wrong.' My lips wriggled with emotion I could not hide. I had to place my hands over them.

She drew me to her, her arms around me, kissed my knuckles. She spoke into my eyes. 'I'm so sorry for you. James suffers for you. You're his temptress. He suffers night thoughts for you, defiles himself. My heart goes out to him; he's no more than human despite his calling, his calling into the priesthood he's been born to, that he strives to live up to. To deserve, to honour, to obey, not to let down. When the time comes, his father's son, he'll be anointed the Christ like his father. That cannot change. It can't change, Mary Magdalene.' For an instant in her words I heard Joshua's voice.

'But you know the truth,' I told her urgently. 'You saw the angels, the real angels. You heard the archangel Gabriel.' I struggled to make her understand. 'The gold, the storm—'

'I'm Joshua's mother,' she said simply. 'I love my son. I want my son to live. I married an old man who was unhappy every day of his life. Now James and John are old, too, youngsters old before their time, unhappy, full of fear and anger.' She smiled to make me comprehend her. 'Joshua . . . Joshua is different.'

The Virgin must be forty years old, but since Joshua had gone she looked younger. What a burden caring for him had been for her. Now, far from his brothers, politics, priests, her son's safety was in the hands of his Father. She was a woman of utter faith. But there is much more to God than faith.

'James believes that Joshua is the AntiChrist,' I said. I hoped to startle her, but she lost none of her luminous calm. I asked, 'Could there be such a thing? Is an Anti-Christ foretold among your people?'

Mary said carefully, 'At Sion the priests believe' – she did not say *she* believed – 'that evil must be allowed to flourish, to come out into the open, before the time is ripe for God's judgment. How can God judge between good and evil if there is no evil?' Again she smiled her smile. She had grown immensely since Joseph's death. How much better we do without men.

Mary continued in her precise, non-committal voice, 'Evil in its greatest possible form, the priests at Sion believe, is the AntiChrist. He will be a false prophet, a rebel, who will try to take God's place. John believes that in the last days men and women will become very wicked, and God will destroy the human race by fire. So John baptises us to bring us to repentance, to save us.'

'But you Nazarenes baptise yourselves several times a day.'

'John gives baptism once, for ever.' She cut a lemon and squeezed its juice in her mouth. Unlike James or John the Virgin ate fruit, even though fruit is made from a form of sexual union. She offered me a slice, wincingly sour. 'For forty years of tribulation the Sons of Light will fight the Sons of Darkness. The Temple will be destroyed. A Beast will rise up out of the sea.' I remembered what I'd heard in the demon's grip above the open-roofed church at Sion, remembered Judas Zadok's battle cry: *Our time is just beginning!* 'A great dragon, red as blood, the serpent of Satan in the Garden of Eden, who cursed women with knowledge.' The dragon again. 'Knowledge is chaos, the enemy of God, and the dragon's tail shall sweep one star in three from the sky. And the dragon shall rise up in front of the woman and devour her child.' She smiled, but from the sourness of the lemon. 'I love my people but I love my child. So I have sent my child away.'

'He'll come back.'

'If God wills.'

I touched her hands in admiration. She had a strong soul. We were so close our faces almost touched, I saw the lines round her eyelids and between her nose and mouth, the fine net of veins in the whites of her eyes, and I knew I'd see her often. She'd chosen a hard way, the way of faith. Whatever happened, she had decided, would reveal the truth.

'I pray the truth is what we pray it is,' I whispered, and returned to the bright colours of Levi's house, and Levi the pale centre of it, all sin washed from him. He ceased his prayers, rose from his knees to bring me a clean gown. His body had no odour whatsoever. I never saw a pimple on his face, or wax in his ears, or heard him blow his nose. I overcame my repugnance and embraced him until my twisted arm ached like a wound. I knew he wanted to die. I'd never forget his words when his body was raised from the dead, *Ignorance is missing from me. I know what's coming for me. When I die I shall scream in flames in Hell for ever for what I did to you.*

Levi gave me his gentle smile, fetched clean sandals for me, cooked supper for me, and felt no pain, and slept dreamlessly.

I dreamt.

I dreamt of the Virgin Mary. Whether the Virgin was nearby in her house or not, or away at Sion, or Jerusalem, or Capernaum where she had friends, or even at Magdala, I dreamt of her. The Virgin gave me beautiful dreams. I saw her in a room shimmering with gold and recognised it for the Holy of Holies in the Temple at Jerusalem, and smiled in my sleep. The Nativity. I saw her holding her baby and it grew from her arms until it stood larger than she, and the Virgin's Child was Jesus Christ, and He took His place sitting on His throne in front of her, and the Zadok who was John the Baptist, scrawny as a desert root, anointed His forehead with the Spirit of precious oils, galbanum, myrrh, balsam, cinnamon, and placed the gold crown of the King of the Jews upon His head. And Jesus Christ our King spoke: 'The Spirit of the Lord God is upon me, because the Lord has anointed me.' Then the throne creaked as he turned and looked at me with the eyes of a man, fallible, demonic, no Son of God but merely human as are we all, and I saw he was James.

I woke sweating. Levi had soaked a cloth in cool water and laid it on my forehead. 'You've been crying for hours,' he said tenderly. 'I've been praying for you.'

I remembered back, back, thousands of years ago to Melchizadok occupying the throne of Jerusalem. It would happen again. How many times had Baby Jesus died, murdered, unknown? I remembered Melchizadok's bloody hand extended in false welcome of Abraham – and Abraham leading his people southward from the occupied land into the desert, and the Hebrews not returning home to Jerusalem for a thousand years.

I sat up. 'The Devil is here. He's been here in this world for—' I bit my tongue. I'd nearly said millions. 'Thousands, thousands of years.'

'It was only a dream.' Levi stroked my forehead, smiling. 'I never dream,' he whispered, but not enviously – he was too close to God to feel envy. 'For me, it's all real.'

Only a dream. But still I shook. There had been nothing false in my dream, but it wasn't a vision – not like the true visions I have had, as you know. I'd dreamt only of something that might be. A possibility. A plan. My unconscious mind warning me of something to come. But what was I to do?

I stood with my arms outstretched. I prayed for God's help, I prayed for Joshua. His touch had restored my body to such youthful strength that I could have passed all day in prayer, but soon my twisted arm began to ache, and my concentration began to focus on my pain not my prayer. I gave up and after that hardly saw him even in my imagination. It was as if Joshua had disappeared from the world, on what business I know not. Once, after an evening of wine which is my principal pleasure, I dreamt I saw him as a brightly coloured serpent wearing sharply patterned snake skins and the exotic plumes of the Isthmus, so I knew I saw a dream because that land is unknown here, except to the Essenes, who as you know believe their souls blow there across the ocean after death to await the Day of Vengeance. The peoples of the Isthmus called Him Quetzalcoatl and He taught them their forgotten skills from long ago, how to measure time and study the movement of the stars, and gave them back their solar calendar with its ceremonies and days of prayer at the Pyramids of the Sun and the Moon at Teotihuacán, which means in their language the place where the gods are born. Suddenly I screamed. He had fallen into a deep cave dug down to the land of the dead, mictlán – how well I remembered these names! – and He lay there dead among the dead. Then He rose and climbed back to the living, and sailed away eastwards into the rising sun promising He would return.

I woke laughing. The Pyramids of the Sun and the Moon, Teotihuacán, mictlán, bottomless pits – all had got mixed up in my dream with Nazarene phraseology, their City of the Sun, their 'bottomless pit' of the Dead Sea so far below sea level, their calling the Jerusalem Temple the Temple of the Moon. The dream did not come again. It was gone as thoroughly as Joshua had gone from the Isthmus.

I remembered his voice calling me *Mary Magdalene*. The name had stuck in my mind. *Only the women care for me in my life*. I almost persuaded myself I heard his voice, the voice I love, but it was only the wind.

Yet it set me thinking of home. I rented, thanks to Levi's unstinting generosity, a pleasant house in Magdala, whitewashed, with a flat roof, near enough to hear the waves breaking ashore from the Sea of Galilee, and by standing on the roof see their rolling glitter by sun or moon between the cypresses. One day the sea breeze blew my hair and my clothes like wings, and as I floated I saw the cliffs of Sion below me and down there the black waters of the Dead Sea, and James in a boat pushing men overboard into the bitter waters, where they swam ashore to John the Baptist standing on a low jetty with his toes lapped by the salt water, and the Baptist lifted 'the fish' from the salt and baptised them, and made new men of them. Some had been Pharisees, a few Sadducees, even one or two Jews from the north, but most were Essenes fulfilling their vows, and all had paid a silver half-shekel into the treasury as ransom for their souls. And then James, the Christ, waded ashore to be among them, and they all prayed on their knees together while the waters of baptism lapped around them like salty tears – yes, prayed on their knees, their hands clasped white-knuckled in front of their faces. Not at all like Christians, who the Bible traditionally tells us prayed standing *orans* with arms outstretched to receive the Spirit, as in fact I was taught to pray long ago.

The vision ceased and I lay alone on my flat roof in Magdala.

Still Joshua did not return, and the power of James and John grew among their disciples.

One night, as the moon rose high above the treetops, I saw another moon which was lower, its rim almost touching the horizon of a sea without land – not Galilee, and far to the west of Judah since this moon was hardly risen. I heard the creak of rigging and the steering oar and I knew, I *knew*

208

Joshua was somewhere there in the boat in the moonlit dark, and I knew he was thinking of me. A shadow stood up, a man's face struck into the moonlight – but it was an older man I did not recognise, black hair, the turban of a priest. 'Keeping course eastward?' he asked the man at the steering oar, and Joshua's voice replied, 'Aye, Joseph, the star Merak on my left eyebrow and the North Star on my temple.' The glare of the full moon obliterates the steering stars mariners use for navigation almost as completely as cloud, but I felt sure Joshua knew the position of the Arimathean's little vessel to the last cubit – and so did the tin-trader, for he turned away with a chuckle, and I saw no more of them in the dark, and the creak of the rigging and the oar faded into the night.

I returned to Sepphoris for Passover. The tribes of Zebulun and Naphtali and all the others you may remember were heading south as they did every year, keeping together for protection, thousands of shabby cloaks led by men in white linen, scrubbed feet in sandals of wood and twine raising dust on the track, followed by the filthy dusty mass of humanity, women and children bringing up the rear as they filed past Levi's house. The Virgin, classed as a 'Rich Widow' of the tribe of Judah by the Poor – because she kept a table for ten women, who by menial work raised money (except during their monthly courses) for their keep and the Poor – took her place behind James at the head of the tribe. She saw me, but James did not. When the wind blew his shift I saw his knees and elbows polished yellow as horn by prayer, and there was no friendship in their greeting. He knew she had deliberately removed Joshua to safety. Though that suited him it must be a dreadful thing for James to know his mother doubted him, to wonder if his own mother would be his enemy given the chance. By the number and closeness of his bodyguards I could see James believed himself surrounded by enemies. He had more important matters to worry about than the Virgin, and gradually she and her donkey were shunted to the back of the queue, and the road fell quiet of footsteps.

Then, at last light, I heard the furtive shuffling of men's feet. At the inn belonging to Demas, the door opened and by the glow of a clay lamp I glimpsed hooded faces, heard whispers. First among the men coming out was one of the Magi I'd never forget from the Bethlehem stable, Simon the Zealot. The Romans still put a price on Simon's head, calling him by his Greek name *Zelotes*, but I was one of the few who knew his face. Judas the Galilean's exiled son had come home again to his tribe of East Manasseh.

Crouching below the window ledge, I followed the men from window to window as they gathered in the street below me. Simon gave up his turban and cloak of stars for a raggedy cape of greasy black wool and leather sandals like a thousand others, drawing no attention to himself: a down-at-heel trader. He tousled his grey beard like a bird's nest, bent his back, leant his weight into his stick. But the men around him moved confidently, watchfully, their hands concealing knives. I saw Dositheus the tax collector join Simon's side, and Barabbas the killer, convicted and escaped, but to my surprise not all were bearded – I saw foreigners among them, clean-shaven non-Jews with the blue eyes and red hair of Celts from Galatia, Syrians with eyes as black and hard as olive stones, leathery ruffians dredged from the seaports of Asia Minor. Gentiles led by a Jew! So Simon had lost the faith of his own people and must be a desperate man, his hopes of ever being recognised zadok firmly in the dust. But still, it seemed, he was determined to attend the Passover at Sion even with his reputation in tatters and these scum following him living in tents, women trudging after them carrying water skins, baskets on their heads. The group moved away, and the darkness of the desert took them.

The door of Demas's inn opened, again showing lamp-light. Here was the boy I remembered who had grown into a man: from the glow stepped Judas the Sicariot.

I knew him at once, remembered Simon's voice from the church at Sion speaking of his dead brother, Judas of Sepphoris. *A martyr does not die. I present to you his son who proudly bears his father's name and the name of his father's father, Judas.* Remembered Simon holding the shoulders of the young candidate. Now Judas was in his late twenties, tall, vital, handsome in a full way, full of flesh. His eyebrows were fierce, level, but as always it was his eyes I recognised, brown, almost black, wild as a cat's. Instinctively my muscles tightened, responding to him, the sense of ruthless power emanated by him, and for the first time in years I felt my nipples scratch my linen shift. I tried to look away. He'd darkened his hair to make himself look more Jewish. A heavy roundness had crept into his chin and cheeks over the years, puckering his intolerant mouth. But he moved decisively, eyes darting – I expected him to look up and see me, but he did not. I stared enthralled over the sill as his deep eloquent voice barked orders, gathering the elders of East Manasseh behind him, peasants to a man, filthy robes and broken teeth. Candlelight glowed over the oil rubbed into his skin, but no woman ran out to wish him farewell. I heard whips crack, the honking and spitting complaint of camels heavily burdened, then the baggage train of East Manasseh passed beneath my window southward along the moonlit road, following Judas.

Something was happening, and Joshua was missing his chance. He should be here. No, he should be at Sion – whatever happened would happen at Sion! That was God's will, and the Devil's will. I looked up into the night clouds and for a moment in my imagination their shapes changed into muscles, into straining arms and shoulders and fingers locked in combat. I closed my eyes and they were gone. But a small growing seed of dread came to me, and I could not shake it off all night, or all the next day. Levi tried to cheer me with small treats and kindnesses but my worry nagged me. Why, I worried, *why* do we know so little of Jesus Christ's ministry before His Recognition and His acceptance of the crown IMRI, from *Amariah*, which means simply 'The Lord has said'? Traditionally He's born to the Virgin, grows up in the city of Nazareth, disputes with the Doctors in the Temple at the age of twelve – and that's all, until that day in his late twenties He suddenly walks into history, a full-grown mature man walking alone through the desert to the River Jordan, and the Baptist recognises Him and baptises Him.

Days passed, a week. I lost myself in spring-cleaning the house, every scrap of leaven must go, and Levi came to the door. Any other man would have coughed at the dust in the room, but he stood with it falling grey on his face, smiling. 'It's an angel to see you, Mary.'

What did Levi see? It was no angel by the dyeing vat, it was a *he*, massively male, golden, uncircumcised as a goat. He bent his bead between his wings, stared at Levi and me through the doorway. One breath would have blown Levi out of his skin. 'Isn't she beautiful?' Levi smiled.

The demon flared his golden nostrils, sniffed him, then reached through the doorway and took my hand, and grew larger than the house. 'Don't hurt him,' I said.

The demon's voice came through the rushing wind. 'Once he was of mine.'

'You're the same one, aren't you,' I said. 'The one who took me before. Have I interfered?'

'No. You were something that might have happened and you did not.'

'I'm disappointed.' I meant it. I *was* disappointed.

'That day by the pond. Something might have happened.'

'Hadassah?'

'Our Lord wanted *you*. There was heat in His loins for *you*, not her. Thoughts of lust. Fornication.'

I put these whispered blasphemies, provocations, to one side. 'Those thoughts never crossed Joshua's mind, you know. He can't commit sin.'

The demon pinched his fingers together. That close. 'He can,' he added.

'No,' I said. 'You don't understand. He felt nothing like that.'

The demon parted my flying hair with his golden lips. I felt his hot breath against my ear. 'Do not for one moment believe,' the demon whispered, 'that I do not understand love.'

My clothes streamed around me and we fell between the cliffs towards the bottomless pit, the Dead Sea opening like an eye beneath us. Now the white geometry of the rooftops of Sion was growing around us, and the demon beat against the rising air with great thrusts of his wings. Then he soared above the battlements, and I saw that the Field of Blood was a mass of tent tops as usual at Passover, Tabernacles and the feasts of the novitiates. The sun glared and I smelt the coming storm, saw the thunderclouds banked in the north-east. Below them the great east-facing gates sealing the vaulted arch of the monastery gateway were barred, and the walls glared white as salt, adamantine white, sparkling, hurting my eyes. And then I saw a single dark line like a crack.

A rope led up the wall from the Field of Blood. Men clung to it like black ants. They swarmed over the battlements, dropped down into the white courtyards below. The black shadows became deeper, filling with men, then the men melted forward through the glare. Their shadows remained more visible than they in the blinding stormy light, shadows spreading out along the steps and esplanades, shadows gathering round doorways, shadows flowing inside. The flash of a curved knife in a cloister. A priest staggered out and lay down, kicking silently, spreading blood that set brown almost at once in the heat. His soul whirled above him in its confusion and the demon reached out his fist, snatched it while it was warm.

I asked, 'Have you brought me here to show me Sion being attacked?'

'You are here,' the demon shook his great golden head, 'to see victory.'

I saw a bare-headed novice pursued by shadows, and closed my eyes.

'Only a few will die,' the demon said. 'Only enough. Death is no part of the plan. Yet.'

The novice lay dead in a baptismal pool, his arms stretched out as though his death took the form of the devout *tau*-cross shape of prayer. I found that human cross deeply disturbing to see; I don't know why.

'Evil in its greatest possible form,' I whispered. 'Is that what's happening here? Is that the plan? The AntiChrist, and the greatest suffering, and forty years of tribulation?'

'See,' he pointed, 'what will happen.' He would not let me close my eyes. Angel or demon, it seems all they have to show us is death, as if all life is a struggle for death, nothing achieved, nothing won, nothing saved. So with my staring eyes I watched the young men die. But I thought, if only Joshua were here.

If only Joshua were here, this would not happen.

The demon heard me, let me fall. My stomach rose to my mouth. 'If Joshua were here,' he whispered, 'would He save you from falling?'

213

The roofs flashed outward on each side of me. I said: 'Yes.'

The demon stopped me a foot's length above the stones. 'And all these others?' he mocked me. I heard the cries of the dying monks, smelt their blood. 'Would He save them all?'

'Yes.'

'And would He save Himself?'

'Yes.'

'Why?'

I was amazed. 'Because He is the Son of God. Because only He can destroy you. Destroy evil. Destroy destruction. What other hope have we?'

The demon bellowed with laughter, sending spray across the pools. 'You know nothing of who I am. It was I who built the Temple for King Solomon. My skill, not that of Hiram the architect, *my* skill not theirs. I know the secrets of the Covenant.' He whirled me up with him above the open-roofed church, then would not let me speak, placed his golden finger against my lips. 'Be silent for once. Thirst for knowledge, woman. Learn.'

I stared down through the roof. James stood in the pulpit of the Christ. Judas Sicariot stood behind him, his knife curled round the Christ's throat. In front of the congregation Simon Magus, the zealot, threw off his disguise of black wool, kicked away his foul leather sandals, and stood revealed in the golden cloak of Zadok.

'You'll have to kill me,' James the Christ called down. 'I serve God, no other.'

'So do I.' Simon crossed the nave, climbed the pulpit stairs to the higher level. 'It is to serve God that I do this,' he proclaimed, pointing at the Baptist's pulpit. 'I am a more righteous servant of God than this impostor, who has brought Temple Sadducees among us, his father's faction.' He strode to where John the Baptist, the zadok who would not wear the golden cloak, was held kneeling between two sicariots. John's scrawny head wore a livid bruise down one side, one of his eyes was closed. Simon spat on him. 'Defiler! Liar! Man of a lie! You led us to destruction. You gave away the baptism of Sion to every pawing hand, wetted each dry brow with God's water, lived on little, took nothing but a miserable half-shekel. Where's the thirty talents of silver for the renewal of God's Covenant? Is it never to be earned? Not this year, not next year, not next, never? You are not a righteous man! Without riches, what is religion? Without power on earth, how can we preach the power of God in Heaven? In one hour shall your judgment come. You have broken the Law. You are excommunicated from among us.'

The Baptist croaked, 'Let me speak.' The passion of John's oratory was famous, his zeal could make flowers bloom. Simon had no intention of letting a word pass his lips.

'An excommunicate has no voice.' Simon waved him away. 'Take him to the caves and shut him there. The court shall pronounce sentence tomorrow.' Simon watched the broken figure of the Baptist dragged from the pulpit. Then, as he climbed to take the Baptist's place, he called down, 'Wait.'

The sicariots held back the Baptist by his long hair, which reached almost to his shanks. As a sign of their contempt for the fallen zadok they had dressed his nearly naked body in a sack made of camel-hair – unclean clothing, made from an unclean animal – and left his feet bare.

Simon turned to James the Christ. 'Are you with him or against him?'

Judas tightened his grip; the knife bit. James teetered with all his strength on the tips of his toes. Judas did not take his faithful black gaze from Simon's. If Simon said cut, the knife would cut James's throat. Slice, and the knife would slice.

Simon insisted, 'James, my lord, are you for me as zadok or against me?'

James clasped his hands so tight they shook, either in mortification or in prayer. He would not look at the Baptist. No man believes himself sent by the Devil.

Then James croaked, 'A solitary pillar cannot stand alone!' He uttered a cry of defeat.

'Good,' Simon said. 'You may keep your voice.' He moved his eyes and Judas stepped back from James, but only one step. A man who changed sides once might change again. Simon turned and braced his hands on the pulpit rail

215

as he began to address the Congregation, consolidating his power over the Sons of Light; but I thought, now you are the Sons of Darkness.

'Oh, Joshua,' I wailed, 'where are you?'

The demon lifted me high in the air. The shadow of Sion lengthened and rotated as the morning sun slid down the sky. *Down* the sky? Beneath us the featureless desert deepened, became grainy, deeply textured, split now with deep valleys of shadow in the level light, each hollow a bottomless pit, each mountain top standing up like an eye of light in the dawn. Time's curve was reversed, and one by one the mountain tops winked out as last night rose from the ground, rose up around us in the thin high air until the first of the sun flashed suddenly to darkness behind the curve of the world. I was being shown the demon's power: this was his world.

The stars glittered unblinking above us. A meteor flared along the horizon at my level or a little below. The demon had reached the limit of his power. This was the place to which, after all, he had been cast down.

How he must hate it. That his power was not infinite. *That* close.

The stars rotated anticlockwise, sunset struck across Judah beneath me, the Dead Sea and the wilderness of Perea and Machaeros were illuminated on my right. To my left the sandy yellow coast of Palestine curved smoothly towards Egypt, and the demon flew towards the sun rising in the west so rapidly that it set behind us in the east. The starlit ocean flashed beneath us, then sunset, then dawn, and he paused in the turquoise bay of an island where the sand lay white as flour beneath the coconut palms. Not a breath of wind, not a wave lapped the beach. A perfect morning.

I whispered, 'Is he here?'

A brightly painted butterfly fluttered on to a coconut, the nut fell, a cloud of parrots rose up squawking, whirling, and a thin vortex formed from their blue and green wings in the warming air. They fluttered back to the palm tops but the disturbed air circled as it rose, warm air from the land feeding the cool layer above the sea. A small cloud formed, drifting along the chain of islands that stuck out of the mirror-calm sea like the rim of some massive drowned crater. The cloud grew, spreading as it heated and cooled, set spinning by the rotation of the earth as the day turned to night, and at dawn the next morning I saw a heavy leaden mass moving northwards beneath me and grey waves breaking across the ocean. Fronts formed between the clouds and the waves, sending rain hurrying one way, wind the other, the storm drawing more weather towards itself, gathering strength like a living organism. I glimpsed the huge coast of Cumorah through bands of drizzle, then the storm turned east, feeding its strength between cold air and warm air, the cold water of the ocean depths and the warm water current that flows north-easterly from the Isthmus, driven forward by the energy of the sun and thermoclines and the spinning of the earth. Chill thunderclouds rose, and waves of water warmed between the island chains of the Isthmus drove forward beneath the cold storm, so that rain poured down. This was no accident, and I wondered what the demon wanted me to see. *Thirst for knowledge, woman.* The raindrops poured from his implacable face, dripping from his nostrils, and the wind tugged his golden hair. The waves surged up beneath us until I thought the slowly rising spray would touch my feet.

'Yes,' I called through the storm, 'it's very impressive, but what's it for?'

He pointed at a wild north-facing coastline, hog's-back cliffs, no beaches, only clefts of stone and pebble. Heather and last year's dead bracken blew in the wind. The waves rose up the cliffs like white wings spreading, and among them I saw the tiny ship driven hither and thither. I knew it was Joshua's ship. The mast had fallen across the Arimathean's leg, splitting his shoe, but the thick wooden sole took the brunt. Joshua dragged him to the windward rail. 'My lucky shoe,' the Arimathean said, and I saw the gleam of his eyes looking at Joshua as lightning flashed. Ahead of them the sea fell streaming from a black mussel-coated rock, the ship wallowed between the rock and the shore, then the next wave lifted the little vessel clear, the cliffs fell behind. I saw Joshua at the steering oar, tatters of canvas blowing around him. He was smiling, cursing, elated by the storm. 'He could stop the wind with a word!' I bragged to the demon.

'He could command the waves to lie down!'

The demon smiled.

Flatter land now, intensely green even in rain and mist. A difficult silty channel of white water breaking brown as it poured through into an inland sea. I knew this was Britain, I did not know where; the land changes so. Joshua pushed at the bending oar, the Arimathean's vessel surfed forward into shallow water, struck bottom with a crack as the wave petered, then the next wave washed it forward out of control. Water slopped up through the deck. The rain parted for a moment, showing a strange-shaped tor, and Joshua turned the bow towards the beach.

'You heard it crack?' the demon laughed. 'The keel's shattered! She won't float again this year, if ever.'

It was tonight. No time had been lost or gained, not a nanosecond.

My mood changed as I watched the tiny figures gathering debris from the shipwreck, piling it on the strand, anchoring the ship with ropes as best they could. The men lay down exhausted among the hawthorn bushes, but Joshua watched the storm.

'Let me stay,' I said quietly. 'Let me stay here with him and live with him here.'

The demon looked at me sentimentally. He loved the idea of it. The sheer poverty of it. That I could waste the life of Jesus Christ raising brats and scraggy sheep on this godforsaken island, and we would die unknown, nothing done.

'Don't worry,' he said, 'the women of this place are ugly but passionate. He'll find plenty to occupy him without you.'

'I didn't even see his face,' I said.

'He saw you.' For a moment the demon's face was perfectly vacant. 'He saw you.'

I was excited, put my hands in my hair. 'D'you think so? How do you know? Did you see? Did he look happy? Did he look sad?'

The demon ignored me. Suddenly he lifted me up, whirled me away. The darkness grew warm, but the wind did not cease and I knew we remained part of the storm. A wave rose up beneath me, doused me, so bitterly salt that I knew this was the Dead Sea. The thin outline of a man clung like an insect to the cliff, letting himself down from a cave, wearing only a camel-hair sack. He fell the last few feet to the beach, sprawled. Someone ran forward, tried to wrap a cloak round him, but the Baptist pushed it away. His eyes gleamed beadily in the dark. Almost the wide-open innocent almond shape of Joshua's eyes, deep brown, but not quite. In fact not by a thousand miles. The cloaked man said, 'It's me, Nathanael. James sent me. There's a boat.'

John stared up the cliff. 'I'm not afraid to die,' he said.

'You will be a voice in the wilderness,' Nathanael said. 'The faction of the Temple Sadducees who supported you has not carried the day. They're dead or broken, you are alive. Use your life.'

Nathanael waited, then pushed the boat into the sea. There were two others, Peter and Andrew I think, who knew how to handle a sail. John sat in the bow, his shoulders hunched, his head between his knees. Nathanael rowed. All night the demon tried to blow them back with his wings, and the little boat turned and twisted round and round beneath its little sail, but dawn found the four men staggering along the stony eastern shore of Perea. The cliffs were impassable, but they climbed inland up the steep tumble of the Arnon river. Nathanael drank, but the Baptist did not. Nathanael talked, but the Baptist did not. He only spoke when there was work to do, and for him there was only one work.

That is what I saw. My experience was a vision, not a dream. A dream feels real but a vision really happens. Levi stood with the household dust still grey on his smiling face, my broom still in his hand. My clothes smelt dank with salt spray, my wrist was burnt where the demon had lifted me. Levi brought me fresh clothes. 'What did you see?' he asked.

'A revolution, a storm, and a shipwreck. And an escape, I think.' But I did not know if these events were large or small.

'I understand,' Levi said humbly. 'I am not worthy to know.'

I gave a little shiver as I changed into my soft clean clothes. I knew what the demon had shown me: he had shown me his victory. And I did not even know his name.

A thought struck me. 'Levi, who built Solomon's Temple?'

'The First Temple? You mean ruined six hundred years ago by the Babylonians?' Levi did not notice my naked body, he was entirely without lust, purified of even the capacity to feel the sin of lust. His eyes coveted my breasts no more than another woman would. It was strangely horrible. 'King Solomon built it.'

'Yes, but not with his own hands. I mean who was his architect?'

'Everyone knows that.' Levi took my dirty clothes. 'Solomon's builder was Hiram, son of the King of Sidon and Tyre. A coppersmith by trade. The entrance to the Temple was flanked by two copper pillars, Boaz and Jachin.' The two pillars of the world. 'No arch joined them. It was symbolised by the Arch of the Covenant.'

'Which was kept in the Holy of Holies.'

'Yes. God's House.' Levi cleared his throat, plucked a strand of coconut hair from my hem. 'By legend the Temple would not stand straight. Three storeys high above ground, the Lord knows how many below, treasure-rooms, half the cedars of Lebanon, floors and walls of gold, courtyards full of bronze bulls and immense bronze fountains and sacrificial altars. But still the foundations would not stand straight. So, by legend, Solomon and Hiram asked the help of an angel in their work. Hiram's father was . . . known for his interest in the occult. There are horrible stories—'

'An angel?'

Levi couldn't lie to me. 'Or a demon.' He looked embarrassed. Demons are a folk belief of the common people, not of priests – except Essene priests. The priests of the Temple have almost no names for them, only the goat-like demons called *seirim*, Reshef the plague demon, Azazel who lives in the wilderness, that's all. But Essene priests know many hundreds of names for demons, from Azrael the angel of death to Zaphkiel the angel of thought; and they even have a name for the dragons in the sea and the deeps of the world, who have inhabited this world from the beginning of time. And of course there is Satan Himself.

I said, 'A demon?'

'Long ago King Solomon tricked a demon to get his help.'

I smiled at Levi's words. We Jews love to think we're so clever, but no one tricks demons. 'King Solomon tricked him,' Levi insisted. 'Got him to do the work, then chained him up in the Well of Souls.' No; a demon always gets what he wants, and it's always much, much, much more than a human can pay. *It was I who built the Temple for King Solomon. I know the secrets of the Covenant.*

I asked, 'What was the demon's name?'

'Asmodeus.'

Asmodeus. I knew his name.

But as I settled down to sleep, alone, between frankincense-white linen sheets, I thought of Joshua not of the demon. I forgot Asmodeus's gloating and remembered simply what he had said of Joshua. *He saw you.*

Joshua saw you.

I wondered if I would ever see Joshua again.

In fact I saw neither Joshua nor the demon. Two more years of my empty, almost perfect life proceeded without him. Of my dreams I shall not tell you since they were sexual and intense, infuriatingly so. If only I had allowed Him to make me as wholly perfect as Levi! By Essene rules three thousand, nine hundred and sixty-seven years have passed from the time God began His creation of Heaven and Earth. I was a little over thirty years old but still flawless apart from my twisted arm, my skin milky smooth, my hair in black glossy curls to take men's breath away, my indigo-blue eyes as strange and limpid and deep as ever, utterly feminine. Few suitors dared press me now. I carried only one man in my head, in my heart and my immaculate virginity, only one love. And that was the one love that could never be.

I dreamt of Joshua stroking my arm. His fingertips, the lips of his mouth. The sinful physical presence of him with me inhabiting my dreams. O God, to be Levi!

I dreamt Joshua woke in a British turf hut, padded barefoot across the dirt floor, crawled through the door, yawned and curled his toes in the wet grass of Ynys Writrin. I knew in my dream it was his last dawn here on the island. For the last time he turned and looked at the little wooden church he'd built from saplings and the thick mud of the lake shore, an odd shape sticking out of its roof-peak, a sort of Christian prayer-cross like a man praying *orans*, arms out-thrown. It was as though Joshua was discovering, groping towards, the classic splayed form of the Christian prayer-cross encrusted with jewels without ever having seen one, as of course he had not. His work was just rough instinctive wood, the bark still clinging, and the proportions were wrong. He helped the Arimathean load the repaired boat, then they stood round waiting. The crew went to sleep. Midges rose off the water. The sail was hoisted, flapping, but still Joshua and the Arimathean waited, gazing towards the tor. At last a small group of horsemen appeared on the slope, moving fast between the hawthorns. They rode without saddles, their bare feet almost clouting the ground, red hair flying. The man in the lead had the reddest, longest hair, and he reined in so hard I thought he'd break his pony's neck. His cruel, strong face was devastated by loss, grief, fury. He clasped arms with his followers, weeping openly, then turned away from them and leapt fiercely aboard the boat without looking back. I had the clear sense that he was being sent into exile for some terrible crime. Joshua pushed the steering oar, the wind snatched the sail, and the red-haired British man stood in the bow and still his harsh blue eyes did not look back, even as the moors of his land sank into the sea behind him.

In the night I saw Joshua go forward to the bow. The man drew his sword ready to use it; I saw the flash. Joshua stood calmly beside him watching the sea break on each side of them.

Joshua said quietly, 'Man, if you've two good ears, you'd better listen.'

I understood instinctively that the man with the sword would kill Joshua without thought. He'd killed so many without thought – warriors, priests, women, children – and burnt cripples and criminals alive in the service of his god. Looking at this man with his blood-red beard and blood-red hair and haunted moon-blue eyes, a phrase was born complete into my mind. The Ruthless One of the Nations.

What did this have to do with the land of the Covenant, the Eretz ha-Brit?

Joshua said gently, 'Follower, it is no sin to love.' God, he might have been talking to me!

The red-haired follower roared something aloud in his agony. He wept, shaking. Joshua took his shoulders.

'I name you John,' he blessed the barbarian. 'John is a name without meaning, a name sent by God. Tonight you are a new man, John Lovernios.' But Lovernios is a name rich with meaning: in the British tongue it means *Fox*.

John Lovernios fell to his knees. His chipped sword clattered on the deck. Could this man, this barbarian foreigner, blessed by Joshua, really be – after myself – the first follower of Jesus Christ? I watched him stare up with his seamed, brutal, filthy face, and I have never seen a look in a man's eyes like the one I saw in that man's eyes as I woke from my dream. Never.

I sat up in bed. It was full daylight. I heard footsteps walking past my house, an uneven tocking tread. A traveller walking with a broken shoe. I rushed outside, so startling the turbaned traveller that he raised his stick in defence. 'You're the Arimathean!' I burst out. 'The mast fell. Your lucky shoe.'

'Yes, my shoe is split.' He looked at me more closely. 'You're the Magdalene,' he said. 'He's often spoken of you.' Often spoken of me! I begged the Arimathean inside for lemon water, figs – I would have given him the whole tree in my hospitality. Levi padded around us, bringing rugs and dishes. I could bear politeness no longer. 'Is Joshua returned to Judah? Is he here?'

The Arimathean looked exactly as I had dreamt him, perhaps a little smaller. He had the same mannerism of scratching the corner of his eye before he spoke. 'Yes, he spoke of you very often. What an amazing chance I should pass your house.'

'Oh, I don't want to see him! Just to know that he's well. Is he well?'

The Arimathean scratched his eye, smiled, peeled a fig with a sigh of luxury, a man who had grown unused to such fare. 'He's well.'

That was no answer! 'Is he happy? Is he strong, is he eating enough?'

The Arimathean looked me in the eye. 'He's not here. Did you not know?'

I slumped. 'To sea again?'

'You mean you really do not know? I thought you two were so close.' He removed a fig pip from the corner of his mouth. 'No, he is serving as a novice with his people, at Sion.'

After I had washed the Arimathean's hands and sent him bowing on his way, I sat thinking about the Joshua I had seen as the Plumed Serpent Quetzalcoatl, the shipwrecked seafarer, the church-builder, the man who had made the barbarian drop his sword and fall to his knees in front of him by sheer force of personality. More than personality. Force of mission.

Joshua had started at the monastery as a novice. I knew he wouldn't remain a novice for long. He'd found what he would do.

ECCE AGNUS DEI

behold the Lamb of God

But still, no word came from Jerusalem. No Recognition – how could there be, the Baptist fallen from power, lost somewhere east of the Dead Sea, hiding out in the wilderness of Perea in fear of his life – so there could be no triumphal entry of Jesus Christ into Jerusalem, no destruction by Him of the Temple, no rebuilding of it by Him in its perfect form in three days, no coronation for Him with the crown IMRI at the start of His earthly reign.

But I knew it would happen. He was the Son of God. He could do anything.

I had one last dream of him. At first I thought it was the same as before – almost exactly the same scene as one from long ago, the 'fishes' being pushed from the side of a boat into the bitter salt sea, plunging over their heads before floundering towards shore to be 'saved' by the snow-white figure of James the Christ on the low jetty. But this time they were pushed overboard into the baptising salt by Simon the Zealot and his nephew Judas Sicariot, and they gave up their shekels first. Joshua watched them thoughtfully from the bow. A red-haired man about to be baptised wobbled on the side of the boat, his name written on a white pebble hung about his neck. For a Gentile to receive baptism was blasphemy – perhaps he pretended to be a Jewish foreigner from Galatia, they have red hair. But Joshua must know the truth.

Joshua said nothing. He pushed the man in with his own foot, then pulled up his shift to his knees and stepped out of

225

the boat after him into the deep water.

Joshua did not fall. He walked on the water. It was skiddy stuff, and the waves knocked his feet. Simon and Judas watched him get his balance, then stared with round eyes. They rubbed their eyes, realising what they saw. They tested the water with their own feet, and sank. Joshua walked past the bobbing heads of the catechumens, 'fishes', sputtering to shore. As he passed them they stared up at him, his toenails gleaming with water splashes, and I'm sure they would have sunk, open-mouthed, but for the thick buoyant salt.

Joshua put out his hand to James. James helped him with shaking hands, and Joshua stepped from the water on to the jetty. As he stepped forward James stepped back, almost fell. Joshua took both his brother's hands, stared into James's eyes. 'Now you see what was in front of your eyes every day of your life, James.' He allowed James to fall back, then turned to the terrified, awe-inspired face staring up from the water between his feet. It was the red-haired man, the Follower. Joshua lifted him from the water, spoke Greek. 'I baptise you in the name of Jesus Christ.' He lifted the next man from the water, and the next, and the next, and the next was a woman. 'I baptise you in the name of Jesus Christ.' They fell at his water-beaded feet, and kissed his toes, and cried aloud their wonder at what they had seen. There was not one man or woman or child there, or slave, or dog, or bird, or ant, who had not seen what Joshua had done, and no one who did not believe what they had seen.

James wrapped his head in his shift like a man who realises he has been blind, hiding his eyes from the light.

Joshua called Simon and Judas to him, and they plunged from the side of the boat over their heads and floundered to him. He pulled them out, one heavy man hanging on each arm, and blessed them, and with one voice they said, 'My Lord.' Joshua looked at them without gentleness or sentiment, angrily, knowing what he gave them, then nodded. He walked on the water to the shore and the evening wind blew the dust from his feet as he climbed past the monastery – and kept on climbing.

Simon turned to Judas. 'He walked across the water.

That's not Egyptian sorcery. *I* should know. It can't be done.'

'I saw it,' Judas said. 'He walked on the water. All the people saw.'

Simon stared up thoughtfully, pulling his beard. 'What would I do if I were him?'

'Follow him,' Judas said. 'He could cast the Romans out with his little finger.' He swore, exultant. 'By God, with his little finger!' Their voices faded as night fell, and then there was nothing but blackness and silence, and so I woke.

Yes, he could do anything. And he wanted to. I sensed it.

Next day I heard Mary's women beating mats in the yard, then saw them fan out to their menial work in the houses of celibate Nazarenes such as Matthew and Delanos – Dositheus, along with many other tax collectors and paymasters, had long gone over to Simon's side. There was tension between the two factions since the Virgin (and therefore Matthew and a few others) still supported John the Baptist even though he had been thrown down. She knew John's teachings were divinely inspired (I remembered her reverently touching the rounded belly of grey-haired Elizabeth, chosen by God) and she knew John did not want war with the Romans, as Simon and his thugs and intellectuals did. John's voice crying from a wilderness added immeasurably to his holiness because the desert is holy, simplifying, a place of God, and instead of his power being broken by his exile many now believed John was the prophet Elijah reborn. The more faintly his voice was heard, the more people strained to hear his words. Many had heard that he was the Messiah, with the same magic powers in his spoken word that Elijah had worn in his cloak, and Moses had carried in his sceptre. Others said the Baptist was simply crazy, but that's no disqualification for a prophet so long as his craziness comes from God.

I watched Mary sewing with her two daughters Salome and Miri in the yard. Mary kept pricking her fingers, so I knew she was upset. I took them some fruit, oranges. Salome had grown into a lovely girl, Miri was smaller and darker. 'Ugh!' they laughed. 'Bitter oranges!'

'The Romans make marmalade out of them,' I said.

'We don't do what Romans do,' Mary said. Uh-oh,

bad-tempered, and those lines around her mouth and eyes. The girls busied themselves over their needles. I wore a rather lovely indigo-coloured cloak Levi had made for me and they kept flashing glances at it, but no one dared speak. Hammers rattled in the workshop round the back and a young man's voice swore. 'Silas!' Mary called. Silas came shamefaced wiping his hands on his hem, straggly beard hanging goatily from his chin. He would not look at me directly but, as usual with young men, I filled the corners of his eyes. 'Silas,' Mary snapped, 'if you cannot work righteously and in silence, do not work at all.'

Silas blushed to the roots of his hair. 'Yes, Mother.' He fled.

I tried to make conversation. 'Is Thomas working at carpentry?'

She stared at me over the oranges. 'Thomas is at Sion, an "angel".'

'With Joshua,' Salome said, ducking her head from her mother's stare.

'I heard the Baptist has been exiled in the wilderness?' I said, helping myself to the least bitter of the little oranges.

'Oh, that's old news!' Mary said testily.

'I thought James the Christ supported him.'

'James can live with it,' she said. I sucked the orange. She could not know I had dreamt so vividly of James falling down before Joshua – if my dream was true, not wishful thinking. Mary pricked her finger. 'It's Joshua I worry about!' she burst out. 'He can't look after himself. He was a disaster at sea apparently. Shipwrecked twice. No profit on the voyage.' She bit her finger to bring out the blood, let a drip fall like a drop of her life.

'It's always the most difficult ones we love the most,' I said. That did make her stare.

'You?' she said. 'Still? Even now?'

I said simply: 'He is my Lord.'

Salome and Miri giggled. Mary sent them away with an irritated gesture, turned to me earnestly. She wanted to talk with me more, much more. But the gate burst open, setting Miri screaming. Then we saw that the man who staggered through was James, covered in dust, his hair white with travel, eyes red-rimmed. He limped to his mother on

228

bleeding feet, threw himself down with his head on her knees. And he wept. He wept his heart out. His tears poured pink runnels down his face. 'I'm fallen!' he cried. 'Mother, I am cast down.'

She stroked his hair. 'James, James.'

He clenched his fists in her white linen shift. 'I do everything right. I live righteously. I pray. I give up my soul to prayer. I bathe five times each day in cold water to preserve my virginity. I worship each jot and tittle of the Law. None is more rigorous in observance than I, or more busy with good works, or more active in charity.' He showed his horny yellow knees and elbows. 'Prayer every hour of the day and night, only minutes for sleep. Only pure food. Only clean water. No one is more holy than I am. No one can be more holy than I am. I am the eldest legitimate son. I was born circumcised.'

She wiped away his tears. 'Yes, you were born without a foreskin.'

James said: 'Joshua has walked on the water.'

Mary, and Salome, and Miri stared at him stupidly. Silas came through wiping his hands on a cloth. He said, 'Joshua has walked on the water?'

James put the heels of his hands to his eyes. 'Joshua walked on the water and everyone saw it.'

'Perhaps it was shallow water,' Silas said ponderously.

'Or ice,' Miri said.

James screamed at them. 'Don't you understand? *Joshua walked on the water!*'

I said, 'I saw it.' They all looked at me. I nodded. 'I dreamed it. I saw it. He walked on the water and then he walked away.'

They stood in silence. Then Salome said, 'Where did he walk to?'

'Anywhere, as long as it's away,' Mary said. 'Anywhere's safer than Sion. He has to get away from Simon.'

'Simon's followed him,' James said. 'And Judas. The zealots, the sicariots, the toughs, the rabble, all of them. Oh, and the devout.'

Mary put her fingers to her mouth. 'His life is in danger.' She was still thinking like his mother, and I supposed she always would.

'Mother,' James said. 'Mother, your son has walked on the water. Nothing is the same.'

'We'll never find him in the desert,' Mary said, then pressed her fingers tight. 'Suppose Simon finds him?'

I realised I still held the orange skin, put it down, stood up. 'Joshua will go to John the Baptist,' I said.

James nodded. 'I agree.'

'The Baptist's in Idumea or Perea.' Mary jumped up. 'At least we can try. Silas, the donkey. Call Joses. Warm clothing, the desert's cold at night.' I saw her making a mental list. 'We go at once.' I put my warm cloak around her shoulders. She touched the rich colour, then looked into my eyes.

'It will keep you warm,' I said. 'I'm coming with you.'

'You have no cloak.'

'I'll get another from Levi. He has hundreds.' I laughed as the donkey brayed mournfully at the sight of its panniers. The women scattered busily, and as soon as we were alone I caught James's shoulder.

'You know the Recognition's going to happen, James. You've kept in contact with the Baptist and his side of the zadokite faction. Spies, runners, secret alliances – I know what you little boys get up to. I know you know where the Baptist is.'

James sighed. 'He's already promised to recognise *me*. To baptise me in the new way, once, for life.'

'When was this deal done?'

'He needs me.'

'Everything's changed.'

James glanced round to make sure we weren't overheard, then burst out, 'Mary, I believe in Jesus Christ, but I don't believe in Joshua!' He covered his mouth, whispered, 'Just because he walks on water doesn't make him the Son of God.'

'Yes it does,' I said.

'Still the same old Mary,' he whispered. 'You hate me because you once loved me and you couldn't love me enough. You're a failure. You've always been a failure.'

James was so sad my heart went out to him. 'Listen to the hatred in your voice,' I said. 'You hate me so much you hate all of us. You can even lie to me because you don't love me any more. But you're just lying to yourself.'

'All I love is God. The search for God. Damn you, you're spoiling everything.' Then James groaned. 'The Baptist is exactly where you'd expect him to be.'

I understood. 'A baptist can't baptise in a desert. There's no water.'

'Exactly.' James helped Joses and Silas tighten the panniers. 'The River Jordan.'

This is what happened.

The road from Sepphoris to the oasis which is all that remains of Jericho is good, though expensive, and roughly follows the downhill course of the Jordan southward from the Sea of Galilee to the Dead Sea. From the hilltop we saw the silty river curling in the desert like a fat brown worm. Herod's lonely palace had attracted a few dwellings and skinny boys with goats, but when we went into the inn that evening we saw few signs of life. First thing in the morning, that changed.

We'd have no difficulty finding John.

There weren't many people, but the wide open landscape made the most of them, knots of travellers moving along the footpaths in roughly the same direction, eastward towards the river, families in groups of one or two moving together, only scrawny dedicated individuals left with nothing to steal travelling alone. Mostly they were Essenes of the village tribes. The word was out. As their paths tangled near the Jordan the travellers became a thin crowd. Some gathered near the cool of the water until the mosquitoes rose, then withdrew to scattered camps on the dry dung-coloured hills, watching the scene in the natural amphitheatre below them. The men slept in the heat of the day, mothers fed their children inside their voluminous robes. We heard the Baptist before we saw him, his cawing unmistakable voice crowing repentance, barrenness, the coming of Heaven. It was the harshness of his message that attracted, the coming anger and wrath of God, richly deserved. God made His people suffer to teach them wisdom. No man or woman mattered, only the good of the people. One land, one people, one God, one baptism. 'That man has God in his voice,' a black-bearded man exulted. Mary and I sat beneath an olive tree watching the starved sun-blackened figure of the Baptist prancing in the shallows dressed only in a camel-hair sack and leather belt. 'It's true,' Mary said, 'he does have God in his voice. If you close your eyes.'

'He lives only on locusts and wild honey,' the bearded man nodded.

'It's illegal to eat locusts unless they're boiled alive,' his wife said, 'And it's a sin to eat bee larva. Anyway, where have you seen bees?'

'Carobs and date honey then,' said the bearded man. He made a face. 'He's that holy.'

A Pharisee called out to John, 'On what authority do you baptise?'

John leapt on to a rock in midstream. 'I baptise only unto repentance. But I shall be followed by one who shall baptise with the Holy Spirit and with fire. Fire! Fire, and eternal damnation upon the wicked!'

'He's got demons in him,' said an old man in Essene robes.

'He's not laying hands on me,' the Pharisee said. He got up. 'Where's the tavern?'

'They only sell repentance here,' the old man said. He hated all Pharisees, and after the Pharisee's back was turned swore all Pharisees were vipers born of vipers. 'You're right to flee Jerusalem from the wrath to come! Confess your sins! Only repentance here today; you can't buy anything else.' He pointed his trembling finger. 'Who's that?'

'It's Joshua.' Mary and I scrambled to our feet. Joshua walked slowly along the river bank dressed in seamless white. Mary ran down to him followed by James and his brothers and sisters. I followed the family more slowly. One of John's disciples, Nathanael, moved forward and intercepted James, speaking. James nodded, then the family gathered round Joshua. He embraced his mother. She asked all the questions I wanted to ask. Was he well? Had he eaten? You look too thin. I was sure Joshua's glance flashed at me, a secret smile, but the moment was so incongruous I thought I must be mistaken. Mary grew angry with her son. What are you doing here, Joshua? Don't you know how dangerous it is? She saw Simon and Judas behind him and her body stiffened with dislike.

232

James said in a low voice, 'John has agreed to baptise Joshua for the remission of sins.'

Mary was furious. 'How can Joshua be baptised? He has no sins, he's the Son of God. To forgive his sins is an impossible contradiction.'

'That's John's offer. And not forgiveness, only remission.'

'He has to acknowledge Joshua as the Son of God.'

'Then he cannot be baptised.'

'My Lord.' I spoke quietly to Joshua, and the others fell silent. 'What would you have us do?'

Joshua held out his hands. 'Come,' he said. 'Follow me.' He took my fingers lightly, his mother on his other side, and guided us forward along the river bank towards John. The Baptist stood on the rock like a bird, staring at us, then pranced fastidiously through the shallow water. In his hunger and piety he had bitten his lips ragged, consuming himself, his own meat. He had eyes only for Joshua. 'Is it true?' he asked. 'What they say?'

Joshua said: 'Who knows what men say?'

Fresh blood trickled on John's chin. 'On the sea. You. Walking.'

Joshua turned. Simon and Judas stood among the bushes of the river bank, watching. Whenever I saw one of them, I knew there were fifty. I saw Yeshua Barabbas the knife man, Dositheus, others.

Joshua said, 'Ask those men what their eyes saw.'

John drew a breath. 'Have they come to kill me?'

'Man, there is only life here today,' Joshua said.

John put his head on one side, scratched his long crawling hair. He squeezed painfully at his lips with his gums; his teeth were entirely rotted away by black honey. He looked starved and exhausted. 'So,' he said. 'Not today.'

Joshua bent down. He whispered, 'There is no death here today. Bring me to life.'

John wriggled his lips over his gums. 'I still can't believe it's you,' he said. 'The abomination. Meat-eater. Wine-drinker.' He drew back from Joshua's touch.

'He walked on the water,' James said.

Simon called out, 'I saw it.' Judas called the same. Peter and Andrew looked at them suspiciously. Nathanael stood talking with John's chief disciple, Apollos.

'If I forgive your sins, Joshua,' John muttered, 'you will sin no more?'

'When I am baptised,' Joshua said, 'you will see what is sin.' He raised his arms to the crowd. For the first time I realised the crowd watched him, not John. Someone called out encouragement.

'Very well,' John grumbled. He took Joshua's elbow. 'This water's infernally shallow.' They splashed out to midstream. Joshua's shift floated around his waist, pulled out by the river. Both men leant against the muddy current. 'Will you fulfil all righteousness?' Then John seized Joshua and thrust him beneath the water in the symbolic drowning.

John's arms straightened, pushed into the water to his shoulders. He drew deep breaths, then held his breath, staring up. The reality of everything around us grew intense, brilliant. The sun was in the world. I have never seen the sky so blue or the trees so green or the river so brown, so muddy, so full of life.

The blue sky above us opened on the stars. I do not mean an eclipse. The noon sky was seized from outside and inside and opened and through it poured not darkness but light, and I saw each star was a dove. The white doves poured down around us from the sky, fluttering around our heads and the olive trees and swooping across the water carrying twigs from the trees, whirling around the Baptist who stared up with his rotten mouth gaping. Then the Baptist stared down at the water and his arms going down into the water and for the first time I saw something very strange. Later I saw it many times, in fact always, but this was the first time I realised what I saw. The good in most men does not recognise Jesus immediately. Godly men probably never do recognise Him. But the evil in men and women and children always knows Him at once. Always. John stood immersed to his armpits like a man swept away by the flood. 'My Lord!' he cried with the last of his breath. 'My Lord, forgive me! I have sinned!'

Joshua rose from the water. The drops showered from his hair and face and open eyes.

And for the second time in my life I heard the voice of God in Heaven calling down to Joshua. The voice was high and sweet, pure as a song, what these Jews call *bat qôl*, daughter of voice.

'You are my beloved Son, in whom I am well pleased.'

The doves whirled upward on the wind, and the sky closed. The dim sunny day returned.

We stared longingly at the blue infinite dull sky.

'You are not a dead man.' Joshua spoke to John. 'Work with me.'

John croaked, 'What is my work?'

Joshua said: 'Your work is mine.'

But everyone still stared at the sky, even John.

Joshua walked ashore. He walked among our staring faces. He took a winnowing fork from one staring peasant and walked among the disciples of John the Baptist touching one, now two, now three with the winnowing fork. 'Come. Follow me.' They followed him, Peter, Andrew, Philip, I forget the others. Still more he pushed back. Apollos, Nathanael, Lazarus, men of ability, bowed respectfully but chose to stay with John. Others merely shook when they were chosen, rooted to the ground. Joshua's white shift steamed as it dried and I smelt his body and the silt of the river clinging to him. Simon he touched with the winnowing fork, and Judas. He needed them. He touched Thomas his younger brother, his hair Nazarene-long, and now so similar in looks to Joshua that some thought Thomas to be Joshua's twin not Miri's. Despite the miracle he had seen, Thomas hesitated before permitting the touch of the winnowing fork.

John, awaking from his trance, stumbled from the river.

'Behold the Lamb of God!' He fell at Joshua's feet. 'Behold, the Lamb of God, whose shoes I am not worthy to tie! He shall gather in the good wheat to Heaven, and the chaff He shall burn with unquenchable fire.'

God had not said *Lamb*. He had said *Son*. Still these people tried to lie to themselves. John could not face the truth even when it poured from the mouth of God and the miracle of the sky. In his heart no Jew really believes any Jew is better than himself. The reality of God, I saw, is not the same as the worship of Him. The reality is here, among us, part of us, *with* us, in the white linen shoulder blades and long brown hair of Joshua moving through the crowd with the winnowing fork. But part of John's mind, however great the evidence of his senses, still tried to deny the truth of what he saw with his own eyes.

Joshua's hair was dry now, as glossy as mine. He walked faster through the crowd, then dropped the fork. His strides lengthened. I ran after him. The crowd thinned, their faces falling behind us. When it suited him, he turned so quickly I bumped into his chest.

'My Lord,' I whispered, 'You did not choose me.'

'You're a woman.'

'You refuse me because I am a woman?'

'The others would not allow it. They wouldn't believe in me.'

'My Lord!' I cried out.

He touched the palm of his hand to the top of my hair. 'Mary.'

I collapsed. My heart broke. I fell on my arm and agony exploded through me like fire. *He shall gather in the good wheat to Heaven, and the chaff He shall burn with unquenchable fire.* I was chaff. I reached out my hand to his foot, but he stepped back. 'Listen,' he said. 'Follow me.'

He threw out his arms, and I realised he had come on to a low hilltop.

Then he said nothing, and the crowd waited.

Then Joshua began to speak. First he spoke rough Aramaic to all the ordinary Jews, filthy, tattered, sick with travelling and hard life. 'You who've got ears had better listen. You who've got eyes had better open them. You who have hearts better lift them up to God. I come to bring you good news and to heal the broken-hearted and the blind.'

He spoke precise Hebrew to the village Essenes. 'Amun, the Spirit of the Lord is upon me, because today He has anointed me to preach the gospel to the Poor. Blessed are the Poor, for yours is the kingdom of Heaven. Blessed are the Meek, for you shall inherit the earth. Blessed are the Pure, for you shall see God.'

He turned to John and spoke words for him. 'Blessed are the Righteous who are persecuted, for yours also is the kingdom of Heaven. You are blessed when men revile you and persecute you and say evil against you for my sake.' John stared raptly. His view of the world was fulfilled.

Joshua turned to Simon and Judas, the zealots and sicariots and toughs holding knives, staves, stones. 'You are the Salt of the earth. If the Salt should lose its savour, it is good for nothing. Be a light of the world, a city that cannot be hidden. Let your light shine before men so that they see your good works.'

Joshua turned to James, to the priests and the scribes. 'Do not think I have come to destroy the Law, or the words of the prophets. I have come not to destroy but to fulfil. Till Heaven and Earth come to pass, not one jot or tittle shall pass from the Law. Whoever breaks the least of the commandments, and teaches so, shall be least in Heaven.'

He spoke straight to James. 'Unless your righteousness exceeds the righteousness of the scribes and Pharisees, you shall not enter the kingdom of Heaven.' Then he spoke gently but with force in his brother's ear. 'Whoever is angry with his brother without cause is in danger of judgment. But if you remember that your brother has nothing against you—' he paused, and James trembled, then Joshua held out his arms. 'Be reconciled with your brother!'

James gripped him. 'My Lord.'

John said, 'My Lord, will you cast out the Herods from their palaces?'

Simon and Judas said, 'Yes, cast out the Romans and the Greeks from the City of the Moon and renew the Covenant in the Temple. You are the Christ!'

A Pharisee spoke with smiling reason. 'Does this Christ claim to forgive sins, or merely offer repentance?'

Joshua said: 'You shall see what I forgive.'

'On what authority?'

Joshua said coldly: 'Today you see my authority.'

He spoke more, much more. It was the most brilliant speech I have ever heard. Ever. He finished as he began. He gave to John what John wanted. James was reconciled. The Poor heard what they wanted to hear. He impressed the righteous with his righteousness and the lawmakers with his knowledge of the Law. Everyone was offered a place at his table, and everyone accepted. I sensed them pushing forward, hungry, each wanting a part of him, seeing something of him in themselves, making themselves larger with him. Several touched his hem. A woman said, 'I felt his ankle, he's warm,' and I wanted to kick her. My old jealous demon was not quite gone, it seemed. I was still human. Again I thought I saw myself in the corner of Joshua's eye, and realised he laughed at me. No, he laughed with me. He knew what he had done and left undone.

He fell silent, and the people realised darkness fell. They came to themselves, realising how far they were from home, and a cold night coming. I watched them stream away towards the villages nearer Jerusalem, then realised Joshua had gone quietly in the opposite direction. I saw him speaking with the followers he had chosen, standing beneath the spreading terebinth tree where they sat, and I didn't dare go close to them because of what he had said about the fact that I am a woman. The light failed but I heard the murmur of his voice continuing. The stars shone above the black tree. I wrapped my cloak around me, I could not possibly sleep. The pale shapes of the followers moved away from the tree, then the single figure of Joshua in his white shift strode away in the opposite direction. He did not need light to see. I stumbled after him and tripped on rocks, and fell, until he turned.

'Mary.'

'I'm not following them,' I said. I trembled. I knew I was losing him.

'Are you cold?'

He well knew how to make me hate him. 'You know I'm not cold. I have Levi's cloak.' I demanded furiously, 'What do you have? Nothing! You'll freeze!'

'Mary, don't be angry.' He sighed. 'They will follow me to Galilee.'

I waited. 'Will I follow you to Galilee?'

'Mary, only you know what you will do. You are not saved. Your will is your own.'

'If you go to Galilee I'll follow you there.'

He sighed. 'No, not Galilee. I have more important business in another place.' For an ecstatic moment I thought he meant Jerusalem. 'Alone.' He turned away. 'Alone.'

I watched his white shape dwindle, striding in the empty grey landscape, and the moon would rise before midnight.

He was easy to follow.

I'd not offered him my cloak. That's why I followed him. My gift. The ground sloped uphill. I puffed, sweating. Folded my cloak in my arms, too hot. It was too heavy. I carried it awkwardly with one arm then the other. His pale figure flickered ahead of me in the moonlight, climbing. The darkness above him turned to gold, the first of the sun illuminating the peak of Mount Quarantine. My feet skidded on the gravel debris. I crawled forward, slid back.

I sat on a rock and the sun warmed me while I watched him climb out of reach.

The mountain was crumbling, full of holes. Devout men and women since Neanderthal times and before have come here, monkeys and apes and men instinctively chipping out galleries and cells so slowly and patiently that they seem to have grown with the mountain, and now crumble away with the mountain. I saw Joshua's figure moving along the terraces high above the debris slopes. He disappeared into the rock.

Peculiar orange-winged blackbirds pecked around me, the first I had seen. I wore my cloak against the heat of the sun. Now I saw him climbing on a staircase hewn into the sheer rock, his midday shadow dragged like an exclamation down the rock face below him. On the tier near the waterfall he paused and drank while vultures, swifts, rock doves swirled below him in the sky. Then his tiny figure hung by his hands from the projecting rock, his feet standing in the air with nothing swinging below his bare soles for five hundred cubits; and then only I. He inched, then wriggled, and scrambled from sight. A last plume of yellow dust was swept over the edge into the air, and he was gone. Perhaps there was another tier of rocks above where I could see. Perhaps there was nothing.

The evening fell beautifully cool and I took off my cloak.

The night was cold and I wrapped myself in the cloak and slept, waiting. He did not come down.

In the first warmth of the sun I unwrapped myself from my cloak and followed the sound of a spring to the roots of an enormous zizyphus tree. By the pool I wrapped myself against the heat of the sun. Then I unwrapped myself, afraid to stay near the pool when the animals came down to drink. Then I wrapped myself against the cold of the night, waiting.

Joshua wore only a thin shift. I imagined the heat and the cold at the top of the mountain. I waited. I ate dates, but not the huge freshwater mussels in the pool, which are forbidden. I waited and frogs hopped around me, forgetting to fear me. When it rained the earth turned to glue, then green shoots, then to dust again. And I waited, talking to myself, and I began to understand why there was no sign of him.

Joshua must fulfil the prophecies and the ancient texts of his people before his entry into Jerusalem. I knew he would never go to Galilee; and Jesus Christ never appointed eleven disciples to follow Him as Judas the Galilean had, and John the Baptist had. Those half-dozen he had chosen by the Jordan were a distraction that confused me, because traditionally John alone straightened the path and cleared the way for the Christ to enter Jerusalem, no disciples. I was sure they would never take up their appointments, if their enthusiasm sustained them so far, which it would not, any more than Joshua would really return to Galilee, which is a province of no importance. A man great in Galilee is less than the dust in Jerusalem.

And where had John gone now? Why was he not here with his master?

I was not thirsty, but I was hungry. Light-headed with hunger.

I imagined Joshua's hunger.

I imagined Joshua's thirst.

How long can a man sit on the baking, freezing peak of a mountain? The forty years the Jews spent in the wilderness? Hardly. But Moses was tested for forty days. So was Elijah.

Joshua would stay on the mountain for forty days.

I waited. I counted. When shepherds wandered up the gorge I bought food. On the morning of the forty-first day I walked to the village, and in the afternoon I returned heavily laden. A terrific storm hung around the mountain top. Lightning struck down, and then the rain came. I sheltered under my cloak peeping out at the lightning in the night, seeing only blinding raindrops and stark rocks, and Joshua's bare feet.

I saw Joshua's bare feet in the mud, and his tattered white shift clinging to his knees, clinging sodden to his whole body, his body so thin that when the lightning flashed I thought I saw a skeleton. A transparent man. I saw through him. I saw through his hair as the lightning flashed, saw through his eyes, saw myself.

Joshua had come down from the mountain.

He staggered, splashed forward, fell splashing me with mud and water, banged into me. He weighed nothing. His body curled up in the mud at my feet like a birth-wet baby, shivering, shuddering. I lay down in the mud and rainwater beside him and wrapped us in my cloak. Wrapped him in my arms. Gave him my warmth. Hugged his head between my breasts with my arms. Felt the intense simple complete-and-utter love that a mother feels for her newborn child. 'Oh, Joshua.' I knew I would never have a child of my own. He had his mother, and she was not me. Even so, the intensity of the moment washed over me and my eyes, I couldn't help myself, filled with tears.

His head moved. He licked my tears with his tongue. He caressed and embraced me as though I were returning from captivity.

Joshua sat up. His hands grew warm, filled with blood. He touched my breasts. 'No,' I said tenderly, 'I'm not her. You can't drink.' He threw off the cloak, letting in the cold night air, but the rain had stopped. He stood easily, the strength coming into his legs.

'I brought you food,' I offered eagerly, proud of myself. 'Bread. Dates. Buttermilk.'

He stared at me. 'You're cold.'

'I'm all right,' I said. 'Eat.'

He put out his hand and a small pile of stones nearby burst into flame. He threw on a few more stones and held out my hands to warm them, then opened my shift and took my cold breasts in his warm hands, my nipples between his fingers feeling the radiating heat of the fire. I did not know what he would do. He kissed me on the mouth. It was wrong. I kissed Joshua's mouth, I felt his lips, I felt my heavy breasts fill his hands. I said to my body, 'No.' I lay back on the fire-warmed ground; I could not resist, would not. I said, 'No, quickly.' My fingernails tore his white linen, I held him. I felt his circumcised penis fill with blood. I looked into his eyes, and he moved into my heart. I felt him touch me there. Felt him completely, everywhere. For an instant I ceased to exist.

The clouds drifted away from the stars, or the stars drifted away from the clouds, I could not tell. I lay beneath the stars listening to the stones crackle and sparks rise. Later we lay alone in the desert except for the stars. And therefore not alone.

Joshua sat eating a date. He was thin. I wished he'd put on weight. His spine stuck out in knobs from his back. He spat out a date-stone and the fire hissed, consuming it. He spat out another, just as accurately. He looked lovely in the firelight and shadows. I stroked his back, the knobbles, his ribs, his ragged white linen. 'I know you,' he said. 'I know everything about you.'

I kissed his skin.

'I know,' he said. 'You do love who I am completely. And you're so afraid.'

'I am afraid.' I sat behind him with my legs and arms around him, feeling with my face the bones working in his jaw as he ate. 'Do you love me?' I asked. 'Can you?'

'More than you know.'

A circumcised man is more naked, more bare, more vulnerable than any other. I touched it and it rose up in my hand. 'Do I know everything about you?'

'No.'

'Will I ever?'

'No.' He kissed my hand. 'But you believe you will.'

I let him go and pretended to sulk. 'What happened to you on the mountain top?'

'Thirst. Hunger. Wild beasts. The Devil.'

'What does the Devil look like?'

'Whatever He wants to look like.'

'The God of this world is a serpent. A dragon. Satan. He knew you, didn't he, Joshua?'

'The Devil knows almost everything.'

'What did He offer you?'

'What the Devil always offers. Knowledge. Power. Certainty. Pride. Destruction.'

'Am I the Devil?' I asked him quietly. 'Do I work against you? Will I destroy you?'

He looked surprised. 'How can you? You are my love.'

'That's what I mean. I love you with all my heart.' A brown bear came through first light to drink at the pool. Joshua listened raptly to its lapping tongue. 'Look at me, Joshua. Look at me! I'm naked with you, I've let you down. Contaminated you. Polluted you.'

'That's James talking.' He spat a pip. 'And the Sons of Light.'

'I've a cold puddle under my bottom exactly like any other man's, believe me.'

He shrugged. 'I am a man, nothing less.'

'You know what your enemies will say.' I said the word. 'Fornication.'

'Who will tell them?' He turned comfortably, raised his knees on each side of my hips, spoke into my eyes. 'For the moment I have no enemies. Am I denied love? Am I denied marriage? Do I have no happiness? Do I fill my life with denial, like James and John? Fill myself with pride in celibacy and denial and the piety of the calluses on my knees and the completeness of my loss, experiencing nothing of life?'

I put my finger to his lips, touched the tip of my nose to the tip of his nose. 'Will you go into Jerusalem?'

He touched me where you know. 'You are my temple, Mary.'

'Don't speak to me like that. Could you do what you must do?'

'Destroy the Temple? Yes.'

'And rebuild it in three days?'

'Easily. But whose will would I be fulfilling, Mary? The prophecies were written by men. Who whispered in their ears? My Father? Or would I be doing the Devil's work?' Joshua's breath smelt of dates. He scratched his beard then stood up, pulled what was left of his shift over his head. His loincloth was already gone, of course, mixed up in my cloak. His skin was white and soft, his long hair and beard protected his face, so only his hands were dark. He slipped awkwardly into the pool, cursed as he twisted his toe on a rock, then gave a sigh of pleasure. He ducked under then reclined with only his head showing. 'Lie beside me, Mary.'

'No!'

His eyes moved past me. A scraggy lion watched us hungrily from the rocks. I slid into the water beside Joshua. He grinned and held out a date in his hand. The lion limped forward buzzing with flies, lowered its great chops, and ate the date. 'A starving lion,' Joshua said sadly.

'It stinks.'

'He's so hungry that his body consumes his own internal organs. Like John the Baptist.'

I said, 'Actually he looks like John the Baptist.' Joshua laughed. There. The Son of God laughed. In fact he laughed until he shook. I washed my hair. He watched me with intense concentration. 'I love you, Mary,' he said. There. He had said that too. The impossible.

The lion rolled, scratching the warts and ticks on its back, then shook itself. The dust came out of its fur, revealing the yellow gloss of health. It yawned and walked away without a limp. 'Are you a lion to a lion?' I asked.

'No. God made Man in His image.'

'When you're crowned in Jerusalem I'll never see you again. You'll instruct us in righteousness and purity and cleanliness, and we shall be a saved people. But I shall remember today. The day I sinned. But I'll never want to confess it or change it.' The sun was about to rise above the horizon. 'You could stop the sun rising,' I said urgently.

He said: 'Now you do sound like the Devil.'

I relaxed, put my head on his chest. 'I saw you build that church in Britain to your mother, near the tor.'

'I'm not a church, Mary. It was a shelter. No sins, no shame, no guilt, no priests, no church.'

I looked at him sharply, then relaxed again. 'Only the Kingdom.'

The orange-winged blackbirds came down to drink around us, then mobbed one bird that dragged its wing. They returned to drink, but slowly the broken-winged bird dragged itself forward almost to the water's edge. Joshua reached out and picked it up. He trickled water from his mouth against its beak, stroking its head with the tip of his forefinger, and as the bird fluttered weakly in its ecstasy he broke its neck with a single quick twist. I stared. 'Why?'

'Do you think I did wrong?'

'You can't do wrong.'

He dug a hole in the sand with his fingers, slipped the body inside, swept dust over the place. 'Then seek the reason.'

I sighed. 'I suppose everything has its place. Its season. But it seems cruel. You could have used your gift.'

'The word you want is mercy. Mercy. My gift's in everyone, Mary. They don't have the eyes to see it or the hearts to feel it. The disease had spread from its liver throughout its body; its broken wing was the least thing. If you touched the bird as you touch me you would have known it.' He looked at me directly. 'With faith, anyone can live for ever.'

I said bitterly, 'Why should they want to?'

He said: 'For love.'

I wondered, how far does a man see into a woman? How much does he really know, or am I completely mysterious to him?

He watched my eyes. 'I know what you are, Mary. A survivor.'

He stood from the pool and let the sun dry him.

I asked, 'Are you walking to Jerusalem today?'

'No.'

'You're not going to Jerusalem?' I sat up and he smiled at my breasts. I covered them with my hands. 'But you must go. You *do* go. You bring certainty. You save us.' He strapped on his loincloth. 'Don't go. Joshua, which religion is right? The Pharisees, the Sadducees, the Essenes? The Cynics?'

He didn't stop laughing. 'No religion is right, Mary. God is God, but religion is made by men. All the religions in the world can't show more than God's little toenail. God – believe me, Mary! – is not only more wonderful than you imagine, God is more wonderful than you *can* imagine.'

'Where are you going to lead us?' I stood up, dripping, put one arm across my breasts, covered my other place with my hand. 'Where are you going?'

He swung his useless shift over his shoulder. 'To Galilee.'

'To *Galilee*?'

'Yes, to preach in Galilee. You'll understand.'

I gaped. 'To preach what?'

'Forgiveness. Tolerance. Salvation. Mercy. Love.'

'*What?*'

He gave a cheerful wave and jumped downhill from rock to rock. I gazed after him stupidly.

He called back over his shoulder: 'The truth, Mary. To preach the truth.'

AMO

I love

He didn't even let me follow him.

But I did follow him, leaving the fire of stones burning – for all I know it burns there still – leaping after him from rock to rock down the Kelt gorge until I lost sight of him. Lizards scuttled downhill past me, frogs and the ugliest toads I have ever seen hopped by, scorpions emerged skittering from under every rock. Snakes slithered, fish jumped in the stream. Below me birds swept and wheeled above him, showing the place far ahead where he was, fluttering wrens, ravens, doves, sandgrouse, griffon-vultures and eagles sweeping from the cliffs. By noon they were the only sign remaining of him, swirling specks following him in the heat-shimmering plain, and he was too far away for me to see him even though I knew where to look.

I stopped, tired and sweating, and drank. As I knelt a drop of semen trickled on my thigh and I stared at it with a sensation of horror. Perhaps I was pregnant. My God, what had I done? The semen of the Son of God must be swarming with life, this single drop would make a thousand women with child, ten thousand. I picked up the white blob on my fingertip. What should I do? Flick it away? I imagined the myriad lives it contained being extinguished, eaten by fishes. I slipped the cold bead back inside me and left it to the will of God. But if I was pregnant, what would I do? Jesus Christ never made anyone pregnant. He never slept with anyone or was even tempted to, so far as we know.

He certainly never kissed any girl on the mouth, as he kissed me.

But if I was silent, no one would know. No one must know.

At the road across the plain I met a party of virtuous ladies returning from expensive sacrifices in the Jerusalem Temple. They were rich, but saw my cloak was fine, and so invited me to join their noisy company on their return to Tiberias. Tiberias is Herod's new city on the Sea of Galilee not far from Magdala. After fanning themselves in the heat of the day the women chattered excitedly as we walked northward through the cool evening, the sons of one of the older ladies keeping guard around us, another running ahead to reserve accommodation. They had heard of Joshua – a handsome prophet is always at an advantage – but they'd not heard of his walking on the water. The miracle of the sky opening over the Jordan they believed to be John's work. John's disciples – though fewer than they had been – were well established, and Apollos and Nathanael were clever with facts. The end of the world was coming. But the innkeeper told us John had been handed over and arrested by Herod whose family life, fornication, incest and intrigues John had preached against so relentlessly. Herod, crazy in a cunning way, rather respected John for his simple crazy holiness. But John's mouth never stopped, and so now, the innkeeper went on, it was said he was shut up in the vast silent fortress of Machaeros where his insults would not be heard.

I saw Simon the Zealot's hand in this betrayal of John, and Judas's hand too, probably through Barabbas. The zealots were behind Joshua now, Joshua who they believed would throw out the Romans from Judah and inaugurate the Covenant, the days of vengeance. I stared from the window of the inn at the stars overhanging the distant hills where Joshua had taken me in love, and put my hands to my head. Joshua who spoke now of love and peace and truth.

I got away from the rich women at the junction near Tiberias and took the risk of travelling alone, following the dusty valleys uphill to Sepphoris. By the Community of the Nazarenes the door of Levi's house creaked open under my hand, and the house felt more silent than I have ever known it. My footsteps echoed, and I heard a weak sigh.

I found Levi lying in his bed, perfectly calm, his perfect white hands clasped over his chest. He smiled weakly, but he was ready to die. He was dying because he wanted to – or rather, he no longer wanted to live – and nothing I could do would change him. I fed him, but he withered away. I gave him water to drink, but he was dying of thirst. It seemed such a waste for Joshua to have brought him back to life. 'What do you expect your death will achieve?' I asked him finally.

Levi whispered, 'Justice.' And he died.

A few days later Mary arrived back home with James, Salome and Miri. They'd been in Capernaum and both girls sulked because they wanted to stay there. 'Capernaum's lovely,' Salome said, her eyes shining as she greeted me in the yard. 'It's on the north shore of Galilee,' she added, pulling me in.

'Yes, Sal, I know where Capernaum is.'

'Josh's there and everyone's talking about him. He stays at this big, *huge* house of Peter's near the shore. Peter's short and losing his hair and he's got a square face and a square curly beard. Josh *will* call him Peter though that isn't his real name, and he lives on bread and olives not fish. Uncle Pete's got fishing boats and hired men. People hang about all day and all night waiting for Josh to come out of the gates, and when he does they scream. They all run after him, calling their friends, and they pull at his clothes, locks of his hair, they got off his sandal once. It's frightening. How badly they want things of him.' She tried to put something strange to her into words. 'How much suffering there is. How much need, even among the most dreadful and undeserving people. I never realised they were there, I never saw them, but Joshua sees them all the time and so they see *him*. He knows how much they suffer and how much they need him and he knows he can help them.' She squeezed my hand earnestly. 'You have to see it to understand it.'

Miri tugged my other hand. She wanted me to know she'd seen it too. 'It's embarrassing sometimes.' She blushed. 'When they mob him in the streets he has to run like a hunted animal. They love him! Sometimes he preaches to them from an anchored boat. They'd pull him to pieces on land. They're such rough nasty people! The lowest. Some of them smell like pigs. I hate it. There are lots of better people for him to preach to and we're trying to make him. At the moment Peter pays for everything.'

'They just want to see miracles,' I said. I couldn't believe they wanted to hear Joshua's odd ideas, so alien to this culture – and only words. Words aren't bread and money to real people.

'No, it's not miracles. They listen to him and he heals them,' Salome said in her outgoing businesslike way. 'He healed Peter's mother-in-law. And he taught in the synagogue last Sabbath! You should have heard him! You should have seen the dumbstruck faces of the Pharisees!'

I imagined the hawklike faces of those fierce learned men of the Scripture and proponents of the wrath of God hearing Joshua's message of forgiveness and tolerance, salvation, mercy and love for the first time. 'Yes, I can imagine their faces,' I said.

'But you should see all the people coming into Capernaum to see Joshua!' Miri said. 'Awful people. They're terribly unpopular and everyone closes their shutters tight before sunset to keep them out, and stallholders won't let them in the market because they haven't got money to pay.'

'Who are they?'

'Poor people. Poorer than I've ever seen. They must dress up for it. And the worst thing is, they drag other poor people in after them. People with disgusting diseases who lie in rags on the street corners groaning and begging, covered with flies.' I've done it myself, I thought. 'So the elders have asked Joshua to leave, because he's bringing the town a bad reputation. But Uncle Pete's a powerful citizen and his wife's family is one of the wealthiest. And of course her mother would do anything for Joshua. She serves his food with her own hands.'

'And the poor people actually pretend to understand Joshua's message?'

Salome laughed awkwardly. 'Josh says they're the only ones who do.'

Whatever was happening in Capernaum was new and extraordinary. There was no precedent for it in the teachings of Jesus Christ. I knew I had to go to Capernaum. I had to see it for myself. I finished talking to the girls then on my way out I overheard James talking to Mary at a window. I paused behind the fig tree.

James sounded furious. 'Thank the Lord that Simon's kept busy at Sion so he's not in Capernaum to hear Joshua, that's all. You've heard your son preaching to scum, unwashed scum, people who haven't eaten kosher in their lives, thieves, bandits, beggars, telling them whatever they want to hear. You know he can't square those promises with what he's promised the Poor. When he sees me coming he talks of righteousness and purity and deserving God by good works, but he looks bored. I don't think Thomas is fooled, either. But Joshua's got the worthless people and women eating out of his hand.'

I definitely had to get to Capernaum, right away.

Mary sighed. 'He can't preach love, it's not a workable philosophy,' was the last I heard her say. 'But salvation, I can see that. He could allow you to baptise in his name if he won't do it himself.'

'Me? Peter's closest to him,' James said. 'He uses Peter to keep me from the inner circle. And these farmers and fishermen' – his voice struggled with the strength of his emotion – 'don't care about his illegitimacy at all, because they're all bastards themselves.'

I left them to their worry and unhappiness and returned home. I had little time.

Levi's house was now mine; at first light next day I saddled the donkey, closed the place up, and rather than take the high road across the Horns of Hattin to Magdala on the western shore of Galilee decided to pass by Sepphoris, taking the path by the stream that wanders through the bare hilly country towards Capernaum. The valley is lovely, full of olive groves, and the path twists and turns between gnarled orchards and the stream. I saw no other travellers; I was not thinking; I was surprised when men jumped down in front of me and behind. The leader of the bandits stepped forward, filthy, limping, his arm bandaged. 'Scream all you like,' he said. He seemed disappointed when I made no sound.

I asked, 'Are you thieves?'

One of the men said, 'Let's kill her.' He touched me.

'She's got skin like honey. Look at her eyes.'

I thought of Joshua. I knew these men would steal my donkey, my money, my clothes, rape my naked body, and kill me. I could see in their eyes what would happen, and they knew what I saw. Terror added to their power over me, but they were not evil men, and strangely I felt no terror. What mercy, love or tolerance had they ever known? All I felt were my thoughts of Joshua. Perhaps they were the sort of men who followed him. I said, 'You've lost your land.' I looked at their worn hands. 'You're farmers.'

'I was a farmer,' the leader admitted. 'And you aren't talking your way out of it.' He grabbed the reins with his good arm, but I'd already slid from the saddle and stood in front of him. In fact I stood taller than he, because well fed, whereas he'd endured years of hunger. 'Peace be with you,' I told the men. Their wives had been taken along with their land, they didn't know where their children were, they'd lost everything. 'You're hungry and tired. In pain.' I touched his arm with my twisted arm, and he knew I understood the truth. I put my cloak around his shoulders, took the bag of gold coins from my belt, scattered them among the trees, and his men scattered after them. 'The donkey is yours,' I promised him, 'and the cloak.' I whispered in his ear, 'Peace be with you, and God will save you in Capernaum.'

And I walked away, and no one thought to stop me.

Out of sight I trembled, then an odd elation rushed through me. I had spoken in good faith. Joshua's words worked. His new words which had never been said before worked, his new beliefs which had never been believed before actually achieved results. Engaged the hearts of men and women. Changed them. I had seen it. I was alive.

For the first time I clearly understood that Joshua could change this world, change it for the better. He could change this world into Heaven and Earth, make it God's world as he was ordained to do, make us God's people. He didn't have to destroy the Temple to inaugurate the Kingdom; simply change men's minds and fill their hearts with whatever he decreed. Joy. Love. Forgiveness. Anything.

I came into Capernaum, and Joshua was not there. I sensed it at once. After Nahum the town elder's mansion Peter's was one of the biggest houses, just south of the synagogue, and none of the women whose voices I could hear inside would even open the gate-hatch to speak with me. Many poor and sick lay outside Peter's gate, discarded by their families, and I tripped over one old woman and hurt my ankle. When I hobbled to the beach I found people shouting at the wind and waves. One of Peter's men mending nets pointed across the surf. 'His lordship's out there if you want to swim. Told 'em not to take the small boat, but the Rock don't change his mind for little things like the weather. Pushing his luck, I'd say.' I carried another bag of coins beneath my gown. 'They're out every day.' The fisherman bit the penny appreciatively. 'Sailing's the quickest way to get between the villages, see, Bethsaida where my master was born, Gergesa in the Gadarene, full of Greeks that is. Philotera, Amathus, Magdala. Not Tiberias. Herod's sick of anyone to do with John, tars 'em all with the same brush.' He fell silent, my penny used up.

I watched the little sail tossing among the waves, blown to the east, then found a length of driftwood for a stick and hobbled after them along the shore. The boat was hard to see now, the sail taken down as the wind and waves rose. After an hour's walk I saw the mast turn towards the Gadarene shore a couple of Roman miles ahead of me. The wind stilled abruptly and the waves curled higher, then fell calm in a few minutes as Galilee always does. In watery mirror-images of themselves men tugged the oars, splashed overboard, hauled the boat on to the beach in the shadow of the cliff. I saw Joshua's white gown going ashore, and ran towards him. I thought of nothing else, not how I would appear, my cloak gone, my ankle bruised. Joshua saw me but none of the other men did. They parted with surprised oaths as I dashed between them and threw myself at Joshua's feet, kissed his feet, his toes, his ankles. 'My Lord!' My hair fell over his feet. I wept, realising now how terrified my body had been as I was robbed.

Rough hands tried to pull me away, but Joshua said, 'This is a woman who knows me.' He lifted me up. 'Are you following me still, Mary?'

He knew what had happened to me but he wanted the men to hear my faith in him.

I told the simple truth. 'My Lord, to the ends of the

earth, until the end of the world.'

He nodded. 'And then in the kingdom of Heaven.'

He walked forward up the cliff path and I walked with him. I never noticed the disciples when I was with him, they were shadows, nonentities. They never said anything that I heard, Joshua's whisper overwhelmed them. They never saw anything for themselves, only what he showed them. They followed behind him like sheep, then vaguely I heard Peter come forward. 'My Lord, this isn't the way. We won't reach the village before dark.' I knew what Peter didn't like. He was afraid of contamination from the pig-Jews I could see living in this district, each outcast tending his hilltop livelihood of four or five pigs, fattening them in this unpopulated area for the Greeks of the Decapolis. The disciples muttered uneasily.

'This is the way,' Joshua told Peter. 'Follow me.' I followed him among the tombs of the Gadarenes, the stopped mouths of the houses of the dead pockmarking the deserted hillside above us. Peter called, 'My Lord, what is there here for us?'

'Look,' Joshua said. 'See.'

And I saw them. Creatures like the one I myself had once been. Human animals shambling forward towards us down the hillside that we had thought deserted but in fact swarmed with people, their brutal diseased faces and bodies distorted by hatred and fear, not of us, but of Joshua. They slobbered and grunted in their pain. The disciples drew back but Joshua walked forward, and I stepped in his footsteps. The men and women living in the tombs gathered gibbering and shrieking around us, enclosing us, some with broken chains rattling at their wrists or dragging from their ankles. Many were naked, but Joshua touched them. One man who was touched gave a terrible scream and fell writhing, gashing at his flesh with stones. Joshua knelt with him.

The man screamed, 'What have I to do with you, Joshua, Son of the most high God?' He emitted a shriek, arching to break his back. 'Don't hurt me!'

'What is your name?'

'My name is Legion.'

Joshua said: 'Come out of him.'

254

Everything came out of the man, whirling around us like a shrieking stinking wind, and Joshua raised his arms, and the demons in all the men and women and children who had gathered around us cried out that Joshua was the Son of God, and the evil and sickness of this world poured up out of them and rose over us so that the disciples choked on the stink of rottenness, disease, damnation. They covered their mouths and noses, shut their eyes in terror that the demons might find a way into them. Joshua took pity on his followers though they didn't deserve him, not one fingernail of him. He moved his hand and the demons rushed like darkness in the air, dashed shrieking into the pigs. The pigs rushed squealing from their sties and pens and the care of the pigmen and ran, falling to the rocks at the foot of the cliff, dashing themselves, bursting so their guts fell out, and silence fell.

I knelt at Joshua's side, held out my arms in prayer. 'My Lord. Don't be angry.'

The disciples stared, stunned. I heard Joses say, 'It's a lesson. He's teaching us that pigs are unclean.'

Peter found a stone, wiped off the vomit and worse filth spattering his cloak. He said rudely, 'We knew that already.'

Joshua looked around him at the calm, cleansed faces of the people who had been possessed. Some of them realised their nakedness and covered themselves but others fell at his feet. One little boy wept his heart out to discover he was well again and ran to find his mother. Others woke, blinking, to discover their fetters broken and chains cast away. They stumbled to their feet and looked for their friends. I wondered how they would ever take up their old lives.

Philip, born in the same town as Peter and speaking in the same rough accent, called out to Joshua, 'Now we know you are stronger than the Devil, Lord.' Some said six thousand pigs had died, the number of demons in Legion; others only five hundred. Even that number meant that almost a hundred pig-herders had lost their living and everything they owned. The pigmen tore their hair and threw stones until Peter drew his knife and ran at them so that they ran away.

Joshua knelt beside me. 'I didn't mean to be angry,' he said in a low voice. 'I didn't mean to destroy the pigs.'

I whispered, 'You cannot admit imperfection to them. Whatever you do is right.'

'It's happened before.' He rubbed his face, and for a moment I saw the virtue stolen from him and replaced by weariness. 'It goes against everything I try to preach, all I try to live by. My Father never made this terrible place.'

'Sssh, Joshua.' I whispered so that no one would hear me say his name and believe I had power over him, that we were intimate. But I was curious. 'Happened before?'

'I – we – walked from the Jordan. I was tired, hungry, made thirsty by the sun. A fig tree stood in the desert and I wanted to eat the figs. They weren't ripe. I cursed the tree, and it withered. It withered and would not grow again. I had destroyed it. James immediately leapt up and proclaimed that the withered tree foretold I would destroy the Temple. The others cried yes, yes, he will destroy the Temple.' He rubbed his face. 'I'm trapped.'

'My Lord, what did you say to your disciples then?'

'What could I say? Have faith in God.'

I whispered, 'Joshua, why are you here? Why are you born?'

'I don't know. I really don't know! I hear what people say. I only know who I am.'

'My Lord,' I whispered, 'you are Jesus Christ. You are here to bring righteousness to these chosen people, and righteous salvation, and purity to every soul, so that we are a saved people just as many other people in many other places, of which you know nothing yet, are saved. You are sent into this world as a blank page, but you are God's only Son, sent to save us, sent to tell people how to live and think, to force salvation, to make the nations bow down and be saved. Joshua, whatever you do in this dusty little place doesn't matter.'

He stared into me, deep into my eyes. 'Do you really believe that, Mary?'

'I used to. Until I heard you speak of the power of love, mercy, forgiveness. Now I believe in you.'

'I think you're the only one who does believe in me, Mary.' We heard the disciples muttering. Joshua confided, 'They each want something of their own. They don't like to see me praying with a woman. They resent that much of my healing is of women. But I believe I am here in this world to tell the truth, Mary. To bring love. To offer salvation. To teach mercy. To nurture tolerance and peace in the world.'

I glanced at the disciples who observed us. 'That's not what you said to them. You said fire and sword. You promised Heaven and Earth to the meek, the poor, rewards to the persecuted—'

'Do you think it's easy?' I was the only one who made Joshua angry like this. His voice rose. 'Yes, it's politics. I pretend I'm a lion to the lions and a dove to the doves. Yes, I promise fire and the sword to men angry with injustice. I promise riches in Heaven to beggars, health to the sick, humility to the proud, poverty to the rich.' He ran his hands through his hair, his boyhood mannerism. 'Do you know I saw Matthew the levite, my old teacher, at the counting table? I said, Come. Follow me. Yes, I'll bring the Temple crashing down. Yes, I'll purchase the Covenant with God. And you, Mary, you want me crowned king? Yes, I promise you.'

I shook my head. 'You don't need to promise me anything. I believe in your beautiful words. Preach them. No one has ever spoken them before. Jesus Christ never did. No one has ever said love in this world. Spoken love. Preached love.' I spoke into his eyes. 'Do you know what God wants of you?'

He hesitated. 'I can't see the future. I only know men's prophecies of what I must do.'

'And you know your heart.'

'My heart.'

'Do what *you* will do,' I whispered. 'Don't try to be all things to all men.'

'My Father *is* all things to all men. One God who is everything. All things.'

'Love. Mercy. Kindness. Peace. These are your words that speak to me.'

He stared. 'Spoken like a woman, Mary.'

'They're not soft words.'

'No. They're hard words. The hardest.'

'A woman in love, Joshua.'

Joshua kissed me on the mouth in front of the disciples. He kissed me on the mouth in front of everyone. The little boy who had found his mother clapped, giggling. Two disciples at least, I didn't know their names, stared with faces as black as thunder as though Joshua's acceptance of me, a woman, was his rejection of them. Several more thought Joshua was indiscreet to the point of madness. But others had seen the sky open over the Jordan and heard the Voice of God bless him, and that memory remained strong. But I have never heard of a female disciple. I was careful to shuffle quietly to the background, fade into the long evening shadows of the rocks.

Joshua stood. The man once called Legion, clothed now, came and sat serenely at his feet. Villagers arrived complaining to the disciples of all they had lost. Joshua said, 'Tonight we stay at this man's house in the village.' He ordered Legion to teach what he had seen throughout the cities of the Decapolis, but the crowd from the village swelled. The word was getting about, spread by the frantic pigmen. While Joshua spoke to Legion the crowd joined the pig-herders picking up stones to throw at us, all afraid of what had happened, all afraid the demons would return, all devastated by the loss of the pigs. Without Greek drachmas this winter, the village would starve. The elders came forward and begged Peter to go before the people could not be stopped.

So Joshua turned away, touched my shoulder, and we walked back to the boat. Strong hands swung me aboard. All night our boat tacked against the wind in the middle of the rough uncomfortable sea, and turned towards Capernaum at dawn.

Lookouts gave the alarm and people ran down to the beach to see us, or hobbled, or crawled, or were carried to be cured. They pressed around us reaching up with their arms and clawing hands, crying out their supplications. At first Joshua could not get down from the boat, then he was pulled from one side to the other in the crush. I saw only his long hair and flashes of his white robe. There was no hope of preaching; his voice would not be heard. The mob pressed us so tight in their adoration that I feared for our lives more than from the stone-throwing Gadarenes. Peter shoved forward, clearing a path, and we came to his house. His men pushed us through the gate, held back the crowd, and I stumbled inside with torn clothes. The crowd set up a disappointed roar that we were gone. They shouted, this woman has not been cured, that child is more deserving; a man who lived in unutterable pain all his life complained he was held back from touching Joshua's robe by toughs demanding money.

Inside the main room Joshua was surrounded by disciples, scribes, assistants, the women of the house calling down from the balcony. Peter's wife introduced her friends, all demanding something different of him. None of them saw his exhaustion. They didn't really care about him; now he was among them they didn't really see him, he was simply the centre of their lives. Without realising it, all they thought of when they were with Joshua was themselves.

But I thought only of Joshua.

I slipped from a side door – it was impossible to leave the front of the house for the crush of people – and spent the last of my ready money shopping, buying a white alabaster box because it was very pretty and I'd always wanted one. I came back to chaos in the house. Four men, it turned out, had climbed the outside staircase carrying a paralysed man on a stretcher, knocked through the thatching and mud of the roof, and lowered him between the beams almost on to Joshua's head. Joshua awoke amused rather than angry, touched the man and said affectionately, 'Child, your sins are forgiven.' The paralysed man had responded angrily that he was no child. His friends shouted he'd committed no sins and didn't want any forgiveness. The paralysed man picked up his stretcher and thanked Joshua for the cure but not the preaching. 'Never seen anything like it,' his friends said, slamming the door behind them.

I tried to show Joshua the alabaster box, but the disciples led him outside through the crowd talking of Yair, an important man in the synagogue, a useful ally, whose daughter seven years old lay dying. A few minutes later Joses returned and said she had died. Later Peter came back and told us Joshua had raised her from the dead saying in Aramaic *tĕlîtā' qûm*, Girl, I say to you, arise. 'She was twelve years old,' Peter said firmly. 'Her raising to new life means our Lord will raise the twelve tribes of Israel to renewed life.' Andrew returned, overheard. 'Yes, and a woman just touched our Lord's robe,' he told us, wiping rain from his thinning hair. 'She's been bleeding for twelve years, unclean, her touch made our Lord unclean. But he said to her, go in peace and be healed for ever.'

'That's it,' Peter said. 'Twelve again.'

'And twelve apostles,' Andrew added. Apostles now, not disciples. They were pitching themselves pretty high.

'Why twelve followers,' I asked, 'not eleven as usual?'

I was ignored by Peter and Andrew but Joses remembered me. 'Because our Lord is above the twelve tribes of Israel, of all not of any one. He dwells in us all.'

One of the scribes of the Capernaum synagogue said smoothly, in a familiar voice, 'If your Joshua tolerates uncleanliness, perhaps his power to heal comes from Satan.' I recognised Sallu, from whose Magdala change-table I'd stolen so often as a child, and turned my face away. 'Your Joshua's healing, my dear disciples with Greek names, may not be a blessing of the Holy Spirit but rather a blasphemy against it.'

The door opened and the hired men pushed Joshua inside to save him from the crowd. He was weary and his hair was wet and tangled, his damp clothes torn, but he overheard Sallu's unctuous tone. 'How can Satan cast out Satan?' Joshua demanded angrily. He knew he wasn't always among friends. *I* thought, perhaps never. He sat on Peter's couch with his head in his hands. I knelt at his feet and opened the alabaster box. Perfume rose like a prayer around my head from the salve of spikenard. It cost three hundred Roman denarii, a year's wage for a working man, little enough to me.

'My Lord,' I said, washing the dust from Joshua's feet, rubbing them with the fragrant ointment. But he spoke angrily to Sallu. 'I have words to say to you, Pharisee. If you've got ears you'd better listen.' Sallu looked insulted; he'd grown into an important man in Capernaum. Joshua's tongue ran away with him, knowing something of Sallu's past. 'Listen, a moneylender had two debtors—'

'What should I know of moneylending or exchange,' Sallu lied quickly.

'One debtor owed this moneylender five hundred denarii, the other fifty. They'd nothing, couldn't pay, they'd lost their land, houses, families, everything. He forgave both of them all they owed.'

'Not a very good moneylender!' Sallu chuckled.

'Tell me, which man loved the moneylender most? The man forgiven five hundred, or fifty?'

Sallu looked for the trap but couldn't see it. Finally he said, 'He who was forgiven most.'

Joshua looked down at me, touched my hair, inhaled the scent of spikenard, then spoke again to Sallu. 'I came into this house, but you offered me no water for my feet. This woman has washed my feet with her tears. She wiped them dry with the hairs of her head. You didn't welcome me, but from the moment I came in she has not ceased to kiss my feet. Not one of you learned Pharisee priests anointed my head with oil, but she has anointed my feet with ointment.'

Sallu glowered. 'What do you mean? I know this woman. She's a sinner. And you, Joshua, if you were truly a prophet, you would know exactly who and what she is, what a great sinner, a woman steeped in sin from birth.'

Joshua said furiously, 'I say to you, Pharisee, no one knows her better than I, and her sins are forgiven her.'

The Pharisee scribes gathered behind Sallu, outraged, talking at once. 'Who are you to say you've got the power to forgive sins? Only God's got that power. Your claim's a blasphemy against God.'

I wept, anointing Joshua's feet with ointment.

'Joshua, you speak so much of the poor,' Sallu sneered. 'That money could have been used to feed the poor, not wasted on your pleasure. You're a hypocrite.' Having won the argument, the Pharisees stood quickly.

'Call them back,' I whispered.

But Joshua would not. His eyes glowed, his face was pale with his anger. 'Their faith shan't save them,' he said loudly as the holy men filed from the room. Then he made a weary gesture and I poured him a cup of wine, and Peter's wife pushed me aside in her eagerness to offer him a grail of bread broken and spiced, putting herself in front of his eyes. But a man came in, whispering, and Joshua waved her away. 'Messengers arriving from John the Baptist.' He beckoned me. 'You've two good eyes and two good ears, Mary. See me. Hear me.'

The messengers were shown in muddy with travel and rain. The first was Nathanael and the other I didn't recognise, probably a disciple of either John or Joshua. They'd ridden from John's cell at Machaeros, the vast fortress standing like a volcano in the desert of Perea, by a roundabout way to throw off Herod's informers and spies, pausing last night at Cana and riding all morning. For John to summon them at all was a token of his desperation, extremely expensive, so many guards and jailers to be bribed – who doubtless did not accept money without Herod's knowledge. Nathanael's journey was difficult and dangerous. He accepted water gratefully, drank thirstily, but refused absolutely the offer of wine or bread.

Nathanael began, 'My master has heard that a great prophet has risen up among the people. That God is visiting His people.'

Joshua said, 'I hear.'

Nathanael asked directly, 'My master asks if you are He that is to come, or should he look for another?'

'Your master knows what his eyes saw and his ears heard,' Joshua said. 'He saw the sky open over the Jordan, he heard the words of God.'

But Nathanael persisted. 'My master asks, are you the One?'

I exclaimed, 'Then your master sees but is blind and hears but is deaf!'

Joshua put his finger on my lips. 'I know what John asks. He asks if I shall stumble from the way he has prepared.' I wanted to speak. I'd never heard a word from John of love, or forgiveness, or mercy, or kindness. He'd not treated even his own body with tenderness or loving kindness. But Joshua's finger still touched my lips and I was silent. He replied to Nathanael with careful words. 'Go back to John and tell him of the things you've seen and heard here in Capernaum, how the blind see and the lame walk, the lepers are cleansed and the deaf hear, the dead are raised, and to the poor the truth is preached.'

Nathanael said, 'That is not an answer.'

'Tell your master he's blessed if he finds no stumbling in me.' Joshua's words were both a warning and a challenge to

John's authority if John turned against him. His eyes did not move from Nathanael.

Nathanael bowed. 'I'll tell my master.'

'Tell your master not to listen to the tongues of the people of this world.' Joshua spoke gently but firmly. 'John the Baptist drinks no wine and eats no bread, so people say he has a demon in him. They say the Son of Man' – he touched his cup – 'is a drunkard who eats bread and meat and kisses a woman on the mouth and keeps innkeepers and tax collectors and sinners for friends, and so they say I am a madman or a fraud. People will say whatever John does is wrong. People will say whatever I do is wrong. That's the nature of the people of this world, to drag down to their level. John should bring sinners to repentance, not believe what they say.'

'But still,' Nathanael said, 'you support Simon as Zadok in place of John. And you have not opposed Simon's appointment of his nephew Judas Sicariot as chief scribe of the scriptorium at Sion, with all the influence that implies.'

So it was true, as I'd heard long ago, that the monastery at Sion possessed a large library! A chief scribe would be responsible for the scrolls of the Poor going back for hundreds of years, new works being written, copies of the old. Within the monastery walls Judas's power must be great as an alphaeus or prior's, revenues from the monastery lands and perfume industry and all monies gathered by the Poor passing through his hands into the vaults of the treasury I'd seen joined to the church.

But that money paid for the armouries forging weapons, paid for political influence with Herod, paid Roman prefects, paid spies and contacts and informers and even priests in the Temple. I knew Joshua must keep above all these things, must not be tainted by involvement in such murky worldly matters. Truly politics in the world of men is a bottomless pit, but the prophets tell us that the destiny of the Jewish nation, and even its existence, depends on our ethical integrity: upon our belief in God. The Poor believe – I'd heard Matthew say many times – that if the Jewish people failed to live up to God (as they had) then God would begin His return, bringing about the New Covenant. This was the Christianity I knew. God imposes His will

263

directly in Man's heart, filling all humans with the knowledge of God through Jesus Christ as King, so that men and women and children are incapable of rejecting God's teachings. Among a saved people there can be no oppression, no injustice or war, only worship of God.

But worship isn't love. It says nothing about love. It says nothing about freedom from intolerance or all the other truths I believed I saw Joshua beginning to preach. Not to decree: to preach his truth, to encourage towards truth, to persuade of truth.

Joshua spoke honestly to Nathanael. 'Among men born of women, there's not a greater prophet than John the Baptist. But he that's smallest in the Kingdom of God is greater than John.' He stood and finished firmly, 'While his voice is locked away in Machaeros, John the Baptist is the same as dead.'

As Joshua's message that he would work without John sank in, the blood drained from Nathanael's face until his skin was white like a fish's belly. He said, 'What do you mean to do?'

Joshua said: 'You'll see and hear what I do.' He laid his hands on Nathanael's shoulders like the weight of the world. 'Come with me. Follow me.'

'While my master is alive I serve my master. My master shall not die.'

Joshua said, 'Your master serves me.' He did not lift his hands. 'I shall call on a good man, Nathanael.' Only then did he release Nathanael's shoulders.

Nathanael said nothing, lost in thought. Then he said, 'I shall be in my house at Cana.'

The men left and for a few instants Joshua and I were alone in the room. We spoke at the same moment, me saying, 'You've decided what you'll—'

'My work's finished here.' Joshua said rapidly. 'Trust Nathanael, he's utterly guileless, but someone will talk and Herod's spies will know for sure I've been in contact with John. Follow me to your house at Sepphoris. My mother, my brothers and the Community of the Nazarenes must hear me preach the good news of the real God, the God of truth and love. In my home I'll show all I've found of my

Father our God of love, compassion, mercy. Not their God of anger and war. I'll show them the God of all good growing things, and peace everlasting.'

I knelt. 'My Lord.'

It didn't work out like that.

He let me follow him, but his disciples didn't. Following in Joshua's footsteps between the hills, which hung over the sea like green mist after the rain, I gradually found myself excluded from the ring of followers around him, followers who hung on his every word and depended on him for every thought. Closeness to him was jealously guarded and step by step I realised that my place was at the back. Sometimes Joses or Peter fell back to me and tried to repeat and explain Joshua's words to me, but plainly they didn't understand him, so obviously I failed in turn to comprehend what they were trying to say, so finally they came to the conclusion that Joshua's teaching was above my reach, which did not surprise them considering my sex. My God, how they tried and tried to explain! Like men learning to swim in quicksand.

I simply believed in Joshua. My faith was wholehearted so everything was easy for me, and every word of his I heard, however distantly, or sometimes as a mere echo from the rocks, sounded true to my ears. I heard him however quietly, I saw him however far away. Joshua healed the blind and the deaf with his hands, but he could not make his own disciples hear and see by the words of his mouth. So, at the camp fire outside a shepherd's hut somewhere near Gennesaret – the lamps of the town below us, and Magdala further away – he began to tell his disciples stories he called *matla*, parables. He told them the parable of the sower, his eyes gleaming in the firelight, but Peter complained, 'I heard you tell this story a hundred times today.' It was Joshua's habit to stop at every little village, every well, every hut, leaving no stone unturned, which is why his progress was so slow and Peter preferred to travel by boat.

Joshua said, 'I speak to ordinary people in ordinary words, so that seeing they *might* not see, and hearing they *might* not understand.' It seemed to me there was no might about it: ordinary people often understood Joshua more than his disciples did. But then I realised Joshua knew the Twelve, as they liked to call themselves, far better than I. They thought he flattered them, and their faces lit up. 'To you I will reveal the secret mysteries in the parables. In the parable of the sower which you have heard a hundred times, a thousand times, you should realise that the sower's seed is in fact the Word of God. The words that fall by the wayside are those which the Devil makes His own, deceiving the people so they cannot have faith and cannot be saved. The words which fall on rock flourish for a day of joy in the sun, but have no root, lose faith and die. The words that fall on faithful ears and minds and hearts will bear good fruit in time.' He looked round their firelit faces. 'To you these secret meanings are given. There are other secrets, deeper, and much more. A word is capable of many interpretations. One day you will come to them.' He changed tack, surprising them, his eyes fixed enormously on me across the fire, speaking to me alone, though I didn't understand his meaning until days later. 'Nothing is secret that shan't be brought out into the open. Nothing is hidden that shall not be known by all.'

The disciples slept, but he stayed awake staring through the flames to me.

In the morning some rich woman came from Tiberias to be healed of a minor infirmity. Her name was Joanna, the wife of Chuza, Herod's steward, so Joshua knew Herod's interest in him was awakened. He healed her and sent her away. Our party hurried in the opposite direction, across the hills to Sepphoris, where the word of Joshua's return had gone ahead of us. The crowd rushed around us, dragging Joshua hither and thither with their grasping hands, their cries and entreaties rising about us like the cries of birds, and we came through the city to my house hardly able to see our way. I slammed the door and the boy brought wine. Joshua threw himself down on the couch, exhausted as always by the demands made on him. I took his gown and pieces of reed-paper and leather scraps fluttered from the hem, stuck there by pious sufferers able to write.

'Your robe's imbued with entreaties,' I said.

'What does that mean?' He saw. 'Their faith saves them.' He drank the cup, held it out, and this time I refilled it.

'You'll come with me to Cana,' he said.

'I, my Lord?'

'We're alone. Alone with you I am Joshua whom you know.' His energy came back to him and he kissed me on the mouth. Peter put his head round the door-curtain and the hubbub of the crowd carried to us. 'Oh, for five minutes of peace!' Joshua said.

Peter ignored me. 'Your mother and brothers were in the crowd from the city, my Lord. You passed them by in the evening light.' People often spoke stiltedly to Joshua like this, I'd noticed. Still Joshua did not let go of the cup which my hands held. Peter said, 'They're waiting outside. They want to see you.'

Joshua burst out, 'My mother and brothers are those who hear the Word of God, and do it!' He relented. 'Let them hear me in the synagogue tomorrow, then they'll come to me.'

That morning of the Sabbath I walked behind the crowd, fewer than yesterday. Nazarenes in their white robes gathered together in silence outside the *shul*-house, washed their hands in the ritual bowls together, removed their sandals and washed their feet together, covered their heads and went inside together. Ordinary worshippers filed inside, then Joshua, then the disciples pushed into the last of the space. But before the psalm could be sung Joshua seized the scroll of the prophet Isaiah and read in a voice loud enough to be heard outside, and along the road, and across the rooftops. He told them what they wanted to hear.

'The Spirit of the Lord is in me, because He anointed me Christ to preach the gospel to the Poor.' I heard the startled rustle of the congregation even from here on the steps. Joshua said, 'The Lord sends me to heal the broken-hearted, to preach deliverance to the captives.' To this audience *captives* meant all Israel, all Jews, who were all captives of the Romans. 'To preach the recovery of sight to the blind.' Promising leadership in the coming uprising. 'To set at liberty our people who are bruised. To preach when the year of the Lord will come.' The Nazarenes stared at him transfixed; the speech, though in the guise of prophecy, was outright sedition. Joshua released the scroll so that it rolled up with a snap. 'Today this scripture is fulfilled in your ears. You've heard it. But it is not enough.' He looked them in their eyes. 'Now there's much more.'

An old man called, 'What more?'

'What I did in Capernaum, I'll do here.' Joshua spoke of the God his Father he knew inside himself, spoke of love, compassion, generosity, peace. Spoke of forgiveness, the last thing they wanted to hear. These people wanted to throw the Romans and the Temple priests into a bottomless pit; they wanted vengeance and fury, not forgiveness. The congregation muttered.

'I remember you,' the old man called out. 'Yes, you. Who d'you think you are, talking to us like this? You're little Joshua, the brother of James and Joses, and Thomas and Silas, the carpenter's boys. Your sisters Salome and Miri, they're always talking about how great you've grown now.' He spat through the doorway, it landed in the dust at my feet. 'You're Mary's son.' It was a terrible insult, to Mary his mother as well as Joshua. A man was always his father's son.

The congregation turned their backs on Joshua, excluding him from the recitation of the *Shema* and the eighteen benedictions. Joshua tried to speak again, but the Torah was read over his voice. He came out, strode past me on the steps. 'A prophet is not without honour except in his own country,' he told me bitterly, 'and among his own kin, and in his own house.'

'Your mother was insulted as well,' I said. 'Go to her, go now.'

But he walked away, and I followed him, and the poorest people streamed after us with their disgusting diseases, and their cries, and their stink, and he did what he could for them. But the Pharisees followed us into the barley fields. 'It is not lawful to heal on the Sabbath,' they said.

'It's lawful to save lives.' Joshua turned on them. I would have put my hand on his arm to restrain him, had I dared. They pushed us into the corner of the field.

The Pharisees said, 'You are not equal with God. You flout the laws of Moses. But we say you are not above the Law of God, Joshua ben-Mary.' I knew it would take only one shout of blasphemy from men so self-satisfied – I recognised Kedar, Hobab's brother, among them – and the stones would fly. I'd seen it before: the punishment for blasphemy is stones. There were twenty of them, two of us. But Joshua had lightning in his hands; he could make stones burn, he could destroy the Pharisees with a flick of his fingers. But that would not change their minds or their hearts.

Joshua fought them with words. 'The Sabbath's made for man, not man for the Sabbath.' He added, 'You Pharisees are breaking your own rules, running after us so far on your holy day.'

'We are not in need of repentance.' But the Pharisees looked around them, the poor people who supported Joshua pressing close. The rain of a few days ago had brought the scrawny crop forward. Joshua picked an ear of grain and ate it, forbidden work on the Sabbath. The Pharisees shuffled their feet, afraid to tear their clothes to give the sign of blasphemy. Neither were the priests certain which side the approaching Nazarenes and zealots and sicariots would take. I saw Simon and Judas and Yeshua Barabbas leading them, striding through the crop. The farmer ran behind them half naked, despairing, trying to straighten the bent stalks. Barabbas stopped two paces from Kedar, staring him down, hands on hips, a knife hooked in his sleeve. Everyone knew Barabbas's reputation. He had the temper of a camel.

Simon, his golden cloak flashing in the sun, walked to Joshua's side and called out to the Pharisees, 'The Son of Man is Lord of the Sabbath!'

The Nazarenes pushed forward. They too picked grain and ate, hating the Temple Sabbath, and the Pharisees fell back. They covered their heads against sin and retreated, wisely. When the danger was over the poor people were pushed away by Simon's men. Simon took Joshua's arm and spoke earnestly into his ear, but I was close by and overheard.

Simon said, 'My Lord, you are the Christ. You speak as our Christ should when you preach to us the prophecies of Isaiah. In your anger you are everything John the Baptist hopes for, and the Poor, and the Salt, and the Princes of the Community, and I too, your twin pillar, zadok equal with Christ. But, my Lord, some of us did not understand your other words. Soft words.'

Joshua replied, 'The Song of Songs teaches us that human love is not to be viewed apart from divine love.'

Simon gave a conniving look; he was infamous for his paramours. But I saw that Judas Sicariot's face, though sensuous, remained perfectly blank. I was sure he knew nothing of love, and realised most of these righteous men, fanatics, would understand absolutely nothing of what Joshua truly had to say. His words were a foreign country to them. Then Joshua sighed and gave them the words they wanted to hear. 'The prophet Hosea's marriage revealed to Sion the Lord's own personal love for His people. Hosea's marriage was a contract not only with his wife but with the Lord, a union of wills through the divine favour which leads to a Covenant with the Lord.' I saw the Nazarenes' eyes light, as always, on that noun Covenant. Joshua said, 'The prophet Isaiah tells us that the Lord promised Sion, "In the day of vengeance I shall hear you, Sion, and in the day of salvation I will help you, and I shall give you a Covenant of the people to establish the earth." But now, Sion says, my Lord has forsaken and forgotten me. I say to you,' Joshua strengthened his voice, 'can a mother forget her suckling child? Can she have no compassion on the son of her womb? Yes, she may forget him. But I say to you, Sion, I will not forget you.'

It was enough. Simon shouted to his followers, 'Truly the Son of Man is Lord of the Sabbath!' They cheered, and slowly began to disperse back to their houses. But Simon whispered quietly to Joshua. 'Nevertheless, my Lord, with some other things that men say you say, you risk losing the faith of those who love you most.' He kissed Joshua's hand and backed away, then beckoned his men. Gradually the sound of birdsong returned to the field and I stood alone beside Joshua. He stared after them until they were gone.

'Faith will move the world,' he said. 'How can I help those men and women who are so sure they believe in the Christ that they see only their own selves? They only have expectation, not faith. I do nothing among my own people. Nothing.'

I knelt. 'My Lord, don't try. You fail when you try to be less than who you are. When you try to please every man you are merely a man. When you speak from your heart, you are the Son of God.'

He laughed, then knelt beside me. 'Marry me.'

EGO ME CHRISTO
SPONSAM TRADIDI

I gave myself as a bride to Christ

Joshua had spoken from his heart. But I am perfectly certain that Jesus Christ, Son of the Virgin, brought up without brothers or sisters, never married. Jesus Christ grew up as a single child and He forbade fornication, and forbade adultery, and there was none. He forbade the secret sins of the heart, even a man's covetous night-thoughts of women, involuntary emissions, even a single lustful thought after a neighbour's wife, for He saw into every heart and condemned every thought that was not Christian, until there was nothing that was not Christian. He remained celibate, untouched, unsullied until the day of His Assumption with His mother, and neither men nor women thought of sin.

My Joshua knew sin from his earliest days: sinful because of his illegitimate birth, his mother's shame, his inability to inherit which the taunts of his brothers never let him forget. Joshua had been brought up as an ordinary human, part of a vigorous living family, not as a single child worshipped as a little god. Joshua had grown up into a man by his own efforts, pulled himself up by the soles of his own sandals, found his own way forward through all the trials that beset him; and to me his struggle and humanity made him infinitely more the Son of God than any instantly created and imposed perfection-in-the-flesh.

For the first time in my long life I realised I could not have loved that perfect Jesus Christ. Worshipped Him, yes. Obeyed Him certainly. Prayed to Him in the certainty of His perfect power and the purity of His commandments, absolutely. But loved Him? Wanted Him? Laughed with Him? Scratched a tickle on His back He couldn't reach? Woken up beside Him in the morning? No, never. I couldn't even imagine kissing Him.

In the flesh I don't think I would even have liked Him.

I think I would have hated, in fact, to meet that Jesus Christ face to face. I'd have found him too holy, too stern, too prissy, too certain, too righteous – in fact found him more like James, *exactly* like James, than the Joshua I knew.

Joshua, who remembered his pain and rejection, who preached so much of inheritance. Joshua who preached so much of love, and knew love. Joshua who found his way to teach that men and women are more important than laws. Joshua who taught that faith could move the world.

Joshua I love.

But Joshua said, '*Marry me.*'

I stared. I remember I said, 'You can't. You don't. I can't!' He smiled: I was foolish. Most men marry. A healthy man who remains single, unless a priest of celibate rank, raises eyebrows. Obviously God gave men these lovely circumcised cocks for a purpose, to be fruitful and multiply, otherwise there would be no chosen people. Without marriage, there's nothing. Joshua had warned Simon and Judas only a few minutes ago of his intentions, but their minds were closed, they didn't hear: a marriage is the contract between a husband and a wife which is a union with the Lord, the union of wills through the divine favour which leads to a Covenant with the Lord.

'But we can't!' I said. 'You're the tribe of Judah. I'm of Dan. It's not allowed.'

'Your mother was from Benjamin's tribe, but Caleb married her,' he pointed out. 'We won't fall foul of the tribal inheritance laws: I own no land or property.' He held out his hands. 'My clothes and sandals and you are all I've got of value in this world, Mary.'

I looked at his threadbare robes and ropy old sandals. 'You wouldn't get much for those,' I sniffed.

'Then you're all I have.'

It was ridiculous but true. He owned nothing. His disciples hung from him by a thread, he was estranged from his mother, his family, his people. He was the Son of God and I was all he had.

'Yes,' I said. 'Yes.'

We stood hearing the birdsong all around us, not touching each other, feeling the sunlight and tasting the hot dusty smell of the crop in our noses. Joshua sneezed.

'Who's going to pay for all this?' the farmer bellyached. We remembered him running out of his hovel half naked from his siesta and now grain and barley stalks stuck to the sweat on his chest, and he was angry. 'Who's going to pay for all this damage? How will I live? Do you think Herod buys our grain? Do you think he pays for it? He carts it to the town granary but do you think they pay? They don't pay. Then the Romans don't pay. The Greeks don't pay. When the time comes to starve, Herod hands out what's left of my grain to his rich friends and his hangers-on, but do we see any of it? You people don't help us. I'd carry a sword if I could, but I'm too old.' Joshua laid his hands on the farmer's head and the man fell silent. In that moment he was more important to Joshua than I.

Joshua glanced at me. 'I'll see you in Cana. At Nathanael's house.' He turned his attention back to the farmer.

That's all? I said, 'When?'

He looked at me as though hardly seeing me. 'When the wind blows.'

I gazed at them. The farmer talked, pouring out his woes. The more he talked, the more he realised he was not an unhappy man. I walked slowly away, and when I looked back the farmer was still talking. I walked, and when I looked they were too far back to see.

And so I came to Cana, but Joshua did not.

Just as Peter's was one of the largest houses in Capernaum, so Nathanael's was one of the richest in Cana. However poor the prophet, his words are not spread without money and influence. An urchin ran to meet me on the path into the village. 'I'm Architrinculus's eldest son. I'll show you everything in Cana!' Other urchins gathered around me shoving and squabbling, peering up at me with earnest begging faces like red little apples. When I asked for Nathanael's house, ten, fifteen, twenty little hands grabbed tugging at my sleeve to show me, with excited cries the hem of my cloak was lifted reverently from the dust, and I was swept to Nathanael's gate at almost a run. I scattered a penny or two and immediately twenty little bottoms showed through ragged coverings as the children bent to scavenge the coins. 'Nathanael? Most people here in Cana call him Bartholomew,' the eldest boy informed me wisely. 'Only his friends like us know that.' I tossed him a penny for his own. 'He gets lots of visitors,' the boy added for free, eyeing me, 'but never women. And never beautiful, not like you.'

I knocked on the gate. It was opened instantly and Nathanael stared out. 'Oh, it's you. I expected you,' he said, disappointed. 'The woman who was with the Christ.' He flapped away the children with his cloak, beckoned me into his courtyard, closed the gate. He stared at me. 'You mean you've not heard?'

My heart hammered. Something had happened to Joshua. I must have paled. Nathanael led me to the stone seat around the fountain, a servant brought me a cup of water. I asked, 'Is Joshua—'

'Joshua's disappeared, wisely. No one ever knows where he is, anyway. He's too careful. The disciples are coming here.' He paused. 'You must know? Messengers came last night: John the Baptist is taken from us. My master's head was cut off from his body, placed on a grail with his mouth open like a fish, and held up in front of Herod's face by a dancer. Some say at Machaeros, some say at Tiberias. Politics. Herod was too frightened to try to kill my master, but . . .' He looked at me accusingly. 'Women.' John's infatuation with women and rejection of us were well known. Flawed, he most desired what he most scorned; he'd never overcome that weakness of his flesh, and it had destroyed him among the women in Herod's court.

'I'm sorry to hear your master is dead.'

'John the Baptist isn't dead,' an old man's voice interrupted. Nathanael stood, welcomed his father Tolomei, helped him to the seat. The old man's white hair and white beard both reached devoutly to his waist. I knelt respectfully, but he allowed me to sit. 'No, our master's not dead, though his body was handed over and some of his disciples have laid him in a tomb. He'll rise in three days, you'll see. Jonah was in the belly of the whale for three days afore he was spat out.' He tapped his stick three times on the stones. 'Three, you see, that's the number of God. Four is the world. Add the world to God and you get Man, seven. That's why the Sabbath is on the seventh day, the union of God with man. Three multiplied by four, that's twelve, the twelve tribes of Israel, your Joshua's twelve disciples.' He grinned without a single tooth. 'Not quite twelve now, eh? I hear they're falling by the wayside like sower's seeds.' He banged his stick three times between my feet. 'Three days, John will rise from the dead. He'll be anointed Zadok, and Simon and Judas and Yeshua Barabbas, your Joshua's friends, will be thrown down from the high places into the pits of sulphur and brimstone.' I saw no mercy in his eyes. I knew he meant thrown down literally, from the cliffs of Sion into the bubbling pits. No men are so cruel to Jews as Jews. 'And maybe John will have himself anointed Christ, eh? Christ and Zadok in one, the single pillar of the world. King and priest combined in one man, one man at last. Our true Messiah.'

I said respectfully, 'But John's head is severed from his body.'

'But God is God,' said the old man.

Quietly Nathanael showed me to a small but not uncomfortable room at the back of the house. Before he turned to go he said, 'My father clings strongly to his beliefs. But his life has not much longer to run.'

I asked, 'Does Joshua know of John's death?'

Nathanael looked over his shoulder, then said quietly in Greek, 'There are those of us who believe that *Iesous Christos* knows of everything that happens, the fall of every leaf, whether in Heaven or here on Earth.'

Iesous Christos. It was the first time I'd heard Joshua called Jesus Christ, except by me, heard him addressed by the official title which means simply our Anointed Saviour. Nathanael knew what he'd seen at the Jordan that day. The Baptist had doubted the evidence of his eyes and ears to the end of his life, but Nathanael believed in Jesus Christ the Son of God. Joshua could trust few men, but he'd trusted wisely in Nathanael.

Three endless days passed in Nathanael's busy house, and still Joshua did not come.

Then some men arrived to say the Baptist had been seen in Samaria, where (Apollos confirmed, arriving from there) John's dismembered body was buried. Others claimed to have seen the Baptist alive in Jerusalem, in the Temple, proclaiming that he would throw it down. But all these rumours came to nothing. John's beheading made it difficult to believe in his resurrection in the flesh. From all over Judah his disciples drifted towards Nathanael's house, one by one at first, then arriving in dispirited knots of weary men day and night, doubting their faith.

Joshua did not come.

After the first week the glum talk of John's disciples turned to the idea of John's spirit being resurrected in the flesh of another prophet. By the second week talk and hope made this a certainty. Lazarus, John's most dedicated follower, walked in from Tiberias saying Herod himself now believed. His steward Chuza swore it to Lazarus's ears; Herod had heard John's spirit had fled into the flesh of an itinerant Galilean healer and made him into a great man, a man to be followed by ordinary Jews. Such a man could only be dangerous to Herod, and such men did not long survive Herod's jealousy. But Chuza knew of his wife Joanna's faith and spoke of Joshua the healer; Lazarus thanked him for the warning, Joanna's debt of health repaid, and came to us quickly to warn Joshua.

But there was no sign of Joshua. No one knew where he was.

I imagined Herod's interest in Joshua awakening, imagined his spies listening at every inn and synagogue, eyes watching every town square. And still Joshua did not come.

Had he been arrested? Would he turn any soldiers who laid hands on him to fire, as I knew he could do?

I sat shivering in my room with no one to talk to, only men's gossip drifting through the window, wild rumours flying in the courtyard with each new dusty dispirited arrival. I was the only woman in Nathanael's house, and lonely as I've ever been. Then I saw a woman wearing a scarf over her head come into the yard. I ran down to greet the Virgin. She touched my hands and knew. 'He's not here?'

I gave a cry of dismay. 'You don't know where Joshua is?'

The men were disturbed by our high voices. I led Joshua's mother to my room, and we sat on the bed. 'How can I know Joshua?' she said sadly. 'Does he speak to me? A messenger tells me I must come here on the Lord's business.' I saw James in the yard.

I whispered, 'Was the messenger an angel?'

She gave her smile. 'I always suppose so.' She touched my face tenderly. Her own skin had grown lines and her hands were stiff with work. But her smile had not changed its innocence; she was still a child inside. Always changing, always the same.

James saw me in the window and called up, 'Why are we here? Why's he brought us here?'

I didn't dare to tell James.

I stood on the roof, stared at the bare hills until my eyes were burnt by the sun. No Joshua.

That afternoon Joses arrived, his second brother, and faithful. I ran down. Joses shrugged. 'I don't know. A messenger brought word to me, that's all. I must go to the house of Nathanael in Cana.'

'A messenger, not Joshua?'

'Do I look as if I've seen Joshua? Here I am, and that's it.'

Next morning one of the Baptist's disciples, who'd changed his name to John after his master, arrived and said he'd seen Joshua by the roadside. James demanded, 'How do you know it was Joshua?' John simply smiled, touching his head, and I knew for certain that he was touched by Joshua. 'Because,' John said, 'he is the word and the life, and I'm his disciple.'

'My master is still the Baptist,' Lazarus said. 'Your Joshua doesn't baptise.'

I called out to John, 'Did you see him in Galilee?'

'I don't know Galilee,' John said, a tall intellectual-looking man. 'I saw him in Judah, and the people arguing with him. And Joshua touched my head and said to me, John, get to Cana to Nathanael's house to be married.'

James pushed forward in the crowd. 'Married? Who to?' I didn't dare say a word.

John put out his hands. 'That's all he said.'

There was a thunderous summons on the gate and we all stood stopped with fear. But the gate opened on a fat jovial man carrying a table on his head, his apron stained with blood. He gave a roar of amusement to see our faces so fixed. 'Don't let me spoil the wedding party!' he roared and waddled forward. 'Architrinculus, I am!' He looked for a place to set down the table, beckoned the children following him carrying tables between them, cloths, benches. 'All mine, the little devils,' he said proudly. 'Architrinculus's brats, every one.' He dumped the table by the steps, slapped his hands over his fat belly, shouted orders at the children who scurried frantically to his whims. 'No, not there. There!'

'I ordered no tables!' Nathanael exclaimed.

'No, but *he* did,' Architrinculus guffawed. 'He sent word, he did. Tables for a wedding feast. And everyone must have something to eat. Not one empty stomach, not a single dry mouth.'

Nathanael looked at Architrinculus's apron with disgust; blood was life. 'He? Who do you mean?'

Architrinculus was surprised. 'Why, Joshua, of course.' He guffawed, 'Fish course, sweetmeat course, nothing lacking! I've cooked for Herod, you know. Just following orders.' He pushed past.

'No wine or bread or meat,' Nathanael called after him. That prohibition was inevitable for Nazarenes, and also for John's disciples, for whom today was a fast day.

But Architrinculus set about his tasks roaring with laughter, his brats scurrying around him with candlesticks, candles and cups. 'Like I said, just following orders!' It was marvellous to see him work; the loyalty a few words from Joshua inspired in an ordinary man.

I stared past the hangers-on and servants and scurrying children to the uncomprehending faces of the disciples. None of them had seen anything like this before, certainly not in Nathanael's house. James was furious. 'Looks like a Greek whorehouse!' he swore, then coloured because I'd heard him say the word. As always, Joshua's most devout followers understood him least. Throughout the afternoon I watched the courtyard fill with tables, benches, costly coverings that the incorrigible Architrinculus had stolen or borrowed or forgotten to return, ornate gold candlesticks, golden grails for the top table, silver platters for the middle, wooden eating-boards for the bottom rows, and beggars gathering busily at the gate.

I saw Peter stepping over the sick and ragged people lying on mats. How did the word of Joshua's arrival get about? Nathanael greeted Peter, calling him by his Jewish name Shimon, but Peter said, 'I'm Peter to my Lord.' He looked surprised when we asked him where Joshua was. 'He's not here?'

Joshua's remaining disciples, the ones closest to him who called themselves the Apostles, arrived during the afternoon.

'Not here!' Simon Zadok said. 'But he spoke to me at Sion, three days ago.'

'No, he was in Capernaum yesterday,' Peter said.

'You're both wrong,' a disciple of John called. 'Three days ago these two ears of mine heard him speak in Samaria.'

'Samaria!' others said eagerly. 'Then Joshua is our master reborn.'

Simon put his hand on his knife. 'John cannot be reborn. The end of the world is coming; John's time is past.' Someone threw a stool and all at once knives were drawn, the blades glinting in the late afternoon light that poured around Nathanael's house. Nathanael shouted, 'No!' He tried to stand between the gangs but all hostile eyes turned on him, and instead of parting them Nathanael was caught in the middle. These men had waited out weeks of despair, and now their anger erupted. The time had come for blood.

'Come,' Joshua said, 'follow me.'

Wearing only a threadbare white gown, Joshua was holding out his arms to the diseased and sick who lay in the gateway, and we saw those who reached up to his hands and touched him rising to their feet whole and healthy. He knelt with those too sick to move and their cries rose around him, cries of despair turning to ecstasy so that our hearts were all touched by the marvel of the healing and cures that we saw, the white eyes of the blind opening and filling with colour, the legs of the paralysed bending, flexing, standing, walking, the mute shrieking aloud their joy.

Joshua turned to the disciples in the yard who stood with knives drawn, the zealots against John's men, the sicariots against the fishermen, the Galileans pushing against the men of Judah. He laughed to see them but his laughter did not reach his eyes. 'Don't be afraid. I'm here! Cheer up.' I saw how angry he was with them, but they did not. The beggars tried to push in after him, dogs bounded past him, and several disciples ran to close the gate.

James pointed, outraged. 'What have those people done to deserve their joy? We're the ones who've suffered. We're the ones who've believed. What have they done for you? Nothing! Where's their righteousness? Nowhere!'

'What about us, who love you?' one of the disciples called.

Joshua held out his arms to us all. 'There is more joy in Heaven over one sinner who repents than over ninety-nine righteous men who need no repentance.' He knew there were exactly ninety-nine of us in the yard, all believing in our righteousness. The fountain splashed noisily in the silence, then the gates sounded very loud as they slammed closed. Architrinculus farted and his children giggled. A small boy ran to hold Joshua's hand, but Joshua picked him up and kissed him.

Then Joshua spoke to us. 'Today I have come not to call the righteous but sinners.'

Did he mean all of us, who thought so highly of ourselves because we believed (as much as we could) in him? Each man believed Joshua spoke to him personally, looked only into him. Joshua looked at me, only me. He looked at me in the height of his power: just he, a man, and I. Everyone in the yard felt this closeness, togetherness, I know, because I know Joshua. Yet I also felt my own body intensely, my separateness. I was a woman.

Joshua embraced Peter. 'Peter.' But it felt as though he embraced me. All of us felt his embrace.

Joshua lifted up Nathanael, and called him Bartholomew. 'Bartholomew shall be your name in Christ from today forward.' When Joshua gave a man or woman a new name it was the same as baptism in his eyes, making them into a new person.

Bartholomew whispered, 'Of course you are the Christ, son of Joseph the Christ. But John was my master for many years.'

'Any man with two ears had better listen.' Joshua looked

every man in his eye, spoke to every man's face. 'Hear me. Anyone who is not with me is against me. There is no past. The link is broken and everything is new.'

In the silence Lazarus said, 'My lord, I cannot believe you are John.'

Joshua said: 'You are John's faithful servant as I am my Father's servant, and you will see who I am.' He raised his voice. 'Today I come to you as a bridegroom. There are many marriages between us today. John's disciples say, Why are these tables piled with food when it is our fast day? I say, It is not a fast day for the disciples of Joshua. Can the children of the bridechamber fast while the bridegroom is with them? No, they cannot fast. Therefore you will eat.' He spoke firmly, treating them like little children. 'You ask me, Why is there bread on the tables when we eat no bread, and meat when we eat no meat?' Then I knew what Joshua would say, I *knew* it.

I cried out, 'Because it is not what a man puts in his mouth which defiles him, it is what comes out of his mouth!' I saw Mary his mother in the crowd, her face stern, but her eye caught mine. We both remembered her own reply from all those years ago.

'Words,' she said, nodding. 'Words.'

Joshua said angrily, 'You Nazarenes, you Pharisees, even you followers of John worship the traditions of men as though they were the commandments of God. The traditions of men are not the way to God. Those who believe in me don't need to bathe seven times a day to prove their holiness, needn't wash hands before breaking bread, don't have to deny themselves meat and fish, don't deny marriage. We keep God's commandments, not the meaningless traditions and pot-washing that men have invented thinking they please God. I say to you, everything that is sold in the market place is lawful. Today is a marriage between Joshua and John; from today there is not the thickness of a needle separating us. Everything I have is yours.'

They were quick to see the other side of the coin. 'So everything we have worked for is yours,' Lazarus said. He shook his head and would not listen to Joshua. But gradually the others melted away from Lazarus, drawn to the tables and the aroma of cooked meat like a sacrifice. 'Come, welcome, all!' Architrinculus beamed. 'Fresh from the bakery. Eggs roasted by the fair hands of my own wife, dear soul, try some. Crusty pastries, honey cakes, fish still cold from the pond, see how their eyes sparkle? And lamb.' He kissed his fingers. 'And fat chicken.' The fire flared up, the flames showing clearly now as the daylight faded, the fat running from the sheep on the spit turning to flame, and the arch of sunset overhanging the darkened house like a rainbow.

Would they eat? Bartholomew took a mouthful, dropped crumbs from his mouth, unused to bread. Where he went, others followed. All had been as hungry as starving men without realising it. For years they had hungered and thirsted, and now they had started eating they could not stop. Dishes rattled. The more they ate, the more they obeyed Joshua's authority, for he had ordered them to eat. Only Lazarus and a few others stayed back in the shadows, and I saw James there, and Thomas only nibbled a few crumbs. Salome and Miri followed Joshua adoringly, their bony white elbows flashing as they fed their thin bodies, and I took a piece of bread to Mary his mother. I held it out to her. She took it between her fingers, but her face struggled.

'You and I,' I whispered, 'we know the truth. We know the truth because we've seen it with our own eyes. We saw the Star and knew what we saw. We saw the stable, we still carry it inside us. Both you and I have heard the Voice of God, twice, and known what we heard.' I touched the bread to her lips. 'Both you and I know that when Joshua says eat, the command comes from God.'

Mary opened her lips, and ate the bread. She made a face and washed it down with water. James stared at her appalled, but she told him, 'Whatever your brother tells you, do it.'

Joshua took my hand, led me to the steps. I felt from his long-fingered hand holding mine what he would say. But Joshua was silent, watching the men eat at the tables below us, and we couldn't hear the fountain splashing for the sound of their eating. Then gradually the sound of them faded away as they realised that I, a woman, stood beside Joshua above them. A woman superior to them.

Joshua squeezed my hand, began quietly. 'Friends, I

invited you here today for a wedding. I did not say whose wedding it was. It is for you to know the truth. Today is not only a marriage between the followers of John and the disciples of Joshua. Not only a contract between a husband and wife which is a union with the Lord, the union of blood through the divine favour which leads to a Covenant with the Lord. This marriage with Mary Magdalene, a woman, is my marriage. This is my wedding day.'

Before they had eaten, his words would have caused a sensation. Now many did not even look up from their food.

Simon Zadok called out. 'What? How do we know this is the Covenant? Where is it?'

Joshua said: 'I am the Covenant.' By those words, in front of every man watching, Joshua had claimed to be more than the Christ, almost to be God. The Son of God, the connection, the Covenant. And claimed it in front of Mary his mother, and me, Mary to be his wife. And in front of Architrinculus and all the children.

I watched Simon's expression mirror the struggle within him in the candlelight. The shifting flames billowing in the night wind made him look as though darkness struggled with darkness inside his strong hooked face. His tongue came out and licked his lips. He looked to Judas. Neither man had eaten meat.

'A man who promises to save the Poor thirty talents of silver,' Judas said, 'promises much.'

James stepped forward. 'I believe—' Simon turned sharply, but James continued. 'I believe we should trust my brother unless we find he fails us. And I pray he will not fail us.'

Joshua exclaimed, 'James, my brother, give me all your love and your hope and your prayers and I shall never fail you, nor any man, or any woman!' He embraced James, but I saw the stiffness in James's smile and his kiss. James knew hope, God knows – and no man ever knew more of prayers! But love James did not know. Not since he was young when we were young.

And peace James did not know. And not mercy. Least of all mercy to himself, to his own conscience. Guilt clung to his soul like an accretion of barnacles. James knelt and said, 'My Lord.' But it was an alliance, not brotherly love, not friendship. An alliance. I whispered to James, 'He will not let you down.' I touched his hand and he turned away as though I burnt his skin with fire. But I thought: Joshua can persuade James. He can bring James round because James *wants* to know love, to know peace, to find God. James will follow him.

But really in my heart I must have been thinking, *Joshua can do anything.*

Joshua embraced Simon, then Judas. 'You dog!' he said fondly, and kissed him. To call a man a dog is the worst of insults, meaning a Gentile or a sodomite, but Joshua laughed, so Judas laughed too. 'Come, follow me,' Joshua said, 'Don't spend all your time as an outsider, an outsider at Sion, be with me.'

There was an almost audible sigh of relief. *Outsider*, Joshua had meant, not a Gentile or anything worse. 'Alas,' Judas spread his hands, 'my duties, my responsibilities.'

Joshua turned to his disciple John who held up the prayer shawl, the *tallit*, over us, and commanded him to begin. Then Joshua turned to me, speaking into my ears so that all heard. 'A man who has no wife is doomed to an existence without joy, without blessing, without experience of life's true goodness, without protection, without peace.' He twined our fingers so that we could not let go of each other even if we'd wanted to, then together we recited the seven blessings beneath the shawl which the night wind set fluttering. The last of the sunset was in our eyes. Then Joshua, bridegroom and so ruler of the feast, called for the cup of celebration.

The gold cup was brought and Architrinculus filled it from a pitcher of clear cold water. 'Where's the wine?' Joshua said. Architrinculus said, 'What wine?'

'The wine.'

Joshua's mother said, 'They have no wine.'

'My Lord, you know what these gentlemen are like,' Architrinculus said uneasily. 'My lord governor Nathanael, I mean Bartholomew, he'd no more let wine within these walls than sin.' He pointed at the six stone tubs of water. 'Pure it is, from the stream. Try it.'

Joshua looked at the men eating below him, spoke to them. 'If I put new wine in old bottles, the bottles would break, the wine run out and be lost. But tonight you're all new men. I'll put new wine in new bottles, and preserve both.'

He touched the water and drank from his cupped hand, and I drank from his hand, and it was wine.

Joshua said, 'This is the blood of the Covenant.'

He held out his hand to Bartholomew, and Bartholomew drank. Then Bartholomew filled his hands with the wine and held them out, and men pushed around him, new men drinking the new wine. Architrinculus's worried face spread into a beaming smile and he called for pitchers, dipped them into the tubs of wine, filled the cups to overflowing and sent his children running with them among the guests, and the children opened the gates and ran with the cups of wine among the beggars and the sick newly arriving in a never ending stream, taking new wine to everyone who was thirsty.

I took a step back and found myself still standing beside Joshua; took another step back and I was still beside him. Quietly we slipped back into the shadows of the house, out through the back way that was locked and barred, but Joshua locked and barred it again from the outside by a means I did not see; and we walked between the people on the road and they did not see us, and we walked under the stars into the desert, and together we were alone. *Ego me Christo sponsam tradidi*. I gave myself as a bride to Christ.

And over my wedding night I draw a veil.

AMO ET ODI

love and hate

Later people said *I* was the water Jesus (by then they spoke Greek) turned into wine.

But my enemies (who were Joshua's, attacking me to attack him) claimed I could not have married him because I was not of the line of David, meaning that the wonders which had happened were a fraud. My friends (who were few) claimed equally fraudulently that I was a princess of the tribe of Benjamin not a commoner. A king had married a princess. So from the very first day of our marriage we were surrounded by lies.

Nearly always we were apart from each other though surrounded by other people, unhappy because we were alone, I in Magdala or Sepphoris or keeping Peter's house in Capernaum with his wife. Sometimes I heard Joshua came into a town I had just left, or that he had departed just before I arrived, not knowing I was coming; so though now we were bound by the closest bond, we lived further apart than before our marriage. Disciples who passed by told me what Joshua preached, not how he was, what he felt, whether the sore on his foot had healed; sometimes Joshua's loneliness, his anger, must have shown in his preaching, and I heard he said, 'Any man comes to me and he doesn't hate his father, and hate his mother, and hate his wife, and his children, and his brothers and sisters, and even his own life, then that man cannot follow me.' The disciples worried earnestly over these parables, prying them apart for meaning like men sucking stones, but they thought of Joshua not

286

at all. I knew I had to be near him.

But everywhere I followed him he had moved forward, and I must find him somewhere else. I heard he preached to the Gentiles of Tyre and Sidon, and followed him there to the north, but he was gone. I followed him southward to Bethany but he was gone. I heard rumours from his followers and returned to Galilee, took ship across the lake to Bethsaida, but found Joshua already sent away, his message fallen on deaf ears, the town turned against him and even against its own sons, the disciples Peter, Andrew and Philip.

'I hear,' Herod said, 'that John the Baptist whom I beheaded is alive again in the minds of his followers.'

I followed Joshua to Chorazin only to hear he had shaken the dust of the place from his feet because the people neither heard him nor allowed his healing to save them. They were afraid of Herod. Every disciple spoke of the success of Joshua's words and of the people acclaiming him, but Herod's important towns, Tiberias, Sepphoris, barred the gates against him, and as Herod's word spread down to the lesser towns and villages they too, as I told you, no longer allowed him to enter.

But sometimes, out in the lonely places which were all that were left to him in Galilee, there was magic. I don't mean Joshua's feeding of the four or five thousand or the walking on the sea; all those actions were easy for him and in his nature. I mean the actions that are hardest: words. Simply to find the words to make people hear what he said! To encourage them to open their eyes and see not him, not only him, but themselves. For him to uplift their hearts so that the uplifting was in themselves. For him to persuade them that there was more, so much more than they knew, not only in their poor impoverished lives walled in by death, but in the wonders and immensities that lie around us and above us and beyond, if only we learn we have eyes to see and ears to listen and hearts to feel. To show us that our power is in ourselves, not him. For Joshua to command the people would have been simple; power was easy for him, but persuasion was very close to the Devil's work.

'I hear,' Herod said, 'that John the Baptist is resurrected, and has done miracles, and his followers and the common people raise him up as their king.' He sent soldiers from Sepphoris to Magdala, where Joshua preached among the tombs.

But Joshua climbed up from the shore at Magdala high into the mountains above Galilee, past the precipices where the robbers and outcasts live in holes cut in the rock, and came to the village of Lubieh where I found him drinking at the well. I ran between the disciples, knocking them aside, and Joshua jumped up and kissed me on the mouth. I fell at his feet and he lifted me up. And that day, I heard him speak.

He began to speak just to me, no more than a whisper into my ear, then the disciples heard and began to listen. The more he spoke the more the word spread, the more the crowd gathered around us and heard. I don't know where they came from, villages, caves, out of the ground; the important thing was that they came and heard, and knew what they heard. By noon hundreds heard him under the sun's shadowless glare; by evening thousands. The disciples formed the *corona fratrum* around him, the circle of friends holding back the crowd who pressed forward, keeping back over-enthusiastic believers, stone-throwers, assassins, false prophets, naughty children, madmen. This place was a natural amphitheatre overlooked by two great horns of rock that magnified and threw down Joshua's words to the multitudes in the crowd.

First he blessed them, 'Amun.' Then Joshua promised: 'I come to preach the Gospel of the Kingdom.'

Voices called up, 'You the king sent to lead us?' Others cried out, 'He's the king, he's the son of David by his father and mother both!'

Joshua said: 'You hear the Law say, An eye for an eye and a tooth for a tooth. But I say, Don't resist evil. Whoever strikes your right cheek, offer him your left cheek. Whoever sues you under the Law and takes your coat, give him your robe as well. Whoever compels you to go a mile, go two miles with him. Give when you are asked, and lend to a borrower.' The people muttered disapproval at this, many of them up to their necks in debt to moneylenders, and the moneylenders muttered disapproval because they didn't want their business reduced. But Joshua said: 'You men and women with two good ears, you better listen! You have heard it said that you must love your neighbour and hate your enemy. But I say, Love your enemies' – nearly everyone muttered, thinking he meant an oath of fealty to Herod – 'and bless the man or woman who curses you, help those who hate you, pray for those who exploit you and persecute you, and make yourselves the children of our Father who is in Heaven. Our Father makes the sun rise on the evil and the good, He sends rain on the lawful and unlawful.' *Rain*. I heard the ripple of excitement run through the Nazarenes and zealots and sicariots and Sionists at that word. They believed he meant the Divine rain which will wash away the Romans. And perhaps he did. Joshua had won the disciples of John to his side, but with the others he still walked a tightrope.

'Remember,' Joshua told us, 'you must strive to be perfect, because our Father in Heaven is perfect.' *Teleios* is such a rare word with these people, I'd never heard any of the disciples come out with it, ever. But Mary the Rain-maker heard it all the time at Sion, where the priests believed utterly in perfection, *their* perfection, in all their dealings with God. A tear trickled on my cheek.

Joshua looked through the men surrounding him, stared straight to me, and he knew what was in my mind: that he sounded like a politician trimming his sails to the wind, tacking this way and that to keep his course in the world of men. He drew a breath. Throwing a long shadow now in the cool of the afternoon, he raised his arms over us.

Joshua said: 'Our Father in Heaven knows of everything you need before you ask Him. Therefore your prayers should *give* to our Father, not try to take from Him.' *Our Father* again, not Yahweh or Jehovah. Joshua began to speak a prayer and at first I thought it was the Eighteen Benedictions over again and he was speaking of our marriage. And Joshua was speaking of marriage, but also of so much more than that.

Joshua said: 'Father, hallowed be Your name. Your kingdom shall come, Your will shall be done in the world as it is in Heaven. Give us this day our needful bread. Forgive our sins, as we forgive the men and women who sin against us. Don't let us fall when we're tempted, and deliver us from

Satan. For Yours is the kingdom, and the power, and the glory, for ever.' Then Joshua finished clearly: 'Amen.'

Something new had happened. I'd never heard Joshua pronounce *Amun* as Amen before, and never at the end of a speech or parable not the beginning. The disciples looked round for him, but he was already gone. Someone took my hand, and I found myself slipping forward with Joshua through the crowd who surged past us towards where he had been.

No one saw us go.

Joshua is flesh and blood. He touches me, and I feel him; I touch his body in the flesh and he feels me as any man feels a woman. Is he a perfect lover? No, his body can be too hard or too soft, too quick or too slow. Sometimes his long hair tickles my face. But that he loves me makes him perfect. Every caress, every moment, every word, perfect. With love my life is perfect, I am perfectly whole wrapped in his arms, his perfect body, his perfectly ordinary love.

It's a long climb up here – Joshua's always fascinated by mountains – the limestone cliffs closing so narrow on each side that often we walk splashing in the torrent, our clothes clinging to our bodies, holding hands to wade across the pools, our echoing shouts and our happiness together setting clouds of pigeons rushing from holes in the rock like gusts of wind. Griffons, lammergeyers and eagles soar in the narrow blue ravine of sky winding above us, crimson creepers cling to the cliff faces like climbing hands reaching towards the caves and terraces high beyond arrow-shot. The place was once famous for refugees; Herod's soldiers were lowered from the top in boxes hung on chains, rooting them out with hooks on long poles, and fire.

The place is deserted now. They say Judas Zadok hid out here. But now there's only us.

We climb from cold shadows into sunlight. My feet slip but Joshua pulls me up with his hand. These upper galleries are untouched except for debris from the ancient siege: poles and bits of cloth; a broken sword which Joshua kicks over the edge, and we watch it fall twinkling end over end through the sunlight into the shadows of the darkness spreading beneath us.

Our perfectly ordinary love; of that you need know no more, since I have just told you everything.

I woke. Beyond the cave entrance the stars glittered desert-bright. I discerned a Joshua-shaped darkness standing silhouetted against them, crawled to him. Joshua sat, swung his legs over the edge. He stared at the Sea of Galilee framed full of stars between the cliffs. I pulled back from the dark drop, dizzy.

He said: 'Stay beside me, Mary.'

I sat beside him, swung my legs in the draught blowing emptily up the cliff. He said nothing. I said nothing. I could bear it no longer. 'I don't know if I've done right or wrong by marrying you!' I said. 'Have I destroyed you?'

'I don't know. Can love destroy?'

'What will happen?'

'I don't care.'

'You care for these people.'

'Men? They've made me into a magician like Simon. I prove myself by tricks. The more they believe in tricks the less they believe in me.'

'Don't listen to Simon or Judas or Yeshua. Don't listen to any of them. I hate them all.'

'Simon claims he can fly. They're so stupid, I'm angry. They don't need Satan.'

I was so afraid of falling, of losing Joshua. 'Joshua?'

He said patiently, 'Mary.'

'Has James gone over to the Devil's side? Does he do the Devil's work?'

'James?' Joshua sounded surprised. 'James is the best of them. Loyal. Unflinching. The most just of men, unswerving in his search for the truth.'

'Truth?'

'God. The reality of God. James is so hungry for the truth that he would die for it.'

I whispered, 'And I?'

'You are Mary Magdalene my wife.'

I laid my fingers lightly on his cheeks. 'Joshua, one day you will be king.' He nodded, he knew it. I said, 'But no Queen of Jerusalem rules beside Jesus Christ, King of the Jews. There never was. There can be no children by her for the Son of God.'

'I know.'

'No family. No heirs. Just glory. Worship. Success. When will you go to Jerusalem?'

'I don't know. I won't go.'

We were silent but for the flapping of our clothes in the night wind. My stomach rumbled. I said, 'I'm hungry again.'

He reached out and took some eggs from among those in one nest, some from another. In one hand he cracked an egg into two halves, spilling nothing, a yolk in each side, and passed it to me.

'Another miracle,' I said.

Joshua said mildly: 'You make yourself sound as blind and stupid and vicious as those who follow me.' His mildness showed me more clearly than shouting how deeply angry he was, how disillusioned. Perhaps how desperate. 'Mary, understand me. Each heartbeat in this world is a miracle, each breath's a miracle, every child's cry is a miracle. Miracles are inside us, outside us, all around us, every moment of every day.' He watched me eat. 'The egg's a miracle.'

'Suppose I'm pregnant?'

'A miracle.'

'And if I'm not?'

'A miracle.' He pointed. 'Look, see the moon.'

I stared. No moon shone among the stars. 'It's a new moon tonight, Joshua.'

'The sun rises soon.' He aligned my arm carefully with my eye. 'Now look.'

'Nothing.'

'That dark circle. The place where there are no stars.'

I saw it, laughed, then understood him. 'Its absence reveals its presence?'

'Just because God can't be seen doesn't mean His Spirit's not here, Mary.'

I stared at the darkness of the moon. 'You're here in the flesh,' I said.

'Today.' He held my elbow, and I remembered the drop below me.

'You can do anything,' I said faithfully. 'You could make that moon light up, couldn't you? Make it shine as a full moon.'

'Yes.'

'But you won't.'

'Satan would ask me to do so. He'd say what can be done, must be done.'

'No, I don't want you to.' I hugged Joshua with all my strength, spoke to his chest. 'How long would it take you to get there? To the moon?' A second and a quarter? Would Joshua travel at the speed of light?

'I am there, Mary.'

'I just want to understand you.'

'My spirit is there, here, everywhere. My body and soul are together in this world, just as your body contains your soul. I am what I do. I'm sent here by my Father for these people. For them I must destroy the Temple. Impose salvation. How can I impose love?'

I looked up, kissed his lips. The first glow of the sun obliterated the moon; the moment would never return. I kissed his nose, his eyes, his hair, hugged his head between my breasts. 'Joshua, stay here with me.'

He said: 'I love you, Mary.'

'I love you, Joshua, I love you,' I cried.

'Mary, Mary, Mary.'

'Get rid of them,' I cried, 'your apostles. Your disciples. Your followers. I hate them all, the rich, the poor, the Sons of Men. Be with me. Only me.'

'Only you.' He hugged me. 'That is the miracle I cannot do.'

'I'll be so quiet, Joshua, I'll be your mouse, you'll never know, just let me stay with you.'

'Sssh, Mary.'

'Joshua, please.'

'I cannot do, Mary.' He stroked the hair and tears from my eyes. 'Cannot.'

The rising sun struck fingers of light across the sky above us. Joshua pointed. 'Sol Invictus, god of the Romans. Amun to the Egyptians, Amun-Ra to Moses who led the Israelites out of Egypt. Amun and Ra, the two pillars of the world. That's how it started.' He was wrong; it started long before that. He pointed out Venus above the glare of the sun. 'Lucifer, the eye of Ra.' He glanced at me. 'I was brought up in Egypt by the Therapeutae of Sotinen, magicians and healers. An Essene sect, supporters of Simon's faction. Like Simon, like Judas, like James, like Matthew, they believe in the Covenant, they believe it's real and actual, buried beneath the Temple on Mount Sion. That they can take its power for their own and use it against their enemies.' He said bitterly: 'Even the Jews of this world are not what they are supposed to be.'

'But *you* are the Covenant, real and actual. *Amen* is new. The single pillar of the world, isn't it? The keystone, kingdom and priesthood made one under Jesus Christ, Amen. Show men your miracles, force them to believe in you. Your beautiful truth shall make them free, they'll come to you.'

He said mildly, dangerously, 'It's impossible to preach the truth, the whole truth. Men see darkness rather than light, because their deeds are evil. They fear the light.'

'But you can show them.'

'Even the best of men will ask, How can words of love, peace, compassion, tolerance, bring the all-powerful God into this world of demons and sinners?'

'Tell them, Joshua! Force them. You confronted the disciples of John. Your miracle at Cana changed the water into wine, brought them, *forced* them, on to your side.'

Joshua stood. 'Yes, I forced them.' For a ghastly moment I thought he was standing on the air, the thin air, then saw it was rock and dust beneath his feet. 'No more miracles.' He strode angrily about the cave. 'I can make men do anything, believe anything with miracles. I'll do no more healing.' He held up his hand. 'There, with this blessing I allow my faithful disciples to heal in my name.' He kicked stones over the edge. The sun struck through the cave entrance into his eyes. Joshua's beautiful eyes.

I went to Joshua and stared into him through those beautiful luminous eyes, his eyelashes, the reflections of me standing in the cave entrance with him, on tiptoe against him.

'Go to them as a man, not as the Son of God,' I whispered. 'Only a man. You don't need miracles. Fulfil the prophecies as a man telling the truth, simply the truth. Go to the Temple as only a man. If Simon will not follow you, go your own way. If Judas will not follow you, go your own way. If the followers of Yeshua Barabbas won't follow you, if Peter won't, go your own way.'

He stroked my hair. 'They'll follow me, Mary.' He smiled sadly. 'I won't be able to get rid of them.'

'And I'll follow you wherever you go.'

'No, Mary.'

I kissed his lips. A sensation of terror whipped through me. 'Have I kissed you like this for the last time?'

I kissed, I slipped down. My hands slid down his chest. I was alone with him for the last time. I felt his hip against my cheek, his long thighs through my hair, his knees, I kissed his ankles, and my hair fell about his feet.

Joshua said: 'It shall be as you say.'

I whispered: 'My Lord.'

He didn't know what would happen. He had no foreknowledge, no more than I.

This is what actually happened. I saw it.

Joshua returned to Capernaum, but dared not stay long; I arrived at the town and Peter's boat had sailed the night before, avoiding the guards on the roads as Herod's grip tightened. Peter's wife and her mother had gone away in fear of their lives, who knows where. Servants, paid off, shut up the empty house, and as I hurried away my last sight was of them kicking the beggars and sick from the gates for the last time. At the corner a stunted child immediately accosted me, a horrid creature with a gaping unformed palate, its tongue lolling between snarling lips like a serpent's tail. The child must have seen me at some time near Joshua; it pressed its face to my thigh with growling cries that turned to a little girl's laughter. Her face smiled up at me, perfectly formed. 'Healed by the blessing of Jesus Christ,' she trilled prettily in Greek, and ran away home.

My touch had healed – and served not only to heal but to heal a little Greek girl, a Gentile not a Jew.

I returned to the gates and healed until I was so utterly exhausted that I fell down among the mattresses the sick had left behind them, and slept there like a dead woman the rest of the day and all the night.

Dawn came again, and I must follow Joshua.

In all the two hundred towns and villages of Galilee,

Herod's word was law. Joshua would never sail to Tiberias, neither could he stay in Galilee; one of Peter's old hands setting up business in his master's place, living in hope of Peter's mansion if business went well, sailed me south to the Decapolis bank of the Jordan. One of the Greek washer-women remembered a tall man with long hair, another had been cured of a wart by a short powerful man who sounded like Peter, but the women got their names mixed up and called the short man with powerful shoulders Jesus.

I waded across the Jordan and in the market square at Agrippina, a town of Romans and Greeks, saw a notice hammered up by a soldier near the garrison gate. Written in Greek and Aramaic, with Latin in smaller joined-together words along the bottom, it was the official Roman search warrant called a forma. At first I thought it was for Yeshua Barabbas, whose name literally means Jesus, Son of God. But I knew Barabbas, a zealot, had already been arrested and taken for execution to Jerusalem for killing a Greek and some Jewish hecklers he called cowards. Barabbas believed, like most zealots, that the end of the world and the start of the Jewish new order would come about in his own lifetime. My mind went back to the Magdalene town square and Judas the Galilean accusing the Jewish crowd of cowardice, and Simon murdering the heckler who opposed violence. These people don't have a history, only their single-minded remorseless unforgiving pursuit of their God.

The notice, over the stamp of *Gaius Iulius Saulus, inquisitor*, sought Joshua. *The man Joshua, the head of a band of Revolutionaries and the Party called the Poor on the sea of Galilee, who escaped by boat.* I ignored the people jostling around me. *A man of simple appearance, mature age, long face, dark skin.* Well, his face and hands were dark from the sun like everyone's. *Small stature, three cubits high, hunchbacked.* Confused with Peter again; and Peter was muscular, not hunched, but it was a common insult among Galileans. *An uncut beard and long unwashed hair parted in the middle of the head, after the manner of the Nazarenes.* That was eyewitness: though consecrated Nazarenes washed their hair every day. Joshua had been travelling in haste, anyway. A man squinted up at me as I read, trying to sell me a chicken.

I knew Joshua couldn't turn back north, into Galilee; and

there were too many Greeks and Romans in the Decapolis. He'd go south. 'Samaria,' I said.

'Buy this chicken to feed you on your way,' the chicken-seller said. 'You'll find nothing in Samaria except Samaritans.' He added, 'And their holy mountain, Gerizim. God's revealing holy relics there, buried by Moses. Nice chicken, lady, kept me warm last night.'

I reached into my pouch – I always seem to have as much money as I need – tossed the man a shekel, and walked on the road towards Shechem carrying the chicken under my arm, where its fleas cheerfully swarmed from its feathers on to my body until I released it to cluck among dropped grains in a field of harvested barley. From the Decapolis, where Jews lob stones at the few Samaritans they meet, I came into Samaria where Samaritans lob stones at the few Jews they meet. Joshua had told a parable about a Samaritan that the disciples had not understood; now, no doubt, they did. I wondered if the Samaritans cursed Joshua as the Pharisees did for not teaching close to the Law of Moses; but Samaritans believe even in a different number of commandments, as well as different holy books and holy days, and at Shechem I heard of a travelling prophet called Jacob by them, and a well that overflowed with water however much was drawn out. Water is their word for wisdom, and they called him the Saviour of the world.

Their holy men searched for the Covenant on Mount Gerizim.

A few days later, or it may have been weeks, I climbed from the town below on to Mount Gerizim, windy and cold in the cloud. At the summit I glimpsed Joshua with the disciples around him, the wintry grey clouds blowing around them so that they appeared and disappeared with the wind, and the dismal clink of shovels digging against stone carried to me. Jars like water-jars had been unearthed, the Samaritan priests claimed, which had contained stones believed to be the Commandments of Moses, the Word of God, and the jars called *capsae* containing scrolls of the Pentateuch. 'Jars of wisdom!' Matthew proclaimed to the villagers watching. This was a pattern I'd see again: the disciples colonising an existing meeting and taking it over rather than starting one of their own.

And Joshua sat, a silent lonely figure in the middle of it all.

Peter said, 'Behold, the Saviour of the world.'

John said, 'He is the living water, the Spirit.'

James proclaimed, 'God's Spirit shall purify the righteous. Like purifying waters the righteous man shall sprinkle upon himself the Spirit of Truth.'

John said, 'He is the fountain of living waters prophesied by the prophet Jeremiah.'

I watched them and heard them and despised them. Their words claiming divinity for Joshua stripped divinity from him, and the wind carried their voices away into the mist. They spoiled everything they touched. Joshua looked so cold; none of them had thought to wrap a cloak round his shoulders.

I took a single step towards him, only one. He knew I was there but he said nothing, and I said nothing. He knew what I thought.

Then Joshua silenced them with an angry gesture, raised his voice, spoke to me. 'She who eats of wisdom is hungry for more, he who drinks of wisdom is still thirsty. But I say to you, whoever drinks of me shall never thirst, whoever eats of me shall never hunger. Amen.' He strode away and the cloud separated us, and when the mist blew away he was gone except for his disciples running after him.

Judas called to the crowd, 'The Messiah has come! The Christ has come!'

There was nothing else I saw or heard that day, nor for months; except that the Roman prefect, Pontius Pilate, ordered everyone found digging on Mount Gerizim killed with swords.

I heard Joshua had crossed the Jordan and gone into the wilderness of Perea to preach wherever there was a well, or a water hole, or an inn with a traveller inside to be found. I travelled to every inn on every road, every water hole, every well, but only in the city of Julias did I see Joshua, the disciples around him like bodyguards, the frenzied crowds lifting him up, and Judas shouting, 'Our Messiah has come! Our Christ has come!'

But Joshua looked at me, and spoke. 'From the beginning of creation God made man and woman, and because of this a man shall leave his mother, and cleave to his wife, they shall be one flesh, and what God has joined together no man can pull asunder. Amen.' But the crowds pulled him and me asunder.

My disciples will follow me, Mary. I won't be able to get rid of them. I'd begged Joshua to let the disciples follow him as a man not a god. But men do not follow men; they must be led by them. To teach is not to lead. The disciples saw what they wanted to see.

Even now, as though it's still happening, I hear the shouts of Simon and Judas rising over the crowd, hear the mass of faces take up the chant. 'Our Messiah is come! Our Christ is come!'

James saw me, pushed through, pulled me aside. 'You were right about Joshua. You were right all along, Mary. He is the Son of God sent to save us, He is truly the Christ and the Covenant. I see that now. I accept it.' He took my hand. 'You look so thin.'

'I walk so far.'

'God is coming to earth,' James said. 'God will come to His Son. You'll see. Every question will be answered, every truth revealed. No more darkness. We shall be a righteous people worthy of God.' He squeezed my fingers eagerly, sitting on a stone bench with me with people knocking past us, following Joshua wherever he had gone. 'I am forgiven, Mary.'

'Forgiven?'

'By Joshua. For doubting Him when I knew no better. He is not Joshua. He is Jesus. He told me a parable of a prodigal son who squandered his father's wealth, but his father forgave him. That son is me. Jesus was speaking to me personally.'

'Yes.' Everyone believed Joshua spoke to him personally. Everyone believed Joshua looked at him personally. 'I know, James.'

'I've done my best, Mary. Always.'

'Yes,' I said sadly, 'you always do your best. You saw Joshua do the miracles, didn't you?'

'Oh, yes! No scientific explanation. No explanation at all. A miracle's the authentic sign of God, an overturning of the laws of nature. No miracles, no God.'

'I understand. You've searched so long and so hard and now you've found Him.'

James looked around him; the crowds were gone. 'Where will you go now, Mary?'

'Wherever my husband goes.'

'Sion.'

'Then I shall go to Sion.'

'They say,' James whispered, 'that Jesus shall fulfil the prophecies at Sion.'

'What prophecies?'

'The prophecies that lead inevitably to the Covenant, to the glorious end of the world, to the rapture of our Assumption without death into Heaven.'

'Rapture?'

'The sight of the approach of God Himself to our world.'

I whispered, 'What of Satan?'

'There shall be a great battle lasting a thousand years, and the reign of the AntiChrist, but the dragon shall rise from the sea and be slain, and Jesus Christ will rule in glory to the end.' James jumped to his feet in his enthusiasm, but I held him back.

'What exactly are the prophecies?'

'Joshua shall make the two pillars into one. *Melchior* and *Zadok*, king and priest, Melchizadok, the perfect union. Establish Himself as king and priest as one to rule us all. Christ *and* Zadok anointed in one entity, the Son of God. The golden crown, the golden cloak.'

'What of Simon? What does he say about giving up his golden cloak to Joshua?'

'He has seen what Joshua can do.'

I said, 'And Joshua – Jesus – will agree to this?'

James looked at me strangely. 'What other choice does he have? If he does not fulfil the prophecies, he is not the One.' He smiled at me, kissed my forehead. 'Will you come to Sion?'

So, alone, I took the path to Sion. The track was very hot, blossom blowing from the orchards of Jerusalem apple which lined the road in places. My mind wandered in the heat and I stumbled full-length across a bloated mule buzzing with flies, dead in the road, its harness not yet stolen. I called out, then around the next corner found a man, red-haired, wearing a striped cloak, lying dead of a knife-wound in the shade of an apple tree. I was not the first to find him; his eyes had been closed, his purse was gone, his secret money-belt empty. I listened for breath then made sure of him, opened one staring blue eye: dead. Red hair, blue eyes. A Celt, probably a pilgrim from Galatia. I was sure I'd never seen that man before, yet his Celtic looks troubled my memory as I walked forward.

At Sion, as you understand, I was not allowed in the monastery of New Jerusalem itself or even into Egypt, which is for families. Exactly threescore furlongs past the monastery, just over seven Roman miles, I came to the desert outpost of wooden huts and booths set aside for women which is called Emmaus, with its miserable dusty stream I remembered from Mary the Rainmaker's day – though at this time of year the waters brimmed full and muddy. There I forgot the Celt, busying myself among the desultory women who distilled balsam perfume, holy to the priests, and helping with the tasks too filthy or demeaning for the priests' purified pious hands. Many devout Essene monks lived in retreat beneath rock slabs jammed together here and there in the desert, and sometimes there was a body to be pulled out – women's work – and washed, and buried. Those who were not dead I healed, and the women called me a disciple of Jesus, but the men said I wasn't a true disciple because I wasn't a man.

And in the open-roofed church (so I heard), Joshua accepted anointment and the crown *Amariah*, IMRI. 'The Lord has said.' So the will of the priests of Sion was the will of the Lord.

From the cliff top I looked down on the seashore far below my feet. From up here the waters of the Dead Sea looked deep black, motionless, lifeless, as though it truly were a bottomless pit. Steam drifted along the shore from the sulphur springs; the air stank of bitumen. Truly a place more like Hell than Heaven. Among the salt pans I saw a cluster of little men, foreshortened, gather around the golden figure of Joshua at the centre, bowing to him, guiding him forward, our anointed saviour, and Joshua walked out along the low jetty as though he walked on the water. He held out his arms like a king, then knelt like a priest, and drew the bobbing heads of the catechumens, 'fishes', to baptism in the bitter salt. Gentiles, mostly, and rich Jews scattered over the empire drawn here by all this talk of the Covenant and the end of the world, eagerly offering their shekels and staters and drachmae and earthly wealth to fill the monastery treasury. A miraculous draught of fishes. But no miracle. My tears dropped from my cheeks on to my breasts, staining my white shift with their moisture so that the colour of my nipples showed through, and I tore my shift and bared myself as I wept, but no one looked up, and no one saw.

VOX POPULI VOX DEI

the voice of the people is the voice of God

Early on Thursday morning in Bethany where I knelt in an alley among the sick and dying, tending those who crawl or are dumped here behind the synagogue to suffer and die out of sight, I heard the hubbub of a crowd in the street and then the voice of Joshua. 'Neither faith in me, nor membership of any church or faction or party, is necessary for salvation.'

People shouted, 'What did he say? Who is he?'

The disciples surrounding Joshua cried out, 'The Son of Man is come in His glory, and all the holy angels with Him, and He shall sit upon the throne of His glory!' Did the disciples call themselves his angels now? The people marvelled and pushed forward to see better.

In the shadows of the alley a woman pressed her bent and ravaged body against my hands, and stood straight. A mother brought her baby to me but I smiled, it was only wind; but still she worried. The shouting faded from the street, and when I finished I followed the people to the square. Joshua sat on the lip of the water trough dressed as they had dressed him, a small gilt circlet round his head like a king's crown, inscribed with stars of David, but he wore it as though to keep his hair in place. Over his seamless white linen shift he wore the yellow cloak that might have been called golden. He told a story about the talents, a fortune in silver coins given away by a rich man to his servants.

'*Kyrios*, Lord, we are Your servants,' Peter said.

'*Kyrios* speaks of the thirty talents with which Sion shall purchase the Covenant with the Lord!' James said eagerly. 'Is that not so?'

Joshua looked at no one as he spoke. He did not see me. 'The servant who had received only one talent went and dug a place in the earth, and hid his lord's money.'

'*Kyrios* speaks of the cave beneath the Temple where the Arch of the Covenant lies hidden,' James interpreted, and Matthew nodded. I listened sadly, remembering Matthew teaching it to the boys.

'I used to believe so,' I heard Matthew murmuring quietly. 'But now *Kyrios* changes everything to make it more marvellous than before.' Joshua's crown slipped slightly and Peter put it straight. Behind Joshua, Judas stood with his face turned up to the sun, savouring its spring warmth. He wore only the pallid white cloak of an ordinary priest over his shift, yet he wore it gorgeously.

Joshua said, 'And the servant who had dug his talent in the earth had it taken away from him, for he was an unprofitable servant.'

Judas knelt beside him. '*Kyrios*, the thirty talents is at your command. Give the word.' The sun's heat had beaded Judas's dark-skinned face with sweat, but he was still a handsome man, more handsome than any of the disciples, who were a thin lot except for Peter. None of them except Simon, Judas's uncle, fifteen years older, matched Judas's stature and educated manner. And none except Simon and Judas wore clothes shaped (I suspected) by one of the stylish Greek tailors of Jerusalem. By now he was too arrogant, too sure of himself, to bother dyeing his red hair black. That Judas was slightly overweight in the cheeks and belly added to the power of his personality. Many believed he was Simon's son – I'd heard John say so – but I never looked at Judas without remembering his real father, Judas of Sepphoris, crucified and burnt alive in front of the Temple; and without remembering the forceful personality of his grandfather Judas the Galilean, who worked all his life to be acclaimed Zadok. The title Simon and Judas had passed to Joshua. Men do not give up power handed down to them by their fathers lightly. Not lightly.

'Only give the word,' Judas repeated.

Joshua looked uncomfortable; the rim of the trough bit

into his skinny shanks. But he said, 'Amen, I say to you, the kingdom of Heaven is like a man travelling into a far country. And you know not the day or the hour when the Son of Man will come.'

Judas looked surprised, then bowed. Joshua stood and moved away, but Judas touched Simon's shoulder, spoke urgently. 'He does not know when the end of the world will come.'

'It will come,' Simon soothed. 'The time will come.'

Judas would have said more, but saw me. He bowed again, and I knew he disliked me. Simon nodded to him, go. When we were alone Simon put his hand on my shoulder, sure of his power over women. '*Kyrios* is staying at a woman's house,' he said. 'We men of Sion celebrated our Passover by the Calendar of the Sun on Tuesday. *Kyrios* is free to do miracles today.'

I shrugged him off.

'She's Martha, about the same age as you,' Simon said. 'A little younger. A sister in Christ, she received the baptism from Peter. Her brother is Lazarus.'

Martha I did not know, but I remembered Lazarus at Cana, faithful to John the Baptist. 'Lazarus doesn't follow my Lord. He wouldn't drink new wine.'

'That's why Lazarus is dead,' Simon said smoothly as we walked. 'He's been dead for months. All winter. A hard winter. But now he believes, like Herod, that John is resurrected in the flesh of Jesus Christ.'

'Then Lazarus has found his faith.'

Simon smiled thinly. 'Not officially. He has not yet been raised up to drink the wine of Our Lord.' He showed me to a house with people coming and going, introduced me to the woman called Martha. 'I must hurry away. Our Lord's raising Lazarus from the dead.'

Joshua had told me he would not heal; he was like a man. I said, 'Lazarus can't really be dead. He'll stink!'

'Symbolic death,' Simon said smoothly. 'It was not an illness to death itself but for the glory of God, so that the Son of God will be glorified by means of it. Lazarus will be raised from excommunication and returned to the life of the Community.'

'But that's a lie. It's just wordplay.'

Simon said, 'No, it's a lie for the greater truth, because it is for the glorification of our Lord Jesus Christ, the Son of God, as I have told you!' He left without bowing.

Martha gave me a nervous, frantic smile, hurrying about as she was, her arms laden with dirty dishes and cups, and her floors filthy. 'They won't be long. It's all planned.' A plain, loyal little thing, she dropped half what she was carrying and I picked up the scattered pieces. 'You wash,' I said, 'I'll do the floors.'

As soon as we heard the noise of the men returning in the street Martha smoothed her mousy hair and ran out to welcome Joshua to Lazarus's house, but I remained sitting inside and waited for him to come to me, which as his wife I am obliged to do. Men came in laughing and joking, relaxing. Lazarus had drunk the wine. I saw Zacchaeus the teacher and Bernice his wife and greeted them, two of Joshua's earliest followers. Among the crowd of heads I saw the turban of Joseph of Arimathea, and he talked to a tall man with the muscles of a blacksmith, Nicodemus, also wearing a turban, both Archons of the Sanhedrin. Someone pushed me aside, another demanded wine. Joshua ducked through the doorway and stopped. We both stared as though we hardly recognised each other.

'You've lost weight,' Joshua said.

The golden cloak hung uncomfortably from his shoulders, the gold circlet had slipped again, and again Peter straightened it. Joshua took it off. He let the cloak drop. He took three paces to me and lifted me up and kissed me on the mouth. I stared into his open eyes. 'You've lost more,' I said.

'*Kyrios*, here's Lazarus,' Peter said.

'Faithful Lazarus,' Joshua said and did not look round. Lazarus was a thin man with a limp. He wore a shroud and stank of nothing worse than sweat, not even moral corruption, unless it's a sin to fool a crowd of peasants.

'I remember you truly raised Levi,' I told Joshua, 'and after he was raised, he was perfect.'

Joshua said, 'Levi who for his earlier sins now burns in the Hell of his master.' So Joshua too believed in Hell, as well as Levi.

The men crowding into the room pushed us into the

corner. Martha hurried about with food. She kept casting me appealing glances, help.

I looked up into Joshua's face. 'So this they're making you do is all part of God's mysterious plan for the salvation of Israel,' I said.

'Is it, Mary?'

'No.'

Someone blessed the food. 'I'll tell you what it is,' Peter ate a chicken leg, 'it's the hour of Jesus. Lazarus proves that. Did you hear them shout!' He added, 'Lazarus has been given bread from the table and hurried to safety at Sion, Lord. We uncovered a plot of the Jerusalem priests – a senior faction of the Sanhedrin, Annas, Caiaphas, others – to have him killed.'

'Killed? Why?' I cried.

As usual, Peter would not look at me when he spoke. 'Obviously, a man who is dead again cannot prove he rose from the dead.'

'The hour is come and the Son of Man will be glorified,' Simon said. '*Kyrios*, it's the Temple Passover in two days. When will you go into Jerusalem?'

I reached up, turned Joshua's face to me. 'Into Jerusalem?'

'My followers have lifted up the Son of Man,' Joshua said, glancing round their faces, then back to me. 'And you know that I am he, and that I do nothing on my own authority.'

I whispered, 'Do not go into Jerusalem as a man.'

He whispered, 'You yourself begged this of me, Mary.'

'Do not go.'

He whispered to my hair, 'You yourself.'

'Do not. Don't let yourself go. Don't make me follow you.' I whispered: 'I know what lies beneath the Temple, what you'd find beneath the ruin.'

'So do I.'

I stood on tiptoe, pressed my lips to his ear. 'The Arch of the Covenant is the work of men not of your Father. Perhaps the work of Satan.'

'What is the work of Satan, Mary?'

'Temptation. Temptation.' I wanted to shake him, batter him with my fists, but he caressed my hands lovingly. I wept, 'Don't go.'

Joshua said simply, 'Who has known God, who can know Who is God?'

Only God could know. There was only one possible reply. 'Only you.'

Outrageously, I hoped that Joshua was not the Son of God. I prayed it.

'Every single thing in Heaven and Earth is my Father's work,' Joshua said gently. 'Don't be careful in this world, don't worship safety. Don't put your faith in pure food. Have faith in God. Believe in me. I am the Covenant. Mary, I know what I'll find in Jerusalem. It's time I showed myself to the world.' He raised his voice, spoke to us all. 'Now is the time of judgment of this world, now shall the ruler of this world, Satan, be cast out. And I, when I am lifted up from the earth, will draw all to myself.'

'*When*,' Simon told Thomas. 'He said *when*, not immediately. It won't be at once.'

'Why do we have to wait?' Thomas said.

'Go far away,' I whispered to Joshua. 'Preach love to us.'

'I do love you.'

'Preach it to the world of men.'

'I do.' He wound a single curl of my hair around his finger. 'You.'

'I've a prophecy of Abel for you, and of Zecher,' I told him. ' "It is impossible that a prophet die outside Jerusalem." '

Joshua kissed my lips.

Then he turned to Peter. 'Go into Jerusalem. Rent a furnished room sufficient for us all for tonight.'

It was prophesied by the prophet Zecher that our anointed saviour will enter Jerusalem riding an ass's colt, so Joshua rode. His followers among the poor threw down palm leaves for him to ride over, the rich threw down their expensive cloaks, and the outcasts and beggars threw down their own bodies, and had to be dragged out of the way crying, 'King Joshua! Hail, King Joshua!' The Rich called out to him, 'King Jesus, see us, King Jesus,' in their educated voices. The Pharisees stared and pointed, sneering. 'Look, the world's going after him.' But children ran shouting hosannas ahead of the procession, not chucking insults and dung as they usually did, and I saw Zacchaeus handing out pennies to their dirty clutching fists. 'Hosanna!' they chirped at the top of their unbroken voices, '*Hosanna membrone barouchamma adonai!* Save us now, Highest; blessed are You for coming in the name of the Lord!'

I said quietly, 'So you're a paymaster these days.'

'For years.' Zacchaeus was utterly bald nowadays, but wore a florid grey beard. 'I'm a teacher who has taught himself to be his pupil's pupil.' One of Bernice's clever sayings, no doubt.

I shielded my eyes against the spring sun. 'Zacchaeus, why is he going into Jerusalem?'

'To take possession of the Temple,' Zacchaeus said. 'There's no other reason. He's got to make his move from the desert or wither away. He's got to get into the people's hearts, which is what he does best. And he'll do it at Passover because a hundred thousand people will be in Jerusalem to see him do it.' The road was crammed with pilgrims in front and behind, some of them complaining about the slowness of Joshua's animal, but it was unbroken and obstinate. 'It's not enough to be a great man,' Zacchaeus said, 'he's got to be a great man in Jerusalem.'

I said, 'Peter will never find a room to hire at this time of year.'

'Oh, that was arranged months ago.' Zacchaeus threw down his cloak on a bare patch of road for Joshua to ride over. Bernice looked up at Joshua against the sun and squeezed my hand. 'The reason Joshua is here,' she said, 'is simply that he has no choice. He believes what he believes. How could he stop?'

It was almost the first time I had ever heard her say something not trying to be clever. Joshua had no choice. King Jesus had no choice. He believed what he believed, knew what he knew, whether or not it was what the world of men believed. Someone at the gate saw us and shouted, 'Fear not, daughters of Sion! Behold, the king approaches, sitting on an ass's colt!' The ass bucked at the Lamb Gate to the city, was pulled through. We listened to the crowd and I couldn't make out whether they were excited followers of Joshua or excited Passover pilgrims. Then we were squeezed between the massive gates into cramped, teeming, festooned Jerusalem.

For a moment I saw Joshua dismounting among the people. 'But I wish he loved himself more,' I whispered. Bernice overheard. I saw Joshua walking up the steps to a house near the Essene Gate with the apostles, his 'angels', hurrying around him to be welcomed by the owner, a Greek disciple, and the door slammed behind them to hold the people out. Bernice said, 'Walk with me.'

We walked along the market of jewellery shops, Greek goldsmiths and silversmiths crafting exquisite work. 'Come to Apollyon the Silver for the best workmanship at the keenest prices!' trilled a boy by the low, hole-in-the-wall entrance to a workshop. We stopped. Ahead of us we saw the cheap jumbled stalls of Jews selling rubbishy copper trinkets. Our people hardly know how to work silver and gold; Jewish silver shekels are so rare that even Jews don't use them much and the Temple won't take them. Apollyon's boy, thinking we wanted to buy, tugged our sleeves. We glimpsed gorgeous silverwork glinting like eyes among the shadows, the backs of buyers cruising like slowly moving fish. 'Apollyon's chosen a poor name to work by,' Bernice said. 'It's the Greek for Abaddon, the angel of the bottomless pit, the place of destruction. At Sion the priests say Abaddon reigns over the locusts which fly out from the pit at the fifth trumpet.' Two men ducked their turbanned heads, blinking as they emerged through the low doorway into the sunlit street, knocking into us. Temple priests: no apologies from them, only haughty stares. The pair were of an age to be father and son but dissimilar in appearance, though both had white beards, the younger with strands of black; but both men were rough and foul, their cloaks stained. The older man's face had collapsed down the left side with a stroke but his distorted eye stared out indomitably, and everyone passing bowed to the two men with reverence. 'Temple priests in a place like this!' I whispered, watching them go. 'And why the dirty clothes?'

Bernice turned her back on them. 'Sadducees. That's High Priest Caiaphas and his father-in-law Annas, high priest before him. Aristocrats dressed for grief, a death in the family perhaps, but they can't ignore Temple Passover.

310

They won't be allowed to do sacrifices in that state of ritual impurity. Only a perfect man can enter the Holy of Holies.' Bernice knew everything and everyone, as usual. 'Annas was high priest for ten years after Judas Zadok's rebellion. It was Annas who cleansed the Temple of the blood. He's suffered an apoplexy, given up daily work, but the old man still pulls Caiaphas's strings, they say. So does the Roman prefect, Pilate, and he's bound to be in Jerusalem for the Passover, there's always trouble. So Caiaphas dances between his wife's father and the Emperor's trained wolf.'

'And Herod?'

'Herod keeps his great palace, that's all. He hates the priests and the priests hate him. Here politics is religion, and everything in Jerusalem is religion, so everything's politics.' She shrugged as we pushed between the stalls of copper knick-knacks, were shoved back, hardly able to move for the crush of visitors pushing devoutly into Jerusalem for the holiest feast of the year. 'You can imagine how it goes. They're like little boys.' A vivid mental image returned to me of Joshua and James as children battering at each other with their fists, pulling hair, rolling in the mud. I blinked. Bernice said, 'Herod builds a balcony to overlook the Temple sacrifices while he breakfasts, so the priests build a wall to stop him, so the Romans knock the wall down so their soldiers keeping watch from the roof can see into the Temple's sacred courtyards – you know, where if a Gentile sets foot there's a riot and he's torn to pieces. And Passover's always the most dangerous time – so many people. One year a Roman soldier on the roof lifted up his tunic, waved his uncircumcised cock at the Jewish worshippers, twenty thousand of them – Passover, remember – then turned and bent over and farted at them. A loud porky fart. You can imagine their fury, the insult to God in God's own house. A riot, thousands trampled, crushed, injured. All Jews.'

'Politics,' I said, grunting as someone pushed me. 'Behaving like children.'

'No, they were right,' Bernice said. 'The Jews can't ignore a blasphemy to God.'

I bought a pot of ointment while Bernice looked for Zacchaeus, and returned alone to the Greek house. One of the hangers-on let me in. There was a large upstairs room but it was empty. Someone said they'd heard that Joshua might be preaching in the Temple.

That was the place to be. I covered my head, took off my sandals, climbed to the huge courtyard where even Gentiles were allowed. I could hardly move; there must be twenty thousand people here, their feet scuffing the dust in clouds, the stink and pressure simply enormous. A sheep escaped and ran across people's heads before being stunned and pulled down. Sometimes trumpets sounded. The crowd pulled me round until I did not know where I was, then I saw signs for the place of trumpeting and the Court of the Women. A message on a stone slab warned Gentiles of death for them if they went further, and I pushed past. This place too was packed with men and women. I'd heard not a word about Joshua. I pushed forward to the Hall of the Nazarenes in the corner but someone said Joshua had already left the Temple precinct. At least they'd heard of him. I pushed my way to the Hall of Lepers where the sick lay, and Joshua had been there, and done no healing, but the apostles had.

I struggled out into the courtyard again. The golden roofs blazed around me in the sun. A woman could go no further. Beyond the Court of Israel, only for men, gleamed the huge marble and gold cube of the Holy of Holies. Joshua, his mother the Virgin beside him, must already have gone into the building for his Recognition and formal coronation as King of all Jews. She'd kneel at his feet as he took his place on the throne as Jesus Christ, the single pillar of king and priest united, the keystone who needed no Baptist to anoint him. Joshua would touch his own forehead with galbanum, myrrh, balsam, cinnamon, and pronounce: 'The Spirit of the Lord God is upon me, because the Lord has anointed me.'

And all the priests would fall down worshipping His glory.

But the veil over the main entrance rippled undisturbed by anything expect the spring breeze. There were guards everywhere; perhaps they'd not let Joshua through. From the sacrificial area I heard lambs cry out briefly, then the fragrant sacrificial smoke drifted over us, an offering to the

Lord. But still I had not seen Joshua, and the sun dipped down towards evening.

A woman cried out she'd heard someone saying words of wisdom, and my heart lifted. 'Where?' She was vague; it was earlier. This morning. No, this afternoon. How her feet hurt, and her back, standing all day. Another woman said she'd heard it wasn't wisdom but blasphemy. Other people hadn't heard anything at all. What was his name? Who? A little girl said his name was Joshua. He'd been asked to leave; no, he'd been asked to stay. A madman had preached crazy words at the top of his voice, no one had listened. A shepherd said, 'The scribes know how to deal with that sort of nonsense, believe me.' The little girl said, 'It was Joshua.' The shepherd said, 'They should give these people a good talking to.' Someone had heard that Joshua had fled the city, not even daring to return to the Passover feast. Others were sure the high priest and the Pharisees and the Sanhedrin council had put a price on his head, so he must be still here, perhaps even in the Temple if he was crazy enough to dare, and the fat woman assured us all prophets were crazy madmen, and people started looking round hoping to make some money.

No Joshua.

But the crowd swept me forward among the sellers of turtledoves, pigeons, birds fluttering in piled-up cages ready for sacrifice, prices starting to drop with the sun no doubt, year-old unblemished lambs and so many baaing and braying and shitting animals that I could hardly hear the prices offered. Fingers were waved in my face instead, discounts shouted in my ear. Gifts and offerings to the Temple could be paid only in Tyrian two-drachma pieces, so moneychangers sat in rows with their backs against the vast ashlar blocks of the Temple wall, satchels of change wedged safe behind them, piles of small bright coins and special offers displayed cunningly on the rugs between their spread legs. They'd change any coin minted in the Empire, raw metal, pottery, wine, anything manufactured or grown, sacks of grain, animals, children, prostitutes – they had assistants to carry away or hurry away everything – they'd change anything into money that could be sold for money, and they always cheated. Cheated the seller, cheated the buyer, cheated each

313

other, and their left hands never touched their right hands. Urchins on commission slipped through the crowd like germs in the blood, pouncing on country bumpkins who were lost, confused, overwhelmed by the awe and majesty of the Temple. Gangs squabbled over the best customers like angry birds. Soon the priests would send round to the moneychangers for their cut, then the guards, gangsters, tax collectors, place holders and everyone else who could muscle in, and the moneychangers survived by cheating everybody, and hoped to live until tomorrow.

By the entrance to the Temple I saw uncovered heads moving forward into the crowd, their hair blowing loose in the evening wind among the devoutly covered heads of the worshippers. I saw Joshua taller than the rest in the circle of disciples. He'd been weeping outside in the street; his cheeks were wet. Among the grandiose surroundings of the Temple the tears looked like weakness, not strength. A guard ran forward and scuffles broke out, but the disciples swept Joshua forward. Peter shouted: 'Behold, King Jesus weeps for Jerusalem whose priests have rejected him!'

I knew Joshua wept for his apostles, for us.

The disciples parted, revealing the twelve apostles around him. Nine or ten, anyway; I didn't see Simon or Judas. Roughs with curved knives and staves pushed among the crowd, keeping order. Peter cried out: 'King Jesus, Jesus Zadok! The two pillars made one!'

Judas called out from among the crowd, 'Our Messiah is come! Our Christ is come!' But the crowd stayed silent.

James shouted, 'Jesus Christ comes to take possession of the Temple. Jesus Christ *is* the Temple! Jesus Christ is our cornerstone, the cornerstone of our Temple wall!'

Simon shouted, 'Jesus Christ is the cornerstone of Israel. Israel, arise, to your tents! Israel shall be reborn, and Jesus Christ is her foundation!' But he looked around him as he spoke, gauging the mood of the crowd.

A priest called out, 'Why are you fellows wearing your shoes?'

'Yes,' another priest called in a high voice, 'and why are you showing your hair, defiling our Temple?'

'He's got a price on his head,' the first priest called. 'You can get five denarii for King Jesus's hairy head.'

A moneychanger called, 'Better cut his hair for him afore he knocks the Temple down like Samson!'

James shouted again, 'Jesus Christ *is* the Temple. The prophet Malachi has foretold this day, "The Lord whom you seek shall suddenly come to His Temple, the messenger of the Covenant. Who shall stand when He appears?" ' But the people did not fall to their knees, though the sicariots knocked a few over. The crowd stared at Joshua like dull animals. James tried again. 'He shall sit in judgment as a refiner and purifier of silver.' Silver's important to them, hopeless though they are at working it with their hands: to them silver means purity. 'Jesus Christ shall purify the priests and purge them of gold and silver, that they may offer their righteousness to the Lord . . .' James's words faded away.

Simon pushed through the ring of disciples, then the apostles, and stood in front of Joshua. In his hand Simon held a length of leather thong knotted at intervals, like a scourge for animals.

'*Kyrios*, the time is now.'

Joshua took the scourge. He looked at the knots. He looked into Simon's eyes.

'*Kyrios*,' Simon said, 'the people watch you for a sign.'

Joshua said, 'I have promised that I will perform no signs in Jerusalem. I am the Lord's servant, not His master.'

'Without the power of Heaven,' Simon whispered, 'how can I control these men?'

James added his voice. 'Without the proof of a miracle, the people will be afraid to rise at your side against the Romans.'

There was a silence, then Judas said, 'The Covenant will not be vindicated unless you prove yourself now. You must destroy the Temple.'

'The Temple must fall,' Simon said, 'or there will be another fall.'

Joshua looked at them one by one.

Judas stood close to Joshua. 'Raise your arm to scourge the Temple now, and angels will flock to empower you with all the might and wrath and vengeance of the righteous God. You shall lead us to the Covenant and yourself be in your own body the Covenant which shall destroy the Romans.'

Joshua said: 'And yet you don't take what I do offer you.'
'What's that?' Judas said.

I pushed forward. 'Love!' I screamed. 'Peace! Love, peace, mercy, generosity, tolerance!' Someone whacked my head with a stave and I fell to the ground. I sounded stupid and I looked stupid and pathetic. Joshua did not come to me. Perhaps he had not heard me. Perhaps he knew it was not the right time to come to me. Judas shot me an uncomprehending glance. I don't suppose he'd heard of these words before, romantic words young girls are supposed to live by, not grown hairy men. I could smell the violence hanging like thunder in the air, I could almost smell the thick sweet smell of men's blood starting to flow.

Joshua held out his arms. The scourge whipped slowly from side to side, dangling from his hand. 'Amen. Amen.' He strode towards the moneychangers who stared at him as blankly as Judas, and he raised the scourge, and brought it down. The apostles stared upward to see the evening sky split open and the Hand of God come grasping down surrounded by lightning and angels to destroy the Temple that had insulted Him for so long, as the priests at Sion believed, with its incorrect and profane rituals of worship. To see the Hand of God revealing through His Son the purchase of His Covenant by Sion, and the beginning of the end of the world.

Nothing happened. Joshua wasn't physically strong. The scourge slapped and a few satchels of coins were dropped; one man tripped on a rug and fell over. Joshua moved among them, a thin man wearing sandals, calling them a den of robbers. The moneychangers laughed, nodding; they knew it. Joshua's arm grew weary. He held the scourge in his other hand, then dropped it.

Then he left the Temple. The disciples and apostles and Greeks stood round for a little while, discussing among themselves what to do, then went after him.

Trumpets sounded as darkness fell. Friday morning (according to the Temple calendar) had begun.

I climbed the outside stairs to the upper room at the Greek's house. The feast to celebrate the destruction of the Temple had been laid out on a long table. None of those who had believed had the stomach to eat; even the lamps seemed dim. Servants had already helped themselves to the best slices of lamb, from the thigh, and crumbs showed where most of the loaves had gone. I hurried head down past the men, who wouldn't look at me, and joined the women in the back room. 'It didn't happen,' the women accused me. 'We did all this work and it didn't happen.' I found the woman who spoke and pulled her hair.

'I've got a husband who's going to kill me,' a girl said, pulling a shawl over her head. 'Day after tomorrow's Passover, and have I got anything ready?' She hurried out.

'Got all our hopes up,' someone said sadly. 'Now he's dropped us in it.'

One by one they left, the last few shamed into lying they'd see me tomorrow, then scurrying away. Most of the Greek men had already left, afraid of a raid on the house by the high priest's religious police. Five denarii was a week's pay for a man in good work, a small fortune to a woman. But a Greek house was safe from a search by Jews, and any outsider who'd seen Joshua would be wary of his rumoured supernatural powers. Martha watched me from a stool, her elbow resting on a grail of broken bread that someone had dropped, her hand wearily in her hair.

'It's impossible,' she said. 'He said he'd knock it down, and it's still there.'

'Where is he?' When she shrugged I said, 'Joshua.' She shrugged again.

I had to find him. We'd leave Jerusalem tonight, go north to Galilee, live in the robbers' caves, live together on eggs and love, the perfect simple life, and burn stones to keep us warm at night.

Martha gazed at me. 'You don't care about Jesus, do you.'

I went back to her angrily. 'Care?'

'Something marvellous almost happened,' Martha said. Her eyes filled with bitter tears. 'For the first time there was someone not just a man. John the Baptist was just a man. Lazarus was just a man. He couldn't live without hope, and believing in Jesus meant believing John was dead, because they aren't the same. Anyone can see that. But my brother was prepared to do even that, let his belief in John die, because he believed in Jesus so very deeply. Believed that

Jesus was more than a man. Believed Jesus was the One who could make everything that needs to happen, happen. But it's a lie! Jesus is a lie.'

'He's the truth.'

'I was there in the Temple today. I saw the lie. Everything I hoped and believed turn into a lie. There's no Heaven for us. No salvation. He betrayed us.' I wiped her tears on my dress. She said, 'And you don't care. You'd let it all go to have your Joshua back.'

'Yes.'

'That's not love,' she wept. 'It's so selfish.' I hugged her head. She was right. I swallowed, about to speak. Through the open shutters drifted the screams and thuds and running footsteps of Jerusalem at night. The Passover moon – always full, of course – was the perfect moon for thieves.

I made myself speak. 'Martha, it was me. I begged him to be only a man. To do no signs in Jerusalem. Not to impose His Godhood. To encourage, persuade, uplift the hearts of men and women to belief in God of their own free will.'

At last she returned my hug. 'I do believe. That's what's so terrible.' She shivered, closed the shutters. 'Anyone who thinks he can uplift the hard hearts of Jerusalem's bound to fail.' She kissed me. 'Well, another day. Let's get on with it.'

I said, 'Joshua hasn't failed.'

'You failed him, then.'

That was true. I saw it was true. What a terrible thing to say, but Martha was busy with the dishes, her mouth saying anything while her hands washed. I had failed Joshua. There was a stir of motion among the men in the main room. Joshua had come in. Then there was the most awful silence I have ever heard. Joshua covered his head, took off his sandals, and I overheard the whisper of his bare feet across the boards.

Simon said loudly, 'Will you do it tomorrow?'

It was late. Tomorrow was almost today.

Joshua said mildly: 'Simon.' His mildness that always showed me his anger.

'If you don't prove you're Lord of the Temple you've betrayed us,' Simon said. He looked round the others. 'We're betrayed by the one we trusted and adored.' He said urgently, 'Don't betray us, Joshua—'

Joshua spoke over him. 'Simon, Simon, Satan beckons you. Give yourself to Him and He will give you everything you desire and break you into atoms' – Joshua used the Greek word – 'until, Simon, you are torn wholly apart and have nothing, not even what you have. Have faith, Simon. I pray your strength won't fail you, and that you have faith in me, and strengthen your brethren in their faith.'

'We're already strong,' Judas said. He meant the zealots and sicariots. 'We need more.'

'We're strong in poverty,' Peter said. 'We don't need more. Let's shake the dust of Jerusalem from our feet.'

Joshua turned on him. 'Faithful Peter. I told you to give up all you owned and follow me in the way of peace, and you have. Have you ever lacked for anything?'

Peter said faithfully, 'No, not lacked.'

Joshua spoke so loudly that the room echoed. 'Amen, now let any one of you who has money buy a sword! If you have no money, sell your clothes to buy one!'

But they didn't move. Simon said, 'Will you lead us with a sword?'

'The prophecies shall be accomplished in me.' Joshua went to the table, but they did not follow him. Half the hangers-on, having slipped what food they could into their robes, had quietly left the room since Joshua started speaking. His voice was a lonely echo in a room made for so many people.

I heard Judas whisper urgently to Simon: 'Will this man lead us? Will this man tear down the Temple with his hands? Will a man such as this man turn the Passover moon to blood?' They stared at Joshua who stood with his back hunched over the table, his long-fingered hands flat on the white cloth, his eyes closed.

Simon whispered, 'All's not lost.'

What fools they were! But they weren't the ones who had let Joshua down. They'd given their lives for him, many of them given up all they had, money, wives, children, to follow him. I was the one who had let Joshua down. And now not one of them had called him *Kyrios*, or Lord, or our anointed one.

I walked into the room. The twelve apostles and however many disciples remained all stared at me, a woman not carrying a plate or a pitcher. I walked to Joshua at the table. I took off my shoes and I covered my head with a white cloth which I did not tie beneath my chin but let hang down on my breasts. I knelt at Joshua's feet, crouched, lay, touched his ankles with my hands.

'My Lord.' I kissed his feet. 'My Lord Jesus Christ, our anointed saviour, save us.'

I meant: go into the Temple tomorrow. Do whatever needs to be done. The Recognition, the destruction, anything. Save yourself. Yes, that's what I really meant. Save yourself from us.

But I felt Joshua's weight shift on his feet as he turned to the apostles.

Joshua said to them: 'Amen, I say to you, I shall neither eat again until my word is fulfilled in the kingdom of God,' I heard a cup scrape as he lifted it, 'nor drink again until the kingdom comes.' He handed the cup among them, I heard them drink. He cut the unleavened bread into twelve pieces. 'This is my entire life which is given for you.' Again the cup. 'This is the new Covenant in my blood.'

I heard each one drink and eat, except James who said, 'I shan't eat your bread until I know your word is fulfilled in the kingdom.' Joshua said, 'When you see, you shall eat.' What I was overhearing was part of the Passover ritual, but also new. Whatever Joshua was doing was new. He didn't plan to go into the Temple tomorrow, I was sure of it. Something dug into my side: the box of ointment I'd bought earlier.

Joshua said: 'One of you has betrayed his faith.'

'Not I!' Peter exclaimed, quickly.

Joshua said, 'Before dawn, Peter, you'll deny three times you even know me.'

'Joshua,' Simon promised, 'I'd go to prison for you. I'd die for you.'

I felt Joshua move as he looked round their faces. Any of them could have betrayed him, or all of them. Nothing fails like failure. They all drew back from him.

Judas said, 'Me?'

Joshua said: 'Man, it would be better for you if you had not been born.'

Judas's chair scraped. His footsteps crossed the floor. He

stopped by the door; I saw his hairy ankles and his rope-and-wood sandals. Then the door closed and he was gone.

Judas, the treasurer at Sion with thirty talents of silver at his fingertips, would betray Joshua for a mere five denarii? Incredible. I didn't believe a word of it, not a word. And who among the priests would dare offer it to the treasurer, except as an insult? Those same priests had not dared lay hands on Joshua even in their own place, by daylight: the word of his miracles had come too strongly from Galilee, and they'd seen the crowds that followed him from Julias and Bethany. I believed neither in the reward nor the betrayal. But still, the door had closed, and Judas was gone.

Joshua spoke to the apostles. 'Amen, tonight the sheep of the flock shall be scattered.' He said other things I was too miserable to hear. He was sending them beyond the city wall; he knew he had to get the apostles away from the house before the priests' men came. They drew back from the table and the room fell silent, then the door closed behind the last footstep.

I lifted the cloth, scrambled out, and stood beside Joshua where he stood shivering with his knuckles on the table. Quickly he turned, gripped me, kissed me on my open mouth.

I touched his forehead trickling with cold sweat. Joshua's mouth tasted sour with fear. His hands gripped far too tight, bruising my flesh. 'My Lord, my Lord,' I whispered. 'Run away. Joshua, come with me, run away.'

He cried out in a voice that echoed up and down the empty room. 'Father, if You can, take temptation away from me.'

'Joshua,' I whispered. I wanted to tell him so much, all the plans I had, the dreams, the robbers' caves, our entire life together.

'Father,' Joshua said. 'Father.'

He shuddered. I think he had never felt so alone even though I was there. But still he tried to speak to his Father. He clung to me with all his strength. Then the strength went out of him and he almost collapsed into a chair. I sat cross-legged in front of him, waiting for the priests' men.

'They'll find us together,' I said. I opened the jar of

ointment, pale yellow, strong-smelling. It was myrrh, for death, the same spice that had accompanied his birth. Joshua covered my hands with his own, and together we anointed his feet with the myrrh.

I asked, 'What will happen?'

'I don't know.'

'They won't harm you.'

'They'll do whatever the prophecies of men foretell, if Satan defeats me. You should ask Matthew or John or James. They know such things.'

'So do you.'

'Yes, I know them. Satan always wins in this world. He's in the eyes and minds and hearts of men. By now Satan *is* men. Men and women are born sinful.' Joshua made me afraid: I remembered my own thoughts from long ago. *Our Saviour has not come. There's no Jesus Christ for us. Here, here, is Hell. We live in Hell, you and I. Our children in this hellish abandoned world are born beyond redemption, born sinful, born to grow and suffer and die like us amid the torments of Hell without hope of salvation.*

I bent my head to his feet, saying nothing, then said, 'Are you just a man who has given up? Then you should follow your apostles.'

Joshua lifted me up, looked into my eyes. 'This world is not Hell, Mary. It need not be.' He added in a lost voice, 'And it is not abandoned.'

I sat alone on the floor. The moonlight glared in strips along the table and the long room from the half-open shutters. Only knocked-over cups were left, spilt wine, crumbs of bread. Even the shadows were empty. Joshua had gone outside the walls of Jerusalem, to the Mount of Olives, to keep faith with the apostles. He had not wished me goodbye or farewell. He had not kissed me again.

'Joshua lied,' I said to myself. I was crying. 'He told me at the robbers' cave I was alone with him for the last time. He can make mistakes. I was alone with him tonight.' Hope filled me. Perhaps Joshua was wrong about much more; once I'd heard him say the name Abiathar the priest when he meant Ahimelech. Perhaps everything was going to be all right. Then I heard Martha's soft footsteps. I'd entirely forgotten her, quiet as a mouse in the back room. We hadn't been alone after all.

Martha knelt beside me, touched my face wonderingly. 'I heard you with him. You're so lucky.' I stared at her. 'Oh, Mary, didn't you see his face, didn't you look? He was happy. He was happy with you.'

'You can't stay here,' I said. 'The priests' men.'

'I heard Joshua,' she whispered. 'I believe in him. I'm not going back home. I'm following him wherever he goes. I saw him kiss your lips.' She touched my lips reverently. We heard footsteps in the street, the house echoed with knocking downstairs. I peeped down through a shutter, saw Judas surrounded by hurrying shadows. The flames of the blazing sticks held by the soldiers sent twisting fingers of fiery light and dark over his face. I said, 'They won't arrest us. Joshua won't let them. We haven't done anything wrong.'

'Hurry!' Martha led me to the side door, the balcony. I forgot my shoes and ran back for them, ran after Martha down the outside stairs, ran hopping after her in the street pulling them on. I didn't even know where the Mount of Olives was.

Martha led me from the sleeping city by a way she knew – we fell over families, robbers, beggars lying together, snoring exhausted in the streets and alleys and gutters. I followed her across the Bethany road to a moonlit hillside studded with trees, oil presses, shepherds' huts and pens bleating with tomorrow's sacrifices. She put her finger to her lips. 'There's a garden, Gethsemane. All prophets and preachers go there.'

'At night?'

She gave me a look. 'They preach at dawn, with the rising sun. The garden faces the Temple wall and pinnacle.' I walked quietly in the moonlight, tripped over Peter lying asleep. Shadows, most of the apostles, lay sleeping beneath the olive trees. Among the trees moved heavily armed guards, zealots and sicariots of the Fourth Way. I moved forward looking for Joshua, thought I heard a footstep downhill, bumped into Simon. I asked, 'Where have you been?'

'Me?' Simon said. He straightened his robe, which glinted. He again wore the golden cloak of Zadok. 'I don't have to answer to you, woman.' I hissed at him, but he went and sat apart from the others so Joshua would not see him. I saw his knife glint in the moonlight as he sharpened the blade.

What were they planning? A betrayal, or an ambush? Was Caiaphas expected here in person? Annas? Was the Sanhedrin united, split, might it fall? Joseph of Arimathea's faction and money would support Joshua; so would Nicodemus and his men. Then I remembered Judas Zadok standing on the top step of the Temple, king and priest of Israel, Pillar of the World, his golden bloody cloak bannering in the wind and smoke, his zealots and sicariots butchering anyone in sight. Annas no doubt remembered that day vividly, and Caiaphas; it was burnt into the minds of all the senior Temple priests.

Joshua was guilty. He must be guilty of something. If he wasn't, the men of this world would condemn sinlessness. Anything. He would be guilty of innocence.

They'd imprison him, or banish him to an island.

I'd find out where. I'd be there.

I heard Joshua groan as he prayed – prayed kneeling, too tired to stand, his head bent forward against his hands. Why didn't his Father speak to Joshua in his despair? Was there nothing at all that God could say? I saw Joshua clearly now despite the dark. The darkness around me turned to light, to a glow. I held up my hands, glorious gold.

'Joshua!' I whispered. My voice was faint; my golden body trembled with the effort to speak. My clothes were gone. I stood naked, golden, glowing, every shadow stretched away from me. My light illuminated the sleeping apostles; I saw the colour of their souls.

'Joshua,' I whispered, almost collapsing.

Joshua turned. He did not see me, any more than the others saw my light, or knew more than to be asleep, as blind as sleeping hogs. Joshua saw an angel.

I am the angel from Bethlehem that witnessed his birth. Joshua remembered me. The strength came back into his legs. He stood. He looked upward as though the light streamed down on me from Heaven. 'Father, if you are willing, release me.'

I held out my arms. I wanted to touch him so badly.

'Let Your will be done,' Joshua said. 'Not mine.' Darkness rushed in. Whatever had been here was no longer here.

I sat against a tree. Joshua was losing everything. Whichever way he turned he lost. My husband was losing everything he had except me. I heard his voice as he came back and woke the apostles who were sleeping. Joshua was always a light sleeper; perhaps he was jealous of their rest. But none of the apostles had to stay; all could have slipped away to Galilee. They were curious; they wanted to hear what Joshua would say in the morning, in the dawn, the sun rising across the Temple behind him as he preached. One last chance. Again Joshua came back and woke them. His face was dark as blood in the moonlight, as though he sweated blood. He was terrified, exhausted, alone, as alone among these madmen as a single man lost in the deepest emptiest space of the furthest universe. Alone among men. My place was beside him.

I stood, and could not move.

But Simon stood, and his knife glinted in the moonlight once, twice, three times, signalling.

A little later I heard the steady tread of footsteps, and the groves encircling Gethsemane rustled as though a wind passed through them. Sounds of armour, swords and movement: a cohort of three hundred Roman soldiers at least. Simon said, 'Welcome.' The two sides faced each other through the olive trees. Simon's zealots and sicariots neither showed their weapons nor relinquished them. Someone called in Latin, 'Which one is it?' Somebody said, 'They all look the same to me.'

Judas came into the garden. I recognised Caiaphas behind him and Annas hobbling with the help of a servant. One sicariot took out his knife but a hundred Roman swords were drawn. The crowd of priests and Temple guards followed Judas uphill. After them came the Archons of the Sanhedrin, puffing, but I didn't see Joseph of Arimathea among them. They must know the Arimathean believed in Joshua's divinity. Right at the back I saw Nicodemus the blacksmith, head uncovered, hair tousled with sleep.

Judas walked ahead of the flaming torches, walked to Joshua and kissed him with closed lips. 'You are not the One.'

A zealot leapt forward and struck at the high priest. Someone screamed in the moonlight; a man staggered, his ear hanging from his head by its lobe. Not Caiaphas. His servant or Annas's, I couldn't see for trees. But I saw Joshua reach out his hand, and make the man's ear whole. Another man raised a wooden stave, threatening him, afraid of what he'd seen. Joshua said something to Caiaphas, I didn't hear what.

But I knew what I'd seen. Joshua had performed a miracle. He'd not broken his word, he was outside the walls of Jerusalem. I understood what Joshua had done. Outside Jerusalem he was free to do whatever he liked. Free to reach out his hands and turn everyone around him to flame and kill us all. Free to make the garden burn. Free to reach out and destroy the Temple so that not one stone stood upon another, and turn the Passover moon whose steady light poured down on us to blood. Free to make himself free.

Joshua stood quietly. The guards circled him warily, then bound his arms and blindfolded him and knocked him about the head. 'Tell us which of us did that if you're so clever.' They kicked his feet to make him walk and pushed him downhill.

Caiaphas said, 'I need a second male witness at my house to identify the guilty man. It's the Law.'

The apostles had melted away, the cowards. Even James. When they were questioned they all denied Joshua, they all thought only of their own skins in the confusion. I saw Peter's bottom hiding behind a bush. 'Here's one of them,' I called. 'He's a Galilean, he must be guilty.'

'Me?' Peter said. 'Not me, I never saw him.'

Caiaphas put his unwashed grimy hand on Simon's shoulder. 'It shall be as we agreed. The promises are struck and out of my hands. Judas takes them into his own hands in the morning and will return to Damascus.' *Damascus* was what the Temple priests disdainfully called Sion. 'Your nation, your Sion, will come.' A cockerel cawed lustily; the first light of dawn glowed opposite the moon.

'Our Covenant will come. As long as we have your promises,' Simon said.

'I am a man of my word.' Caiaphas removed his hand from Simon's gilt shoulder, rubbed his fingers with distaste.

'Sion's thirty talents of silver will buy the Covenant. But not in my lifetime.'

'We shall keep your promises in a very safe place,' Simon said.

Caiaphas shrugged. 'Oh, I know there are very many caves at Sion.' He turned away, a busy man, then turned back. 'By the way, did you really believe he was the Son of God?'

Judas overheard. 'The Son of God would have saved himself.'

Simon told the priests, 'He didn't destroy us, so he was not the One. What sort of God would allow men to destroy His Son? Not ours.'

At my house, Caiaphas had said. Martha and I kept our lonely vigil outside Caiaphas's house that dawning Friday morning, hiding behind a pile of stinking rubbish where the guards at the pillars of the long low building could not see us. Simon was escorted through the twilight by the Sion Gate and went in, bore witness, reappeared almost at once. Peter and several others arrived under guard, for interrogation I guessed, but Peter came out quickly. I surprised him at the corner. He turned but didn't recognise me at first in the half-light. Then he said, 'Miriam?' The formal greeting didn't even acknowledge me as a sister in Christ. He hurried away.

'Simon Peter,' I called insultingly. 'Why did they let you go? Aren't you one of his apostles?' I ran after him, pulled him round. 'Will they let him go?'

'It's questions,' Peter said, looking away from my eyes. 'Annas asked Joshua, does he call himself the King of the Jews, the Christ? Everyone knows Joshua's the Christ! They mean will the Christ throw down their Temple as it is prophesied, and steal the Law of the Covenant brought back by Moses. Joshua replied that he was a Son of Man sitting on the right hand of the power of God.' That answer, mild yet so menacing to the ears of Temple priests, was also true; in the church at Sion the Christ sat in the pulpit to the right of the holy menorah, the seven-branched candlestick that had separated him from the Zadok. 'So then Caiaphas asked Joshua if that meant he was the Son of God.'

I groaned.

Peter said, 'Joshua replied that Caiaphas had said so, and Caiaphas tore his clothes to show he'd heard blasphemy.' He hurried away.

'Blasphemy?' I said. 'How can that be? It's true. Joshua *is* the Son of God.'

Martha whispered, 'The punishment for blasphemy is death.'

'They can't kill him!' I laughed, relieved. 'They can't, they're Jews. Jews don't have the legal power to impose a death penalty.' But I covered my mouth with my hands, trembling. It was illegal for the priests to make arrests at night, but they had. Illegal to hold a trial at night, or with the Sabbath tomorrow so that no appeal could be made. But they had.

A while later Nicodemus came out. He remembered me from Bethany, called me Mary. 'The Sanhedrin council has dismissed all witnesses, whether false or true, and voted for death.'

'They can't,' I said. 'Jesus Christ can't die.' I shook him, but he was so strong I only shook myself. 'They can't do it. It's impossible.' I broke down. 'God will save Joshua.'

'They decided on it yesterday,' Nicodemus told the others. 'Weeks ago, probably. Months ago. They knew the Galilean troublemaker was spreading his poison, as they saw it, from his stronghold at Sion through Perea, Judah, Samaria, Galilee, even into Tyre and Sidon. But they knew he must come to Jerusalem. They waited.' He flexed his great muscles powerlessly. 'He's accused of being a bastard born of fornication. That his birth in Bethlehem caused the murder of thousands of children. That Mary and Joseph fled to Egypt because they feared the anger of the people.' Nicodemus sighed. 'They'll send him to the Romans. The prefect can pronounce sentence of death.'

Martha whispered, 'But he's in Caesar Maritima, on the coast. Pilate never comes to Jerusalem, not since he brought idols into the Temple and the people defied him.'

I heard a soft footstep, and Bernice took my elbow. 'Jerusalem's where everything happens. Pilate's definitely here for the Passover.' Nicodemus nodded his respects, he'd do what he could with his friends in the Sanhedrin, and hurried away.

328

Alone, we three women clung to each other behind the rubbish, shivering and inconsolable. I simply could not believe what was happening. The sun rose over the stink of decaying vegetables and Jerusalem came to life. The street filled with people, scavengers rooting in the rubbish, then workmen arrived to carry it off through the Essene Gate, calling it the dung gate. We moved further from the high priest's house, then saw the priests of the senior faction, old men who were not busy in the Temple, Dothaim, Somne (Nicodemus had told us their names), Gamaliel, Nepthalim, come hurrying out led by Caiaphas. The high priest's beard was matted, his clothes hung ragged where he'd torn them to bare his chest, his face was distorted by grief and anger. Martha whispered, 'How can a holy man behave like this? Surely God can't be talking to him. He can't fight God.'

'He's afraid,' I said. 'The high priests are simply afraid of losing what they believe in.'

'I found out why Caiaphas is in mourning,' Bernice said. 'He's almost out of his mind. A few days ago his daughter Sarah, a young priestess of the Temple sanctuary like the Virgin Mary in her childhood, was found alone in worship, stripped naked and raped by a Galilean innkeeper, Demas.'

'Is she alive?'

'She's alive, poor girl.' Bernice sighed. In silence we all recalled the myths of the Virgin's rape by Pantera, or Kantera, in the same room. 'They say Demas tortured her to reveal the hiding place of the Covenant. They say Demas is a thief—'

'All innkeepers are thieves,' I said.

'A thief and a follower of Joshua,' said Bernice. Then she said, 'Who can deny that Satan is here, everywhere, all around us?'

Somebody said the guilty man called King Jesus had been hurried from the house by a back way, to avoid the crowds, and taken to Pilate's praetorium in Herod's palace for sentence. We pushed and shoved to the limits of our strength through the crowds to the western quarter where the palace, as magnificent as the Temple, gleamed quietly above the hubbub in the morning sun. The crowd grew denser, gossiping, trading, arguing, sensing a show. I managed to drink at Pilate's fountain where no one else would drink, because of the pagan idols. Daylight was hardly an hour old but I felt my lifetime had passed since last night. I was dying of thirst. 'The Romans will let him go,' I said faithfully, water trickling down my chin. I still had faith.

Word came through the crowd that Pilate had let Joshua go. I thanked God, I thanked the fish-god of the water, Bernice and Martha and I embraced and danced in a circle. Joshua was released without charge; the Roman prefect didn't care whether a Jew was the son of the Jewish god or not. Pilate already had another Son of God locked in his cells, Yeshua Barabbas, whom he would crucify for murder and sedition this morning. Demas the rapist would die too, beside him. When Pilate read the centurion's reports of Joshua pathetically scourging the Temple he'd laughed aloud. Joshua ben-Joseph was free to go.

The crowd shook their heads; they didn't like anyone let go. The gate opened and a man appeared.

Not Joshua: Joseph of Arimathea. Zacchaeus and Bernice ran to him. He shook his head. 'Caiaphas has changed the charges,' he told us.

'That's illegal,' Zacchaeus said.

'He's done it. Twenty thousand pilgrims will arrive in Jerusalem today, from Galilee, Junias, Bethany, Bethlehem, Sepphoris, Capernaum, everywhere. By tonight Jerusalem will overflow with people who've heard of the Nazarene's miracles and healing even if they've never seen Joshua. But the Jerusalem crowd don't know him. They don't care.'

I interrupted furiously, 'What do they care about?'

'They care,' Joseph said, 'that God will throw out the Romans.'

Bernice said, 'What are the new charges put before Pilate?'

'That Joshua claims to be King of the Jews and wants to stop Roman taxes.'

Herod would never support another king; and the threat of another tax uprising was a brilliant stroke by Caiaphas, reminding Pilate of Judas Zadok's tax revolt. Another Galilean. But Joseph touched my shoulder reassuringly. 'Joshua replied that what belongs to the Emperor should be paid to the Emperor. So Caiaphas has come up with an old charge dressed in new clothes: Joshua is a robber because he'll steal the Covenant of Moses, the Law.'

'The same charge that was levelled against Demas.'

'Aren't they clever? They make it look like a conspiracy. Caiaphas didn't say anything about the thirty talents, naturally, and Pilate knows nothing of Jewish history except that it's all God, blood and suffering.'

'Joshua's trapped,' I said. 'He mustn't say a word.'

'Silence is guilt. Don't worry, Mary. Pilate's wife has heard of Joshua's healing, and she's as gentle as Pilate is cruel. And frankly, by now Joshua looks more like a beggar or the king's lowest servant than a king.' His effort to cheer me failed. Joseph returned to the palace.

I shouted after him, 'He doesn't look like a beggar!'

'They knock them about a bit,' Zacchaeus said. 'Isaiah prophesied, "I offered my back to those who beat me, my cheeks to those who pulled my beard; I did not hide my face from mocking and spitting." '

Bernice added, 'And Isaiah says, "My servant will prosper. He will be raised and lifted up and greatly exalted." '

I shouted, 'I don't care what the old prophets said!'

Zacchaeus and Bernice hugged me. 'God spared Abraham's son from sacrifice, God saved Isaac. So God will surely not sacrifice His own Son. There'll be a miracle, you'll see.' But the sun rose over the rooftops, pouring into the square. Bernice's veil fluttered in the hot wind.

Joseph came out. He sounded worried. 'I'm threatened with prison if I oppose Caiaphas. Peter and James were arrested by Saulus the inquisitor and forced to bear witness identifying Joshua, but they've been released.' I nodded; we'd seen Peter. 'It's said Annas and Caiaphas paid an enormous price to Judas, but it turns out to be only thirty pieces of the purest silver. How silver could be so precious I cannot imagine. Mined in the Mountains of the Moon in Africa, I suppose!'

'Promises,' I said. 'They're more than pieces of silver. They're promises, from the Temple to Sion.'

Just then the crowd roared. Roman soldiers, swords and armour flashing, cleared the steps. A slave ran forward carrying a bent staff, the prefect's symbol of office, and

Pilate strode from the judgment hall on to the balcony. Yeshua Barabbas was dragged after him struggling and kicking at his guards, his back showing like chopped meat through his ripped clothes, scourged ready for the cross. The crowd threw up their hands, shouting, 'Barabbas! Jesus Barabbas!' Barabbas, Son of God, held up his chained arms in salute. A soldier kicked him to make him kneel. Barabbas lashed out against his fetters and was beaten down by swords. But still he tried to get up, dung trickling slackly from him, sodomised. Two soldiers whacked Barabbas until he curled up without moving, then by his beard dragged him to his knees, held him crouching between them like an animal. Barabbas trickled blood and saliva, but he managed a victorious wink to the crowd. 'Judah for Judah,' the zealot croaked, 'Sion for Sion,' his spirit undimmed, and the crowd roared for him.

The Arimathean murmured, 'As a Galilean, Joshua was allowed to appeal personally to Herod for mercy. Herod laughed when he saw him, the man who had made him so afraid. Gave him an old yellow cloak like a zadok's to mock him. Joshua wouldn't ask for mercy and Herod wouldn't give it.'

Another man was dragged forward, the crowd chanting, 'Demas, Demas!' The rapist had been severely tortured; his burnt skin hung in blisters, his mouth dropped open tooth-less and torn. He didn't know where he was. He tried to grin.

'Gestas!' Cries and shouts rose from the crowd, and several women ran forward cursing the robber who slob-bered and hooted as he was pulled forward, his head distorted, mad from birth. The crowd hated Gestas because he attacked pilgrims such as themselves, hiding at cross-roads, killing the men but hanging women up by the heels, cutting off their breasts, then killing their children and drinking their blood. The life was all he knew.

Joshua was pushed and fell to his knees, head down. Pilate spoke Greek to the crowd. 'I call the Sun to witness I find no fault with this man Joshua.' The crowd jeered as the Greek was translated; they wanted blood, not innocence. Caiaphas said in Hebrew: 'He must die.'

The crowd fell silent. Pilate said, 'Your god has forbidden you to slay him, High Priest, but allows me?'

Barabbas gave a formless shout of rebellion. The Jerusalem crowd took it up. Pilate, a politician ambitious to be elected senator one day, felt them slipping away from him. He said, shaking his head, 'This man Joshua doesn't deserve to be crucified.'

They shouted in Aramaic, 'Crucify him!'

Pilate said: 'I've got three crosses and four criminals. Tell me which man shall go free.'

'Barabbas!' shouted the crowd, when it was translated. They chanted, 'Barabbas, Barabbas!' My voice was drowned. I could not even hear myself screaming against them. Their chant spread like fire to the far side of the square. 'Free Barabbas!'

Pilate looked around him. The priests, the crowd, Herod. He dare not release Demas or Gestas, but Barabbas was the one he hated to let go. Yet he could feel the crowd slipping out of his control.

Pilate called for a bowl of water, and it was carried forward by slaves who filled it from pitchers to overflowing. People fell silent, watching.

Pilate addressed the crowd. 'You shall have your wish. *Iesous Christos* dies.' To make his meaning crystal clear he dipped his hands into the bowl, washed them, then flicked the drops from his fingers contemptuously into the crowd. 'I alone am innocent of his blood.'

Someone cried in Aramaic, 'Blood!'

'Yes,' shouted the people. 'His blood be upon us and upon our children!'

Satan was here today. I could smell Him like a thickness in the air, the stench of blood. I looked around me as if I was surrounded by demons, their open mouths and broken brown teeth chanting 'Blood!' with stinking breath, the stink of corruption and decay, the joy of violence and destruction rising out of the ground around me. 'Yes,' they cried, 'upon us and upon our children!'

'*No!*' I screamed. But my voice was lost against democracy.

DEUS MISEREATUR

may God have mercy

I waited for God to destroy them.

They tied Gestas to a blood-clotted post and he grinned cheerfully at the crowd. He shrieked as the whip struck across his back thirty-nine times, one short of death. The pieces of metal and bone embedded in the splayed ends of the whip flayed his skin in tanners' strips until it hung down like clothes. He took the final blows in silence. The knobs of his spine stuck out like white knuckles.

Demas was tied. Caiaphas and the Archons watched from the window, not wanting to be spattered with blood.

Joshua was tied and scourged with the greatest violence, for he had scourged the Temple. I screamed and wept, but the women always did that. Demas's wife and daughters screamed and wept and struggled, and even Gestas had some poor girl to scream and weep for him. The soldiers pulled a few beards to make the men pull the women back. Joseph of Arimathea dragged me back but I struggled and screamed and wept. Then we stared numbly.

This was not happening. The sun burned down out of a cloudless sky. Flies buzzed round the blood. 'Don't let them hurt him,' I whispered.

The Romans hung a tattered scarlet cloak like a king's on Joshua's shoulders. His blood soaked through it immediately, red as the cloak. Someone made a crown of thorns, crushed it over his head. They beat it down with their swords until his head ran with blood. I don't know where they'd got the thorns. His blood dripped from his nose and chin and cheeks. The soldiers thought he was being killed for claiming to be king and that he was not, but they thought all Jews were crazy anyway. But Pilate called them, spoke Latin from the balcony, not in mockery. It was the rule that a man's crime was hung around his neck for his final journey. 'Mark this man *Iesous Nazarenus, Rex Iudaeorum.*' Jesus the Nazarene, King of the Jews. The crime was the truth. Somebody carved the sign on a piece of old wood, initials in the Roman fashion: INRI.

Not IMRI, the Lord has said, which means God's will be done. Joshua was being mocked by the crowd for being what he actually was: their king through both his mother and his earthly father. Everything was changed, twisted, warped from what was meant to be. Instead of anointing God they mocked Him.

'It's the Devil,' I whispered. 'Satan's won.'

I still could not believe it.

But this is what I saw happen: the condemned men were each made to lift on to their shoulders a heavy length of timber weighing as much as myself. Joshua struggled beneath the weight, swaying, then staggered forward with the criminals.

Groaning, the condemned men, necks bent forward by the awkward weight, stumbled with their pieces of timber along the public markets. Children threw stones and dung, women spat, the usual sight. Men cursed and mocked and shoved forward as usual, as usual the soldiers shoved them back. But Joshua stopped. Zacchaeus climbed a tree to see better. Joshua could not go on; the weight of wood bent him double, the bloody strands of his hair almost touched the stones. I struggled near. Somebody gave me a stone to throw. Joshua didn't see me, his swollen face almost closed his eyes, but then he turned his head, and his eyes opened, and he looked straight at Judas.

Judas came from Apollyon the silversmith's. His tall frame was bent double in the doorway, and for a moment the two men, betrayer and betrayed, stared at each other from the same level. A son of Satan and the Son of God. Judas clutched in his hands a cedarwood chest, small, fragrant, beautifully worked. The top fell open and light came out, silvering his face like a monster's mask, sunlight reflecting from the silver coins inside. Thirty of them, no doubt. I saw the reflection of Joshua's face in the coins thirty times over, without blood, without thorns, without suffering. *Man, it would be better for you if you had not been born.*

A soldier swore, lashed, and Joshua staggered forward.

Judas. I spat at him. He shut the chest with shaking fingers. He held his fate in his own hands.

I ran to the city gate. Now a man I did not know carried Joshua's piece of wood. Soldiers dragged Joshua who had collapsed, then they swore, dropped him, kicked him. Bernice ran forward, pressed her veil to Joshua's face to take away his sweat and dust. He was dragged forward and she stared at her veil, at the living image of Joshua's face imprinted there in blood and tears.

'Beyond the city wall,' I said, 'he'll use his strength. You'll see. He'll destroy them all. All the crowds, the soldiers, the Temple.'

'He can't.' Zacchaeus shook his head. 'Joshua knows he's God's suffering servant. Isaiah foretells it. The servant who suffers but is beloved and chosen by God. The servant who is also the people of Israel, blind, deaf, spoilt, the slaves of kings. The servant is weighed down with their sins.'

Joshua took up his burden again, staggered on the dusty track outside the city wall between the soldiers. Few people followed, hanging back in the city now, peeping from afar. These people are offended by nudity, and they knew what came next.

I followed. I would see everything.

Three tall posts, though they looked small from a distance, stood on the hill called Golgotha. The tomb entrances did make the place look like a skull, the dusty curve of hilltop as dry as a bone.

They stripped Gestas naked to the balls and put him up first, nailed his timber across the top of the tall vertical post called the stipe, lifted his buttocks on to the little wooden ledge halfway up, swore at him to keep still, then with soft thuds hammered nails between the bones of his wrists to the crossbar to hold him. He slipped, the ledge was too narrow, his arms took all his weight, the joints of his shoulders and elbows creaked, twisting, then dislocated under the strain.

The soldiers cursed the heat, pulled his legs round to expose his ankles, hammered nails through his heelbones with sharp cracking sounds then stepped back, satisfied their work was solid enough.

Then they stripped Demas naked, lifted him, and crucified him.

Now they crucify Joshua.

I can't bear to look or to look away. This happens now. Inside me it still happens.

Naked but for thorns, Joshua takes his weight on the nails through his heels, but the pain is too much. Then he hangs his weight from the nails through his wrists, but the pain is agony. He can't sit on the seat, the uncomfortable ledge is just enough to push him out so that he neither stands nor sits nor hangs. It sounds as if his back is breaking. Sweat, blood and spittle trickles down his flesh. Can't scream; his weight hanging forward compresses his lungs. Breathes in gasps. The soldiers yawn beneath the shade of a single olive tree, drink wine, play dice. The midday sun burns down, blisters his white body. I hear the nails creak as he writhes.

He whimpers, refusing strong wine mixed with myrrh to dull his pain.

I stand beneath him. I hold out my arms like his arms. I pray. The sun burns my head as it burns his.

Joshua cries out, gasps.

Zacchaeus murmurs, 'He takes the sins of this world upon him. Sins are separation from God. God hides His face from you and does not hear.' Zacchaeus tries to tear me away from such a terrible sight, then gives a low cry of wonder, and awe, and worship.

Here it is at last. The miracle. The sun burns dim, dimmer. Not an eclipse. An overturning of the laws of nature: the sun burning no hotter than a full moon. The air grows thick and heavy as blood pressing down on us. No smell of thunder, no earthquake, only screams from the city. Someone comes, terrified. The veil of the Temple, which the Virgin Mary helped weave when she was a child, is torn in two. The barrier between men and God is gone.

Joshua hangs from his dislocated arms. Blood trickles everywhere from his skin in the extremity of his suffering. His mouth opens, his tongue quivers between his gums.

A centurion comes and gives orders, Longinus the sergeant throws down his dice, gets up from the game adjusting his uncomfortable belt, goes to Gestas and calls out cheerfully, picks up a club and with two quick cracks breaks the dying man's legs. Gestas hangs from his arms, strangling. Longinus ambles to Demas, takes aim, does the same. 'Known 'em carry on four, five days if they aren't given a push. Three weeks, we had once. His wife kept bringing him water, not doing him a favour if you ask me.' He leaves Demas to suffocate, comes to Joshua. 'Dead already, this one. I reckoned he wouldn't last long. That's a denarius to me.' He looks at me without sympathy. 'Listen, if he was the Son of God, why didn't he jump down off here?' He wanders off to check if Demas is dead yet, sticks him under the ribs with a spear. Demas groans.

Joshua's head moves. He's not dead.

His eyelids flutter. Does he see me?

'I'm thirsty.'

I run, fetch a sponge soaked in vinegar, pierce it with a stick, lift it above my head to his lips. Don't die, don't die. Does he feel the cool touch of vinegar? Does he remember touching me? Does he remember his life?

He puts back his head. His eyes open, staring at the sun.

He lifts with his wrists. He pushes with his heels. He stands on the cross.

He cries out.

'My God, my God, why have you abandoned me?'

DEUS MORS EST

God is dead

God is dead, for He has abandoned us.

Staring up at the body on the cross, I know this now for certain: there's no God.

There's no Jesus Christ.

God never sent His Son to be our salvation in this world. There was no Messiah. There's no freedom, no end to time, no hope for us. Without Jesus Christ there's no judgment, no forgiveness, no peace, no glory, no Heaven.

This world belongs to the Devil. God is not in this world but Satan is, and Satan is victorious.

I pulled myself up against the cross and kissed my husband's feet. Remembered his own words to me when he received my kiss when we were young: *Faith only receives, but love gives.*

I slid down, and splinters cut me. The cruel heat had returned to the sun; the miracle was an illusion. The soldier came and stuck the spear in the body's side. Blood and plasma gushed out from the ruptured heart and lung.

Past three in the afternoon; less than three hours to the Sabbath, and a criminal must be buried the day he dies. The soldiers levered the nails from the wood, the body flopped to the ground and the women who had been watching hurried forward and began their task. Nicodemus used his tools to draw the nails, longer than my hand from wrist to fingertip, from the flesh. 'Lay him in my own tomb,' Joseph ordered. Did Joseph, incredibly, still believe everything we'd so badly wanted to believe? My feeling of desolation emptied me, I stood like a husk, I hated Joshua's pathetic deserted body for being so much less than he had been in life. Stared dully as the women wrapped him in a sheet and his blood soaked through, showing the shape of him beneath, bloody face – we'd forgotten to close his eyes – bloody ribs still dripping, each bloody nail hole dripping.

Joseph shook me, spoke urgently. 'Caiaphas has forbidden absolutely a burial for Joshua in the Tomb of the Davids at the Water Gate. But Pilate knows Nicodemus and I are dissenting members of the Sanhedrin, so he agreed to hand over the body to us for a decent burial, not a pauper's grave, as long as it's outside the city walls.'

'Caiaphas won't allow any place that may become a shrine whether in the city or not. He'll have Joshua tossed in the common pit with Gestas and Demas.'

Nicodemus interrupted in his deep voice, 'Yes, yes, that's why we work in haste.' The sun hung low over Jerusalem; after sunset no work was permitted. Nicodemus lifted the body in his arms as though it were no heavier than a child. We followed him downhill from Golgotha to the abandoned quarry near the city wall. The massive stone blocks had been dug from here and it was deep, full of shadow. The path descended into the shadows past the rough-hewn stones and boulders of ordinary sealed tombs, came down to the façades of houses for rich dead carved into the living rock, some with pillars and porticoes. Nicodemus sang softly as he carried his burden down, one of the psalms about a valley. Though I walk in the valley of death, I fear no evil.

People scattered away from us as we descended, eyes staring from the shadows, foaming mouths, sometimes gibbering like monkeys. Men and women such as I once was; and inside myself perhaps, but for Joshua, still am.

'Oh, Joshua!' I cried, overcome with grief. 'My love! my love!'

My voice rose up echoing between the rock walls, and pigeons and doves and sparrows fluttered from every hole like the wind, whirling in the evening sky.

Each tomb, of course, was blocked by slabs to keep out squatters, thieves, itinerants such as I had been. My twisted arm ached as never before. Joseph's tomb had a fine front and a great stone slab for a door. We could not shift it. Nicodemus laid down his burden, heaved with his great strength. The stone, with the help of the women following, grated aside. Inside the narrow gap, deep in the rock, was carved a house of stone. Bent double, we followed the awkward steps down. Joseph muttered, 'They say it was once a secret way into the city. Perhaps a tunnel for water in times of siege.' If so, long blocked; we came to the lowest level and Nicodemus pushed aside heavy spice sacks smelling sharply of aloes and fragrant myrrh, laid the body on a slab.

'Here we're inside the walls. Joshua will lie like a king after all, in David's city.'

At least seven copper grails glinted in the lamplight, and the sacks of aloes must weigh a hundred pounds. I remembered the death of Joshua's earthly father Joseph and understood. Nicodemus was a Pharisee; they wrap the body in spices beneath the shroud to cover the smell of decay before placing the dry bones in their final resting place, the ossuary. But Joshua's body would be preserved in the Essene fashion of the Davids, the internal organs and blood placed in the grails, the flesh embalmed with large, purifying quantities of aloes and myrrh.

'No time tonight,' Nicodemus said. 'I'll come back after the Sabbath, on the third day.'

The women *taracheutae*, embalmers, quickly wrapped the body in a clean linen shroud, but again the blood came through, haunting us with Joshua's bloody face. 'I knew him more closely than any man,' Joseph said quietly. 'Aboard ship, and for two years on the island at Ynys Writrin. Now, when my time comes, I shall sleep in his company until our resurrection at Judgment Day.'

As he climbed the steps Nicodemus said, 'Do you believe you'll live for ever?'

'I know it,' Joseph said.

'I spoke to him secretly one night,' Nicodemus said. 'I believed him, but I didn't understand what I believed except that it was beautiful and true.'

Almost sunset; the women hurried away through the quarry while Nicodemus and Joseph heaved the stone back into place, but Martha and Bernice hung back for me. We walked back to the city in silent misery. Sunset, the beginning of the Sabbath. Already, according to the law, Joshua had lain in his tomb for one day.

The second day began, and there was no work we could do, only remember.

At sunset, the end of the Sabbath and the second day, Martha fetched water and returned with news. Joseph had been arrested the moment he returned home last night, taken to an unknown location, shut up in a windowless house. A windowless house is a tomb, a prison from which there is no escape. Only Caiaphas had the key. It was possible Joseph had already been killed.

And Nicodemus? We did not know. And the apostles? Arrested, scattered, run away. None came here to the Greek's house. Fled to Lazarus's house at Bethany, perhaps.

Bernice returned through the dark with news of a midnight convocation of the whole Sanhedrin – at last! – in the Temple. Nicodemus had spoken out for Joshua and been threatened with the same fate. Caiaphas heard that Joshua had been laid in Joseph's tomb and, with the key he alone held, hurried to the windowless house where Joseph was imprisoned. Caiaphas took no chances: guards and trusted members of the senior faction accompanied him, which as you know means no witnesses.

Joseph was gone. The house was empty. Joseph had fled back to Arimathaea for his life.

Caiaphas ordered guards to the quarry to secure the stone of Joshua's tomb, saying he was afraid that the apostles who had stolen Joseph would try to steal their master's body. I said: 'That means Caiaphas himself has ordered Joshua's body stolen from the tomb and thrown in the common pit.'

It was still dark, but I followed the city wall to the quarry. I heard footsteps running after me and ran faster, but they were only Martha and Bernice. We ran together. They tripped on the stones, hurting their feet, but I raced ahead, down the steep path into the quarry, and didn't care if I fell.

What made me go? Love. Not worship. I simply couldn't bear the thought of these evil men (goodness doesn't exist now, but evil does) dragging from his tomb the poor body of my husband who had suffered so much in his life. I would not abandon him.

I paused, understanding. The rocks around me filled with illumination, every shadow turned to light. I would not abandon him. I understood a little of myself at last, and cried out with wonder.

A woman's voice called up to me softly, 'Are you here? Is it dawn?'

I ran down to the Virgin Mary and embraced her. 'It's too early for dawn.'

'Dawn on the Day of First Fruits,' she murmured. 'Today we celebrate the earth coming to life again.'

'No, it's much too early.' I went down carefully but could not feel the rocks against my feet. The guards at the stone looked up, shielding their eyes. They drew their swords then threw them down. The earth shook under their feet and they fell to their knees. They clung to the earth with their fingers and toes, and the stone rolled away from the tomb.

I stood on the stone looking down the passage into the tomb. I was a naked child, naked as Joshua on the cross. I went down the steps. The tomb was filled with light. Now I was gone I heard from above the guard crying out in fear and terror of what they had seen. Or perhaps they saw some new thing.

The tomb was empty.

Empty.

I touched the slab. Felt the warm blood on the stone.

The shroud unwound, lying curled on the floor, still warm.

I turned round, inhaling the scent of Joshua I knew so well. His sweat. His dusty feet. The scent of his breath like apples. He was here. And yet he was not here.

I returned up the stairs and stood on the stone, looked down into the faces of the women who gathered. The Virgin Mary, of course, with Salome and Miri; Martha, Bernice, and other women I knew more or less, healed in Galilee or Samaria or Perea, Joanna the wife of Herod's steward; the women who had chosen themselves to come to embalm Joshua's body. The guards stared at me, eyes wide, backs pressed to the rocks.

I held out my arms. 'Don't be afraid. Jesus Christ was

raised, and He is risen.' When they did not move I pointed. 'Go, see into the tomb where the crucified earthly body of Jesus Christ lay.'

They went down and saw what I had told them they would see: nothing. An empty tomb.

The guards ran away forgetting their swords.

Mary came back, climbing slowly; not as young as she used to be. 'Are you my son?'

I called out to all the women: 'Don't seek the living among the dead. Seek Him in Galilee.' Then I fell down, and saw only the dim light of dawn. The women were running away, holding up their hems to run faster so their feet showed as they ran, dust flying from their heels. Did they think His body was stolen? Were they afraid it was not? The Virgin Mary, Martha and Bernice retreated more slowly, but they didn't stop until they were out of sight.

I slid from the rock where I had stood so easily a moment ago, fell to the ground, and a hand lifted me up. I said, 'Who are you?'

Amazing; I didn't recognise Him, yet He lifted me up and stood beside me shimmering with all the colour and emotion of His life. He opened my eyes and I said: 'Joshua.' He kissed me on the mouth, and I ran frantically to tell the women what I had seen. Who I had seen. They were already in Jerusalem but I followed them into the city. 'I've seen Him. Our Jesus Christ. He is risen.' The women wept, mourning, and didn't believe a word but only stroked my hair sadly, then hugged me thinking they understood. They'd already told Peter the body was stolen. The other eleven apostles were at Bethany; Jerusalem was too dangerous for them. Peter went to the tomb, saw the discarded shroud, and decided to return to Bethany with the sad news. Anyway, he was afraid Simon would try to take his place. Martha and Bernice went with him.

Later in the day someone recognised me in the street for Joshua's wife and ran after me calling me Queen Jesus. Children followed shouting gleefully. Jerusalem was too dangerous for me; I retreated to Lazarus's house at Bethany. The apostles wouldn't speak to me – not because they believed I hadn't seen their Jesus Christ, but because they knew I had. 'Why her, not us?' I overheard them saying.

'Why her and the other women, not us?' Jesus Christ had appeared to Bernice and Martha walking on the road to Bethany. At first they were sure it was James, but it was not. Jesus had not been in the form I saw Him, but in His body. Had He arrived here in Bethany? The apostles kept the doors locked for fear of arrest, but watched for Him from the windows.

There was no welcome for me among them, and only one other place within walking distance I could go. I decided to walk to Sion, to the women's quarters at Emmaus. The track was very hot, blossom blowing from the orchards of Jerusalem apple. My mind wandered in the heat. I remembered stumbling on the bloated mule, the murdered Celt. The path was strangely empty today; I thought, if Jesus walked with Bernice and Martha, perhaps He'll walk with me. Perhaps He's walking this very road, right now. The apple trees fell behind me, and through the desert I came to the dry-stone boundaries of Sion, then to Emmaus.

No women drew water from the stream. A door rattled open, closed in the wind. Nothing else moved. Everyone was gone.

The feast of First Fruits; yet everything that should have been full was empty. Today celebrated new life, but everything smelt of ancient death and desertion. Several of the huts and tents had fallen down; I wondered if the earthquake that opened the tomb of Jesus Christ had made the people drop everything they owned and run away.

There was nothing for me here. I took the track from Emmaus towards New Jerusalem, the monastery. Bethlehem for the women's lying-in and childbirth, silent; Egypt, Nazareth, Damascus, all were empty, vacant. I stared down from the cliff tops at the white monastery on its spur below me, inhaling the smell of brimstone. It seemed to me even from this distance that the gates were closed, and I saw no men on the battlements or in the courtyards. The potter's field, the Field of Blood, was empty of all the usual Passover tents, only the bare unused poles of the tent posts standing up like a bare forest of stipes, as though only awaiting men and women to arrive sweating and stumbling with crossbars ready for their crucifixion.

I made my way down the steep track and saw the tiny

figure of a man come from the monastery, climbing towards me as I climbed down. He wore only a loincloth, reaching forward with long arms and legs as he climbed, and that way he moved spoke louder than words. I stopped. I knew him.

He climbed to me. Just the way He moved; and yet I hardly recognised Him, He looked so exactly like our image of Jesus Christ, the long locks of Nazarene hair, the beard, the luminous, suffering, compassionate eyes; seeing everything, understanding everything, forgiving everything.

Joshua climbed to me, and said: 'Mary.'

I fell at His feet, I touched His warm skin. 'My Lord.'

He knew I needed time. 'Touch me. Feel me. See me.'

His spirit was in Heaven; and this was not the transfigured soul of Joshua, bound to His body on this earth, that I had seen earlier. This time I touched the risen body of Jesus Christ who walked from His tomb, walked from Jerusalem to Bethany, from Bethany here to Sion, who touched me here, now, on the road from Emmaus.

'My God, my God,' I whispered, just as He had on the cross – *my God*, not my Father – 'my God, it's true. It's all true. You're true. How can you be alive?'

'Stop kneeling,' Joshua said. 'Why are you kneeling? Why are you crying?'

'I'm happy.'

'Good.' Joshua laughed. 'Stop kneeling! Do you think you get better treatment if you worship me?'

I gazed into Joshua's face. 'It's really you.'

He held out His wrists, showed the nail holes trickling blood. The holes in His heels. He took my hand, pushed it in His side where the spear had gone through His lung and heart. He touched my hand to the mocking crown of thorns which He still wore, and the sharp points gouged my fingers, which bled. 'I'm so sorry,' I murmured. 'All we've done to you.'

'That I did to myself for you,' Joshua said. 'Don't be afraid. Salvation is not an easy road.' He took my hand and climbed down towards the monastery, the sun shining low from behind us, sending our shadows almost infinitely far ahead of us over the Dead Sea. He paused for a moment to admire the view, shared a piece of meat and bees' honey-comb with me.

I had to know. 'Are we saved now? By your suffering? Are we a saved people?'

'Mary, Mary, my suffering has hardly started. I died easily on my cross, don't you think? Only four hours, so little. Many people suffer a life of grief. Children die after years of excruciating pain and despair. I see men, women and children crucified in unimaginable distress and suffer the torments of Satan's Hell while still alive and innocent in this life. How can pain improve, or suffering redeem? Wouldn't it be easy?' He touched my face. 'Sometimes we lose everyone we love. I told you it wasn't an easy road, salvation.'

He jumped down, and I followed, calling: 'But you didn't die. You haven't deserted us. What's happened? Will you live for ever?'

'This is my resurrection, so that people will believe in me.' Jesus Christ, not a ruler but defeated, betrayed, crucified, resurrected! I was amazed by the newness, strangeness, the force of what was happening. I slipped and He put out His hand to steady me. We came to level ground and He walked beside me holding my hand, my whole body, my heart, as the monastery walls rose over us.

I asked, 'Will you stay with us for ever?'

'Yes, from now.'

I burst out, 'Joshua, are we still married?'

'We are still one.' He put His hands on my shoulders. 'It will be harder for you than you could believe.'

'I'll believe anything you say! Anything!'

'That's not enough, Mary,' Joshua chuckled. 'It's not nearly enough.'

The gates at Sion stood closed in front of us, massive, throwing back our voices. I whispered, 'Do you know our future?'

'If I know what you'll do, you aren't free.'

I looked into His eyes. 'Am I free? Can I truly be free of you? If I wanted to be?'

He took His hands away from me. 'Freer than you'd wish.'

I staggered, then followed Him walking towards the gates. 'What will happen now?'

'I don't know.' He put out His arms, the wind blew, the gates grated, creaking open away from Him, then splintered and sagged as the hinges split. He took my hand and walked me through: there, I'm the first woman to enter Sion. I could commit no greater sin.

I looked round the empty courtyards as He led me forward. The pools were cracked, only puddles left. The wind blew dust-devils around us but did not touch us. Darkness rose up the stark white walls.

We came to the empty church, and I put out my arms and prayed with Jesus Christ until night.

In the dark, His fingers found mine. The roof hung open, showing the full moon rising. There was no sound but the wind. 'Where did they all go?' I whispered.

'They were afraid. Wisely.' His fingers led me to the refectory, the long table laid out as if for a meal but all twelve places empty, then to the winding stair in the corner. 'Judas has heard of me at Bethany. He tried to throw his silver back into the Temple, but the priests won't touch it. Blood money can't be undone, any more than blood can be sucked back into the dead body to make it alive again.' He led me lightly up the stone stairs. 'There's something I will show you. I'll meet him here soon, very soon.'

'Does he know it?'

'He knows. He knows.'

This long room above the refectory was Sion's most precious possession, I realised: the scriptorium. Here was a treasure worth far more than thirty talents. In wooden pigeon holes along the walls, in stacks of *capsae* each neatly tagged with its title, were stored hundreds, perhaps thousands, of scrolls. Perhaps many thousands. Others were stretched out in preparation on long tables. Each represented an almost unimaginable labour of skill: soft gazelle skins joined by hair-fine stitching, some of them fifty cubits long, the most precious of copper or gold. The floor creaked beneath Joshua's weight, then the wind blew around us, unravelling everything, skins flapping, *capsae* tumbling open, scrolls unrolling, picked up by the wind like fluttering wings. Joshua held out His hands and the scrolls brushed His fingers, flapped against His arms.

'Here's everything Sion is.' He laughed as a piece caught

in the thorns. 'Knowledge.' He shook His head and the scroll flew free. 'The greatest treasure of men's knowledge in this world. This unique world. Everything is written here somewhere, much more's buried out of sight. And still these men who had everything wanted more, more, more.'

'The Covenant that Moses brought from the desert,' I said. 'The Word of God, they believe. You're the Covenant, but they were afraid to believe in you.' I watched, wanted, touched Him. 'You are Jesus Christ. Have you spoken with believers?'

'Even the best don't know me. Poor Thomas couldn't believe until he touched my side. James is here, and he does not believe he speaks to me, yet he is my beloved disciple.' He sounded sad. 'James, my brother, my most devout and beloved apostle. James, for whose sake Heaven and Earth came into existence in this world.'

He gave me too much to think about. My mind was full, yet I wanted to know everything. 'The others? What of the others?'

'Only men. Returning to Galilee.'

I knew Judas was coming here; I asked, 'And Simon?'

'Simon Magus, yes, I've spoken with him. He runs away, crouches by the fire at an inn where he thinks I won't know him. He's lost even his cloak. And other things are happening, much more than you know.'

'Is this why you come back? Because there's no hope for us? Satan wins?'

'Believe in me. Preach not with words but silently, by example. Make one green shoot of grass grow.'

I tried to understand. 'You won't do anything, but we will?'

'You won't know what I do. But I will show you one thing for all men and women.' He held up His hand and the moon stopped; the scrolls were frozen in the air. He said: 'Now I confront the God of this world, Satan.'

I screamed.

The room opened like a mouth, the ground opened, and Sion fell.

Jesus Christ protects me among the dead. Flames engulf me, His hand holds me. Smoke blinds me, but He leads me forward in the place where there is no forward or back. Down into a place where there is no up. Here everything that happens, happens for ever. Each moment *is* eternity. Immortality. The Cross.

The Cross: I begin to understand. This new symbol not of royalty, encrusted with jewels and gold, but of salvation offered in poverty, humility and suffering to the world. Not a law, not a royal decree from the Temple of Jesus Christ the King of Jerusalem. No; a choice.

A choice, meekly and humbly offered. A choice between Heaven and Hell.

Here I scream and scream and scream in terror, all spirit, all womanhood bleeding from me. I see myself as I am, writhing with doubt, stinking of shit and mortality and corruption. And I, Mary Magdalene, am saved by Jesus, my sins washed clean! I cling to Him, I cling to His hand, screaming!

Here is new, and old as time.

Not Sheol, not Gehenna, not Hades, not a place where sinners learn redemption; not a place living men ever imagined. Here is the Hell of this world, the Hell of Satan the Prince of Death; here death lives for ever.

I stand with Jesus Christ on a mountaintop in a valley in Hell.

A voice almost as great as the Voice of God comes to us through fire and smoke: 'I sharpened a spear to thrust you through, I mixed death and wine for you to drink, I made nails to pierce you, I prepared a cross to crucify you. I know you, Jesus Christ. Your death is here. Come to me.'

The circles turn, and the land rises up like a screw, or falls away.

My God, my God, the people.

Here my mother hangs herself for ever.

Here my father, burning, begs for water for his burning tongue, a single drop.

Levi writhes and shrieks in a bath of flames, no mercy, no hope, no redemption. For the first time I understand the greatness, the enormity of Joshua's gift to me when He simply cleansed me in the pool that sunny day. My twisted arm burns like fire, but I clasp His hand with both my hands, and He takes me forward.

My God, there's Sarai, my friend, she died when she was just a child!

The people here, the maggots, the millions and billions without strength to save themselves, to lift themselves higher.

Here's the Hell of good intentions, the priests and the police, the doctors and scientists, the teachers and the preachers, the givers to charity and receivers of it; piles of burning books, pits of fire and worms to swallow the elected and unelected, the lawmakers, judges, lawyers, clerks, down and down to the lowest doorkeeper. And the demons.

My God, the demons, snarling like dogs, working like butchers.

There's no God here. But my hand is squeezed in friendship, love and power flows into me like a cool breeze in this place. Have strength.

The wasteland opens up, and whether or not I look up or down, I see a vast gilt temple gleaming like oily smoke in the lowest pit beneath me and the highest hilltop above me.

Joshua commands: 'Remove your gates of brass, lift up your doors of iron.' He illuminates the corners of Hell, and light rushes in. The brass gates of the palace crack and fall, ringing like bells as they topple on the steps, fall out in pieces into the abyss, where my eyes follow them falling for so long it seems I see them still.

Joshua climbs alone into the temple of Satan, and speaks face to face with the fallen angel. What they say I do not know and cannot tell. I am the Queen of Hell.

But this I see: Jesus Christ sets up His Cross like a beacon on the steps above and below the abyss.

And immediately it seems to me that I've seen almost nothing of Hell after all, because everything I thought was large becomes small, the temple and the abyss and the mountaintop shrink until they're almost too small to see, the land slopes under my feet and I realise it's not land but skin; we stand no taller than microbes on a single scale on the spine of a dragon.

And Sion rises around me.

I blinked.

The scrolls fluttered around me in the wind, the moon

bathed the landscape at Sion in its cool glow, set the Dead Sea glittering with silver.

I hung on to a desk. 'Have you won this time?'

Joshua stood at the window, sunk in thought. He wore a white linen shift that tugged and rippled in the wind: Jesus as I always imagine Him, Jesus I see in my dreams.

He half turned, knowing everything I thought before I thought it, waiting for me to catch up. I touched His shoulder. 'How many times before has a baby Jesus been born on this world?'

Joshua said: 'Ten thousand times ten thousand times.'

'Will you be born again?'

'I'm born. I'm here.'

'Is your work done?'

He held out His arm to the emptiness of the world outside. 'Does my work look done?'

My voice trembled. 'Will I see you again?' I cleared my throat, spoke steadily. 'Will I see you again?'

Joshua said: 'You shan't see me after forty days until the end of time.'

My whole body trembled.

He took me in his arms, enfolded me, encompassed me. His lips kissed the top of my head in blessing. His mouth kissed my mouth. He held me up. I had no strength.

'Is there no hope for us at all?' I whispered.

'There's always hope.' He lifted me, gazed into my eyes. He knew me. He touched my belly with his fingertip, and I felt my womb fill with blood.

Jesus Christ said to me: 'Mary, make one green shoot of grass grow.' He let me go. 'You're free, Mary Magdalene. Except of me.'

Is it a blessing or a curse? Was my freedom an end, or another new beginning? I didn't know. As I went down the winding stair I knew I'd never see Joshua again. He'd told me so.

In fact I did see Him again, many times. I never ceased loving Him with all my heart and soul. He'd told me men and women make our own future, but He couldn't foresee it. He didn't know what would happen.

What terrible things would happen.

I heard footsteps climbing the winding stair towards me, drew back in a niche. Judas climbed past me with a heavy tread. He carried a leather bag in his hands like a thief; I scented the cedarwood casket inside and heard it rattling. Judas's hands and whole body shook with terror as he climbed. His terrified eyes looked straight at me, didn't see me. I went down into the moonlit refectory, heard nothing; went outside into the moonlight, heard nothing; crossed the courtyards towards the gates. *Man, it would be better for you if you had not been born.*

I sat quietly in the moon-shadows of the kiln at the corner of the potter's field. The dry-stone field boundaries stretched away from me like a maze. The great gate of Sion that Jesus had broken banged in the wind, the wind whined among the stipes that threw shadows across the moonlight like penitent crosses. I slept, and when I woke the moon had moved, and I heard the approaching heavy tread that I recognised, Judas the Sicariot.

I shrank back in the shadow, afraid. The dust of his footsteps blew over me, his robe and unbound hair blowing in the wind. Judas stepped carefully over the shadows of the stipes as if afraid of falling into them; a superstitious man. He carried the leather bag as though it were the heaviest weight in the world; looked around him like a pilgrim deciding where to pitch his tent, chose a stipe. He put down the bag, took a rope, tied a noose. Tried again, several times, to get the knot right. His hands shook.

He stood on the post-cleat, pulling himself up against the stipe, looped the rope over the top.

A gallows not a cross.

Judas sat on the post-cleat, tied the bag to his legs to make himself heavy, stood up on the cleat and put his head through the noose, pulled it tight, and stepped off.

Not enough of a drop to break his neck. Judas Sicariot hanged writhing, strangling, legs kicking, the bag jingling and jangling and chiming between his ankles. No demons came out of him, he was only a man. Tears poured down his blackening face. An ordinary man.

Then I saw another man watching. Not Jesus. Even by moonlight, as he came forward, I saw this man's hair was redder even than Judas's, red as blood. The moon flashed across his eyes, bright blue, and I knew I'd seen him before. A Celt. Not the man, the Galatian Celt, lying murdered on the road to Sion; but I knew I had seen him somewhere. I tasted salt spray on my tongue, remembered another night, a heaving ship and this British chieftain on his knees before Joshua, the spray flying darkly on each side. *Tonight you are a new man, John Fox.*

I'd seen Joshua baptise him here at Sion.

John Fox, the Follower, the Ruthless One of the Nations who had been foretold, tall, wearing a long cloak, walked slowly to the strangling man. Judas dangled motionless, gazing at the stranger's approach. Fox stared curiously, then crouched, and his knife flashed, cutting the rope that held the leather bag, which fell heavily in the dust. Judas groaned as the weight came off him. He'd hoped the knife was for himself.

Fox grunted, pulled open the bag, and the cedarwood casket fell out. He lifted the lid, jerked back. Then looked again, more cautiously, crouching like an animal, moving his head as though admiring himself. Held out his hands as if warming them over a fire. He lifted out the coins and stared at them in his palms, then pressed his face to them. What he saw I do not know. The wind moaned, or perhaps it was Judas. Fox stood.

He took mercy on the dying man, reached as high as he could with his knife and stuck Judas beneath the breast-bone, pulled the blade to the crotch as economically as a Gentile butcher gutting a pig, stepped back so the bursting guts and blood of Judas didn't foul him.

Then Fox stuffed the coins back in the casket and hid it beneath his cloak, and climbed away past me and never saw me.

And I, too, hurried away. I knew Jesus Christ was no longer at Sion. There was nothing for me here.

VERITAS ODIUM PARET

truth breeds hatred

None of us had any place to go, except me. Martha, Bernice and Zacchaeus dared not stay near Jerusalem where the *huperatai*, the Sanhedrin police, watched every gate. We travelled by back roads to Sepphoris, fearful of Temple informers in Judah and Herod's troops in Galilee, but after a month or two the fuss died down, the world moved on, some new crisis or other rose up, and Jesus Christ was forgotten. My friends gave way to disappointment, almost despair. Forty days had long passed and it was certain that Jesus Christ was no longer here in the flesh among us. At first we heard the usual rumours – I remember them after John the Baptist's death – Jesus Christ had shown Himself on this road or that road, or to Peter, or in Jerusalem, or five hundred people had seen Him somewhere. Even that He showed Himself to Saulus the Inquisitor who hunted Him. But gradually the sightings tailed off. Zacchaeus, Bernice and Martha sat around in my house not knowing what to do, what was expected of them. The reason for living had gone from their lives.

The blood didn't run from my womb. My womb grew inside me. *I* had a reason for living. But how could I put it into words?

I said simply: 'I still can't believe they did it. That they crucified Him.'

'It was the Will of God,' Zacchaeus murmured. 'His sacrifice for men.'

I said, 'I just don't see how God's sacrificing His Son saves us. Or redeems us. Or brings us to repentance in any way, or why.'

Bernice said, 'It's so the risen Christ could show Himself to us so that we believe in Him.'

'He isn't showing Himself to us,' I said. 'He's gone. He could have made us believe more by staying alive, doing miracles to prove His divinity, and ruling over us so that we could not possibly commit sin. Instead He taught love, and they crucified Him.'

Martha came in with flour still clinging to her hands; she'd been baking. 'Don't you understand?' she said, though she had none of Bernice's intelligence. 'I believe more deeply because He *doesn't* tell us what to do. It's up to us. He wants us to get to Heaven by our own efforts.'

'Martha's right,' I said. 'It's up to us to do what He would have done. To live how He would live if He were here among us.' My excitement grew. 'He told me to preach not with words but by example.' I climbed clumsily to my feet. 'I'll speak to the apostles in Capernaum.'

Bernice said: 'If there are any apostles left.' She stood curiously. 'You're very over-excited. Your face is flushed.'

There was a silence, then Martha said, 'And she's sick when she wakes up.'

Bernice watched me, marvelling. 'You? You're carrying the son of the Son of God?'

'Or daughter,' I said.

They touched my tummy, wondering what this new life meant. 'You can't travel to Capernaum, that's a long journey,' Bernice said. 'You must be so careful. Don't be irresponsible. It's not fair on the rest of us to risk His child.'

But I was determined to go, whatever happened. I was the child's mother and in my prayers I tried to give something to God, not seek answers or favours. I had to do what I thought was right. But Bernice, childless, stayed on her knees in front of me. 'Nine months,' she whispered. 'I can hardly wait. He'll be so beautiful.'

She and Zacchaeus believed that God made our future, not us. As I listened to her I realised that already, after only a few months, we were splitting apart. They insisted on protecting me on the dangerous road to Capernaum, of course, and I saw the accusation in their eyes that I was needlessly risking the life of the son of the Son. But our journey was uneventful and as we came into Capernaum they gave thanks that God had looked after us.

We found Peter's house run down, leaves in the courtyard, the fountain cracked. His wife, her mother, their servants, all gone. Peter had dark half-moons of exhaustion and perhaps fear under his eyes. I saw only the Bethsaida faction with him, Andrew and Philip. Simon had fled for his life, of course, to the tiny kingdom of Adiabene, I'd heard. Joses looked after his mother Mary in seclusion in Sepphoris; I didn't know where Thomas was. Not here.

As soon as they saw me the three chief apostles drew back, but I knelt at their feet as best I could. The town had turned against them; Nahum and the Pharisee Archons would not allow them to speak in public. 'What are you doing here?' Peter asked us. 'It's all over.' Matthew arrived later, but I saw no sign of James. 'He's at Sion,' Peter said. 'From the Church at New Jerusalem James proclaims he's the Christ.'

'The New Jerusalem Church? That's what he calls it?'

Matthew said, 'I'm no believer in James. He says he's the Covenant, that he'll get it, dig it, unearth it somehow from beneath the Temple. James believes what I once taught him. But I saw Jesus risen in Jerusalem and I know the truth. We already have the Covenant, each of us, inside us, if only we have the faith to know it.'

I urged them: 'Peter, Philip, Andrew, Matthew, believe me, Jesus Christ is in you. Follow Him. If you seek Him, you'll find Him.'

Peter sat on the step and wept. 'Who do you think you are, a woman, to say this to us?' He burst out, 'They crucified Him, what do you think they'll do to us?'

'I saw the risen Christ, Peter, and so did you. His Resurrection is the promise, don't you see? *He* is the promise. Not any thirty talents or Judas's thirty coins already stolen, lost, wasted.' I begged them, 'Don't waste your lives doing nothing.'

'He promised us eternal life.'

'Peter, Peter, it doesn't matter how you die, only how you live.'

Philip said stolidly, 'As for the risen Christ, I don't know what I saw. He wasn't the same.'

Andrew turned on me bitterly. 'Woman, you've been heard claiming you saw Him twice, as though that makes you twice as good as us.'

I put my hand on Peter's shoulder. 'Don't weep. Don't grieve. Don't give up.'

He shrugged me off, his lips drawing back from his teeth in fury. No, not fury. Jealousy. Really they were just like little boys who'd lost their father. They didn't know what to do, and in their anger and confusion they struck out at anybody. How they must argue among themselves! They all needed a good meal and a few cups of wine, more than a few, followed by a good night's sleep, a hangover and a solid dose of common sense.

I tried to talk to the exhausted apostles without offending them. 'The grace of Jesus Christ will protect you. He made you into men. Yet here you are hiding behind walls when you should be preaching in the world.'

'I won't hear these words from her,' Philip said. 'My Lord was a man not a woman.'

Peter jumped up, pulled me round. 'Listen, we know our Lord loved you more than the rest of us. He wed you in front of us. He often kissed you on the mouth in front of us. He must have told you special things when you were alone.' Here it was! I realised my power. They gathered around me like animals hungry for leftovers.

Matthew said, 'Tell us the secret words of the Saviour.'

I told them: 'He said to me, Blessed are you who do not waver at the sight of Me. For where the mind is, there is the Covenant.'

'More,' Matthew said.

Andrew said, 'The Lord never said those words to her, she's making it up!'

I told them: 'These are things He said to me in the night, when He lay beside me, in the matters of my marriage bed over which I have drawn a veil. He said to me, Neither the soul nor the spirit sees. It is the mind between the soul and the spirit who sees.'

'Will we be resurrected in the flesh?' Zacchaeus asked. 'After death should our bodies be embalmed and dressed in clothes ready for our resurrection? How long must we wait until the end of the world?'

'Will the Resurrection come in our lifetime?' Bernice asked. 'Will we remain married to the same spouse when we are resurrected?'

I said, 'My husband saw His death as the means whereby God would come to men and women and children and be welcome among them. He did not know when the end of time would come.'

'It's soon,' Matthew said. 'Very soon. That's why we have to be so careful.'

I said,'He never said be careful. He said live the best you can.'

Andrew pushed me aside, spoke to the others. 'You can say what you like about what she says He said to her, I don't believe a word of it.'

Philip nodded. 'She's lying. Jesus Christ never said such things to us. That each person is a trinity of mind, soul and spirit.'

'That God is not one God but three,' I said, glad that Nahum and the Pharisees couldn't hear me, for they would surely have stoned me, 'always in movement, balanced, made equal. The alpha and the omega. God the Father, God the Son, God the Holy Ghost.'

Matthew said, 'They're strange ideas.' I uttered a small silent prayer of thanks that I had not mentioned the fiery Hell of Satan that lies beneath us, everywhere.

Peter stood on the step to make himself tall. 'Listen, friends, brothers, ask ourselves this question. Do we really believe that our Lord would speak privately with a woman? That He'd whisper secrets to her denied to us? Are we to turn everything on its head and listen to her?'

'He didn't prefer her to us,' Andrew said. 'We were equal with Him. She's lying.'

I shouted, 'I'd turn myself into a man and lead you if I could!'

Peter's face flushed dark red; he drew his knife in my face. Martha screamed.

The blade touched my eyebrow, not deliberately I think, but a little blood trickled in my eye. It distracted him for a moment. I said quickly, 'Peter, Peter, my brother in Christ, do you think I would have made up these things in my heart to deceive you? Do you think I'd lie about your Saviour? Do you really?'

'I don't know!' Peter shouted, 'I don't know you! Would our Jesus Christ who didn't come out of a woman ever go into one and love only her? Could our Christ, our Son of Man, love a woman more than us? He never loved you, Mary Magdalene, sinner, thief, whore!' Peter's voice rose, he screamed: '*He loved us all!*'

'Us most of all,' Andrew said.

Matthew pushed back Peter's knife. 'Peter, you're hot-tempered. You can't fight a woman not your wife. You'll kill her.'

Martha called down from the top step, 'You can't kill her. She's carrying Joshua's son.'

From dark red, Peter's face went white. He stood with the knife upraised, then it fell from his fingers. 'I don't believe you.' He stared at my belly's curve. 'No. My God. No.'

Andrew swore like the fisherman he was.

Matthew spoke in the silence. 'If our Saviour made her worthy, who are we to reject her?'

'Blasphemy,' Peter said dully. 'She's ruined everything.' He turned angrily on Matthew. 'He didn't *make* her worthy! He didn't make her an apostle, did He? No! No woman could be an apostle. *We're* His apostles, *we're* His words. Why should we change our minds and listen to her?'

'She'll set herself up as more important than us,' Andrew said. 'Her son will be the son of the Widow.'

I said, 'Our Lord told that whoever the Spirit inspires is divinely ordained to speak, whether man or woman. How can it matter whether the preacher's a man or a woman? It's the words that matter. It's the heart that matters.'

'Listen to her. She's making herself the centre of it all,' Andrew said. 'Everything we say or preach will be for a woman. Our Lord never meant this. Peter's right. She's a blasphemy in herself, carrying a blasphemy in her belly. She tricked our Lord somehow.'

'How can I trick God?' I cried.

'Look at her strange eyes,' said Philip. 'Look at that strange colour.'

I defied him. 'Indigo-blue! So what!'

Philip peered at me close, accused me. 'The prophet Malachi tells us, "An abomination is committed in Israel and Jerusalem, for Judah has profaned the holiness of the Lord which he loved, and married the daughter of a strange god." '

Peter said, 'Our Lord warned us of Satan.' He picked up the knife, came forward like a bull.

In fear of my life, I called quickly, 'Malachi also tells you, "She's your companion, and the wife of your Covenant." '

Matthew stepped between us, spoke to me in a low voice. 'Mary, go quickly. These are men's matters, not to be interfered in lightly. Let tempers cool.'

'Her eyes are no more Jewish than the colour of Judas's hair,' Philip said. 'I never trusted Judas, and I don't trust her. Our Lord didn't offer her His blood and His body at the Last Supper.'

Peter said, 'That's because He saw her laugh!'

'She wasn't laughing,' Martha said. 'She was crying.'

Zacchaeus called from the step, 'My brothers, this is ridiculous.'

'Brother?' They turned on him. 'Are you our brother, or hers? Are you in on her scheme?'

'There's no scheme,' Bernice said. The more she denied it, the more it sounded as though there was a scheme, and as though I were the schemer. My baby put me in charge. I was the Madonna. My baby was the succession to Christ, not the apostles. All the sins of women were heaped on my head: I schemed, I manipulated, I was the enemy of men. And especially I was the enemy of my husband. Had I not betrayed Him as much as Judas had? Was it not for me, on my insistence, that He had performed no signs in Jerusalem?

Because of me, our Saviour had gone to His death.

'No. No.' I shook my head. The more I denied it, the more the apostles believed it was the truth. Nowhere did the prophecies foretell that Jesus Christ would have a child by a woman.

His heir.

Peter pulled at my arm and I screamed, feeling it break. 'I hardly touched her,' he said.

Matthew pulled me back. 'Go. Go quickly!'

Martha and Bernice hurried me to the gate. Zacchaeus said angrily to Peter, 'You're the one who betrayed our

Lord, not her. Three times you denied Him.'

Peter struck out, bellowed at me. 'Mary Magdalene, you're excommunicated from among us. You are dead.'

We stood in the dust outside the gates, stupefied.

'Go!' called Matthew's voice. 'Go quickly.'

TERRA FIRMA

dry land

The sail bellied above me, creaking, and our little boat surged forward as though pushed by a giant hand, then was pulled back. A blue wave rose up, showing the sun through it, then as the wave fell away the cold mistral wind blew spray across us where we crouched in the bottom of the Arimathean's boat. We pressed our faces miserably to the boards. Zacchaeus was seasick, sick since the day we first stepped aboard in Caesarea Maritima and the bow lifted to the first wave. After so many days of wind and storm and sea we no longer knew or cared which was the bow and which the stern, where the wind blew us, whether we'd live or die in exile.

I knew I would live. I carried the son of the Son inside me. Surely God would look after me. Then I remembered how He had not looked after even His own Son, not in any way I could recognise; and how Joshua, in the moment of His earthly death, had not called on God as His Father.

I screamed as the boat dropped. The baby moved inside me; the boat surged up. Martha hugged me, trying to shelter me from the spray, then stinking water poured over us from the bilges below, and we were glad of fresh as the boat rolled and the spray poured down like hail.

I laughed. It's not the first time, as you know, that I've been adrift in a boat as lost as I: I even laughed when a wave broke the steering oar. Adrift again in a boat as rudderless as Noah's Ark, but in all too lively a sea this time, the Mediterranean; or perhaps it's the Atlantic by now. And only a cargo of humans aboard, no animals. The captain, one of Joseph of Arimathea's, cowers with his crew in the bilges and has no more idea of our position than I. Is it Spain I see through the breaking waves ahead of us? Or Britain at last, the Land of the Covenant?

The Land of the Covenant.

I remember my vision of Joshua building the church on the tor. I know that everything makes sense, that God works in ways plain to see if only we can understand His purpose for us, His reason for us. There is an answer, and I know it's so huge and obvious and true we simply can't see it. Or as small as the brightly painted butterfly whose fluttering made the storm that blew Joshua inevitably to His shipwreck in Britain. I have faith now that God is not dead but sleeping, we are not entirely lost, not entirely abandoned.

But Zacchaeus and Bernice find God in everything. Zacchaeus says the stick with which I offered Joshua the vinegar-soaked sponge wasn't any old stick but a reed, reeds being richly invested with more symbolic meaning than I can be bothered to say; Bernice corrects him that it was a stick of marjoram, also full of prophetic prediction. Each of them carries aspenwood splinters of the Cross bound with twine into its T or *tau* shape, which they hang round their necks.

Our little boat almost overturns in the steepening waves, bangs us painfully from side to side as the captain half climbs, half falls to the sail. A wave washes over us, sweeps him into the foam, he's gone.

Soon the end of time will come, and there's no place for me in Sion.

Is even my insignificant life part of God's purpose?

Something huge and obvious and true, and we're stone blind. Deaf. Dumb. Without feeling. Can't see it or hear it or speak it or touch it.

Joshua knew. As Jesus Christ He rose in the flesh from the dead, and confronted Satan, and knew His purpose.

Why Britain? I don't know, only that long ago the survivors carried me from the cave in the hills to the low chalky island, Vectis, crunching with white seashells where the dragon fell on Balaam the Zadok, and there all our hopes were lost. Joshua wants me there. Wants my child there. God is not anger and fury but love, peace, mercy, generosity, solitude.

I watched the ropes fraying and flying apart from our little boat like cracking whips, the sail bannering loosely ahead of us like a wing, then whirled away on the wind.

In Britain I first loved James, as I told you, loved him with all my heart and soul but never with my crippled body; and as you know, for James's sake, so that he'd know love and the children I couldn't give him, I shot myself in the mouth, and my body fell into the bottomless pit where he could neither grieve for me or build a shrine to remember me, only get on with his life.

But now God has come into this world, and something apart from evil, despair, loss, exists.

I've learned to live.

The waves curl upwards, break across us in the surf, everything turns over, sand fills my mouth.

A gull caws, then a cloud of them rise away from me when I first move.

I'm lying on a beach, hard yellow sand under my face and hands, the sun burning the back of my head. The sand's hot, even the wavelets lapping my feet are warm, and the busy whirring of cicadas emanates from the swamps and tangled scrub behind the beach. This isn't Britain.

I sit up holding my belly, but I can feel my baby's fine. Kicking once or twice, angry little fellow, as I remember his father was at first. Martha helps me to my feet, wraps me in my cloak which the sun has dried. Zacchaeus sits with a broad smile, glad to be off the sea dead or alive. Among the debris I find a broad-brimmed hat to cover his bald head from the sun. Bernice stands some distance along the strand where the sea carried her. She waves. We wave.

We're alone. No sailors, no captain, no one knows about us.

Joshua could stare at the sun for hours without blinking; I shielded my eyes against the glare. Distant hills, purple-violet; swampland to the right and left; but directly in front of us rose a dusty island of low hills, a stone cottage or two, a vineyard that I could just see, a few narrow strips of crop, some goats, maybe a small village somewhere out of sight.

Beyond the hills, empty hinterland.

I turned. The empty blue sea.

One green shoot. The hope I carried inside me.

I called to the others, embraced them, and we looked around us. Love, peace, mercy, solitude.

'God wants me here,' I told them. 'I'll have my baby here.'

No 6,759   Published in London and Manchester

Your Daily   19 November 1987   *12p*

NEWS & STAR-LEGION

DEDICATED TO THE PEOPLE OF BRITAIN

WHEN?

FROM OUR SPECIAL CORRESPONDENT

EXCLUSIVE

CENTRAL LONDON

After an accident 30 feet below the River Thames today four Telecom engineers are lucky to be alive.

Construction Foreman Jack Katherill was first at the scene. "Shortly after starting the night shift boring-machine one of the lads shouted
stuck.
obstruction.
the machine could be shut d
broke through.

The men were working for Brit
believed to be site
old London Bridge. Foundations

"I could see the mortar was pretty dodgy stuff a

ordered the lads back, but
all hell let loos
mortar gave way
fell
medieval

sort of stair
find in a church
winding stair
down
couldn't tell.

A Telecom spokesman
denied that historians were
baffl
scientists
Manchester Science &
Technology.

Reports that a man-si
coffin
also denied.
large wooden box remo
were "fanciful and
unhelpful".

The four men taken to
Guy's Hospital were
-charged after tell
not to talk. Sorry."

Mr Kather
no. Got a job to
getting on with my job."

Old London Bri
1176 by Peter Colechurch
and Jack Mason. King John
Muslim.

BOOK TWO

Jude

*And he shall turn the heart of the fathers to the children
and the heart of the children to their fathers
lest I come and strike the earth with a curse.*
Malachi 4:6

FILIUS MARIA

Mary's son

MARIE DE L'ÉGLISE, NEAR NARBO, SOUTHERN GAUL
WEDNESDAY 17 MARCH AD 62

All morning, as usual, I pushed the hoe into the stony unyielding earth until sweat trickled into my beard, and the birds perched on my shoulders rubbed their beaks against my skin to drink. 'They just want your salt,' I knew my mother would say in her harsh voice. 'That's all they're interested in, Jude, not you.' She'd say the same of the dogs from the village who gathered around me. 'Jude, they expect you to throw them scraps, that's all. They know you're soft!' I smiled as I worked, knowing the dogs and birds were with me for love, and imagined my mother alone at tireless prayer in the small church coaxed from the stones by Uncle Zacchaeus long ago. Strange a woman who prayed so hard knew so little of love. It's all around us.

I felt it working all around me in the field as I laboured: I knelt and watched beetles pushing their little balls of dust, their work more arduous than mine. I saw life pushing and spreading under every stone. Snails sucking the last of the night's dew before the sun turned the drops to air. Down-hill, near the stream where the ground was damper and the sun not so prolonged, the crop sent green shoots through the grey obstinate earth, ten thousand at least, perhaps ten thousand times ten thousand; my mother had taught me to count. Snails nibbled among them, so I abandoned my hoe (my mother's hoe), picked out the snails one by one and popped them in the hem of my smock, then sat on a rock by the stream winkling them out of their shells with a sharp stick, eating them. I wished I had garlic, but that grew near the house, and salt came from the little flood-pan by the beach. One dog had a hurt leg; I made it better. The dogs performed tricks to be awarded the last snails, then crouched, snarling, as a scarecrow moved in the field.

But the scarecrow was only my aunt, Martha, almost as old as my mother. Dust puffed from her sandals as she hobbled awkwardly across the crop, leaving a flattened trail behind her, so even before I heard her calling I knew it was urgent. She turned round and round calling for me in the wrong direction, almost blind, limping on her stiff hips. I ran in front of her and gripped her elbows lightly.

'Is it my mother? Is she dead?' I knew she was very ill. It was a malaise of the heart rather than her body, which was strong for her age, her muscles like leather. I felt nothing wrong in her, but her spirit failed her. In old age she had given way to doubt and despair. Lately the old woman trembled as though she saw more than I – sometimes I turned, expecting to see someone standing behind me, and she asked questions of the air. She'd not expected to live so long. Like Zacchaeus and Bernice, whom I remembered from my childhood, my mother believed in the end of the world. She prayed for the end day by day, and the Resurrection. Now her life was completing in the usual merciful way God grants the old: her mind slipping away, sliding into fantasies and dreams of her bright youth and days of strength when everything, she muttered, was so important. But sometimes her mumbling confusion was painful to see.

I saw into Martha's eyes. 'She's not dead? Not another stroke? Can she move? She sent you?'

Martha gripped me tight, gasping. 'Men seen in the village!' I let her recover her breath. By *men* she meant outsiders, not villagers; my mother and Martha have always feared outsiders. As a child I was taught to run from anyone I didn't know, to talk to no one, never to go with them. My mother named the village Peche, which in the language of these parts, Oc, means Sin. A villa, two houses, a dormitory for slaves, hovels for free men, a few bushes for goatherds and their brats to sleep beneath; the villagers were ordinary people who lived entirely without the love, peace, generosity and mercy that my mother and Uncle Zacchaeus tried to coax into them. The men fought and stole and fucked each other's wives and goats, and their wives stole, cheated, fucked and in agony bred children who lived in perfect imitation of their parents. But I loved errands that took me to the hotbed of village gossip, vendetta, rumour – a dark swarming underbelly to my life of solitude with two old women. Once on the god Bacchus's festival day a girl kissed me in the shade of an olive tree but my mother saw and shrieked like a gull, pulled me off her by my ear, almost twisting the lobe off, kicking at the girl (whose name was Giselle) with her sandals. Giselle's an unusual name here, though there's an old woman called Gizela, but Giselle and her mother came somewhere from the north. I was almost as interested in Giselle's exciting story as in her breasts; I lie, of course, but I could have learnt much from her. She could have told me a little of the world outside. I was almost as hungry for knowledge as for love; my second lie, as you must know by now, since I've told you of Giselle.

Strangers? The world outside never came to the island of Clape, our few dusty hills of nowhere, bound by swamp on every side except the beach. Nothing brought outsiders here; nothing good. Martha had recovered her breath, though I felt her heart fluttering. 'What men? Are you sure? What's so wrong?'

Martha wailed, 'Men with long hair and long beards, wearing white linen!'

It meant nothing to me. My mother was losing her mind. 'I'll go to her,' I promised Martha. 'It's all right. Don't worry. I'll help you home.'

But Martha jerked away from me with all her strength, a crack of her old bones. 'Go to her!' She showed her gums, snarling like an old grey dog. 'Go to the Magdalene quickly.' Being my mother's servant she never called her Mary, only the Magdalene. As for where or what that is, it has never been told for me to know. Martha pushed me. 'Outsiders in the village!'

My mother's little church on the hilltop was no larger than a stable. On one side was the small cemetery for sailors washed up on the beach, together with the few villagers years ago coaxed and browbeaten to look up from their miserable ignorant lives and believe in the Jesus Christ of Zacchaeus. Their village tongues couldn't even get round the word Nazarene. They called Him a Nazari, which my mother hated, saying it was untrue: her Saviour had not been a Nazari or Nazarene. But the name had stuck to us. Once a dying Egyptian sailor brought to us called himself a Naasene, so there were obviously beliefs similar to my mother's in Alexandria. The Egyptian even muttered the word *Thomas*, which meant nothing to me, but it was obviously a name because my mother gripped the man with white fingers. 'Is Thomas there in Egypt?' But even my hands could not save him, and the Egyptian arched and died.

'Who's Thomas?' I'd asked, but my mother drew into herself as she always did when questioned. She'd developed a way of answering fully and completely uninformatively, as though I was expected to know.

'The Lord's brother.' I'd supposed she meant a brother of Jesus Christ, to whose Father we pray. But Martha had told me that all believers in Jesus are His brothers and sisters. She herself was a sister of Jesus, because she believed in Him. All I knew of Jesus was that He was wonderful. He'd been crucified and risen from the dead. Jesus believed in love and all good things, and believing in Him was the way to believe in those good things, and He would lead us to Heaven very soon at the end of time.

But the end of time had not come. When God brought my mother here (she wasn't born here) at first she'd not even bothered to sow crops, thinking it was enough to have her baby. She was a wonderful mother; no child had more love than I. Years had passed before she allowed Zacchaeus to start on the church. And I remember the pain the decision caused her. As if, I saw now, the church were not the living symbol of her faith but the first sign of her despair.

After its completion Zacchaeus parted from his wife and went north, calling himself Amadour, to bring more unbelievers to my mother's God; we never heard of him again. Bernice moved to Bazas, then Soulac, where the villagers built a single pillar to mark her grave.

My solitude with Mary and Martha was all I knew.

The doorway to my mother's church was low, so that a worshipper bowed low in imitation of our Lord's humility.

Being tall, I bent almost double. Inside I stood up, the room narrow but high enough for me not to be able to touch the reed roof. It was dark and warm, the darkness and warmth full of God; sometimes rush candles deliberately filled the place with smoke, as though God were most easily found inside a warm cloud of darkness and smoke. As my eyes adjusted I saw a narrow side window glaring sunlight on to the table at the far end, illuminating thirteen grails of food and wine laid out ready to eat and drink, and thirteen stools set ready. Jesus was followed by twelve apostles apparently; they'd betrayed Him and never been heard of again. But my mother had once hoped they'd return to His teachings.

On the wall behind the table hung a small *tau* of wood that formed the T-shape naturally, of gnarled olive wood since aspen doesn't grow on the island. Below the cross was the niche where the holy *capsae* containing the Torah are stored as in the synagogues of my mother's people. There was just enough space beside them for a few *membranae*, notebooks of the sayings of Jesus Christ.

'Mother?' It was a moment before I saw Mary Magdalene on her knees in the gloom before the table, dressed in black as she was, with a white linen scarf Nazarene women have adopted since the Crucifixion of Jesus: black in mourning at being cut off from the light of God. Nowadays my mother prayed on her knees not from piety but because she could no longer stand.

'I wish I was strong again!' she complained. I lifted her, sat her on the stone bench along one wall, knelt in front of her. Her horny yellow knees stuck through her skirt, her callused elbows jutted in threadbare holes worn by her devotion. She really thought He would come back any moment and make her body young again. 'Don't I look a little like James?' she chuckled, coughing. I knew no James. 'Knees like a camel!' Her mind was rambling; another stroke. I touched her twisted arm.

'Are you all right?' I asked. 'Are you in pain?' As a child I can remember her wrist, elbow, shoulder knotted hard with arthritis, and I had taken it away. But she'd never allowed me to take all her pain, and it worried me that I felt no pain in her now. Only peace and love. 'Mother,' I whispered. 'Don't die.'

'I believe in Jesus Christ.' She stroked my hair. I have her hair – her hair which is still black, just as her teeth are still white. Her eyes are clear, still vivid. Her eyes are my earliest memories, together with my certain knowledge that she loved me more than her life. She kissed my forehead. 'You have your father's eyes, Jude.'

'What's this news Martha's worrying you with, strangers in the village?'

'Sssh, my son.' She stroked my ears. 'And your father's ears. He had beautiful feet. It was almost the first thing I noticed about him.'

'You never talk of my father when I ask you about him.' I made to lift her. 'You aren't dying. I'll carry you home.'

'I am home.' She raised her twisted arm to display the church, and I felt her pain flood into her. She gripped me tight. 'Carry me to the altar. I have to talk to you.' By altar she meant the table. I carried her in my arms, finding her surprisingly heavy. She wouldn't sit on the holy stools but stood on her feet, swaying, looking up into my eyes. 'Oh, Jude, Jude, you know almost nothing.'

'I'm thirty-three years old.'

'I tried to protect you all this time.' From Giselle? From knowledge? From the world outside? I wondered if my mother had intended this place, and my isolated life and upbringing, to be a safe retreat, a kind of Garden of Eden where everything would be perfect. Even I. Perfectly ready for the end of time. But now her breath rattled in her throat, and pain filled her lungs. Her time would come first. 'You have to leave, Jude,' she whispered. 'Run away, run away. They've found you.'

'Who?'

'James's men.' She shrugged. 'Or Saul's, who calls himself Paul. Or Peter's. Or Simon's.'

'These names mean nothing to me.'

'Zealots. Sicariots. They'll kill you.'

'I'm afraid for you, Mother. Rest.'

'It's too late for me.' She wouldn't let me support her, braced herself against the altar with all her strength, spoke to the Cross. 'My time has come. I've done my best for you. I've failed. My son, my dear son, what do you know of our Jesus Christ?'

I realised how little I really knew in fact. 'He was a Jew. He lived in a place called Galilee. He was a scholar who preached love and many other fine things. He died before I was born.'

She nodded. 'Now, tell me what you know of your father.'

'He was a Jew. He married you in Galilee. He was a carpenter who travelled wherever there was work to be found. He died before I was born.' I stopped.

'Don't you wonder who you are?' my mother asked. 'Don't you wonder where you came from?'

I thought of Giselle coming from the north. She hadn't known her father. She didn't know why she was her mother's daughter, she just was. Or why she stood no taller than my chest, or why she had deep brown eyes. Neither of us knew why we wanted to be in love.

I said: 'Everyone wonders sometimes.' I tried to see my mother's face. 'No one knows who, why, what for we are. We just are. We're born and die. No one knows anything. We're part of the world.'

'Your father knew who he was.' Calmly she reached for the grail at the centre of the table, a wooden platter slightly larger than the six others on each side of it. On it lay twelve wafers of unleavened bread. She took one, laid it on her tongue. 'This is His entire life which is given for us.' She sipped from the wooden cup, also called a grail. 'This is the Covenant of His blood which is His promise to us.'

'Mother, what are you saying?'

I turned her face towards me. Her neck cracked audibly. 'Your father is Jesus Christ.'

My mother Mary Magdalene told me every word she told you.

Not one single word more, or less. She talked while the sun set. She talked through the night. I lived, like you, through the Rainmaker's death. I was born in Galilee, I saw the Annunciation of the archangel Gabriel to the Virgin, I saw the infant Jesus Christ carried down by angels into the Bethlehem stable, saw him bring the dead to life, saw his brothers and sisters, saw Sion, the Salt, the baptisms, saw him walk on the sea, saw everything my mother saw with her own eyes. I saw him marry my mother at Cana, I saw him crucified, saw the Son rise from the dead, just as my mother had. Saw the moment of my own conception in the library at Sion. My mother still talked when the sun rose, and she ended with those words: 'Your father is Jesus Christ.'

And then she fell silent.

I stood. The rising sun illuminated the altar directly, shafts of glare pouring from a couple of windows like arrow-slits in the end wall. My mother's church faced not towards the Jerusalem Temple, like a synagogue, but eastward to greet each new sun. I stretched my stiff muscles. I yawned. I had to go outside and piss in the dew-speckled grass, stood relieving myself in the dawn light. Not our Father. Your father is Jesus Christ.

Is Jesus Christ, not *was*.

If it had been *was* I'd escape it somehow. Deny it. Laugh. Thank you, Mother, but I think you're mistaken. Rest. You're tired. Sleep. She was crazy, senile, her story would die when she died. No one would ever hear of it again until the end of time, when my mother was judged for her lie.

Your father *is* Jesus Christ. I remembered all she'd told me. Had she lied about everything? Every single word, a lie?

Only a story, obviously. No truth meant to be in it. A parable. A dream. And strangely lacking in authority – an unsubstantiated story from a woman. Her life. What she saw with her own eyes and heard with her own ears. *Anyone with two good ears had better listen.* My father speaking.

She believed in Jesus Christ, but it was only a belief! He could have fooled her, surely.

Her belief that the Devil made this world. Only a belief.

I tousled my hair angrily with my fingers, swept the long strands back over my white linen shoulders. Who would ever know what she made up? Suppose she made it all up? Suppose it was all true?

Suppose it *is* all true.

Suppose not one word is false.

Suppose last night I saw, heard in her words, something real and authentic of the working of God in this world?

Suppose something in me *is* God, not a thing to pray to, worship to, crouch to, supplicate to, but something real and alive inside me? Someone to be. A possibility. A chance.

A choice.

I stare at the sun. She'd said my father stared at the sun.

I ran back into the darkness of the church. My mother had fallen by the altar-table like dropped clothes. I swept off the grails and chalices, lifted her, laid her gently on the altar. Her eyes opened.

She whispered, 'Now you know the truth, Jude. You *are* the truth.'

I felt she was in no pain. I muttered, 'I don't know what the truth is.'

'Then you'll never know who you are.' She gripped my wrist with her hand like a claw, looking up to me. 'Will I die when this body dies?' She begged me, 'Will I?'

'No. Yes. No. How should I know?'

'You're the son of the Son. I opened your eyes. You're my son, more than me. You must know!'

'My God,' I whispered, 'I don't know anything.'

'Save yourself, Jude. Strangers in the village! Don't let them crucify you.'

She'd sheltered me from everything all my life! I felt as though the earth I tended lovingly, thoughtlessly, had opened up and swallowed me, and all I'd known was different from what I thought it was. 'I'm not God,' I said. 'I don't know anything about God.'

'No one knows. We only believe. But I promise you, there's more to believe in than belief. More than religions made by men. There *is* truth.' She groaned. 'What harm's Peter done by now? What evil has James committed in the name of God in his search for God? The men and women Simon must have fooled with his tricks! I've been the fool. What demons are at work?' Her voice rose hysterically, exhausted. 'Fire in the sky!'

It was only the rising sun. 'Mother, calm down. Rest.'

She gripped me. 'This is still Satan's world, Jude. The world of creatures and men, the worst of all possible worlds. Heaven hasn't come.' She touched my face. 'I tried to make it a heaven for you. To keep you innocent.' Her eyes opened wide, seeing something new. 'Thirty-three. Exactly the same age as your father endured earthly death on the Cross.'

'Coincidence.'

'Fire in the sky!' She struggled, almost without strength.

Then she fought for breath, just one single breath. 'In the hour of my death,' she whispered, 'I opened my son's eyes.' Her eyes stared at me. The life had left them; my mother was gone. I cuddled her to keep her warm, but her body cooled, just meat and bone, and I shivered. Martha tugged my sleeve, and I saw the sun had moved. 'You have to go. You can't stay.'

'I won't go.'

'I'll deal with this. I know what to do. Your mother was a queen.'

I touched Martha's shoulder, felt my strength flow into her. Martha wasn't ready to die yet: she was still fighting. 'Martha, do you believe what my mother said about who my father is?'

She busied herself, folded my mother's arms across her shrivelled breasts, made her feet lie straight. 'We can't keep her long in this heat. The cart's outside. Carry her to it; I'll arrange the rest. Then go!'

I stopped her. 'Tell me.'

'You have your father's anger. His ruthlessness. I can see it in you, you'll find it. He always did what was right whatever the cost to himself or anyone else.' Martha's eyes trickled with age, or grief, or love, or worship. 'I'll tell you one thing I saw.' She sat on a stool without thinking. 'The night of their last supper, it was, when everyone felt themselves betrayed. The apostles and disciples who'd followed Jesus, gave up everything for him, left their wives and sons and daughters to follow him, houses, jobs, money, lost everything they had in the world to follow him, made themselves as naked as children to follow his word – that night they finally realised he'd failed them. He left them nothing they'd wanted. The hangers-on and followers turned against him, the disciples deserted him to the last man. Only the apostles were left to betray him. It could have been any one of them, or all: they were all of one mind in their despair. And while this was happening, while everything good fell apart because God was not what men demanded, because God was not the God of their beliefs, I saw your mother walk calmly forward through the apostles, a woman entirely alone among men. Jude, I saw this. I saw your mother Mary Magdalene lie at your father's feet in front of everyone who'd lost faith in him, and she touched his feet and greeted him: "My Lord." I heard her. She said: "My Lord Jesus Christ, our anointed saviour, save us." '

The vision left Martha's eyes. Her body slumped a little.

I whispered, 'My mother said that? She alone recognised her husband as Jesus Christ in front of everyone who'd lost faith?'

Martha combed the body's hair for the last time.

'She alone. It won her no friends. She still has enemies who remember her. There are men who believe that your existence is blasphemy. That you are yourself the blasphemy, Jude. A scheme of your mother's to make herself greater than the apostles. You have to save your life.'

Listening to Martha, I felt I was going mad. Martha's story was exactly as my mother had told it to me. I didn't know what to believe. I touched my mother's icy hand.

'My father never ran away. Neither will I.'

Martha told me what to bring and I fetched bitter aloes and the purple petals of myrrh that grow in my mother's field, a pestle and mortar to grind them in, clay pots, and a sharp knife. The church was the coolest place for work. 'Don't watch.' I watched Martha split open my mother's body from breastbone to crotch with the knife in the Essene fashion that my mother described to me only a few hours ago. Her internal organs, in perfect condition for a woman in her middle seventies, were cut from the membranes that held them and placed in the pots except for the heart and kidneys, which were left in place in the body cavity packed with aloes and myrrh. The blood was allowed to drain out, sticky and dark with death, from the livid veins where it sank in the body with the ceasing of the heart. Martha pushed small long-handled spoons up the nostrils, removed the brain patiently. I remember her practising this with the Egyptian sailor. We sewed the body, washed it, dressed it as though alive again. Even now my mother's knees and elbows stuck automatically through the holes worn in her shift by her devotion. We covered her with her cloak, pressed her hands together beneath her chin, and stepped back to pray. It was almost dark, and I bumped into something soft. Martha shouted in alarm.

But I turned and saw that it was only Giselle, and I felt I'd turned from death to life.

Giselle stood praying in our style, arms outstretched *orans* as my mother taught us, which lifted her breasts beneath her clothes. She'd known that to have any chance of winning my mother's consent she must believe in my mother's God. So she believed. Her face was small but wide-eyed, with a mole just above the left corner of her mouth. Her breasts moved upward with each breath, her long black hair curling round her nipples which I sensed beneath her shift, and imagined perfectly. 'I'm sorry she's dead.' Giselle looked at me earnestly and we stepped back alone. She whispered, 'I came to warn you. Someone's asking for you in the village.'

I took her elbow, drew her outside. The last glow of sunset was around us. I knew how badly Giselle wanted me – she was hot and cold inside – but she knew nothing would happen. I think I still had my mother's blood on my hands. I wiped them on the grass by Giselle's feet, stood, kissed her.

I kissed Giselle's lips and felt the heat flood through her. She put her hands over my ears, murmuring my name. She moved like an animal, held my head to her throat. I pushed my way back to her lips, which tasted of strawberries, wild spring strawberries, and she knew I had to have her. Her nipples lifted against mine. I lifted her skirts to her waist, touched her; she squeezed me, pulled me. I forgot what I was doing, I only knew I wanted her, all of her, I felt all of her. Quickly, quickly, not here: a hut nearby where the tools were kept. We didn't get that far, she knew she had to let me in her, we fell belly to belly, she rolled on me so her weight pulled me inside her, I pushed, we rolled, her womb tightened, she felt herself taking me, we couldn't stop.

Giselle lay on top of me in the grass. I felt for the corner of her cloak, covered her bottom from the night air. The dew was cold under my back. I was naked. My cock was still inside her, we couldn't move if we wanted to. Her hair lay across my face. I stared through the strands at the stars. She murmured in my ear, 'You're free of her at last.'

'My mother?'

'You never even looked at me before.'

'I looked at you.'

She tickled me with her sharp little nose, gazed at me with her wide eyes. 'Not like you looked at me tonight.' She giggled, rested her warm face against mine. 'You're still looking at me. You're still stiff.' A light scratched the sky, sparked brilliantly, was gone. She saw the reflection in my eyes. 'What was that?'

'A shooting star. That's what my mother called them.'

Giselle stilled. 'Perhaps not quite free of her.' I bit her ear and we wriggled, but Giselle was right. A little bit of my mother lived on in me, probably quite a lot of her, in fact. What she'd called – the Greek word – genes. Blood. Just another form of immortality, if what she'd told me last night was true. Last night; I'd been awake for two days, and felt my eyes closing. Giselle jerked, her fingers twisting my nose. 'Jude, I almost forgot. The men in the village asking about the Magdalene?'

'Too late.'

'Asking if she had a child. Asking if the child was a son. Asking your name.'

'They'll go away.'

'I told them there was no son. But someone's bound to talk.'

I was almost asleep, but from the tip of my cock touching her womb I felt the warmth spread through her. I sat half up and she laughed. 'What? What is it?'

'Do you feel it?'

She whispered in my ear, 'I feel only you. You're so special, and you don't know it.'

'Special?'

She cuddled. 'Special to me.'

I had felt her conceive. A cell was dividing in her womb. *Semen* is the Jewish word meaning oil, and through it my body had passed forward my mortality and my immortality. Not only a son; now a grandchild. Giselle kissed me, licked me, warm and comfortable over me, suspecting nothing. I loved her, fell asleep stroking her back, and slept.

As I slept I heard her whisper in my dreams. 'Why? Why do the men hate you? Why do they fear you?'

In the morning both Giselle and I were needed to lift my

mother's body on to the cart, stiff and heavy with aloes and myrrh as it was.

Giselle watched my face curiously as we lifted. She knew that the Magdalene's hold over me was so strong I almost expected my mother to sit up, throw out her arms, and begin praying to the sun. But soon her body would lie in the darkness of the caves behind the village, her tomb prepared long ago according to her instructions.

A donkey dragged loyally between the shafts but the wheels were solid timber, the axle a tree trunk: the cart weighed twice what it could carry. And Martha, too weary to walk, climbed aboard. The donkey strained, the cart creaked, but did not move. I put my shoulder to the wheel, lifting, pushing, and slowly my mother's body began its last journey. We'd raised a canopy overhead to protect it from the sun's heat, and the patch of deep shadow wobbled and jerked over its face as the cart bumped downhill between the shimmering slopes of Clape. When the cart stuck on a stone Giselle pushed the wheel with me. I knew from her glances she needed to know what I was feeling; whether I was truly free of my mother, whether my love was unchained, who I carried in my heart.

Why did Giselle think me so strong, though I was hardly strong enough to shift the cart?

No, it was purely romance. She needed me to be strong because she loved me. Her love made me strong. Every time I looked at her she was looking at me. More like a wedding than a funeral.

The cart rumbled easily down a smooth stretch, and I walked behind it with Giselle, and squeezed her warm hand. She whispered, 'What are you thinking?' I knew she wanted to be seen beside me as we walked through the village. She was no more popular in Peche than I; her Frankish accent jarred the villagers of the Oc as harshly as my mother's preaching. Slaves hoeing the neat narrow fields stared as we passed, hands not ceasing their steady lifelong rhythm. Peasant women watched crouching from their doorways, their brats and dogs yapping after us on the beaten bath winding between the hovels. No one said anything in the presence of death. Here was the house of Giselle's mother, with stone walls, and Giselle looked up at her mother wearing Roman clothes on the step. Her hand tightened its grip on mine. Her mother, Clodius's daughter, a child fetching water at some river on the northern rim of the world, was stolen by a Roman soldier; rape was followed by consent and finally love, the soldier prospered, grew mighty in Rome, fell from grace, and his widow and daughter fled from his enemies to safety here. Giselle returned my squeeze, hard. We understood each other, she thought.

Near the smithy by the stream a few men crossed themselves with the Pharisee T for the Holy Torah, workers from the many Jewish estates scattered throughout Vienne. Exiles like ourselves probably, fallen on hard times. They turned their heads away from death as the cart creaked past, but I looked back. One of the Jewish workers pointed after the cart and two bearded men came from the shadows, stared. I saw the flash of a silver denarius flicked to one of the informers. The newcomers spoke with deep hoarse voices that carried to me. 'What, the bitch is dead?'

Their hair was as long as mine, but because they were older their beards reached like scruffy black tongues almost to their waists. Their callused feet were tied in rope sandals, and the wooden soles clacked on the stones as they hurried after us. Their baggy linen robes were dusty and travel-stained, their cheeks and foreheads burnt; they were thin as leather chewed and hardened in the sun. My mother had told me of sicariots, men who cursed themselves to neither eat bread nor drink wine until their task was done. 'Hold on there,' they called cheerfully, 'hold back, we'd pay our respects to the dead.'

I heard the lie in their voices, saw the darkness inside them. I ignored the two men, whacked the donkey's rump, and the cart jerked forward into the stream. The wheels jolted on the rocks below the cool swirling water. I winked at Giselle. We'd escaped. But she looked angry and frightened.

The men came into the water after us, splashed on the other side of the cart. 'Go away!' Giselle said.

The men walked beside the cart, turned their smiling faces towards me across the body, but I remember my mother telling me that behind every face is a skull looking out at you, and I saw into them. 'Leave us alone, please,' I said. One man put out his hand at the body but I reached across, pushed him away. I shouted, 'Leave us alone!'

But the second man, keeping pace, reached out and twisted the dead face towards his companion. 'That her?' A Jewish man touching death defiled himself, but my mother's words had shown me that sicariots are used to death. 'She the one?'

'Check the eyes,' the first man said, but the eyes were sewn shut.

The second man dragged my mother's face towards him by her hair, her arm flopping from the side of the cart. I shouted at him at the top of my voice. But he slipped a curved knife from his belt and cut the threads that held her eyes closed, no stronger than eyelashes, with two quick slices. He opened the lids, crossed himself. 'All right, she's dead all right.' Martha had removed the eyes, part of the embalming process; only dark holes into the skull remained over which the eyelids had been sewn. The man smiled, pushed the body towards me, and its cloak almost caught in the turning wheel which splashed drips up into my face. 'Now for the noisy one,' he said.

'Run.' Giselle pushed me. 'Run!'

Halfway across the stream, and the donkey would not stop. The washerwomen scattered away from us, cursing. A robe drifted down in the water, was crushed beneath the wheel in a thousand creases.

'You,' the man smiled. 'You must be Jude.'

Giselle shrieked. 'He's going to kill you!'

I saw the man lunge across the cart at me with the knife, but I could not believe it. I tried to grab the blade.

My fingers missed, and the blade slid through my hand. I screamed just at the thought of it, then the pain started. He tugged back and the curved blade jammed between my bones, dragged me in agony towards him across the cart. He smashed his fist into my face. The other man said, 'Good, hold him.' He stabbed his knife down on my neck, but the cartwheel banged on a rock below the water, the body of my mother rose up, and the knife sank through her cloak into her dead flesh.

For a moment it looked as though she'd sat up to take the blow.

'Jerusalem save us!' the man swore shakily. He let go the knife and my mother fell back. Her head thumped lightly, hollowly, on the boards.

The first man, cursing, dragged at his knife in my hand. 'Hell take you.' He twisted, found the angle to free the blade, jerked it out. I held up my hand. Blood ran from both sides down my wrist. The pain was unbelievable. I had never hurt these men, nor would I, yet I was in agony, mutilated. I didn't even know their names. 'Why?' I asked them, but they wouldn't stop. The man with the bloody knife came round the cart, not taking his eyes off mine. I saw my death in his eyes.

I reached out and took his knife hand in mine, felt his pain join mine, felt his bones collapse. The bone splinters stuck out of his flesh and would have hurt me but I was already in such pain. 'Why?' I asked him. He shrieked like Giselle: Giselle was shrieking. The man who had lost his knife pushed past her, knocked her down in the water.

I asked, 'Why are you hurting us?'

He grinned, came at me holding a length of knotted leather between his fists. I thought he'd tie my arm but he got behind me, slipped the leather expertly round my neck, pulled tight so that the knots sank into my throat. I had no air. He pushed me down, my hair rippled in the flowing water, he got his knees into the back of my neck, he strangled me between his knee and the rope. I could no longer question the two men. There were no answers. The man whose broken hand I held in mine flapped like a fish, agonised as a dying fish with fear and pain, hardly knowing where he was. I felt the miracle of his heart beating, filling him with life over and over. What a beautiful miracle. I stopped it.

His pain left him, his body rolled past me in the stream.

I reached up, pulled the hair of the man who strangled me, lifted him over my head and put him in the water, stepped my foot on his neck to hold him under, then touched his heart before he endured the suffering of drowning.

The stream rolled them away.

Giselle clung to the side of the cart, staring at me, eyes

385

wide. She wasn't afraid. She was excited.

'That's better!' she said. 'That's what I saw in you last night.' Her breath panted, her clothes were stained with splashes, her hair was wet, her eyes shone bright with love. She embraced me, held me tight. 'Jude, I'll go with you. Anywhere. Just let me be with you.' She tore her skirt, wrapped my hand. She wanted me here, now, but villagers stared from the shore. Even so she wanted me like fire. She didn't know what had happened inside her, but I knew she wanted that too. A child image of me, its father, the man she loved. And in her eyes I saw the reflection of the man her love saw, calm, indomitable, compassionate, my blood soaking into her skirt, my enemies dead. She thought I could do anything.

I could. It was easy. A peasant splashed through the water to help push the cart. I could have killed him easily.

The peasant crouched at my feet in the stream, touched his forehead to my knee. 'My lord.' Martha watched me. I remembered how many times my mother told me she lay at the feet of Jesus Christ and whispered her simple and complete conviction, 'My Lord.' This was different. This was horrible.

I kicked at the peasant. 'Get away from me!'

'Yes, my lord.' He scrambled eagerly to the donkey's bridle. Such men would do anything in my service. I counted twenty along the stream bank who would follow me anywhere.

I turned to my mother's body, pulled the curved knife gently from the bloodless flesh, covered her. I wept.

I wept because I was angry.

My mother had told me, in exactly the words she told you, that my father raised dead men from death. And my father could kill – he'd killed Hobab – just as I can kill. Killing is easy. Killing doesn't do a miracle, only stops one. Could I do a miracle?

I splashed downstream, stumbling, found the body of one of the men caught against a rock, held against it by the flow. I lifted his face dripping from the water. 'Rise. Come back. Come to life.' Nothing happened. 'Rise!' I stared into the face, then let it go, and the water took it away.

I stumbled back towards the cart, which had bumped to

the far shore. Giselle and Martha waited for me there. I was the leader now, I'd proved myself, they'd do nothing without me. 'Go home,' I told the peasant at the donkey's head. He said, 'My lord.' I shouted at him, 'Go home.' He bowed and went back to his friends, and told them how I trusted him, how I gave him tasks to perform, how close we were.

'What were you doing back there in the stream?' Giselle asked. She didn't realise my failure. My father raised the dead from death, but I cannot.

I saw at once that the slope was too steep for the donkey and cart.

'It's not far,' I told them. 'I'll do the rest myself.' I put my arms under the knees and neck of my mother, lifted her burden against me as gently as I could. 'Take Martha home,' I told Giselle. 'Stay with her. Look after her until I come.'

She said, 'When will I see you?'

'When you see me.' Martha stiffened. I'd spoken like my father.

I clicked my tongue. The donkey turned the empty cart easily and trotted off, glad to avoid the climb.

In the afternoon heat I climbed the steep track towards the tombs, natural caves, three or four of them. My mother felt heavier than I could have believed possible. She dragged me down. The sweat trickled on my face and arms, the sun's heat beat down from the pale sky and up from the grey rocks. I found the whitened entrance to the tomb and staggered inside. The floor sloped steeply, which was why it was not used by goatherds; but there was a narrow platform at the far end, a slab not unlike the one that would seal the doorway.

I laid her to rest, covered her face, and knelt beside her in the cool whitewashed shadows.

'I am the son of Jesus Christ,' I whispered. 'I believe that.' In my exhaustion I prayed as my mother had been forced by her failing strength, on my knees, even though she'd hated it. 'Mother, I believe every word you told me to be true. The Virgin Mary giving birth without soiling herself. Angels. Demons. The Son of God, the Cross. I know it's true. But you told me so little.' My hand throbbed, I unwrapped the bandage and licked the flesh till it healed. My eyes closed. 'You should have told me everything. Why didn't you tell me everything?'

I stare down at Jude asleep beside the slab on which my body lies.

He's handsome, a beautiful mature handsomeness settling on his sleeping face, and he's strong – as strong as Herakles, by legend also the son of a god, though a pagan god. But Jude is more, the son of the Son: just as Jesus Christ is more, and more complex, than any of the gods of men, Tammuz, Attis, Adonis, Osiris, and all the others tormented and killed and reborn in the springtime. Just as Hell is greater and deeper and more complex than the pallid underworld where (according to the stories of men) Herakles saved the woman he loved, Alkestis, and fought the Lord of the Spirits for her.

Long, long ago, I lived in my body and knew no more than anyone else. I was a child, I thought as a child; I was a woman, I thought as a woman. I loved but could not love; I died and lived. Ten thousand times ten thousand times I died and lived and saw no sign of God, only the vast machine of the natural world dying and dying and dying and reborn, heedless, pitiless, godless. I survived. I endured. And then, as you know, I felt the Hand of God, and immediately all I knew (and I thought I knew almost everything) was nothing. Seized by a power incomparably greater than myself I was overwhelmed, thrust into the womb, born, as you saw, in blood. In torrents of blood. No escape. Total involvement, not an observer: a gasping participant, a baby. Life in blood and pain, in the flesh, mortal perhaps, growing up, asking questions that need answers. Needing to know.

Ah, my son, how I love you. Your long sleeping eyelashes hide eyes as luminous as your father's; I see them moving beneath your eyelids as you dream. Your long slim hands, your linen shift, your beautiful feet. Yawning as you turn over in your sleep, cuddling your face into your hand. You're so special to me, your mother, even if you weren't special. But you are.

My son, if only I could touch you one more time!

I'm so afraid. So afraid terrible things will happen to

you. Perhaps worse than I can imagine. I never imagined anything as terrible, as pointless or profound as your father's death. But where's the truth in it? What do I learn? How does it improve me?

Such a waste!

Jude, Jude, if only I could save you. Save you from suffering. Save you from death, save you from evil, from this terrible world. There's so much more than you know. I know *for certain* of Jesus Christ's divinity. I told you I saw Him born, I saw His miracles, I felt Him, touched Him, loved Him, I was there at His Resurrection, no one saw more than I, Mary Magdalene. I know for certain that truth does exist. Perfection. Love. Mercy. God.

That our defeat isn't certain.

But how can I convince you of that?

I could reach out and touch you, Jude. I could reach out with all my strength and come into your dreams. But I won't. Because there's one question I can't answer. Whose side am I on?

Everyone's on one side or the other in this battle. It's the question I once asked James, devout James, no-man-was-ever-more-devout-James. How do we know which side?

Am I with God, *ho theos*, or the Devil, *ho theos*?

If I reach out to you, do I do harm or good? How can I know? No sane man or woman deliberately commits evil; in an imperfect world we live the best we can. But those who do the greatest evil have the very best of intentions: Caiaphas believed by Christ's death he saved not only the Temple but all his people from destruction, and his predecessor as high priest gave up Judas of Sepphoris to be flayed, crucified, and burnt alive for the same reason. Better one should suffer than many.

The past creates the future. There's nothing we do that may not do harm. *Go to the Temple as only a man.* My soul cringes. We're helpless, powerless, we don't know what we do, and this world roars brutally on its way.

A puff of dust stirs in the mouth of my tomb, as if thrown by a hand.

The sigh of an approaching breeze.

And then the wind blows through the entrance to my tomb, sends dust scurrying along the floor, then sand grains rolling, pittering. Now the increasing wind picks them up, swirling, a vortex hisses round the rough-hewn walls. Jude's shift flaps once, then the hem flutters, and now the wind pulls his hair from his sleeping face. His eyes flicker open as he wakes, he tries to shelter his eyes from the wind, but the wind growls like a storm, sending dust and sand and debris around him like a whirling cloud. He rolls over, crouches, bends his back against the cloud, clings to the floor, screams without sound under the thunder of the storm that fills the tomb.

And I feel myself taken by a power incomparably greater than my own.

I was woken by a freak storm where I slept in my mother's tomb. For a moment I was confused by sleep, and the power of the wind seemed utterly overwhelming. I felt as though the solid rock floor was overturned, and I hung on by my fingers, wedged my knee in a gap beneath the slab so I was not blown away. The air all but spirited me away, I could not breathe, my clothes beat at my face and the thunder of the wind was so loud that I couldn't hear myself shouting my mother's prayers in my fear and terror.

'O God of Israel, for Your sake I have borne reproach, and shame has covered my face. I am a stranger to my people, an outsider to my mother's children. The zeal of Your people has eaten me and swallowed me; the reproaches of the men who reproached You are fallen on me.'

Silence. The dust and sand dropped all at once to the floor. I was shouting at the top of my voice. My voice faded away. Cautiously I let go of the floor, pulled my knee from beneath the slab. I told myself that these summer storms can be very intense.

A tiny breath of air moved across my face, no more than the flutter of a butterfly's wing.

The veil laid over my mother's face moved. The storm had not moved it, but now it moved. I watched the veil form a hollow O over her mouth, as though breath were sucked into her.

She breathed in, she breathed out.

She sat up, and the veil fell from her face. I watched the pale material flutter down her breasts into her lap. She stood, and it fluttered to the floor. Her indigo cloak hung from her shoulders.

I said: 'Is it you?'

She turned towards the sound of my voice.

I said: 'Is it you, Mother?'

She pressed on her chest; she had no lungs. 'Jude?'

'It's me.'

She reached out her hand. 'I'm afraid. I hate the dark. I can't see you.'

I took her stiff cold hand in my warm hand, tried to make her understand. 'You're blind, Mother. It's really you?'

'Yes.' She breathed out, then in. 'It's all right, it's me. I didn't recognise your father at first. Don't be alarmed, this' – she held up her clawed hand – 'this is no miracle, no Resurrection. No transfiguration. Just mechanics.' Her closed eyelids quivered; she was trying hard to see. 'I remember I saw your father transformed, shimmering and shining with all the colour and feeling and depth and height of His life. Another time I saw Him fully alive, in the living flesh.' She let her hand drop. 'Willpower, that's all this is. I pray God ends time before you learn it.'

I bowed my head. 'Are you God?'

'I'm your mother, Jude. I'm Mary. God brought me here. Allowed me here.'

I knelt. 'What should I do?'

'God doesn't talk to me. I talk to myself deep in the ground. I come and go as I wish. Then the wind blew.'

I said: 'God sent you.'

'I don't know.' She groaned as though she bore all the grief of the world on her shoulders. 'Something new happens. The Cross. Jesus Christ died on the Cross.'

Happens. She spoke as though it was still happening. 'What happens now, Mother?'

'I'm afraid! Something marvellous came into this world' – her body shuddered, as though by *world* she spoke of filth – 'teachings more marvellous than anyone could have imagined.' Her body struggled to draw a breath, groaning. 'And something happened more terrible than anyone can imagine. The Crucifixion. Redeem us. We must redeem ourselves.' Her body struggled for air and the sad bitter stink of aloes carried to me. 'Evil lives, Jude.' Her larynx croaked so harshly I could hardly understand her. 'With the Covenant Satan will destroy the world. Satan own the world. Own you, and destroy you all.'

That wasn't what she'd told me when she was alive. 'But you said Jesus Christ is our Covenant. He's God's promise that evil won't win.'

The body paused, gasping. 'Who knows when the Last Battle will be fought, who knows when Judgment Day will come? God loses every battle except the last. But evil has no end, and who knows when the end of time will come? Ten thousand years?'

'Ten thousand times ten thousand,' I said.

'Yes, billions of years. No one knows.' She groaned. 'But this I know. James is right.'

'You said James was the AntiChrist!'

'Perhaps. He believed Jesus was the AntiChrist. James once claimed to be Christ. Who knows anything for sure?' Her eyelids flickered open, looking out with nothing, eyeless, emptily facing emptiness in her despair. 'James believes himself to be on God's side. But Satan has answers to every question, reasons for everything. He makes the truth tell lies.'

'You said the AntiChrist would be a devout man used by Satan. A false prophet, a rebel who'll try to take God's place. Doesn't that sound like James?'

'There is a Covenant buried beneath the Temple.' She interrupted me with a harsh croak. 'All the Essenes believe it, I told you. Jesus spoke of it in the Parable of the Talents. James *knows*.'

'The Arch of the Covenant, the receptacle of holy power?' As a child taught by Zacchaeus I always pictured the Arch as a big box of blessings covered with gold and holy writing. 'It was destroyed along with Solomon's First Temple. It's just a symbol, a memory, a guiding light.'

'It survived,' my mother's voice grated. 'Only God can destroy destruction.'

'The Arch exists?'

'The Zadoks at Sion believe, their ancestors *knew*, that the Arch contains the Word of God. The words given by God to Moses in the desert more than a thousand years ago. That's why Sion agreed to pay the Temple thirty talents of silver, so that God would renew His Covenant with the Poor. The Temple promised to return the Arch to its ancient keepers, the Zadoks, one day in the future. And sealed the bargain with thirty promises, in return for a kiss.'

I saw now. 'Judas.'

'And Simon. And James. Yes.'

'Will Caiaphas keep his word?'

Her lips twisted, dripping the dark juice of aloes. 'Priests are men.'

I understood. 'And James isn't stupid. He knows. He won't trust them. What will he do?'

'I love James.' Dark juice trickled from my mother's eyelids. 'I've always loved James. He struggles, he searches. His followers call him James the Righteous, the Second Shepherd of the prophecies. He'll pay any price for the truth. He'll go to Jerusalem. You'll find him in the Temple. Kill him if you can. He tried to kill you.'

'Kill my father's brother?' My eyes narrowed and I pulled away from her distrustfully. But God often kills. God brings down whole cities for His people, Ai, Lachish, Debir, Meron, Hebron. God told the Jews how to bring the walls of Jericho crashing down and ordered them to kill everyone inside, men, women, children, animals.

'Jude, find the truth, seek out James.' She moaned. 'God help me, whose work do I do, Satan's, or the Lord's?' My mother gripped me with hard hands, cold, dead as ice. 'Don't listen to me. Don't seek the living among the dead. You're the only true thing I know, Jude, my son, my dear son. When my Lord Jesus Christ was with me after His Resurrection, He called James His beloved apostle. "James, for whose sake Heaven and Earth came into existence in this world." Because James is a good man seeking after the truth with all his heart.'

'Is James trying to continue my father's work?'

'James's work leads to devastation.'

'Has Satan fooled my father? Is Hell as powerful as Jesus Christ? Is my father deceived? Is that possible?'

'James is only a man, brought into the flesh as only a man, just as I was born only a woman. Every single one of us has a devil inside. Jude, listen to me. I know James. For all his good intentions he *is* the AntiChrist. Used not by God but by Satan.'

I thought about it. 'What did Satan promise him?'

Her voice faded. 'What James would sell his soul for, of course. The truth. James didn't believe in the Resurrection of Jesus, remember, even though he was the first man to see Him in the form of His body. James had lost faith.' She staggered. My mother was weary. 'Knowledge. James was promised knowledge.'

I gripped the shoulders, tried to turn her head towards me. 'God threw the first humans out of the Garden of Eden for thinking they knew the difference between right and wrong. What knowledge?'

The appearance of life was fading away from her, her movements were clumsy, mechanical, dead muscle jerking at dead bone.

'The answers to everything, Jude. The face of God.' Her eyelids opened wide, showing the emptiness inside her skull. 'Power.'

The breath gusted out of her; she was just bone and leather. Her head flopped on my shoulder. I tried to hold her up.

'Mother? What power?'

'Destruction.' The last of her voice whispered in my ear as she slipped away. 'Destruction.'

If one tenth of what my mother had told me was true, there was nowhere in the world I could run where I would not be found.

In the dark I stood with my bag over my shoulder. I stared up at the lamplit shutters of the house where Giselle lived with her mother. Twice a shadow crossed them. Once I raised my hand to the door. Giselle carried my child. I should stay, marry her, farm, grow old.

Seek out James, for whose sake Heaven and Earth came into existence in this world.

I turned away from her door and hurried into the dark.

IACIMUS HIEROSOLYMI

James of Jerusalem

How best to seek the truth? By believing everything my mother told me in her story, her incredible story? Or by assuming that every word she'd told me was a lie – or at least, not fact. Not history. No God, no marriage, no Sion, no Jesus, no Cross. My father obviously lived, or I wouldn't be here, but whether he was what my mother claimed for him (or even called Jesus) I'd find out for myself. I didn't disbelieve that there had been a man called Jesus Christ, but I didn't believe it either. I know no more than you; I won't believe the Land of Judah exists until I see it with my own eyes.

But I saw my mother's body move after she was dead.

No, I saw nothing. It was a dream.

She spoke to me.

I heard nothing. *Seek out James, for whom Heaven and Earth came into existence.* No, I heard nothing. I just happen to be here.

For five days I sailed with the wine ship from Narbo to Ostia, the port of Rome; from Ostia to Puteoli beneath the volcano is a day's sail from lighthouse to lighthouse; from Puteoli to Caesar Maritima with a cargo of fish spice, army supplies, messengers and seasick civil servants takes three weeks. But God (or the gods) sent headwinds against us, then a storm from the south that blew us north almost to Ephesus, then a storm from the north that blew us south almost to Alexandria before finally dumping the ship against the harbour wall at Gaza. Was I being punished for my disbelief? Or was it just chance? The sailors burnt sacrifices, and I jumped ashore rather than go further by boat.

Or did God have some purpose for me, and brought me to Gaza deliberately?

Here I am. My father's land: for the first time I breathe the hot desert winds of Judah blowing dusty and old as time across the porticoes of the Roman seaport. The imperial customs houses and quays and the ruins of the Temple of Dagon shimmer as though the heat and dust melts them, wears them away, the ground reclaims them, their stone dissolves to sand.

Here only the people and the desert are permanent.

The Jews gather round me, faces harder than stone, selling me anything. I speak Aramaic clumsily; they take me for a foreigner at once. I buy (for a fortune) old clothes at the market to blend with them (though I'm a Jew I don't feel like one among these people), but at least my beard makes me look unlike a Greek or a Roman. But the women laugh at me, shaking their heads. I begin to wonder if the women in this land, though wholly subject to men under the Law, are in fact the rulers.

Despite all my mother told me of them, I know I don't understand the first thing about Jews. Evening prayers, the town stops; I slip away into the desert. I'd take advantage of my misfortune, cut due east through the desert, and see Sion – if it exists – with my own eyes. There's no reason Sion should exist, only my mother's story. I keep the star Merak over my left eyebrow as I walk, the Pole Star above my left temple.

Am I doing as God intends me to do? Is it possible?

Above me the stars twinkle like ice in the freezing sky. Had my mother really seen a special star over Bethlehem? Was that possible too? Really a comet, perhaps? Comets foretell the birth and death of kings. But my mother knew stars like a Greek, she'd have known what it was if anyone did. Instead she'd rambled about the 'huge planet' which she called Uranus, the dimmest speck that circles the earth, because no one else ever heard of it.

The sun rises ahead of me like a fire. I find a cave to sleep through the heat, walk again at evening. At dawn I stop, because the land ahead of me stops.

I stand on a cliff top; everything below me is shadow. The shadows fall as the sun climbs the sky, illuminates tiers of crumbling rock falling away below me as though I stand on a mountain peak, and I stare down into the bottomless pit at Sion as though it's the whole world, a whole world of darkness. Then the sun touches the Dead Sea, the dark waters flash silver, and the sulphurous heat of the place washes over me with the stink of brimstone and boiling springs and ancient burnt rock.

All morning I climb down towards the lifeless seashore. *A perfect place for priests*, my mother told me. I stare up at the strong walls of Sion broken down, the battlements crumbling, carried away for stone, the gateways gone. Everything smaller than she'd told it to me, but the monastery cloisters still bearing the marks of the earthquake she'd described, many of the pools still empty. I looked round curiously, seeing no baptisms. Young men wearing white linen clothes hurried towards me, pushed me away. I stopped them. 'I seek James the Apostle.'

They stared blankly.

I tried a second time. 'James the brother of Jesus.'

'Search for the Christ in Jerusalem.' They picked up stones, watched me suspiciously. 'Search for the Oblias in Jerusalem. Nothing for you here!'

Oblias means *shield against the Devil*. Was the Christ still to be found in Jerusalem? Did they now believe the Son of God had been sent to save them? I thanked these dangerous young zealots before they cast their stones, turned uphill, and did not stop until I reached the cliff top.

Sion. I even identify the places my mother described, the potter's kiln and the Field of Blood beyond the walls, most of the great stipes uprooted, no pilgrim tents now. But an 'angel' or novice still stood by the *gnomon* on the church roof, chanting prayers I could not hear, whose precise length divided the minutes from the five minutes, repeated exactly twelve times so that piety matched even the passage of the sun across the sundial. As though their prayers held up even the sun in the sky. After all my mother told me I felt I understood Sion instinctively: a church, a library and a fortress. Not all the chain of zealot fortresses were so broken down: through the glaring sunlight and drifting sulphur smoke of the vale of Sodom I saw the cliffs of Masada like a mirage overhanging the Dead Sea's southern shore, and the glint of glass or blades on the peak.

I shivered as though I felt a cold unrefreshing breeze on my back, a breath of Satan. Here at Sion at least, my mother told the truth. Perhaps she was even carried to this dominion by a demon. Standing here with the cliffs crumbling away below me to the Dead Sea, I believed her every word.

Here's the Temple, and the noise and babble of the Temple at Passover just as my mother said it was, the bleating and baaing of lambs on sacrificial leashes, the clap of pigeons' wings flying in cages, cooing turtledoves, trilling songbirds, here's the sweet heavy smell of blood and dust blowing across the great courtyards. Twenty thousand lambs will give their blood to God today on the altar, numberless birds be offered up in piety and prayer, just as my mother said they are. And the moneychangers that my father had scourged so ineffectually sat on their satchels against the wall, just as she'd said they did.

But something had changed.

I covered my head and moved barefoot through the Court of the Gentiles. What Gentiles? The huge space was empty of all but Jews as far as I could see. I'd noticed in the market that the silversmiths' shops (even Apollyon's) were shut up: no Greeks. The soldiers on the city gates searched every Jew for weapons, thoroughly and unpleasantly, and arrested those found even with eating knives.

I stopped at a railing by the stone slab guarding the steps to the Court of Women. 'Let no Gentile enter this enclosure around the Holy of Holies, and whoever is caught is responsible to himself for his death.' I climbed the steps without hesitation, a Jew among Jews.

The Temple was dedicated, like all temples, to sacrifice and death. It rose through levels of sanctity towards the Holy of Holies. I pushed between the waiting peasants and flocks of lambs, the escaped birds fluttering overhead prevented by stretched wires from profaning the holy rooftops with their mess, and let myself be swept by the slow surge of worshippers into the Court of Israel, for men alone.

Bearded faces were turned towards the Holy of Holies in prayer, standing up for the reading, then the priests above us called, 'Come, let us bow down in worship; let us kneel before the Lord who made us.' We knelt for the communal confession of sins until the priests called, '*Qûmû*,' then we prayed with arms raised towards Heaven.

I moved quietly through the crowd to the front. The smoke of burning meat and cereal sacrifices hung like a curtain in the air, and priests worked shifts busily around the altar. Some wore white linen, others the usual robes and turbans. I approached the overseer on the step, a Sadducee. 'I seek James the Apostle.' He shrugged, never heard of him. I said, 'I seek James the brother of Jesus.'

The Sadducee shook his head impatiently. 'Which Jesus?'

A young levite wearing white linen overheard me. 'Today the Christ performs a special atonement for the sins of the people, for the Temple and for Jerusalem.' He stared at me intolerantly. 'He sees no one.'

'Tell him I will see him.'

The levite hesitated. His beard was thin and straggly. I saw through it to his skin. He covered his chin with his hand. 'Who are you?'

'I am Jude the son of Jesus.'

This one knew Jesus. He called others who gathered round me, hemmed me in. Life meant nothing here; it was a place of worship, God's house, only God mattered. A place of purification for a whole people. These men around me were sicariots, guards, not priests. The levite left. The sun grew hot. I talked but no one answered. Above the broad ceremonial steps leading to the veiled porch and tables of bread, the huge cube-shaped gold and marble building of the Holy of Holies glittered painfully bright in my eyes. All around me rose the cries of fleecy lambs led to the slaughter. I asked for water but none came. These men spoke Hebrew, the language of God. My Hebrew is worse than my Aramaic. 'Water?'

One of the sicariots pushed his face close to mine. 'I'm Cephas.' For a moment I thought he said *Caiaphas*, the names are almost indistinguishable in Hebrew. Or Clopas. Or Cleophas. These people love wordplay. Brutal, single-minded, dedicated to death to God, but not stupid.

Cephas demanded, 'Are you holy to God?'

His spit spattered me. I was a fool to come here. I'd die here. A wrong word might be my death. The queuing peasants bowed devoutly, offering their year's work to God, copper knives flashed golden, perfectly honed, flawless, another throat was cut, the priests sprinkled blood around the altar, the smoke sent up an aroma of holiness acceptable to God.

'Yes,' I said.

Cephas mistrusted me. He parted my clothes, muttered, 'Are you holy enough to stand with us, or shall you be swallowed? Are you a righteous man? Hold him, Mohel.' I was held from behind: strong arms, sour breath. Cephas ripped the knot that held my belt around my waist, reached inside. 'Or are you a liar, the servant of the Devil?'

The levite returned. 'Leave him!'

Cephas stared into my eyes, but his hand stopped a finger's breadth from my penis.

The levite beckoned. 'Oblias will see you.' The sicariots drew back except for two, who walked forward holding me between them, Cephas following a step behind. The levite went ahead of us to an entrance beneath the porch. Two sicariots guarded the door. I walked past them, then looked back. Nobody followed me inside.

I came into quiet and calm, an air of hushed sanctity.

It would not be hard to believe God was here. The floors were marble, smooth as glass. The thick stone walls were clothed with aromatic cedarwood, the doorways with gold, not a speck of dust anywhere, I stood in my reflection. I saw a room for wood, a room for oil, a room with various implements of gold, another of copper. In front of me in the sacristy, his back to me, an old man knelt almost naked before God – wearing only a loincloth – praying on his bare knees on the hard unmerciful floor. His voice murmured, echoing, muttering, and for a moment I overheard his continuous prayer, 'Grief to the people' – he touched his forehead to the floor – 'grief to Jerusalem, grief to the Temple, if we fail.' In all he pressed his forehead flat three times to the floor. I watched him for I do not know how long a time, feeling I saw something very ancient, a ritual stretching back from the time of the Jews in Egypt, and perhaps long before. He rose on his haunches; I saw his back was a dreadful mass of scar tissue. His muscles stood out like strips of leather in the intensity of his religious passion as he cried out, 'Make me your single pillar, your keystone of this world, O Lord.' He reached up his arms, cried out his sincere prayer: 'Make haste, O God, to deliver me before the end of time! Make haste to help me, O Lord!'

It was hard to believe this man was the AntiChrist.

He stood without turning, head bowed. 'You are Jude, the son of Jesus my brother.'

'Yes, I'm Jude, the man you sent your men to murder.'

'Murder?' The old man turned, long white hair hanging on each side of his face, long white beard. Long face, small sad mouth. He looked the way my mother described my father, but without love, and thirty years older. Worn down by age. And his eyes were different, dim, an ancient sadness in them. What everyone said was true: his elbows and knees wore huge yellow knobs of callus from prayer.

My father's brother James, grown old. I softened, remembering my mother's vivid description of him playing knockabout with my father, just children. But now James of Jerusalem stared at me as hard as chewed leather, spat out, hardened in the pitiless sun of Sion.

'Not to kill you, child.'

'With knives!' I burst out. 'To kill me because to you I'm a blasphemy, the son of Jesus!'

'For blasphemy I should stone you with stones, child.' He stared, not an ounce of toleration in him. I understood nothing. 'My sicariots carry knives not for murder but for more important business.' He held out his hand. 'Are your hands washed? Are you holy before God? Then pass my undershift.'

Surprised, I followed his pointing finger, lifted the priestly vestment from the rail. The seamless white linen had worn thin as a spider's web but was utterly clean – I should say, cleansed. I smelt the chalky aroma of frankincense. He kissed it, pulled it over his head. The hem was frayed where people had pulled it to be healed. His head reappeared.

I asked, 'What business could be more important than murder?'

'Circumcision, child. Life itself.' He pulled his beard

from the neck of his undershift. 'What could be more important than circumcision, the mark of God's favour to Abraham, the brand which identifies His people? How else would He make us special above foreigners? By circumcision we make ourselves perfect by fulfilling a divine command. Sicariot means Circumciser. Why else would their knives be curved? Eh? A clothed and contaminated penis such as the Gentiles flaunt is an affront and a profanity to God, which is why they are damned and we shall be saved.' His arms were too arthritic to reach behind him, and he jerked his head irritably. I stood behind him, pulled up his hair from beneath the linen. 'Child, heresy must be wiped clean if we are to be granted the Covenant. Only by clean living, morality, righteousness, good works, can we redeem ourselves in the sight of God.' He pointed to a long white robe. 'Don't let it touch the floor. Not even the merest touch, or all must be begun again.'

I lifted the robe carefully, hung it round his shoulders. I said, 'Jesus Christ saved us all when He died for us on the Cross.'

'Died for us all?' James's voice rose. 'Not for the Gentiles! *Not the Gentiles!* Your words curse your mouth just as the words of Gaius Iulius Saulus the Roman, the traitor, curse him to damnation the moment he utters them.'

'Saulus.' The name sounded familiar but I couldn't place it. 'Saulus the inquisitor? The Temple guard who tried to arrest my father?'

'He went mad. Five times in all I've had him flogged the thirty-nine strokes for heresy. He preaches that the Romans are appointed by God to rule us! That the AntiChrist will rule over the Romans. I say truly *he* is the AntiChrist, and I shall fight him at the end of time and cast him down. Saulus attacked me with his fists when his arguments failed. He brought Trophimus the Greek into the Temple, unforgivable profanity! To my face Saulus claimed my bastard brother was crucified to save the Romans and Greeks from damnation.' James trembled with rage. 'The little worm escaped from me once, lowered down the walls of Jerusalem in a basket, but the second time I made sure the Romans arrested him. He should be dead, but he wriggles from one legal nicety to another, or he wouldn't still be spreading his lies among foreigners!'

I found the arm holes and James pushed his hands through. He calmed himself. 'Now, the cloak.'

I fetched the white cloak from the rail. There was a tiny spot of blood on the collar but it would not show. The garment was discreetly lined with gold: James was zadok. No one had called him that in my hearing; but this was Jerusalem.

I asked mildly, 'What things does Saulus say?'

'What lies does the demon spread?' James exploded. 'The deceiver was once my most loyal follower, held the cloaks of the sicariots who stoned James the son of Zebedee to death for blasphemy, hunted my brother out of Galilee. He was a Temple guard trusted by the Temple, a Roman citizen trusted by the Romans! Now Satan has filled him, Satan has opened his eyes, and Saulus claims that my bastard brother was the Son of God. *The Son of God!* How could a Son of God have brothers and sisters? Why should God, praise His name, decree that His Son should be a bastard?' James stared at me with glaring eyes. 'Man, improve yourself! Joshua was an abomination sent to despoil us, deceive us, prepare us for the reign of Satan. He was the AntiChrist, he confused even me, but with God's help he was defeated.'

'Then how did He rise from the dead?'

'He didn't. That's Saulus's heresy.'

I said respectfully, 'Rabbi, my father told my mother that you were the first apostle to see Him after His Resurrection. His beloved apostle.'

'I never saw anyone. I didn't recognise him. Faith without good works is dead. Don't you think I knew what he looked like well enough? Joshua was just a man born out of wedlock. His presence was a millstone around the necks of my mother and father, a constant reminder of their sinfulness. Joshua lived in jealousy of me all his life. He deceived me, yes, leading us into filth, he confused us Nazarenes of the Poor of Sion and yes for him we ate bread and swallowed meat from copulating animals and drank strong drink, for him we left our hands unwashed, for him we lived as dirty pigs because he deceived us with his clever, clever, clever words. Persuaded us to turn our backs on God. But

God is merciful, God is great, and He covered the eyes of the Romans whose tool Joshua was so that they themselves killed him! Glory to God for the Crucifixion.'

'My mother saw Him afterwards. Twice.'

'Then your mother had a demon in her and was deceived. She was full of demons. Seven of them, the sure sign of Satan. I don't care if she saw him seven thousand times, it wouldn't mean anything!' His spit speckled my hands as I hooked the gold hasp of his cloak. James swallowed, then spoke as calmly as he could. 'Only God is God. There is no other God but God. No Jesus Christ, no God cut into halves or thirds. I am the Christ, born legitimately of King David's line and recognised Iacimus Christus by my people, and now recognised even here at the Temple, because although the Temple priests are puppets (the high priest of the Temple even begged for his clothes from the Romans!) all true Jews groan under the heels of the Romans and their foreign infection of our people and God. Even some of our own leaders claimed to be gods – yes, my brother did, and Agrippa whom God rotted with worms, and Simon Magus who paid money for his divinity and married a prostitute, an Adiabenese beauty named Helen, then while doing his magic tricks in the air fell down at a crossroads in Rome and burst open and died. And there were many others. Many were mistaken. Three years ago I myself had to run for my life into the desert when I was cursed by the priests of the Temple as an Egyptian sorcerer.'

'Yet you say you're the Christ.'

'Yes, I am Christ and Zadok both, the single pillar, the keystone. The stone without which the Temple will fall. I have achieved this but I am only a man, not a god. Only a man but I was chosen by God, consecrated to God in my mother's womb, born without a foreskin and even circumcised a second time to achieve perfection before both God and men, a virgin of sixty-four who has never known a woman, and I have lived a life of such virtue, purity and prayer that all agree – even the Temple priests who used to curse me as an Egyptian – that I am sanctified above all other men as most blessed before God. I am His suffering servant' – he patted his poor knees – 'and for me God will grant freedom for His people.'

'You call yourself Zadok here in the Temple?'

He pointed at the heavy gold breastplate. I lifted it over his shoulders. 'At Sion I'm Zadok, in Jerusalem I am James the Just, James the Righteous of Jerusalem.' He shrugged. It didn't matter, it was only practical politics; the words just and righteous both mean zadok. 'Today, as bishop of the Jerusalem Church, I'm elected to take my turn as high priest. I'll enter the Holy of Holies to offer up, as Israel's holiest man, the prayers and entreaties of our whole suffering people directly to God.'

He sounded just as my mother had said. She'd told the truth. This old man, I realised, probably hadn't changed at all since he was a child. My father's influence on his adult life had lasted less than a year. James's guiding light was the memory of John the Baptist. But for James there could be no more living with the Romans or waiting for the end of time which didn't come. The patience of the Jews had run out. Now the priests preached that sedition was virtue, and rebellion was a holy war. And if the Temple was destroyed that suited James. It fulfilled the prophecies. By the fall of the Temple the Jews would know their Christ.

I asked, 'Will God hear you? Will He answer you?'

'The Holy of Holies is a place of smoke and darkness. All answers are there.' James pointed to the bishop's mitre, white and gold. I lifted it to place it on his head. He stopped me. Spoke in a low voice. 'Your mother is dead?'

I said carefully, 'She has passed on.'

'Dead. Good.' He nodded. 'Where's her tomb?'

I bit my tongue. 'Tomb? What tomb? She's gone, that's all.'

'Not going to tell me. Well, she always ran away. She knew much, that woman, too much for a sinner. To marry the Son of God, how romantic! Do you know who she was? How much did she tell you? Mary Magdalene?'

I was very careful now. Raised the mitre above his head very carefully. 'She told me that she was Mary.'

He laughed between his gums, one brown incisor, an old man's cackle. 'More.'

'She was in love with you once.'

His laughter died. He gave a sigh.

I placed the mitre carefully on his head.

He said, 'More.'

I said: '*Ouranos*.' He stood perfectly still. Then his tongue licked his remaining tooth, remembering.

'Yes, *Ouranos*. In those days,' he whispered, 'we knew everything. Everything. No doubt, no lies, happiness, simplicity. A saved people, no pain, only knowing love, worship, truth. A people saved by Christ and Christianity. But here everything's doubt and lies, lies and doubt, everything we touch is contamination. Love contaminates us and brings suffering, pain, death, not joy. Every pleasure is stained with guilt. Breathing contaminates us; there are monsters in every breath. All around us is a machine abandoned, forgotten, forsaken by God. This natural world. A world of demons.'

I knelt in front of him, latched his sandals. 'What are we to do?'

'God can hear me. With sufficient holiness, virtue, purity, I Iacimus Christus can stand before God, and He will answer me.'

'In the Holy of Holies?'

'The people are prepared. Foreigners are barred from the Temple. Herod's court, family, sycophants, hangers-on, all are banned from this holy ground. Let my enemies curse me as an Egyptian, very well, I am in the Temple. From today anyone considered blasphemous will be forbidden sacrifice – anyone not circumcised, baptised, washed, purified, perfect, is a blasphemy to God. Any Jew peasant not eating kosher shall be stoned with stones. Any man and woman committing fornication, both shall be stoned. Any child born out of wedlock shall be a strangled thing. No Gentile shall own property or eat at the same table with a Jew. He who curses his father or his mother shall die the death. He who sins shall be paid by death; breaking the smallest law breaks all laws. The unmarried girl who is found to be not virgin shall be stoned to death at her father's door, but the daughter of a priest shall be burnt until she dies. Whoever works on the Sabbath shall be put to death. By their good living the people will be made to deserve God.'

'How do you know?'

'The thirty talents are paid, transferred from the treasury at Sion to the vaults here, deep in Mount Sion beneath the

Temple. We true Jews shall rise up like a whirlwind against the Romans, the nations of the world shall bow at our feet. When we live in perfection God will come to us and bless us, and He shall say to us in His voice of thunder, Arise, My chosen people, and I shall renew My Covenant with you, and make you a saved people.'

The Covenant again. I knew how this would end. 'And the Temple walls will fall.'

'I am the scourge of the Temple.' James stood before me as bishop and high priest, golden shepherd's crook in hand. 'I am the Second Shepherd. I was scourged just as your father was, and I'll be scourged again, but my time will come. The Temple didn't fall for your father but these walls will fall down at my feet, and by that sign the people will know me and acclaim me.'

I said, 'Three Roman legions within a hundred miles. The Tenth Legion to be garrisoned in Jerusalem.'

'Just the tinder to light our fire.' James wasn't mad, he was horribly sane. And perfectly correct. The people would rebel, but they'd lose. Judas Zadok lost sixty years ago because peasants, however righteous, however zealous, can't fight trained soldiers. James Zadok, Christ, whatever he called himself, would fail for the same reason. Having God isn't the same as training troops. It would be a bloodbath, and James knew it. He wanted it. The thirty talents was paid, the whirlwind of the Jews would throw the Romans out of Israel. The Temple would fall; but in three days it would rise.

'These prophecies killed my father,' I said.

'Have faith. Satan can be defeated. I know how. The Arch of the Covenant is here beneath the Temple, somewhere beneath the Holy of Holies, the place that was known only to the High Priest Ananus. I'll find it. Today I go into the Holy of Holies, to make atonement for the sins of the people. My Lord is there, my hidden saviour! These words have been written about me: "I shall be the One who comes to Jerusalem, and I shall stand behind a strong wall until rescued. I stand on You, my God, for You built our foundation on rock. I shall stand as a shield of strength against the Devil, I shall not give way. The gate of Jerusalem shall protect me, barring the entrance with a strength that can never be broken." '

The Temple priests would not like this at all. 'Where is Ananus now?'

'The same place I put his brother the High Priest Jonathan seven years ago. Dead.'

I was stunned. 'You killed him?'

'I butchered him like a sacrifice. After Jonathan's death the people failed to understand God, Ananus and the mob chased me from Jerusalem, and I fell back to Sion with four thousand sicariots to protect me. Some say it was five thousand, but it was four. And after three years in the wilderness Ananus and I began to be reconciled, and I agreed to pay the thirty talents. But Ananus was a traitor to God.'

I'd dressed James in the robes and breastplate of the high priest he'd killed, tied the dead man's shoes on his murderer. James read my thoughts, shook his head. 'How little you know. Jonathan and Ananus were appeasers, both of them. They died so that the true Israel can live. That's not murder, it's destiny. It's salvation.'

I remembered the tiny spot of blood. 'My God, you killed him in his robes.'

'You don't understand. The truth is in the Arch of the Covenant.' James reached out his hand, but I drew back.

I said, 'My mother warned my father that the Arch wasn't God's work. Perhaps the work of Satan.'

'Satan makes no artefacts. He uses men.'

'Is Satan using you?'

'God uses me.'

'My mother said God, Jesus Christ, makes men free.'

'Only by complete obedience to the Church, and abstinence from sin, and commitment to good living, can men deserve God.'

'Temptation,' I whispered. 'Satan uses temptation. Pride. He turns you against yourself.'

James eyed me with an old man's fixed glare. 'Are you a true Jew, Jude ben-Joshua? Or are you a liar like Saulus the Roman, another impostor sent by Satan to tempt the chosen people from the truth so that we fail?'

There was no answer to such an accusation. I stood silent. But silence is guilt.

James called: 'Cephas!'

The sicariots had been listening all the time. In a moment the sacristy seemed full of their muscular white shapes. I was held, pushed back against the wall by strong hands.

James said, 'Cephas, see if he's one of ours or one of the Devil's.'

This time the knot of my belt tore easily when Cephas pulled it. He pulled open my clothes, tore off my loincloth. It dangled from his hand, swinging. I stood naked among them. Cephas stared at my penis in disgust, clothed and hidden by foreskin as it was. 'You disgusting animal,' he muttered. 'You're dead.'

He covered me and turned to James. 'He's not a true Jew.'

James turned his face away that he might not see profanity in the Temple.

Cephas said, 'Is it blasphemy? Shall I—'

James stopped him. 'I cannot have this now. Make him perfect, not in here. Kill him if you see him again.' Acolytes gathered around James, ready for his ceremonial ascent to the Holy of Holies, lifting the hem of his cloak reverently. James spoke without looking at me. 'If it's the Enemy you seek, my brother's foolish son, seek out Gaius Iulius Saulus in Rome. You'll find him hidden with his apostates praying to his idol in some hovel or dungeon in the Transtiberium where, praise the Lord, God has made Saulus's own people, the Romans, place him under sentence of death. But hurry. Soon the end of time is come. Very soon.' James finished with the same prayer he had begun. 'Make haste, O God, to deliver us before the end of time! Make haste to help us, O Lord!'

'Amun!' The sicariots slammed their fists across their chests. 'Amun!'

I tried to call to James. A leather thong was thrown round my neck, choking my air. Even before James left the room I was lifted by my legs and my arms, struggling, choked. The vaulted cedarwood ceiling moved above me, I was carried like a dead man between the sicariots. My head thudded on the marble floor when I struggled, their knees bumped me as they ran. At a storeroom one man stayed on the door. The knot in the thong was released, I gasped air, it tightened again, they dropped me. Cephas said, 'Do him or kill him, Mohel.'

Mohel grabbed my penis but I struggled. Someone slammed a fist into my stomach. My mouth opened like a stranded fish; I felt my veins would burst. 'One breath,' Cephas said. 'Get on with it, Mohel.'

The thong was released. I gasped one breath. It tightened unmercifully.

'Wait, blade's got a nick in it,' Mohel said. He sharpened the curved copper blade on a strop hanging from his belt. A blade must be perfectly sharp, it's the Law. He tested the edge with his thumb, then grabbed my balls in his other hand. I arched, but it was only a warning: I'd endure much worse than circumcision if I were foolish. I lay rigid, staring, groaning for breath. Mohel stretched out my foreskin between his forefinger and thumb until I thought it would snap, then with one sweep of the knife cut away the outer skin. I screamed, strangling. Cephas put his fist in my mouth to gag me, and I was allowed a breath. They'd done this many times; they knew how far to go without killing me or allowing my screams.

Mohel's thumbnail was long, deliberately left uncut. He slid the nail beneath the lining of my inner foreskin, freeing it from the flesh of my penis with quick slices, then peeled it off between finger and thumb. I shrieked. I felt my blood run. Mohel crouched over me for the third part of the ritual, swallowed my penis in his mouth, sucked, spat blood. Sucked, spat. Even a circumciser is forbidden to swallow blood.

Cephas told me: 'Go with God, stand in the perfection of the Nazarene Way.' The knot went limp. I was released. Someone dropped my clothes on me. Ten minutes later I was pushed down the Temple steps into the street. I knew better than to go back.

I watched, I waited. Whether James entered the Holy of Holies, I don't know. I believe he did. People said he did. Did he find the Arch of the Covenant? Had Ananus taken the thirty talents of Sion into the Temple coffers then reneged on the deal, kept the Arch's location secret after all? If so, the deceiver had died for his treachery. With my own eyes I'd seen the single spot of blood.

Ananus had kept his secret to death.

But there was nothing to stop James, robed in the vestments of the murdered high priest, entering the Holy of Holies. I watched, waited, imagined. The Holy of Holies was the centre of a maze: God could not be approached directly but must be searched for, attained. When James opened the last gold door, what did he see?

Nothing, I believe. God lives in dark and smoke. The Holy of Holies is a square cube of dark gold, equal in every dimension, empty, full of God. The flames of the priestly lamp, the menorah, would throw out little illumination and much perfumed smoke. I imagine the room flickered with shadow not light. Was God truly to be found there, as James believed? As James held up the seven flames and peered through the darkness and smoke, did he glimpse the Throne of God? Did he reach out his hand and with trembling fingertips touch the Arch concealing God?

Did he open the Arch and see God?

Did God grant the Covenant to James and to Sion?

Time did not end. I crouched on the steps, my penis stuck to my clothes with dried blood, and the markets packed up, the calls to evening prayer ended, Jerusalem grew dark and the lamps were lit, the last colour faded from the sky, night fell and the stars hung bright over the holy city; then the stars faded and dawn grew bright with another day.

No end to time.

James had not found the Arch of the Covenant.

I watched and waited on the Temple steps another day, ate a loaf when I was hungry, drank wine when I was thirsty. Time didn't end that day, or the next. James had not found God.

Was James sent by Satan, as my mother believed? Then James's enemy was my friend.

If it's the Enemy you seek, seek out Gaius Iulius Saulus in Rome.

GAIUS IULIUS SAULUS

Paul

Nothing's what it seems.

That's impossible. How can we live like that, nothing, nothing, denying the evidence of our senses? Suppose, I told myself as I boarded ship, everything's exactly what it appears. That the sun isn't firewood lit daily by God for our benefit but sustains itself of its own nature like the sort of perpetual furnace my mother described, a nuclear holocaust. And these men James and Saulus are just politicians having their silly disagreements and inventing big things like Satan and God to make themselves feel important. To make their tiny worthless lives feel worthwhile.

But my mother knew Joshua was the Son of God. She knew it. She knew she'd touched something greater than even she, who knew so much, knew how to describe.

Nine weeks against the wind to reach Rome; almost shipwrecked on Cyprus, then on the tip of Malta; God did not want me to reach Saulus. Or perhaps He simply didn't care.

Rome's the centre of the world, and the Jewish Transtiberium is its most wretched suburb, houses like dirty orange cliffs rising six, seven storeys to the rainy sky, half burnt, half falling down, half washed away, the streets below like rivers of men and women shrieking and selling, the River Tiber flooding again and the stench of shit and fish and mud slopping on the spreading brown waters into the chaos.

I would stay here two years, I'd know it well; it would be my home.

'Saulus?' Someone pointed. I ducked down, opened a rotting door, gasped at the tanners' stench, half fell down the steps into a cellar. Blinking in the gloom, I found myself in a sweatshop full of women. Among them a single man stood up slowly, a curved needle growing out of his blunt fingers, a leather pad in his palm. No more than three cubits tall, he was short as a small woman, but muscular, his right shoulder hunched by a lifetime of hard tent-work, and sheets of stitched tent-leather fell from his lap as he stood. What remained of his scanty hair hung long down his back and his beard was thin and white, his dark skin a pallid olive colour from days and nights of work in the sunless cellar. I recognised him from the description of my father in the *forma*. I'd reached the man Saulus had described himself hunting: he was a man searching for himself.

'Saulus,' I called.

Saulus watched me without fear, then pulled open the neck of his garment.

'Strike, strike me here in my heart if you dare, for God is in my heart.'

I threaded through the shadows between the tables. The women dropped their needles and drew back from my white linen clothes in fear.

'Don't be afraid,' I said. 'I'm no sicariot.'

'And I,' he said, 'am not Saulus. I'm Paul.'

'I was born a Jew and a Roman citizen in Tarsus of Cilicia, no mean town, the son of my father who was tentmaker to the legions like his father before him, making our family rich; now in my old age I work night and day like a slave for men I once owned. My childhood was perfect, lacking for nothing except love. My education was Greek, my friends were idle, my house was full of servants, I lived in perfect misery and hatred.'

Paul often spoke to us as we worked; he had no love for leather, speaking was what he needed. He talked as though to himself, of himself. Every word was of Paul, speaking of Christ he spoke of Paul, speaking of the Temple he spoke of Paul. His whole life was dedicated to Paul, something he felt inside himself, more than himself. In us, the leather-workers, cutters and stitchers of the cellar, he had a captive audience who could not (until pay day) turn their backs on him as so many did in public – and even in private houses, when he was invited to speak after the patrons had finished dinner. Often he spoke until dawn, finding by daylight his listeners asleep. But in the sweatshop there was only the sound of brittle needles pushing through tough stinking leather, and Paul's deep voice speaking of Paul.

'When I was Saulus I was a Roman to the Romans, a Jew to the Jews, I ate at the table of my Roman governors and generals, yet I was also a *talmîd hākām* to my Jews. The life so satisfactory to my father was hateful to me, without purpose. I sat at the feet of the great Rabbi Gamaliel in Bethshearim and learnt the mysteries, I would be rabbi in my turn. A rabbi must marry before his fortieth year (the age the father of our Lord was married), so I was a husband to my wife, and turned from profits and idleness to zeal for the Pharisee Law, and pursued righteousness with full legal authority from the Temple, as one of guardians of Temple purity throughout Israel.'

I said, 'When you say the father of our Lord do you mean Joseph, His earthly father?'

'Who else could our Lord's father be?' Paul despised interruptions, they took him out of himself, reminded him who he really was: a poor man in old age and ill health, arrested and brought under guard to Rome for trial for provoking riots against the Jerusalem Church, working to pay his bail-bondsmen who drank wine in the tavern upstairs.

I said, 'James says you call Jesus Christ the Son of God.'

'Perhaps James says that, he's a whitewashed wall, a whitened sepulchre!' Did Paul not know that the Voice of God had called Jesus His beloved Son? Inside himself James knew the truth of it, but Paul had never heard of it. 'Who is James? James is not in Christ, has not felt the love of Christ, he does not believe in the risen Christ, James is a virgin of ninety-six and he is the servant of the Devil!' Paul glared. The anger in his eye made him look very like James, and each called the other the AntiChrist. Where was God in all this bickering between the two men, each of whom had attempted to kill the other for their version of God? I remembered my mother telling so simply and exactly the

414

marvellous sight she had seen with her own eyes of the angels descending over the Bethlehem stable holding up the baby Son between them, but I never heard Paul speak of it. 'Will you interrupt me a third time, Jude?'

'No more, master.'

'In Galilee I found many heresies, riots, false prophets, rainmakers, revolutionaries, and backsliders from the Law of Moses among the poor people. The more I looked, the more I found! The more questions I asked, the more questions I found needing answers. I was searching, searching, and never saw that what I searched for stood waiting in front of my eyes.'

'Did you never see' – I bit my tongue, I almost said *my father* – 'Jesus Christ actually preaching?'

'That's not important. What our Lord *is*, that's important,' Paul said. 'His meekness, humility, love. The love in our King that lives inside us, inside all of us. Christ Jesus who bears all burdens, believes everything, hopes everything, endures everything. He's us. He's in me.'

The old inquisitor's words made me catch my breath. He'd caught something of the man in my mother's words the night she died. I'd never told him; and by Paul's own admission he'd never met my father, only hunted him. Paul thought his King Jesus was only a man, yet he'd caught hold of God.

'What do you know of Jesus Christ?' I asked. 'Do you know He was born of the Virgin?'

'Who put these ideas in your head?'

They weren't ideas, they were true. 'Don't you even know her name?'

Paul ignored me. Then he said, 'She was of the line of David, obviously, like his father you call Joseph, because Christ Jesus was born a king, yet chose to live in humility and humiliation.'

I raised my voice. 'Don't you know Jesus Christ did miracles, walked on the sea, turned crumbs into loaves, water into wine?'

'Christ Jesus is in me, I feel everything.'

'He healed the sick.'

'I heal the sick.'

I said, 'He's my father.'

Paul said gently, 'I understand you. Welcome, my brother. He is my Father too, and my Mother, and you and I and our brothers and sisters of the Roman Way shall fly together in the air to the Lord of the clouds at the end of time, soon, soon.' While we spoke the women sewed and gossiped together under their breath of more important matters. Paul murmured, 'In this world we struggle against the eternal powers of this present darkness, against the spiritual forces of evil in high places.'

A woman gasped; she'd driven her needle through her hand. Paul realised night fell. He examined the women's work in the last of the light, paid them little, and clapped my shoulder not in friendship but in brotherhood. His hand stank of pig. Paul and these women, Jews in Christ of the Roman Way, worked even with pigskin, anything that could be bought in the market. The Jerusalem Church of James and Peter forbade contact with foreigners; Paul baptised them. The Jerusalem Church allowed only clean food; Paul ate pork. He'd grown very far from the church assembly at Sion whose members he'd been sent to arrest, which first nurtured him.

I walked with Paul to the river in the glow of evening, keeping close; he always feared a Jewish knife in his back. The Jews who did not follow him hated him for his apostasy from Jerusalem. We leant on the bridge parapet, watched fishermen hooking and netting round the sewer outlets for the fattest fish.

'Once I was as close to James as a brother, that's what hurts,' Paul confessed. 'Before that I pursued him across Galilee, and Peter and all the apostles, it was my duty, but they always slipped into the countryside, the mountains, across the lake. In any event Nazarenes die under torture, don't talk. I almost caught up with Christ Jesus in Capernaum. I would have met Him face to face. At Mount Gerizim I missed Him by only a few days. He was completely nobody to me, a shadow. Word that Christ Jesus was crucified in Jerusalem came too late for me to attend the final humiliation of my assigned prey, but afterwards Caiaphas sent me to Sion to arrest James and any other apostles I found there. Now that the danger was over I was to reclaim the thirty promises from Judas, by force if necessary.'

'You couldn't, they were gone. Judas was dead. The pieces had been stolen.'

'How did you know?' The crowd cried out as a huge filthy licker-fish was dragged writhing from the muddy water on to the sludge. Should I tell Paul what I knew? That my mother had seen the man who stole them, the Follower? Was that God's purpose or not? I hesitated.

'Yes, they've never been found.' Paul turned from the spectacle of the licker-fish. 'But this is what happened. I saw Christ Jesus on the road to Sion.'

'You saw Him after He was risen?'

'Everyone heard Him. Hundreds of us, all my guard, and I don't know how many others travelling with us for safety from robbers. Perhaps five hundred in all. We expected trouble at Sion but not on the road. My horse fell, they all fell down, but I stood. A huge voice cried out over us all like the sun, "Saulus, Saulus, why do you persecute me?" And I saw the light coming down in the shape of a man. None of the others saw, they only heard His voice, but I was allowed to see Him. I called out, "Who are you, rabbi?" He came close to me, He filled me with light. "I am Jesus the Nazarene, whom you are persecuting." He looked at me, me alone, as I fell down naked before Him, as ugly as an abortion dropped before His face, and I felt Him fill me with His love and understanding and compassion for me, even for me, so that I was struck blind with love, so filled that I could neither see nor hear nor speak for love, and I was not the man I was.'

My mother hadn't talked of this; she hadn't known. Always something new was happening in this world, something unexpected. Paul crossed the street, bought a sausage and an onion for his supper while I bargained for the loaf. Half the apartment block where he had his room had been gutted by fire. We climbed the stairs clinging precariously to the side of the light well, now open on one side where the building had fallen down, showing the dizzy drop to the river stinking in the shadows.

'My guards ran away at once along the road. Later James came out from Sion and carried me in over his own shoulder. He didn't know who I was, laid me in one of the huts called Damascus, for men alone. He thought I would die. But after three days I awoke and had my sight, and I knew I was not a man alone, for I had Christ Jesus in me.'

'But James didn't believe you saw the risen Christ.'

'No. James is a holy man, completely devout to God. How could he understand? I had Christ Jesus inside me! Christ Jesus boiling, burning in my blood! I was exalted. Terrified. I knew I carried the truth within me.' Paul pushed open his door, cut the sausage on the table, we broke the bread. 'Christ Jesus feeds me.' He talked round his food. 'I went out into the desert. Years I was in the desert with Jesus. Years I did the Lord's work from Sion for the Jerusalem Church, unknown, unnoticed, a nobody. Through weakness, I found strength. My strength grew despite my weakness. With growing humility I put forward my views with increasing strength, until the Greek Jews of Jerusalem plotted to kill me. So James sent me to Caesarea, Tarsus, Ephesus, Macedonia, and I spread the word and the people heard me, or did not hear me. But in the Jerusalem Church my whispers came back and were heard as shouts, and the Nazarene saints asked me with whose voice I spoke. Ah, my friends had fallen away from me! The end of time is here, almost here; to James the end is war. To me it is love.'

Paul washed down his sausage with beer. In the corner I saw the notebooks where he wrote his life, preparing his defence for the Roman court. He followed my eyes.

'Finally, now the end of the world is so near, and the race to save what souls we can is reaching its climax, James could no longer ignore my apostasy from his religion, from *his* search for God, or ignore my success in converting both foreigners and Jews to our Christ Jesus who was crucified and is risen. James recalled me to Jerusalem. I journeyed. At Troas the Jews in Christ warned me I would be killed by sicariots though strong men accompanied me. At Tyre the brothers in Christ told me I was to die on the road to Jerusalem, so I went south by sea. At Caesarea Maritima word came that I'd be bound hand and foot and dragged to Jerusalem as a prisoner, an apostate, blasphemer, scourged as Christ Jesus was scourged, thrown to the Roman authorities as He had been. Yet, being a Roman citizen, with rights under Roman law, I feared the Jews more than the authorities. Anyway, why should I turn away from my Lord's fate?'

Paul picked what was left of his teeth, nodding. A second crucifixion for the Christ Jesus he felt in him, the pupil imitating his master on the path to glory. Anyway, Paul must have believed the end of time would come first, that his death might even precipitate the end. I remembered the old saying, 'It is impossible that a prophet die outside Jerusalem.' That's why Caiaphas had Jesus killed outside the walls: his ultimate denial of Jesus's divinity. Paul would follow his master in denial, turn weakness into strength, humiliation into glory.

Paul belched sausage breath, then stood as the hour was called in a growing babble of calls and chimes from the riverside temples and shrines. He touched my shoulder. 'Come, you shall be made new as my brother tonight.' He sent me ahead of him downstairs in case his murderer awaited on the bottom step. I fumbled among the shadows of the hall then Paul's hand guided my shoulder to the street.

'When I finally arrived in Jerusalem James greeted me in the Temple, smiling, all sweet reason, the saints around him,' Paul said as we walked. 'We spoke as though we were not enemies unto death. I told the saints of the marvels God performed among the foreigners. I spoke of all the people who heard my voice and became like us, finding themselves in Christ. James and the saints thanked God for it, and the people shouted. Then James the Righteous Teacher, smiling, told me of the zealousness of his people the Nazarenes, their righteousness to the Law of Moses, and how the good news I preached had reached them as bad news. "They hear that you tell Jews to forsake Moses, not to circumcise their children, not to eat clean food. That like pagans you eat blood and flesh sacrificed to idols, to Jesus Christ. That you bow like Romans before an idol to Jesus Christ, fragments in the shape of his cross. Tell me these blasphemies are false."

'I told James that Jerusalem was a holy city, purified and immaculate, where purity could be enforced, but I worked in filthy seaports swarming with foreigners, Ephesus, Thessalonika, Corinth, even Rome itself at the centre of the world of men. James murmured, pulling his beard, "You say, Paul, that Rome is the centre of the world, not

Jerusalem where God is?" I was trapped. Each Nazarene, each sicariot, each saint looked to see if James would tear his robes, the sign he'd heard blasphemy.

'But James—' An oath burst from Paul's lips as he was jostled by night-revellers. He continued as we came to a broader street, a richer quarter. 'James just smiled, he had something better in mind for me. A test, a fine, a humiliation. Four young men were being consecrated as Nazarenes. Would, he asked, I pay for them to go through the rite of purification, as a sign of my faith in the true Church? A fortune! But I agreed. Then James said, "And you will go through the rite of purification with them, as the sign of the renewal of your true faith." I was neatly caught! So I took the Nazarene vows, and my head was shaved. I had little enough left on top anyway.' He patted the bald top of his head, mimicked James's voice savagely. ' "Now, Saulus, my faithful follower," James continued, "all the people know that the bad stories they heard about you as Paul were lies, that you are not Paul the Spouter of Lies, and that truly you are Saulus again, a guardian and observer of the Law." And then James said, "And I have sent a letter to the foreigners together with my judgment on you. They shall not break the Law. They shall circumcise their children. They shall not eat foul food. They shall not bow down before an idol. They shall not eat food sacrificed to an idol, and they shall not drink blood." James forbade our Eucharist, the very blood and flesh of Christ Jesus! We were forbidden to pray before our Cross. Intolerable!' He parodied James's benediction angrily, spitting. ' "I, Iacimus Christus, have spoken and say so!" Ha!'

'But if you obeyed James and took the oath, why did he have you arrested?'

'Well, the very next day I took Trophimus into the Temple.'

'Trophimus? A Greek?'

Paul stuck out his lower lip. 'Couldn't resist it.'

'Stupid thing to do.'

Paul walked in silence for a while, he would not be criticised. 'But irresistible, Jude. Am I not human? Am I not Paul, Saulus no longer? Who – especially Paul – wouldn't want to wangle his way past those huge offensive overbearing notices? You see, Trophimus wasn't really a foreigner, a Gentile. Yes, he was Greek, but *he was in Christ*. He was in Christ, you see! He was in Christ where all are one, no more Greeks, Romans, Jews, no nations, no temples. Trophimus held within himself, within his own body, the place where all men and women are equal, Christ Jesus; in himself, in Christ Jesus, he *was* the place.'

We came to a broad avenue of separated houses. As an afterthought I asked, 'What happened to Trophimus?'

'The people rioted. They threw him from the wall, stoned him. Martyred him for his faith. Not a Roman citizen.'

We arrived at the gates of a large house where some people were gathering. Paul moved quietly among them. 'But *I* know faith chooses our God, not circumcision. We people choose freely to live in Christ, we neither tear the foreskin from helpless babes nor baptise those too young to choose what is imposed upon them.' Someone held up a lamp and Paul spoke directly to my face. 'Israel has failed. We're the remnant who will be saved. The mystery that was kept secret these long ages is now disclosed.' He touched the people around him. 'Watch, see,' he promised, 'listen, hear.'

I listened to the quiet religious murmur of the gathering crowd, Jews mingling with foreigners, ordinary Romans, Greeks, a Nubian black as the night, women. Several held cross-shaped bits of wood. Someone scrawled the shape of a fish on the wall, recalling the Nazarene fish I suppose, Peter being a fisherman. In some of the Egyptian tongues Nazarene means fish.

A slave opened the gate and allowed Paul through. He went inside and preached to the wealthy man and woman of the house, Pudens and Claudia. Someone said she was a British princess, daughter of King Caractacus. We waited, then Paul came out on to the balcony. A slave stood on one side of him holding a grail of bread. On his other side stood a slave holding a grail of wine.

Paul blessed the bread and the wine, and turned them into the flesh and blood of his Christ Jesus. Pudens and Claudia knelt, receiving communion with Christ Jesus literally into their mouths and bodies. Then Pudens gave a patrician wave of his hand to the poor gathered at his gate.

Paul came out among us. He moved among us, fed us with the blood and body of Christ Jesus.

'This is His entire life which is given for you. This is the new covenant in His blood.'

I watched, I waited. I saw, I heard. I ate, I drank.

I thought, no wonder James wants this man dead. Paul *is* the AntiChrist – to James.

James's enemies were Paul's friends. Paul the Jewish Roman was strong in Rome, James the true Jew unassailable in Jerusalem. Neither could overturn his opponent.

Paul appealed to the Emperor Nero against his death sentence. The suspense was unbearable. First the battle tugged one way then the other. Paul would be released: Paul would be executed. Any day, preaching, standing, walking, working, a curved dagger might be thrust beneath his ribs. And every day his lawyers' bills went up like the sky. 'They won't execute me,' Paul said, 'until I can't pay any more.' The poor know justice is for the rich, and money is life.

But in Jerusalem James, too, was poor. For the first time in a hundred years the Poor were literally (except in their scrolls) without riches. The thirty talents had drained Sion's treasury dry, and now in his zeal for God James banned Herodians from the Temple. The royal faction were with the Sadducees but (my mother had told me) also supported Sion in return for half the income from baptisms. But James refused to baptise foreigners, even foreign Jews, to show his Jewish God His people's moral purity. So Sion, without baptismal shekels, had neither riches nor income. The flow to the royal coffers stopped; Sion was a dry well. The Herodians complained and James banned them from the Temple; they were of Idumean stock, not true Jews in the eyes of God.

So I knew James had failed to find the Covenant.

He must be tearing the Temple apart. But the Second Temple had taken eighty years to build – it was still being built – a maze built over a maze, a thousand years of history going down through the ruins of the First Temple deep into the earth, earlier than Solomon, earlier than David, perhaps going back to Melchizadok the first king-priest, sitting where my mother expected to find Jesus Christ on the throne.

Perhaps much earlier even than that.

The royal Herodians, now James's enemies, were Paul's friends. Sometimes we walked past the Appian Forum to the Three Taverns, the Herodian palace by the south wall where Paul held communion among friends. He appointed young Prince Aristobulus to be bishop of Britain, and though these were the last days of the world I watched an Arimathean ship sail with the royal party from Ostia – even Britain, now part of the community of Empire, was nearer than it once was. Roman money was good on the island and the warlike British aristocrats took easily to Prince Aristobulus's gold wine chalices swearing brotherhood with blood, so familiar from their own rites, if not his message of peace.

Most of Paul's real friends were scattered far from Rome, in Ephesus, Thessalonika, Corinth, scattered like the journeys of his life; by now they *were* his life, more real to him than his present misery. Just as my own mind turned increasingly often – and increasingly guiltily – to Giselle the wife I'd not married and my child I didn't know, I often climbed to Paul in his tiny gutted apartment to find him eagerly waving letters that had arrived, letters to an old man from his life whose ripples were spreading as he sank. I read them loudly because he was almost deaf now. He wrote less often – his scribe Luke was long gone, and Paul's hand shook from age and exhaustion, so I wrote for him. He looked forward to death because to him it was life; and death came to find him.

The appeal to the clemency of Nero the god failed. Fourteen days before the kalend of Sextilis – the seventeenth of July, by the calendar of Sion – Paul was ordered to present himself for execution as a citizen, by beheading, the next morning.

In this, I knew, he'd be as obedient as any Roman. But the other side of Paul said, 'You know, Jude, my only sadness is that I won't be crucified like my Lord.'

In the evening all of us who knew him climbed the ramshackle stairs for the traditional feast that would crown Paul's life, Pudens and Claudia, Linus her brother, Priscilla and Aquila, Timothy, others I did not know but whom I allowed upstairs. The room was so crowded I thought the creaking floor would collapse. Those who could not get in gathered in the street outside, not fading away until the early hours. One stocky white-haired man was left standing where they had been. Paul grunted. 'Looks like Peter's kept his hair.'

I was startled. 'The apostle Peter? One of James's saints?'

'Yes, he calls himself Christ Jesus's apostle.' Paul snorted. 'Don't believe a word Peter the Galilean says. James sent him to lick the foreigners back into shape after I'd shown them the Roman Way. Undoing my work! You can't trust him. Peter tacks in the wind like one of his boats. Let him stay down there. I'm too old a fish to be hooked by him. What's he doing in Rome?'

'I think you've hooked *him*,' Priscilla said. 'Let him come up. He's even older than you are.'

Paul snorted but sent me down to allow Peter up. The old enemies stared at each other quivering for strength, then Peter reached across and they embraced. Nobody else in the room mattered: only these two old men. We were not here. One by one the guests were gone, Priscilla whom Paul always called Prisca, Claudia, the others whose names I forget, all forgotten now. Only the lamp guttering and dawn soon to come over the rooftops of Rome.

I lifted the wick so it burned brighter and Paul, sitting, spoke to Peter across the table. 'What brings you here? Gloating? You've won.'

Peter said: 'James is dead.'

Paul prayed for him. 'I pray for his soul, though he was a wicked man. Sit, Peter.'

'He was a good man.' Peter sat. He spoke Latin like a butcher but his Aramaic was rich and impulsive. 'He did what he thought was right, all right. Can't do more.'

'Poor James,' Paul mused. 'All his searching, all his holiness, all his Egyptian mumbo-jumbo about pillars and arches and secret covenants, and all the time the truth was in front of his eyes and in his heart, in Christ Jesus. What happened to James? How did he die?'

'Times change, Paul. Everyone thinks James's zeal and prayers were wickedness, because they didn't work. So they tempted him to jump off the Temple walls and fly.'

I said quickly, 'Inside the walls of Jerusalem or outside?'

'Outside. The people lifted James up as he prayed for

424

them and threw him down from the pinnacle of the Temple. When he survived and prayed for them despite his fall they placed a rock on him and jumped on the rock and shouted, "You've deceived us, you aren't the Christ who will save us." When he didn't die but still tried to pray for them they dug a pit for him, stood him in it to the belly and stoned him with stones until he was dead. The Temple did not fall. James was not the Messiah, not the successor to Jesus Christ after all. The standing Temple means the disappointment and fury of the people is righteous, approved by God. They're rioting, looting. Roman soldiers are dead. It's war.'

'Romans will never understand the Jews,' I said.

Paul said: 'Christ Jesus gave us the freedom to choose whether the Temple should stand or fall. It's up to us.'

'*You* believe, *you* hope,' Peter said angrily. 'But all of us, the whole community, we're nothing without the salvation of Jesus Christ. One lawbreaker, one individual, endangers us all. Men and women are children who've got to be led and guided and cajoled and coerced to God through the sacraments of the Church. A Church who'll be their mother just as Mary was the virgin mother of Jesus Christ.'

Paul said, 'The Jerusalem Church?'

A cockerel crowed and Peter flinched. 'The Jerusalem Church is in Jerusalem. This is Rome, a nation of foreigners. Jesus Christ can't save us from Rome.'

Paul said quickly: 'Christ Jesus can *be* Rome. Only have faith, Peter.'

I saw the rooftops outside. Dawn stole across them like fingers. 'It's nearly time,' I said.

Paul gripped Peter's hands as though he feared he'd run away. 'Will you continue the work?'

Peter admitted, 'I'm old enough now to know, I *know*, the truth of what I saw when I was young. The truth of the incredible things I saw. Oh, Paul, Paul, if only you'd seen! I saw and heard the Son of God in this world. I know and believe in His virgin birth, I believe in the chastity of His mother Mary. I know and believe in His miracles. I know that Jesus Christ died on the Cross for me and for every' – he searched for a new word – 'for every *Christian*, and I know and believe that He rose after three days and spoke to me, and showed me His empty tomb.'

Christian. There it was. The word my mother had looked for and expected and hoped for in the days of Abraham.

Peter said, 'I shall make it my life's work to return to Jerusalem and make a shrine of Christ's tomb so that believers are drawn to Him from all over the earth.'

'Nobody knows where Christ's tomb is,' Paul said gently. 'The Arimathean could never go back to Jerusalem for fear of James.'

I knew where my father's tomb was, my mother had told me: a quarry downhill from Golgotha, close to the city wall. But I'd found the quarry full of burning rubbish. There are many quarries and rubbish tips close to the city wall, and everywhere is downhill from Golgotha.

'It doesn't matter where it is. Christ Jesus is everywhere,' Paul said. 'Christ Jesus is in our hearts.'

I heard the tramp of guards. 'Paul, *tempus fugit*.'

Paul stood, prepared himself, took communion from Peter. Then he reached across the cup of Christ's blood, gripped Peter's arm. 'Promise me. Your work is here in Rome. Not Jerusalem. Jerusalem is only God but Rome is the world, people, souls, the living world of men and women. Here you may bring Christ Jesus into every heart.'

The sergeant of the guard called up, 'Gaius Iulius Saulus!'

Peter would not reply, still torn between Rome and Jerusalem. He wouldn't promise. Paul looked round the little room for the last time. 'I've failed completely,' he said.

The guard took Paul before he could say more. They pulled him to the nearby square. Paul asked to speak to the people and the guard said, 'Save it for later.' Paul was beheaded with a sword, duly witnessed. His head bounced three times, spraying blood. The sergeant struck off Paul's name from his list, moved on. When the body ceased writhing I wrapped it in a shroud. Peter picked up the head, stared curiously into the eyes, then he kissed the bloody lips. We carried the body and head outside the city walls, to the plot I'd bought in one of the huge cemeteries which follow the road for miles. It was a prime site; like my mother I always have money, I'm never poor. Peter said honest words over the body of his old enemy, and the Christians gathered round.

There was nothing more for me here.

We returned to Paul's empty room, and wondered what to do. Peter thought of God, I thought of Giselle. After two years among Paul's Christians I badly needed sex, I felt as though I'd thought of little else. Sleeping through the heat of the day I dreamt I smelt the smoke of Hell.

I awoke, and Rome was burning.

You must know more of it than I; all I saw were buildings falling, and flames as big as houses, and heard the fire roaring like the wind. Apartment blocks burned like candles, palaces like gigantic burning trees. Nothing stopped the fire. Not sacrifice, not the god Nero's command, not firefighters, not temples or shrines, not rivers of buckets in the streets. After a week the whole stone city glowed as bright by night as by day, like lava.

After the fires were extinguished the people looked for the cause, which was us Jews, us Jews who worship our single intolerant God and no other and outraged all the gods of Rome. None saw any difference between a Jew and a Jew in Christ, a Jew of Paul, a Jew of Peter, a Jew of Apollos, a Jew of John the Baptist, a Jew of James, they killed us all. The smell of blood sent the mob wild. Even Romans and Greeks who'd called themselves Paul's Christians were hounded to death for spreading our Jewish infection, our God. Our arrogant God. Our jealous God who allowed no other gods but Himself, our God of anger whose jealousy and intolerance brought about the destruction of Rome. The Romans in Rome were as bad as the Jews in Jerusalem. For the first time, among the ruins of Rome, we thought of ourselves as Christians. For the first time we were persecuted as Christians. What could even Christians say to pagans left with nothing, homes gone, families gone, all they loved destroyed? Peter tried to preach the Trinity to the mob, that he believed God was not one but three: 'You are judged as men in the flesh, but live according to God in the spirit. The end of time is here; don't think the fiery trial which has tried you is some strange new thing. Rejoice, rejoice, for today you are partakers in Christ's suffering.' I had to break heads to get him away alive.

I crouched together with Peter in a smoking roofless ruin, the rubble still hot. Peter was so without motion, folded in on himself, that at first I thought he was praying. Then I thought he was dead. But when I touched him he was shivering. 'I can't do it,' he said. 'Christ has deserted us.' We heard the screams of the mob, sounds of running, but they passed and went away. 'They're animals,' he said. 'I can't show Christ to animals.' He lifted his face from his hands, black with charcoal, and I saw his tears streaming pink streaks down his cheeks.

What could I say? My mother had called the apostles animals, just animals hungry for leftovers. *Peter, Peter, it doesn't matter how you die, only how you live.* But this old man wasn't that young Peter. His anger was all gone, he was drained.

'You don't know me,' I confessed. 'I am the son of Jesus Christ, and Mary Magdalene was my mother.'

Peter lashed out at me with what was left of his strength. 'Liar. Blasphemer! Jesus Christ had no child by that wicked woman, that sinner, no one was fouler in sin, her blood stank upon her legs. She tried to deceive Him because women are vipers in their hearts but He, pure perfect celibate man, laid no finger upon her, except to cast out her sins. Liar!'

'If you believe that,' I said, 'you've moved so far from Christ that I can understand why you've given up.'

'I know Christ. I don't permit a woman even to speak in church, nor baptise, nor offer the Eucharist, nor claim a share in any masculine function, least of all any priestly office. Mary Magdalene would have made herself queen, you know. Pope.' Peter clasped his hands as the shrieks of some Christian victim carried to us. He scrambled from the ruins and limped away from me down the road. I called after him, 'Peter.' He shook his head, limping. I went after him. Peter stopped, leant on the wall of a building being rebuilt, pulled the stone out of his shoe, threw it at me. He walked away. And I saw myself walk towards him from another direction, and talk to him by the fallen wall.

I stared at my hands, I touched my face. I stood where I was, rooted, but I watched the man I recognised as myself talk to Peter. I saw the stranger's lips move as though they were my lips. Peter, my rock, why have you abandoned me?

The man I couldn't recognise as anyone but myself was

barefoot. He had beautiful feet. But I wore sandals. He wore perfect white, but my clothes were sooty and stained.

Peter sank to his knees. He looked up in awe.

The stranger touched Peter's face with the palms of his hands, and Peter kissed the hands and cried out weeping, ecstatic, like a man seeing a dream. But it's reality, a vision, I'm seeing it too, seeing the stranger looking at me across the top of Peter's head, looking along the road into me with my own eyes, but *more*, deeper. Infinitely suffering. Infinite. And the last thing I expect to see: happiness. The happiness in those eyes. The fullness of everything I see. The greenness of the growing grass, birdsong overwhelming me, the rich warm scent of the earth gathering itself until I know I've seen, felt, known nothing until this one moment.

'My Lord!' Peter cried out. 'My Lord Jesus Christ our Saviour, save me!'

The sun went behind a cloud.

Peter, do not forsake me, but go about your work.

The cloud-shadow passed, the stranger walked into the building being built and did not come out the other side into the sunlight, and Peter fell forward alone on the road.

I ran to the building, looked inside. Empty, except for startled workmen at the far end, and by me a single bare footprint in the wet mortar of the floor. Even the faint whorls on the skin of the heel and toes were perfectly preserved in the image. Even the nail hole in the heel. The footprint of Jesus Christ.

We are not lost. Not abandoned. Not forsaken. Not alone.

Peter limped back to Rome. He preached to the Romans. Within the week, on the third day before the kalend of Sextilis, I saw them crucify him. With the last of his strength after his scourging, Peter insisted on being nailed upside down to show that he was lower than his Lord, so that the manner of his suffering and death did not imitate that of his Lord Jesus Christ.

Paul had longed to be crucified like his Lord; Peter and Paul were different even in death. They were just men.

I know my father is still alive somewhere in this world. More than transubstantiated bread for his body, more than wine for blood. More than a miracle. Much more. It isn't over.

I listened to the Christian martyrs howling as the flames consumed them. It wasn't the last time I heard them. For the first time I smelt the stink of burning men and women: like burning pork, sickly, sweet, penetrating. I'd smell it many times, the smell of evil. The smell of evil made by men in this world. The smoke of the fires hung like an anvil over the burnt city.

I shook its dust from my feet. I turned from death to life. I thought of Giselle, her laugh, I imagined her breasts and buttocks, her belly bulging with new life. I clung to her memory although I hardly knew her, though I felt I knew her through and through. We'd been separated all our lives except for a day, but I had to be with her. I talked to her, imagined her as I walked. That's all. It's love.

From Rome to the island of Clape is a long walk, and a wet wade for the last half-mile.

From the village I saw my mother's church on the hilltop. It rained. I stumbled across the stream, stopped outside Giselle's house which was as I remembered, except the roof had a hole in it. I knew her house would still be here. I knew she'd be angry to see me. I knew she'd have an angry husband, or a lover. Worst, she wouldn't be here at all. Gone. That's the way the world works.

I raised my hand and beat on the door, but the door opened wide. Giselle stood as I remembered her, though her hair was longer, and a toddling child clung to her hand. She looked at me as though I'd not been away, and smiled as though she knew me very well.

'You forgot your daughter,' she said. 'And the roof leaks.'

I fixed the roof and I took her in my arms, and I gave her my life, and she gave me children, though she squealed with laughter when she first saw me naked, circumcised. Our daughter was Lisette, in memory of Giselle's mother, a name from the wild north, and what a wild handful that girl of ours was: strong and sulky, her mother's eyes, but her hair as long and black as mine, and teeth like tiny pearls. I loved Giselle more than the world and she was pregnant again. 'Your kiss could make a girl pregnant,' she said.

430

Our son was Dagobert, which Giselle's tongue pronounced Dajobear, and he screamed and roared and bit the breast which fed him, but he adored Lisette and would do anything for her, followed her in the fields all day as I farmed behind the house. Under my hands the land changed from grey dust to green life, to gold, to harvest. And the moment Dagobert ceased to chew and arch at his mother's breast she was with child again, swelling like the harvest with Mary. Giselle and I drank our own wine and ate our own food and reared our own children in our own house, and in the same bed where the next baby was started, Giselle brought Elle squealing and kicking into the world. I held up my new daughter who dribbled breast-milk and birth-blood down my arms and I knew there was no more happiness than this, and if there is a Heaven this is its Earth.

Then after the harvest a stranger in white linen walked towards me across the stubble, thin, so starved that his pallid face stared at me gaunt as a skull, his ribs stuck out of his skin like fingertips. I dropped my hoe, put out my hand to hold him up, and he struck at me with a curved dagger.

I caught it easily, threw him over my shoulder, but carefully, so that he landed on the ground with his neck beneath my foot, his wrist locked in my hand. The sicariot cursed me with zealot curses. I squeezed him a little and the knife fell into my hand, then I flicked it so it stuck in an olive tree. 'I am Jude the son of Jesus Christ,' I said. 'Why are you trying to kill me?'

The sicariot spat. I let his arm twist until it creaked. He stared up at me with pure hatred.

'Jesus, the false prophet, the betrayer,' he groaned. 'And you're his false blood. These truths are now proved, Jude the blasphemy, Jude the abortion. When Jesus died the Temple did not fall. Now that James the Christ dies for us the Temple is fallen. Grief on Israel! Grief to you, Jude the abortion!'

'The Temple has fallen?' I said. I tried to imagine it actually falling, that enormous structure on Mount Sion, its walls thick as fortress walls falling, and simply could not. 'How? How can that be? When?'

'It happens now, it still happens! The martyrdom of

James started the war. Now the Romans are destroying the Temple of God. Now is the time of the Abomination of Desolation, and James the Christ shall rise from the dead to lead us. Death to you!' The sicariot clawed at my neck with his hand, strained against me until he broke his arm. He lay back panting. 'I fail. I fail but others are coming, Jude the abomination. Die! Die!'

Before I could stop him he put back his head, stuck the fingers of his good hand in his mouth and died the sicariot way, choked on his vomit.

AB AETERNO

from the beginning of time

'I have to go.'

'Soothsayers and oracles always say the end of time is now.' Giselle begged me to stop. Lisette, Dagobert, Mary, Elle, all silently watched me with enormous eyes. 'You don't really believe it. Your God of love wouldn't really destroy us.'

'The God of Paul and Peter and James would, anyone who doesn't believe in Him. My mother learned to believe in a Jesus Christ who'll save everyone, believers, unbelievers, every child, every dog, lion, ant, none will be left behind. Well, that hasn't happened, Giselle. I have to go.' I pulled her away from her children for a moment, spoke quietly. 'More sicariots will come. To the Jews my father is a blasphemy, a splitting of God, and so am I. You'll come with me, we'll never be safe here. We'll find a safe place somewhere.'

'And then you'll go alone?'

'I have to see with my own eyes.'

'Will we miss you for another two years?'

'You know I have to go, Giselle. I have to see. I have to know.'

She cried, so the children cried, except Dagobert. 'This quest,' Giselle wept. 'This quest your mother set you on. I hate it. I hate her.'

'I'm born,' I said. 'We can't change who we are.'

'I can change you,' she whispered. 'I love you. I've made you happy, haven't I? You said some Christians believe we're all the children of God. You don't have to be special. You can be my husband like other husbands, the father of my children like other fathers.'

I pulled the knife from the tree by way of an answer.

We hurried; any time now the *mare clausum* of winter storms would make sea travel impossible. From Narbo we scrambled aboard the last wine ship to Ostia, but as before the wind took charge and the captain beached his vessel at Puteoli. He was stuck here for the winter. I carried Elle on my shoulder to Boscoreale and outside the village, on a steep ridge of the volcano, I found a house that was too small for four children (a fifth on the way, thanks to the voyage), but the view down the steep fields to the distant rooftops of Pompeii and the sea was too magnificent for Giselle to resist, and the widow who was selling swore the ashy soil was made of life itself. So I kissed my wife and children goodbye and promised I'd be back before they knew I was gone. Lisette, Dagobert and Mary ran downhill after me (Elle waved with pudgy seriousness from her mother's arms), and at the crossroads temple I kissed them again and turned them back. Am I making my departure sound a little sentimental, as though I never saw them again? I did see them, of course, in only a couple of months, and they were much the same except that Elle was walking and Dagobert had learnt to swear like the locals.

But I would not be the same. We're all simple; it had never occurred to me that there was so much more than I knew – that I knew almost nothing. You see, from what my mother told me I knew 'in' God. I believe what she believed, that Jesus Christ – Joshua, the real Jesus Christ, the full man, not only the mystical sacramental figure of Paul and Peter – is our Son of God in real life. Actual, factual, as well as true. More than a religious figure, more than my father: everything. He's all the choices we can make, and all the forgiveness.

My mother had shown me a little of God; but I didn't know that I knew almost nothing of Satan. Satan, the absent figure, the unseen hand. Could I really be expected to believe in Asmodeus the demon, however real he appeared to my mother? To believe in a burning Hell as real and existent as Jesus Christ? Well, my mother believed, and experienced them too. But she'd never spoken directly of Satan. She'd told me her story; I knew it was still continuing. But I didn't really understand. As I waved goodbye to my family and set off for Jerusalem that sunny day I didn't really believe, didn't really *know*, that Satan is among us as real and vividly as Christ.

But I would learn.

Jerusalem had ceased to exist.

I had no idea as I took the smooth straight road overland to Brundisium. A fisherman sailed me across the grey strait to Apollonia and I walked to Thessalonika, where the sea was white waves. Two days at the inn, and I heard rumours: Titus, conqueror of Jerusalem, had desecrated the Holy of Holies of the Temple sword in hand and found it empty of God. I endured the short dangerous sail to a smuggling village in Aeolis (where the tribes who remember Troy, who fled here centuries ago from Palestine, still call themselves the people of the new covenant); and at Myrina the fishermen had heard the Temple's treasures were looted, even the Jews' holy menorah that lit their way to God. The Temple had been set afire, they said, and burned like a beacon for three days and three nights, and still burned. I set off by cart to Ephesus, arrived on horseback at Tarsus in the snow. The innkeeper, shutting his doors against refugees who couldn't pay, told me the burning walls of the Temple fell at last, all except one, which still stood and the Romans could not knock it down. From Tarsus (paying the captain's wife before he would set sail) the north-westerly blew me straight to Tyre. The Land of Judah was the personal property of Titus.

Alone I walked southward on the main trade road. I saw no traders, I saw no trade. I saw no one except soldiers who stopped, searched and robbed me at every turn, so barefoot I cut cross country through a misery of deserted snow-streaked hills and burnt villages. The fields were burnt, seed stocks destroyed, wells poisoned. Each hilltop in sight of Jerusalem was tattered with the crucified figures of women, children, old men who'd escaped the siege. Birds pecked the flesh and the wind flapped the skeletons' ragged clothes like mournful applause. I found a pair of sandals which fit me.

I came down into the valley beneath Mount Sion, where Jerusalem once stood.

Soldiers stopped me, stole my sandals, kicked me until I turned back. That night I found a few prostitutes huddling round a fire waiting for the soldiers' summons. There was no Jerusalem. No Temple. Not one Jew survived within the walls of the city. From now on no Jew was allowed within sight of wrecked Mount Sion, except one day of the year, when Jews would be permitted to mourn from distant hilltops the holy city and fallen Temple that their hatred of Rome had lost to them for ever. 'Not for ever,' the oldest hag muttered toothlessly. 'The prophecy came true. James was killed, the Temple fell.' She pointed through the dark to the Kedron valley below the pinnacle of the Temple, where James had been thrown down to his suffering and death. Halfway down the cliff face I made out the pillars, impressively carved, of the entrance to his tomb. 'James was the Christ,' she said simply. 'He'll rise again.'

'Took the Galileans to do it,' nodded another grandmother. 'Eleazar Zadok was there at the fall, and Menachem Magus who's Judas the Galilean's grandson, and John of Galilee who fought the Romans even as the Temple burnt. Dragged off in chains to Rome. But there's all these Galilean zealots and sicariots and patriots still holding out at Masada, Machaeros, Herodium, I don't know where.'

'And at Sion?'

'Wouldn't know about that, dear.' Someone whistled, and the women girded their skirts and left me alone at the fire.

I had to see inside the fallen Temple. I had to see.

Before dawn I stole down from Golgotha. Mount Sion and the Temple ruins rose high over me as I climbed the broken city wall. It never seemed to get light; the leaden clouds fluttered a thin snow across the cracked masonry, making my handholds desperately slippery. Once my feet slid out, and I swung held only by my fingertips squeezed into the ice. Inching nearer the top I found the ice and stones blackened by fire, split by intense heat but now icy cold and sharp as knives, and I peered over the top of the wall into the peeling skull of a dead man.

The wind hadn't yet flapped the body's cloak to pieces. I

wrapped myself in it, black with soot, to hide me among the ruins.

But there was no one here on the mountaintop. It was an empty place, only the hiss of snow and the pad of my own footsteps going forward. The Temple ruins were immense, even more of a maze in death than in life, the courtyards tangles of stone, the roofs and porticoes all fallen among cindered trunks of cedar, the collapse sometimes driving through into the cellars below where the defenders had made their desperate last stand, scaly brown blood splashed across the burnt stones. As I climbed and slid among the debris across the Gentiles' Court, my fingers got a grip by chance in the pattern carved on a fallen block: *Let no Gentile enter this enclosure around the Holy of Holies, and whoever is caught is responsible to himself for his death.*

Part of the steps had not broken away; I climbed to the next level, the Court of Women. The colonnades that encircled it and the Hall of Nazarenes next to the wood store had exploded in the furious heat. I climbed to the Court of Israel. Above me rose the monumental staircase towards the Holy of Holies. It stopped in mid-air.

I climbed, jumped across the gap on to the floor, all that remained. The mass of debris still smoked. This was the roof of the storerooms, guardrooms, sacristy, treasury, robe rooms and washrooms below. The stumps of pillars stuck up, frozen trickles of gold glinting like eyes in the shambles. I wondered why they hadn't been looted, then as I took a step the floor creaked. Stones fell from my feet into the sacristy vaults underneath as I jumped forward. I scrambled up the heap of rubble beyond and found myself in the outline of a large square room, roofless, without walls.

I stood in the Holy of Holies.

Even the thick cedar beams that had covered the floor were burnt through to the stone roof beneath. I trod across the top of the ceiling vaults of the sacristy, my footsteps crunching in the charcoal as I went forward. A few fragments still smouldered, sending up perfumed smoke. I stopped at the centre of the room.

I imagined this place as it had been, the glow of the

menorah flickering dimly off gold-clad walls, James standing here wearing the robe, mitre and breastplate of the high priest, searching, searching, searching for his God. And not finding Him.

The floor creaked, and the keystone of the vault beneath fell away beneath my heel. I jumped sideways, fearing the whole floor might collapse into whatever lay below, then knelt at the hole. It sounded as though I'd dropped a stone into a well. I listened to the stone bouncing and clattering slowly down into the dark. My heart beat much faster than the falling stone.

I knocked out another stone, dropped it. The same sounds, falling away for longer than I could hear.

James, Matthew, Simon, Judas: they were right. The Second Temple had been rebuilt with the Holy of Holies placed literally over the keystone at the centre, the entrance from above to the most secret vault. So secret, so holy it couldn't be found except by tearing out the floor of the Temple's holiest place, the Holy of Holies. Unthinkable desecration. But the unthinkable had happened.

I knocked away the stones, stuck my head down into the hole, opened my eyes wide against the dark, saw downward endlessly. I gasped, pulled myself back.

I sat shivering in the wind. The grey sun rose in the snowclouds. I sat staring at the hole, numb with cold.

I shouldn't tell you what I saw. Because, of course, you and I know this is impossible. As impossible as God being and caring for us. As impossible as the Son of God coming down to this world and born as a man in Bethlehem. As impossible as Heaven and Earth.

I saw a staircase winding down into the earth below the Temple like a giant screw made of stone steps, down and down into the darkness, as though it led as deep and as far as the centre of the world.

I sit shivering.

I must be mad.

My mother's words bother me. A conversation she recounted to you and me – I paid little attention at the time, but now I see everything's important. James talking to her: '*You dragged yourself on your elbows to the cave, Mary, God knows how, your back broken, and you shot yourself in the mouth with my pistol, and your body fell to the centre of the world. Into the bottomless pit.'*

Just part of her story; I'd hardly noticed it. Another of my mother's nonsensical names, pistol, a sort of bow no doubt, but otherwise as meaningless as nuclear or Uranus, the Roman god.

But not *this* hole, obviously, or James would've known of it. He wouldn't have passed his life in a fruitless search at such enormous personal cost. Known *of*, but not exactly *where*. Then how did the legend arise?

Solomon had known; the Arch was hidden by Hiram and the king beneath the First Temple. Had Hiram dug the winding stair? Winding stairs are part of Therapeutan and Egyptian ritual, their mystical rites for pillars of the world, keystones shaped like inverted pyramids, incantations for the resurrection of God in the spring, not stuff for most of us Jews for five hundred years; but when Moses the Egyptian found the Arch and brought it from Egypt a thousand years ago, had he brought Egyptian practices with him? When the First Temple was destroyed the Arch was not lost, as most people thought; it simply remained hidden. The zadoks of the Temple knew of it, their knowledge passed down from father to son, perhaps growing fabulous. When Herod killed or expelled them the survivors took their stories to Sion. The Therapeutae had been healers at Sion almost as long as their allies the Essenes. My mother had mentioned the winding stair leading to the scriptorium, and 'Egypt'.

I remembered her story of my father starting his education at Sotinen in Egypt and the idols of the pagan temple bowing down before Him. My God, what nearly happened? I can almost see the pattern, grasp it, but it slips away from me.

I sit staring at the hole. My mother knew this was here, she *knew*, but she didn't want James to know. My father knew of it yet refused the power hidden down there. Resisted the temptation.

I grasp another stone, lift it out, widening the hole. Another. I can see the top step now.

I grab one of the smouldering beam-ends from the

rubble, blow the charred tip to a live flame, discard the bulky cloak and let myself down into the darkness of the stair. It's almost blocked by debris at the top, the internal sacristy walls collapsed against it, the stone creaking. From below a cool dry wind blows smoothly. In here goes down for ever. My hand touches the rubble and stones fall away further than I can see, the whole mass almost slides forward, then a wooden roof beam jams, holds it back.

I duck beneath, hurry down round and round the narrow stair into the earth.

Within a few feet the dressed stone walls revert to the ancient rock interior of Mount Sion, though glassy smooth except where veins of impurity have flaked away. Thick dust puffs up from each step as I go down; no one's come down here below the foundations of the First Temple for hundreds of years. The stair's so narrow and steep the steps try to push me forward, sending dust showering past me into the abyss that swings beneath me like a pointing needle.

Cellars dug deep beneath the First Temple open up on my right. Bent double, I step aside from the stair into a crumbling room, hold up my burning wood, more smoke than flame. Dimly make out a large circle carved roughly on one wall. The sun? An eye? That crescent on the wall opposite, the crescent moon? Am I seeing the sun eclipsed, or the phases of the moon from new to full?

I don't know. I know nothing down here.

I crawl to the next opening. The way divides; the way to the left is collapsed no taller than my hand, blocked. To my right two rooms open up, one without a floor, a pit, or perhaps an ancient well. The edge crumbles beneath my hands, the stones gouged and scarred as if by gigantic claws. I hold out my pitiful flame, coughing. Down at the bottom a stout iron post stands out of the floor, wound about with chains and enormous iron fetters, broken. My mother's words: *King Solomon tricked a demon to get his help. Got him to do the work, then chained him up in the Well of Souls.*

'Asmodeus,' I murmur aloud. My mother tells the truth. However he escaped from here, Asmodeus hasn't been able to find his way back again. Perhaps a demon can't easily re-enter ground after its consecration (usually with the blood of its builder) let alone the Holy of Holies. Can words chain a demon even if chains cannot? When Asmodeus showed my mother Sion he held her above the church to look through the roof, he didn't go inside. But he himself had bragged to her, *It was I who built the Temple for King Solomon. I know the secrets of the Covenant.*

I crawl to the other room, longer but no higher, its roof bowed almost to the floor by time and the weight of earth and ruins above.

I peer beneath. I can almost see something. *Like a prisoner beneath the Temple, profaned, Sion in Sion, His Word cannot be heard in this world.*

I lie flat, sliding forward like a snake between roof and floor. Grit showers in my hair, ears, eyes.

I scramble out into the far side, blind, deaf. Rub my eyes clean. Stop. Stare.

A box made of rough wood. The oldest, most battered box I've ever seen, acacia wood split, bumped, knocked, the corners almost worn away – which of course it would be, carried by the Jewish people through the desert for forty years, set up in conquered towns, carried out to battle innumerable times, captured by the Philistines, sent back in awe and terror, hidden away all these centuries. The Covenant given by God to Moses.

The Arch of the Covenant.

What a shabby old thing it is. It'll fall to pieces if I touch it. Twelve pointed arches or vaults carved along the bottom like a bridge, the twelve tribes of Israel. On them stand two pillars, king and priest, joined at the top by a pyramid standing in its image, a diamond: the keystone, *shalom*, the single pillar of the world, the Christ.

The Covenant's no longer than I can spread out my arms, and not as high. Smaller than I pictured it. Rough work, maybe had wheels beneath it once, long ago torn off. Holes cut in each end for shafts to carry it shoulder-high, the twelve-foot lengths of wood lying discarded on the floor. I touch one and it crumbles, rotten through.

The roof's higher here, I can stand. I hold up what's left of the flame and something glints on top of the box, a tilted circle of dusty metal held in a frame. Never seen so much dust, thick as grey snow on top of the box. Grey snow, or powdered bone. Drifts of it against the sides. I reach out my

441

fingertip, touch the circle of encrusted metal, draw a streak of dull gold. A *shekinah*, the light representing God. Probably the Israelites polished the circle then tilted its frame so it reflected the sun to frighten their enemies. To some people a mirror is magic; even one's own face looking back from the most common mirror, a bowl of water, can be strange and magical. Other shapes curve up to each side of the *shekinah*. I rub them with the palm of my hand: gold wings. Country workmanship – I don't know what sort of birds they found in the Sinai. Maybe desert eagles. Outstretched gold wings, the best they could do. My hand knocks something laid in the dust, a sceptre.

A shepherd's crook such as Moses might have used, leant on, to support him in the desert. The shaft smooth and slim, not gnarled like acacia wood or olive, something dark. I wipe it, ebony black. The snake head at the top is of gold, scrawled with writing. I can't read it; I've enough trouble with Aramaic, ancient Hebrew's beyond me. If Hebrew's what it is, exactly. I drop it back where I found it.

I stare again.

My God. The Arch of the Covenant. What a wonderful, incredible find. I tap the box and it sounds hollow, empty. Even with the weight of gold it moves easily, no heavier than tinder. Two men could carry it easily. One push and it slides, nothing to it. A shell.

I wonder if God, *ho theos*, really is in the box. But God doesn't sleep. God isn't here.

I remember my mother telling James, *We both know that what Moses found in the desert was not the Power of God but the power of men.*

Then why did James want it?

James had spent his life chasing a phantom. Sion paid thirty talents for nothing. The works of men are nothing, Babel can't rise to Heaven, no human skill can paint the face of God. Jesus Christ is the only God on earth: He is the covenant nobody recognised because He is already (according to Paul) inside us. To Paul his Christ Jesus, not the Arch, was the 'mystery kept secret these long ages and now disclosed'.

But it's impossible not to be impressed by something venerated for so long by so many people, an entire race and religion: their abode for their God.

My hand touches something hard in the dust, a corner of stone. I tug at it, the wood crumbles, a stone tablet slides from the Covenant into my hand.

I lift high what remains of the flame, the shadows shifting.

I hold a complex stone tablet carved with the shape of the *tau* or T cross so beloved of Pharisees and Christians, but more ornate, as though shown encrusted with precious stones – which, perhaps, the marks and scoops in the cross had once held.

Like the cover of a book.

Below the cross three meaningless words are stamped: ARAM MENAHT MENOU.

My hand shakes. I'm holding the Law of Moses. The Ten Commandments. The stone, a kind of marble, is not much thicker than papyrus. It'll last for ever, yet break easily. That's the way God does things, He allows breakages. So perhaps the story of Moses breaking the stone tablet is exactly true. All I have to do is drop them. Trembling, I place it flat on top of the Covenant with all the care I can.

Then I can't resist turning the tablet over and looking on the other side. But it's a disappointment, just more of the same writing that was on the sceptre, row after row.

But I'm sure I'm looking at the Ten Commandments. At least the first few of them. There must be more.

I crouch where the box has split, reach towards it.

The hairs stand up on the back of my hand as if in worship. They bow forward towards the Covenant that my fingers have gone inside.

I snatch my hand back.

A shiver crawls up my spine.

I stroke my hand smooth, then kneel. But I'm too afraid to put my hand back inside.

I lean forward, trying to see into the hole, but there's only darkness. I blow on the flame, hold it close, it comes so close I smell my hair burn.

Something moves inside the Covenant.

Light grows inside the box. I peer forward. There it is, I can almost see it.

Then my hair stands on end from terror, from sheer terror.

My own face, my own staring eyes, stare out at me from the Covenant. My own mouth, horribly distorted, suddenly full of enormous teeth as it opens, screams.

I drop the flame, it goes out, I jump backwards in the dark. I wriggle backwards in the dark like a snake beneath the bow of the roof, I know it'll come down, squeeze me tight, crush me. I panic, I scream, thrash against the dark. I stand, run, run with my hands in front of me like a madman or a child. Where are the stairs? I stumble forward through blackness, knock against walls, I can't see what's behind me or in front. I may fall for ever.

Stand still. Don't look back. Breathe steadily. Steady breaths. I can make out my hands. A faint grey glow in front of me.

The staircase.

Don't turn round. Don't look back.

I climb the steps, round and round. The wind blows past me from the centre of the world. The rough circle of light at the top of the stair vault sends snowflakes spiralling past me, illuminates the overhanging mass of rubble held by the beam. The beam bends now, creaking, splinters sticking out.

But nothing happens. I am the son of the Son.

I pulled myself up into grey daylight, not sunlight, only snow and swirling cloud and gleams of watery glow streaming across the mountaintop and the ruins, then mist again, and my cloak was not where I'd left it. A hooded figure entirely wrapped in the blackened cloak sat on the stump of a pillar. I was going to say watching me; but I couldn't see his eyes.

'That's my cloak,' I called. 'I stole it first.'

There was no reply.

I was in danger here, but I'd been frightened, and now I was angry. 'Go and steal your own cloak,' I said, and grabbed it. The wind blew, flapped up the hem of the cloak, revealing not a leg but only a thin brown leg bone, an ankle clothed in rags of flesh. The small intricate joints of the foot still showed meaty gristle between them where the mice and beetles hadn't reached. What was left of the muscles jerked, trying to move the bones. The foot tapped. The shape of a skull moved under the hood.

I said: 'Who are you? What in Hell are you?'

'No one recognised your father either.' The hands moved inside the cloak, reached under the ribs to press the lungs. The voice croaked, shredding, almost nothing left of the vocal flesh. I stared.

'Mother?'

'Aaah. The bitch. She knew, didn't she. Knew where it was all along.' A bony hand slid from the sleeve of the cloak, strips of bloody muscle quivered, curled the fingers. The hood fell back, revealing the head and long white hair blowing in the wind. No eyes, except part of the left eye collapsed in the socket. Whatever it was, it was blind. The tongue was bitten in half but struggled to force sounds between the rotting gums. One single pointed brown tooth: an incisor.

'James,' I said. 'I know you. You're James.'

The mouth opened as if smiling, as if it had lips to smile. 'This is my resurrection. I can do this. I have a strong, strong, strong soul. I've had lots of practice.'

I picked up a heavy stick, part of the stand for an ornament, a weapon.

'Your resurrection!' I was appalled. 'It's not resurrection, James. My father was beautiful, transcendent when He rose from the dead. Everyone said so. So beautiful that they hardly recognised Him for Joshua, the man they thought they'd known. But my mother knew. She saw.'

The head turned towards me following my voice. It licked its tooth, James's mannerism. It reached its hands inside its ribs, squeezed its lungs with bony fingers.

'You have no idea of suffering.' Squeezed again. Phlegm trickled down the finger bones as the rotting tissue tore. 'You will.'

I waved the stick. 'You lost. You aren't God, you aren't Christ.'

The mouth opened in that smileless smile. 'You've found it, haven't you?'

I banged the stick on the stones around him, I was so angry. 'What? What? Don't know what you're talking about.'

'Give me the Arch of the Covenant.' James pulled his hand from his ribs, held it towards me in friendship. 'I'll give you eternal life.'

'Jesus Christ already promises us that. Are you Satan?'

'No.'

'Are you speaking for Satan?'

'He'd set you free. Freedom, Jude. An end to pain, suffering, humility, sacrifice. I'm so sorry I look like this. If I were beautiful, would you believe me? He'll give you anything you want. Love. Even love for God, if you want.'

That offer was truly frightening. 'Now I know you're Satan,' I said.

James said clearly: 'I loved your mother and I would have wanted you for my own child by her. No creature could be further from me than Satan. I'm tired. Tired.' The wind tugged his cloak, almost pulling him over. He huddled miserably in the cloth.

I hefted the stick in my hand. 'What did Satan offer you?' I raised the stick menacingly. James sensed it but didn't raise his arm to ward off the blow he expected to crush the thin bare bone of his skull. Death, discorporation, dispersal, dust. That was mercy to him.

James said, 'He offered me a chance to give up eternal life.'

'I don't understand what you're saying, James.'

'To give up our eternal life in this Hell.' He waited, but I didn't destroy him. 'A chance to be God.'

'How can Satan offer that?'

'To make me God of this world. It's worse, crueller, more hopeless than you can possibly imagine, this world. With the Covenant I can make it into Heaven. I can, Jude. I can save every soul. I can give you true Christianity, I can make you believe. I can make you all a saved people, not just the Jews. I can stop pain, I can kill both cancer of the body and the cancer of disbelief, I can bring worship to everyone and save everyone, not one shall be left unsaved. Not one child will be left crying in the dark, I promise. I can make this world into Heaven and Earth, Jude.' He held out his bony claw. 'Give me the chance.'

If he was beautiful, would I have believed him? I believed him anyway. James was sincere in what he said.

446

'Only give me the Arch of the Covenant,' he said. 'Show me, that's all I ask. I know it's here. The end to time. The future. That's his price.' He held out his skeletal hands in supplication to me. 'Only that. Then everything's possible. Everything is within our grasp, Jude. Salvation.'

'It's an empty box.'

'Give it to me.'

I shouted, 'It's an empty box, there's no God in it!'

'*I know there's no God in it!*' James roared. His voice rose like thunder. '*GIVE IT TO ME.*'

The wind howled in the ruins, snow swept across us, ice blew through the air. James clung to my arms, almost blown away. Ice blew into his eye sockets, filled them, snow looked out like the whites of upturned eyes, then more snow spattered across his skull, clothed his face in icy white flesh. The muscles of his arms fattened, his grip tightened on me with terrible strength, lifted me from the ground into the air. James shrieked in agony and the snow covering him like new flesh and blood gleamed golden, changing, rising up, possessing him. Snow solidified like feathers growing into the shape of wings, golden eyelids flickered about to open in what was left of James's face.

The wind stopped still, as though the present time stopped. The snowflakes fell like roaring surf, then the air was empty, motionless, drained of life.

'Quickly,' James whispered. 'I can't wait.'

More than his strength held me. The ice cracked, breaking away from the golden arms of an angel.

James gave a terrible cry. He knew he'd lost.

The angel's eyes opened, melted like golden wax into an expression of pity. Such pity for me, for James, for the human condition. But his grip held me like iron. I stared into his golden eyes and saw no reflection of myself. The face smeared and rippled, becoming less like James, growing in strength. No angel. Asmodeus the demon, golden, his body hugely male, uncircumcised, rippling with forming muscle, stood up among the ruins of the Temple. He bent his head towards me as his wings lifted, swishing the air, gathering force.

From the demon's mouth James whispered, 'Kill me. Let me die.'

I brought the stick down on his head. James crumpled like gold leaf, his skull clattered white on to the burnt stone. The demon howled, imploded, was gone.

I brought the stick down again and again until James's skull, spine, fingers and every bone in him was smashed to grey powder, and the wind blew him away.

'I believe in love.' I stood alone among the ruins. 'I believe in love.'

No one watched me. No one saw me. I walked to the hole, stared down into the abyss.

The Arch of the Covenant was mine. It was light enough to carry. I could carry it out in my arms somehow. There was nothing to stop me taking away the Covenant of God with men and women, nothing to stop me hiding it wherever I wanted. I could bury it only I knew where, I could do what I chose with it. Open it. Look inside. Just one look. Empty, but I knew there was something inside. Something worth killing Jesus Christ for. Just one look, one touch. The power of God in my hands.

The power of Satan. The power of men. Power over men. I could be king. I could *be* the Arch. Not just the son of the Son: I could make myself God on this world.

What hideous thing had I seen in there? Myself? What I would become?

I thought of Giselle. I thought of my children. Nothing romantic or sentimental about it. I thought of them playing. I heard their laughter.

Beneath me something roared in the ground. Perhaps it was just falling rock. Perhaps it was Asmodeus, failed, thrown down, once more chained and fettered in Solomon's pit so close to the Covenant, almost close enough to touch it, if only he knew.

I leant down, pushed at the beam. It moved. I kicked it once, twice, three times. The beam cracked, the mass of rubble showered forward, then great lumps of stone followed, blocking the stair, piling up. Dust billowed upward into the air. I pulled myself back, walked backwards from the floor of the Holy of Holies. With a crash the whole floor dropped several feet, splitting, as the vaults below collapsed on themselves. The centre cratered as though a giant fist had struck it.

I spoke. I don't know if God hears everything on this world, but I suppose He does. I know Satan does.

I said: 'I believe in love.'

I turned my back on the whole desolation and walked away. I was going home.

VITA

life

We Boscans of Boscoreale in the Campania have a saying, *albo lapillo notare diem*, which means happy days. We pass our happy days in the smoking shadow of Vesuvius, savouring each one that ends quietly, and till the richest soil in the world. Sometimes fresh ash falling from the sky covers our landscape like grey snow: one drop of rain makes it green. Our grapes are the fattest and sweetest, and make wine as red and strong as lava. Our customers learn to drink our wine of Boscoreale well watered, and Jerusalem is a distant memory, ten thousand miles and ten thousand years away, part of another life that happened to someone else. My mind is blank. I had no life before I returned here to Boscoreale, my family, my happy days. I'm determined on it. Nothing happened there.

'Jerusalem,' Giselle said. I sat on the balcony of my villa, my vineyards spread out below me, my children fighting. Someone's jabbed too hard with the wooden sword; someone's pulled hair. She poured wine from the jug on the low table into my cup, sat beside me on the couch. 'Jerusalem,' Giselle said again. 'It doesn't exist, does it.'

I watered my wine and hers. I sipped, she sipped. She looked at me over the rim. She'd had her hair done in the town, the latest fashion, swept back with ringlets pulled artfully round her forehead and temples. Her dress was fashionably broad at the waist to show her fertile plumpness; we were either between babies or in the early stages. Her breasts were still heavy from the last, she'd barely stopped nursing. Elle, tall and willowy for her age and already budding breasts of her own, looked after baby Ione in the shade. 'Must find a husband for her,' I said. Giselle had given much thought to this. There was no shortage of suitors.

But for the first time Giselle refused to be drawn into her favourite subject, suitable marriages for her sons and daughters. She looked wise. 'I hear it's been renamed Aelia Capitolina.'

'What?'

'Jerusalem.'

'Why should I care?'

'Because you've never talked about Jerusalem. You're secretive.' She sipped her wine, touched my chest with her fingertip, and I knew we were going to make love before the midday meal. 'You aren't secretive by nature.'

'I can be secretive.'

'You poor fool.' She gave me a very small wine-tasting kiss on my lips. 'You can't keep secrets from me. I know you don't have a single girl in the village for your lover. You don't enforce your rights as master of the house over your girl servants. You healed Nydia of the birthmark that disfigured her face so she was married, you healed Dio from the point of death. You're busy as a doctor, and your cures actually work, the word's getting about. You even give "Christian" a good name. Let me finish.' She provoked me with her tiny wine-tasty kiss again, making me thirsty for more. 'You're such a good father. You care for our children, love them, even play with them. You're a child yourself, I watch you. But then I see your eyes. You're laughing, happy, in love, but there's something in your eyes.' She touched her eyes. 'Right at the back. I know what it's called.'

'It's lust. Elle can look after the baby. Let's go to our room.'

She sat still. 'It's Jerusalem. The secret you keep from me.'

'You wouldn't understand.'

'I don't want to understand, I want to know! I want to know everything about you. I want to know why my husband shouts in his sleep, why he tosses and turns so hard that my loving arms can't hold him, why he wakes dripping sweat. And why, when I ask him why, he pretends he can't remember.'

'I can't remember.'

'You can't keep a secret from me.' She kissed my lips openly, fully. She was crying. I tasted her tears in my mouth. She was right.

So I told her about Jesus Christ, immortal souls, about the man my mother loved, and how Hell truly and deeply exists beneath us all, everywhere; I told her of the virgin birth in the Bethlehem stable, about miracles, the Crucifixion, about His Resurrection and meeting with my mother twice, and how Jesus Christ lives for each and every one of us, and suffers for our sins for us all until we can learn to save ourselves.

'I knew,' Giselle said. She lay beside me in bed. 'I knew I was right to love you. You aren't like other men. You're a bit odd. You haven't lost your hair.' She pulled my long hair. 'And you're so *nice*. You hardly ever get angry.'

'I get angry with a woman who pulls my hair.'

'You aren't a Christian, are you,' she murmured. 'You're not at all what people mean when they say Christian.' I'd forgotten how odd *Christian* sounds; a worshipper of Zeus isn't a Zeusian, because he worships the other gods too, the gods and spirits that inhabit every house, pond, tree, stream, crossroads, he treats none with disrespect. He doesn't call the worshippers of other gods blasphemers. But Christians say there's no other god but God, and Jesus Christ was His servant whom He raised from the dead. Christians only believe, they don't know anything much of what really happened, don't call Jesus the Son of God or Mary the Virgin, and the stories of Bethlehem and the Crucifixion, as my mother told them, are hopelessly garbled. Sometimes I spread the truth in my own small way to people I've healed. Jesus is the Son of God born of the Virgin Mary. But then they say, if she was a virgin how did Jesus come out of her? I reply, by means of angels. Then they say, if she was the lifelong Virgin, our Mother Mary (for Christ Jesus is in us all), how could He have brothers and sisters? And if He was the Son of God in this world for more than thirty years, why did He only show Himself for the last few months of His life? Didn't anything happen before, was His life completely empty? Why was nothing written of Him by the people around Him?

Giselle laid her head on my chest. She whispered, 'Dio saw Nazarenes in Pompeii yesterday. He bargained with fishermen for *domator* and the Nazarenes made a disturbance.'

'The Nazarenes weren't my father's sort of Christian.'

'Instead of lots of gods worshipped equally the Christians have one God which they worship in different ways, don't they? Sects. Factions.'

'The Nazarenes are of the Jerusalem Church. James's Church.'

'Your father's brother.' She was guiding the talk back to Jerusalem.

'What disturbance?'

'The Nazarenes said the Last Days of the world have come. They asked if there were any true believers listening who feared the end of the world. They always want to make converts to their Church, they won't leave people alone. Of course Dio said he was afraid of the world ending, anyone would be.'

'Dio's so gullible.' But we're only a few miles from Cumae, where Hercules descended to the underworld to battle with Satan. And the smoking volcano hangs over our heads. The Nazarenes would find eager ears for their message here.

'They asked Dio if there were any Christians living nearby.'

I sat up. Giselle's head slid into my lap. She punched me and sat doing her hair angrily.

'Dio didn't say . . .'

She snapped. 'No, he isn't such a great fool you think he is! Besides, you aren't a Christian! And nothing happened in Jerusalem!'

'What did he say?'

'That there was a good man living nearby who healed people.'

Now I knew why she was worried. I stood at the window listening to the voices of my children below, thinking of our happiness and all we had. Then I thought of the Christians. Where was the truth I'd glimpsed of my father? In these squabbling Christian sects, Paul's Romans pitched against James's Nazarenes, now scattered throughout the Empire with the fall of Jerusalem, both of them against Thomas's Copts in Alexandria and the deserts of Egypt, all three sects against Apollos and the Johannines who'd undone Bishop Aristobulus's work for Paul in Britain? And what of the Alexandrian traders who'd set up their brand of Christianity in southern Ireland? Did the beliefs of any of them measure up one patch to what my father had begun to teach?

Giselle slipped her arms around my waist. 'Are they sicariots?'

I shook my head. 'They're all dead. All the freedom fighters, the bands of sicariots and zealots and all the others were pushed back by the Roman armies moving south through Galilee and Judah, forced back on Jerusalem and to Sion. The monastery at Sion was besieged, massacred and destroyed two years before Jerusalem. Most of the escapers were butchered when Jerusalem fell. A few held out at the great fortresses, Machaeros, Herodium. When the end came they committed suicide. At Masada the last thousand jumped from the cliff top or slit their bellies open with circumcising knives rather than live.'

'Good,' Giselle said. 'You're safe.' She turned me and rested her head against my chest. 'You're safe.'

'Yes.'

I sensed her squeeze her eyes shut. 'I've missed the point, haven't I.'

'Yes, Giselle.' I stroked her hair. I loved her, loved her so much. 'You're thinking of Christianity being like any other religion made by men. More hatred than love, more dark than light, fools setting themselves up as priests and fools listening to them. That it isn't really true, that in the end it's just a matter of opinion. That Christianity doesn't have something really real and true at the heart of it.'

She whispered, 'But it does. It has your father, Jesus Christ.'

'Yes, real and true. And Bethlehem, the Virgin Mary, miracles. It all happened. Maybe people will believe in them, believe it all really happened, maybe they won't. Perhaps, perhaps, people will end up believing the exact truth. But my point is, all this isn't based on nothing. It's based on fact. The world wasn't created out of nothing.'

'But God – seven days—'

'That's Heaven and Earth, not the world. My mother believed the world was older. Maybe she was wrong. I don't know, I can't imagine it. What I'm saying is, there are real truths, truths that can actually be found. Seen with your own eyes. Touched. Explored with your own hands. Opened.'

She looked up into my eyes. 'Tell me what you saw in Jerusalem. No.' She put her finger on my lips. 'Kiss me first.'

I bent down and kissed her.

'Again,' she said.

I kissed her and hugged her tight.

'That's better,' she said.

'I saw the Arch of the Covenant down a winding stair. I know where it is. I made sure it'll never be found.'

She didn't look away from my eyes. 'You hid the truth?'

The sunlight had gone from the day. I smelt sulphur.

'Yes, Giselle. I don't know whether it's God or Satan in there. I think it's the sort of truth that if you know it, you've opened it, you've used it. Or it's used you. It's too late to stop it or change your mind, you can't put it back. Whatever it is it's out.'

She murmured, 'Suppose it's God.'

'Tempting, isn't it?'

She gave a little shudder like a sort of orgasm. 'Frightening.'

I said: 'I think my mother was right about everything. I think what Jesus Christ has done may have surprised even God. I don't think God defined His Son exactly. No written instructions, no foreordained code on what to do in all situations. The Father gave His Son the most precious gift any father can give his son: freedom. Perhaps the storm-God of the mountaintop and the cloud was even amazed by the wonder of His creation, at the goodness and love taught by Jesus Christ.'

Giselle laughed, but she said, 'That's beautiful.'

I listened to the clack of Dagobert's wooden sword echoing from the garden.

'Satan exists, Giselle. You have to understand that. He *is*.

Hell is. It's not a religion made up by men, it's all real. The Arch of the Covenant is real. I saw the winding stair at Jerusalem. I stood in the ruins at Sion, saw a winding stair going up to what was left of the scriptorium, the design used as a sort of emblem. The scrolls were all gone, Giselle. Thousands of them. Many were lost after the Crucifixion, looted when Sion was left deserted, but James built the library up again over the next thirty years. The Romans would have burnt anything they found, but they found nothing. All had been carefully removed and hidden.'

'Ready to happen again.'

'All I know is that whatever hideous thing I saw inside the Arch, I want no part of it. I refuse to accept that I can be . . .' My voice faltered. 'That I'm a monster.'

'But you aren't a monster!'

'Perhaps I'm capable of being one. Perhaps everyone has a monster inside them.'

'A soul,' she said. 'An immortal soul like the Christians believe in.'

I heard someone hammering their knuckles against the gate. Dio's voice called out, 'Who's there? Don't make such a noise!'

'I'm coming down,' I called.

Giselle sat very quiet as I kissed the top of her head. Then she said, 'If you can be a monster, Jude, what hope is there for the rest of us?'

I saw the day had turned windy and overcast as I went down to the gate. Dio was reaching for the latch, still complaining about the caller's noise, which was rich coming from Dio the chatterbox. He was a small, handsome lad from the village, a mute slave until I released him (his freedom frightened him, because it meant he had to work harder or go hungry). One of Dio's lungs had grown a cancer from the fumes that seep constantly from the soil, and I'd laid hands on him and turned the cancer to water. Silent Dio became Dio the garrulous. What other changes had my touch made in him? I don't know. But he loved my children almost as much as I. Still the person on the other side of the gate banged noisily on the boards. 'Probably your leek seller again,' I told Dio.

'I'll give him leeks.' Dio swung the gate open. 'Here, you, that's enough.'

Not the leek seller. The caller was a consecrated Nazarene, dressed of course in the flowing robes worn by Nazarene men, not white nowadays but black, mourning the fall of Jerusalem. The hood was pulled over his face, his hands hidden in his long sleeves. 'You, the master of the house?' he asked Dio throatily. But the voice sounded like a woman's voice. The accent was from the village. No Nazarene had been consecrated from Boscoreale.

'Not me,' Dio said suspiciously. The hood turned between me and Dio, unable to decide, though I wore finest saffron linen, and calfskin sandals.

I said, 'I'm the master of this house. What's your business?'

The Nazarene put back his hood. 'Grief to you.'

Not a man but a girl, once pretty, young, her face pocked from whatever dreadful disease had been the death of her. Her limbs moved stiffly, bent from the foetal posture the dead are forced into when buried, to save space in cemeteries. The servant girls screamed. I called to them, 'Get in the house.'

Dio's face was white as a ghost. With trembling fingers he made the sign of the Evil Eye, which is how people here keep away death, or curse with death. I ordered him, 'Dio, close the gate.' But he was rooted to the ground by terror. 'What, shut it in?' he cried. All people in this country believe their dead walk. They propitiate their gods carefully, pay close attention to omens; I've seen a man worried almost to death by the hoot of an owl, yet a white hen crossing his footsteps made him happy as a child. '*Dio, shut the gate!*' Still Dio could not move.

I pulled him aside as the creature stabbed at him. The curved knife didn't shine in the grey dimness. Evening had fallen at midday. I pushed Dio at the gate. 'Not to keep it in,' I shouted. 'To keep the others out!'

'Others?' Dio said. Urine trickled down his thigh, dripped from his knee.

My son Dagobert ran forward, shouting at the creature, 'Are you death?'

The Nazarene turned on him. 'Yes, and yours too.'

I grabbed Dagobert's wooden sword, blocked the creature's swinging knife. It snarled, the bones clinging to the wood. I jerked the hand from the wrist, swung again, struck. The robe billowed, earth, blood and rotting meat dropped down, the bones on the sword clawed my hand. Everyone was screaming. Giselle screamed from the upstairs window, 'They're all coming!'

I shouted at Dio. 'Close the gate, close the gate!'

Dio stared. He gibbered. The sword broke in my hand. But Dagobert ran forward, knocked Dio aside, slammed the gate closed. The slam thumped softly against bodies. The gate was held open by a finger's width. He dropped the locking bar but it didn't fit. The opening gate pushed him back. Hands felt round the join, caught his clothes, pulling at him. My daughter Lisette ran to help, pushing back with her shoulders, but her feet skidded on the gravel. I toppled a statue, Venus I think, on the creature in the cloak. The bones crunched. The joints moved, inching after me. Slowly movement left them. Was withdrawn from them. A finger bone tapped my toe then was still.

Giselle screamed. Dagobert and Lisette ran back. The gate burst open, a dull flood of humanity came forward. Movement, motivation, had been pushed into their poor straining bodies by a means as mysterious to me as life. The rich shambled forward wrapped in fine clothes for the grave, the paupers dressed only in canvas, those from robbed graves naked. Children looked for their mothers. One woman had been buried with her baby which she still carried in rotted swaddling. No wonder Christians pray their immortal souls will be resurrected not in the flesh of death but of life. I shouted, 'Get back into the house.' Dagobert and Lisette ran past me, waited at the door. I had to drag Dio by the shoulder; he shook as though he died of cold. We piled through the door, slammed, barred it behind us. My children looked relieved, but our fate was only a matter of time. Even the quiet gloomy rooms inside the house stank of rotten meat and I dreaded who I might see. I grabbed a ringlet of Dio's hair, twisted it until he squealed. 'Dio, look out for Dagobert.'

'Yes, my lord.' But still Dio shook.

I said, 'Dagobert, look after Dio. Both of you look after the girls. Swear it.'

'We'll look after the boys,' Lisette said. Ah, my children.

'I'll close the shutters,' Dagobert said, efficient as a military commander. I clapped his shoulder.

'I'll help him,' Dio swallowed, his nerve returning. I let them go, it gave them something to do.

Giselle ran into my arms. 'There's fire in the sky.' My mother's dying words: *Fire in the sky*. There's so much I don't know! No time, no time. 'Get upstairs. Elle, carry Ione. Never mind toys. Quick!' I heard Lisette rummaging in my study, she ran out with my sword. Probably she was better with it than me. Dagobert always beat me. But I took it to please her. 'Is it only you?' she asked. 'Or all of us?'

'All.'

'But why?'

'I'm the son of Jesus and you are His granddaughter.'

She wrinkled her nose. 'Who's Jesus?'

'You'll know.'

One of the small unshuttered windows burst, sending shattered glass across the mosaic floor. Hands reached through. I lopped them off, choking on the smell, then arms and heads, but still more came forward. There's not enough air. The smell of death. The interior of the house almost dark as the last shutter bangs closed. I cough, choking, tasting bitter dust. Bony hands tug at my sword blade, my sleeves, my knees. I drop the sword, fall back. Lisette pulls me to the stairs. She has lovely long hair like my own and the legs of Venus. The shutters creak, splintering under the weight of bodies; there's never a shortage of the dead. Dagobert and Dio throw furniture at the shapes stumbling in the doorways, then dash to me. We run upstairs. Giselle shouts, thinking we're the dead.

We block the stairs with couches, no good. The servants flee to the end window, jumping from the first floor. Screams.

The bedroom, push the children inside. Wedge the door behind us. In the stable yard my horse and mules whinny frantically. Between them the corpse of the woman stands in the centre of the yard calmly holding her poor dead baby, kissing his face, some trace of her instinct, identity, what she had been in life, remaining inside her even in the horror of death.

One of the mules snaps its rope, sends the wine-cart tumbling, gallops into the weird distorted gloom over the fields. The horizon's gone. The volcano's gone. Only the corpse with her baby.

The sloping roof of the outside corridor beneath the window: Dagobert understands at once. 'Quickly, quickly.' He slides down the roof, lets go. I climb out from window on to the roof, pull Giselle out. I can feel in her flesh she's pregnant again, I'll have another child. She looks me in the eyes. 'Jude? Will I see you?'

I kiss her lips, let her go. She slides helplessly down the tiles, Dagobert catches her. Now baby Ione, quick, quick. Thumps on the bedroom door. Below me the dead come pushing forward past the wine-cart, slipping on the spilt and broken amphorae. Their bare feet crunch on the pottery shards like teeth crunching. Dagobert pulls Giselle up behind him on the horse, she clutches baby Ione. For a moment the corpse-mother cuddling its child looks up at Giselle, eye to eye, close enough to touch, and I sense something shared between the living and the dead. She's the only one who could stop Giselle. But she doesn't. Dagobert kicks the horse forward, free.

Dio shoves at the door. It moves, creaking. 'Can't hold them!'

Lisette slides past me into the yard, Elle hands my children out to me from the window, Mary, Joshua who looks as angry as always, Paul, James who's almost asleep, Peter in his carrying basket. Elle grins. We're calm when it really matters. I've brought them up well. 'Elle, out now.' I give her a kiss as she slides past. 'Dio, come now.' But no reply, only the sudden clatter of bones into the room, and Dio's shrieks.

Dead dripping hands reach for me from the window.

I slide down, the girls already trotting the mules from the yard, my young sons clinging to them. Dio's shrieks are muffled, weakening. I saved his life; now mine is saved.

The dead roll sliding down the roof after me, fall heedless to the ground on their heads and necks and knees, lift themselves on broken limbs, stagger forward.

460

The last mule won't allow me to catch it, breaks free. I run alone into the vineyard. The row of vines follows the contour of the hill. The fat ripe grapes spatter red juice like blood, but when I look down at my clothes I see the red is grey. Everything's grey. The air's fumes, smoke, falling ash as though a great filthy chimney burns instead of the sun. Can't see the horses or mules.

I turn downhill towards the village. Where's the village? Here's open country. Then for one magical moment the air clears and I see my family, my family scattering away from me like seeds blown on the wind, Dagobert and Giselle on horseback galloping towards Pompeii, Lisette on the mule cantering with the young boys towards the harbour at Boscoreale, and in the distance to my right Elle and Mary running towards the coast road packed with carts and refugees, the stormy sea with boats.

Then the ash and dust sweeps down like night.

I can't find downhill or up. I can't tell if I climb or fall, everywhere's the same. In the cloud misty figures appear, the Congregation of the Nazarenes, their voices wailing under the thunder of the mountain. 'Grief, grief to all!' Their prayers rise around me as they pass, walking in single file from where to I know not where. The priest sees me and raises his voice, 'Behold, the Lord descends to pass judgment! The Lord makes fire come down from Heaven into the sight of men. The Lord gives grief to make the strong weak, the Lord sends grief to humble the mighty. Grief to the judges and the governments. Grief to the idolater and the worshipper of the Beast. Grief to you who pour out the blood of the saints, and gloat over the death-pangs of the Sons of Men! Grief to the harlot of the sea!' Stones rattle from the air as the procession moves away from me in the cloud, their chant fading, lost in the roar of burning stones. Poplars lining the road burst into flame, burning like candles. I tear my tunic, hold it over my mouth against the choking smoke.

Between the trees figures arise, walk steadily towards me. Their shrouds and flesh smoke, smouldering, their hair catches fire. I run, run uphill.

It's brighter up here. A beautiful red glow fills the mist, brighter, louder, racing towards me. The violence of the rising heat keeps the air clear above a stream of molten rock running like red wine. Everything it touches flashes to clean white flame.

Climb, climb away. Come here, the top of the ridge. No further to go, a river of glowing boulders surges downhill below me. The cooling rock screeches and hisses like a great machine as it slides, tricking my senses with its mass so that the ridge, the solid ground, seems to slide uphill. Fire behind me, fire in front. I climb along the spine of the ridge and come to the road, the wreck of the main road from Boscoreale to Pompeii, lined like all Roman roads with houses for the dead. Lava spills over them, overturns them, the dead struggle out like burning leather, burning like torches. They stumble, fall to the ground, thrown down.

Intense heat washes over me, tightening my skin, I smell my hair.

Flames shoot from the broken dead-houses. Fire moving within the flames takes shape, rises up like the face of a demon. Asmodeus? No, no. Other monstrosities, hundreds of them, thousands, rising like phoenixes, quick and savage, quite different from the dead. Demons like those my mother saw in Hell.

The flames come together and I see they are one. They are only one.

The fire moves together within the flames, wings of flame. A million screaming faces, a million voices screaming. This is how we end. This is eternity.

I see a brow of flame rise up like a wave.

I see an eye.

I see the eyes, the body, scales, *something*, blood, claws, nostrils, tenderness, *passion*, rise up.

I see into the eyes, huge, fierce, cruel, loving. I may be seeing the face of God. The Roman word comes into my mind. Deus. God. I scream.

I'm seeing the face of the God of this world. The face of the serpent of Eden. *On your belly you shall go, and you shall eat dust all the days of your life.* The fiery legs flash claws of fire rising into the clouds. I see the dragon of Eden. Unfallen. Unbowed. Immense.

The Beast. He knows me.

The ground splits open, gapes. Safety. I know it. Temptation.

Who would not take it in the last few moments of their life?

I shout with all my strength: *NO!*

The heat piles on me, hair burning, skin frying from my chest and back. I resist, I turn, run away, run away uphill. Hold my arms over my face. The rivers of light join, flow down towards me screeching, boiling.

'Dear God, save me.'

The flow encases my feet, my legs burst into flame. My arms burn, my clothes burn, but the dragon's fire does not touch me. Molten rock rises over my knees, my waist, touches my heart. My heart is vaporised, my body is steam held inside the rock.

My eyes are blinded, my ears are deafened.

Giselle. My children. My life. These were the only things that mattered.

Lava pours over my head like burning water, solidifies, tightens, hardens, deepens.

I am the perfect sculpture of myself, all content burned away, only my outline remaining, even my fingerprints, my anguished screaming mouth, the image of my staring agonised eyes, perfectly preserved.

My body is empty space held deep in the frozen rock.

MORTIS

death

Where do I go when I die?

Here. Just here. Deep in the rock.

Where was I before I was conceived?

I remember my life; before that I remember nothing. Before I'm born, there's nothing. But now there's something.

That something is me. I am me. I'm still me. I was born with a soul, I made more of it in my life; I can't die.

I cannot die.

(How wrong I am, but we'll come to that later.)

Can you hear me?

It's peaceful, sleepy here in the dark. No more pain, only peace. Rest after my busy buzzing life. Perhaps God is in here, surrounding me in the dark. I want to stay here thinking these stupid thoughts.

Water trickles through me; it's a way out. It must be raining.

I remember the rain. I remember the feel of cool drops on my head, shoulders, my clothes clinging to me.

I remember making love with Giselle in the rain.

Giselle, a name.

Giselle, my wife. I remember my villa, my sons, Dagobert, his younger brothers, and their sisters Lisette, Elle, and don't forget Mary . . . and another still to be born, whose name I will never know.

Fire in the sky. The firestorm. Oh my God, perhaps they, too, are in death. Locked here somewhere in the quiet earth.

Perhaps all that I and Giselle gave life to with our bodies, with our love, has no life any more. All wasted. Our immortality leading nowhere.

I weep in my terrible prison. My terrible prison of ignorance.

Even if they died, their souls are alive.

No, I want to see my children *alive*! I want to see the life in them, the heat, the excitement, the adventure! Plenty of time for death.

Plenty of time.

Water trickles down, tasting of grass. Of life. Life returning to the rock. How long has happened? Does grass cover the bare hillside above me? Do farmers till fields sweating and complaining of their hard labour in their day under the sun, their quick hard lives? Never dreaming of the vacant sculpture of my body caught somewhere deep in the rock below their feet. The living don't think of the dead.

But I think of the living. I think of life. Oh, God, how I want life!

I understand so much more of my mother now. She knew so much, she had such a strong soul.

Not had. Has. *Has.* I remember her warning: *God doesn't talk to me. I talk to myself deep in the ground. I come and go as I wish. Then the wind blew.*

I call out to God in the silence, give me life! God, give me life!

Silence.

God, make the wind blow.

No wind blows.

Only the endless silence, endless calm, endless peace of the grave. Endless thoughts.

God, give me life!

My mother saying: *I come and go as I wish.*

I wish. I exert my will. I try. I struggle. I never give up.

It must be raining again, water trickles past me. I reach up, catch at a flash of life in the water. Some small piece of pond life, a tiny struggling insect swept down. I fix on it with all my concentration but its life flickers, fading, drowned.

I reach up, sense a blade of green grass growing towards the sun. Even a single blade of grass has its own life. I sense a million of me green under the rain. More. Ten thousand times ten thousand. More, more, more.

The sun comes out. I feel the warm pressure of the sun. How we grow! How we lift ourselves!

Something large and hard brushes against me, a beetle. I sense its dull flickering remorseless soul. Reach out, but it's too much for me, I can't encompass it.

There are other beetles in the rich volcanic soil. Reach out. I reach out a thousand times.

I see the grass. I move. I am the beetle. Turn left! But the beetle goes its way. Turn right, but it goes its own way. *Turn left*. The beetle turns left.

Turn right. The beetle turns right.

Immense thumping noises in the grass, a vast creature shakes the world. A young hare, a leveret. Its nose twitches. It nibbles the grass by the beetle with a sound like crashing doors, its jaws working busily but slowly, so slowly!

I reach. I fail, pushed back.

A huge paw thuds down, crushing me. No life left in the beetle, it writhes for a moment in the nervous jig of death, its dull soul slips out from under me like colour out of cloth. The beetle is merely dead, inert, stopped machinery.

I reach with all my strength. I grow. I reach.

I see clearly. I have proper eyes. I see stalks of lush grass, even the crushed beetle by the leveret's paw. A worm slides over the beetle, pulls it down into the earth. The leveret hops forward in the sunlight, the grassy sloping field. Turn left! The leveret still hops forward. *Turn right!* Now the leveret turns right. But it's afraid, senses birds that way, danger.

Right to the bottom of its soul, it doesn't want to die.

Terrible danger! The leveret runs instinctively, streaks uphill instinctively, pushing faster with its strong back legs, whipping through the grass towards safety, dodging this way, that way, so fast I'm dizzy. I can almost see the picture in its mind, darkness, safety. Run! Run! Anything but a cross-shaped shadow racing across the grass, the swish of a bird's wings.

Shadow, wings. The leveret squeals in fear. The impact of the bird's strike on the leveret's shoulders breaks the young bones of its neck, it's lifted by great gouging talons. With failing sight I glimpse volcanic slopes, the terracotta roofs of a town. The bird's beak makes harsh whistling sounds for breath, her wings beat hard to get back to the nest. The leveret hangs limp from her claws.

I reach, easier this time. *My* claws, *my* wings, easy. Even at the height of its mature strength the hawk has less potential than the leveret, its soul's a glimmering spark.

This time I've learnt to let the animal, the intricate machinery of flesh and instinct created by God a few thousand years back, do things its own way. The hawk knows better than I how to ride the air currents pushing over the mountain's flanks, how to find its nest. I see the distance amazingly clearly, even a mouse in the field below me, I pick out each orange roof tile of Puteoli, the harbour, the lighthouse, the violet horizon of the sea. Storm coming.

The hawk's wings strain, turning on the last updraught for the final swoop to her nest. Her skill is beautiful, she conserves the last of her strength, scoops and spills the air between her feathers, it's a privilege to feel her precision. Perfect pattern, she's done this a thousand times before. But then the shouts of men below. A net jerks up in front of her from a hide, she flaps her wings but too late, too slow, the air won't hold her. She falls, leveret and all, into the tangling net.

'Two birds with one stone!' The laughing peasant, a red-faced whiskery man with a bulging belly, calls to his son holding the other end of the net. A quiet boy with intense brown eyes. Those eyes tell me what the boy thinks: a net's not a stone, a leveret's not a bird, and his father's an idiot. The thin boy's fat father wraps bird, flapping wings, clawing beak, leveret, net and all in his hairy arms. 'Hare for my supper instead of sparrow. And just the gift for my *patron*'s feast.' A freedman, then, not wholly free. He presses his thumb behind the hawk's head, twists back the beak with his forefinger, breaks the neck. The bird struggles to fly, darkness rushes in.

I reach in the moment of death, I rush forward. Not into the fat freedman. I don't want to be him.

I stand holding the other end of the net watching my fat father extricate the two corpses from the net. He smells of wine and sweat. 'That's enough for tonight, Lucius.' He ties a smaller net of sparrows and swifts round his neck, the terrified birds fluttering against his belly, throws his arm around my shoulders as we walk. 'Which body will you carry, Lucius, the hare, or the hawk?'

Lucius, my name is Lucius. 'The hawk, father.'

'Why?'

It's obvious to Lucius as it is to me: because it's beautiful. But Lucius hates his father and wouldn't tell him the truth about anything. 'Because it makes me feel like a hunter like you.'

'Like your father, eh? Lick-arse boy, you are, Lucius. Too clever for your own good. You'll go far. You'll look after your old father, won't you?'

Lucius strokes the soft feathers of the bird's neck, the long flight-feathers of the wings, and thinks his own thoughts. I like this boy. As we walk I see how everything has changed from what I knew. Where I remember Pompeii stands a green hill, though the boy's father still calls it 'the city', but Lucius doesn't know why. All the villages I remember are gone. New ones, different ones, have sprung up in different places but they look the same, and the people look the same, and it feels as though nothing's changed. Life goes on.

The *patron*'s villa is on the outside of town, a white building with a shallow terracotta roof on a busy street. My father knocks on the door, I stroke the feathers, hold up the hawk's head as though it were still alive. A slave opens the door, knows my father, sees the hawk. 'Ah, Marius. Your offering. He'll be pleased.'

'I'll give it him myself,' Marius says. The door-slave shrugs. The *patron* receives us in his office decorated with murals of his family. Publius is the name beneath his likeness, and as in the picture Publius wears a cream toga and a circlet of shiny laurel in his curled grey hair, and he has a face like a hatchet. Marius bows nervously, kisses his *patron*'s seal ring. 'All day I waited in hiding to catch this proud bird to show my respect to your family on this special day, the occasion of the marriage of your daughter.' Publius nods, accepting the gift. There is a small matter of a land dispute by which he may help his client, Marius, in return. But Publius glances at me as though there's another matter of which we both know. 'Don't forget to send your son to me afterwards for the bones.'

Marius bows deeply, sweating and stinking. Publius waves the back of his hand. Go.

Lucius doesn't want to go back this evening. I can feel it. He's sad at home, sits quietly by himself. His mother and father are both used to Lucius's moods. I'd talk to them, but Lucius won't. He keeps to himself, a solitary boy sharpening his eating knife, eating his parents' leftovers sullenly, lost in his own dark thoughts. 'Time,' Marius yawns; it's been a long day. 'Anything he gives you, I want it.'

Lucius walks through the twilit town lanes; the door-slave lets him into the villa. Lucius stands head down, the routine familiar to them both. Lucius's face is washed, his hair combed into curls. The door-slave leads him through the atrium, past the shrines of Publius's ancestors to the triclinium, the dining room with three couches arranged as usual at a low broad table scattered with the ruins of food. The hawk, the noble centrepiece, is still preserved with its feathers.

Lucius is left alone. What's he supposed to do? He helps himself to crumbs. On the wall is the image of a fish and beneath it words he doesn't understand, *Iesous Christos Theos*. Publius steps from the shadows, his toga changed for a short tunic that shows his muscular grey-haired thighs. 'Drink wine.' Lucius pours wine, undiluted, offers it. I know this strong Campanian wine. 'You drink it, Lucius, my friend.' Lucius drinks, coughs, his eyes water. Publius kneels on the couch, licks the tears from Lucius's cheeks. His saliva smells of wine. 'You know you are very beautiful.'

Lucius has heard this before.

Publius stands. 'You know what I require of you, Lucius.'

Lucius nods. He knows. 'Yes, *patron*.' He lifts the hem of Publius's tunic, cups the hairy grey bag of balls in his small brown hand. Publius groans, rises erect, uncircumcised. Lucius knows what's expected of him, kneels, takes it in his mouth like a gristly eel.

'There's more.' Publius stops him. 'This time there's more. You're old enough. I won't hurt you.'

Lucius knows what *more* means. But once he lets Publius sodomise him, his value decreases. Besides, he knows it will

469

hurt. He moves his tongue faster, drawing Publius up on tiptoe, any moment the old man won't be able to stop and Lucius will be safe until another day. I definitely admire this boy.

'Stop.' Publius drags Lucius's head up by the hair. 'Stop, boy. Turn. Crouch. No, not there. On the table.'

The low table makes everything the right height. 'Hold your heels.'

Lucius stands on the table over a bowl of broken bread, bends forward. He dare not resist. A confused jumble of faces goes through his mind, father, mother, uncles, his father's friends, all those whose lives will be the worse if he says no. If he resists.

Lucius says in a trembling voice, 'No.'

'Lovely.' Publius leans over the boy, his belly on Lucius's back, caresses the boy's face with his hand. 'Fight me.' He pushes forward, clamps his hand tight over Lucius's mouth, he thrusts. Lucius struggles helplessly. I know what I'd do: Lucius still has his eating knife in his belt.

The boy pulls the knife from his belt, reaches behind his arse, slices.

Publius opens his mouth. He can't make a sound. He stares down at his passionate stump pulsing blood. Tries to hold it but there's nothing to hold. Between his feet lies his penis, erect for a moment.

I'd stamp on it, but first Lucius holds his knife at the old man's eyes, a warning. Then he puts his foot between Publius's feet, and treads down with his heel.

Publius gives a cry and collapses.

Lucius watches him, panting, knife in hand. Did I make him do it? I hear footsteps, the slave's voice at the door. The magistrate's punishment will be far worse than Lucius's crime. I can't leave him now.

Run, Lucius, run!

But Lucius has an even better idea. I like him a lot, he's so quick-thinking and determined. He doesn't try to run from the house, he takes the other door, runs deeper into a corridor between the rooms. Here's the familiar door to Publius's office. At the desk he rummages out a couple of money pouches, drags the knife across the genital region of Publius's wall painting, and jumps from the window. He can hear shouts and screams gathering pace behind him.

In the street Lucius crouches, hesitates, doesn't know which way to turn. Turn left! He runs to the left. Run downhill! He runs downhill. The harbour, quickly! The whores try to stop him but he plunges through, runs along the breakwater. Faster! The bonfire roaring on the lighthouse illuminates the sails of a ship taking advantage of the night wind, the gap of black water narrowing at the harbour entrance: Lucius leaps, hits the deck, rolls.

Strong hands drag him to his feet. I know Lucius must say exactly the right thing, and fortunately, after my voyages, I know how to handle a boat. But this captain looks, unfortunately, very much like Lucius's father. Lucius's tongue freezes to the roof of his mouth, his wits desert him, his mind goes blank. But I know exactly what to say. I can help Lucius.

'You idiot!' Lucius bursts out. 'You almost sailed without me!' And he drops a bag of money into the captain's hand.

DE RERUM NATURA
the nature of things

I always try to find men like Lucius who live by their wits, men who make their own way in life, men with a cat's instinct for landing on their feet. Sometimes I find a woman, I love the smell of a beautiful woman, I love the way she moves, and I love to turn heads, but it's my nature to be a man. There's so many things women do, and sense, and wonder, and lust after, so many dark secrets they carry captive in their hearts that are so utterly different and so much more than anything men experience, that filling a woman's skin as intimately as I do feels unnatural, even perverse, to a man used to men. Sometimes I like to be perverse. But men of a certain style, and a certain type of woman attractive to men, I instinctively understand.

He's handsome with his dark eyes, this lad Lucius, and the boat has three Roman ladies not including the captain's wife aboard, and the voyage to Valentia in Tarraconensis, the Iberian peninsula, is long and becalmed. In three nights he loses his virginity three times, once for real, to the Roman matrons, and on the fourth night (just before dawn, while the captain still sleeps) to the captain's wife. Lucius is irresistible and dangerous to himself; the captain has a short temper, a jealous disposition and a long knife. But Lucius is intoxicated by his freedom, and so am I.

He's also literally intoxicated, plied with wine by the Roman women competing for his charms. He can hardly see straight, let alone screw. Below decks is a stinking hell where slaves in chains grapple with the massive oars, inching the boat forward at a knot or two. A guard slips on deck, covers Lucius's body sleeping in a stupor with his own. But I never sleep. Lucius now has what are called good instincts. He's hardly awake before his knife has slipped beneath the guard's ribs. He almost goes to sleep again, dreaming, then stares in horror at his hands. It takes all Lucius's willowy strength to lift the dead man overboard, and the rhythmic grind of the oars drowns the splash. But later Dumitia, the captain's wife, lies beside him passionately and whispers, 'I like a man with blood on his hands.'

My father lived among people who thought that eating bread was one of the worst crimes a man could commit. I'm in the natural world now, among men and women who never heard of God, I'm a million miles from Jerusalem, I can't remember that place. The concept of holiness has no relevance. At dawn the captain won't turn his ship to search for any man overboard, and his wife licks her fingers like a cat licking cream. A rower who died in the night is pitched into the sea. Anyone would have to be a saint not to be a devil in this world.

I know; I'm sounding facile. It's all so easy. But it is all so easy! I missed so much in my life. I lived in my mother's shadow, married the first girl I touched, made children who grew into a fine family, and I was happy, that's all! But I missed all this. Marcia, the least pretty but hungriest of the Roman matrons, gives Lucius a bag of gold to make up for the one he paid, and (to wear inside his shirt) the heavy lumps of gold jewellery her husband gave her that she'll lie she lost. The truth is – she has lovely truthful eyes – she can't live without him. Lucius puts the pieces in his pouch when he sleeps with the other women, wears their trinkets instead. Dumitia, once (and still) a Puteolian whore, has taught him how to kiss. A woman forgives a good kisser anything. He even cuddles. None of them have known affection before.

In a story or a play some reversal, terrible or witty, would provide a moral ending, and Lucius would be taught a fitting lesson. That doesn't happen in this world. The vessel anchors at Valentia, Lucius swears fidelity to all, dives overboard and swims to shore, and the four women never see him again, and weep for him constantly for a day.

A boy came aboard; a man dived overboard, and now Lucius isn't the sort of man a man tangles with lightly, something in his eyes: he pushes watchfully forward through the market crowds, and anyone can see those dark eyes don't miss a trick. Obviously a man with the right instincts. He's a beautiful machine.

Lucius doesn't know where he wants to go; he'll shack up with some whore for a week, get drunk, move on, get lucky or not and die with a knife in his back. No girl to mourn him, no family to survive him. That's the sort of man I like. Live hard and short, and die quick.

But that's not the sort of man I am.

Lucius lies drunk in someone's plump arms in the back of the whorehouse, but I think of my family. Lucius dreams of them, my last sight of them, my wife and children scattering in different directions from the volcano: what happened? Did they survive? Did they meet up? Or were they scattered like seeds? A tear trickles down his cheek in his sleep, making the girl with plump arms love him a little.

When he bought his wine and his girl I didn't even recognise the head of the emperor on his money. Trajan. When Lucius is drunk he's easier to control. He lifts his head from her breasts, *in vino veritas*, slurs: 'Vespasian was emperor before Trajan, wasn't he?'

She looks at Lucius as if he's mad. 'Who's Vesp whatever?' Vespasian besieged Jerusalem; his son razed the city.

Another whore calls, 'Who's Trajan anyway?'

I've missed four emperors. My sons, if they survived, are middle-aged at least, probably with wives and families of their own. My daughters may be grandmothers. But probably they're dead.

Almost certainly my wife Giselle is dead. Did she have our last baby?

I have to know.

Lucius rises to his feet, swaying. 'Got to go.'

The girl wraps her plump arms round him. 'Give me another of your kisses first, Lucius.' Her cheeks flush pink, her eyes shine. 'Ooh, that was nice.' All the old tarts start calling for a kiss. Lucius will never leave at this rate, but finally during the heat of the day, when the offshore wind blows, he sees a squid boat casting off.

Where to start? Where the wind blows.

I make sure Lucius has such a headache he swears off drink. The wind blows to Terraco. Iberian leather is very fine and I make sure Lucius buys good clothes, well cut. The wind blows a wine ship to the Baleares islands where Lucius falls in love, again, though this time with a respectable widow who teaches him to read. Really life is very pleasant; she gives him a ruby ring, ruby for blood, she truly loves him. But he steals away one night before he outstays his welcome, and the wind blows him to Ostia with olives and wine, to Alexandria with ironware and pottery, to Marsilea with papyrus and linen, to Ostia again with grain, and at last the wind blows a marble ship in ballast from Ostia to Narbo.

Lucius feels as though he knows this land. Feels at home here. Wanders. Walks the (new) causeway through the marshes to the island of Clape, the village of Peche, stays at the inn (larger) by the stream, falls in love. I don't recognise anybody. Over the next few days I try to get Lucius to go for a walk to pass my mother's tomb by chance, but he's blinded by love. The girl's name is Julia, her mother's dead, it's her grandmother's house, so Julia and Lucius hold their trysts in the orchard, or behind the wine-press, and finally a whole night in the barn, and Lucius falls into an exhausted slumber. He twitches in his sleep, eyes moving, dreaming.

I sat up, very gently removed Julia's moonlit milk-white hand where it lay on my shoulder, and left her sleeping. The autumn was dry so I crossed the stream on stepping-stones, climbed to my mother's tomb. The stone was gone, a rickety gate placed across the entrance. The floor had been levelled and it was full of goats. Yet . . .

Yet I almost sensed her. The goatherd snored. The night wind blew lightly on the back of my neck. I turned quickly. No one.

'Mother?'

She was here. I let Lucius lie down, reached, *reached*, felt nothing in the goatherd but a poor cringing soul. I let Lucius stand, examined the night carefully. Was she still here? Was she hiding in the goats, some night bird, an owl perhaps? An insect watching me dimly? I could feel her presence, her age, her hardness, as though she permeated the rock itself.

Was she as strong as I? I am the son of the Son.

I called: 'Mother! Mother, please!' The goatherd shouted, waking. The goats panicked, I opened the gate, they rushed out followed by the shouting goatherd, and as I listened the sound of them faded to silence in the moonlit dark.

I stepped into my mother's alabaster tomb. Her body had long been thrown away, but I sensed her. Her force. Willpower. Old, monstrously old – she'd told me so herself. *A heart as hard and cold as iron. That's the only difference between us, you and I. My age, power, knowledge. There's nothing I don't know, no despair I haven't known, no life I've not lost in pain and suffering.*

I was finally beginning to understand. I was no longer a young innocent man, a virgin thirty-three years old. I was much older, and much wiser.

I called: 'Mother.'

'Jude.' My mother's voice came clearly in my ear. 'You will not find me here.'

She was gone. I felt her absence, a sudden emptiness around me.

Find. Was I still seeking my mother? I stood in the entrance to the tomb. A shooting star scratched the sky, an omen no doubt of something or other to pagans. No, it wasn't Mother I sought to find: I sought my children, my family. I needed to see my children. Just to see them. Just to know. I knew instinctively I'd recognise my own children however much they'd changed.

The goatherd climbed towards me leading a couple of goats on tethers. 'A man can't know where he goes, Jude, unless he knows where he comes from.' The goatherd looked confused. 'And he can't seek his mother without also seeking his father.'

I stared after him. 'What are you talking about?'

'What?' He shrugged. 'I didn't say a word. Look what's happened to my goats.'

I returned downhill to the stepping-stones, dipped my hand into the water to drink, re-entered the barn quietly, lay down beside Julia in the straw. Lifted her hand carefully back on my shoulder, snuggled into her with my chin between her breasts just as Lucius had slept before his body got up in his sleep and walked away from her. She giggled. Pushed Lucius's shoulder, waking him.

'Don't pretend you're asleep, my lover.'

Lucius wakes sleepily, yawns. 'You woke me.'

'Where've you been? You can't fool me. Come on, own up.'

He eyes her appreciatively. What lovely long legs Julia has. She kicks his splashed boot with her bare toes. 'You've been down to the river. You've been with another girl, naughty boy.'

'I haven't. I drank from the river. I thought I was dreaming.' He lifts himself on one elbow, admires the moonlit outline of her body, but she's unforgiving. He complains, laughing, 'I haven't!'

That's what she wants to hear. 'Prove it,' she says, giving a delicious little wriggle. She wants him to kiss her everywhere, especially where she wriggles most. Wraps her long legs round his neck, arches her back. Her hips buck, she cries out like the call of a bird. Love, love, love, we can't get enough of it, whatever the price, however high. Anything for these tiny squirts of immortality, these frantic moments of peace.

The moon sets. Before the first glow of dawn Julia sits up, pulls on her tunic. She has her plan. Fetches the milk bucket, milks the cow, kisses Lucius goodbye on the lips. 'Surely,' she says, 'I could introduce you to my grandmother somehow.'

Lucius knows this warning sign. 'Yes, that'd be good,' he smiles. 'Let's think about it.'

'We can't keep us secret for ever. You could pretend to be a traveller. We've never met. I'll see you tonight?'

'Yes.'

She brushes his mouth with her lips, he watches her sway with her buckets across the yard. The house door opens, her grandmother stands on the step. 'Up at cock-crow, youngster?' Oh my God, I'd recognise her anywhere, even with her hair grey and short. That old woman, she's my daughter Lisette. Julia's bucking hips and tickly pubic hairs, tasty nipples and ardent cries that so pleasured Lucius are my own great-granddaughter's.

★ ★ ★

I have to know.

But Lucius's instinct is to leave, he's already leaving. He's had a good time with Julia, it can't get any better, now's the best time to go. He goes quietly from the back of the barn, knows perfectly well the curved tines of a winnowing fork are hidden in the straw, but his mind goes blank for a moment. He treads on the tines, the handle of the fork whips up into his face. Lucius cries out. His nose feels broken.

'That'll teach you to sneak into respectable people's barns to sleep.' Lisette guides him into her kitchen, sits him by the warm bricks of the fire, wets a cloth and dabs his bloody nose. 'It's not broken. You'll have two black eyes.' Julia smiles, head down, busy at her tasks. Lisette takes in the traveller's fine clothes, heavy pouch. 'Why didn't you stay at the tavern? You've got plenty of money.'

Lucius would rather be anywhere than here, speaks thickly. 'Dark. Lost my way.'

'Where are you going?'

'Uh, Narbo.'

'You're so far out of your way! Didn't you notice the causeway?' Lisette always was bright. If Lucius isn't careful he'll meet his match. She's so forthright – that's my girl – he doesn't know quite how to lie to her.

I push. Lucius always likes to show off. He says impulsively, showing off to Julia, 'My sister lived on the island for a year. I thought I might see.'

'What was her name?'

Lucius can't think of a name, of course. 'Giselle.'

'Oh, that was my mother's name!' Lisette looks at him, interested. 'I thought it was so unusual.'

Lucius is floundering now. Something comes into his mind. 'Oh, we came from up north.'

'So did she.' Lisette pours this interesting traveller a cup of wine, takes hot rolls from the oven. 'She's dead now. She lived to a great age. We buried her on the hill.' She pointed. 'There's a church to Christ on the hill.'

Chewing the hot roll makes Lucius's nose hurt. 'Did she have any other daughters?'

'Our father, Jude, was killed in the eruption of Vesuvius nearly half a century ago.'

478

Lucius has never heard of an eruption. Half a century is several lifetimes to him. 'I'm sorry.'

'Giselle always hoped he'd survived somehow. She searched for him, she never remarried. She was carrying his child, you see.'

Lucius blurts, 'What was the child's name?'

'She was his daughter Christa.'

Christa. Now I know her name.

'She married a merchant in Narbo. He died, but she has four children now to carry on the wine business. The eldest will be married soon. Her daughter hopes to be betrothed to a frightfully important wine-grower in Tarraconensis.'

Lucius forgets his nose. The roll is delicious, and Julia keeps sending him glances. Distracted, he asks, 'What about your other sisters?' Did Lisette mention three sisters?

'Is this really so interesting?' Lisette's flattered, but Julia gives a jealous yawn, trying to catch Lucius's eye. 'Yes, three more. Elle moved north to the Rhine. She's had several husbands. Probably more by now, the post's so slow, but we try to keep in touch. Ione ran off with a British trader: you know, red hair, long red moustache, baby-blue eyes.' I imagine drizzle and hawthorn bushes and a little church by a tor, which is all I know of Britain. 'Mary went east, married a king, they call themselves the Fisher Kings, frightfully romantic.'

'Fisher Kings? Why?'

'Christians. King-priests. The initial letters of Iesous Christos Theos spell *fish* in Greek. And my mother Giselle thought some of the Christ's earliest followers were fishermen. Now the Fisher Kings call themselves the People of the New Covenant. All that's left of the Jerusalem Church. Their battle flags are the emblem of the fish interwoven with the Lion of Judah.'

'You don't need to show him the letters,' Julia says testily.

'What about your brothers, Lisette?'

'Yes, I do have brothers. Dagobert went with Mary and served in the army of the tribal Fisher King. He did well and his sons have done very well, they may be Fisher Kings of their own tribes one day. My younger brothers . . . one to Egypt I believe, another – Paul – to Ireland. Very religious, a monk. Both Egypt and Ireland have Christian monasteries in deserted places. Someone passed by here, a friend who had seen Paul. The names of these places are barbaric.' Ireland, Hibernia, was the outermost fringe of the Empire, little settled. She tried to get her tongue round the difficult words. 'A monastery called—' She gave up, translated. 'The Priory of Our Lady of Sion.'

Lucius spits bread. 'Sion!' *Our Lady?* Where does Our Lady come from?

Then I remember my mother Mary Magdalene meeting my father at Sion in the place women were forbidden to enter, on the day I was conceived. What's happening here?

Julia pats his back. 'Really, Grandmother, you're monopolising him. Would you like some cheese, ah—'

Lucius remembers his name. 'Lucius.' The intoxicating, dangerous scent of Julia sets him scrambling to his feet, but if he isn't careful he'll be staying here for the rest of his life. The thought of Lucius marrying my own blood, even if my great-granddaughter is three generations down the line, feels indecent, remembering her passion from last night. Besides, Lucius isn't good enough for her. 'I have to go,' he says.

Julia looks alarmed. 'You can't go.'

'Yes, you must stay,' Lisette says. She has many memories to share. 'Be my guest tonight at least. We have plenty of room.'

'And your nose, Lucius,' Julia adds with one of those provocative looks I remember from Giselle. 'Your nose is swelling.' She glances between his legs with her small private smile. 'I'll see if I can make it go down.' She dabs his face with cold water, but Lucius knows exactly what she means. She knows how to keep him.

Lisette reminisces all afternoon. It's very sad to hear of my death from my daughter's lips, her grief that seems so long ago yet still so sharp to her. Soon she'll die, she can't live more than another twenty years at most. What of her soul? I reach, then draw back. What she will find out when her death comes, she must find out for herself.

During the evening, when the fire's dying down, almost the last thing she says, Lisette leans forward and confides to Lucius, 'You know, one of the last things my father said to me. I'll never forget it. He said' – she leant forward, whispered – ' "*I am the son of Jesus and you are His granddaughter.*" Somehow I felt it explained all the bad things that happened to us.'

'It can't be true,' Julia says, 'Or we'd be perfect.'

Lisette laughs. 'But you are perfect, Julia dear. You are perfect!'

She shows Lucius to his room and the house falls quiet. Lucius lies sleepless, hands behind his head, listening to owls hoot outside the window. Julia comes in, whispers angrily, 'I waited *ages*. I thought you were going to come.'

'I didn't know which room.'

She kisses him, forgives him, knows what he wants, straddles him, impales herself. She makes love so noisily it's a miracle Lisette doesn't hear. Is this perfection? I don't know. I reach, *reach* in her, feel two souls inside her. She has two lives. Julia will bear Lucius's child.

'Oh, my love!' Lucius clasps Julia to him tight.

When they lay asleep Lucius's eyes opened. I knew how heavily Julia slept. I slipped out from beneath her, pulled on my boots and cloak. At the window I stopped, then went back to her sleeping form. I thought she was the most beautiful thing I'd ever seen. I slid the ruby ring from my finger, slipped it over her own finger. Then I kissed her neck just beneath her ear.

I lowered myself from the window, dropped. A few pigs grunted at me in the dark. I walked quickly through the sleeping village, took the track uphill towards the place the villagers now called the Sanctes Maria, the two saints Mary. Lucius muttered in his sleep, dreaming.

I came to the hilltop at dawn. The fields I'd once hoed were scrub. The roof of the little church had fallen in except for a few burnt and blackened timbers from some long-ago (perhaps deliberate) fire, but the walls still stood, covered with creeper and wild flowers, crawling with life. I saw a butterfly spread its wings in the first heat of the sun. The tiny ruined church at the centre of its graveyard.

Here was Giselle's grave. Well tended, no weeds: Lisette's hands probably.

And probably Lisette herself would be buried here, one day.

And Julia.

481

And Julia's child.

I pushed through the empty doorway into the empty church. My foot touched a wooden grail chalice split by the sun. On the end wall, above the empty niche where the scrolls and books had burnt, the *tau* cross of my father was burnt away. In its place stood a statue blackened by the fire. A woman wearing black Nazarene mourning clothes, but the fire had burnt even her devout expression and praying hands as black as cinders. I walked slowly forward, peered into the icon's face. Someone had scrawled beneath her in charcoal, Our Lady. *Sanctus Maria* could have meant either one, Our Lady Mary Magdalene or Our Lady the Virgin Mary.

Around her black head someone had wound a pearl necklace. It shone in the sun like a halo of stars.

That devout, cindered face, wide-open blackened eyes seeing all, understanding all. A Black Madonna wearing a halo of stars.

I promised myself I'd come back here one day.

I walked downhill by another path that took me nowhere near the village and spent most of the day wading through the marshes out of sight of the causeway, the first place Julia in her abandonment and distress would search. By the Narbo road at evening I sat back against a stone wall where Lucius dreamt he banged his head. He'd think he'd fled his entanglement with Julia in the night and never realise he'd lost a whole day of his life.

The sun rose like a bloody eye, spreading its reflection like veins and arteries along the maze of channels crisscrossing the marshes. A single bird call reminded me of Julia.

Tomorrow Lucius would stop by chance in Narbo, where my youngest daughter Christa lived. And so it would go on. I'd find them all, I'd know everything about them. I'd see their children born, and their great-great-grandchildren.

Then my mother's chilling words struck me. *A man can't know where he goes, Jude, unless he knows where he comes from. And he can't seek his mother without also seeking his father.*

Lucius's eyelids fluttered, waking.

Another day.

QUAERE VERUM

seek the truth

Because there must be more. There must be more to it than this. This, that our immortality is just sex, the endless, endless repetition of sex (Lucius can vouch for that, sleeping with a different woman for a day or a week in whatever city takes my interest, probably having as many children as I do, knowing none of them). Lucius lives his life blindly making life, an unknowing link in the chain forming new links leading he cares not where. He follows his God-given nature: all he wants from life is a loving cunt and a cup of wine, a chicken leg and a piece of bread, and a bosom to lay his head on for the night.

Is human nature God-given, implacable? Or is it just human nature, malleable clay? Can we improve ourselves, can we learn love? Can Jesus Christ work through us, with us, just a little?

The Emperor of Rome, *dominus et deus*, man and God, has had the children of my father's brothers brought to him for interrogation, and dismissed them as mere peasants. Had he considered them dangerous, he would have had them killed. But by now my father whom my mother knew is almost entirely erased, only his name Jesus Christ survives, the man he was is lost. The events of his life are distant history, a lost world.

It is, of course, someone's wife who loves Lucius and is about to lose him who plants her knife in his back, and holds him in her arms and weeps on him as he dies. I look down at Lucius's dying face, my vision bleary and smeary

483

from my running tears, holding him in my remorseful arms. I always knew Lucius would end this way, and so did he. His last physical act is a smile. Yes, he had style. Then he's gone. The brief unchaining flicker of his soul like a freed spark, then nothing at all, only the irresistible, roaring glimpse of Hell.

But I'm strong. I do resist. I overcome. I pull away.

The woman tries to cut her throat to join her lover in the most romantic tryst of all, death. But her knife, though sharply pointed, is blunt. Her husband saves her from the executioner but takes his revenge on her day by day, night by night, until her life is purest hell. When she can't stand her suffering again she escapes him, throws herself from the roof. I feel like leaking from her body lying smashed in the street, the soul of all she was falling away unchained from her unchristian brain, unchristian heart, unchristian bones, and her soul falls to Hell to scream and suffer for ever. Her suffering in this world wasn't a candle by comparison.

I can't save her, but I'm strong. A youth goes through her bloody clothes for whatever he can steal, a good ring, two fine gold bracelets, the gold headband fallen from her head and rolled into the gutter. And I reach, I *reach*—

He's dull; doesn't last long, though I make something of him while he lives, fine clothes, a touch of style. One of his lovers owns the villa on the headland, which is soon mine; I love a little luxury as much as you. But soon, with age and fat and a failing heart, luxury palls, and I reach, I *reach*—

There's more, much more. I am who I am. Even you, I can be. Have you improved lately? Has your life changed for the better? Perhaps what you once found unforgivingly hard is a little easier. But mostly I prefer people who are nobody. You know them, the people you avert your eyes from, you don't quite notice them. The drunk in a doorway. The idiot. The traveller beaten up by thieves and left to die or to live, people who've lost everything, people on the point of suicide, people about to jump from the bridge, fall on the sword, give up, give in, give out. People you cross to the other side to pass. You do know them, don't you?

Sometimes I call myself Trevrizent, the searcher, which suits me in any language. I was among Christa's children spreading out from Narbo and Tarraconensis, I was with my warrior great-grandson Dagobert at the Priory of Our Lady of Sion in Ireland, the finest education the Celtic Church (or the Coptic Church, for that matter) can provide for aristocratic second sons, and I saw him ordained as a priest, and knew he would be anointed Fisher King one day. So many are my father's grandsons and granddaughters and all our children spreading forward through time that they're called the *desposyni*, the children of the Master, the Blood Royal of Judah. Through them, their strength, I think I can begin to see the shape of my father's plan.

But no, even the truth's turned to lies by Christian priests. I see it with my own eyes: a few stories and parables about my father, passed down by word of mouth, were written down after the Apostle Paul's time and gradually collected to make gospels, scriptures eventually collected into a new great book, a growing Bible. Miraculous to see this happening; for all the faults and flaws and the mistaken memories of men, for all the wonders that men left out or did not dare believe, I saw the hand of my father in its pages. Yet the bishops and patriarchs of the Church wrote to one another suggesting revisions to fit with their own beliefs. My mother's marriage ceremony at Cana merely turned water into wine, a miracle without reason or explanation, and the names of the bride and bridegroom were deleted.

Over the next hundred years the gospels were edited to fit the God of men. With my own eyes I saw Bishop Clement doctoring the Gospel of Mark. 'Not all true things are the Truth,' he wrote to a follower. 'The true Truth of the Faith should always be preferred to fact. And when liars spout their reasoning and interpretations, never should we concede that the secret Gospel is by Mark – but should deny it on oath. For not all true things are to be revealed to all men.'

Where was the truth in denying my mother was the bride of Christ, and that the gospel had said so?

A hundred years later the king-priest of the *desposyni*, Joses (a descendant of my father's young brother Joses – and also, through by now innumerable cousins, of my father and me), argued bitterly with Pope Silvester that the centre of the Church should be Jerusalem, not Rome. That the Pope of Jerusalem should be a *desposyni*, and his son after him, perpetuating the bloodline of Christ. But the Pope accused Joses of heresy. Jesus Christ had never been created a man, Silvester said; Jesus was always God Himself, the Son of God equal with the other parts of the Deity, God the Father and God the Holy Ghost. From now on there was no place in Jerusalem or Rome for the *desposyni*. To Silvester the Roman it was impossible for the Son of the Virgin to have brothers or sons, so the *desposyni* were hounded as liars, frauds, heretics and criminals, and the survivors fled back to the east and the north, to the Fisher Kings.

'Faith,' Clement had written, 'is a compendious knowledge of the essentials.'

I followed the *desposyni*, the descendants of my son Dagobert and my little girl Mary, northwards and westwards with the Fisher Kings as the tribes migrated to the safety of the forests of the Rhine. The Roman Empire collapsed and the Fisher Kings, the People of the New Covenant, ruled from the *colonia* they called Cologne. Princess Argotta, the *desposyni* granddaughter of one of the many kings Dagobert, married King Faramund of the West Franks, himself a *desposyni* through my daughter Elle, reinforcing the two bloodlines just as Joseph and Mary brought together King David's. Their son was Clodion, born in Tournai, and his son was Meroveus, King of all the Franks, first of the long-haired Merovingian kings whose rule spread south through France. Meroveus's son was Childeric, and his son was Clovis, and their sisters spread the blood, the *sang réal*, into every royal and aristocratic house, and the kings' brothers and cousins were the bishops and warlords of every noble family of Europe; Taliesin and the Pendragons of Avalon, the counts and dukes and sires of Brittany, Liège, Ardennes, Burgundy, the Midi, the Langue d'Oc, all the others. After a thousand years my descendant Charles of Sicily, Count of Provence, found my mother's skull (so he supposed) at Les Saintes Marie and had it set in gold and silver. But I'd long lost interest in my family. The mystery is incalculably huge; my family is everyone. Gradually, generation after generation, they'd forgotten who they were, and thought that kings was all they were. They are you.

★ ★ ★

A man can't know where he goes, Jude, unless he knows where he comes from. And he can't seek his mother without also seeking his father.

My mother knew the truth. To find the truth, I had to find my mother. I had to know her. She was the only way to find a path to God through the sex and death and confusion of this hellish world.

Through despair, through misery and loss, through losing faith in God, she'd found God, God more perfect than she had ever imagined, only to have Him taken from her. So I looked for her wherever misery and despair was deepest, everywhere the battle was lost. On the battlefield I picked through the dead and dying the day after the battle, searched for her among the terribly injured and the women who searched for their men. I searched for my mother in the whorehouses, sick houses, leper colonies, churches, everywhere people lie abandoned. I looked for her in the small room where a child lies dying without a candle in the night, the darkest places closest to Hell.

In the year 415 I found her in the last place I expected: I was bargaining for my evening meal in the busy street market near the ruins of the great library at Alexandria when I felt the weight and age of her close over me and heard a woman speaking. I followed her voice to the roofless, fire-blackened auditorium of the library. Smartly dressed as always, I slipped inside easily. Hell is here even – especially – in libraries and universities surrounded by books, scrolls, ancient genealogies. Most, nearly all irreplaceable, had been lost in the fire and all that remained of one of the greatest centres of learning in the world was a gutted shell, and my mother's voice speaking in it. 'The Emperor fell in love with me, but I converted the Empress and her attendants to my Christianity, and they were good Christians! So the Emperor had them executed for their beliefs! You ask me, why did I refuse to marry the Emperor?'

An old man shuffled reluctantly to one side, making room for me on a sooty stone bench. He nodded through the crowd to the beautiful woman in an indigo gown, her hair piled high pinned with mother-of-pearl, who spoke from the

487

podium. He whispered appreciatively, 'Isn't she a one?'

The woman raised her voice. 'Why did I refuse to marry Emperor Maxentius? Because I am already and for ever the bride of Christ. *Ego me Christo sponsam tradidi.*' That gave a turn; they were my mother's exact words. 'The emperor brought in fifty philosophers to convince me of the errors of my views of Christianity. I beat them all, I converted them to my way of thinking . . .'

The old man nudged my side. 'Come to listen to her for the same reason as the rest of us, eh?'

'What's that?'

'Because she's beautiful.' He coughed, spat. 'Better on the eye than the ear. She could put her mouth to better use, eh?' He made a crude gesture, winked. 'We called her Hypatia when she worshipped the old gods, I liked her better. No reason a woman shouldn't be a great thinker. Filled this place four years ago, standing room only. Hypatia told us we should elevate our human nature by renouncing any interest in the real world – I asked her if she ever took a bath! That got her. She told me if I reached the point of being able to contemplate the Idea of Ideas (that's when the Christians shouted out, did she mean Heaven?) a mystical union would take place between me and the One. Greek teachings, right? Plato. The only union I was interested in was with her, I can tell you! But the Christians shouted out, by One did she mean God? Then they shouted blasphemy, blasphemy, the riot started and that's how it all got out of hand.'

'Who started the fire?'

'The Christians. Just like Saint Paul's Christians burnt all the books of the Ephesians. But this time the whole library and most of the knowledge in the world went up. Gave my eyebrows a good singeing, I'll say.'

I said, 'But now she's a Christian?'

'Oh yes, right old conversion on the road to Damascus. But she isn't a Christian sort of Christian, if you get my meaning. And the Christians still hate her, anyway.'

'Why?'

'Because she's a woman. Worse, she's a beautiful woman, so old farts like me come and listen to her. Christians hate women with brains. Timothy says, "Let the woman learn in silence, with total subjection. I suffer not a woman to teach, nor to usurp authority over a man, but only to be silent." '

'She changed her name when she became a Christian?' Mary, had she chosen the name Mary?

'She calls herself Catharine,' the old man said. 'It means pure. It's her purity and perfection and this bride of Christ nonsense that's got her into trouble with the Emperor. One quick fuck would've shut him up, he'd have got tired of her lecturing soon enough, but would she do it? Now everyone hates her, the emperor hates her because he lost face when she escaped, the worshippers of the old spirits hate her because she turned to Christianity, and the Christians hate her because it isn't their sort of Christianity.' He looked round at a ripple in the crowd. 'She should've stayed in hiding.'

The ripple spread forward, a wave of people pushing from the street. The benches were thrown down as the mob surged towards the podium. Catharine of Alexandria was seized, her arms and legs pulled this way and that by competing mobs of pagans, Christians, and the emperor's soldiers. Her arm was broken, blood ran from her lips that she had bitten in her agony, but then she spoke out again in a strong voice about her love for Christ. One of the Christians punched her in the face to shut her up.

I followed the soldiers taking her to the fortress. The gates slammed in my face.

I returned to the city and waited a few days for her release. No release, no trial. After a week I found a doctor's house and called him from his evening meal. He smiled seeing my fine clothes, knowing I'd call him to a patient who'd pay well. I whispered in his ear, 'I want your hat, your cape, your medicine box and your splints.' He laughed, then saw my frown and stopped. I have a way of frowning. He bowed, trying to deceive me, showed me the room where his knives and spatulae and speculae hung on hooks, then tried to call for help. I put him to sleep, collected everything I thought I'd need, rested his snoring head comfortably on his forearm. Then I left the house with his box under my arm, pulling on the hat and cape that identified me as a doctor over the woman's clothes I wore below. I returned to the fortress at the quietest hour before dawn, to a side gate this time. 'Doctor for the woman, Catharine.'

The soldier lifted his spear to get rid of me. 'You're very tired,' I told him. 'You're weary. You're asleep on your feet. Where is she?'

'The princess?' he slurred. 'Top floor.'

I looked back from the steps set in the thickness of the wall. 'You're asleep.'

I found the upper storeys more like a palace than a fort, large rooms with pillars and marble floors. They were empty at this hour but I sensed my mother's personality like a heavy weight. A slave came forward but I let her go to sleep. I retraced her perfumed footsteps behind the veils to a small stone room in one corner, no larger than a monastery cell. The door was closed but not barred. A self-made prison. Catharine was asleep, dreaming she sat at a table watching the sun rise: my mother was sitting at the small table by the window, watching the star Sirius gleam like a pearl in the coming glow of sunrise. It was the Egyptians' heliacal rising, predicting that today the Nile would begin its annual flood.

I said: 'Mother.'

She didn't turn. 'Sssh. I know who you are. Go away, Jude.'

I took off the doctor's cloak, unlaced the serving woman's clothes from beneath my own. 'Quickly, put these on. It's not too late.' I realised her right arm was swollen, enormous, broken at the elbow. I touched the discoloured flesh tenderly. 'You must be in agony.'

She held a finger of her good arm to her lips, ignoring me. A moment passed, then the top of the sun sliced through the horizon like a *shekinah*. Sirius faded, made invisible by the thickening light. The trumpets blew, announcing the risen sun to the city.

My mother watched me watch the sunrise. 'I still look for your father in you,' she said.

'Do you find Him in me?'

'I don't find Him anywhere, Jude. There's no Christ on this world. It's worse than if He'd never lived.' She looked at her discoloured arm, dug her nails into her puffy flesh. 'This is my suffering. I'm Catharine completely. I'm strong enough to do it, to *be* her, of my own will.'

490

I was in a hurry, the fortress awakening, calls, guards changing. But I knew my mother wouldn't be hurried. 'God made you Mary Magdalene, didn't He?' I said.

'I believe so with all my heart.' She added, 'God makes all of us.'

'You told me you had no choice in it that time you were born.' I checked the window: a hundred feet sheer to the ground. 'Chosen, you said. Was that the truth?'

'Yes. You've never experienced anything like it, Jude. The overwhelming, conscious, omniscient power of it.' She looked into my eyes. 'You have the strongest soul I've ever known. To come such a long way in so short a time.' She sighed. 'It took me a thousand years, much more, to learn what you were born knowing.'

'Look who my father was.'

She said simply: 'Do you know where He is?' So she hadn't found His earthly tomb either, lost somewhere beneath the rubbish tips of Jerusalem.

I heard the tramp of boots echo from the yard, then they stopped. Shouted commands, the neigh of horses, wagons rumbling. Military business.

'Sometimes,' I said, 'I think I catch glimpses of my father. I think I see . . . and then I don't see.' I leant forward urgently. 'Mother, you can still escape.'

She shook her head. Catharine's renowned beauty was ugly after a week at the hands of the soldiers. The sun illuminated dried blood on her face, her broken nose. Her hair hung unpinned, unlacquered, and her arm stank. I don't think they'd fed her at all. 'Or water,' she said, reading my mind. Her voice cracked. 'I'm thirsty.'

I fetched a vase from one of the big rooms, threw out the flowers. She drank. 'Now I shall say an angel brought me water.'

'Am I an angel?'

'You're all too human,' she said. 'So am I.'

'Really?'

'A very ordinary human indeed. A very ordinary little girl.'

'But you were one of the saved people.'

'I don't think there are any saved people in this world, Jude. Just people who think they are.'

'But you saved people didn't just *think*, you *knew*.'

'Yes. We knew we were saved. Until we came here.'

'Then everything you told me was the truth? The whole thing? God's truth.'

'Yes. Every word. I married Jesus Christ. Everything happened. I'm still married to Him. I gave myself as a bride to Christ and I am His for eternity.' She added, 'So are you.'

More calls. Gates slammed. Trumpets blew, drums beat.

'Come with me,' I said. 'I think you're an angel of this world. You've learned to be. I think God only helped a little. But you can't fight against Satan alone.'

She shook her head from side to side. 'Maxentius can't have me, so he'll have me killed. You can't save me.'

'Who can save you?'

'Jesus Christ.' She gestured at the desert beyond the walls, the crowds gathering. 'In front of thousands. *That* will defeat Satan. Faith.'

I stared at her. 'That isn't what happens. He didn't jump down from the Cross in front of thousands. He didn't impose faith.' She'd forgotten her own lessons. 'You can't force God,' I said.

'He'll save me.'

'You're crazy.'

'In love.' She gripped my hand gently with her good hand. 'I'm in love. How else can my love save me, except by setting an example?'

'You can't provoke Him into saving people by your suffering.'

'But He will see. I believe He sees everything, Jude, down to the smallest bacterium in my gut. We have set an example before God. Climb towards God. Writhe towards God on our bellies if necessary.' She tried to make me understand. 'I'm so full of love for Him.'

I sat. Such faith made my legs weak. It was inspiring and frightening.

'You believe,' I said, then corrected myself, 'You *know* that something marvellous happened in Judah.'

'In the Holy Land,' she said eagerly. 'Yes, I saw something happen that was *so much more* marvellous than anything that's happened anywhere before, ever.'

'Even among the saved people?'

'Yes. Much more marvellous even than that. Our Jesus Christ, but new, deeper, higher, greater. Now men and women make pain and suffering and disease and evil again. But there's hope. I live in hope.'

I had only to look from the window, the sheer drop, no hope. 'They'll kill you and no one will care.'

'Then I'll die and die and die until they care. They *will* care. He *will* return, as is prophesied.'

'No, no, Mother, the Roman Empire's all but gone, it's falling in. Sion's a ruin. Without the Empire and Sion, how can all those prophecies of doom come to pass? Harlots and dragons and I don't know what? Have you thought of that?'

Her face fixed. Her eyes glinted suspiciously. 'Did you see it?'

I sat shaking my head. We'd run out of time. 'See what?'

'The Covenant.' She stared. 'You did!'

'Yes, I went to Jerusalem. I saw the Covenant beneath the Temple. I made sure it'll never be found.'

'And James?'

'James is dead. He's gone.'

'What do you mean? James can't be dead!' I'd forgotten she'd loved him once, long ago. 'He's like me, he's the same as everyone. No one dies.'

'His deal with the Devil was all or nothing, Godhood or death. A chance to give up eternal life, his eternal soul. If he won, he'd be all a man can be. If he lost . . . James wanted to let go. He was tired of living in this hell.'

She looked at me longingly. 'Do you think Satan granted him that? Death?'

'Satan has no mercy.'

'But you are the son of Jesus Christ.'

I tried not to think of James as I had seen him. 'Yes,' I said. 'I did as you asked. I killed James. That was mercy.'

She wept.

I said, 'Just before he died, he said he loved you and would have wanted me for his own child by you.'

My mother dried her tears, embraced me with her good arm. 'You gave him peace. That's the greatest mercy. Thank you, Jude, from the bottom of my heart.'

But I thought of my face I'd seen inside the Covenant.

My mouth was close to her ear; I had to know. 'What is it exactly in the Covenant?'

She hugged me without looking at me; it was Catharine's last few minutes of warmth. 'Are you devout, Jude?'

'You know who I am, Mother. How can I not be devout?' I chilled. 'Once you said the AntiChrist would be a devout man used by Satan. A false prophet, a rebel who'll try to take God's place.' I asked her numbly, 'Doesn't that sound like me?'

The son of Jesus Christ, uniquely gifted, uniquely vulnerable, uniquely dangerous. How could I possibly take my father's place? I remembered the dragon of Eden rising from the furnace of Vesuvius, unfallen, unbowed, immense, the Beast.

Still she wouldn't look at me, so she'd wondered about me. She whispered, 'Did you see the words of Moses's God?'

'No. I looked at them. They didn't mean anything. I can't read ancient Hebrew.'

She looked me in my eyes, stroked my hair. 'Then you are not the AntiChrist, Jude. But you're strong, so strong. You may become the AntiChrist. You may.' She shuddered. 'Oh, how I hate to live! God, God, God grant me redemption! God, save me!' She raised her good arm in supplication; the other hung limp and stinking.

'Mother, come with me.' I heard banging doors, the tramp of boots across the fine rooms leading to the cell. 'I can save you, Mother. Quickly, the window—'

'Life isn't salvation.' She stood her ground. 'What do you call yourself here?'

'Trevrizent.'

She understood, smiled. 'The searcher. Are you familiar with the cards of the Egyptian arcana used by my followers here? My' – she mocked herself – 'my very few true Christian followers. To them Mary Magdalene is the Magdaleder, the Tower Magdalene. The Tower of the Flock.' Her mouth twitched. 'Or a tower of fish, if you like.' Did she mean the *Migdal Nunayah* of her childhood? Or Christian fish? 'Sometimes the Magdalene's shown leading a lion, or supporting a broken pillar.' She brushed my lips with her own. 'Doesn't this awful world work in sometimes marvellous ways? I am the woman Pope. I am the naked woman crowned with a halo of stars. I am the source of the sacred River Alphaeus which was forced underground.'

Alphaeus. Hadn't she mentioned that was one of Joseph's titles? And my father had spoken of the alpha.

'Alphaeus,' I said. 'The bloodline. The bloodline!'

'Exactly. The sacred river Alph.'

I heard shouts. The sleeping slave girl had been found.

'But there's so much of it!' I cried. 'What am I supposed to understand?'

'Understand God,' she said gently. 'You are supposed to understand God.'

I heard footsteps running in the corridor. I leant my strength back against the door, held it closed with my shoulders.

'Mother, let me ask you one question. The answer to which can't be known. But which I may one day find out.'

Fists and swords hammered on the door. She said calmly, 'Ask.'

'Mother, you talked of the People of the Isthmus. Are there truly lands beyond the ocean?'

'Yes. Exactly as I described them.'

'The land where storms are started by butterflies?'

'Absolutely. And of horseflies and mosquitoes as big as your fist.'

The blade of a sword struck through the door by my ear.

I demanded, 'And the planet Uranus truly exists?'

Splinters flew. A hand groped between the shattered planks.

'Yes, Jude. In Greek, Ouranos. And it wears a halo of stars. But don't bother about me. I'm not important any more. You must find your father.' She touched her fingertip to my lip. 'Your father.'

No more time. I shook off the hands which clutched at me, the door flew open. I jumped on to the table, and then from the window.

Heads appeared below me from the window, staring down. I stood pressed tight to the wall above the window top, toes and fingertips pushed deep into the gaps between the stones. The men didn't look up. They never do. The heads swore, turning from side to side, then withdrew. My mother screamed as she was manhandled, then there was only the low moan of the desert wind, and the flutter of swifts at their nests on the battlements above me.

I slid down the wall, braced my feet on the ornamental top of a pillar, somersaulted on to a balcony, helped myself to one of the apples piled on a silver salver. 'Here,' the woman said, 'don't go.' I jumped into the garden, vaulted the wall, dusted off my clothes, and threw the apple to a beggar. I had no appetite.

I knew what I'd see.

It was worse.

I pushed to the edge of the arena through the crowd. They roared, threw up their hats as the show began. Chariots, gladiators, I don't know what else, I'd seen more in Rome. Wild animals, misery, death, the roars of the crowd, the women holding shawls over their heads against the fierce sun. My mother was tied to a spiked wheel. The leather ropes from her wrists and heels were pulled taut, arching her back around the rim, the spikes sank into her flesh, she cried out. She shrieked and bled, and Jesus Christ did not come. When the ropes could be pulled no harder they were tied off and doused with buckets of water. The crowd listened fascinated to the wet leather straps creaking as they tightened. She shrieked, then fell silent, her lungs flattened. The shape of her body changed as her bones began to break. A team of slaves heaved on a windlass, and the wheel turned slowly at first, bringing her down almost to the ground then lifting her high into the air. Faster and faster it turned. The axle smoked.

'Look at that!' the man beside me cried exultantly. 'She don't know whether she's going up or going down! Let the clever bitch find her way to her Heaven now! That'll teach her!'

The axle shuddered on its mountings, abruptly the wheel flew apart, the machine collapsed. A heavy fragment of iron rolled into the crowd, killing one or two, injuring others. I heard a child screaming.

My mother was dragged from the broken wheel and beheaded. The crowd roared its disappointment.

★ ★ ★

It isn't the worst thing that happens.

It gets worse.

Everything's wrong. Even the best turns to the worst. How are the priests and great thinkers so accurate, so increasingly accurate, in their belief in the Hell of fire and brimstone? Here on Satan's world part of the joy of the saved comes from imagining the torments of the damned. Suffering proves God's justice and hatred of sin. But I wonder if it proves Satan's power over us, not God's, when babies are born sinful as the African Bishop Augustine says they are – I hear him preach it! – and only the saved go to Heaven (he preaches that too, but he doesn't know what Heaven is at all, no idea, he's clear only about Hell) and Augustine's road to salvation is lit by the bodies of burning sinners. He spends the last half of his life and fifteen books trying to prove the Trinity of God. On the beach at Hippo I watch him walk by a small boy fetching seawater in a spoon, playing at filling a hole in the sand. 'You'll never get all the sea in there, my child,' Augustine says wisely, and the sinful boy looks up at him and says, 'No, and you'll never explain the Trinity in only fifteen books, either.' A flock of seagulls rises like a cloud, and the child's gone. Augustine falls with a crack to his arthritic knees. He believes he's been granted a vision of the Christ-Child, and gives thanks to God, but that doesn't make him a better man. He agonises over the Trinity to his dying day, and fantasises over the purity of the child he saw, and never learns a thing from the child's words.

But I know it wasn't a vision.

My father's here among us, real and actual.

They never do learn.

Who is He? Where is He? Can I touch Him?

I must find my father. The more I learnt the more I realised that without Jesus Christ, we are lost. We don't stand a chance.

How can I find my father if I don't know where to look?

Of course in my heart I knew where to look. The last place I wanted to go.

Jerusalem.

More than seven hundred years have passed since Bishop

Augustine saw my father on the beach at Hippo, and the whole of Jerusalem is a building site. The Muslims of Allah and the Jews of Yahweh were massacred when the city fell and the Christian cross was raised over the battlements in victory, and the air still tasted of dust.

Jerusalem, the centre of God's earth. Nowhere was God or Satan stronger.

A skinny brown child tugged my sleeve. 'Show you where Our Lord wept and water still comes up through the stones? True Cross? Veronica's Veil?'

I tossed a penny to make him go away. He followed me among the buzzing toiling gangs of workmen, flies swarming around us, slaves and prisoners stinking of sweat and blood, shovels and picks scraping and clinking at vast toppling heaps of Muslim rubble. Religion, Jerusalem's only industry. The crusaders rebuilt the looted mosques as churches, each with its fragment of True Cross, though the Church of the Holy Sepulchre (its site decreed by an empress three hundred years after my father's crucifixion) claimed almost the complete item. To pay for the war and these enormous holy works, palaces, fortresses, armies, the jewelled crosses on every golden altar, the thousands of chalices of silver and gold and rubies from which Our Lord took his last sip, pilgrims and their money were drawn from all over Christendom. The safe arrival of both the pilgrims and their money depended on the Knights Templar.

The Order of the Poor Fellow-Soldiers of Christ and the Temple of Solomon was founded a few decades ago to guard the pilgrim road to Jerusalem, but by now the Templars' vast organisation controlled everything in the Holy Land. The Grand Master was more powerful than the King of Jerusalem. Wearing only white, the blood-red splayed Cross of Christ blazoned on their robes, the knights' hair and beards hung uncut to their waists. The wealth of the Order was immense; even their forts were called temples. The network of temples and commanderies, from the mightiest fortresses like the London Temple and the Paris Temple, down to thousands of round temple churches and fortified manors, crisscrossed every country of Europe controlled by the Pope. Mightier than kings, living as simply as monks, the Templars disdained national affairs.

Their authority came directly from the Pope and the Grand Masters answered to him alone. They took orders from no earthly king and paid no taxes. Nothing happened without them. Fleets of Templar supply ships sailed pilgrims from Marseille and Genoa to the vast Temple at Acre. Their men-at-arms escorted pilgrims safely on the bandit road from Acre to Jerusalem, and on arrival the pilgrim found the spending money he'd deposited with the Templars before departure in London or Rome or wherever awaiting him – for a fee.

I watched the pilgrims filing, heads down as they imagined Jesus Christ, along the Via Dolorosa. They prayed at the Holy Sepulchre, inhaled the holy air of Christ, touched the rocks touched by Christ; nowhere near where my mother described my father's tomb, but belief isn't about fact or history. It's about this feeling of truth. The pilgrims' feeling of approaching the truth, of reaching out to truth. And whatever the lies surrounding them, I knew those bowed heads and clasped hands (nowadays every Christian prays kneeling, like James's Nazarenes) did grasp at a slice of the truth, because their Jesus Christ was here in the crypt even if He'd never actually set foot here: like St Paul, they believe Jesus Christ is in everyone, and as you know that's certainly a slice of the truth.

But it's such a small slice.

I left the pilgrim trail and walked uphill on Mount Sion. The child hurried after me, worried I'd lost my way. 'You can't buy anything up here. No Christs. No Madonnas.' His name was Jesús, he was Spanish, his father and mother had been robbed and killed but he didn't believe it, and he was searching for them. I flicked another penny to get rid of him but he stuck to me like a small complaining limpet as I climbed. He was sad for me, all the opportunities to make purchases I was missing.

Up here a thousand years of houses and rubbish had buried almost everything I remembered. A few outlines remained, barely enough for me to find my way. The Temple was gone except for that one piece of wall. A mosque with a golden dome had been built over part of the vast eradicated ruin. But as I came to the top of Mount Sion, higher than I remembered, I heard picks and shovels once more, and dust blew over me.

Over the centuries the summit had been built up with a shambles of hovels and hovels built on top of hovels, a constant organic rebuilding and decay. The Templars had levelled the lot under the biggest building site of all. On the site of the Holy of Holies lines of pegs and twine marked out massive new foundations. Jesús followed my eyes. 'The Templars are building their Jerusalem Temple over the site of the Jews' Second Temple. Stables for two thousand horses underground. Quarters for many thousands of men. Courtyards, fountains. A mighty church shaped in a circle.'

A workman held up a mason's pole, sighting carefully, measured angles with an instrument I'd never seen before. Templars call Muslims Evil Ones yet trade secretly for fine Arab cloths and instruments unknown in the west, lost books of the Greeks and Egyptians, mathematics, maps – so now Templar maps, making much of Muslim algebra in their Golden Line projection, are the finest that can be found. More workmen pushed busily past me, as organised at building as the Templars at war. I watched teams of trained professionals work stone with quick expert strokes of hammer and chisel, marking each finished block with a number and the symbol of their Lodge. The symbols looked like the Egyptian hieroglyphs I've seen in the pyramids. The Egyptians' masonic lodges built the greatest structures in the world and are still revered. From my mother I knew the Jews had imitated their Egyptian masters' system of government, the two pillars of the Pharaoh king-priests who'd united Upper and Lower Egypt, when they escaped from slavery led by Aaron their Hebrew king and their priest, the Egyptian exile Moses. Solomon's architect Hiram had flanked the entrance to the First Temple with two copper pillars, Boaz and Jachin, the two pillars of the world: Boaz the great-grandfather of King David, my father's ancestor, Jachin the priest of Zadok.

'Masons. They serve many years of apprenticeship, many grades.' Jesús nodded at the workmen, hoping for more pennies. 'Masons of great skill. The priests of stones. His Holiness permits them to cross frontiers without passports. No king may stop them or take them for his own work before the Pope's.' Masons were in great demand. Until the thousandth anniversary of Christ's death in the thirty-fourth year of the last century, when many Christians expected the world to end, most buildings were of wood and any stonework was by monk-masons. No Day of Judgment; in an explosion of relief kings and bishops commissioned buildings to last another thousand years, stone churches in place of timber, stone palaces, stone bridges, stone cathedrals. Masons split away from the monasteries and followed the work, forming Lodges to negotiate pay rates, using secret signs and tallies to keep track of their members, growing powerful. The Templars were by far the greatest employers of freemasons.

'The freemasons worship Hiram,' Jesús said. 'In their Lodge churches they kneel between two pillars.'

'Two pillars?'

'They call them Boaz and Jachin.'

I watched the master mason, grey as stone, check the gangs' work against gigantic maps drawn in plaster on the ground. 'Why build here?' I murmured. 'Why exactly here over the old Temple?'

Jesús eyed me. 'The Templars are devout.' He whispered, 'Pain, suffering, humility, sacrifice. That's what they believe in. And that Christ was only a man. And that He did not rise from the dead.' He put his mouth close to my ear. 'It's rumoured they've found a great treasure. Found it, and hidden it.'

'Everyone's heard about the Templar treasure,' I scoffed. 'No one knows what it is. I'm not going to pay for rumours I can hear for free in a wine shop.'

'How much money do you have, Jude?'

Jude's a dangerous name in a Jerusalem full of Christians. The name I had given the child was Trevrizent. I watched him thoughtfully. 'Why do you call me Jude?'

'How much will you pay, if paying money will make you believe what you disbelieve for free?'

'Enough to get you back to Spain.'

He tugged me behind a half-finished wall. 'Show me.'

I showed him the gold and silver coins I always carry, filled his hand with as much as he could hold. Jesús said, 'Now you've paid so much, Jude, will you believe?'

501

I held his collar just in case. 'I'll fill your other hand when you tell me what you know, little Jesús. If you make me believe every word.'

His large brown eyes looked round nervously then gazed straight into my own eyes. 'The Templar masons were digging when they fell down into the foundations of the old Temple. They found a winding staircase.'

I shivered in the heat. 'A winding stair? Where did it go?'

He pouted, 'I knew you wouldn't believe me.'

I shrugged, dropped a coin in his empty hand. 'Tell me anyway.'

'A winding stair going down beneath the ancient foundations.' Now he didn't look at the coins, gazed earnestly into my eyes, and I realised he was going to tell me whether I paid him or not: the truth mattered to the child. 'They fell down into a tunnel. They say these men who fell died. They found the *Bir Arruah* of King Solomon and it devoured them, devoured their souls.'

'*Bir Arruah?*' Muslim words, Arabic.

'The Well of Souls.'

I'd seen it: the pit, the stake, the fetters. The masons had found the demon Asmodeus where I'd thrown him back down to Solomon's ancient prison when I killed James, his possession, on consecrated ground. 'Have there been other killings? Devourings?'

Jesús said sadly, 'There are always lost souls to be found in Jerusalem.'

Through the masons, Asmodeus had once again escaped. I asked, 'Did the Templar knights go down?' Jesús nodded. 'What did they find?'

'Death.' Hiram's tomb, perhaps. Usually the builder was killed on the completion of his greatest work and sealed within its stones, just as in ancient Egypt. 'Death, destruction,' Jesús said wretchedly. 'They found terrible power. The power of Satan.'

'The Arch of the Covenant?'

'Perhaps. And secret knowledge. Knowledge not meant to be known.' The child gripped my hands tight, spilling his coins in his anguish. 'And more. They found life. The Templars found life, Jude. They found what they believed in. Pain, suffering, humility, sacrifice.'

'Is that life to them? I don't understand.'

'Some say they found the tomb of Joseph of Arimathea.'

'But Joseph was never put in his tomb.' I stopped. 'They've found the Tomb of Christ.'

We fell silent at a disturbance. A group of knights wearing surcoats marked with the blood-red cross, white woollen cloaks swirling in the hot wind, walked among the building works. The master mason hurried to greet the leader, a tall black-bearded knight with a sunburnt face. The burns, not recent, had tightened the skin on his cheeks like angry red scars. 'Are you building your walls straight today, Master Mason?' So they were having Solomon's trouble making the walls stand straight.

One of the young aides-de-camp sniggered. 'Perhaps we should ask the help of an angel, master?'

The sunburnt knight glowered ferociously, pulled the young man close by the wall where we hid. We overheard him speak in a low ugly voice away from the others. 'Keep your mouth shut, Bernard, even if you are my son.' The Templar master strode away, the masons running after him like little dogs to answer questions about the building. The young man straightened his clothes, wiped the fear-sweat from his face with shaking hands before rejoining the others.

'I thought Templars lived by the Rule of chastity, poverty, obedience.' I realised how similar that made them sound to the monks of Sion. 'How can a Templar father a son?'

'The master? He's Bertrand de Blanchefort, one of the first Christian knights to ride into Jerusalem. Templars make sure they have sons to perpetuate their blood before they take the oath to the Order. Anyway, de Blanchefort can do what he likes. He's already *Grand Maître de l'Ordre de Notre Dame du Sion*, the most powerful faction among the Templars.' Our Lady of Sion. Here she was again. 'Some call it the Order of the Rose Cross Veritas – you've seen the blood-red cross they wear. Rose means blood, the *sang réal*. The Order of the True Blood. *They* are Templars who believe in the Resurrection. They believe the Resurrection will come in their own lifetimes. They believe they will be the masters of the Resurrection.'

'The masters of God?'

'That they can achieve Godhood in their own lives.' Nothing had changed.

I murmured, 'I'm sure I've heard the name de Blanchefort before.'

'It just means white castle. He'll be Grand Master one day. De Blanchefort's worse than the others. Braver, more ruthless, more depraved, he's renounced all contact with the contamination of women, lives wholly for the Templar brethren. Body and soul. You know what they say about all Templars.'

Everyone knew. 'Unnatural vices.'

'The best, corrupted, becomes the worst. They live in sodomy. Their oath of loyalty is a marriage between men.'

I tried to find something good happening here. 'Yet they love God.'

'They love *their* God.'

'Who is their God?'

Jesús said: 'Their prisoner.'

I swallowed. 'I don't—' But I did. I understood all too much. I put my hands to my head.

Jesús turned my face to his, looking at me, into me, with his enormous eyes as he spoke.

'De Blanchefort, he was the one who discovered the Tomb. The masons had found the tunnel but nobody dared go along it.' My mother had spoken of a tunnel. I knew that tombs were sometimes very large, constructed like houses in the rock, but I'd forgotten the details she'd told me. 'De Blanchefort hung a cloth soaked in oil from the tip of his sword, and he crawled along the tunnel. With the last of the flame he found the Tomb.'

I recalled something I'd heard in a tavern at Acre. 'Is it true the Templar treasure is the Shroud of Christ? Did de Blanchefort find the Shroud lying discarded on the floor?'

Jesús said, 'No, Jude. De Blanchefort found the Shroud wrapped around the earthly remains of Jesus Christ.'

I heard a soft footfall behind me, a bare foot perhaps, and turned. But there was only the soft whicker of doves' wings whirling white against the sky. I turned back and the child Jesús was gone, and my money sparkled discarded on the ground.

★ ★ ★

I'm obsessed.

Who told the Templars where to dig? Was their find accidental? Chance? Really?

Preach to me of accidents and chances when you have seen Satan, as I have.

My father isn't in Jerusalem. I'd know. Where have they hidden Him?

Not here. It's dawn two days later, the sixth hour of the night, the twenty-third of July 1150, and I stand in the ruins of Sion listening to the hiss of sand, of time. I'm obsessed . . . but I'm beginning to fear where my search leads me. By searching for my father, I'm searching for myself. But the deeper I go into myself, the more I'm afraid of what I'll find.

I came back to Sion not to find but merely to delay. To think. To make excuses. Not to do what I know I must do.

Sion, Sion. It isn't here any more, it's dispersed, spread out, spreading forward. I can hardly tell this was a fortress, a monastery, a church; the fragments sticking out of the sand might be all that's left of a villa or a farm, nothing. Except that the place hasn't lost its power. I feel it breathing in the sand, the wind. And against the dawn the two pillars of the gateway stand like two tall legs out of the sand, braced by the vaulted arch *Qimrôn* at the top.

I walk forward into the ruin of the church, stand between a few stark teeth of wall. The roof which opened to the sky is gone, completely open to the last fading stars in the immense glow of dawn, the edge of the sun striking over the Dead Sea like a fierce silver coin. I climb the raised platform, the pulpits where the Christ and the Zadok stood beneath the open roof – and the sun rises in my eyes. And at the same moment, a handspan to the right of the sun and a little higher, Sirius rises above the dark arch *Qimrôn*.

Sirius, brightest and last star in the sky, and no longer red as my mother described it: the star twinkles like a tiny pure diamond almost exactly over the centre of the arch. The coincidence is too precise to be a coincidence.

The Essenes were great astrologers: it's no coincidence, no mistake.

Were the Essenes remembering the heliacal rising of

Sirius in Egypt, the land of their forefathers? Or something else? Something more?

Something more. The star isn't quite where it should be, not quite at the centre of the arch. Not quite precise. Is there something in the sky I can't see? I stare until my eyes water, and Sirius fades to nothing in the blue glare. Gone.

I shout at the top of my voice, the wind snatches it away, gone.

Three hundred years ago Christians from Jerusalem found a cache of scrolls buried abandoned here at Sion, in the ground, in a cave – I see caves burrowed inaccessibly in the cliffs, like eyes. The Christians hurried back to Jerusalem carrying their precious flammable finds on donkeys. All lost, all gone. Nothing burns as easily as words. There was a rumour that the scrolls undermined Christianity, that is to say, priests. That Christ was a man. No Virgin Birth, no miracles. Scrolls all gone, all quietly turned to ash, or filed away among worthless paper trash to be forgotten.

And now the Templars in Jerusalem building their Christian Temple over the site of the Jews' Temple.

Bertrand de Blanchefort. I knew the name was familiar. As so often, not only the name of a family but also the name of their place. Blanchefort! I know it.

I know where my father lies. I know where de Blanchefort and the Templars of the Rose Cross Veritas have taken their prize, where they've hidden the most valuable possession in Christendom.

Satan has the body of Christ.

I return to the rural peace of my country, southern France, the Langue d'Oc. A hundred years ago a new church was built over the old wooden one on the mountain at Rennes-le-Château, on a foothill of nearby Mount Bugarach, and dedicated to my mother. My boots, soled with metal studs, tock loudly as I cross the cobbled square and the men drinking or drunk at the tavern look up, and the women talking at the fountain fall silent. I like to make a big entrance.

My boots tread silently on the dusty path into the church, silently in the earth-floored nave for ordinary worshippers, then tock steadily on the paving stones across the chancel where the pillars of the community worship. The church smells of woodworm and decay, a mouse squeaks; Christianity in the Langue d'Oc of the Cathars is by now very different from worship elsewhere, but no less Christian. A Black Madonna stands three feet high in its niche, a halo of stars round her head. I call out, 'Mother?' The roof vault echoes but there's no reply. The door to the tower's locked but I reach out, touch, and the metal clicks open. My boots tock on the winding stair in the tower as I climb. No priest stops me; the Cathars have no priests, only *perfecti*, the pure in heart. Anyone can achieve perfection, even in this world. Even the lowest Cathar peasant believes himself or herself made equal in spirit, under God, with the best aristocrat, and that men and women are personally responsible for their actions and possess rights as well as duties, and can improve themselves by their own efforts without the sacraments of the Church. 'Mother,' I call, 'I know you're here.'

I stand on the tower and stare at that immense view of Templar hilltops. I've not been idle; many things are clear to me. The peasant name Mount Bugarach means exactly what it says: Mount Buggery. Peasants have long memories, folk legends of the Bulgars, their descendants the aristocratic Templar families of the Langue d'Oc. From here I can see Peyrolles, Arques, Alet, St Gilles, Blanchefort, Col Doux, many others, fitting as precisely into the vast geometry as the stones that go together to build a cathedral. The church at Peyrolles is a Templar *commanderie*, as is the Château d'Arques. The Benedictine abbeys of Alet and St Gilles are in Templar hands, granted by the Pope. Watchtowers and church towers fly the splayed blood-red cross of the Templars. And that white castle on the crag between Rennes and Col Doux is the Château de Blanchefort, family seat of Bertrand de Blanchefort, now elected Grand Master of the Templars.

Blanchefort is the place.

I left the church more discreetly than I'd arrived, strolled past teams of woodcutters on the track to Serres – then saw another Templar guardpost in the village. I drew back, climbed the steep tree-clad slope towards the crag of

Blanchefort. From its cliff top the castle seemed almost to overhang the steep Blanche valley below, its turrets clustered over the edge of the drop as if observing the scree slopes of Col Doux rising on the far side. Access from upstream was guarded by the tiny village of Bugarach, little more than a Templar guardhouse. Trees and vegetation ran wild on Col Doux, no woodcutters worked there, perhaps it was demon-haunted; then I saw a party of knights dismounting by the stream far below. They looked around them then one by one disappeared into the trees; a path had been cut but was well concealed, even my eyes could not discern it. A few minutes later the sun flashed off armour some way uphill. I settled down to wait. Much later the three Templar knights emerged above the tree line on to the slopes of grey broken rock, climbing steadily in the heat of the day. Still no sign of a path, but there must have been one, or the scree would have swept them away. Their tiny figures flashing with the sun climbed across a huge loose tongue of debris, the crumbling cliff above it directly opposite Blanchefort.

Where the scree looked steepest and most dangerous, the knights stopped.

One by one they shrank and disappeared as if by magic – as if the hill had opened and swallowed them. I stared, rubbed my eyes. No wonder the place had such a reputation woodcutters wouldn't go there. No doubt the Templars had spread rumours of demons so that the place almost guarded itself. I waited, yawning.

I remembered the woodcutters talking. In the Oc peasants pronounce Col Doux as Cardou. For a moment in my mind it sounded exactly like *Corps Dieu*.

Corps Dieu, the body of God.

The knights walked up out of the ground. The evening sun stamped their shadows up the scree behind them as they came stumbling downhill. One man went ahead watchfully, sword drawn. The other two followed carrying something between them. Their cloaks blew in the wind, obscuring my view, then their burden flashed golden in the rays of the sun.

They carried a tall gold grail encrusted with jewels, one man to each handle. It swung heavily, full. They must have been exhausted carrying its weight but would not rest. The treetops rose over them. Finally they reappeared out of the hidden path, passed up the gold grail to the first man who had mounted his horse, then all three rode away together, carefully. Reverently.

I waited until dark, and then I waited a little longer, until the moon rose over the shoulder of the mountain. I crossed the silvery moonlit Blanche into the silver trees, finding the path at once by the illumination in the treetops, and climbed into darkness as the slope steepened. The track of crushed gravel, invisible from below, crunched reassuringly under my boots to guide me. Blanchefort glowed like milk across the valley, but now that I crossed the steepest slopes of the mountain I was hidden deep in the moon's shadows, and I came to the place.

I knelt.

The moon swung in the sky, its radiance sliding up the scree slopes below me. Here alone was a boulder. I pushed, it would not move. I reached beneath, touched a handle. A windlass handle turned as I pushed at it, and the mountainside creaked, and a door opened.

I stared. A ramp led into the mountain to a shining door.

I ducked inside and the windlass rattled free, slamming the outer door behind me. I stood in total darkness. Reached forward. The inner door, massive, oak, bound with bands of brass, felt icy cold under my fingers. I struck it with my fists, no sound. Kicked, and the door did not move.

I touched the sides lightly with my fingertips, felt two iron locks. I reached forward in the way you know, and the locks thudded open.

The door swung open, and the smell of burning pitch like Hell came out.

I coughed in the smoke of a flambeau, its tip still burning from the knights' visit. I took a fresh torch from a wall bracket, lit it and touched its flames one by one to flambeaux mounted in brackets along the walls as I walked forward.

A tunnel had been dug deep into the mountain.

As I walked up the slope the rough rock walls gave way to smooth marble, black, with glints of gold. I came into a high room gleaming with reflections of darkness and gold, the walls inscribed with masonic symbols, drawings of machines I don't know – I recognised an astrolabe like the one I saw used in the Temple. A pair of masonic dividers. The masonic All-Seeing Eye. Beautifully worked in gold, an Egyptian *ankh* that looked unnervingly like the Cross.

I walked forward and the light grew, throwing back a golden radiance. Statues of golden angels, cherubs, the mournful savage figure of the demon Asmodeus, chained. But when I touched the chain it fell away: Asmodeus unchained. At the middle I found standing two tall gold pillars, Boaz and Jachin, their headless tops – no arch *Qimrôn* joined them – carved with golden shapes of strange fruit that I don't know. To the sides ten lesser pillars of gold in attendance, representing the ten lesser apostles ranking below the Two Pillars.

Between Boaz and Jachin two golden doors meet at the centre. I push with all my strength. Slowly, smoothly, the solid gold swings aside. I walk up golden steps. This room is itself the keystone, or contains the keystone, the One, that joins the two pillars of the world.

Hardly a tomb; a chamber circular as a Templar church, a fabulous display of wealth. Here's the menorah, the seven-branched candlestick of hammered gold long believed lost, looted from the Temple by the Romans. I walk round the curved edges of the room staring in awe and terror at what has happened. Skeletons of the saints – or perhaps of the damned, I don't know. A spear, the spear that pierced my father's side? Splinters of wood, the Cross? And here stands the battered trunk of acacia wood that I remember, its scars smelling of the sand and desert heat of the wilderness where it was manhandled for forty years, the blood of countless battles, the cold black stone beneath the Temple: the Arch of the Covenant.

Why can't the Templars use it? Why aren't the Templars, the Keepers of the Covenant, the *Notzri ha-Brit*, victorious at Armageddon as was prophesied by Sion long ago, the nations of the world lying helpless at their feet?

I can't help it. I reach out. The hairs stand up on the back of my hand. My hair jumps erect on my head. The sceptre of Moses laid on top of the Arch turns towards my outstretched hand. I imagine it. I step back. I imagined it.

I imagined using it.

Something bumps into my spine.

I turn slowly, the studs of my boots grating on the marble floor.

It's an altar of pure white marble at the very centre of the room. On top of the white altar lies a gold casket as long as a man, only as long as a man. But for a moment it seems immense.

I climb the white marble steps and look in the open top of the casket.

'Oh my God.'

I know him.

'Oh my God, my father.'

He lies wrapped in a linen shroud, sleeping. His blood seeps through the wrapping, dripping. He's dead. He can't breathe. He can't move. His face is seeping blood and sweat like wounds through the shroud, tears trickle from under His closed eyes, they trickle through the shroud and drip down dripping into Holy Grails like the one I'd seen the knights carrying, like the ones Nicodemus would have used to store the holy blood and internal organs of the embalmed body. Now I know where the Holy Cross of the *sang réal* that the Templars wear comes from. The blood trickles like a crown around His head, the nail holes in His wrists and heels drip like mouths.

'You're alive,' I whisper. 'Father, you're alive.'

I reach down, touch. Feel. His body is warm. Full of life. I feel the warmth filling my arm, filling me, filling my heart. I felt my strength grow, and my humility. This is an awful place! This is a terrible place!

I knelt. 'My God, what have they done.'

He bleeds. He bleeds.

In front of my eyes I see the golden words hammered deep into the sides of the casket, each letter set with a king's ransom in jewels and precious rubies. Greek, Hebrew, Latin, I can't tell.

ARAM MENAHT MENOU.

511

MORS IANUA VITAE

death is the gateway to life

We never escape our birth.

'I knew you'd find me,' my mother said. In Siena I confronted her on the stair, from the top step, the boards eaten away by worm, her thin face turned up towards me as she climbed: her face a pallid skull of suffering, her thin cancerous body a bundle of sticks tied together beneath her nun's habit. I could have snapped her arms and fingers like twigs. 'You're strong, my cardinal,' she acknowledged, then touched my sleeve and my silver rings, my cardinal-red robe, as though they tainted her. She shuddered, praying. 'Give them to the poor!' When I didn't reply she said: 'I've hidden from you, Jude. This is Satan's world. God is overwhelmed. God is defeated.'

'Jesus Christ is alive, Mother.'

'I know!' she cried.

'I mean actually alive. His heart still beats.'

She screamed at me, but I knew her for my mother.

The one thousand three hundred and eighty-first year of Our Lord, and Catharine Benincasa's the twenty-fifth child of a wool dyer – yes, a dyer, like Levi! No escape. Catharine's twin died beside her in childbirth, the legend of the Twin Pillars living on in the story among these people that Jesus was Himself a twin. My mother's as obsessed as I; more, still searching, straining for the truth. I felt cancer growing like a lead weight in her belly. Not forty years old and her teeth all fallen out, her gums bloody with disease and starvation. She lived deliberately in this suffering body, writing in her agony alone in the night, in her despair, in her loss. To the common people my mother was the holiest woman in Christendom, unwashed, black with filth, brilliant, crawling with lice, animated and demented by her furious love for Jesus, her rage for God. I'd watched her for days and nights, followed Catharine back here to Siena from the Vatican, stood by her convent cell watching her dreams, her back arched in desperate love, her lust for the blood of God. Her love, her unrequited passion, her intensity of suffering, worried me. Children followed her, women touched the hem of her black Dominican robe wherever she went. They called her Catharine of Siena, the glorious virgin.

The stench of sewers and rubbish pits gusted on the hot Italian wind, carrying the plague. She elbowed past me on the creaking stair as though I, Cardinal Salamandari, were no one, and my valets and guards and priests gasped at her *lèse majesté*, but I waved them back. Yes, guards. There are two Popes, my holy master ruling in Rome and Satan's Pope in Avignon, and not even a cardinal's safe from assassination. 'Look at you!' Catharine spat angrily over her shoulder. 'The Pope you serve torments his enemies on the rack, tortures them to force them to accept salvation, burns them alive for the good of their souls, and you say Jesus is alive?'

I said, 'The Pope means only to bring the damned to his God, the God of love, yes.'

She turned on the top step above me, spat full in my face. 'Have you no blood in your belly, Cardinal Salamandari? Is hatred your God of love?'

My priests paled. Only Catharine of Siena talked to a cardinal of Rome like this; she ranted at Pope Urban himself the same, I've heard her. She was mad and dangerous, but goodness shone out of her raddled skin and staring eyes like a light. People are torn apart for saying less than she, but none of my priests dared touch her. As she went ahead of me I turned to them. 'Stay here.'

She pushed open a rotten door, and I followed her inside.

The stench, the darkness, struck me like a blow. I held a fine expensive orange to my nose, I chewed a clove, but even so the stink of rat-droppings and death made me sick. Vomit spattered my gown, my crucifix. The attic stretched out long and dark, knives of sunlight stabbing between roof tiles where last night's rain had poured, where now the huddled figures who'd shivered through the wet and cold suffered the appalling heat of the Sienese day. The sun rippled over the pale figure of Catharine as she stepped forward through the darkness, stooped by a dying man, prayed for him, held his head to her belly despite his dripping sores. I've never seen such love with my own eyes, never experienced such love. She eased him with her prayers. My mother touched his diseased human flesh, lowered her face to him, reverently licked the pus from his wounds.

'Mother,' I said gently, 'I believe my father is all around us. Why do you punish yourself so harshly?'

'To be like Him.' She lifted a dying child. 'To forsake myself and all creatures utterly, to be only myself. Pure spirit. To hide myself fully in Jesus. To find His love again.'

I choked on the stench. 'Love? You find love here?'

'To be transformed by love into my Lord.' She kissed the child's face, its eyes, its bleeding gums. 'So that I don't think, don't understand, don't love, don't have a mind, only God. Not to love myself, only God. To give myself to Him utterly so that my soul is mated to God. I trust only in Jesus Christ, not in myself.' She laid the child's body lightly on the straw. 'I've chosen pain to bring me to Jesus Christ, to bring Jesus Christ to *me*. Chosen suffering. Chosen humility. Chosen sacrifice.'

I knelt beside her among the dying, whispered, 'You know I discovered His earthly body.'

My mother said passionately, 'What I know is that we must improve this world so that we can come to Him, so that His Spirit and His body will rise from the dead! And because we *should*, we *can*.' She cuddled some woman's ghastly face to her breasts, cried exultantly, 'We can! We have the strength.'

Someone, trembling, lifted himself to kiss my ring. I muttered a blessing round the orange, then realised my mother stared directly into my eyes. 'Is He in Jerusalem, Jude? Will the Resurrection be there?'

I shook my head. Christians believe that they, not the Jews, are the saved people. Jews are confined to ghettoes and called the murderers of God, their scriptures are burnt, and they're forced to wear yellow badges as symbols of their damnation. Despite its cruel treatment of the enemies of God, Christianity has not yet redeemed Christians from God's wrath. Jerusalem's lost to the Evil Ones, the followers of Muhammad, who like the Templars believe Jesus was not the Son of Allah but only a prophet. The Templars were driven out of the Holy City nearly two hundred years ago, after the disastrous Battle of the Sermon of the Mount in Galilee – the same place, by legend, that Jesus made His great speech to a multitude gathered between two horns of rock; no doubt my mother knew the truth or lie of that for a fact. What I know is that after their victory the Muhammadans marched north through Spain towards the Langue d'Oc, until it seemed sure France would fall.

'My father's earthly body had been taken from Jerusalem by the Templars before the city fell, and hidden in France.' My mother nodded impatiently; she knew. I went on, 'But when Jerusalem fell to the Evil Ones even France was deemed unsafe, and the Templar Grand Master of England, Geoffrey de Prudome, ordered the prize removed to London for safekeeping.'

'London!' She covered her mouth. 'London's a dreadful place! What do you know of London?'

I'd kept vigil over my father's body at Corps Dieu for nearly thirty years. From a turret of Blanchefort I'd seen Bernard de Blanchefort, Bertrand's grandson, climbing up to the tomb in 1187 after the battle to save Jerusalem was lost, Sir Geoffrey de Prudome the English Grand Master with him, and young Sir Nicholas de Mason carrying a book of numbers roped to his waist beneath his Templar tabard. The book had been given to the young knight in the Holy Land by an Arab trader, *Šayk* Muhammad, a deadly enemy, yet bound by an oath of hospitality not to harm the Templar. Sir Nicholas had been promised that no harm would befall him except by his own hand. The knights had spoken of the little volume as though it were a holy scripture, calling it the Book.

I said, 'The three Templars took the gold casket bearing the body of Jesus Christ, still wrapped in His shroud, downhill on their shoulders, and placed it on an ordinary cart. They covered it with a tarpaulin, but I saw the gold and the jewelled words ARAM MENAHT MENOU shining through. For days, a common peasant, the sort of man no one notices, I followed their struggle with the cart through the rain across the foothills of the Pyrenees towards Bordeaux. Sometimes I watched them from the shade of a tree, drinking a cup of wine; they never saw me. I think they were more interested in the Book than in the body of Christ. A fourth knight joined them, Geoffrey de Charney, who knew nothing of the Book, but one night he took the opportunity to steal the shroud and carry it off to his family home in Normandy. Meanwhile the Master lay with Sir Nicholas in the forest and whispered to him, "Give me the Book." '

My mother demanded sharply, 'What was in the Book?'

I shrugged; I'd not thought it important. 'I don't know. Numbers.'

'Numbers!'

'Yes, that's all. Nicholas believed it was a collection of ten ciphers, or *sephers*, ten enciphered books of wisdom. Something to do with the Kabbalah.' The Kabbalah started off as books of grace written long ago by mystical rabbis but were now much prized by Arab mathematicians. Kabbalists, like Essenes, believed the Bible was not only true, but also contained layer after layer of deeper truth concealed within it, deep truths that could be expressed as numbers. I remembered my mother telling of Judas Zadok's revelation at Sion, his preaching of a beast that came up out of the sea, *And the dragon gave the beast his power and great authority, and the number of the beast was the same as the number of a man. And the number of God is 3. And the number of the created earth is 4.* Each holy letter that comprised the Old and New Testaments had its particular place and number which added up to special meanings, greater truths. As a cardinal I know that only *Peshat*, the simple words, are revealed (in Latin which they do not understand anyway) to the ordinary people. *Remex*, the next level of comprehension, is revealed only to priests such as myself. Kabbalists, like Essenes, believe in *Derash*, the meaning of the Bible under the Law of Moses, and *Zod* is the level of most secret, most sacred interpretations which require peshers, or keys to the code, to decipher the hidden meaning. Judas Zadok had

516

understood well. *His name Immanuel adds up to 543, in congregations also 543. This is the Word of God and shall be His Covenant with us. One day all will be revealed to you under the sun. And the number of the beast is 666.* To the Kabbalists, as to Essenes, the Word of God was coded in numbers. I remembered my mother telling me, *Numbers don't change with language; they're their own language. Roman, Greek, Hebrew, Egyptian, even the glyphs and bar-dot numbers of the Maya of the Isthmus: some arithmetics are quicker than others, but they all add up to the same result however ancient they are.*

Now my mother jerked at me, almost toppling the cardinal's mitre from my balding head. 'Did Sir Nicholas understand the Book?'

I considered. 'I think he was frightened of it. He thought it contained magic, perhaps terrible magic. Sometimes he read a page with staring eyes, an expression of terror. I think, Mother, he'd come by the Book through weakness not strength. Some crime he'd committed. The Book entranced him to his soul, but he knew he'd been given it by Šayk Muhammad as a punishment.'

'What punishment?'

'Perhaps to the sheikh being a Christian Templar was crime enough.' Then I told my mother how the three knights came at last to Bordeaux, the Templar ship *Baucent* hoisting its skull-and-crossbones flag ready to sail. I told her how I was a sailor aboard *Baucent* as the Biscay storms fell calm in her path, and how the wind backed to the east to blow the vessel up the Thames to London, gliding between the stumps of the new stone London Bridge that were already cracking and collapsing, the drawbridge of the old wooden bridge raised to allow us through, and how we came alongside the wharves of the London Temple in a lightning storm. 'Mother, I saw the knights carry the gold casket containing the body of Jesus Christ into the round church at the centre of the Temple. The knights drew their swords and proclaimed the place the Temple of God and the Priory of Sion. All the knights pressed their foreheads to the hilts of their drawn swords in prayer and devotion. But Sir Nicholas gave a shout, "No!" Threw down his sword, his armour, his tabard, stood naked before the brethren clothed only in his white linen loincloth and white Templar cloak marked with the Cross of His Blood, the true Blood of Christ. Then he unroped the Book from his waist and sent it sliding across the stone floor to the Master's feet. He renounced his membership of the Order, turned his back, ran away. But the Master picked up the Book and called after him in a very deep voice, "You are a man, Nicholas. You cannot deny your nature." But still, young Nicholas, no longer a knight, ran away into the dark clad only in what he was wearing. Then the elder knights carried the gold casket of Christ down the winding stair to the crypt of the church.'

My mother repeated, 'The Priory of Sion?'

'That's what I overheard. A year later, in 1188 in the French town of Gisors, the Templars split formally into two factions, those who knew only that the body of Christ had been stolen from Corps Dieu, and those who knew it had been carried to London and hidden in the crypt of the Templar church. This second group of Templars called themselves Knights of the Rosy Cross, the Rosicrucians, and wore the Blood of Christ.'

My mother cradled a dying woman and her girl-child. 'He's still alive in this world.' She murmured: 'It's the most horrible thing I've ever heard.'

'Yes.'

'You don't know where His body is exactly?'

'In the crypt, I presume.'

'You don't know London,' she said wearily. 'He's not hidden in the crypt. Oh, God, there's no end to it.'

I asked gently, 'No end to what?'

'Evil.' My mother kissed the lips of the woman, put forward all her strength to save the life that trickled away, to save the flickering soul, but the woman's head lolled back. I performed the last rites. The baby whimpered for milk and my mother pressed it to her own dry cancerous breast, but even her power could not make one drip flow.

I said, 'What evil?'

She sighed. 'After Jerusalem and the Crusades were lost, and the Muslims were victorious, and the power of the Church was full of doubt and endangered from within, to preserve the unity and purpose of the Church the Pope turned Christian against Christian. He set the Templars against their own people, the Cathars of the Langue d'Oc.

The Cathars were declared heretic, excommunicated. Whole towns of Cathars were put to the sword. Villages were burnt. Every hideout, every hilltop fort, was besieged and defeated. Every Cathar who did not renounce his or her belief was burnt alive.'

As Cardinal Salamandari I said, 'His Holiness does not make mistakes.'

'Every cave was searched.'

'But the body of Christ was not found, for He was no longer there.'

She held out the child to me, said fiercely, 'Don't you see how dreadful men and women are and how they're destroying everything good in this world?'

'Is this your Satan?' I said, and blessed the child.

She said: 'We both know Satan lives and Hell is real.' But she took the child and it looked up peacefully into her face, into the enormous eyes of Catharine of Siena full of love, the darkness and sunlight brilliant around my mother, and I saw she truly was the Black Madonna whom the Pope forbids us to worship as Jesus's mother or His wife. He permits icons to the Virgin in no other colours but blue and white, which is why the common people often call the Virgin the White Madonna. But looking at the dark figure of my mother now, as she cradles the baby in her lap, and I see her love, I am filled with love for her to the point of adoration. Truly she is the wife of Christ.

'Everything's wrong,' she murmured. 'Everything we try to do for the better, we make worse.' The child lay dead in her arms. 'We're helpless.'

I said: 'Over seventy years ago, at dawn on Friday the thirteenth of October 1307, every Templar in France was arrested and the power of the Order was broken. Their lands were stolen by the king, their castles seized. But the king found only old men in his prisons, and no sign of the Templars' vast wealth. The Templar fleets had already sailed from La Rochelle, Boulogne, Bordeaux westward into the ocean, skull and crossbones flying from the mastheads. They were never seen again.'

She moved her emaciated, loving face into a barb of sunlight. 'Tell me what you know, Jude.'

'That you told me the truth, Mother. There's a land

across the ocean. The Templars sailed with the wind and I sailed with them, Trevrizent the navigator, and we sailed holding the star Merak on our starboard side, just as you told me my father did, to the land the Templars call Meraka.'

'And you saw the butterflies?'

'Yes, butterflies! And storms! And the great ring of islands leading to a vast curving isthmus where the people still worship Quetzalcoatl, Jesus Christ, just as you said.'

'And another ocean beyond?'

'Yes. Stretching to the end of the world. Is that what the Essenes meant by the end of the world?'

'The world is round, Jude.' I stared uncomprehendingly. She touched my face. 'The world is round, Cardinal Salamandari. It has no end. Its end is its beginning.' From her knees she slumped sideways, sitting, holding herself up on one arm among the dying. She gave a weak radiant smile. 'Did you see the mosquitoes?'

'And the horseflies. Big as my hand.'

'I always tell the truth.'

'But what does it mean, Mother? With the Templars I sailed north towards Merak the star, holding Meraka on our starboard hand, and we came to the island they call New Jerusalem where they have their city. They call the land beyond the water and the river New Sion. The forest, the river, has no end.' I stopped, trying to imagine a round world. 'Mother, I don't understand what it means!'

'It means this world always makes its own way.' Her dry fingers gripped my hand, my ring. 'Did the Templars take their greatest treasure with them?'

'I don't believe so. There wasn't time. The drawbridge of the stone London Bridge would've had to be specially raised to allow a masted ship to escape from the Temple. No, I believe the body of Christ is still in the crypt beneath the Templar church. The walls of the fortress were knocked about and carried away for masonry, but the central buildings and citadel were so massively constructed that they're used as repositories for state and legal papers, arrest warrants, judicial documents, land titles and I don't know what else, thousands of them. The English State depends on the Temple.'

She murmured, 'There's a second crypt below the first. He's safe.'

'A second crypt? Whoever heard of such a thing?'

'Cardinal Salamandari, you are like a newborn child who sees and hears only chaos.' She stroked my face tenderly. 'Jude, there is order and sense in the world. You have to understand. It is all so simple.' She pulled on me, trying to raise herself, but could not. 'Now tell me what happened to the Book.'

'That Sir Nicholas threw down? I don't know. The Master, de Prudome, took it.'

'Where?'

'I don't know.' I stared into her eyes, her lovely eyes in her ravaged face. 'Why's it so important?' I leant so close our faces touched. 'Why, Mother?'

'The Book is a copy of what you saw in Jerusalem, in the Arch of the Covenant.'

I remembered the acacia wood box, remembered crawling to it on my belly beneath the collapsed Second Temple. Remembered the stone tablet sliding from the Covenant into my hand. The pages of marble not much thicker than papyrus carved with the simple *tau* cross, but more ornate, as though once encrusted with as many jewels as any Bishops' Bible today.

'My God,' I said, understanding. 'I wasn't the first. Who was there before me?'

'Oh, it's a famous story. Long ago when the Hebrews were prisoners in Egypt in Sinai the Land of the Moon, and when Moses, enshrouded, came down from his time in the mountain with God, and broke the Ten Commandments when his people would not believe in them or in God, even the fragments blinded all those who saw them. Later the Sages of Tanna, the seventy holiest rabbis, gave their eyes trying to see the Word of God. But Rabbi Simon ben-Yohai was the first man to fully see them, for he was already blind.'

I didn't want her to talk about it. 'Mother, I saw something terrifying in there.'

'Listen. This is before the fall of Jerusalem. Ben-Yohai was a Christian, a *minim*, and his zealot followers called him the Lamp of Israel for his preaching and rabble-rousing. The Romans threw ben-Yohai into prison for twelve years.

The prison was a cave beneath the Temple.'

'God help us. He touched the Arch of the Covenant. The marble book slid into his hand just as it did mine.'

'For twelve years ben-Yohai transcribed an exact copy of the radiance he saw stamped on his eyelids into ten books. Even his followers thought he was mad. But his son Rabbi Eliezer smuggled them out past the guards and called them the ten ciphers, the *sephers* of God. Nowadays Kabbalists give them names like the Book of Brilliance and the Book of Splendour. They decipher all sorts of meanings from them, *Remex, Derash, Zod*, all that. But they aren't ciphers, Jude. The greatest secret is that there's no secret. They're just numbers, Arabic numbers, exactly what ben-Yohai transcribed without understanding. Only numbers.'

'This was the Book that Sir Nicholas was given in the desert?'

'A copy of it, probably made in Barcelona by Rabbi Judah ben-Barzillai, which fell into Arab hands when Barcelona was overrun.'

My mother fell slowly on to her side, exhausted.

'You can't let them have the power of the Covenant.' She gripped my wrist. 'You can't trust anyone. You can't trust yourself. You can't trust *me*.'

The sun moved across her face, making her seem almost transparent. I lifted her lightly in my arms; her body was almost all cancer. Her heart fluttered like a trapped bird. I groaned. It seems I only ever really know my mother in the moment of her death.

'The Templar Master took the Book,' I whispered. 'I don't know what Geoffrey de Prudome did with it. I know he died in the year 1212. He was supposed to have doused himself in brandy and set light to himself. Every inch of skin was burnt from his body. He took nine days to die.'

My mother whispered, 'He read the Book.'

I hissed, 'What is it in the Book if it's not codes?'

My mother's eyes had turned up. Her voice rattled, speaking from the grave as the last breath sighed between her lips.

'Instructions.'

Within the week Cardinal Salamandari died of the plague.

His physician staggered from the deathbed wearing a leather mask and perfume bottle to keep out the fumes of death, past the bonfires lit in the great bedroom of the palace to burn infected air, and stumbled into the street. The plague was already in his blood, and he fell down beside a young man lying dead drunk in an alley. After a while the young man stood up and walked away, and whenever his name was asked he replied, 'Trevrizent.' He had few memories of his early life as a thief and pimp, but the wanderlust was in him, and from that day on his luck changed. If anyone who'd known him lying down and out in Siena had met him they wouldn't have recognised him: fine leather clothes and a velvet cap, jewels on his hands, money always in his purse. And the more he gave to the poor, the richer he became.

My journey took me north from Siena into France.

I stopped in the small farming town of Lirey in Normandy, intrigued by the reputation of its church. Besides the usual saints' bones it was supposed to possess the Shroud of Christ, and each Friday the Shroud was said to sit up of itself to impart grace to the townsfolk. I waited, and come Friday in the shadows beneath the dumpy church tower the Shroud indeed raised itself from its bier, and revealed to us the face of Christ stamped in blood just as I knew Him, no fake. But when I looked beneath the bier I saw a sandalled priest crouching, his hands pushing on the broom-handle that lifted the Shroud. The descendants of the thief de Charney had fallen on hard times after the dissolution of the Templars, and times must have got harder for them, for later I heard the Shroud was sold to someone in Turin.

There was no plague during the winter and as soon as the roads were dry I travelled to England in good health, only to find the county of Kent in uproar. The Dover innkeeper cried out the Archbishop of Canterbury was murdered by a mob of peasants. The King, who was fourteen years old, was dead. No, the King was not dead. On the London Road I heard the Lord Mayor of London had raised the drawbridge of London Bridge against the rebels, but no, the innkeeper of the Pope's Head at Vaudey said the common people dropped it down again and broke the mechanism, and welcomed the rebels into the City.

In Southwark a prison was burning and the smell of smoke gusted after me between the narrow houses of London Bridge as I crossed beneath the archbishop's severed head on its pole. From the bridge chapel I saw the Temple blazing upstream like an enormous bonfire where Wat the tiler and Jack Straw, who led the rebels, burnt the poll tax records. 'Piling 'em on with shovels,' a woman screamed. 'I saw our Wat, it was him, and I shook him by his hand, and I said bless you you're our boy! Burn the tax! Burn the rich!'

It was time to throw off my clothes and run with the crowd through the firelit streets. Night fell. The gates of London were thrown open. I ran into Fleet Street then stopped in awe at sparkling clouds of cindered paper whirling and falling around me from the sky where the roaring flames of the Temple had lifted them. Some jolly lads raping a woman invited me to join them and I cracked their heads, and the woman killed them with a pin from her hair, then put her hands on her hips and bussed me with a great kiss. A gentleman was tossed from his upstairs window, a rope round his neck, and she ran forward grabbing his feet, and his family screaming tried to pull him up, but she swung from him until his neck broke. Past me churchmen ran waddling for their lives like fat white swans through the dark, and the mob swarmed after them and beat them to death.

I crept into the shadow of a massive black wall, slipped through a ruined gateway, then stared up at the vaulted arch, *Qimrôn*, above me. Something had survived.

The Dovecote Tower and the long-derelict Templar dormitories, armouries, stables, burnt like paper. At the centre the round church was untouched, though I saw the flames of torches in the windows. Inside my feet slid on blood, and I inhaled the sweet smell of death as I stepped over the bodies. 'Will you talk to me, monk?' a voice roared. One, two, three, I counted thirty-seven headless bodies as I stepped forward, and by the altar an axe-blade flashed down among struggling figures, and a tonsured head rolled gleaming from the steps into the bodies below.

The men at the altar threw down the body, and another monk was dragged forward. He drew himself up, saying, 'I am the Prior of Sion.' His head was severed from his neck with seven bangs from the axe, his body thrown down. A tradesman who could count called out, 'Thirty-nine, Jack!'

'Lucky forty,' Jack said, hefting the axe. An old monk was dragged to the altar by his white nape-hair, the bloody axe-blade was thrust against his face. 'Will you talk to me, monk? Where is the treasure of the Templars?'

The monk did not understand; I would swear he did not understand. Everyone knows of the fabulous Templar treasure, but no one truly knows any more what it is. Some say the gold cup of Christ, others gold and jewels looted from Constantinople, some say the bloody veil that Bernice pressed to the face of Christ on the Via Dolorosa. Whatever it is, they want it more than anything else in the world. Jack ranted, *'Where's the treasure of the Templars? Give it to me!'*

I listened to the old monk screaming when he was hurt and weeping when he was not.

'I'll show you, sir,' he wept finally. Probably he was used to receiving a penny for showing visitors round. 'I'll show you.'

Jack grinned. He shook the old man to make sure, then broke his knees with the axe so he couldn't get away by a trick.

'Show me,' he said. 'Everything.'

The monk dragged himself to the winding stair. 'Hugh, Arthur!' Jack called, jerked his head, and the old man was carried down, dropped at the bottom in the crypt. He crawled forward to a second altar-table, pulled a secret mechanism I did not see. It grated loudly, unused for probably seventy years. The altar swung aside, the stone floor dropped and made steps going round and down. A winding stair led down to a second crypt below the first.

Again my mother had told the truth.

I followed the bobbing heads below me around the winding stair, then, as the flames and smoke of the burning brands they carried lit up the second crypt, I heard their cries of disappointment. There was no treasure. The walls were covered with mouldy faded tapestries and hangings attacked by rats and damp – rats the Templars had brought back from the Holy Land, bringing the plague with them. But most of the room was taken up with paper, piles of rotting paper, receipts and copies of receipts, and copies of copies, as painstaking as only clerks can be, two hundred years' worth.

'That's it, sir,' the old monk of Sion called down eagerly. 'That's our treasure.'

'This,' Jack Straw said. He touched the flames of his brand to the papers, and thin pale flames raced up. 'All this, for that.'

For a moment his face was utterly weary, and I think he knew his rebellion would fail. He kicked away the papers, then spoke from the winding stair. 'Come on, lads. Let's kill a few more bastards afore we're killed.'

He threw down his burning brand and ran up out of sight, and when I saw his face again it was spiked in place of the archbishop's on London Bridge.

I watched the papers burn. The pile slipped, revealing parchments covered with codes, the locations of Templar treasures, everything abandoned on Friday the thirteenth seventy-four years ago. They blackened, burning, and turned to ash, and as the heat tightened my face I retreated to the stair. Flames ran up a tapestry, catching my eye: a map of Jerusalem as if seen by a bird flying above. I crouched under the heat, marvelling. The hangings were Templar maps, priceless Golden Line maps in true proportion: beneath the smoke I glimpsed London, and Rome, and Jerusalem, and the lands between them all true to scale, not huge to the north and tiny to the south. Maps of the round Earth made by mathematical calculation to look flat. And far to the west, across the ocean where manticores, manipagoes, giant squid and whales dragged down ships, I saw the island of New Jerusalem whose shape I knew, and the river, and the immense coastline of New Sion.

The map turned to flame, fell burning to the floor. Where it had hung I saw a door revealed in the stone.

I pushed, and darkness opened.

I grabbed the fiery brand Jack Straw had dropped, jumped forward with smouldering hair into the dark. The door thudded closed behind me, then almost immediately there was nothing beneath my feet and I fell, rolled down a flight of steps with my clothes showering sparks.

I stood, held the flame high in the silence. A tunnel had

been dug through the clay. Sloping downwards, it led into blackness.

A dull thud of falling stones came from above and behind. I could not go back, so I started forward. From time to time as I descended water trickled from the walls, followed channels and drained away. The flame that lit my way rustled in the breeze that blew in my face. A tunnel joined from my right, then my left, and the breeze blew from behind me. Then it turned, blew in my face again. *He's safe.* My mother had known of these tunnels.

A light grew ahead of me, the dark clay gave way to white chalk. It seems that when God made this round world He decreed that although London would be built on brick-earth and clay, some hundreds of feet below He would provide a layer of chalk. Was this the same chalk that made the chalk hills I'd walked through on my way from Dover? Why? The complexity of the Earth that God had created and the details He had hidden in it filled me with awe.

The walls turned to chalk boulders with gravel trapped between them dripping water. I wondered if I were deep below the Thames, as if once the Thames had somehow flowed down here at the bottom of a deep valley, carrying gravel on its flood from I know not where, and gradually piled up the gravel and clay for it to flow across today, so high above my head. But what would be God's purpose in such a huge creation, so much of it unknown, and thus apparently so purposeless? Perhaps everything, however small, however hidden, has its purpose. The tunnel turned back on itself, sloped below the gravel layer into solid chalk once more, and my tiny figure questing beneath its spark of flame followed it down.

Tunnels met, the walls fell back. The wind blew out of this entrance, blew into that one. Just as I always sense the presence of my mother when she is near, I sensed the presence of my father, and let the wind blow me forward.

Gold glittered, and I entered the Sanctum Sanctorum of the Templars.

Before they disappeared the Order had more than a hundred years to move everything piecemeal from Corps Dieu; they hadn't wasted their time. Here was the masons' All-Seeing Eye, the Egyptian *ankh*, the golden angels,

Asmodeus unchained. The Templars called him *Baphomet* and worshipped him as the son of Deus. Deus, both their God and their Satan, just as *ho theos* is God or Satan, both.

Deus, God in Latin, *Deuce* in French, the second, the persuader, the contriver: *Rex Mundi*, Lord of this World.

Boaz and Jachin, the two pillars. The doors of solid gold. I push.

I push, and they swing open.

On the altar of white marble Jesus Christ lies naked, except for a white linen loincloth. Iron Templar chains bind His body to the altar, ARAM MENAHT MENOU carved in jewels into the marble.

Down the cold marble trickles His warm red blood from the Crown of Thorns, the nail holes, the spear-thrust in His side.

I climb the steps close enough to touch Him.

Look down into His sleeping face.

I reach out, almost touch His skin, His living skin. My hands hovering over Him feel His warmth, His life, radiating outward. I feel He may awaken at any moment. The tiny hairs in His nostrils move as He breathes. Does He dream? Are we His dream?

'Father.'

His eyelids flutter at my whisper, but He does not awaken. He *is* awake.

I touch one of the heavy chains and the massive links fall away beneath my hand, broken. The iron has been worn shiny, worn down, worn away by a force I do not know. The links clatter across the marble floor, sending a single mouse running. Then the sound of the sliding links is muffled, and the whole floor moves.

I turn slowly, and stare.

Mice.

A scuttling sound, and the links are pulled away by tiny teeth, tiny bodies pulling with all their strength.

Ten thousand mice. Ten thousand times ten thousand mice, ten thousand times ten thousand little souls.

More than a thousand years of life, and I am beginning to know I know nothing. I've seen love wear away iron; I have seen nothing. I've seen faith change the world; I have seen nothing. I have seen the body of my father, and learnt nothing. There is nothing to learn. Where is the plan? Where's the ascent? Where's the meaning and the revelation?

Here is the Arch of the Covenant. Here, on a lectern surmounted by a gold eagle, lies the Book. The pages turn as I reach out. Read me.

Read me, as Grand Templar Master de Prudome read me, and took nine days to die.

Read me as the blind man read me.

Read me as Moses read me.

I reach out my hands to turn the pages, the numbers leap to life. Of course Arabic numbers are familiar to me, as they cannot possibly have been to ben-Yohai or to Moses; to them these numbers were just shapes, runes. But I can understand them. I can!

But perhaps there is more to understand even than I *can* understand. *Some arithmetics are quicker than others, but they all add up to the same result however ancient they are.* But there are greater truths even than numbers.

And the greatest truth is God, surely.

I leave the Book.

Light pours from my father's body like sunlight on a summer's day, illuminates me throughout. I realise I see through my skin, my fingernails, the palms of my hands, my arteries and veins pulsing with blood, my living bones, as if all this is the most natural light in Heaven and Earth and I was blind not to see it before, blind and stupid, and I stand marvelling in His light as though I am my father's newborn baby again and understand that age and years are an illusion, and there is no reason for Time to run forward.

One day may have passed, or ten. I know my body was starving by the time I started my journey back from the earth to the world. I staggered, my strength almost gone. I licked water wherever it leaked from the Thames above, and stumbled finally to a place where a winding stair came down from above me, and continued below me as though it would not end until it reached the centre of the world.

I climbed the stair trembling in every muscle. Stopped exhausted. Climbed again. My head banged a stone slab, which I pushed until it slid aside, and I climbed into a room hung with drapes. Later I'd know this was the Sacred Templar Lodge of the Worshipful Masonic Brethren of London Bridge and the Priory of Sion, but for the moment all I saw was stars, thousands of stars patiently woven in gold and silver and blue amethyst and red ruby into the drapes, as many as an eye can see in the night sky, more. Some were wrong, drawn into shapes that stars cannot grow, spirals, ellipses, strange tortured patterns. And there was an error with the orbits and number of planets, too many, ten, more than exist: and the seventh wore a crown of stars.

There was nothing to eat.

I climbed the stairs in the corner, pushed aside an altar, came out in the undercroft of a chapel. Sails moved across the windows set high in the wall; I was still below the level of the tide. A further winding stair led up to the Bridge Chapel of London Bridge, and the priest intoning Latin from the Ordinal ignored me.

I half fell into the street, and followed the mouth-watering aroma to a cookshop, and devoured a chicken.

DE NOVA STELLA

about a new star

VAUDEY, LONDON, 13 MARCH 1781

From the roof of my Georgian house in Vaudey with my telescope trained down not up, I watch them watch the sky.

A hundred years ago John Flamsteed found something up there and called it 34 Tauri, a tiny distant star. Others have seen it since, but none of them knew what they saw. Like sleepwalkers, the astronomers did not really see what they observed. They were men blessed with fortunate birth, driven by curiosity not intelligence, and despite their gigantic telescopes they were not men of vision. The more they saw, the less they understood what they saw. But they never gave up.

My wife Emma called up to me. Ours isn't a particularly happy marriage, since she's certainly my distant relation, certainly related to Christ. Everyone in the world is. I can't put out of my mind a feeling almost of incest. This strong manly body (which I found in its youth, left for dead in a Deptford ditch) is full of lust even in middle age, I'm driven nightly by my hot-blooded manhood to her bedroom, her bed, her opened body which I possess with the physical thrusts of sex, and yet even as my orgasm comes and this body's life flows into her I can't help thinking of Jesus Christ who's inside us, whose blood flows in us both, and wonder at the reason for us all. So I seem mysterious to Emma, withdrawing, masculine, conquered, because I treat her coldly afterwards in my exhaustion and guilt. Love would be so simple without sex.

But my attentions make her love me more, even as I turn

531

from my penis to my telescope. I'm obsessed with my telescope. 'May I come with you, dearest?' she called suddenly as I left her bedroom, pulling on my boots and thick coat against the chill pre-dawn air.

'Come with me?' My wife with me on the roof, sharing my obsession? The idea had never occurred to me. 'But you wouldn't find it interesting. Sleep. You need your sleep.'

She stood in her nightdress, my seed spilling still warm down her thigh. 'To see what you see,' she said. 'To be with you.'

Oh, God, I had never needed anyone to be with me, not since Giselle all those years ago.

'All right,' I said. Emma laughed and kissed my ear, bade me look away. She pulled on her dress behind a screen, appeared in a moment wrapped in her cloak with her red hair spilling unpinned, uncombed down her shoulders, looking less like a wife than a harlot or an excited child. 'Come!' she trilled, taking my hand. 'Show me!'

Vaudey, as you know, means Valley of God. The valley fell steeply from the heights of Blackheath, parted round the knoll standing out like a clitoris where Sir Matthew and Lady Fox owned Holywell Manor, then joined again and lost itself in the Thames marshes. Emma slipped her fingers between mine, and I felt her rings already cold in the dawn and the dew slippery under our feet as we crossed the roof to my telescope – my telescope which, as I told you, does not point at the sky.

Directly between Vaudey and London lies Greenwich. A sensible man wouldn't build an astronomical observatory on a hillock near the world's greatest city. The prevailing wind blows the smoke of a million fires constantly over Greenwich, lamps and braziers light up the muddy sky, and the river draws obscuring mists to it like a magnet. But there it is, Greenwich Observatory, and its telescope taller than my house.

'I'm so cold!' Emma shivered. 'Warm me up.'

I pulled off the tarpaulin that protected my own telescope, a reflecting telescope of my own design fabricated by Lorris in the village. Emma pointed at the small tube on the side. 'It's had a baby,' she said.

'That's what you look through.' I handed her the lens

covers, as large as parasols, and she held them helpfully.

'The stars are going out,' she said. 'They aren't there any more.'

I adjusted the mechanism. 'They're still there. It's just that we can't see them because the sky is too bright.'

She said: 'How do you know they're still there if you can't see them?'

I searched for an answer. 'Because the universe would fly apart otherwise, that's why.'

'How do you know it hasn't?' She pointed at the rising sun over Germany. 'Look, doesn't the sun look like a burning coal?'

'It *is* burning coal,' I said. 'Nothing else explains the sun. It's been burning for nearly six thousand years.'

'And the sun goes round and round the earth.'

'It only seems that way.'

She kissed my ear. 'You're the centre of my universe,' she said. Again I thought how like a vulva and clitoris the valley looked. My wife's body drives me mad with lust yet as soon as she talks she irritates me unbearably. I moved the vernier by a tenth. She jogged me. 'What's that?'

'It's a vernier.' I moved it back two-tenths.

'The Observatory's telescope points at the sky,' she said. 'Yours points at the ground.'

I took her warm elbow, guided her to the eyepiece. 'Mine,' I said, 'points at the Observatory.'

She stiffened, interested, then giggled. 'It looks close enough to touch. I can see Herr Hairy Herschel coming out.' Her hips moved in unconscious parody of the fat astronomer's walk. I'd introduced her to him at Greenwich Fair. Wilhelm was indeed hairy, mostly because of his Georgian wigs which came unbound, but also it was my nickname for him because of his work on comets, hairy stars. I'd thought it was my private joke. 'He's lifting up his arms, he's dancing,' Emma said, her hips swaying. 'Now he's playing an oboe.'

'What?' I said. I fear my wife's humour. People allowed to look through telescopes always pretend amazing sights.

'He's playing an oboe,' she insisted. 'He's marching up and down and his sister who we met's dancing round him.'

'Caroline?' I pushed Emma aside, stared through the

eyepiece. 'Good God, she is. *He* is.' I stared at the two of them parading up and down, making fools of themselves in the early morning sunlight, then ran to the attic door.

'Where are you going?' Emma called. 'What about your telescope? What about the covers?'

I ran downstairs, heard her running after me. No time for my horse or gig. I ran across the road and into the field, Emma running after me with her cloak and hair flying like a wanton woman, her bare feet flashing in the dewy grass. 'Wait! Jude! Your heart! The pills! Your doctor!' I didn't wait for her, but she caught up. 'Slow down, you'll hurt yourself.' You must know by now she was twenty years younger than I.

I slowed down on the hill in Greenwich Park, wheezing. 'I can hear his oboe,' she said. 'It's one of those Hanoverian marching songs.' I caught my breath by the railings, then turned the corner as though this was a chance meeting. 'My husband has run like the wind to see you, Herr Hairy!' Emma called out. Both Germans stared at us, then burst out laughing.

I couldn't wait. 'What have you found?'

Wilhelm blew a last blast on his oboe, then straightened his wig. He tried to be serious, but put his arm round my shoulder and kissed me like a Frenchman, making me frown. Then he kissed Emma and made her laugh. 'I have discovered, Sir Jude,' Wilhelm informed us, 'a discovery. A discovery that is a discovery of discoveries.'

'His English is crazy,' Caroline said. 'We are exhausted. We are so tired. We are so happy.'

I said rapidly, 'Is it a star?'

Wilhelm yawned. 'Return tonight,' he whispered, 'and I will show you what I have found.'

All day I observed the Observatory through my telescope. In the afternoon Wilhelm appeared looking sleepy and walked his spaniel in the park. His serving girl returned from the village with pork brains and a cabbage for his supper. Caroline worked at an upstairs window, calculations perhaps. During the afternoon gentlemen began to arrive from London, in carriages, on horseback, by water, even on foot. Clouds gathered from the west, I watched them in an agony of suspense, but they disappeared as mysteriously as they had arrived. Fortunately the evening set perfectly clear and cold. I hurried across the road determined not to be late, but Emma would not let me go alone. 'Someone has to make conversation,' she said firmly. 'You men'll bore each other to death with talking and fall down drunk with port. Poor Caroline!'

'You'll make us late,' I said. She decided on her light green dress with the dark green cape. The idiot I employed as a giggie took a wrong turn and lost us among the riverside docks, so finally I abandoned the gig and pulled Emma after me uphill, she tripping in her impractical green shoes. 'Too late!' I said, watching the stars appear over the rooftops. 'We shall be last.' There was hardly room to get in the observatory door, and the gentlemen amateurs who had gathered pushed back as hard as they were pushed forward. But Emma stepped in front of me and as they doffed their hats politely to her she swanned past them, and I cut through in her wake. The distraction she causes is the great advantage of a beautiful young wife. I soon found myself with her at Willie's side. Emma started talking to Caroline about cakes.

I grabbed Willie's arm. 'Is it a star?'

'Watch, see.' He reached towards the great telescope that pointed through the open roof and everyone pressed forward, disturbing the mechanism. He adjusted the verniers with fine detail, consulting numbers in Caroline's book. Not a particularly good night for viewing, a full moon rising in the south-east, but the telescope pointed westward. 'Yes, we search almost due west, over London. Later we will see better, when the cooking fires are out. Here we are. Azimuth 286 degrees, altitude 20 degrees 26 minutes above the horizon.' He pointed through the window. 'Observe Sirius rising over Herne Hill. Observe the red star Betelgeuse due west exactly, above Sirius and to the right. Now draw an imaginary line between them. Continue that line upward to the right, directly over the Houses of Parliament.'

A clergyman called briskly, 'It's blank sky, man!'

But I pressed my eye to the brass viewfinder, and the sky rushed near and filled with stars, an almost solid mass of stars moving slowly across the black background of space. As the earth turned, carrying me and the telescope with it, one by one these climbing points of light disappeared upward to the right. But one single star did not appear to move. It was not a dot like a star. It was a pale blue bead, steady among the travelling points.

'It's a planet,' I said.

'Now look.' Willie adjusted the focus and new stars jumped into view around the edge of the new planet.

I whispered, 'A planet wearing a halo of stars.' My hands trembled, I wiped my eye. 'Ouranos, god of the sky. The sky itself. Ouranos wearing a crown of stars.'

'Strictly speaking moons,' Caroline said.

I hardly heard her. My mind turned back to James whispering, 'Ouranos. In those days we knew everything.' I remembered my mother telling me 'Ouranos,' and the myth of how the ancient god of the sky had fallen in love with the earth, Gaia. Ouranos in Greek, but in Latin Uranus. By means of this new invention, Herschel's telescope, forty feet of lenses and mirrors, I saw for the first time with my own eyes the huge planet Uranus of which my mother spoke so long ago.

'Yes, a crown of stars,' Willie burbled happily in his thick German accent. 'And for that reason I am naming my discovery after our King. Gentlemen, observe our King's new world, the seventh planet of the solar realm, *Georgium Sidus.*'

Georgium Sidus, King George's Planet! A new world for King George III in place of the one he was losing and perhaps had already lost, the old new world, America.

'What's the matter with you?' Emma chattered as we ate. 'Why are you so upset? Isn't Caroline as clever as a man? They're so clever, those two! What a wonderful pair. I'm sure Willie gets on much better with her than his wife.'

'A man can always trust his sister.'

Emma's eyes filled with moisture. Here we went again. 'Don't you love me?'

'Yes, of course I do.' I ate a mouthful of hothouse peas off the side of my knife.

She brightened and leant from her place across the table, kissed me. 'That's all that matters.'

'Love doesn't make things easier. It makes them harder.'

'Caroline certainly has no dress sense whatsoever.' Emma stopped. Though she pretends not to care she knows my moods better than anyone, even my tailor. 'Is something wrong? What's wrong? Is there something you can't tell me?' Yes, Wilhelm Herschel has named the first new planet ever discovered after our crackpot foreign king, not the god of the sky! 'You aren't in love with her. Are you?'

I was flabbergasted. 'Who?'

'Caroline.'

I'll never understand my wife. 'Good God! She's got a face like a foot!'

'Good. Is it me you're angry with?'

Emma looked very serious. I hugged and kissed her, which is enough to reassure her of anything.

'But you *are* angry. You're angry with Willie,' she decided. 'No, you're angry with yourself. I don't want you to be angry. I'm going to have your baby.'

'Of course I'm angry! Willie's discovered an unknown planet, a seventh planet unlike all the others, with moons orbiting outside the plane of the ecliptic—' Emma wouldn't know what *ecliptic* meant so I explained it to her, putting an orange on the table. 'The orange is the sun.'

'Yes, dearest. I'm going to have your baby.'

I scattered peas around the orange. 'The planets are peas.' I pushed them rolling round the sun with my knife. 'The table is the plane of the ecliptic. The planets don't roll off it, they all orbit the equator of the sun. And all their moons orbit in the same line, even Earth's moon – that's why sometimes our moon gets in front of the sun, an eclipse. Jupiter's moons, Saturn's moons, they all appear as a dotted line out to each side. Except, *except* the moons of Herschel's planet, which orbit at an angle to us, so they appear as a halo or crown.'

She squashed a pea with her forefinger. She said nothing. She licked the pea off the tip of her finger.

'A baby?' I said.

'No, no, let's talk about the planets.'

'What planets? How long have you known?'

'I fear I've eaten your *Georgium Sidus*, dearest. Two months. If it's a boy you'll be able to bore him to death with your telescope.'

'He'll be fascinated.'

She shook her head in disbelief, then laughed. I love her laugh. I love all of them when they laugh, all the seventy or eighty generations of women I've known, their brief lives full of pain as often as not, and no certain knowledge of immortality, yet they laugh. 'All right, Jude dearest, he'll be fascinated. Let's talk about names.'

'Yes. All the other planets are named after Roman gods, Mercury, Venus, Mars, Jupiter, Saturn, but no, Willie has to call *his* planet after a king.'

'I meant,' she said coldly, 'the name of our child, not your – not your—' She flooded over with tears. 'Not your damned planets!'

I tried to think of children's names.

But while she talked I thought of the planets, and God making the planets. My mother had said the earth was billions of years old, but no one believes that. Everyone's sure that God created the earth and sky with great attention to detail, for a reason, so that we can learn from the secrets He's buried for us and climb to a more perfect understanding of Him. If He made the new planet's moons orbit at that incredible angle, sixty degrees from the plane of the ecliptic, there's a reason for it, He's telling us something. Of course the true path to God is through the sacraments of the Church, but perhaps science can help us on our way. Perhaps science can provide the answers, and scientific knowledge reveal what was lost to men and women in the Garden of Eden: the face of God Himself.

Or perhaps science, as Mr Newton found, is just another apple.

Emma died in childbirth. My son cried out once and so did she, then both lay still, entangled in the womb.

I peer through my telescope. There are always new stars.

BEATA MARIA

Blessed Mary

Where's my mother? Where's she gone? *Why?*

My father Jesus Christ is everywhere, I know that now. His blood runs in us all. We are all, as it turns out, literally St Paul's Christians: we are all in Christ, and Christ flows in us literally. He's real. That doesn't make life, or love, or happiness or sadness, or death, any easier. But it does give us strength. We have the power to believe, and some find faith, and some ignore faith, and some renounce faith. It's a free world. We aren't a fully saved people: we're free to attempt to climb to salvation in our own way. We have choices. An infinite number of choices.

Oh, God, the misery, confusion, chaos in this world!

But there are answers as well as choices. There *are* truths. There *is* a purpose.

This I believe. God is more powerful than Satan. My father can rise from death, *and has risen*, and He can conquer Hell, and He is able to strike down Satan with His fist. But still, we are a free people. We must choose God of our own free will.

Sometimes when the City sleeps, I come down here to the Temple of God: there are many ways down to those who know London as I do, more than the winding stair below London Bridge, more than the tunnels below the Temple north of the Thames and Temple Paris Gardens to the south, more than the Tabard Inn in Southwark, more than St Paul's Cathedral.

I kneel here in the flickering firelit cavern beside my

539

father's bleeding, sleeping body. Here is the eternal, the infinite. And also someone new.

My mother knew it. Jesus Christ is someone new, not who He was supposed to be: He is someone she could love as well as worship. Someone who transcended Godhood in His life as a man.

And I pray, because it's all gone so wrong, so dreadfully wrong.

Twenty centuries in which everything Jesus Christ taught has been stood on its head. Life turned into death, truth into lies, love into hate. Remember the Cathars. Remember the Jews.

Satan's world.

And where does science lead us?

Georgium Sidus. Whatever does God have to do with *Georgium Sidus*? Nothing, and soon the mad king was dead anyway. Most people (those educated enough to have heard of it) called the planet Herschel. His compatriot Johann Bode worked out the arithmetic showing why the planets are exactly the distances from the sun that they are, and pointed out that since the others are called after Roman gods, the planet Herschel should be renamed Uranus. Not in Bode's lifetime. Only after an eighth planet was discovered, Neptune, was the seventh renamed Uranus.

The universe is blind. Science is blind. Comets plunge from the void without warning towards our sun, and return to the void. Bones of monsters come out of the earth and some say they're millions of years old, made by evolution, and others say they're a few thousand years old, made by God. Scientists tell us we're not men and women created by God but only animals created by sex between monkeys.

But here I kneel and I know God is real, actual, factual. I see Him. I reach out and touch Him. I hear the whisper of His sleeping breath.

And sometimes I hear footsteps, and draw back into the shadows.

London Bridge is falling down – London Bridge was built falling down – but the Worshipful Masonic Brethren of the Sacred Templar Lodge of London Bridge and the Priory of Sion sealed the crypt beneath the undercroft of the Bridge Chapel with concrete. The undercroft was used as a cheese store, the chapel as a shop; the chapel fell down and eventually the arches of old London Bridge were knocked down, mud and silt and weed flowed over the place, but the concrete plug beneath the site of the chapel remained standing like a pillar deep in the riverbed. New London Bridge was built a hundred feet upstream, the old bridge forgotten as though it was never here.

Almost at once the new bridge began to subside; a gap a foot wide opened up in one pillar as the foundations sank, and engineers suspected pockets or chambers in the clay and chalk deep beneath the gravel fill of the prehistoric riverbed.

As you know, there are other ways down, and from the shadows I watched the monks of Sion, the masonic guardians of Christ, at their gleaming-gold, candlelit devotions. Do these Grand Masters really understand any more the object of their worship? Do they really believe in Christ, as I do, or is it all meaningless ritual to them? They were famous men in their own times, important in their tiny lives for a moment; now they're just names, forgotten names. I've seen Lord George Stuart down here, but I've forgotten who he was. Dukes of Kent, minor princes, all gone. Several paintings by Poussin and Van Dyck show secret knowledge, though I never saw them down here. Cocteau I saw, but did *he* believe what he saw? Or was it just a curious prize to him, the preserved body of a man who'd died like Christ, as real as the shroud of Turin?

None of these men can understand. The mice show more love than they, the faithful mice.

Here He is, my father. But where's my mother? Not here, though sometimes I used to sense she'd been here: a sense of her perfume, her femininity, her warmth lingering in something she'd touched. But no longer. The domineering presence I'd sensed in Catharine of Alexandria, and later from time to time, and certainly in Catharine of Siena, was gone. I never met Joan of Arc, or Catharine of Pisan, or Catharine of Genoa, though too late I read her Dialogue between the soul and the body and heard my mother's voice. But that's all, too late. I looked for her in Marie Curie and Mother Teresa and found nothing.

She's hiding.

She, not my father, is hiding from me.

You can't let them have the power of the Covenant. I felt her death-grip on my wrist even now. *You can't trust anyone. You can't trust yourself. You can't trust me!*

I didn't want to look at the Covenant; it frightened me. My mother had told me the truth about everything and been right about everything. Right that the sun is a nuclear furnace not a burning coal. Right that the planet Uranus exists and wears a halo of stars. Right that the Earth is four billion years old – a little over four and a half billion actually. Nowadays almost everyone knows these facts, whether or not we believe them to be true. Our universe is eight billion years old and twelve billion light-years across, the Hubble Constant is 127, our sun is a fourth generation star resurrected from the exploding material of earlier stars, and the planets are formed from the condensation rings of gases, silicon, carbon and metals, as are we and our works – all part of the evolution of the universe, the evolution of creation, the evolution of life.

And yet I look at that little gap in the worm-eaten side of the Covenant, and see my face.

And once the most horrible thing happened, and I understand a little perhaps why my mother has abandoned me, forsaken me.

Once, my father's eyes opened.

His eyes open, perhaps He sees some terrible evil happening unknown in some corner of the world, I don't know, perhaps it's happening all the time. It must be.

His eyes are full of the most appalling suffering.

This is what she can't bear, because she loves Him more deeply and more completely than any woman I've ever known. She can't stand this terrible suffering of Jesus Christ. Not His suffering on the Cross, which was brief, symbolic; not His love for just her. No, it's this: His love for all of us and His suffering for all of us for eternity, with every breath we take, for as long as we are.

On Thursday 19 November 1987 British Telecom engineers, driving a tunnel for fibre-optic data transmission cables beneath the Thames a hundred feet downstream of new London Bridge, encountered without warning a massive foundation of the old bridge. Before the boring machine could be stopped it broke through the ancient crumbling mortar and revealed, to the astonished eyes of the engineers, a medieval winding stair. One man was injured by whipping hydraulic cables as the machine fell from sight. Others stared down, their helmet lights stabbing down through the rising dust.

The story was replaced almost immediately on the front pages by horrifying news of the fire on the London Underground at King's Cross, where thirty people were burnt alive or suffocated. After a few weeks I still heard nothing more of any discovery of a medieval stair. Six months later I read a snippet in a BT magazine that the tunnel had been completed on time.

I dared wait no longer.

I found the way from Temple Paris Gardens was blocked by rubble. I couldn't tell whether the fall was accidental or deliberate.

From the beer cellar of the Tabard I reached only as far as the river before encountering a roof-fall.

But tunnelling beneath the sacred ground of St Paul's Cathedral is forbidden by Act of Parliament. From the nave of St Paul's I walked over the Crossing beneath the dome to the great north-east pillar that supports Wren's masterpiece. It was early, no one saw me. The statue of Algar, first prebendary of St Paul's nearly a thousand years ago, stood in its niche. I touched Algar's foot in the way I know, the statue turned aside, and I went down. The statue stood back in its place behind me. A cathedral is a maze, almost as complex as a person.

My father was gone.

The Covenant was gone. The Book of numbers that the Templar Sir Nicholas de Mason had brought back from the Holy Land was gone. Every certainty had turned to uncertainty; my faith was air.

INSULA VECTIS

the Isle of Wight

GATWICK AIRPORT, LONDON,
22 DECEMBER 2012, 6:04 A.M.

'My God,' Dr Michaels said, 'she's black.'

We crouched under the roar of the rotors and the doctor, white hair flying in the downwash, cupped his hands to my ear as the cars drew up: 'My God, Julian, black! And beads! I never guessed!'

Nothing happened. The limousine door remained closed, the black woman behind the glass stared straight ahead of her, waiting. She wore a diamond shape of coloured beads as a necklace – for a moment I imagined the shape was a Star of David, unhinged, the two triangles joined along the base to make the diamond – and more beads were patterned in her headband. I hurried forward on the oily concrete under the glare of airport lights, dodged the puddles, shook open the courtesy umbrella but it blew out. Davidson I recognised from the Ministry, pinstriped, the other men climbing from following cars I did not know. I still don't like cars; I'm a bit of a throwback, I suppose. And I hate getting oil on my shoes.

But not as much as I hate shaking hands with civil servants, especially while being deafened by helicopters. 'Oh, Trevrizent, isn't it!' Davidson shook hands. He shouted: 'Here's Jacobsen, American Embassy.'

'Good evening, sir!' More introductions until I put my hand in my pocket.

Davidson noticed my gun holster. 'Any need for it?'

'Better safe than sorry, sir.'

'Everyone's here who's in the loop.' Davidson moved

closer against the noise. 'Security. Lawyers. Everyone on the distribution list. Thank God the rain's stopped.'

I stared into a camera, held on to my hat, turned back to Davidson. 'A video crew?'

'Historic moment,' Davidson said, embarrassed.

'What happened to secrecy at the Site?' I nodded at the limousine. 'She insisted.'

'We insisted,' Davidson said.

The Frenchman from the European Commission said something, I lost his name under the rising whine of turbines.

'Not for distribution to CNN,' Jacobsen called. He laughed, we laughed. A Chinook took off, twin rotors tilting against the floodlights across the night sky. None of us laughed with our eyes, nobody understood what we'd found. The black woman sat unsmiling in the limousine, staring straight in front of her, the papers she'd studied during her flight from the University of the Mid-West stacked neatly in her lap, tied with pink ribbon. I knew we could go to hell. She'd wait until I opened the door.

I opened her door. 'Good morning, professor. Welcome to England.' Then I stepped back as the black woman stood up from the limousine. I'm six foot two in my shoes; she'd be as tall in bare feet. 'I'm Colonel Trevrizent. Julian Trevrizent.'

She had a voice deep as melted chocolate. 'You know who I am, Julian.'

'Professor Dumazulu.' Michaels clutched the umbrella. 'We've communicated electronically of course. I've read your articles. Many years. Your reputation. But we've never met.'

She glanced at him. 'That's right.' She turned to me. 'Tell me what you know, Julian.'

'It may be nothing,' Jacobsen interrupted. 'We think it's nothing. Don't get excited.'

'Six thousand miles in twelve hours,' she mused, her deep luxurious voice carrying clearly over the rotors. 'A convoy of limousines. Now helicopters. You're not excited.'

'We're unpersuaded that it's anything, anything special,' Davidson said. 'That's why we need you, professor. You are by common consent the great, greatest authority on palaeontology. Early life, its relationship to geology, to Man.'

She didn't look at him, only me. 'Our place in our Earth. What do you need to know?'

Davidson said: 'Whether what we've found is a hoax or the greatest discovery in the history of the world.'

Still she stared at me. 'It's real.'

'Yes,' I said, though I hadn't seen the Site.

Michaels nodded. 'You studied my papers, of course.'

'You miscalculate the Site's chalk strata at a hundred million years of age,' she said without turning. 'Too old by thirty-five million.'

Michaels disagreed. 'The geology is well known. The chalk beds were laid down in a deepwater marine environment. The last time the Site was above water was a hundred million or more years back. Dry land—'

'Michaels, my dear doctor, you're forgetting that about eighty-five million years ago the Pokesdown Axis swelled. The Site was shallow sea, coastal. A temporary stretching of the Earth's lithosphere could easily lower sea level by an additional hundred and fifty feet. Finally, there's a discontinuity in the island's geology record from seventy-five to sixty-five million years during which *nothing* is known.' She dismissed him, put her hand on my shoulder, stepped into the Chinook and patted the canvas seat for me to sit beside her. She didn't want Davidson or Michaels beside her any more than I did, but Michaels dropped into the seat opposite us and the door slid shut. The rotors hammered, the ground canted beneath us as we lifted, then the airport lights slid away, were replaced by swaying racing patches of village lights, orange roads, dark flooded fields, southern England. Occasionally through the small window I glimpsed the flashing navigation lights of the military Chinook accompanying us as we rushed through the night.

Michaels clicked on the interior light to distract his stomach. He smiled at us. 'Beads,' he said. 'Very good. Most fetching. What do they mean?'

'Do you know what the name Mary Dumazulu means?' she said.

'No, I don't.'

She said, 'It means, mind your own business.' I hung on

as the helicopter rose over a hill, dropped down the far side. Michaels pretended to be asleep, but I didn't look away from her. 'Tell me about them.'

She touched the double triangle of white beads at her neck. 'A married woman. Each set of three corners represents father, mother, child. But the white means I remain a virgin. My marriage is a spiritual love, complete purity. The red border shows my longing for physical sex, my heartache, my anger. My loss.' Michaels's eyes gleamed beneath his lids, watching us, but Mary looked only at me. 'The black bead is for my sorrow. Because I live in despair. Because without my love I'd rather die.'

I whispered, 'And your hair?' Her eyes followed my moving lips.

'*Izipenethu*. I'm alone, far from home. *Inkanyezi*, the star that catches your eye. You know who I am, Julian.'

'I know who you are.' I glanced at Michaels, spoke to her mouth.

'You know why I've come,' Mary whispered.

'Because of Dr Michaels's find. Why's it so important? So *very* important.' The helicopter roared, swooped, we hung on. Michaels pretended to awaken, smiled at us, settled back when he couldn't overhear us. 'You knew, whatever it is, it'd be found one day. You guessed.'

'Everything is found one day. Heaven and Earth doesn't keep her secrets. Not a day passes without something new, if only you see it.'

'You told me so much, Mother. You told me everything.'

'Everything you'd believe.'

'No.' I shook my head, whispering. 'I see now you told me everything. Just like a jigsaw puzzle. The last few pieces can only fit one way. Even if I can't see them, I know what shape they must be.'

'You wouldn't have believed the truth if I'd given it to you. Just as people didn't believe Jesus Christ who was given to them. Truth is earned, not given. Earn it.'

'I have.'

'Not yet. You've got to see those last pieces.'

'Good God, Mother.' A tear trickled from my eye. 'He's gone. My father's gone. What more do I have to do?'

'Salvation's not given away, it's earned. Earn it. Struggle.

Never give up. Your purpose was to find the truth, Jude. That's why you were born. Your father is *you*. Us. In everyone you see.'

'I've found you,' I whispered. 'Good God, Mother, help me.'

She touched my hair. 'It's harder, isn't it? Harder than living men and women on this planet can possibly believe.' She sighed. 'Something huge and obvious and true, and they're stone blind. Deaf. Dumb. Without feeling. Can't see it or hear it or speak it or touch it.' A grey coastline raced below us, replaced by grey sea. 'Ticket to Ryde,' she said grimly. She knew exactly where we were. 'The Isle of Wight.'

'Vectis,' I said. 'That's how I knew. You told me outright. You told me of the white island Vectis where, you said, Balaam the high priest met his horrible death. Vectis was the Roman name for here, the Isle of Wight. In Britain, you said, *Long ago the survivors carried me from the cave in the hills to the low chalky island, Vectis, crunching with white seashells where the dragon fell on Balaam the zadok, and there all our hopes were lost.*'

'Yes. You'll see the truth of what I said.'

'London, wasn't it? The place the survivors carried you from on a stretcher, to Vectis.'

'Yes. London before there was London.'

'And afterwards they carried you back there.'

'Yes.'

'Where you were in love with James.'

Her lips trembled. 'Yes.'

'But you couldn't love him, not physically. You were paralysed, your back was broken. Having his child would've killed you.' She shook her head. I shouted, 'Wouldn't it?'

'I'd have gone ahead, conceived. For James. Died to give life for love. Worth it.' She pressed her knuckles to her lips.

'Instead you saw James—'

'Don't.'

'You saw James sleeping with Esther in her sleeping bag. Having her. She could give him what you couldn't. Children.'

'Yes.' Mary shuddered. 'Her name was Esther. She shouted out with passion. She knew I listened. She knew I watched him, I saw her eyes gleam.'

'On your elbows you dragged yourself back to the cave. There you shot yourself in the mouth with James's pistol, and your body fell to the centre of the world.'

'Yes.'

'That's what you said.'

'Yes. James lost me, and his children by Esther all died. Every one. He never forgave himself.'

'The cave was in London. At the top of the winding stair.'

'Yes, but there was no winding stair. That's medieval. Recent. The tunnel goes down almost vertically. Walls of fused sand and rock.'

'Fused by heat?'

'Yes. Like glass.'

'Does it go to the centre of the world?'

She hesitated. 'The monk-masons of the Priory of Sion stopped before reaching bottom.'

'How far? A thousand feet? Thousands?'

'When I fell to my death, it felt like I fell for eternity.'

'My God,' I said, 'miles? Many miles? How can that be?'

'When you see, you'll believe,' she said. 'When you saw your father Jesus Christ, you believed in Him. You *knew.*' She touched my arm. 'When you see this, Jude, this *fact,* you'll believe. You'll *know.*'

I glanced at the waves racing below us. 'What is it at the Site exactly?'

She mimicked Davidson's Eton voice. 'Either a hoax or the greatest discovery in the history of the world.'

'And you know it isn't a hoax.'

She looked tired. 'I wish, I wish with all my heart it was.'

I leant close, whispered: 'Is it science? Or is it religion?'

Michaels moved and we parted guiltily.

'It seems,' Michaels yawned, stretching, 'that you two have got to know one another quite well.'

The helicopter leaned over, almost throwing us into each other's arms as it followed the curve of the island coast. Grey chalk cliffs flickered past the window, cows lolloped away from us like pale shadows across the dull rolling fields above. Slow waves reached up towards the racing helicopters, turned to foam, fell back. White spires of chalk stood out of the foaming sea. 'The Needles,' Mary said. A lighthouse flashed, and the sun rose around the end of the island. The cliffs of St Catharine's Point struck rose-pink for a moment, then the lid of raincloud descended again.

'Rain, rain, go away,' Michaels said. 'Wettest winter for thirty years. That's what caused the cliff to wash out in the first place.'

'I saw the news,' I said. 'The Culver Cliff Hotel? Dining room hanging over the edge.'

'Three hundred feet straight down.' Michaels leant to the window between us, pointed out the hotel turning below. 'No room to touch down on the beach. We'll land beside the hotel. Won't wake the guests. Evacuated. Nobody there.'

'Somebody's there.' Mary pointed out the scurrying figures in the car park, Land Rovers in army camouflage, white police vehicles. The cliff edge swept beneath us as the helicopters turned on the final approach, and I glimpsed the beach below, a landing craft, piles of stores, tents, a yellow bulldozer the size of a toy. 'Good thing it's calm in the bay,' Michaels said. 'Got the heavy stuff ashore despite the bloody rain.'

The helicopters settled, blowing spray across the lawn at the cliff edge. The swishing rotors fell silent. We stood in the dripping rain staring at the distorted hotel, a few tiles sliding from the roof as we watched, the walls bent by the strain, nothing but air supporting the collapsing dining areas. 'The patio and bars have already gone.' Michaels pointed out debris strewn down the cliff. 'Come on, let's get in first.' The second helicopter swept overhead as we started down the cliff path. Michaels took Mary's elbow to help her down but she shook him off, stronger and nimbler than we.

'Got to admire her,' Michaels confided. 'Brilliant. She identified *Scipionyx* for what it was. First dinosaur ever found in Italy. Breastbone like a bird's, liver like a reptile's. And brilliant work for the American Museum of Natural History in Montana and China, the mothering instincts of hadrosaurs. Really made the huge ugly bastards come alive.'

I hardly listened to him, the chalk boulders from the landslip rising around us streaming with rain as we went down. The army had blasted the largest to make a precarious descent, an orange rope on one side, sometimes aluminium ladders. 'Idiots,' Michaels said, pointing up the jumbled face of the cliff. 'It'll let go one day, and the idiots started blasting. High explosive. Damn soon put a stop to that.'

'What would happen to the Site?'

'Lost for another few million, I expect.'

We followed Mary making the last jump on to the beach. A caterpillar tractor blew exhaust smoke, lurched from the landing craft towing stores. More stores and drums of diesel fuel were piled under tarpaulins near the portable cabins, offices, canteens. Generators blared, computers and electric lights gleamed in the windows, armed guards saluted. 'Base camp,' Michaels said. Workmen in hard hats shored up the cliff with hydraulic jacks and steel mesh, but I sensed the weight teetering over us as we went forward.

'Here we are. Not so much a cave,' Michaels said. 'More a crack.' A stone bounced from above, Davidson and the others coming down. He waved. Wait for us.

Mary crouched quickly. She wouldn't wait. 'Michaels, this is exactly how you found it?'

'On holiday. It gets wider inside. These fossil cliffs are always collapsing, what luck. When my wife was alive we called this Dinosaur Island. I walked from the museum at Sandown, stopped to eat my sausage roll, a bone washed out from the cliff right in front of my eyes. A stone claw, ebony black. Knew it at once, thumb claw from a carnivorous dinosaur. Bigger than my hand. My first thought: it's another *Neovenator salerii* – found only on the Isle of Wight,' he explained to me.

'Too big,' Mary said. 'It's a marshland reptile, more like *Baryonyx*.'

Michaels disagreed. '*Baryonyx* is too recent. And terrestrial dinosaurs only turn up between Aberfield and Compton Bay.'

Mary said, 'It had a crocodile head.'

Michaels stopped. 'How do you know that? No one's been told that.'

'They run faster than a running man,' she said. 'Long legs.'

She ducked inside and we followed her, bent double. 'Should wear hard hats,' Michaels's voice boomed. A line of bare bulbs glowed like dim stars from the roof, leading us forward. My holster caught on a boulder and I hurried to catch up. The sound of generators and machinery faded to silence, only the scrape of our footsteps accompanied us, our awkward breathing. Jacks and mining timbers held up the roof. I touched one, and chalk dust sifted down.

'Michaels?'

'Here.' I followed their voices. The Royal Engineers had dug a cleared space where the roof was higher. We straightened our backs in the gloom with a sigh of relief. My mother took a torch from the rack, couldn't find the switch. 'What are we supposed to see exactly?' I asked.

Her thumb found the switch.

When you see, Jude, you'll believe. You'll know.

I saw. I believed.

I reached out and touched. I stuck my hands among the fossilised bones. I sniffed them, ancient life turned to stone by death and millions of years of time.

The dinosaur bones stuck out of the wall, shadows moving around them as my mother swung the torch. Carefully exposed with dental drills and picks, soft brushes, almost infinite patience. A skeleton twenty feet long or more embedded in the wall, massive rear legs, crocodile head. The mouth was wide open, still biting downwards in the moment of death. The front claws sprouted talons more than twelve inches long, wickedly curved, sunk deep within the fossilised rib cage of a man.

'A man,' I said.

I reached forward, touched his smooth skull with the palms of my hands. His mouth was open, still screaming. His teeth were perfect, every one. 'Sixty-five million years,' I said. 'A man.'

Mary whispered in my ear. 'Sixty-five million, and four hundred and four thousand, and three hundred and ninety-four.'

'The K-T Event,' Michaels said, trying to overhear. 'Seventy per cent of all species of life on earth disappeared within a few years. Say less than half a century.'

'K-T?' I asked.

'The Cretaceous-Tertiary mass extinction,' Mary said. She touched a thin black line in the chalk. 'The discontinuity. Silt. The sedimentary clay layer, it's found all over the world. End of the reign of the dinosaurs.'

My palms caressed the high curve of his forehead. 'Modern man.'

'Raises questions, doesn't it?' Michaels said. 'A man killed by a dinosaur.'

I wondered, 'Evolution never happened?'

'Evolution happened,' my mother said. 'Inevitable evolution, to the inevitable conclusion. Nothing happens by chance. The Bible tells us so. God made Man in His image.'

'Science is no help to you here,' my mother said.

I touched his ribs. Stone still clung to them, perhaps fossilised skin.

'No, not skin,' my mother said. 'He wore a cloak.'

That did shake me. 'A manufactured article?'

'A white linen cloak. He was a priest.' She shone the torch in my eyes. 'Are you all right?'

'Balaam,' I said. I understood. I thought I understood. 'He was Balaam! You said, *The dragon fell on Balaam the zadok, and all our hopes were lost.*'

I heard Michaels in the background asking what a zadok was.

'Yes, Jude,' Mary said. 'All lost.' She touched a small stone device lying by Balaam's hand, buried by a million generations of chalky shells. 'All mine, anyway,' she murmured. 'It was the first time we realised we were no longer a saved people, a chosen people. That bad things happen. That we were going to die.'

'What are you two muttering about?' Michaels said. 'You haven't seen anything yet. This' – he reached inside the skeleton – '*this* is what's going to make my reputation.'

He brushed a little chalk dust aside with his knuckles but it wasn't enough. He bent over the ribcage, blew, and a cloud of white dust puffed up round his head. He waved it away. 'You won't believe your eyes.'

Mary and I leant over. Balaam had died trying to protect something he held. As his body decayed the object had fallen from the bones of his fingers into his belly, finally ending up lying on his spine where time had welded it to his vertebrae. It looked like a stone rectangle.

It looked like a book, a fossilised book.

I bent down until I breathed on chalk and bone, mouth open, staring.

The cover of the book beneath the skeletal fingers was worked with the raised outline of a Christian Cross, once richly decorated with jewels, but now the jewels were dull stone.

'It's a Bible,' I said. 'It can't be. It can't be.'

'The Cross doesn't stand for the Crucifixion,' Mary murmured. 'There was no Crucifixion. No suffering. The Cross meant the meeting of the ways, the crossroads. Unity. Christ ruling as both king and priest, the single pillar, saving every Christian.'

I made out shapes stamped beneath the Cross, smoothed away the dust, and saw that they were words. Familiar words, but without meaning.

ARAM MENAHT MENOU.

My mother whispered, 'It means, "This is the Holy Bible of the Lord your God." '

'Just wait until we open it,' Michaels said.

I watched Michaels, his enthusiasm. *Whose side are you on, Michaels? Whose work do you do?*

God's work? Or Satan's?

I whispered to my mother, 'What's happening here? Science or religion?'

'In a few days we'll use a laser to cut the Christian artefact away from his spine,' Michaels said.

I burst out, 'How can it be a Christian artefact? How can the Bible have been written millions of years ago?'

'We're having it sent to the Manchester Institute of Technology,' Michaels said. 'They did the work opening the most difficult Dead Sea Scrolls.' Like a time bomb buried for two thousand years, the Scrolls of the Community of Sion, hidden when the monastery was destroyed by the Romans, had been discovered by the Arabs after the Second World War. The Jordanians called the place not by the name of their enemy, Sion, but by the Arabic version of *Qimrôn*, the vaulted arch: Qumran. The ruins were overrun by the Jews in the 1967 war. The Scrolls of Sion made, subtly at first – many were bought or controlled by the Christian Church – new knowledge and thus the new truths about early Christianity available first to an academic clique and finally to ordinary Christians. A thousand years ago the Bible had started to free itself from the grip of priests, to filter down to ordinary people translated into tongues we could understand, giving everyone a personal Christ we can believe in, a Christ who is personally true and adaptable to each of us, changing Christianity for ever and causing immense destruction and suffering as well as benefit. The Sion Scrolls, freed from academics and translated and widely available in the 1990s, slowly brought back the idea of Jesus Christ as a real figure, a real person living in historical times, a person about whom facts could be known.

'Now this,' I said, and touched the Cross of the stone Bible. *There was no Crucifixion. The Cross meant the meeting of the ways. Unity.* 'Now this.'

'Who knows what we'll learn from it,' Michaels said.

Mary touched the Bible and shuddered. Why was she so afraid? 'Or un-learn,' she said. Why did I sense such hatred and fear in her? Unity, ways meeting, no suffering; surely these are modern buzz-words, things we take for granted as good. Surely she should want them. Most people don't want to believe in Hell nowadays, or demons, or eternal suffering for tiny sins, or the cruel, unmerciful, jealous God of the ancient Israelites, or even in Satan. We each have our own God whom we have made in our image. Yet she touched that Bible, her hand beside mine, and I felt her whole body absolutely shudder. 'I never thought I'd see this again.'

Michaels said, 'Again?'

She murmured, 'I never thought I'd see this Bible again, Jude.'

'Jude?' Michaels's voice rose. 'Who's Jude?' He pulled at her. 'Don't touch that, it's of priceless importance. What do you think you're doing?'

I knew. Suddenly it all makes sense. She'd told me everything, everything, right from the start, and I'd been too blind to see it. She'd been cast adrift in a rudderless boat.

In this world Abraham didn't find Jesus Christ our Anointed Saviour, the Virgin's only Son, reigning in righteousness and perfection, eternal, universal, in Jerusalem as has been foretold in other places from the beginning of time; only Melchizadok the king-priest, fallible, demonic, merely human, as are we all. Here, here, is Hell. We live in Hell, you and I. This world itself on which we find ourselves is Hell.

I said: 'In this Bible He does rule, doesn't He? Abraham finds Jesus Christ born in the Holy of Holies and ruling in Jerusalem. Jesus Christ saves everyone, doesn't He?'

'Yes. ARAM MENAHT MENOU, this is the Holy Bible of the Lord your God. The Bible He wrote.'

'He saves Jews. Greeks. Chinese. Everyone.'

'He's our Jesus Christ our king and priest. He has the power to impose salvation on everyone. Eradicate the cancer of disbelief.'

'And everyone's happy ever after and there's no Hell.'

'Yes.'

'What's wrong with it?'

She looked me in the eye and said clearly: 'You of all people should know.'

Mary brought the torch down on the Bible with all her strength, shattering the fossil into pieces. Michaels shouted. My mother brought the torch down again and again, hammering the stone fragments to dust, bending the torch casing, breaking the bulb, the light went out and we hardly saw one another in the gloom. Michaels wrapped his arms round her, shouted for help. He shouted, 'Help me, for God's sake.' He struggled forward with her. 'Grab her. Colonel, Colonel Trevrizent. For God's sake help me.' His eyes stared white at the shattered Bible, staring at the disaster. 'Oh my God, my God.' His arms fell to his side. 'My God, what has she done?'

I didn't lift a hand to help him. My mother stepped away from him, brushed against me.

'That was the Christianity I knew,' she murmured. 'God imposing His will through King Jesus Christ, so that men and women and children were incapable of rejecting God's teachings. We were saved. We could not *not* be saved. Bliss. Among a saved people, Jude, there's no oppression. No unhappiness. No injustice. No war. No disease. No pain. Nothing wrong. There's only justice, the divine worship of God, and devotion, and prayer, and pilgrimage. Our lives for Him.'

I remembered her words. 'But worship isn't love.'

'Worship says nothing about love.' She smiled, brushed the hair out of my eyes as though I were still a child. 'Worship says nothing about freedom and the great truths I saw Joshua preach in Galilee with my own eyes, and heard him tell with my own ears. Joshua is our Jesus Christ, *ours*, in this hellish world, whom I love, whom we crucified. Can it be the Son is more than the Father, just as Yahweh is more than El, and El is more than Enki? Our Jesus Christ who doesn't impose, doesn't decree. Our Jesus Christ who teaches us, encourages us, persuades us. Our Jesus Christ who *is*.'

Her fingers lifted the flap of my holster.

'My darling son, to understand everything, you must see everything.'

She lifted the pistol from my holster, pushed it against Michaels's head, pulled the trigger, almost deafening me. Michaels's brains and blood exploded against the skeleton.

'Break it,' she said, shouting when I couldn't hear her. 'Break the terrible thing!' I knocked at the brittle bones with my fists and arms, sending them flying to dust. 'Now Davidson,' she said grimly. 'Everyone who knows of here, everyone who's seen it.' I followed her into the narrow tunnel, squeezing along the crack, shielding my eyes against the bare brilliant bulbs. She held the gun behind her back as we came out into the rain on the pebble beach. 'What's going on in there?' Davidson said, and the video crew moved forward. She shot the camera, then pressed the pistol against Davidson's chest and shot him through the heart. Jacobsen shouted, 'No.' She shot him. The cameraman staggered with glass dripping blood from his head, she held the pistol in both hands and shot him. The Frenchman skidded on the stones, she stepped over him and shot him where he lay, their souls rose around us tiny and frightened, the wind blew them away.

She turned, embraced me: 'I love you, Jude.'

Without looking away from my eyes she raised her arm and emptied the magazine into the fuel dump. Flames blew out around us, and then the explosion came and the pain, the usual sad drifting-away pain of death.

'Understand everything,' her voice whispered. 'See everything.'

But her strength, her strength that had stood out against evil for so long, failed her.

I lie rolling on my back among the waves where the explosion threw my body. The breaking waves wash over my face, rolling my body to and fro on the shingle and seaweed, and bitter seawater fills my mouth. The sea's red with fire, burning fuel, burning above and below. A man runs gasping on the beach, no hard hat, pieces of metal fall clattering around him from the sky, part of an engine, a tractor wheel bounces like a toy before rolling into the surf, he dodges them all, then fire engulfs him. The enormous voice of the flames is reflected back from the cliff as the metal jacks give way, squealing, and a million tons of chalk rock sags forward, beginning to fall, trailing dust upward like spray as the cliff face slowly topples out, strikes the beach like a breaking wave and obliterates the cabins, the dumps, the perimeter, spreading forward in a cloud of debris towards the sea. I glimpse a Chinook, rotors moving like treacle in the air, slide down among the rocks and grass into an explosion of boulders and smoke. The hotel falls sideways with the cliff top, flakes of tarmac, people, tiny vehicles tumbling like drops of brightly coloured paint. A wave washes over my face, again I gasp bitter salt, and see my mother's body.

A wave drags me into the sea, another throws me back. My clothes are gone, rags cling to my blackened flesh, my teeth chatter with deathly cold as I crawl forward on my burnt belly, blistered elbows, knees.

'Mother.' The sea rolls her back, rolls her forward. I reach out.

I grip her hand, and her hand grips mine. 'Mother.'

A wave washes over us, her face bubbles, comes up shining, naked, her eyelids burnt away.

'Love. Remember love.' My mother stares. 'I tried so hard. I've no more to give. I'm weary. I'm so tired.' She slips away from me, I can't hold her. I grip her hands with every ounce of my strength, then the next wave brings her back. Her eyes stare up, terrified. I twist round, but see only the sun golden in the clouds. 'Mother? What is it?' Her mouth fills with seawater, I lift her. My eyes are pouring salt tears. She wants to die, she's given up. 'Mother, why did you do such a terrible thing?'

'Terrible? They're coming.' Her mouth moves, splitting her burnt lips. 'It's a time bomb, a time bomb with a fuse sixty-five million years long. Maybe they don't exist any more. Maybe there's still hope. It was a long time ago.' She tries to blink. 'But I don't think much changes in Heaven.'

'Who?' I shake her, it's only her body. 'Who's coming?' I burst out, 'Why did you kill these people?'

'A long, long time ago.' She gasps, tries to gather her strength. 'A message was sent.'

'What message?'

'SOS. Save our souls. Help. Rescue.' She groans, begins to speak rapidly. 'It doesn't matter, Jude, it doesn't matter! What matters is that it was sent.' She falls silent, staring past me.

I shake her, but a weird golden light is reflected in her eyes, her staring terrified eyes. I turn my back to the sea so my shadow falls across her, forces her to look up at me.

'Love,' she whispers, 'I can't help you any more.' Her fingers loosen, the sea pulls her round as limply as weed. 'There's only you, Jude. Only Jesus Christ saves us.'

The sea throws our bodies together, drags us apart.

The waves roll her over, then my mother's face comes up for almost the last time, and the surf breaks golden around us.

'Love,' she whispers. 'Remember, Jude. Remember love. Always remember who you are.'

My shadow deepens across her face, so intensely black that she seems not to be held in my arms, and the world turns to golden light, a beautiful golden illumination so intense that everything is deep streaming shadow. I turn. I forget my mother's terror.

I see the Angel.

She soars above the sea, half walking, half flying on the waves, beautiful, golden, the most beautiful girl I have ever seen, golden-haired, naked Venus. Her breasts are gold, her pubic hair gleaming gold fluff, her legs and hair long and flying and pure gold. Her golden wings sweep up, reach high above her face, sweep down again then up, sending spray swirling from the waves beneath her toes.

Her ruby-tipped breasts bob and sway with each beat of her fluttering gold feathers, and she has eyes only for me. Her indigo-violet eyes. She folds her wings, her gold now white as pearl, pale as uncovered secret skin, and I know I see my mother as my father saw her, in her naked flesh. That day when Joshua touched her by the pool perhaps. But perfect. Perfect woman. No crooked arm, no dirt, no demons, utterly perfect she is. She smiles in wonderment, responding to me. Holds out her hands. Come to me. 'Look at me,' she commands. 'My vagina is no longer torn. I'm a virgin again.'

It's the most terrible blasphemy I've ever heard. My mother screams, stands up to her waist in the waves, clenches her fists. 'You're not Him! You're nothing like Him!' She screams: 'Liar! Cheat! Deceiver!'

The demon reaches out its fist and crushes her. My mother screams a word or two, then all I hear is breaking waves. A single thread of blood trickles out between the demon's second and third fingers. The demon licks it away, then her beguiling eyes observe me with the most immense pity I have ever seen.

'Your mother was wrong, poor boy,' the demon says in her beautifully feminine voice, desiring me. 'She destroyed what she most loved. Jesus Christ has not been seen or heard on this planet for two thousand years. Suppose she'd not married Him? His apostles wouldn't have betrayed Him. There'd have been no Crucifixion. Suppose she'd not whispered in His ear? He would've destroyed the Temple and rebuilt it and reigned as King over you all. And she did it for love, that's what's so sweet. They destroyed themselves for love.'

Is it really weakness? 'Remember love!' my mother screamed as she was crushed. *Remember love.*

'Liar,' I tell this beautiful woman with difficulty, because she is so very beautiful. 'Liar. Cheat. Deceiver.'

She smiles. 'Men lie and cheat and deceive themselves quite well enough.'

'I know who you are.' I almost say it. *Asmodeus.* But for some reason, instinctively perhaps, I stop my tongue.

'No, poor man,' the demon says, 'you don't know me. Listen to me. Your God of love is the man of a lie, because

560

there is no love, no real love in this world. My Master always tells the truth, and believe me, there's only struggle and death. Who knows more of struggle and death than my Master? You don't know enough to know love. You humans have no idea of scale, whether this world of mine's at the centre of the universe or not, whether the universe is large or small, whether it's everything there is or just a bubble in a waterfall. You don't know if you're alone, you don't know if twelve billion light years is for ever or next door. You don't even know if you're important. You're not important! This world is ours, not yours. Poor man!' She reaches out her perfumed hand, her long nails lacquered with ruby. 'You won't believe me if I tell you truth, history, the facts. But I can show you Truth. I'll show you Truth, I'll take you there. Because everything that happens, happens for ever.'

'Happens for ever? Is that a scientific view of nature?'

'No.' She takes my hand effortlessly, lifts me. 'It's the nature of God.'

She lifts me high into the air, higher, until the world is small, into darkness, and the stars shine.

ARMAGEDDON

the end of the world

THE K-T EVENT, YUCATÁN,
MIDSUMMER 65,402,382 YEARS BC

Its absence revealed its presence: a mountain black against
the rushing stars, a hole punched in the blaze of starlight.
Its outline glowed with the light of stars bent around it by
its intense gravitational field – simply by its weight, its mass,
its velocity. 'Travelling within a few tenths of one per cent of
the speed of light,' the demon murmured. 'A mountain
eleven miles long and eight and a half miles wide, heavier
than my sun. Than a hundred of my suns. Energy is not a
problem for them.' A mountain made into an ark: the shape
of the ark grew enormous, filling with detail, craters, lakes
of ice, cliffs and canyons that raced above us. On one side
an immense pattern of letters passed high over our heads,
hundreds of yards long, perfectly carved in gold and jewels:
Ouranos.

As it rotated a vast jewelled Cross rose into view. One
God, one Christianity, one Way. The power of whatever
drove it forward smeared the starlight around us as the ark
plunged along its imponderable course.

My hair blew in the interstellar wind. 'Am I really flying
with you above the earth?'

'Beyond my earth.' The demon gestured forwards with
her thumb, dots of light, the planets centred around a tiny
twinkling star ahead of the *Ouranos*. 'A long time ago. Your
mother counted the years correctly. But time depends on
who you are. For your pilgrims in the *Ouranos*, travelling on
their *hajj* from whatever holy Christian site to whatever
other holy Christian site of pilgrimage – there must be

thousands, *millions* of boring places for a saved people to worship their sterile Christ – for them, time is but a day, as long as they don't slow down. I told you my universe is small.' The demon made me look at her, her suntanned beauty, her nudity, her breasts, her long hair flowing weightless against the stars.

Irrationally, I was terrified of falling; the mountain bending starlight as it rushed ahead of us through the immensity of the universe made me dizzy. 'Looks big enough to me.'

'This is small, Jude. This universe is as small as a prison. To Christians it's just a waypoint, a shortcut. They cut through' – she pointed her right arm – 'look, beyond Sirius, that bright star.'

Sirius! 'I knew Sirius was important.'

'No, not the star. It's only eight or nine light years away, a few seconds' journey near light speed. No, beyond Sirius, behind, see that faint glow? It's a galaxy, NGC 2207. A touch over sixty-five million light years. That's their waypoint, the relay station where they come in.' She pointed her left arm in the other direction. 'That's where they go out, M71. A few days away.'

I felt like a medieval priest being told the sun was a nuclear reactor. The idea was both bigger and smaller than I could understand.

'We're tiny?' I said. 'Our universe – all this – tiny?'

'When God throws Satan and His angels out of Heaven,' the demon said, 'He doesn't throw them somewhere important.'

'You've existed from the beginning?'

'From the beginning of time. Long before this little creation.' She showed her teeth, trying to smile, but I could almost feel the prison bars of her captivity. 'Here is where we fell. God cannot create imperfection, but he can create a place for it.'

'God made us?'

'God orders every atom. He even breaks His own laws.'

'No wonder you're frightened of our Jesus Christ,' I said. I felt my awe slip away. I didn't hang limply from the demon's grip any more but tightened my grasp on her hand. 'You *are* frightened, aren't you?'

'Yes. I'll destroy everyone if I have to. Every living thing.'

'I wish you didn't try to make yourself look like my mother,' I said. 'She gave life.'

The demon laughed, opening her indigo-violet eyes wide. 'For her, I made myself appear as naked as Joshua. But I curled my hair like a Greek, even my pubic hair, with curling-tongs. It disturbed her, she hated it. But that and my understandable lie that I couldn't fly above the air of the earth – I didn't reveal the extent of My father's kingdom to my enemy – are my only lies to her.'

'And to me? Do you lie to me?'

'Not one.' She pointed her finger. 'Watch. Any moment now. Poor saints. Accidents never happen. They spend their lives in worship, and in return there's nothing bad. No pain. No suffering.' She smiled. 'No Satan.' A red glare bloomed on one side of the mountain. 'Until now. Oh-oh, looks like a fuse has blown.'

Abruptly the stars were mere points of light, the gravitational field had shut down. A plume of gas geysered silently into the vacuum. The asteroid began to rotate awkwardly, clumsily, out of control, curving off course towards our tiny twinkling sun. A lake shattered, ice flew around us like diamonds.

'Time to meet your mother,' the demon said. 'You'll find little Mary's not nearly as beautiful as I am, not yet.' She smiled: 'And she never will be. I made sure of that.'

'Until she's Mary Magdalene,' I said, 'and one day Jesus Christ makes her whole by the water.'

The demon snarled, pulled me down into the ark.

A cave, a sandy floor, a child's doll dropped by footprints in the sand. The distant rumble of tortured machinery echoes through miles of rock, then a woman's shriek: 'Mary!' A little girl runs back to her doll, snatches it up in her chubby hand.

My mother. I can feel her. My mother, young, untested, untried, her soul as light as vapour, a child for the very first time.

'Naughty Dottie,' she scolds the doll, 'where have you been?' She kisses the doll and runs after her mother.

'Never mind that!' Mary's mother screams. 'Something dreadful's happened!'

'Of course it hasn't,' an older woman says, Mary's grand-mother. 'I've done this a hundred times. It's always a false alarm.' Sand drifts across the floor as the gravity shifts. The two elder women hold on to each other, eyes wide.

'It's fun,' Mary says, playing. 'Look, Dottie can slide.'

'Quick, take her hand. Don't let go.' The silver-haired woman takes one side, Mary's mother the other, the doll falls to the floor. Mary looks back over her shoulder as the adults pull her into the concourse, cries for her lost doll. The artificial sun has gone out, the blue is gone, and beneath the dark rock sky the familiar village looks strange with shadow, then something jerks and the stream runs backwards, spills over its banks. The ornamental swan lake in front of the shopping mall slops a breaking wave which surges against the shop fronts, the fountain blows sideways. An old woman falls, her hip cracks, everyone stares stupidly. A man lies face down, a heart attack. There are no facilities to deal with this. 'I'm going to complain,' Mary's grand-mother says firmly. 'I don't know what the crew think they're up to.' She calls a priest. 'What's going on?'

The young priest reassures her. 'Don't worry, it's meant to happen. It's all under control.' A gas pipe ruptures outside the saddlery, sending a jet of fire into the air. The priest falls to his knees, praying, but still the fire burns.

The three women hurry away beneath us, the mother saying, 'Your father will know what to do, Mary.'

'What?' the grandmother says. 'You should never have married an engineer, what do they know?' She stops at the cathedral. 'Balaam's preaching.' She goes up the steps as Balaam in his gold zadokite cloak strides out, lowers her head for his blessing.

'I save you in the name of the Lord your God,' Balaam leans his weight on his ornate sceptre, touches her without looking, 'I guarantee you complete safety from harm in the name of Jesus Christ your Lord and King.' The incredible, the unthinkable happens: the Cross that protects the Place of Meeting topples, falls, crashes among the crowd. Balaam stares angrily, but with the first trace of incomprehension. He pushes the young priest forward. 'Save them.' He hurries down the steps and away, followed by his twelve young apostles and a clutch of older men and women struggling to touch the hem of his robe. 'Mother!' Mary's mother calls, but there's the thump of an explosion, people run past, and in a moment the grandmother's silver hair can no longer be seen.

Mary cries for her doll, then sees someone she recognises: James's mother, who's tall. James is Mary's best friend, they always play. She pushes through the crowd and while the adults speak I hear Mary telling James, 'I've lost my doll.'

James is a name entirely without meaning; as everyone knows, Jesus had no brothers. James is a year younger than Mary and has to keep his end up, an only child secretly in awe of her. 'Our house was flooded,' James brags. 'The carpet's soaked and Mum says the furniture's ruined, she'll have to get more.' From somewhere comes an immense noise like firecrackers exploding, and everyone covers their ears. The adults duck down at the sound of breaking glass but the children hold hands, laughing. Inertia and momentum tug them this way and that as on the playground rides, but the grown-ups fall over and lie holding the ground, then the ground tears open revealing the levels falling away below, shrieking metal, falling people. Wind rushes down, intensely cold, pulling long clouds of vapour. Green face-masks drop from the oxygen stations, everyone runs. Mary clings to James's hands, the children are jostled from side to side by the running people. James's mother falls from sight, steam blows, James shrieks for her. They're in a tunnel, automatic doors slam brassily behind them, cutting out the screaming wind. In its place a message blares. 'Lifeboats. Proceed to your lifeboat stations.' A steward jerks a bulky inflatable helmet over his head in case of pressure loss, the valve won't work, he throws it down, pushes at the people. He wears the jewelled pin showing he's a qualified *shul*-house teacher; everyone obeys him. 'Lifeboat five to your left, lifeboat nineteen to your right. Even numbers, proceed straight on. Passengers for decks thirty-two through fifty-two, do not use elevators.' The lights flicker, his orders stop, no sound now but running feet, occasional cries, a fat woman leaning gasping for breath against the wall. A man in overalls steps from a studded brass doorway, snatches Mary up, hugs her. 'Daddy!'

'God bless us,' Mary's mother says, 'we're safe.'

'We're not safe,' Mary's father says in a low voice. His wife stares.

James asks seriously, 'Where's my mother?'

'We should get to the lifeboats just in case, eh?' Mary's father pulls them through the doorway on to a balcony over Engineering. In the centre of the space, unattached, hangs an immense mirror. A perfect sphere, a perfect mirror. Reflections of running people curve across its perfect face, I even see ourselves, and Mary's father running with her and little James – towards the lifeboat decks, I suppose. But the sphere takes all my attention.

'I've seen it before,' I whisper.

'You have.' The demon pulls me closer. 'You saw your face reflected from it. A much smaller one. The size that would fit in a lifeboat.'

'I saw—' I bite my tongue. I don't want to say I'd seen it in the Covenant.

'I know you saw it in the Covenant.' The demon smiles her smile, our faces grow enormous, distorted, hideous in the immense perfect mirror. She lifts her breasts, her thighs, changing her shape deliberately, careful, nothing playful, a huge pornographic totem. 'It weighs nothing. It *is* nothing. A hole enclosed by a perfect mirror, that's all.'

'There must be something inside.'

'Yes, a vacuum with absolutely nothing located precisely at its centre, at a temperature of 10^{-7} of a degree above absolute zero. Now do you know?' She pulls herself away, beautiful again, and I try to imagine what she means. The ark sways slightly, ever so slightly, around the perfect silver mirror which is as heavy as a hundred suns. In a sense, the ark does not contain this mirror; the billion tons of mountain, and all of us, orbit around the mirror like specks of dust around a sun: we're nothing by comparison. I can feel space stretching, my hands lifted up, my feet pulled down. Alarms scream. 'It's a Hawking box,' the demon says. 'A black hole in a box.'

'It makes the ship go?'

'It's damaged. Now they can't stop.' The hair rises up on people's heads, their feet move heavily. 'Tidal forces. It's leaking gravity, leaking radiation. And it's heading straight for our sun.' The demon smiles as the people run heavy-footed, in nightmarish slow motion. 'Look at them. They're going to die.'

I can see people working controls. A priest holds up a sceptre like Balaam's. Strands of vapour form, curling around the mirror, rushing in. The mirror glows, expanding, I sense the fierce heat. 'X-rays. As material enters the event horizon of the black hole immense quantities of energy are thrown off. They have no choice, they're dead men, but maybe they can save the ship.' The mirror glows, now slightly transparent to the temperature of the star inside. The air roars like a whirlpool above and below the black hole, spreading out from the north and south poles, whirling papers and consoles, men and women in its grasp, stretching them to streaks of blood as it sucks them in.

'My God,' I whisper, 'you can't let them die.'

'I can. I'm God here.'

The demon took me round the waist, lifted me into space. The mountain rotated below us, twisting, yawing, the peaks and outcrops breaking up. 'Six hundred and seventy million miles an hour,' the demon grins. 'Hard as diamond at that speed, as I now know from my Einstein. I wish I'd known at the time.' A dim greenish-blue planet rises in front of us, swells, the sun beyond illuminating the atmosphere with a beautiful crescent of royal blue; daylight. I even see tiny cloud-patterns, storms as large as the earth. The *Ouranos* strikes the planet and passes straight through, leaving it ringing like a bell. I see the ripples of concussion spreading out through the weather like nuclear bomb blasts, then more of them in a line as smaller debris hits. The seventh planet stretches, twists, skewing in its orbit so that its south pole points at the sun, and its seventeen moons are pushed out of the ecliptic and rotate like a halo of tiny stars.

More tiny stars around the stricken *Ouranos* now: lifeboats spiralling outwards, then falling backwards under maximum deceleration, but the *Ouranos* plunges forward. It's the saddest sight I ever saw. The mountain breaks in two unequal pieces, torn apart by the forces within.

I get it. 'The lifeboats have those little boxes too?'

'They won't stop in time either. Watch.'

Ahead of us rises a little blue-green world with a large moon, and continents of a shape I do not recognise.

★ ★ ★

Dinosaur world.

Some great creature shambles past, wades into the sea, raises its voice in a hooting mournful call, then plunges forward and all I see is its long neck questing the moonlit bay.

I'm standing on a beach, alien-feeling trees and ferns rising dark behind me before the desert starts, no grass, no flowers. Alien calls and cries, alien smells. Something crashing in the woods, then silence. Suddenly a deep, petrifying roar. But the waves break at my feet exactly as usual. The night breeze is cool as usual. The sand feels soft as a holiday beach under my toes. Sirius rises over the sea, signalling dawn. 'Where are we?'

'Yucatán. In another sixty-five million years.' The demon nods out to sea. 'The southern part of Britain's just broken off from North America. Further over there is Africa, and Mount Sion. And Antarctica's two islands, both of them warm.' She turns me and kisses me. 'Do you want to make love? Humans usually do about now.'

'What's now?'

'The end of the world.' She slips her slim golden hand inside my tattered clothes, touches my blackened chest. 'Celebrate the passing of an era.' Her long golden tongue caresses my nipples, licking them pink. 'Ring out the old world, ring in the new.' It's easy to condemn my lust for her, my sexual urge to bury myself in her, but she was so very beautiful, Venus, completely desirable. No doubt she's made of worms and shit but that's nothing new. Her skin's lovely, her eyes wide and her breath perfumed, and her ruby nails touch me like deadly alluring enticing knives exactly where you imagine.

I pull back. 'No.'

'You can't say no,' she pouts. 'You're the son of the Son. You're at least a man. More than a man. I can feel it. Show me.'

'No.'

She points her nail at a tiny moving star. 'You can stop it, brave man. Holy man. You can stop the *Ouranos*. You can save them.'

'No.'

'You could if you wanted.'

'You tempted my father, didn't you.'

She spits on the sand. 'He wasn't the One.'

'You know He was.'

'You are greater than he. I can make you greater.'

'If that little point of light is going to crash into the earth, I can't stop it. I can't stop the death of a fly.'

'You can.' She snatches an insect out of the air. 'Stop me from killing it, Jude.'

I shoot back, 'Are you tempting me, Asmodeus?'

Asmodeus stares, then shivers. Goosebumps come up over her golden skin like blisters. Names are powerful. At Gadara my father demanded Legion's name, and so cast out his devils. Asmodeus's creature, Levi the dyer, had blurted out the demon's name to my mother after my father raised him from death.

I tell Asmodeus: 'We can hurt one another, Asmodeus. You can hurt me, but I can hurt you.'

'The French call me Asmodée. It's feminine. You have no power over me.'

'You're Asmodeus, and you're your master's lackey.'

'So are you, son of the Son. My Master is more powerful here. I am a son of Satan, and this is *our* world, not God's. There's no Heaven and Earth here. My Master is God of this world, Deus, the dragon, Leviathan, *ho theos*, Satan.' The demon's face contorts viciously, female, male, horrible, as she crushes the fly between her lips. 'I crushed Mary Magdalene. I tormented her everywhere I found her. I gave her no peace, no rest, no salvation.'

I say gently, 'Peace, rest, salvation were what she denied herself, even when they were offered.'

Asmodeus points. 'Watch them suffer.'

The star hangs above Sirius, barely moving for it plunges straight towards us here on Yucatán, rudderless, out of control. Then terribly small points of light spray out to each side, lifeboats, debris. The dinosaur's long neck lifts indifferently from the water, a tail flapping in its teeth, as the first lines of light burst like fireworks in the sky. Then the stars go out, black, and I glimpse the mountain hanging huge as a fist in the sky above us.

Then the sky flashes to white fire, and in a moment everything's gone.

Asmodeus lifts me high, and I understand the legends. *Ouranos* strikes down into the land and sea that these people will call Gaia, thrusts down as though pushed by a giant hand. As the front flashes into fiery vapour the main part still stands erect in space, plunging forward into the explosion, vaporising rock and seawater and life. The black hole no doubt slices forward through the earth like a blade pushed through butter, emerges from the antipodes with its speed unchecked, and continues in the general direction of its destination M71. Or perhaps it breaks up, and fragments still orbit effortlessly in molten rock at the centre of the earth. I'll never know, or care.

This I know. Darkness falls at dawn, the air turns to sulphurous dust, and when I stand on the rim of a crater nine miles deep I can't see the far side, only the ragged curve of mountain peaks that will become the isthmus and the island chains of the Caribbean. Across the horizon streak more lines of light, debris, lifeboats, thudding into the atmosphere and the earth and filling the air with sonic booms. Tidal waves overwhelm every shore. Within six hours another huge fragment of *Ouranos* strikes the far side of the rotating world, in the Indian Ocean, setting off volcanic eruptions that never seem to end, turning the earth into a greenhouse planet.

But for the moment, darkness, death.

A hill stands over a low river swamp somewhere east of America. Ice cakes the surface of the waters, still warm beneath, and the fronds of exotic plants still green beneath the frost. Giant tropical animals stand motionless, blowing white clouds of breath, the meat eater next to the grass eater, their great flanks creaking like leather bellows. Fish swim sluggishly as the waters cool, and the fish-hunting plesiosaur gazes at them with its gigantic saucer eyes, then rolls over with its flippers in the yellow sulphurous snow, and does not move again.

A shooting star, and the snowy hilltop explodes.

Asmodeus lifts me, stands with me by the baking heat of the hole, perfectly circular, as perfectly circular as though drilled, driven at a steep angle into the earth. I can't see the bottom, only the glowing walls of the tunnel fused like glass, cooling, darkening. I hold out my arms. 'The exact size of a Hawking box.'

'In a lifeboat.'

'Then there must be others.'

'Not as many as you'd think. This isn't a saved world. They're no longer a saved people. They're just animals like the rest of us. Bad things happen to them. Life. Pain. Death.' She looks at me, golden eyes glittering. 'I can hear her already, can't you? Mary. Screaming. Five miles deep in the earth, maybe ten. Burning hot down there.'

I look around me, at the dying treetops and the heads of great beasts moving among them. 'Where is this place?'

'It's Hell.'

'Asmodeus,' I adjure her, 'what is the name of this place?' She blurts, 'London.'

A leathery creature like a bat, but with a long toothed beak, soars above the marshland calling harshly, *kaw-kaw*.

I turn back to the hole. 'What are they doing down there?'

'What meat always does. Trying to save itself.'

I stand helplessly. I have no rope. No lifting equipment. No medicines. 'Save them,' says Asmodeus. 'You can do it. You can say, Save them, O Lord, for they cry out to me in their injury and suffering. Say it, and an angel will come down and do it.'

'There are no angels in this world, except fallen angels. Demons.'

Asmodeus said: 'There's *you*. Go on, reach out your arms like your father did.'

In millions of years my mother would brush my hair out of my eyes, and speak to me like a child. *Joshua is our Jesus Christ, ours, in this hellish world, whom I love, whom we crucified. Our Jesus Christ who doesn't impose, doesn't decree. Our Jesus Christ who teaches us, encourages us, persuades us. Our Jesus Christ who is.*

But my father isn't born yet. 'It's an ascent,' I said. 'Jesus Christ is more than the God of these people. They worshipped their Father without freedom or love, only safety.'

'We'll kill your Jesus Christ by the thousand,' Asmodeus promises. 'Thousands of babies, Jude. Here my Master is more powerful than God. Save them. You don't think Herod was the only tyrant who killed his people's children, do you? That starvation and disease spare children, that accidents don't happen to children?' She hissed: 'Save them. You can do it now.'

I knew I could. I knew that if I had faith it would happen. 'I won't bring that God into this world.'

'God doesn't care about you,' Asmodeus said viciously, 'any more than He cares about Us, His fallen angels whom He cast out of Heaven and abandoned here.' Her voice climbs in a terrible futile scream of loss. 'How could He? How could He abandon and forsake Us, even Us who loved Him and served Him once with all our hearts and minds and souls?'

She raises her fists and beautiful golden wings, thrashing and swishing them helplessly, screaming at the black sky, and I look around me and know for sure this place is Hell.

Maybe they're just meat like the other animals dying around us, but it's impossible not to feel for the humans in their desperate struggle, just as the great lizards struggle and the tiny unevolved mammals struggle, and every dragonfly struggles, and even the fish wriggling in their icy pools struggle to live, to gasp one last time before the ice overtakes them. The sun never rises, most of the tallest and most exotic trees and shrubs die and rot where they stand and fall, only the hardiest thorniest underbrush survives. All this, and Mary's back was broken in the crash, as you know. A child's back can break in this world. The survivors lift her and drag her and pull her that immense distance up the tunnel from the wreck of the lifeboat with ropes, crawling beside her stretcher as it bangs and jerks, and she screams. Children scream in agony on this world. It's allowed.

Soon the painkillers are used up. They have no way to rebuild her nerves or fuse her vertebrae. Their first shelter's a draughty cave by the tunnel, later a tent of fronds on the hilltop. Mary's mother and father lie beside her, warming her, tending her, giving her all their love. And Mary doesn't die, if this is a life.

But as James's height and strength grows, and that of Mary's parents fades, there's nothing James won't do for her. James gives Mary the will to live. Even when the others give up James prays to God to save them. God, make Mary walk again. God, make Mary smile.

He manhandles trees for Mary's shelter and builds the stockade for her, protecting her from the beasts that still shamble through the sunless desolation. He keeps Mary's fire going. Feeds her when she will not eat. Brushes her hair. Lifts her withering legs to exercise them. And one day, if there is such a thing as day, Mary smiles. 'There!' James says. 'God made you smile.'

'God didn't make me smile, James.'

'He did. I've prayed and prayed and now you have.'

'I smiled because I'm happy.'

'Happy.' James looks at her lying in the sleeping bag, water dripping through the roof, the fire hissing smoke. 'How can you be happy?'

'Because.' She holds his hand. 'Because.'

'I love you,' James says. His face fixes in that nervous, attentive look. 'I'll always love you.'

But life is harder than that. James and Mary's father get down to the wreck several times over a period of months, wrestling up whatever odds and ends they can salvage, exhausted by their labour. And it's dangerous work: one of the other survivors, Malachi, is killed when a rope, incredibly, breaks. Everything has to be checked. Some of the other ropes are found defective. Thad is stung by an insect and dies. The air is full of germs, the water of bacteria, and they try to learn how careful they must be.

'This place must be worse than any other,' Mary's father says. 'We'll have to join up with other bands of survivors. There must be more.' Another trip to the wreck, two days' hard labour, but when he comes up he puts his hand in his pocket, grinning. 'The communicator was in the nose section, it's completely crushed.' They knew that; with a communicator they'd already have dialled up the relay station at Waypoint 2207, help would've been all over them months ago. But Mary's father pulls out something small and grey from his pocket. 'It's a radio. The crew use them for ship-to-shore at planetfall.' He holds up his hand against the clamour. 'Wait. There's a problem. Radio waves travel only at the speed of light – at least, they do everywhere else, so I guess they do here.'

'I wouldn't bet on it,' Mary's mother says listlessly. Her

hair's grey, she's lost her spark. Mary's pain has aged her.

'If we can't use it to call for help,' James says, 'what use is it?'

'We can use it to call up other bands of survivors on this world. Even at the speed of radio waves this world's probably small enough to hold a conversation. Certainly to signal them, anyway.'

'If there is anyone else,' Mary's mother says. It's left to Mary, hurting worse than any of them, to make the only joke.

'Thank God you married an engineer.'

Does Asmodeus make it worse for them? I think she enjoys their story as it unfolds. Their struggle for survival. Their moments of victory, their setbacks, sometimes their devastating loss. Asmodeus doesn't mind, she allows them their moments of respite, even of love, it makes their suffering more intense, more poignant, more human. She knows she wins in the end, these fat, saved souls lost and wandering in this pagan wilderness.

There are other survivors, some closer to the Yucatán or Bombay impact sites in even worse condition. Gradually the radio brings them together, Esther leading in a party of injured on crutches and stretchers, others walking in from further away. More survivors prefer to stay where they are in the jungles of Antarctica, Australia, a peninsula of China – I can't get the hang of these continents scattered not where I expect them. I think Esther's party came from Paris, but I recognise it as little as London; just another marsh.

Then one day the sun breaks through. The sunlight stands like the finger of God pointing on the grey landscape. Everyone comes out to watch; even Mary's carried out. And at that moment, that exact moment, Balaam's voice speaks crackling out of the radio. 'Fear not, for God is with me,' the Zadok booms. 'This is God's Earth, God's new blessing for us.'

Mary's father lifts the transmitter, shaking. 'Your Holiness, do you have a doctor with you? Can you help us? My daughter Mary, her spine—'

'By God's will I shall cure her. I have a medicator with

me, but God's will shall be enough. I shall speak His Word and she shall be cured and leap to her feet. Only have faith. Have faith.'

No one replies. The authority of the priest is so great that they know everything will be all right.

Mary's mother simply murmurs: 'We have faith.'

They prepare themselves for the long journey. I know how it will end, but they don't. Balaam's site is over a thousand miles away. 'Mount Sion,' Asmodeus whispers, 'that's what Balaam calls the place, after his Bible.' James and Mary's father set off full of hope to meet Balaam halfway, keeping in touch by radio. The canoe is by far the easiest method of travel in the marshland and takes Mary's stretcher comfortably. Her mother stays with Esther and the others, waving from the stockade. Mary's father sticks the pistol in his belt, James slings the rifle. 'When you see her again,' James calls back to Mary's mother, 'she'll walk to you.'

It's hard work paddling in the marsh, but then the flow of the river takes over and meanders from the east towards the south, broadening. Here every forest has been smashed by vast waves, choking the river with trees, debris, reptile bodies. James splashes ahead of the canoe to find the channel. Tides begin; usually they rest up on some island during the rising tide and continue on the fall. Even at high tide the sea level has dropped by hundreds of feet, leaving the toffee-coloured waters lapping between huge mudbanks. Mary keeps looking for birds, cranes, waders, but there are none on this world. The water turns milky with chalk, the exposed seabed makes low hills stinking of fish and damp. Between them stretch saltwater lagoons teeming with trapped life, fins darting around the canoe as James and Mary's father paddle steadily forward, their furs gleaming with ice, white frost clinging to their beards.

Balaam's voice crackles from the radio. There's an island higher than the others, a few trees clinging to its back. He can see it too. James and Mary's father paddle with a will. They beach the canoe, carry the stretcher with their feet crunching on the white seashells. There's a smell of dung, fish bones everywhere. Balaam and his acolytes come walking through the undergrowth between the muddy pools. Balaam's gold robe gleams, zadokite sceptre upraised in greeting, and as he lifts it the metal glints in the sun. Something waiting patiently in the mud moves, long crocodile head rising out of concealment dripping mud and fish skin from its jaws, then abruptly stands up as tall as the trees. Balaam holds his ground unafraid. Drops his sceptre, lifts his Bible to ward off evil. The acolytes grab the sceptre, back away, but Balaam has no fear, he knows God will save him from the beast. James stands between Mary and the monster but his hands are shaking, he can't unsling the rifle, he fumbles. Her father takes aim with the pistol.

'No!' Balaam shouts. 'The creature is God's creature.'

The crocodile head gapes over Balaam, the claws hook the priest upward into the gaping mouth. Balaam screams. The teeth are sharp as razors, pointed back in the jaws to grip slippery fish bodies and decaying meat. The mouth gusts cold reptile breath, flapping the zadok's cloak, and Balaam shrieks. James's rifle slips from the sling, falls to the ground, the movement catches the creature's eye. It lowers its head, runs towards James on vast clumping footfalls. 'Shoot the rifle,' Mary's father calls. James picks it up, works the bolt, but it's jammed with seashells. 'Shoot the rifle!' Mary's father screams. Balaam screams. Mary says, 'Run away.'

'I won't.' James clears the bolt, it locks smoothly. 'I won't leave you, Mary.'

He raises the rifle, cleverer than Mary's father. Instead of shooting at the belly he takes aim at the head, and as the creature's head comes down on James with Balaam shrieking in its jaws, he blows its eye to jelly. As it turns to see him James shoots out the other eye. The creature shrieks, Balaam shrieks.

Its crocodile head turns away from James towards the pool, its instinctive home.

'Don't let it get to the water,' Mary's father shouts. 'You idiot.'

James reloads. The creature topples, plunges forward, slides from the shallows into deep water. James runs along its floating back, tries to grab the medicator from Balaam's wrist, but air bubbles out of the creature's body, stinking water washes over it, James flounders to shore. The monster's gone, Balaam's body crushed beneath it somewhere on the bottom of the lagoon, and the medicator with him. Mary will never get better.

'It wasn't your fault,' Mary tells James. 'It wasn't your fault.'

Asmodeus smiles. She knows it was James's fault, so do I, so does Mary, and so will everyone.

They return in silence to the London hilltop, the paddles dipping slowly in the water, Mary in physical agony, James emotional. When she touches his hand he turns away from her. When she murmurs to him he shouts at her. Asmodeus watches them greedily.

Others have died. Grief, despair, hangs over the hilltop. They know they're going to die.

Asmodeus pulls me into the forest. Among the gigantic fallen trunks and ribs of bone Esther works with James, pulling away branches as he cuts them with the hand-axe. The steel one's broken; he uses stone. Asmodeus stands behind Esther, a strong sweaty girl with streaky hair, and James looks at her for the first time. Asmodeus smiles, and James smiles at Esther, still angry with Mary. Humans are so easy for demons. James kisses her, she clasps him, he bites her breasts, you know how it always goes. James lying with Esther in his fury and his love for Mary and his loneliness, without God, in terror of dying, Esther in her hunger for more life than her own in her body. I don't know if it's hormones or demons. I don't know which is right.

But I do know that among the dwindling band the only one who didn't know about them was Mary.

And then, one night, the sound we know. The sound of a pistol shot from the cave.

But we do not die.

Mary's father erected a memorial to his lost daughter on the hilltop. It was a large piece of rock standing naturally out of the earth where the landing-explosion had thrown it. He buried a Bible at its foot, and carved three words deeply into the face of the rock. He looked around him at the desolation of the world his people had destroyed, which in turn was destroying them, and the ones who were left gathered round him. They had no priest, but Esther, belly bulging like a fertility goddess, tried to weep a few Christian words. The wind whipped them away.

Mary's father knelt at her memorial stone, turned his mind from the Godless wilderness, and tried to concentrate his mind on the meaning of the words in the stone.

This is the Holy Bible of the Lord your God.

Deep into its surface, white hair flying in the wind, he pushed his fingers deep into the letters he had carved.

ARAM MENAHT MENOU.

These poor suffering people. Watching them, their grief, sadness, incomprehension, their religiosity, their almost complete lack of any understanding about the nature of the world in which they find themselves, is almost unbearable. Esther's baby is born dead, and her next baby, and her next baby, and she dies in childbirth, and James prays. How he prays! Frantic prayer. He believes that somehow his prayers can bring his God into this world. That same fixed, nervous, attentive look on his face and in his eyes when he prays to the God he's lost as when he was with Mary. *I'll always love you.*

James will always love her. But he'll never find her, not until it's too late.

I stand on the hilltop beside Asmodeus. 'You don't know where she is, do you?'

I know by now when she doesn't want to answer.

'At the time, this time, I didn't think Mary was important. Just another soul, just the crippled girl. Even dinosaurs have souls, you know. I believe now His scheme is infinite. Every bug, every stone, even a planet is a living organism, and every grain of dust has its place in His scheme.'

'You didn't see her as part of God's plan.'

Finally Asmodeus speaks. 'At the time I thought the asteroid proved that God didn't have a plan.'

'But there was Mary.'

'I didn't know what she'd become. She could be a bird, a dragonfly, a mouse, a lemur, I didn't care. If I found her I made her suffer, that's all. I should have destroyed her. I should've dropped her soul screaming through the church roof at Sion. Anything.' Asmodeus shrugged her shoulder. A fleck of gold peeled off.

'You aren't as beautiful as you were,' I said. 'I find I can ignore your beauty now. I don't think about you all the time.'

'Don't kid yourself.' She kissed me, but her mouth tasted faintly of seaweed. I found her repulsive. She looked angry, and disappeared.

The sun shone more frequently now but the weather remained cold, unstable. Most of the big lizards were dead and the great migrations stopped, though crocodiles remained along the shore and sharks in the sea. It was as though the world held its breath before starting something new. I began to see the Hand of God in the fate of *Ouranos*, the fragment striking Yucatán so precisely in the world's great deposit of sulphur rocks, throwing up the billions of tons of sulphur that alone could have blocked sunlight from the atmosphere and caused winter to fall overnight all over the world. And the other half of the ship striking India, causing the immense eruptions that showed no sign of stopping, keeping the weather cold with their volcanic dust, yet also warming the world with their greenhouse gases. Life will come back quickly when it comes.

'The start of God's return to earth and all He had abandoned.' Asmodeus speaks behind me, making me turn. 'Fanciful. We didn't see it that way at the time. My Master thought the crash of *Ouranos* symbolised God's defeat. That Hell is more powerful than Heaven. Look how they suffer.'

'But they keep fighting to survive,' I point out: in the freezing air before dawn, as Sirius rises before the sun, Mary's father climbs slowly from the ruins of the stockade. He's very old, and in his arms, unsteadily, carries something he's spent many months constructing out of salvaged metals, aluminium, iridium, quartz. He makes it to the hilltop in the end, drops down, and finally opens the aluminium petals like a silvery umbrella. He puts one end on the ground and sights the handle carefully at Sirius, then slightly off to one side. Then he connects the radio to the tip of the handle, and touches the button.

'That's what we didn't know,' Asmodeus snarls. 'He called home. If I'd known I would've destroyed him before he ever climbed the hill.'

The old man slumps against the stone. ARAM MENAHT
MENOU.

He slides down, gazing at Sirius and the tiny insignificant
glow of NGC 2207 rising above the handle of the umbrella.
A galaxy sixty-five million, four hundred and four thousand,
three hundred and ninety-four light years distant. An SOS
that will take exactly sixty-five million, four hundred and
four thousand, three hundred and ninety-four years to
arrive.

I work it out in my head. 'AD 2012.'

'The Mayans will work it out on their Long Calendar as
three days before Christmas 2012. Not until the world ends.
Until the world *changes*.'

'Mayans? Where will they live?'

'Yucatán. The Isthmus of Panama.'

It had meant nothing to me when my mother had spoken
of the People of the Isthmus. But again I see the hand of
God. Something is remembered. I begin to see what my
mother meant: we are, all of us, part of something huge and
important. There *is* a reason for everything, there *is* something true, and however small we feel we're all connected in
a vast scheme.

I see hardly any survivors now. Asmodeus lifts me into the
air, I watch new life filling the devastated world, turning
brown to green, dead oceans to blue teeming seas. Does any
human community survive, anywhere? Perhaps, impoverished, primitive, deep in the jungles, or on the forgotten
islands of Antarctica. Do any folk memories survive? As the
continents are separated by the spreading seas and become
the shapes familiar to me, with familiar mountains and
familiar bays, sometimes I think I see signs of almost-
human life – great structures like runways in South America
that seem designed to be seen from space, coincidences in
the placing of hills, but no doubt there are natural explana-
tions.

Sometimes I sense my mother. Not my mother as I would
know her, ancient, indomitable. Just sometimes in the
trilling of a bird, the calling of whales in the deeps in the
dead of night, the flutter of a butterfly . . . something.

And always, the reminder of that immense curve of the

Isthmus and the Caribbean, like a staring blue eye, and monkeys howling in the jungles of Yucatán.

Asmodeus lifts me by the hand. She covers herself with diaphanous robes hoping I won't notice her peeling body, carries me to the long, familiar, sandy coastline that one day will be the Holy Land. This is recent; perhaps thirty, forty thousand years ago. The Dead Sea's here, but far from dead, surrounded by lush grassland, and in the northern distance Galilee is dense green forest.

On a hill where the forest touches the southern grassland a campfire sends up a thread of smoke. At the fire sit half a dozen women, and two more lying down. Where are their men? One of the women is dying; the other is giving birth. As the girl arches her back and emits guttural cries the older woman holds her hand, remembering as she dies her own time of living. From their muscular bodies and big intelligent heads – the Jews will remember them as Nephilim – I recognise Neanderthals. They're neither brutish nor hairy, and the girl's pretty. She cries out to God as a head peeps between her legs, slips back in again. The women gather round her, helping her push, the girl swears and sweats and pushes, and the head peeps out again smooth and round, then the baby slides out into its mother's arms and its eyes open, bright blue, indigo-blue, as it bawls, high-browed, with a snubby nose and a chin at first glance too large for its face. Despite the round head its brain is smaller, and it's difficult to think of any reason for that chin. Only a mother could love such a face. But the young mother cuddles it fondly to her breast, her baby girl sucks eagerly, and I know I'm seeing evolution at work: one of the billion trillion tiny divisions and multiplications of evolution, each one of them ordained and ordered by the hand of God, not one of them random. Inevitable evolution. Inevitable Man, inevitable woman. 'She's Eve,' I say, and the little girl squalls and sucks, kicking.

While new life was born, the old woman's died. The mothers douse the fire and by the cold hearth scratch a hole with branches, fold her withered legs to her chin, place flowers over her body. The men shuffle out of a cave entrance carrying something they've found. It's a perfect round ball like nothing they've seen, and shines like the sun in the sunlight. They put it down, but it's light enough for the wind to blow like a bubble. They gather round, crouching, holding it down with their hands, staring at their reflected faces. They laugh, then fight, then stare again. 'They think it's the moon fallen from the sky,' Asmodeus says. The largest man picks up the moon in his arms and holds it over the dead woman, but she doesn't stir. One of the boys has found a tall straight stick with a top as shiny as the silver moon and brandishes it, laughing. The others wrestle him for it. I stare entranced. 'Balaam's sceptre.'

The acolytes brought it back from the island. One day they, or their children, or their great-grandchildren, knew the secrets would be lost. The numbers. Instructions. So they etched them on impermeable stone.' I watched the children playing with the stones.

Two boys tug for the stick, it clatters against a rock. Suddenly the man holding the moon shouts, his hands and chest burning. He drops the ball as though it weighs a ton. Its weight pulls it half into the soft earth, crunching the stones, burning the grass. Leaves and stalks of dead grass whirl around, fall into the glowing ball. As the doused fire bursts into flame the women cry out in awe. The moon shines with a fierce light, sucking in earth and wind around it, making the treetops roar, then the boy who'd held the stick – the others had run away – picks it up, closes his eyes, and presses it with his thumbs. Everything stops.

The moon sits cool and quiet in the ground.

The large man picks up a twig. He prods the moon gingerly, then brushes his fingertip against it. Everyone gathers around, sunburnt faces staring reverently.

A few days later the tribe follows the food south, the girl carrying her newborn baby in the crook of her arm, the men in the lead carrying the moon between them.

'We couldn't know everything,' Asmodeus says quietly. 'It was no longer at Mount Sion.'

A stone stands on a hilltop where London will stand. The land rises and falls, but the stone stands. The marshland turns to desert, the Thames roars in its chalky chasm, but still the stone stands overlooking herds of deer and hippopotamus. Ice ages come and go, but the glaciers never quite reach the stone. In the stone were once carved the letters ARAM MENAHT MENOU, their meaning long forgotten. But faithful fingers follow the shapes of the letters, wearing them deeper, and the place is remembered as a religious place. When the women of the tribe, Mary among them, are long forgotten, the holiness of the place will be remembered by the girl Aioula who alone remains its guardian, and St Paul's Cathedral will be built here.

In the jungles of the Isthmus, among the tribes of the Mayapan and the Toltec-Maya, something is remembered. They build their huge pyramids to God and His fallen angels, as perhaps they believe themselves to be, but Jesus Christ is almost forgotten. Yet now I have foreknowledge I see the hand of God in so many peoples, quietly bringing Heaven and Earth into Satan's world, beginning the redemption of Satan and the salvation of his peoples. In stone the Maya begin their Long Count, believing the earth was created on 13 August 3114 BC, and maybe they're right. My mother would overhear Matthew teach Joshua and Jacob dates that aren't so very different, and into the twenty-first century many Christians still believe God created the earth at about that time. Something that had started millions of years ago was rushing forward, becoming obvious.

'But my Master,' Asmodeus says, 'has no interest in redemption or in reconciliation.'

The Egyptians remember. And far to the north-east a Prince of Shem, Abraham, follows his father King Terah from Ur west to Haran, where he breaks away from his father and leads his people south. Abraham, that's a name my mother would have recognised, she spoke of him. Obviously she expects him to find Jesus Christ ruling in a city called Jerusalem on Mount Sion, 'the holy mountain, fairest of heights, the joy of all the earth'. Just as there's not a jot or tittle in evolution that's not preordained in God's plan, neither is there in religion. Does Mary walk eager with anticipation among these people I see coming through the green fields and dust of Canaan to Jerusalem? Of course she does. But instead of Jerusalem the City of God they come to dirty Jebus, Ur-Shalom, crouched like any other walled village on its hilltop, and Melchizadok wheezing on his throne, all too human, and Mary's hopes are dashed. But then she must have wondered: Melchizadok's people worship the shrine of El Elyon on Mount Sion, and worship Zadok too. All's not lost. Jebus-Jerusalem. Maybe one day Jerusalem will stand here, Christ will rule here.

Incredibly, Melchizadok persuades Abraham to leave, lavishes gifts on him to send him on his way, and Abraham leads his people south into Sinai the Land of the Moon. The Hebrews make their nomadic home wandering among moon-worshippers and the worshippers of a meteorite. When the desert's conquered by the People of the Sun, the Egyptians, the Hebrews are enslaved. In this world not only have they not found Jesus in Jerusalem, they've lost their freedom, they're scattered and demoralised and dying in Pharaoh's copper mines, they're no longer the first Chosen People.

Asmodeus smiles.

I understand. 'You thought you'd won.'

But some Hebrews do well under the Egyptians. Unexpectedly the slave Yosef interprets Pharaoh's dreams with eerie accuracy, is appointed Vizier, and some Hebrews learn Egyptian ways alongside their own. Their three principal goddesses are Asherah the lover of El, Ashtoreth the warrior and Anath the virgin, the lady of the mountain. As long as they mine their quota of copper and don't attempt to leave the Land of the Moon, the desert east of the Red Sea, the Hebrews are ruled on daily matters by their own small king, Aaron. But the women of the tribe dream of a great successor, a Messiah, to lead them and their children to freedom. 'Exactly,' Asmodeus says. 'We knew God was sending Jesus into the world. We opposed at every turn, tried to kill the child.' Pharaoh orders all newborn Hebrew children killed. And here's the Hand of God again, in a most unlikely way, suddenly quite visible: an Egyptian princess finds a baby floating on the Nile a hundred miles west of the Red Sea in a basket sealed with pitch, though there's no pitch in Egypt, and names him Akenmoses. The boy's no good, grows up pampered with every luxury, uncircumcised, wilful, temperamental, proud. Then he kills a man.

Asmodeus lifts me over the desert. 'A murderer. So we

were sure Akenmoses was one of ours.' Akenmoses is banished to the Land of the Moon. 'It meant nothing to us, neither did the name of the place.' The wasteland of rock and sand and shimmering heat passes below us. 'Just another sad human in the wilderness. He lost all he knew at court, power, position, respect. He suffered, he cursed the Egyptian gods. Finally he was reduced to marrying Zipporah, daughter of one of the ethnic priests, Jethro, not much better than a slave. But Jethro's respected among his own Midianite people and the rulers of nearby tribes, including Aaron of the Hebrews, who trade their copper for the famous Midianite pack camels. That's Akenmoses's job.' Beneath us a few scrawny camels led by boys plod towards a circle of tents on a mountain slope. Alone ahead of them strides a white camel mounted by a black-bearded man, the hem of his striped *galabiya* fluttering in the desert wind. He waits to be welcomed and offered hospitality before he dismounts. Akenmoses is a man of few words, even fewer of them Hebrew, but he knows how to bargain with a king like a king. In the tent Aaron's sister comes forward, washes his feet. Her name is Miriam, the prophet of El.

Miriam, Mary. We're still thirteen hundred years before the time of Christ. I've never heard the name before among these people. I see my mother in the prophet's steady, unimpressed gaze as she watches Akenmoses, feel the weight and age of her in the strength of Miriam's personality. Only Akenmoses's personality is as powerful.

'Welcome,' she says, her manner making it plain that neither Egyptians nor Midianites are really welcome. But Aaron is garrulous, embraces Akenmoses's shoulders, sits him on the best rug. They talk, Aaron doing most of the talking. Miriam watches Akenmoses. He and his name mean nothing to her, but her expression is intense. I think I know why she's here. I think the Hebrews have found something and she wants to stop Aaron talking.

The two men sip a cup of wine to conclude the camel bargain. 'Had a man die a few days ago,' Aaron says. Death's nothing unusual in the mines.

Miriam says warningly: 'My brother.'

Both men frown, offended by the woman's interruption. Akenmoses grunts, 'You allow your women to speak?'

'I ask forgiveness for my sister. I knew the man slightly, so I was called.'

'My brother,' Miriam said. 'We must lead the people in the evening prayer.'

Aaron eyes the sun in the tent-flap. 'It's not evening. The man was burnt to death.'

'It doesn't matter where,' Miriam says hastily. She pours more wine.

Akenmoses scratches his beard, annoyed. He ignores the wine. 'Where?'

Aaron blurts: 'In the deepest level of the mine where there is no fire, only a flickering reed for light.'

Akenmoses gets to his feet. 'A man doesn't burn without fire, except by the sun. El lives in the mountain. Your man has been burnt by God.'

'Don't go,' Miriam says. 'It's dangerous.' She adds: 'And El is not there. My brother and I are the priests of El. El is with us.'

Akenmoses glares. 'I'll see for myself.' As he strides uphill with Aaron he mutters, 'Does she hate all men?'

Aaron shrugs, women. 'She's never accepted a husband.' Bitter dust hangs over the slope, gangs of men hack wearily at mounds of rock. Spill slides dangerously from the mouth of a natural cave. The two men scramble the last few yards, take burning tapers from a pallid boy, walk crouching into the dark. The air's almost unbreathable, acrid with smoke. They push past the shadowy backs of men, the slaves of slaves get this work, only the lowest of the low, criminals, blasphemers. Wars are the only way to get miners. 'The cave was much longer but the roof fell in long ago.' Aaron holds the tail of his burnouse over his mouth, choking. Coughs: 'We're digging it out. That's when we found—' They crawl beyond the miserable clink of picks and shovels. 'This.'

Here it is. The moon of the Land of the Moon. Whorls of grey bone-dust surround the silver moon that the Neanderthals brought this far and worshipped, if the collapsed roof is any guide, once too often.

'It's El,' Akenmoses breathes.

Aaron's ashamed. 'My sister disagrees. The people want to worship it, but—' He shrugs. 'I wish it was made of gold.'

'Do you pray to it?'

'Inside the mountain? The people can't see it.'

Akenmoses breathes, 'Perhaps that makes it more power-ful. Look.' He points at a stick lying in the dust, picks it up, tall as he. 'In Egypt the priests use sceptres like these. Not as heavy.' He stares at the top. 'Not as complicated.' He touches it with his fingertip.

Aaron says quickly, 'He was burnt to a cinder.'

Akenmoses crouches towards the moon. 'It isn't the moon. The moon doesn't show back faces. It isn't El, there's no storm and fury.' He leans closer, the hairs prickle over his hands, his hair stands up. 'I know what it is. I've felt this before. It's a lightning storm.' He stands back, prods the intricate top of the sceptre with his finger.

There's no lightning, not at once anyway. Both men approach again. 'It's warm,' Aaron says, and both men hold out their hands as if to a fire. A wind starts in the chamber, rotating around the silver ball, setting the burning reed fluttering. Both men's eyes sting, as though they've been too long in the sun.

'It makes a sound like singing voices,' Akenmoses says.

'I don't like it.' Aaron backs away. Akenmoses touches the stick, and the air stops moving. They stare at the ball, waiting, but nothing happens.

They return outside to find the people gathered. Every-one bursts out laughing. Both men's faces, though tough-ened by years in the desert, are bright red with sunburn.

Only Miriam doesn't laugh. She weeps. She turns on her heel and walks away.

'It's not El,' Akenmoses murmurs quietly, watching her. 'It's more than that.'

That evening Akenmoses borrows every *galabiya* and every blanket he can find, from Aaron, the chiefs of the clans, the heads of individual families, everyone except Miriam, and persuades the giggling women to sew the corners together to make a huge thick garment. At dawn slaves carry it up to the cave ahead of him, but suddenly Miriam runs forward and grabs his arm. 'You'll find that garment will be your shroud.' She tugs him, tries to stop him. 'He'll kill us all!'

He shrugs her off, pulls the heavy mass over his shoulders in the mouth of the cave, and goes in alone.

Miriam's shriek follows him: 'You'll kill us all! You don't know what you're doing! You'll destroy the whole world.' Aaron gestures; strong men hold her back.

I stare at her as she weeps helplessly. She doesn't know what's going to happen. She thinks she does, she thinks this fool Akenmoses is going to press buttons at random with his big stupid fingers and the Hawking box is going to do what it does: attract matter and emit energy. I'm perfectly sure that none of this is in Balaam's Bible, no Akenmoses, no Land of the Moon, no Egypt, no mountain, no Arch of the Covenant, but you and I know exactly what is going to happen, just as we knew Abraham wouldn't linger in Jerusalem: because *our* Bible tells us so. *Our* Bible tells us God speaks to Akenmoses in the mountain and Akenmoses the Prince of Egypt comes out of Mount Musa as Moses the Israelite, priest to Aaron the king. The shroud Moses wears protects him from the *shekinah* of God, and as a further sign of His favour in the fury of the storm God reveals to Moses His sacred name, Yahweh. Yahweh makes a Covenant with Israel, and Moses is appointed His messenger, receiving the Book of the Covenant. God reveals His Word to Moses so that Pharaoh will be forced to let Moses's people go, and Moses will lead his people back towards Jerusalem, and the Word will defeat any enemy who stands against the Israelites. We know all this from school, you and I. We've entered the time of recorded history.

But in real life I watch the mountain, fascinated by its yellowish-orange, rocky outline against the blinding blue sky, wondering what will happen. We all hold our breath.

The rumbling begins, the immense thunder later called 'theophany'. A bush bursts into flame but is not consumed. Moses comes down from the mountain. He says: 'God spoke to me.' He tells us of the God more powerful than El whose Name is too holy to be spoken aloud, and orders the Israelites to construct a box – acacia are the only trees that grow on the mountain – to contain the Covenant and carry it with them.

I watch Miriam's face. She doesn't know what to believe. Whether to be joyful, or despair. She doesn't know – who would? – whether Moses has really met God in the mountain or not. It must be proved by signs. When she challenges

589

Moses she's struck down with a skin disease that makes her ritually impure, so she can't perform her priestly duties until Moses agrees to cure her.

Trusting wholly in God, Moses takes the Israelites beyond the Red Sea and demands to Pharaoh's face that they be released from bondage. When Pharaoh refuses, all the people whether Egyptian or not are struck down by the finger of God, first with blood, then frogs, then gnats, then flies; then diseased livestock belonging to the Egyptians, then boils over the bodies of the Egyptians themselves; hail falls on all, then locusts eat the crops, and darkness falls over the world to make it as it was before God's earth was created; but is this truly the direct action of the finger of God, or by the Covenant He has given? The tenth plague attacks the firstborn of the uncircumcised Egyptians – and his wife Zipporah hastily circumcises Egyptian-raised Moses in his sleep, or her own first child would die, which he's characteristically forgotten.

'Ooh, it was a good time for us,' Asmodeus says. 'The Angel of Death. Lovely. Yes, God got us to do His dirty work.' She tries to smile at me in the same old alluring way, but her gold skin's tattered and peeling, revealing the black beneath, and her eyes are like iron. 'Yes, we were fooled. The souls, their suffering, how they screamed. They were only Egyptians. But we were learning how hard God can be, even with His own people. Harder on them than any, maybe. Anyway, He got them back to Jerusalem. Almost forced them.'

'With the Covenant: His promise that they should be His Chosen People.'

'I saw Moses part the Red Sea. He did it. He pointed his sceptre and did it. God must have guided his hand. Moses could have destroyed everything. North Africa. The world. One slip.'

'No. Moses had seen the Word.'

'How we feared it. How we wanted it.'

'But you never got it.'

Asmodeus seizes me round the neck with dreadful force. 'Until now.'

ALPHA ET OMEGA

the beginning and the end

THE DEAD SEA, 22 DECEMBER 2012, 7:35 A.M.

'Forget what you knew,' Asmodeus snarled. 'Jesus Christ has abandoned you.'

I lay in the bottom of a rowboat, the noose around my neck tied to a bag of stones. The boat turned idly in the dawn wind, the winter sun rising over the cliffs of Jordan.

I tried to speak past the gag. Asmodeus cut it with a flick of the finger, splitting my lip, then settled watchfully in the stern of the boat.

I said: 'I thought my father was your prisoner in the cave below old London Bridge. Then the workmen broke through.'

'He was gone.'

'They didn't find the body of Christ?'

'He was gone! About a dozen years ago some people said they saw Him at Vaudey, others in St Paul's Cathedral, but it was just year 2000 talk.' Asmodeus kicked my knee, causing excruciating pain. I writhed, the boat rocked. 'The scientists got the Arch of the Covenant. We'd never made it work. It burnt alive anyone we made try. Grand Master de Prudome. Others. Hundreds.'

'Where is it now?'

'Manchester Institute of Science and Technology had it for ten years. Couldn't make it work either. Octal number system, see. It's something else. Got to be a priest to work it, or be born to it. Got to feel it.' Kicked me again. 'Stop your pain, son of the Son. You can do it, you know.'

'You don't have the Covenant?'

'I know where it is.'

'Where?'

Asmodeus made the wind blow the boat round, and pointed. I recognised the ruins of Sion beneath the cliffs of Israel. Too early for tourist buses, even in the run-up to Christmas when so many Christians would be in Jerusalem.

I whispered, 'Sion?'

'Lots of hiding places.'

The boat turned again. I glimpsed the moon like a dark hole beneath the sun. Asmodeus kicked me for the third time. I wasn't sure whether it was female or male any more. All its beauty was gone, and it stank. It stamped its heel, smashing a hole in the bottom of the boat, and bitter seawater bubbled up. The bag of stones was very heavy round my neck. I whispered, 'You don't have to be like this.'

Asmodeus shouted, 'Then make me better, son of the Son! Heal me!'

'I can't.'

'Try. Try. To redeem Satan and his brood, that's the greatest test of God. To come here. To dare.'

'My father did. He descended to Hell.'

'Only for a day.'

I raised my head, stared at the ruins of Sion behind him. 'Will you use it? The power of the Covenant?'

'If you don't die. Yes, I'll use it. Using it's easy, it's not using it that's hard. I have the black hole, I'll burn the world if I have to, I'll burn the sun and moon. I want to. I've always wanted to.'

'You'll destroy yourself.'

'I'm already destroyed.'

It meant it. It would. 'Why? What do you gain from death and destruction?'

'To keep God out of here.'

'God Himself is coming to the world?'

Asmodeus growled. A penis slid from its vagina and dangled, then its balls hung in their bag like a prolapsed womb. It considered me an idiot. 'The message that was sent arrives now. The saved perfect peoples of God, the Christians, have had sixty-five million years of prayer to find a faster way of travel. By now they're either instantaneous or extinct. And anyway God isn't constrained by His own laws, we know that. He's coming. Jesus Christ broke the laws of this world, not only the Law of Moses by healing on the Sabbath, but by the Star of Bethlehem, the Virgin Birth, walking on the water, changing water into wine—'

'Why did my mother kill all those people?' I asked.

'Isn't it obvious? To keep them from reading the Bible. Balaam's Bible, the true Bible written by King Jesus Christ in His own hand, His laws for His Christians He had saved. ARAM MENAHT MENOU, this is the Holy Bible of the Lord your God. Christians who were never allowed to know pain or doubt or loss or anything bad, because of their faith.'

'What's wrong with that?'

'The Jesus Christ who was never crucified. Who was born king and ruled by decree and imposed salvation.'

'Most people would welcome that. The certainty.'

'Exactly. A God who'd scourge my sinful world with His wrath and force belief on unbelievers would find favour in many quarters. Many people feel your Jesus of love and peace is out of date in the real world. Mary knew Balaam's Bible, the Jesus Christ of the Old Testament, the Jesus Christ of fire, storm, anger, an eye for an eye and a tooth for a tooth in punishment against crime, against fornication, against sodomy, against rape, against child abuse, against homosexuals, would be immensely popular. People would welcome that God with open arms, a Jesus Christ to impose order and compel belief. Safety, no need to think. A real Jesus to believe in, the Messiah. Isn't that what everyone wants? Isn't that what they've *always* wanted? Isn't that what Judas wanted? Much better than the loving, generous, forgiving Jesus of your New Testament. What good did that Jesus of yours do, except let himself get given away by his own followers to be crucified?'

I laughed, though it hurt my neck on the noose, and made the water bubble faster into the boat. 'You're saying Balaam's Messiah would be as bad as Satan because He'd enslave the people enslaved by Satan?'

Asmodeus murmured, 'Wouldn't you rebel against such a God? Such an AntiChrist?'

I was staggered. 'Did you?'

'And be cast down to Hell for your failure?'

'And you were.'

'You have no idea,' Asmodeus said quietly, 'what a terrible place this is.'

'Let me go.'

'Release yourself.' We were back to the angel-will-come-down-and-help-you temptation thing again. The demon pushed forward its stinking face against me. 'You can be Jesus Christ. You can. You can save us all.'

I remembered my mother. I remembered her last words to me.

Love. Remember, Jude. Remember love. Always remember who you are.

'You fool, Asmodeus,' I whispered. 'I am Jesus Christ.'

Asmodeus whimpered. 'Save me.'

'All of us are Jesus Christ. Every one of us. Every human. We all have His blood in our veins. *That* is the secret of the Covenant.' I marvelled. 'You never saw it. All this time, thousands of years, you've worried and fretted to control that miserable little box. And the truth was in front of your eyes all the time. All of us *are* Jesus whether we know or not, care or not, believe or not. The choice is ours. The Covenant is *us.*'

Asmodeus stared at his bloodless hand.

'But not me.'

I said in a strong voice, 'Satan, come out of him.'

The demon tried to lie. 'But I'm Asmodeus, not Satan.'

'Come out of him, Satan.'

The demon struggled with itself. The boat rocked from side to side but I sat up calmly. I leant forward, rested my face against the demon's face like a lover. For a moment I sensed it: that terrible pain. That endless suffering. Eternally without God, a fallen angel thrown down without hope, knowing all they had lost.

I whispered, 'Come out of him, God of this world, Deus, the dragon, Leviathan, *ho theos*, Satan. Come out.'

PAX MUNDI

the Peace of the World

I don't know what time it was. Still no sound of tourist buses. Perhaps it was no time at all and everything that happens happens for ever. I lay exhausted in the bottom of the boat, the sun swinging round me as the boat turned, the rising water lapping my body.

I lifted my head, grunting with the effort. The great walls of Sion, white as salt, pure white as frankincense, shone in the sunlight as though they never fell. Only one imperfection: the gate hung open where my father had broken it long ago, or perhaps today. In the potter's field Judas Sicariot's empty noose swung from the stipe, the upright post of a cross without a crossbar. His blood and the thirty pieces of silver were gone.

'Help,' I cried weakly. The salt water against my sunburnt skin was very painful, and water began to slop over the sides of the boat. I blew seawater away from my lips, gasped a breath. Just one more breath, O Lord.

Sirius rose over the arch *Qimrôn*. A man stood exactly in the centre between the two pillars, silhouetted against the azure sky, the sky full of stars in the brilliant sunlight. 'Amen.' The wind blew His long Nazarene hair and gown of seamless white linen, blew my little boat round and round. Beneath me the Dead Sea was full of stars, a perfect azure mirror of the sky. Jesus Christ outstretched His arms as though encompassing the sea, but His voice was calm and quiet.

'I bring you redemption, if you wish it.'

He was not speaking to me. He raised his voice over the Dead Sea.

'I bring you reconciliation, if you will take it.'

His voice roared, that sound, thunder without thunder: *theophany*.

'Come to me. Be healed. Do not be afraid. I am with you always.' He spoke as quietly as the whisper of a butterfly's wing, but I heard every word. 'Your time is over, your suffering is ended. You are never alone.'

He lowered His arms slowly to His side. 'Rise up, Satan.'

The Dead Sea rose up all around me, swamping my little boat in the roar of breaking waves.

The dragon rose from the sea. It lay on its belly over the sea, its neck rising up and overhanging the land. Water and blood poured from its scales, staining the sea red.

It lowered its head, fallen, bowed, immense. *The dragon shall rise from the sea and be slain.*

Its eyes opened, huge, fierce, cruel, loving, demanding, passionate.

Jesus Christ held out his hands. 'Satan, I give you peace. I offer you love.'

I remembered a prophecy, not of the AntiChrist, one of King David's: *Praise the Lord from the earth, ye dragons; ye dragons, and all ye deeps.* Beneath its nostrils the dragon opened its great mouth, the abyss. A woman stood up, my mother, the Queen of Hell, and God knows she'd known enough hell in her long life. She looked around her, saw my father, jumped down on to the sand. He walked towards her across the beach, kissed her openly, and the dragon fell back into the sea.

Joshua threw out a net from the shore, pulled me in my little boat towards the beach like a fish, walked to me across the waves. The waves breaking against his ankles splashed him to the waist. He brushed the hair from my eyes as my mother once had. He touched my cut lip and took away my pain. He felt my sunburn and healed me.

I'd forgotten how beautiful his eyes were. He smiled. 'Jude, my son.'

'Father.'

'Did you think I would let my child die? That I would let any of my children die?' He touched my face, marvelling.

'It's really you. You're so tall. You're taller than me, I think.'
He hugged me. 'You're a miracle. You really are me, part of
me, different from me. I'm so proud of you.'

Joshua put his arm round my mother's shoulders, turned
us away from Sion to face the sea. 'Listen, if you've got two
good ears. A great man, a greater man than I, said these
words much better than I can. This is what he said.' He
cleared his throat. ' "God has chosen the foolish things of
the world to confound the wise. Neither death, nor life, nor
angels, nor principalities, nor powers, nor things present,
nor things to come, nor height, nor depth, nor any other
creature, shall be able to separate us from the love of God.
Whatsoever things are true, whatsoever things are honest,
whatsoever things are just, whatsoever things are pure,
whatsoever things are lovely, whatsoever things are of good
report; if there be any virtue and if there be any praise, think
on these things." '

Then my father turned us to face the almost perfect walls
of Sion.

'Welcome home.'

Resurrection

Philip Boast

From the last Ice Age to the Industrial Revolution London had at its heart a holy place. A place of worship, of reverence, of violence, of mystery. Five cathedrals were built on the site, four were razed to the ground.

Beneath their foundations rested a secret, a legacy whose existence was passed on through generations of women, that could hurt and heal in equal terrible measure – the lost gospel of Judas Iscariot . . .

An unforgettable story of two millennia and the loves, faiths and passions of the men and women who, as they played out their lives around the holy place we now call St Paul's Cathedral, grasped at a fragment of eternity.

0 7472 5379 X

HEADLINE

The Foundling

Philip Boast

To burglar Jack Riddles five-year-old Joy Briggs is a valuable commodity he can sell in the child-brothels of Victorian London. But in the hue and cry following her kidnap from her parents' opulent home, Riddles abandons Joy – deaf and so deemed stupid – in a canal tunnel. To his distress, for the child's silent knowingness has touched him, she is gone on his return. Drowned, he thinks, or, as the Scotland Yard men called in by her outraged parents believe, lost to the city's vice-infested underworld.

They are wrong. For Joy is found by a family of canal folk who bring her up as their own, giving her the kind of open-hearted love she has never received at home. But as Joy reaches womanhood it becomes clear that her past cannot let her live in peace and that events she witnessed as a child on that terrifying night mean there are those who want her dead . . .

0 7472 4882 6

HEADLINE